AF496525

Constellation Planet

CONSTELLATION PLANET

A Dreamerverse Novel Published by Monica Moon ©

This is a work of fiction. All names, characters, places, religions and cultures resembling real life are coincidental. This novel consists purely of creations from the author's original body of work.

PRINTING HISTORY

Monica Moon Edition / Hardback / 2019

Cover illustration by Nicolae Negura

ISBN: 978-1-9161287-0-5

A MONICA MOON BOOK©

PRINTED IN THE UNITED KINGDOM

www.monicamoon.co.uk

JASON FALLOON

A DREAMERVERSE NOVEL

A MONICA MOON BOOK

For Monica

We got there in the end.

"I have loved the stars too fondly to be fearful of the night."

Galileo

Oscar

Oscar's First Awakening...

It's a little brighter once I open my eyes.

The sun is setting under what seems to have been a beautiful day. Even though that humid hum of the air urges me to deny it, I still believe I'm homebound, lying on the mattress of my king-sized bed. It feels the same. I'm convinced it does. A soft, spongy, sinking texture – the unforgettable sensation of my brand new mattress. Only a couple of days old. An adulterer to evanescence, that mattress' silk has a perpetual freshness, just as it should (and *will* always) have. No matter how many times I sleep in that bed, there's not a night I fall under those satin duvets where the mattress feels in any way similar to the way it had felt the night before. It's an eternal novelty I can hear from the crisp crunch of the clean sheets, measure from the youthful spring in its depth and even judge strictly on the nostril alone, off the *whiff*. Because whenever I wake, the air simply *smells fresh...*

Then again, that isn't what I *smell* here. What I smell now is something equivalently sweet, but riper, holier, and weightier, as if it isn't *new* at all, but has lingered for some time; a satisfying aroma that reminds me of something I so fondly remember. But what is it? *Aaah, yes—yes, yes, yes! My mother's old banana cakes!* How could one forget the seduction of those inviting bakes? A scent from home. The sibilant delight of them crackling in the home oven was enough to make grown men drool with the dogs...

Dogs? Is that what that sound is too? No... birds, maybe? *Howling* birds?

I sit up...and a heap of sand showers off my back, down my shoulders and from the sides of my head. *Shivering* gate-crashes my submission to the cordiality of my new surroundings. Suddenly, a subdued breeze hits me, unacquainted. I'm soaked to the bone, the chilly wind purely accommodating this uncomfortable revelation. But—*water? From where?* A wave must have flushed over me whilst I've been lying here. A wave? From where? Well, *come on*: from the ocean, of course.

There—I capture it!

A ceaseless stretch of water that spans far beyond the sun-christened horizon, shimmying a thousand currents in every direction. Resolutely bountiful, the aquatic sanctuary showcases a landscape broader than any of the unblemished reservoir resorts I've visited during my monthly vacations. But is it a lake? Can it be? At least, can it be one of the huge and famous ones I've been to, or, even in the slightest aspect, be one of the private, intimate destinations that I remember for all their fortified nostalgia? None of them are comparable, for this can't be a lake in any shape or scope. If it was, I'd be able to see the other end of it, another shore in the distance. There would be trees and people, or boats and little houses. Nope, it isn't a lake. Far more impressive—

—Wave!

I quickly jump up, slipping on the soggy patch of sand on which I've laid. Heart pumping, head throbbing, I'm unable to comprehend anything at the moment. I've never seen the ocean up-close before...*nor have I ever before taken the chance to learn how to swim for that matter.* How my mother had used to urge me into taking regular lessons and I'd been having none of it. I'd neglected every opportunity. And now, here I am, thinking: *She was right about the ocean.* It's a tomb to those who can't swim. She had always been right in the end. Regardless of what it was, her experience always cradled the most sense and quite soon after that wisdom diminished I became a very regretful person. '*A remorseful child,*' Aunt Sibyl would still criticise me on occasions. '*Always the child to make the wrong decisions and rather talented at making the wrong decisions. Behold the son of a Decider.*' That was only *half*-true – like now: how I'm attempting to rub the salty wetness off my calves but only smothering them in a slushy coating of aureate sand; bad idea, but not exactly a gift.

The heat is constant and it's strangling me. No wind. Just mugginess. Very soon, I'll pass out, as I'm already remarkably dizzy after mere seconds. I don't know whether or not to move, for, at this point, I'm unsure if the ground is safe or stable – my legs really aren't at all. So, I take the risk, staggering my way cautiously down the length of the 'beach'. Yes, it's definitely a beach. The sand isn't hot like people have warned me it can be. Instead, this sand is cool. And this entire stretch of the shore is shadowed by the dimness left from the descending sun. As I walk further, the dark, golden sand starts to become more like snow, colder and colder and I'm not enjoying it. (Quite the opposite of what those yakking liars told me). Its depth and thickness works me so stiff that I can hardly respire after each step; I'm rather more dragging my feet along—

—Another wave!

This one is freezing, sending chills up my legs. I sense myself wobbling and decide to let all my hard labour collapse back into the sand. Dry sand—Phew! I pull myself backwards up the shore to save myself from the perimeter of the impending waves, then sigh exhaustedly. With my back in the sand and my legs splayed outwards, I gaze up at the purplish-reddish sky. It's predominantly purple, a soothing shade that causes my eyes to buzz in a state of dreariness. Since the sun is already semi-consumed by the ocean's brink, the colour begins to fade away, divorcing the horizon and shuttering daylight behind an opaque, black oblivion, and that's where the night-sky plunges in. The transition of sunset happens within moments. It's clear—peaceful—jubilant. And all to be seen are the stars. Millions of stars have spawned. My eyes widen at this startling spectacle. Something I've never witnessed in my life. Where I'm from, stars are the stuff of myth. They're the blueprints of dreams. And dreams are full of them. Only, never have they appeared so crystalline as they do in this...

Dream...Is this one?

If so, then why does it feel so palpable? It's surreal, yet it carries an intuitive ambience like some hazy reality. Why is that? Why does it feel so alive?

'Because it is.'

I sit upright abruptly. The voice sounds frighteningly close. Although, it doesn't sound like anything intelligible at all. In the mellowness of the evening – if I can really call this placeless situation 'evening' – the noise rings like a tetchy zephyr chasing the stuffiness out of the air. The words don't really linger like words normally do; they lack weight, riding between the wisp of the sea current and the wind. They're transparent, insubstantial. Shuddered by this discovery, I spin round, expecting to find a face.

'That's because words mean nothing. They're only sounds afterall.'

There it is again—

'They are the primal utterances of cudgel-bearers that many generations of progenies have since strung pretentious meanings to—namely, ***human beings****.'*

And there again!

I swing my glance right around, disturbed. Sparing a breath, I pause—and all to be heard are the rolling waves and the arbitrary chirps of the birds far in the jungle. The jungle? Ah, yes! Towering palm trees, stretching for as far as this length of the beach goes. A classic tropical island scene. That's what it is! I've been marooned on a desolate island and all I have to accompany me is my teetering sanity – which has no means of improving – and my dark, strangely talkative imagination.

'You watch far too much television...particularly ***reality*** *shows.'*

'Ha—ha, ha--No! This isn't a joke! I happen to be lost, if you don't mind!'

'Lost? You're lost, are you?'

'Yeah, I am!' I'm actually *replying* to it – I kick myself.

Gratefully, there's no answer this time. I force myself to think rationally and, in doing so, close my eyes again and try to recapture some sleep. Perhaps then I'll be transported back home and wake up in my ordinarily new bed on my seemingly normal mattress in my magnificently *real* home! I do exactly that. My eyes are shut firmly and painfully. But I can't withhold the strong, sweet aroma of...whatever it is. Banana cakes? MummyMummyMummyMum...

Curiosity holds me hostage. But I want to go home! I want to go back to where I—

'Sure you do! Go! Don't worry about anyone else! It's you who wants to run home—you Selfish Wimp!'

My imagination is starting to get a little feisty with me now.

'I'm not your imagination. And I'm most definitely not your conscience! What are you? A wooden puppet? Feisty...'

Don't answer, don't answer, I tell myself. *I have a bitchy imagination, that's all. What's worse? It's beginning to make fun of me!*

'For the last time, I am not your imagination! You fool!'

'Then, what are you?' I shout.

'Would it help if I gave you reminder of the pecking order here?'

Gave me a wha—?

Something very sharp pinches my cheek.

'ARGH! Why—why—why?'

I open my eyes to be confronted with a bird. But it's not any bird. It's a parrot, cackling a very human laugh from a bulbous beak; its head is cocked back as if mocking the sky above, while its thick neck is chugging hysterics. It has small, dotty eyes and the colours of its feathers are bright, random and prettily immaculate. Also, it's a glowing parrot with its body outlined by a shimmering silver glow – sure, why not?

'Is this a coincidence? I hope it is,' I say, annoyed. 'You…and the voice in my head?'

'*A coincidence? Does this look like a coincidence to you?*' the voice says – but it doesn't seem to be coming from the parrot. '*You are so naïve!*'

'What? Wait, so…this isn't a coincidence?' I must appear so stupid.

'*Oh, I see. You're wondering why my lips aren't moving in sync to what I'm saying. Well, let me just make it obvious to you: I'm a bird; a bird does not have lips.*'

'Well, yeah, I knew that much. But you're a parrot. Parrots can't talk…PROPERLY! They can repeat things, yes, but not have—a full-on, opinionated conversation with someone!'

'*That's a stupid circus trick that everyone falls for. Honestly, I thought you were better than that.*'

'You had better expectations of *me*? You're a bird with a conscience!'

'*What's your name, Dreamer?*'

I hesitate before revealing anything more. The situation is humiliating enough. 'Dreamer?' I respond.

'*Well, that's what you are, aren't you?*'

'What? So, this *is* a dream? Wait! Before I tell you anything, I want to know where the hell I am!'

'*You're not home.*' The parrot's beak is curled as though it's constantly smirking. '*Home is cosy, not a place for thinking on your toes. Anywhere that isn't home is "roaming" and requires some getting to know—*'

'Can you stop talking in riddles. I'm right here, right now and everything seems normal, everything appears real and everything looks—'

'*Alive?*' the 'bird' finishes my sentence. '*Aware? Conscious?*' he utters.

'Where am I?'

'*Well, let's see. You fell asleep and you didn't wake up…yeah, that just about sums it up.*'

'But I did wake up! I woke up here!' I hiss.

'No, you didn't. If you had done, you'd be in your comfy new bed, on your spongy new mattress.'

'How'd you know that?'

The parrot's smirk does not falter. His unblinking glare is expectant like he's been here before and explained this to many.

'Who are you? Do stray parrots have names?' I've got a feeling this comment might ruffle his feathers.

'I'm a Dreamer just like you. But I'm rather more experienced than you are.'

'Experienced? You're an Experienced Dreamer?' This is becoming harder to believe by the second.

'They call me the Steward. I come to inspect the beach for new arrivals. New Dreamers. More people like you.'

'And who are "They"?'

'Dreamers. I just told you that.'

'No. I meant "They". As in, you said "*They* call me the Steward". Who are "They"? The original inhabitants of this island?'

'Original inhabitants? What are you on about? No. There are no "original inhabitants". We're all the same here. We've all come and gone. Only, some have been about longer than others.'

'So, this isn't a quaint, little island?'

'No.'

'Then, what is it?' I sound too eager to be talking to a bird.

'It's a beach. You're on a beach.'

I sigh in frustration. 'You don't give very useful answers, do you?'

'Was that a rhetorical question?'

'Yes, it was.'

'No. I just asked you a rhetorical question by asking 'Was that a rhetorical question?' You weren't supposed to answer,' the bird chuckles – the bird actually laughs (this time it isn't in my head). *'Oh, newbies are hilarious! This can get fun!'*

'Really? Because I'm all for sarcasm, but I'm not actually getting the joke here. Moments ago, I hoped to find myself sitting on what *should have been* my bed-mattress, in what *should have been* my bedroom, in what *should have been* my own living space, but perhaps the actual joke is how that reality was everything it *wasn't* and more! Instead, it was a pit of itching crap that I found myself *lying* in, *dripping*, and *shaken all over*! Like a sow rolling in squalor! My head stings, I can't stand because my legs ache, and now I'm being wised-up by a crackhead parrot!'

'That really helps my job, kid. Thanks a lot for your compliments. Really friendly!'

'What *is* your job again...Mister Steward?'

'Please, call me Stewart,' the bird tilts his head slightly, almost to show that he's flattered to be called 'Mister'. *'I didn't start out as a bird, allow me to just clarify that. And I wasn't one of the first, you'll be happy to know, so I won't be blabbering on all the time like I know every last corner of this place. Like I said, I am rather experienced – more than you, anyhow. I'll leave all the surprises to you.'*

'One of the first? What is a Dreamer? The exact definition.'

'You are a Dreamer! I am a Dreamer! Everyone on this entire planet is a Dreamer!'

'Planet? This is a planet? I'm on another planet?'

'Dreamscape, dimension, planet—this place is whatever you make it. Nothing here's real. It may feel real, but you're only imagining it to be. Think about it, you've never seen a real palm tree before, you've seen the ocean – but never for real – and you've only ever been told what sand feels like by friends, family – those who've been lucky enough to visit a beach over their vacations and haven't been locked up in an urban birdhouse like you. Everything you see, feel and hear are the things which you could only ever imagine.'

'So, I'm imagining that I'm on vacation?'

I can tell by the awkward silence that the parrot is unsatisfied by this answer. It's his way of saying: *'Try again.'*

I do: 'What you're saying is that everything around me, everything I'm imagining, is something I've never seen or experienced before in the real world? I'm only imagining what it must be like from what I've heard and, therefore, that's how it exists...in my mind.'

'Now you're beginning to sound like a Dreamer,' Stewart seems happy with that.

'But—why me? Why am I here?'

'Everyone who comes here comes for a reason.'

'Everyone? Where is everyone?'

'You came at a bad time. Not many Dreamers arrive in the night.'

Is it night already? The sun has fully set and all that remain are the sparkling stars. That was fast.

'Does that make me special then? Is that a bad thing?' I ask.

'What's your name, Dreamer? You're leaving me hanging here.'

'Oscar Philson,' I tell him. 'But I thought you could read minds? You read mine.'

'It's called telepathy. It's how I choose to communicate with everyone. It doesn't make me a psychological intruder with sophisticated mind reading powers. And it's not just you, remember?'

'I hope so,' I say, unconvinced, but the greater distraction of bitter sand itching at my feet reminds me that there are weirder things to care (and worry) about right now. 'Am I only *temporarily* stuck here? And, if so, for how long?'

'I think you'll grow to like it here.'

'So much that I won't want to go home?'

'Stop mentioning home and perhaps you will. Besides, what's left of the world you call home these days, eh?'

He says this in such an unforeseen tone that I go quiet. Suddenly, the waves sound more distant and the birds have stopped harmonising amongst the trees in the jungle.

'My advice to you: I wouldn't lie around here at this time of night. We might not be expecting arrivals, but we are expecting to see some departures.'

The bird glances up. And this influences my own attention to switch towards wherever Stewart is looking. I turn on my belly, so I'm facing the jungle. It's in this direction where I hear mild rustling against the bushes and ivy. In the darkness of the night it's hard to see, let alone witness the line of dark figures approach from between the first trees. As they come towards us, I watch in fascination, for it's soon clearer who they are. None of them are distinguishable faces, only shadows identifiable by the pyjamas they're wearing. Yes, they're all dressed in their pyjamas – some wearing atrociously less than others. And a few wearing garishly more than you'd expect in even the wintriest of alternate realities. Each figure carries a jar out before them, clasped in two hands. Inside the jar is something glowing, a lively agent that lights the way. Fireflies. Of course. *It made sense, fireflies* – more things I've never before seen first-hand in reality, but had in the movies and on the TV screen – *were often caught in jars and kept as temporary pets or boasted captives. It's sometimes done as a hobby.* Unflinching, the pyjama-figures continue to gradually drift towards us. I just about manage to lift myself up onto my feet and stand tightly next to the now fluttering Stewart.

The pyjama-people pass us without noticing our presence. They're all bare-footed with the cold sand covering their grubby toes and their legs continue to sink until they're shin-deep. It's then when I realise that the fireflies aren't only used to paint a pretty picture. They have a function. Each and every one of the pyjama-people comes to a stop in a space somewhere along the beach. There are more of them than I'd first anticipated. Hundreds, in fact. Still, legions continue to protrude from the jungle. Now is when the first wave of pyjama-people, having come to a stop on the beach, place their firefly jars into the sand in front of them. Nothing happens for a few seconds, but then the pyjama-people begin to let themselves fall backwards into the sand. And, subsequently, they vanish in a flash of light. One-by-one, the pyjama-people disappear into the sand. I gape at the rapid decline of bodies, astonished, until none are left to count. The last of the sinking-ditches soaks up and the beach is vacant once again.

'*Finding it hard to believe?*' Stewart asks from beside me. He begins whizzing around, inspecting the shore.

'I'm finding it easy to believe that it's a dream. Is that good?'

'*Don't ask me.*' He's gone to where one of the pyjama-people has left their firefly-jar and starts to peck at the lid. The rim begins to part and once he's covered the entire circumference of it, the lid detaches and the firefly is released.

'Is this what you do?'

'*I'm here to greet newcomers. New Dreamers. Those homebound Dreamers you saw just then were advanced. They were experienced Dreamers. They come and go with little supervision. They don't require my assistance as much. You, on the other hand...*'

'Why were they wearing pyjamas?'

'*What do you think you're wearing?*'

I look down at myself, and gasp, for I've just realised that I'm nude. Completely. From head to toe.

'*Don't worry. Just imagine something a tad more...dignified or...appropriate...or not naked.*'

I stare back up at him, confusedly squinting my eyes. Then I return my sight down to...I'm wearing clothes! Well, pyjamas at least. *My* pyjamas. The blue silk ones I'd worn to bed.

'*I repeat: are you finding it hard to believe?*' Stewart has drifted over to another jar-lid and has started pecking at this one.

'Yes.'

'*Good. Because, you're not supposed to find it easy. Not at first anyway.*'

'Then, what am I supposed to do? If this is a dream...? I'm here now—what reason do I have? What do people do in dreams if they can't take their environment or themselves seriously? If they're inexperienced like I am?'

'Dreamers! You're a Dreamer now. Think, what do ***Dreamers*** *do in dreams? You do have a role here, Oscar. Find it before it finds you—as it did in my case.'*

'People—*Dreamers* come and go. Like guests? This is some sort of…imaginary pit stop? A service station for the mentally disturbed?'

'Oh, I wish it was, son. Just remember: In dreams, things don't always seem the way they are. They aren't supposed to, for your own safety and sanity, because when a dream gets too real it becomes—'

'A nightmare.'

There's an oddly frozen lull as he pecks away at a few more jar-lids. I take this time to look at the stars once more. Their glistening delight is phenomenal. How there must be billions of them up there, watching us as admirably as we gaze up at them. *My mother, could she really be somewhere up there with them this time, watching over me at last, in this place with the pungent aromas that remind me so much of what home used to be…?*

Suddenly, all around, thousands of specs of light shoot up into the air. The fireflies have been released from their jars and they now ascend up towards the sky, twinkling brightly. Each is so fast that I have trouble seizing sight of them all. But then I do, once they unite with the vista of constellations. Up above, there are more stars than before.

'Don't stop disbelieving. Once you start trusting things, the more dangerous it will become for you here.'

'Okay, that almost made sense,' I laugh at his remark, still transfixed on the sky. 'Those are beautiful.'

At first, the bird doesn't reply. Only once the crash of another wave or two has rustled back into the ocean are his words lifted with the sea breeze: *'Scepticism can be your closest ally, but only befriend those who are as sceptical as you.'* The restless sea does not shuffle in her bed again after this is said. Now at rest with the last gales of the evening cuddled close, her silence is when I suspect most that Stewart has truly retired for the night. The parrot has left the shore.

How long has it been since I'd last stuffed down a slice of that banana cake? I ponder, since the smell is growing stronger and the more I continue to think about it – as well as inhale it – the more I think of my mother and how much I miss her and how little I can remember of our past. It was almost half a lifetime ago. I was nine-years-old; I'm seventeen now. At any other time or place, it would've been hard to reconstruct the way she appeared in my mind, but now that my imagination is at its ripest, it's doing me a delicious favour. I can picture her as pristinely as the moon above.

I sit in the sand further up the shore, observing the massive moon, which glooms above the horizon and gives the impression of being sensationally closer than it really is. Its light is invigorating, each beam a chamber, an ignition of cognizance, through which I am slowly led to my senses. My true senses. My human senses. Not my surreal, Dreamer World senses. Although, according to a talking parrot, I'm apparently a part of this strange 'Dreamerverse', whether I like it or not. Where the waves hound you the same as those in the great fabled storms I was repeatedly told about in folktales. Where even the night-sky isn't entirely dark, with the moonlight decolouring the black – and, instead, stirring a lugubrious shade of blue. Where you can appreciate the sun-ironed sand like velvet beneath your feet. Where you can score a sweet taste of hot bananas every direction you go along the shore. Where you can witness the mythic stars in an abundance only the privileged eyes of those once living in a past reality had done.

There's no rationale as to how this can all be happening to me so suddenly, so randomly. I clamber up from the sand in an unintended strop, flicking a lump of sand into my face, into my eyes. I scratch it out, whining inaudibly to myself and questioning how my subconscious mind could be cruel enough to abandon me here. Why trap me in this prism of inhibitions and not someplace where I would be deemed more fit to survive?

Faintish, I dopily turn to face the line of palm trees that shield the entrance to the jungle. The stench of ripened banana soars stronger in this direction. It hits me like a lorry on the motorway.

Timid, I slip through a gap in the bushes. There isn't much to be seen ahead, other than trunks and vines. Also, there isn't much to be heard other than countable tired birds, chattering up in the canopies.

I pass the first row of trees. Broken branches and twigs, which have fallen from unknown heights, scrape my legs and small cuts and scratches quickly manifest on my ankles. This isn't going to be a tranquil walk in the countryside. I stop to gather myself. Collect my strength again.

But something withdraws my attention.

Cooking.

Somewhere close.

A barbeque must be taking place nearby. Could that be? Is that what I'm smelling? Well, it seems to be overpowering the old, hanging banana-stench. So, it must be.

Then, I spot heavy, white fumes rising in the distance. Even through the dark, I can sense a fire at-large. Meat sizzling, sweating on a grill, perhaps? A grill out here? Made of what? A fire formed by sunlight or bow drill? The smoke billows confidently like the fringe of a recently lit flame. But it's the belief that there may be more pyjama-people nearby that really unnerves me.

I follow the trail of smoke that covers quite a generous portion of the jungle. The temperature has dropped drastically and it's no longer humid. Instead, to my surprise, there's a whistling draught everywhere. No animal presence can be heard even as high as the canopies this late. No ambience of insects, not one click from a single cricket. And it's not until I've trekked past sixty, seventy, or eighty palms that I bump into something validly phonetic again. *Someone*, perhaps?

'You! Yes, *you!* Is there any other *you* that *you* know of?' the voice is a husky rasp that stabs at me, though I register an amateurish attempt at vindication all the same.

'Who is that? Who's there?' I question.

'Look up!'

Dangling from a bundle of vines above me is a large, brawny monkey. Its tail has been tied to one of the vines, hoisting him up, and his torso has been twisted so that he can meet my face without his head being inverted with the rest of his body. His eyes are a dark and murky green, terrifyingly translucent in the shadows. Intrepid, they stare objectively. Blind to everything, except me. *Talking monkeys are also on trend here.*

'What are you doing in the jungle after sunset?' it queries like a dutiful detective. 'Do you not know it's *prohibited* to be on jungle sands at this time? It is not safe around these areas. Dreamers fall into trouble during the night far more commonly than they do during the day.'

'Then why are you here?' I retort.

He doesn't expect this response.

'Let's just say, for our understanding, that I know my way around a lot better than you do and it is the irresponsible Dreamers like yourself who need to be watched by someone. Believe me, I have seen with my own eyes that reckless Dreamers don't turn out so fortunate when lurking under these high palms at dangerous hours after sunset. Who dared you? What is your business?'

'I'm new here,' I explain to defuse his doubts. 'Trying to find my bearings.'

'Newcomer—*huh-huh-huh-hoo*,' the monkey scorns. 'A rogue Dreamer frolicking in the jungle this long after sunset…when I happened to watch the last Dreamer depart from Awakening Coast just shy of an hour ago. So now you're lying to me as well, are *you-hoo-hoo-hoo*?'

'*I'm not!* I swear—I'm not!'

'You couldn't have just arrived,' the monkey spits stubbornly. 'New Dreamers arrive at sunrise.'

'I'm not every Dreamer – apparently.'

The monkey lowers himself gradually from the vine, the muscles in his tail working like iron pistons to hold him up. Bragging his strength, he manoeuvres effortlessly to get a better look at me. And with a graceful silkiness, he swings with his tail to another vine and stands there upright on his legs. His hands are firmly on his hips.

'Dreamers can have extremely devastating encounters in this jungle,' he yarns. 'It is not the jungle natives you should fear – the wild beasts, the poisonous plants and critters, or the mysterious monkeys with a knack for popping up from out of nowhere – but the other lost foreigners like yourself, who are scared and bewildered and will hunt and feast on other nomad Dreamers just to feed their starving panic.'

'People can seriously die in an imaginary jungle?' My playful responses are not appeasing this creature. I understand – the baboon wants to be spoken to like a man. He's clearly been misanalysing my motives from up in those treetops and now that my naivety has come clean, he doesn't have the patience for tourists. But I have my own suspicions. I'm just as vigilant of him as he is of me.

'Listen,' the monkey finally gives in, 'to tell the truth, the Dreamers won't eat you, but something will unless you stop clucking like a farmstead chicken. You really must be new around here if you're dumb enough to believe any of the nonsense I just spewed, so I'll give you the benefit of the doubt and let you off this once. But you do have to understand that it is not welcome for Dreamers to gallivant around the jungle alone – especially not at sun-fall.'

'If none of those pyjama-hippies are going to eat me, then why?'

'*Why?* Well, simply because every individual being on this world is cursed from the moment they first step foot on it. It's in the sand, my friend. The curse has been cast into the sand since millennia-*ago-ho-hoo-hoo-ho*.'

'By whom?'

'The Stellar Gods who form the constellations, who regulate the Dreamerverse and this world in it, Constellation Planet. They are the ones who pick and choose who they allow to enter this world. Not everyone or anything is allowed to materialise here. The Stellar Gods only select those who they credit great trust in. A Dreamer must be selected as an individual of broad cranial capacity, must lack the tendencies of narrow-mindedness, and must – most importantly of all – provide a powerful imagination. Without that, a human being would cease to exist here. A vivid imagination is paramount to getting around this lucid paradise.'

'So, are you saying that all Dreamers share the same mentality and, therefore, imagine this place to exist in the same image?'

'Not necessarily through sheer likemindedness. But all Dreamers have to devote their minds to this realm, share lucid determination and entirely block out the other world – their home of reality. Otherwise, their capacity to imagine will be limited and they will not be resilient enough to survive. To help them with this, the Memory Lane was put in place, which is the Void that separates the Dreamerverse and the real world…Where in the constellations have you been? Did the Steward not teach you all of this on your arrival to Awakening *Coa-ho-ho-ho-ho-st*? *That dippy, psychic quill!*' the monkey curses. He snatches a banana from a tree and, in frustration, breaks it in half and aggressively starts to gobble it up. 'Only incredibly powerful Dreamers can breach the Void between worlds – the Stellar Gods were once among this kind – and they are known as Night Dreamers. They are tales of myth and legend, of course, so no need to worry yourself about any of that.'

Little does this baboon know that he's probably talking to one of those 'legends' right now.

'And was it the Stellar Gods who made all these rules?' I trample over the subject of Night Dreamers.

'These are the ways of the Dreamerverse. The Stellar Gods are simply the delegated powers behind them and they are responsible for selecting the individuals who they believe will respect these laws and thrive under them.'

'Who are you? And how do you know so much about all this?'

'Palm Patrol, Lieutenant Bowe. I enforce the Laws of Constellation Planet.'

'So, will you be having to arrest me, officer?'

'Not on this occasion. You are obviously misguided. I believe a verbal warning is more or less enough to suffice your safety. As long as you return to the kingdom and stay clear of the jungle at night, you won't have to worry.'

Kingdom?

'Why did the Stellar Gods curse the sand?' This is glued to my mind above all

else.

'It was the only way they could retain their protection of this world. Decades ago, Constellation Planet was threatened by an impenetrable phenomenon.'

'Extra-terrestrials?' This doesn't ring a bell for the Lieutenant, so I translate it instead as: 'Foreigners?'

'It is unclear what this entity was defined as. But it was unbeatable then, as not even the Stellar Gods were capable of eradicating it entirely. When it came all those years ago, it flooded a massive burden upon the planet. And life here was never the same again.'

'It wasn't always like this here? Something awfully terrible tainted—*this place?*' I say, perplexed. I run my eyes around the dark, along the jungle floor, through the trunks, up to the canopies. Nothing seems out of place to me.

'Apparently. That's how the myth stands. I wasn't there to see it. But enough rumours have led me to believe that it did happen. That event left a terrible scar.'

'I couldn't imagine that. This place isn't far from perfection by the look of it.'

'Don't be so sure of your immediate impressions. Not so soon.'

Before I manage to digest this comment, I realise that his presence has vanished, like an unbearable weight being lifted from my lap. The only *impression* I'm collecting right now is that this jungle must be heaving with more of the likes of him: the so-called "Palm Patrol". I'm crossing my fingers that, hopefully, there won't be any others, because at this rate I'm starting to lose orchestration in, not only my sanity, but also my surprisingly vast imagination.

Are you finding it hard to believe now? The bird's voice is beginning to haunt. Wherever I go, the conversation on the beach follows and I'm leading his voice along on a chain, as shackling and as docile as it can be – the feathered steward on Awakening Coast is my fellow-prisoner upon this hazy exile. And I've let his voice loiter on a chain because it is reassuringly evocative. It increases the likelihood of plentiful thinking and questioning, and right now I'm learning that the *more* I think, the *more* my mind becomes logged and fogged and bogged with things that don't add-up or have been shone on me too soon to make any lucrative sense.

Perhaps, he's *my* conscience?

Maybe he's the source of all this confusion?

The voice of reason in the back of my head is supposed to be the thing relentlessly telling me to wake up. Instead, it uses its power to dig me into an even deeper hole.

I look back up at the stars, scattered in their explosive patterns. I've never been able to depict them at their best. Never at their greatest. Only ever imagined them in the stories, in the dreams. Well, I can picture them now, shining soundly. And they're bona fide.

For me to carry on going, they have to be.

The jungle is seeing to my arrival ceremoniously. Further in, the sounds have become louder and more distinguishable. On the tree-trunks, I've detected large families of crickets and beetles, chirping and ticking harmoniously. Around them, like a disciplined infestation, red ants scurry up and down the bark. Higher up, owls and small, hairy, prickly-eared creatures with gloating eyes, that make themselves at home in tiny holes and burrows in the trees. Their vision is wide, awake for acknowledging their surroundings. My passing seems to have never gone unnoticed and it's clearly unfamiliar with many of these creatures, being the only human mistaken enough to intrude on their turf.

On the ground is a different situation. Most of the noise, in fact, is rising from below, among the fallen branches and palm-leaves. Camouflaged frogs and lizards have begun to expose themselves, nestling within these cuttings or crawling out from beneath the shrubs and undergrowth. Whether they're poisonous or not is a question I have no means of asking. I hold firm and steer clear past them. Far away now, the ocean waves can still be heard whipping the shore – "*Awakening Coast*" was what the Palm Patroller had called the beach I'd materialised on.

Yet this new – and rather dusky – setting doesn't expel my curiosities, as there are many more of those to spare. Oh, yes. And the strongest seems to be roused by the stench that has led me in here. Without the edifying warning from the Palm Patroller at hand, I'd have most likely dashed back to the beach. Surprisingly, I haven't yet had the urge to turn around and retrace steps back to "safety", and no one else has shooed me off so far. *I'll go right ahead. It's only a dream after all.* Maybe such a liberty as the dream's lucidness is making me daft, or turning me into a blissfully intrusive tourist? Or perhaps I've been left to find out the perils of this jungle curse the hard way? Or, forbid, could it be that alluring smell of a burning fire that has battled with my wits and sense and brought me this deep – to a point where I can evidently see faint fumes drifting up from the distance and into the night sky? Somebody's at work down there and they're cooking up a late-night supper. Roasting meat. Sweating flesh, spitting and crisping at the skin.

I'm not only curious now. I'm also quite hungry.

I hunt after the trajectory of fumes, which are spiralling in my direction, wafting away from the source. With less regard to what's actually cooking, I start to think more of why somebody would be having a barbeque in the middle of a "prohibited jungle"? Is it something ritual, or religious? A rite to the Stellar Gods? Or am I being stereotypical? Perhaps, somebody's just famished, but has nowhere to go, let alone cook their meat? Nevertheless, it's leading the way to somewhere at least and exciting my taste buds at the same time.

I wonder whether whoever it is will see me coming and how I might react if they decide to attack me. If this Somebody has the nerve to put up a fire in the middle of a cursed jungle, then there'd be no reason for them not to put up a fight if a stranger invaded their space. In fact, a Somebody like this probably has all their work cut out like a chain of paper-men, perfectly rowed up into a little army. The Somebody just beyond this colony of tree-trunks and at the end of this trail of fumes must be able to put up – not only a fire or a fight – with anybody or thing that poses a threat or appears to be of an otherworldly nature. Like *me*! It is definitely a Some*body* and not a Some*thing*.

It ought to be a Somebody. I mean, I would be very surprised to find a Something that is able to start a fire and cook its own meat. Or, in this surreal situation, would I really be that surprised…?

I guess I've already accomplished losing the plot. Can tick that off the bucket list…mind you, at this rate, I don't think I'll have much time left to write one.

As the fumes stem thicker, I'm now swallowed by an unnatural fog, which engulfs my surroundings and winds around me. The smoke is relentlessly itching at my skin and attracting everything local almost magnetically with its heat. I've invited anxiety to be my last standing companion, now that the trivial urge of hunger has said farewell.

The sizzle and pop of flames at work protrudes from a foundation nearby. The sound tickles my eardrums and causes a plantation field of goosebumps to sprout, flourish and prickle on my arms and legs.

The smoke parts and subsides, opening my vision. I've come to a clearance somewhere at the heart of the jungle. Here, more than two-dozen trees have been severed at the stump and all that remain are several long trunks, laying around the empty ground, none having yet been put to use.

Instantly, my attention has been guided away from the scenery and I quickly realise that I'm in the presence of somebody else – and, yes, it's definitely a *Somebody.*

A girl, in fact.

Her back is turned. She's dressed in purple, flimsy pyjamas, which she's long since grown out of. Her hair is a rumpled cape of dark-red. And most distinctive of all are the gross slippers on her feet. By the looks, they must have been plump and fluffy in the past. But, since being here, it is apparent that stray, bristling branches have had their tear at them and wet sand has managed to seep in via holes in the soles; they are now flat, damp and shapeless. There's something very familiar about her height – that is a lot of person, particularly for a girl.

She obviously hasn't heard me coming.

At the moment, she's attending a large bonfire in the centre of the clearing. The flames bouncing off the branches, twigs and palm leaves spark life into the night, they battle with the stars and flourish in the subtle ocean-breeze. I suppose that is what has become of the timber. Then, I notice the axe lying beside a stump. The long, iron handle is rusted and the sharp edge of the axe itself is crusted with blood.

Perhaps, that's the only tool she managed to acquire? But where from? I can't imagine there being a local supermarket somewhere on this island, selling survival equipment to jungle trespassers.

On the stump is half a coconut shell. Inside the shell are what look like a variety of shrimp, clams and crayfish. *Tonight's supper?* I wonder. No, that definitely smells like meat cooking. Not fish. Most certainly meat.

She shifts, glancing uneasily to the right, as though she's heard movement close in that direction. For a moment, I believe I heard the same mild disturbance, before awkwardly remembering that I'm the one who's not meant to be here. Regardless of what it is that's caught her attention, I'm swift to react. I quickly jump behind one of the tree trunks surrounding the clearing.

When she'd glanced off to the side, I'd only caught a glimpse of her face. It had been shadowed, but I could see that her cheek was lean and rouged. Though thin from malnourishment, there's a blush in those cheeks, which makes me think: it isn't exactly cold out here. There may be a dusky bite, but it wouldn't cause a shiver. Nor is it disconcertingly hot. Something else is turning those cheeks sickly rubicund. A certain emotion. Embarrassment? Shame? Fear? It can't quite be placed.

I peer round at the clearing again to see that she's begun to prod the bonfire with a fat branch. This causes an array of sparks to fly and shrivel in the air. I strategically move towards the neighbouring tree. Cautious. She still doesn't know I'm here and I don't want to make the moment any more extraordinary than it already is. I'm trying to get a better look at the fire, because I'm curious to know what's cooking, before I announce my arrival (*if* I announce my arrival). Unless there's prey (or predators) running about in this jungle, it begs the question: meat from where exactly? And caught how? With an axe? Unlikely. If I'm going to grow some balls, speak up and greet her, I don't want my appearance to seem unwelcoming, like I'd intended to sneak up on her.

Tracking the garish view of the fire from behind the trunk, I observe. Currently alight, a bed of palm leaves has been built upon the flames that guzzle the timber and twigs beneath. I imagine this to be some makeshift grill at first. But then I see that the thing on the bed is too long to be a boar, or a chicken—and the thing is far too large for somebody to consume alone. In fact, it's nothing to be consumed at all...

The burning cadaver has blackened and bygone is the stage of melting. In some parts, the skin that is on the brink of disintegration still glows a fleshy golden brown, and in others the carbonised crisp is molten red, singeing in the ardour of the flames. Skeleton has started to show and it's pushing its way out through the now liquidised muscle. This body is strictly irretrievable. It is absorbing the scorching smoke, soaking up the heat, wilting perilously down to the very marrow of the bone. And the smell is unforgiving, revolting. Stirred with the banana-odour of the cooking palm leaves is the porky stink of hot, thawing flesh, and both are carried in the fumes that amass in the hollow clearing. I feel my stomach contracting when I realise what it is that's burning on this fierce beacon of death. The spoil of meat that has been set alight on this wakeless night is the charred body of a human being. An unrecognisable person. Cremated and historic, his or her remains have joined the atoms of the air. Up with them follow the soul and identity of a person who'd once lived who-knows-how-long-ago. Somebody knows: *She* knows.

The cherry-haired girl watches the bonfire. Her eyes glisten, almost as deadpan as the corpse burning before her. She can't retract herself from the sight. Her emotions are set on the departed – commissary, anger, triumph? I may never know how she feels, only that she was responsible for destroying the remains. For she knows more about this than anyone else. And, hopefully – for the corpse's own peace – she knows more than *it* did before its decease and the respects she now pays it. My heart rate is going again – another surreal encounter, which I will perhaps regret in moments to come. Is this really all an aberration? Am I imagining this?

The girl's arms are crossed. This is especially noticeable, since most of the light is being directed towards her front as the wind bullies the flames. Although her features are still fairly difficult to comprehend, I manage to identify a possible age. She's no younger than around eighteen. Or perhaps she could be older? She has the body and face of a young adolescent woman, whereas, on the other hand, she swanks an upright posture of self-awareness and maturity, with her legs assertively held apart and her neck cocking her head up towards the moon hidden in the canopies – a confident attitude wizened by experience. My view of her facial expression is extremely limited at the moment. From what I've seen of it, when she turned to the right, it had looked completely still, as though I'd caught her contemplating over a severely perseverant situation. The self-effacing scrutiny there is prevalent always, not affecting the interminable determination in her eyes. And those eyes of hers, they broadly disregard me, as well as all her other surroundings. She hasn't blinked once. Until now…

She notices me!

All of a sudden, elsewhere in this strange and hallucinated whirlwind of Who's, Where's, What's and When's, I feel something sharp and pointed press against the nape of my neck. Instantly, I realise that it isn't a loose branch, but the end of a blade—it's a seizing position. I dare not turn! Too tense to do anything, even gesture by raising my hands in surrender. I've never been a man to stand his own ground. And, believe me, a dream is no time or place to be *standing on grounds*, where you can never really be sure whether or not it is *actual* ground upon which you are standing.

'Don't move!' a piercing voice hisses from behind me. It's negligible whether the voice is male or female – I haven't come to that conclusion. 'Why are you here?'

'You tell me,' I challenge, quite bravely. 'You folk seem to know a lot more than I do right now. I'm the last guy you want to be asking questions.'

'Shut up, fool! Who are you? And who gave you permission to be about the jungle at this time of night?'

The point on the back of my neck is close to making an incision.

'You really don't want to kill me,' I say. 'You really don't *need* to kill me.'

'Forget *wants* and *needs*! If you don't give me a proper answer, I'll *have* to kill you! I've done it before and, trust me, killing is really addictive once you get the hang of it!'

'I'm new around here,' I alert. 'Can't you tell?'

'Camson, what have you found?' The girl from the bonfire has finally broken from her daze and turned, stepping away. 'Who have you found? Who is that?'

'Some stalker!' the voice behind me replies. 'Says he's a new Dreamer!'

'And what are you doing to him?'

'He's breaking the rules by coming out in the jungle at this time—!'

'No—answer my question, Camson! What are *you* doing?' she persists. Her arms are still crossed and she's looking blindly into the darkness, facing me, but most probably only looking at the tree in front of me.

Camson doesn't reply.

'Camson!' she shouts. 'Bring him out here. I want to take a look at him.'

Suddenly, there's a knackered sigh from behind me and I'm grasped at the shoulder. It's the rough grip of a man. His nails really dig in.

He guides me out from behind the trunk. I almost trip on a shrub before collapsing onto the flat grit of the clearing. The impact strikes my knees and I gasp in pain. I glance up slowly, trying not to be too capricious with my latest acquaintances. The girl stands over me, unmistakably now, her distance only a couple of inches. Her head is still vaguely silhouetted, but I can see that she has a tanned complexion that's lightly blemished and her hair is a lighter red now that the firelight is screaming at her back, but it's tangled with leaves and tiny twig-cuttings. But one thing is for sure and it's astonishing to say the least: she's undoubtedly recognisable. She has a face I've seen before. Steadfast, she approaches me, but not with the zeal of an old friend.

'Is it true? Are you new here?' she inquires.

'Yes,' I reply honestly. 'Do you have any idea where this place is?'

'This is no "place",' she states. 'We're surrounded by many places on this planet, many worlds expand beyond here. Don't be so naïve.'

'I thought the Dreamerverse was just one planet?' I say. 'I mean—that's what I was told—'

'A Dreamer-*verse*. It's not the same thing as a *world*. It's not the same as being back in the real world, back on Mankind's World. There are fewer limits here, less boundaries, because it's bigger and louder, so the laws have to stretch to apply to much vaster proportions.'

A memorable hand lands back on my shoulder. 'Which means that there's more harm we're allowed do to you.' Without hesitation, Camson lifts me and throws me aside violently. I land, bracingly, on my backside. I turn to find a little muscular man with dark, powerful features storming at me with a long sword. The blade has been generously polished to the degree where it houses my reflection like a mirror. It glimmers at the tip as he swings it down towards my neck.

I successfully roll over just in time to dodge the metal slicing past my collarbone, and it smacks the ground. Immediately, the girl jumps in and prises the weapon from his hand. She grips him by the collar of his pyjama-shirt and drags his forehead to her chin.

'Don't make an idiot of yourself again!' she snaps. 'We're not here to make enemies. Well, I'm certainly not. The sooner you realise that, the better. I sympathise with you, Cammy. You know I do and I want to do everything I can to help you. But we almost got banished from the Kingdom because of you and your fits! Now, I'm trusting you not to cause any further problems. Can you promise me that?'

Camson evaluates this shortly and rather pathetically, rolling his eyes and huffing in disgust. He shoots a look at me, which doesn't fail to read: *This is all your fault!* Then, he *really* says: 'You can rely on me.'

'Brilliant,' and with that, she releases him, tossing the sword off to one side. 'Get something to eat, Camson. Everyone can see you're hungry. Just keep in mind that we're still on the same side. For now, at least. Please.'

Ashamed, Camson strides away viciously, not looking back once.

The girl then pivots back to me. She offers me a hand. I take it. And with one hoist, I'm back up on my feet.

'I'm really sorry about him. We haven't eaten tonight. We needed the fire for other priorities,' she excuses hesitantly. 'He gets a little bit out of sorts when he's missed supper.'

'Is he usually this *hungry*?' I ask with a shade of humour, even though I mean to consider this seriously.

'*No, no*—He's just very, very…upset, I guess.'

She focuses on the fire again, numbly avoiding my attention.

'Why's that? Are you two lost? Because, if you are, then we may have a lot more in common than we think. It isn't at all difficult to misplace yourself out here.'

'It's not that,' she admits. Then she pauses and searches for Camson, who stands at the bonfire, holding a coconut shell in his palm and eating crayfish out of it. When she knows for certain that he's not listening, she continues. 'We lost somebody. *He* lost somebody. His son drowned in the water yesterday. This morning, we went fishing for whatever we could find of his boy. His son was stolen in a flash. We both saw it happen before our own eyes.'

'What did you see?'

'I wasn't on the scene at first,' she whispers. 'I arrived a little after it started. Camson got in a sticky situation in the water, said he could feel something tickling his feet from down-under. He presumed it was just crabs initially. Whatever it was got a lock on his legs and his son, Thuban, went to help him out. I soon arrived to support. We managed to get Camson out, but his son then got caught seconds after. It happened too fast. Before we knew it and before we could do anything, Thuban was dragged straight under. The force was too strong. All we could see after he'd gone was a round, glowing… *blue light* in the seafloor under the water. We've stuck with this idea that it was a beast that lurched up and snatched Thuban. But we don't know. Dreamers being kidnapped in the shallows of the ocean? Have you heard of that before? Is that even possible?'

'I guess anything is,' I say. 'I'm still not quite certain about anything yet.'

'I wish we'd been able to drag that poor kid out. Camson has been in a fowl mood, as you can see.'

I can't keep my eyes off the bonfire—I daren't say anything about it—I daren't even mention it…and yet, that's exactly what I do. 'Is that…is that not the kid's body?'

She looks to the bonfire and, suddenly, I notice that the paleness hasn't left her complexion and her innermost emotions seem to be solemn and reflective. She's stubborn, cautious not to say too much. When she does decide to finally answer, she hardly says anything at all.

'No.' Her voice is still nothing more than a deep whisper. Then, to call closure to the subject, she throws her head back and gazes up at the stars. More of them have appeared and their company is mellowing.

'Where did you come from?' I ask the girl. 'The same reality as me?'

'Of course. Mankind's World,' she replies. 'It only makes sense that a dimension as beautiful as this would never exist back home. It can't even compare. Here, the seas are too vast, the trees are too tall, the mountains are too distant, the sky is too clear and...*they* really do exist here.'

'I'm sorry? "*They*"?' I latch onto this.

'The stars,' she says. 'They exist here. Back home, it's always overcast with grey and gloom and the people below are bound by a glum notion. Even when you rarely do see the stars through a telescope at night or in the illustrated pages of a book, a fantasy, you never meet them for real. And such an experience can't fulfil your deepest curiosities. We wouldn't know what to expect and, believe, when it comes to the constellations. Some others wouldn't even know what to look for, let alone be aware of their existence at all. The few stars on Mankind's World never flirt with your imagination like these ones do.'

'You've got that right.'

'They used to say "*every cloud has a silver-lining*". Well, the clouds back home never do. Don't matter where you look for it. Reality doesn't really have a soft spot. Mankind's World finds simple things too hard to understand. But these embellishments sparkling in the sky are reassuring, aren't they? They're like souls, or even gods, looking down on everything, recognising the flaws among us and the human idiocy we permit and they're laughing at us, the stupid ones who believe everything we see and hear on the stage They created.'

'You're religious,' I jeer with a weak and disappointed huff.

'Nope. I'm just not sceptical like you,' the girl reasons.

I look at her with fascination. The paleness in her face has died and her cheeks are blushing again. She's still gazing up, not realising that she's become quite the glowing spectacle herself. But she doesn't care and that's what's so extravagantly modest about her. That's what I find appealingly different about her and it's something I can't quite understand or put into words.

'How's your life in the real world?' she asks. 'Do you live in the City?'

'Lived there all my life,' I respond.

'Really?' she takes this by surprise. 'I've only just moved there in the last couple of years. Arrived with the narrow-minded belief that the City's *supposed* to be the safest place in all Mankind's World. I'd beg to differ now.'

'What d'you mean? I like to think the City's still a safe place,' I argue defensively.

'After landing in this place? That's where you stand? Still persuaded that the City is a haven?' the girl winces. 'Are you really that vanilla?'

'Not vanilla. Just passionately preferential.'

'Oh—it's because you're *new* here. I guess that's why. Your head is still in the real world. You haven't acclimatised yet and still having trouble feeling your way around somewhere that doesn't have a mall on every corner, a restaurant in every crevasse, or someone that doesn't iron your clothes for you,' she deflates her puzzlement and rolls her eyes at me contemptuously.

'There's nothing wrong with preferring where I come from,' I respond. 'And there's nothing wrong with being a little homesick. Yeah? So what?'

'Some toffee-nosed City-boy you are, aren't you? You probably hate the feeling of sand on your feet, the stink of seaweed, the sight of monkeys, birds and insects. I bet you'd really love to wave your hometown flag right now. Wave it right in my face.'

'I don't see the problem with *preferring* a civilised and highly established urban jungle to this...*jungle*.'

'Do you know how much conflict the First Nation has caused back home? The damage it's constructed in Mankind's World? How much *they've* contributed to the rapid collapse of civilisations? Once that war ends, we'll all be at the mercy of the West.'

'Now you make us seem like the bad guys.'

'I'm not saying the West are the bad guys. I'm just saying they've started most of the conflict by prodding the East from day one.'

'The East loves to play victim!'

'We perhaps shouldn't talk too much about that, anyway,' her grainy voice has shrunk into another whisper. 'He's not too sharp on people from the West.' She discreetly gestures at Camson.

'Not too sharp at all, is he?' I remark. 'Not unless he's a got a sword in his hand, that is.'

'Seriously, no.'

'Why? What's wrong with him?'

'Can't you tell? He's an East veteran. Fought against the West fifteen years ago. Helped to kill over two hundred million of your men.'

'Disgruntled bastard,' I huff. 'I could smell something rotten in him a mile off.'

'I wouldn't tempt him. He doesn't have the time or the state of mind for the likes of you.'

'And where do you stand? In the middle? Because you're "*the likes of me*" too! Living it up in the City.'

'I don't advocate global harassment, so I don't support the West or the City. Keep me out of it.' She begins to move towards the fire, leaving me for dust. I follow urgently.

'Hey—I never said I was all for war!' I call after her. 'That isn't what I'm about! The City's reputation doesn't *define* me! I was just brought up there! I don't know anything else.'

But she doesn't turn. She's ditched her interest in me. My new face has lost its novelty for them both.

'When I said I had passion, I never meant it like that!' I explain to the red-haired girl. 'I'm not proud of where I'm from; I'm just comfortable there! Boy, you have one hell of a preconception when it comes to strangers.'

'I could say the same about you,' she mumbles.

'Okay—fine! Don't we all have perceptions afforded to us by our upbringing?' I say. 'But that's why we're here, isn't it? In this Dreamerverse? We share the same perception! Or, at least, similarities...don't we? So, there must be something we have in common. We're Dreamers and we're all on the same wavelength! I was told this place is one big perception!'

She spins on her heels to assert me abruptly. 'How many times do I need to remind you? This is not a "place"! We're not *placed* here! We just appear and it's as coincidental as that. And it will always be as coincidental as that!'

'Whoever said it was a coincidence? Why can't there be a logical reason behind this?' Nothing I say seems to attract her back to me. 'It isn't an accident why we're here! The Stellar...Gods...select us!'

'If this all really is as much of a "perception" as you say it is, then, why does it feel so natural? To me, this *feels* like it should be home! Not the City!' There's a rattle of condescendence in her tone, like she thinks she's the only one with any sagacity about her. 'I've never felt as much at home and at peace as I do here.'

I glance around, trying to soak up the atmosphere, trying to find her "*peace*"...

'In the jungle?' I utter, screwing my mouth a little.

She gives me a sarcastic glance and then marches off again, away from the bonfire this time. Not mentioning any more, as if she's muting herself for my own good. Have I not picked up on something she said? Am I actually dodging something important here? I don't intend to be ignorant—I'm just struggling to relate. But the glint in her eyes suggests other things. There's so much more that she wants to tell me, but she doesn't feel that we're familiar enough to do so. She's holding back.

I groan. 'What is it you have on me?' I register. 'Have I offended you?'

She doesn't stop. She's headed back for the fire again. I scurry after her still.

I catch sight of the sizzling corpse one more time. And suddenly, the pungency of sweating meat and browning bananas returns to me. 'What about the body?' I urge. 'Who was it? You have to tell me that much at least.'

The cherry-haired girl is helping herself to another coconut-shell – the other half of Camson's – waiting on another stump. Picking at the crayfish, she exchanges a knowing look with Camson. The pair have a very odd bond. The sort of relationship an under-aged female secretary would have with her older male boss – out of the hands and control of the gentleman's estranged wife. They have their secrets and, the majority of the time, it's not a matter of whether they're prepared to tell you those secrets, but rather, a matter of whether you're ready to hear them.

'None of your business,' the girl says. 'Besides, it doesn't matter anymore. *She* doesn't matter.'

I don't know if this is bad news or not. It's definitely a task to digest, as most of the minor and major details have been left to the imagination. The carbonising corpse belonged to a "*She*". They've told me just about the appropriate amount I need to know. For the time being.

And now she's bending over, placing the coconut back on the stump and sucking the fish off her fingers. She passes Camson, who's demented by the fire, and grabs the axe from beside an empty stump.

Then, without further ado, she begins to hack at one of the remaining trees surrounding the clearing.

I'm left standing awkwardly as I watch her do this. But to kill the tension, I open my big mouth again: 'So, what are the pair of you still doing out here? I thought Dreamers were supposed to leave at night? You know...Awakening Coast?'

Camson doesn't answer. He continues chewing the claw of a little lobster. I notice the embroidered patterns of long snake bodies coiled around the sleeves of his red robe. The girl drops the axe and turns slightly, half-facing me and obscurely profiled by the moonlight shredding through the canopies. 'We're not *supposed* to do anything. Our time in the Dreamerverse depends on our conscience. We leave when our minds are prepared to leave. Have you ever dreamt before? Oh, yeah—' she chuckles cheekily, 'I keep forgetting you think you're already living the dream in the City.' She hesitates before taking another swing at the tree. 'But wait...when did you arrive?'

'Just now. An hour and a bit ago. Why?'

'You arrived after sunset?' she turns fully now, discarding her censorship. Her arms are crossed again and she slants on her hips. Her reaction catches Camson's attention and he's sharply seduced away from the fire.

'Yeah,' I confirm. 'The bird mentioned there was something strange about people arriving at night. I just thought that was because sunset was the time Dreamers usually decided to leave. Why? What else does it mean?'

'That's what the damn bird told me!' she barks.

'You met the parrot too? Did you arrive after sunset?' I'm starting to become annoyed by my own dumb nosiness. *But I can't help it!*

'No! He said that was impossible! It never happens anymore.'

'Why?'

'You must be one special guy,' she says bluntly and huffs. 'Nobody arrives after sunset. It's rumoured that only the most capable Dreamers arrive at night.'

Capable? What does she mean by that?

'Capable? I don't follow...'

'It means that you must be a star pupil of the Stellar Gods, specially chosen, that's all,' she says, mockingly. She has trouble pronouncing the words: "specially chosen", trying to dress it up with a frilly imitation of a First Nation accent. Then she cherishes a small grin. She addresses Camson, who's placed his own coconut-shell back on a stump. 'He's from the City. Would you believe?' she sways the subject in this direction once more and towards Camson, as if it's a pending joke she can't wait to share with him.

'The City, huh?' Camson champions this as a chance to examine me. He sticks his nose out at my chest, trying to intimidate me from a foot below my chin, sizing me up shortly before giving his damning opinion. 'You should be used to fixing problems by now, shouldn't you, City Boy?'

'What are you talking about?' I spit back.

'As open as the battleground looks here in your dreams, our grievances haven't been left behind with the Conscious. Not with me around,' Camson warns.

The girl wades into the confrontation. 'What's your name?' she says to me, erratically.

'Oscar,' I tell her. Deliberately avoiding my surname. 'Yours?'

'Samuella,' she does the same: simply first name, no surname. She and I must definitely be *on the same wavelength.* I guess that's what occurs between City Folk. Well…that's the view I've believed for so long. Whereas, I don't understand a word Camson's on about – perhaps, he doesn't understand me either. He has a twisted attitude about him. An unbreakable grudge. Lost his son in a dream and now he seems to be blaming everything on the West again – even though he isn't in the West. Dummy. This doesn't look like the City, but to him it must be the equivalent to such a horror show when he's surrounded by City Folk in a cursed jungle. Those of the East are certainly not on the *same wavelength* as those in the West and the real world has nothing to do with this camp Fantasy Land. *The Stellar Gods must have made a mistake drawing the three of us together.*

'That's a memorable name,' I comment. 'Sort of.'

'Not as funny as yours,' Samuella manages to flip the topic back onto me again. 'There's a smidge that's familiar about you. Something I can't quite spot, but definitely something mutual there. I've seen a face like yours before.'

'I could say the same about you,' I match her confidence. It's an inkling of a notion, a memory. But any hint I can grasp from the real world is a gem for me right now. Nothing has changed in my mind. *I want to go home.*

'I don't recognise either of you. Thankfully.' Camson regards.

'Did you just come straight from the beach?' Samuella says to me.

'Yeah. Where'd you two come from?' I exchange.

'The Kingdom Palace—not long ago,' she says. 'But we were sent on an expedition, you see. Following an order given by the king.'

'An order from the king?' My ears perk up. 'To do what?'

'Well, we were about to be exiled from the Kingdom, once Camson and his mixed bag of emotions started spilling all over the place. But we were told that we could 'redeem' ourselves if we managed to catch and slay the beast. It is believed to be the same beast that kidnapped Thuban.'

'A beast? There's a beast?'

'Some call it a misconception, a humourless rumour, a mythic entity,' she lists. 'Others know it purely as the Drag-in.'

'I might have heard about that,' I murmur, waiting for her to elaborate. 'Something like it.'

'Once we find it and tie it down, we can return to the kingdom. But, until then, we're stuck out in this jungle, living off bite-sized fish.' She looks down at the ground temporarily, then throws her head back and searches, yet again, for the brightest sparkle in the sky. She sighs. 'What I'd give to stay here forever. Imagine that. It makes me reminisce living in the countryside. And I admit, at the time, my little countryside keep had been everything to me. I'd felt lonely and unambitious, but it was enough. On those old fields, I used to dream of the City and its twinkling, majestic lights and its bursting atmosphere of constant excitement.' I notice Camson grunting with mockery. He begins to hum to himself, blocking out her voice. But she continues, not taking any notice. 'Then…once I finally got there for myself, I started to realise how accustomed I'd been to the rural life. Because, in a place like the City, nobody cares where you sow your seeds. You're on your own and I quickly became aware of that. And I still hold regrets about leaving behind the old keep with all of the animals still grazing on the farm – the ones I'd eventually sold to another couple who'd conveniently arrived from the mountains. I never met the new owners, but thought of how happy they would be in my place. Indisputably satisfied. Surrounded by the pigs and the sheep and the cows and awake at the cry of the fowl. The flocks had been my only motivation. It was enough. They were all I needed to depend on, all I had…that and the stars. I do remember the stars. There weren't any more stars left when I got to the City, which is exactly why, when I look up at the sky now, I realise they are all the motivation I have left.'

'Why do you need motivation?' I query. 'If you don't mind me asking.'

'One needs it to be sure of what they choose to believe in life and the decisions they make. For me, having a role in the world that gets me out of bed in the morning and aligned in a routine like the stars in their constellations gives me faith in tomorrow. Albeit, a new purpose will guide me to a place I can call home again,' she answers.

I observe her as she moves for the fire again. She passes it and walks out through the first blockade of palm trees. She disappears amongst the shadows shortly, before returning to the clearing with a large wooden bucket filled with water. She launches the water at the flames, choking the fire. I then see that Camson has appeared with his own bucket. He spurts the fire, managing to kill it.

There is nothing remaining of the unrecognisable corpse. The burning aroma continues to drift up into the canopies and it's within this moment of smoky silence that I hear the last of the Sunset Birds flutter to their hideaways. The ocean waves in the distance are strikingly audible now that the fire has dissolved with the nightlife around it.

'Do you think the king will still be awake?' Camson's voice emerges from somewhere in the new darkness. 'Or will he have already departed by now?'

'He departs via his own private area of the beach, from what I understand. Doesn't like to be seen. So, it would be hard to tell,' Samuella replies from somewhere else. 'Why? Are you thinking what I'm thinking?'

'We ought to introduce him to the king.'

Night, warm and black, is like the cape of a blanket, tucking the world around us. The sound of the ocean fades ever further away the deeper we trek through the jungle and the birds are absent from the palms above. Although that cooked-banana smell has abandoned us, the balminess of smoky entrails picks at my goosebumps.

Camson knows his way through the jungle in the dark. Every narrow track and splitting turn is memorable for him, which gives the impression that he's been exiled out here for a while and his comfort with it is his refusal to go home. Or – according to Samuella's logic – his conscience isn't yet ready to return to the beach. Now I realise that he isn't leading the way alone. The stars are responsible for this. Marked in their inviolable patterns between the palmtops, they retrace us along a jagged trail. Wherever they can be seen, we should be safe.

'So, what is this Kingdom? I thought this was all there was: a jungle, deserted tropical landscapes and telepathic wildlife. It doesn't seem like a very civilised planet, closer to a desolate island,' I address Samuella, who strides beside me.

'To a Dreamer who's only just woken, that's how it seems. But I wouldn't stress thinking too philosophically about this world and the laws of its universe – it's a smidge too sophisticated for our weeny human minds to understand,' she replies. 'Its appearance responds to whatever our conscience is thinking. What we imagine is what we see, remember? So, keep it simple and you shouldn't run into too much trouble.'

'Don't you want to find any reason behind that? Any meaning as to why you were selected to arrive here above anyone else in the real world?'

Finding it hard to believe still? The steward's voice is ringing in my ears again.

'Not for much longer!' I hiss at it. 'I'm getting to the bottom of this Dreamerverse-place, before getting the hell out—!'

Samuella shoots me a look of wild concern. And yet, me talking to myself doesn't seem to bother Camson as much. Regardless of whether he heard it or not, he's pretty good at pretending to 'lead the way'.

'What's wrong?' Samuella says, nervous.

'Nothing. Just…just something I forgot,' I lie.

'What did you forget?'

'I forgot to switch the light off in the bathroom before I fell asleep. That's all.'

'Rubbish,' she debunks, grinning. 'It's impossible to remember anything so minor about the real world here.'

'Oh…is it?' There I go again – another dim blunder from the unpalatable novice.

'There's the mental void that divides both worlds. We call it the Memory Lane. And, because it's there, we can't remember anything vague about here in the real world and, vice versa, we can't remember anything indistinct about the real world while we're here. The only exceptions are the big memories, the ones that punch enough out of the Void for us to see them. This world may be an open battleground – as Cammy likes to put it to you – but it still has its laws and those laws have to be regulated.' Then I remember all the banana cakes hovering about my mind – *aren't they small, and vague, and indistinct? Kind of. So, how can I remember that?*

'By "vague", what do you mean?' I mention. 'Would my bathroom light switch be subject to this Memory Lane?'

'If you were honestly remembering a *light switch* in a dream and not just making things up to hide your weirdness, then, yes, you'd be out of your mind. Besides, it's only the big and obvious things we can remember between worlds. People have faces and they also have names. But a face will always be stronger than a name.'

'The Laws of the Dreamerverse?' I suggest. 'The Stellar Gods really couldn't hold themselves back with that one, could they.'

'Not one bit. But, as a rule, it's a necessary one! Think about it! If we were able to remember things inter-worldly, it would be classified as a sixth-sense. Humans are limited to their senses. We only gather five from birth. Developing a sixth would be physically and mentally impossible.'

'How do you know all this?'

'We've been here a while, haven't we, Cammy?' she admits. 'And I've read into these subjects a lot back in Mankind's World.'

'We all know you have a load of time for that,' Camson notes.

'Yeah—of course…I still make time to read those science articles…when I'm not working my butt off.' Her cheeks regain some colour suddenly and start to fluoresce red. She's embarrassed by this remark. *Maybe she doesn't want to be known as somebody who has a lot of time on her hands?* I try to consider. *But, what's wrong with not being a busybody from time to time? Nobody wants their body to be busy* ***all the time.***

'There's nothing wrong with that,' I say, ignoring Camson's scowl targeted at me.

'You're only a rural girl once,' she declares. 'Especially since nobody has to do anything in the City anymore. Everything's done for them. I consider myself one of the few capable of lifting a finger. Sometimes I have to agree with the fact that the West is lazy. City sounds a lot like settee.'

Camson giggles. 'You can say that again.'

'Are you only grovelling to him because he's carrying the sword?' I look to the long, glimmering blade in Camson's right hand.

Samuella smiles. 'Believe me, a goldfish wouldn't be afraid of this guy. He doesn't even know how to fan a palm-leaf, let alone wield a sword. Did I put enough emphasis on the title "war veteran"?'

'Well, hold on—' Camson tries to slice his way in and save himself some dignity.

'I've seen you attempting to fend off smidgy fireflies with ginormous palm-leaves. Don't try it on with me, Cammy,' Samuella bellows, smiling a little as if she's finally pinned one over the smug little man.

An awkward hiatus in conversation suddenly inserts itself between my captors, with me being the main subject of such verbal caution, sandwiched in the middle. Samuella's intense presence against my back doesn't let up; she's a heavy breather. I steal this silence as a chance to scrutinise Camson from behind. To say that he's five feet off the ground would be a euphemism. Over his pyjamas, he wears a long, red, silk robe. Two embroidered snakes woven into either sleeve boast their heads on his cuffs, their fangs resting just under his wrists. His hair is firmly packed into a field of greasy perm. And on his feet is a pair of opulent leather slippers.

I mean, look at the amount of Balm cementing this dwarf's hair! A head louse would be skidding between an ice-rink and a marble ballroom under that hairline. East Folk, I think disgustedly. Always blaming the West for their excessive greed, and their plunder, and for their horrendous famines, when they're just as equally to blame—if not more!

It would help if they all just stopped fighting, wouldn't it? This voice is new. It doesn't sound like the parrot; this isn't Stewart's telepathy flapping in my head again. It's a new personality that rises from out of the boggiest pits of my brain.

Well, we all know that's not going to happen any time soon, I orate in the theatre of my skull. I peel the subconscious conversation onwards, keen to garner another response from the new lodger in my thoughts.

One day it's going to get out of hand. And then we'll all be sorry. I finally recognise the nature of the voice. With its light and airy echo, I know that the person speaking to me is not here to taunt me, only to advise. I smile warmly.

Before we can better acquaint, however, a flurry of distortion hovers over our surroundings, contaminating the atmosphere, and it suddenly causes everything to seem somewhat darker. Camson freezes in his tracks ahead of us. His head has shifted abnormally in a way that his neck almost arches in a curve and his hand automatically places itself on the handle of his sword. Warrior's instinct. Meanwhile, Samuella has gone for my arm. She grips it tightly, sending spurts of goosebumps up my elbow and forearm. I don't move.

We've all stopped.

High up in the canopies, the last of the fleeing birds have fluttered away in alarm. Once they're gone, it's only us who remain in anticipation.

Nobody says a word. Nobody has anything to say aloud right now. A frosty breeze overwhelms us, and a sibling to this chill is the daunting mist that starts to approach from out of the darkness. Thick fumes of fog and steam fasten around us, weaving in and out of the gaps. I'm short of breath. And this breathless feeling rapidly worsens into choking.

Only now does Camson draw the blade and he swings it out before himself. Then hurries off into the mist, leaving Samuella and me behind.

'What's happening?' I manage. 'What's going on?'

'It found us,' she says quietly, as if not to provoke any more chaos than there already is. 'It was too easy a hunt! The sands are too shallow! The Stellar Gods' curse can't protect us here! It's found us!'

'What is it?' I tremor. '*Tell me—!*'

'Run! For God's Sake! Run!'

Without question. I dash. Drifting seconds fleet into relics of the ancient past. Winding acid industrialises my stomach and a flush of heat has engulfed my head. I'm running so fast that I can't even feel my feet touch the ground. The ground doesn't exist. There's nothing other than a thick mist rising over my knees and ascending taller up my thighs and waist. The sight ahead is limited, clouded. Trees and bursting-roots seem to be out of the question – I haven't crashed into one yet, so I can only imagine that they no longer exist in this region of the jungle. Voices are everywhere. Different whispers are filling my ears. The whispers of ghosts, strangers and anonymous auras. Ethereal taunts so volatile they have become somatic. Something is trying to *speak* to me, *call* to me, using a million anonymous voices and personas to do so.

'*I can follow you home...I will follow you home...even when there is no home for you to go to...I will always follow you home...*'

The only way to escape the harmonic haunting in close proximity has to be to ignore the voices, close off their alluring insights. It's hard to achieve, but I try it. I think of the parrot on the beach and I think of the banana cakes and I think of my mother and I think of hom—

'*Run! For God's Sake! Run!*' Samuella's voice is resonant through the mist. Hearing the echoing of her words, stolen and resounded by the vapour and artificially reconstructed like the imitations of a puppeteer, knocks me off balance. My lungs can't handle the stress of making up for the shortage of oxygen. The smoke is blocking it out, gagging me. Whatever this mist is, or whatever form this creature appears to have taken, it isn't at all compatible with human beings. Dreamerverse or not, anatomy still applies.

'It found us...It was too easy a hunt...Sands are too shallow...Stellar Gods' curse...can't protect us...It's found us!'

I trip on something and fall instantly to the hard and unsympathetic ground. The moment I land, my back collides with the monster-of-a-root that I lost my footing under. I screech in agony and splutter helplessly at the same time. *Is that what tripping on a root feels like? Is that what a* ***tree root*** *looks like? Is that what a* ***palm tree*** *looks like from underneath?* It seems stupid, but this new world couldn't feel any more outlandish than it does right at this moment. The jungle welters into a blur. Soreness in my eyes has made its debut. My sockets feel fiery. I want to bounce up to thoroughly rub them, but I can't. My back is bruised, in conjunction with something else that's pressing my shoulders to the ground, preventing me from moving. *A pair of invisible hands, maybe? Strong, invisible hands.* I don't bother opening my eyes to see; I'm too afraid and my body has already slipped into a gruelling struggle of distressing spasms. More mist fills my eyes, ears and mouth, forcing the upper body pain to become immensely unbearable. Though, in a coexisting mind-set (perhaps while fast asleep in another reality entirely), I am numbly transfixed by the force of those invisible fingers that render my uncompetitive body lingering like a haemophiliac upon a crucifix. But, here in the Dreamerverse, the experience could not be more tangible. The danger could not be more stifling. I caw. I curse. I cry. I do everything I possibly can to break free. But...

'Don't struggle...Don't be angry...' a calm voice pirouettes in the air above me. *'...You're safe, and you're alive, and that's all that matters...'*

This calling is also very familiar. It isn't Samuella. Nor is it like any of the other souls slaving in the mist. This voice is original and boomingly virile. But it strikes a personal note, just like how I recognised Stewart's and the other when they'd spoke in my head earlier.

'...You're safe, and you're alive, and that's all that matters...'

I'm dreary. The fire in my stomach is dying and so is the heat-flush in my sinuses. Instead, my body is getting colder and colder. There's a vicious face in the mist. Something ferocious. The cruel charm in its eyes reduces the flame in my heart to a flicker, as they pop into view above me. It has championed the very soul of the jungle. The anger and the threat and the terror are unhidden in its glowing, silver gaze. And it's looking straight at me. A beast made entirely of smoke. The beast's mouth drops open, revealing rows of long, piercing teeth. Preying on me, the creature doesn't pounce instantly. I dread the instant it does.

In the short distance behind it, the small figure of a man stands broadly and unafraid. His red robe billowing in the riotous wind. The long blade in his hand shines in the dark, illuminating a patch of glimmering light in the mist. He doesn't move either. It isn't clear whether this is because the creature hasn't yet noticed him and he's choosing his moment to take action wisely or because he wishes to do nothing at all. I would shout to him in the hope for help, but I know well that he wouldn't for love or reward. His intentions aren't to save me, his enemy, but to save himself. And this is where the true conflict stands, where the line is drawn.

The figure turns casually, as if taking no notice of my mercy, and leaves. Then, without a gasp left to spare, the head of the beast lunges down and devours me…

The phase of horror has fled when my eyes reopen. The terrible apparition has departed. The smoke has fully receded. And I'm lying on my back again; only, this time there is no monstrous root beneath my spine. Instead, a cluster of fallen palm-leaves form a bed around me. Not exactly my *brand new mattress*, but definitely something creditable all the same. I realise that I'm not facing the night-sky directly, as my head is being cocked up at a right angle by something large and round. I immediately think of *a fruit…a round fruit…a coconut?*

I hadn't passed out, but only been a detainee to delirium. Must still be alive. For *some reason*, I must be alive. Spared by that beast. With the jungle night still everywhere, blotting out my surroundings as thickly as the aggressive smoke had, the thorny motions of ants, woodlice and centipedes under my skin and the infinitesimal mob of moths and mosquitos twirling around my head, remind me that I'm still listening uninterruptedly to the static-buzz of silence, a sonic pool for the loud heaves of a healthy pair of lungs. I am surprised how capable I am of captaining my breathing again.

After several blinks of reassurance, my sight develops the obscure figure sitting on an enormous boulder, a couple of metres in front of me. This time it isn't the little man who'd willingly abandoned me during my final few moments of survival. It's the young lady with redolently long red hair. She now possesses the blade that the little man had wielded. The blade is clean, advertising not a single stain or scratch. Since dragging my body up from the bed of palm leaves, my eyesight has wired-in fully and I can now make out her calm and soporific expression.

'Thought it would be best to wait until you woke up,' she says, 'before we continued travelling. I couldn't imagine Camson or me carrying you anywhere. You're quite a big fellow and you'd slow us down.'

'I thought it killed me? The thing ate me?' I squeak. 'But, I'm—I'm—'

'You're breathing now, aren't you? Without any serious injuries?' she examines briefly.

'Yeah.'

'Well, that's that bridge crossed and we're good to go! Would you mind getting up now? Because we've got a meeting at the Kingdom Palace and you're our only key to getting back in the house of the king. I don't think he'd forgive us it if we were late, let alone if we never thought to show up with *you* at all, Night Dreamer.'

'No, no, no!' I cry. 'I need answers! Long, complicated, understandable, substantial...answers! I need them now! Before we go on! Before I go anywhere with either of you! Also, I'd like to have a chat with Camson! That square-faced twit left me for dead when that creature burst out of thin air and cornered me!'

'I can explain things once we get going. *Where* we're going will be explained once we *get* going.' She slides down the boulder and lands like a feline. She's up on her feet now, swinging the sword around loosely and ineptly. 'Talking of Camson...*Caaam—Caaammy!*'

A distant voice arrives in response to this calling, from somewhere high up. 'Is he awake yet?'

'Yeah! Let's get going!' Samuella demands.

Camson returns. He drops down from some branches above and lands between us, carrying a net of various fruit he's found. 'About time you decided to come around. We've been hanging about for hours, waiting for you to return to the Land of the Dormant. Look! You've even given me time to tie a net and go grocery shopping!'

Magically, and to everyone's astonishment, I manage to flare up onto my feet. Samuella's impressed and Camson suddenly gets defensive, flinching in shock before squatting steadily. Unfortunately, this action-sequence doesn't last—I reach for my back, scouring in pain.

'Would you like to say something?' Camson mocks. Though his face is sombre, settling a little from his brief unease. His cocksure attitude is nauseating.

'Why did you leave me?' I hiss at him. 'When I obviously needed someone's help, why did you leave me there? You were happy to watch that thing tear me apart?'

Camson liberates a callous snigger from his mask of seriousness. 'It's an awkward life we live in, isn't it? You can't stand by anyone, especially when they're about to shake hands with death. If you had even half a clue of what it was really like out on the battlefield – a battlefield that I used to call my home for years – you wouldn't be thanking me for standing-by. If I was killed because I offered *you* sympathy, Samuella wouldn't have stood a chance against that monster, that *Living Smoke*, not alone. Combat is all about numbers – three is better than two, two is more flattering than one, and one is just not an option – *because that's what fighting is all about*. But, sometimes *one* must be sacrificed, so that the other two are at least left with a chance of survival. Kid, from experience, I know what it's like to work it out in a situation like that. The men who you used to call family…all of them dying in front of you, and meanwhile you need to decide whether to save them or save yourself. Most men in my position don't even need to make that decision; it's already been made. You stick by your guns, follow orders and do as you've been told. Afterwards, you start to wonder whether they'd do the same for you, if anybody would be willing to save you and risk their own life for the success of a campaign.

'Now, before you point your finger at me, think to yourself: would I really spare the soul to save a doormat like *you*, if I hadn't even the power to save those I loved most?'

'I'm sorry about your son,' I admit. 'But that's all I'm sorry for. You and I are from completely different worlds and I understand that fully. But I think you need to realise that this world belongs to neither of us. And, one way or another, we're going to need to somehow come to terms in No Man's Land. Which means that you can't be leaving me to get slaughtered by a massive carnivorous beast. Not if there are only three of us. What is the good in there only being two of you? You clearly need all the help you can get. The economy in this is a lot less than in the wars you've fought back home on Mankind's World. There are no other soldiers here. Only three relatively powerless strangers who met by chance and one extremely powerful entity that doesn't even need to take a chance to kill us all. On *this* battlefield, I'm as useful to you as you are to me. It won't do trying to oust me before letting me show what I can offer. In order to get at this thing, I'm afraid we're going to need to do it together.'

Camson hasn't tried to consider this much yet, but he's definitely thinking about something, reading my eyes with his own beady little pupils. 'Didn't say you weren't "useful",' is all he says, shaking with glee. 'You've proven to be a reliable source of bait.'

'So, you're going to help us slay it?' Samuella has only honed in on that one small (and very unlikely) detail.

I turn to her. 'As soon as you tell me more about what we're dealing with and what's at stake here.'

She's smiling now. I can feel the power of her hope uplifting me from within. We're momentarily on the same page again. And somewhere along the line, Camson has been dropped off at nursery and left behind.

Suddenly and without announcement, a loud crashing noise enters the jungle. The crunch of barged tree trunks and leaves being puffed into the air and out of the way has emerged from out of nowhere. Impossible uproar.

There are no more birds left to flee, no insects left to mute, nor any *Living Smoke* left to rip through. So this very placid interval is the perfect time to rouse undisturbed commotion – *it has chosen well.* And this is exactly what these intruders intend to impose. Attention. New light materialises from between the tree trunks. A large object on wheels follows through, squealing and wobbling erratically to a nervous brake. On either side of the vehicle's front are two small fire torches, sticking out wide and exposing the space ahead clearly enough for the driver to realise that he doesn't need to run us over. The vehicle is round and built of wood. Not newly carved, freshly varnished wood, but rotting and damp timber. This vessel has been around the jungle a time too many and it's not too obvious how long – *Very Long* would be my best and only guess. Then, once the wooden carriage has fully rattled to a close stop, two creatures suddenly flash into view at the very front of it, as if revealed from beneath a magician's vanishing curtain. Two huge, sparkling lizards have hauled the carriage, each of them spattering saliva they find difficult to hold in their wet mouths with long, flapping tongues. I squint and twist my head a little, struggling to look at the frightening creatures and the glaring lights face-on, and notice that these overgrown reptiles are salamanders. I've seen them in archived wildlife documentaries – notably slim and flat-headed. These have smooth scaly skins are patterned with a glossy dark-red and orange blend. The lizards are bound to the front of the carriage by the chains locked around their necks.

A tiny block of steps rolls down from either side of the carriage like that of a playground climbing-frame, allowing descent from the carriage doors. Four monkeys in fine armour scurry out urgently. Palm Patrollers wearing round helmets, grilled-chest-plates and massive circular shields attached to their backs. Three wield long, bulky swords and the fourth carries a bow – crossed over it are a duo of arrows, ready to fire immediately (at multiple targets).

The warrior with the steadied-bow runs out before the others. He lifts the weapon. His first direct target is me. Both arrows are aimed at my torso.

Samuella suddenly springs out ahead of me, blocking the Patroller's vision with her sword. She slants the edge of the blade to line it up horizontally with both of his eyes, daring his next move. The warrior freezes, contemplating his actions wisely. He glances at me, then back at the livid Babe With The Blade.

'Are you the ones All Eyes banished?' the warrior questions like it's an open query to everyone not dressed in armour – even the mealworms in the trees and the ants in the sand can answer if they so wish.

Who's All Eyes? I wonder.

'Oh, come on! You're better than this!' Samuella says feistily. 'Would you be expecting to find any other brazen mugs hanging about out here? Anyone aimlessly lolling about in a *cursed* jungle, on a *vastly* uncharted planet, in the *middle* of the night would have to be doddering on lunacy. You can go and tell All Eyes that we need a smidge more time or we won't be playing this game any longer.'

The warrior, humiliated, lowers his weapon slowly. He then wags his hand to the others behind him, ordering them to do the same.

'He's been inferring that you should return with news,' the warrior says.

'Oh, really?' Samuella chortles hysterically. 'Already?'

'Well, tell him that the monster isn't dead yet. It's still having trouble coming and going, but we know it's getting stronger and more capable of breaching the Void the more we dwindle out here, talking to tree-swingers,' Camson insults.

'An intellectual monster? One that can actually learn and utilise the benefits of its abilities?' the warrior with the bow and arrows elaborates interestedly. '*Who-hoo-who*ever said you were required to *wuh-wuh-wait* for it anyway? You were given the task to expel the beast from the jungle before sunset! Only then would you be allowed back into the king*dom-hom-hom-hom*.'

'Well, we did...' The lie escapes Samuella's lips before she can do anything about it and we've all strapped in for the outcome of her sentence, but it never arrives. Needless to say, I don't entirely trust this primate's ability to shoot arrows—let alone *two spearheads in tandem*—so, in my head, my urgency to Samuella pleads: *Spit it out! Spit it out! Spit it out!*

'Did we?' Camson spins his own wheel of uncertainty.

Meanwhile, the warrior has shot Samuella with, not an arrow, but an undertone of his disapproval, reading: *Where is it then, Miss Queen of the Dumb-Dumbs?*

'...We almost did...' she finally clarifies. 'But it was too quick to judge *how* successful we were! We might have wounded it. We definitely scared it off—well, I did—and, like Camson said, it was too intelligent! The creature, it exhales this...this weird condensation, a smoke that fills the air and suffocates its prey. We couldn't breathe! We were dying the very moment it came into contact with us! We couldn't confront it in that condition! Using the smoke to its advantage, it manages to hunt with it, disorienting its victim and overpowering them through contaminating the air!'

'*Living Smoke*,' Camson reiterates.

'Are you suggesting that the beast has no lungs of any sort? It doesn't need to breathe—thence, cannot truly be alive?' the warrior asks.

'I'm not sure whether it breathes or not,' Camson theorises. 'With that substance filling the air, I couldn't imagine *anything* being capable of breathing.'

'From the way it came, it didn't even seem to have taken complete form yet,' Samuella adds. 'It was just an entity, a mist that fell upon us like a freak storm in a random section of the jungle. It hadn't followed us. There was no build-up. We didn't anticipate its arrival at all – it just happened.'

'Perhaps, it's immune to its own condensation,' I remark – then laugh at what I'm really thinking: I mean, being immune to something it produces wouldn't be rocket science, would it?

'Tell the king that we need more time and more men,' Camson demands. 'The task of defending this jungle is too arduous for three strangers.'

The Patroller chuckles at this. 'I think you are forgetting the definition of a punishment, my friend. You were banished from the kingdom for good reason by His Majesty, so you will serve as he instructs you to serve.'

This infuriates Camson in several ways – a few of those ways seem to be more personal than I can imagine; Samuella and Camson have never met these particular monkeys before, but they're used to encountering Palm Patrollers. I can see the strain in Camson's balling fists and the tension in his souring face.

'That was the first time we'd seen the thing in a while,' Samuella swears. 'Before then, it was only ever glimpses we witnessed. We never caught sight of its face. Tonight was the first time any of us saw as much as a glimpse of its body! It was terrifying—the kind of devil nightmares must be made of. Of course, if I knew what the thing looked like in the face, in the eyes, I could draw you a picture of some shape or form.'

'I saw the creature's face,' I declare, timidly.

Suddenly, everyone's eyes are on me. *It's like being on stage back at the Academy, when the Christmas performance was in full-swing and one little boy needed to recite a monologue from an archaic Trivium Testament – he forgot his words and, within the first two lines, the entire audience were shielding themselves from the horrific shower of projectile vomit. And sometime after that, he would keep remembering the bitter taste of those verses and the tickle of them on his tongue would always make him gag.* However, this glimmering reminiscence of the real world is forced from the teetering focus of my thoughts and made difficult for me to remember – as if a pair of scissors are at work through the centre of my brain, parting the vague memories from what I'm currently thinking – and, as easily as I plucked it out of my mind, I forget I even imagined it.

'You did?' Samuella utters this. 'The face?'

'Maybe I *should* have intervened,' Camson regrets, tearing out a feeble simper.

'It definitely looked like a dragon, like you mentioned. It was round and maned and had teeth alone that were bigger than me,' I try to describe it to them in as much detail as I can muster.

'Did it breathe well in the smoke?' the idiotic Patroller with the aching trigger finger asks.

'Well, how the hell am I supposed to know that? I guess so. It managed to speak to me. Does that confirm to you whether it could breathe or not?'

'IT SPOKE TO YOU?' They all shout this at once, causing me to leap backwards and fumble on my feet.

'Just whispers and echoes in the smoke. That's all I really heard,' I clarify.

'It exhales toxic fumes and now it can speak to people?' the warrior shakes his head dizzily. 'Why—that sounds more frightening than the king permitted our imaginations to believe.'

'Tell me more! Tell me more! What did it say? Could you understand it?' the Patroller is eager with excitement.

'I can't remember!' I bellow. 'It said something like…something like: "*You're safe…You're safe…and you're alive and that's…all that matters*".'

Nobody can process any sense behind these phrases; they all just gawk at one another, struck by the idea that the beast could speak at all.

'I never heard it say that to me,' Camson objects.

'It could just be what Oscar heard,' Samuella responds. 'It only spoke to Oscar.'

'The really strange thing is that I could recognise those words anywhere,' I tell them. 'I've heard them before. Stolen from someone in my past, a long time ago. But I just can't remember exactly where I've heard them and who they originally belonged to.'

'Well, I think we should discuss this in the presence of His Majesty, as he has requested all the latest information based on this mission,' the commanding Patroller who threatened to arrow me instructs. 'For the safety of the kingdom and the protection of Constellation Planet, he feels it is his sharpest priority to acquire anything jarringly new on the *Beast of Living Smoke* you describe. After all, he is the omniscient All Eyes.'

'Who summoned you?' Samuella asks the warrior, slightly suspicious.

'We are the Bellator, a contingent of the Palm Patrol who act as the king's leading military force. We initiate ourselves mostly. But we abide to the king's orders when they're declared. On this occasion we were formally requested by the king "*to collect three Dreamers wandering in the Jungles of Camelopardalis and escort them to the Kingdom Palace*".'

'And yet you were still keen to shoot us when you showed up?' Camson argues.

'*And* you told us we couldn't return until the beast was deterred from the island?' Samuella snaps. 'You lied!'

'Precautions, my Fellow Dreamer,' the Bellator Leader with the bow and arrows upholds his dignity. 'I had to be sure it was the right group of Dreamers I was addressing. The reason I didn't tell you about your relief from exile in our introduction was also a part of the test. You have successfully proven yourselves as the Dreamers tasked by All Eyes.'

'But we've been banished from the kingdom. Ejected by His Majesty,' Camson says. 'What have we done to earn our acceptance back?'

'On this occasion, His Kind Highness has requested your company with the news of a New Dreamer present within your group. The newcomer is another to arrive after sunset.'

Another to arrive after sunset? This statement gets me thinking. Am I really the only Night Dreamer—could there be others? Might I not be so "special" after all?

'Excuse my cursed curiosities,' the Bellator Leader says, 'but which of the three of you was it who recently arrived after sunset?'

'I did,' I say quietly, as if owning up to a remorseful crime.

A stunned look fades over the warrior's face – which I've begun to notice is quite young and without sign of a single battle scar. This cute look of inexperience spreads between the other warriors.

'Don't look so surprised!' Samuella snaps at the warriors in my defence.

'Why, I have never been so privileged…' the young warrior drops his bow, allowing the two arrows to roll onto the ground, into the reeds and grass. 'I mean…apologies…' He scratches his elbow, then goes to collect his weapon and ammo from the ground pathetically. His eyes are in a daze and he's not taking them off me.

'Do you have any respect at all?' Samuella's prepared to take advantage of the Patroller's vulnerability, telling him all the harsh, ballsy things I wish she wouldn't. Only, I don't think she's doing it on my behalf. Like Camson, a subtle jealousy at the awe and attention I'm receiving has crept into her tone and I'm the only person noticing it. It's at an instance like this when I start to remember that we're not as friendly as I thought we were.

Then it all starts to become clearer. The Bellator's slip of the tongue: *Another to arrive after sunset*, Samuella's subtle envy…

'You arrived after sunset too, didn't you?' I whisper to her.

'Shut up!' she hisses at me and then whispers back: 'I didn't come to this world for a reputation. I was put here so I could get away from that rancid reality I've been forced to endure all my life. The reality you're so quick to defend, City Boy. I won't let you mess up my only opportunity in this world.'

'Yes, he did arrive after sundown! There you go! Lock him up! Do what you want with the boy?' Camson says straightly. 'To be honest, he never really fit in with us to begin with. Bit of a third wheel, a loose cog. You can have him.'

The East Man repulses me. I want to strangle the disloyal buffoon until his eyes burst from their sockets. However, I'm sensible enough to catalogue the muscular men with swords and arrows and the wicked potential of a hormonal redhead, wielding a sword that is far too big for her.

'Don't listen to him,' Samuella tells the warriors. 'Camson had the unfortunate event of losing his son – and his appetite – not long ago, so he's garbling all kinds of nonsense. Don't try anything funny with him either, because he's grieving and isn't giving into what most of us like to call "optimism". And yes, our friend, Oscar, *did* arrive during the sundown hours. *So what?* Dreamers who wake at night aren't criminals! They can't help it! They don't make that decision! Such a phenomenon is nothing to get excited about – we all have our secrets.'

I respect her tenacity not to taint or obscure the Bellator's perception of me (unlike the ugly, mean-spirited East Man), but I'm getting a vibe that she's trying her hardest not to let a secret of her own slip, rather than defending me from slipping into another naïve rookie mistake. Okay, the warriors now know that I'm the Night Dreamer, although that doesn't appear to bother Samuella as greatly as what she doesn't want to reveal about herself – and she's clinging onto it like a trained funambulist to their ropes.

The warrior cannot prevent his jackpot grin seeping out from under a moustache of fur. 'Dreamers who arrive in the night aren't arrested. They never were! You've been listening to too many rumours. Honestly, His Majesty wishes to meet him. "The Night Dreamer", he calls these folk. A lieutenant of ours addressed the king just a few hours ago up at the palace, where he mentioned about the Night Dreamer he bumped into and how the newbie had been casually strolling in the jungle afterhours. His Majesty responded to the Patroller, saying that Night Dreamers might be our biggest saviours yet—go get them all.'

Deep eventide chases the carriage through into dawn and, gradually, there become fewer stars visible in the sky. The first few rays of sunshine sink through gaps in the ceiling of palmtops and shed speckled pools of light on the jungle floor.

The salamanders at the helm of the carriage register an invisible force, quickly tugging the weight of the vehicle on its way, as if a fixed track is routing it. A tatty wooden wall divides the interior of the vehicle, splitting it into two tiny cabins. In the cabin at the front of the carriage, the king's Bellator warriors are at least pretending to be aware of their chauffeuring, while gossiping drearily between themselves. Whereas, on our side – the back of the carriage, where Samuella, Camson and I have been nestled into a narrow cabin and sit on parallel bamboo benches – Camson is roosting on the bench facing me, gazing out of the window sorrowfully and sucking most of the youthful sunlight onto his unpleasant face (*he obviously hadn't been satisfied with NOT being the land's "biggest saviour yet"*). Samuella has placed herself beside Camson, though being sure to keep a decent gap between herself and the East vet. I've quietly observed she's only doing this for my satisfaction, just so I'm not to feel excluded and antagonised against their already maturing bond. But I can imagine how cosy they'd been when I wasn't around, can still smell it on them, fresh like the drifting smoke of a recently doused bonfire. The sword lies exclusively on her lap. She strokes the gleaming blade with her hand, as her eyes are focused on the scenery coming to life outside of the window. I watch her. She hasn't been disturbed by my staring – not yet.

What is *she* doing with the sword? In that time of crisis, when the smoky beast attacked, how had Samuella managed to prise it from the gobby goblin of a man?

'Where did you get that?' I inquire delicately.

She glances at me. Then she lobs that look straight back out the window. 'I got it a long time ago.'

'I asked where you got it. And *how?*' I nod discreetly towards Camson.

Camson wouldn't have given that weapon up for anything. It's his power of defiance. It's what he stands for. A soldier.

'Does it really matter?' she growls. 'I have it now. We're taking shifts.' Her shaky hand cradles the handle and I decide to avoid sparring about the question.

I spot a glint in her pupils. Something suddenly connects between us. What she said—*Taking shifts?* For a moment, I know who she is. Or, at least, I know who she might be. It lasts for a few seconds and passes like the distant sea breeze. I forget. (*I seem to be forgetting everything; must be the Memory Lane playing on my imagination*).

At last, I've come to terms with the real reason I'm sitting here, **alive**. It's thanks to her. It's no surprise this young redhead sat facing me can assert herself above the lippy, little East Man who seems to have all the pride an imp can ingest without exploding. Credit to her. How she procured the sword from that stubborn cretin is a mystery – it would have, I believe, involved some shouting, some intimidating, some demining, and some patronising (all of which inflate me with supressed pleasure). The sword bears prestige and she's the dominion of its passage; the East Man merely wanders that path, having to labour in and out of the craters of her footprints. The sword in her possession resembles compassion. And so it is because of compassion why I'm still alive. Samuella's attempting to be fair and spare her compassion for both of us – spare a heart for both him of the East and me of the West. How peculiar she is…more than I first imagined.

Now she apparels her face with a cruel simper, one that swaps her shrewdness for bliss. The smirk and the sword are signs that I shouldn't dare to contest her impartiality or her odd discernments. Instead, I should probably follow her suit: grin jauntily out of the carriage window and pretend to be pitiless and shallow.

As the carriage shudders over the last few sticks and stones of the jungle floor and carefully shuttles between this and a kinder terrain, it's apparent that we've finally slipped into totally new territory. I'm peering out of the window and see a magnificent floral landscape. The diversity of flowers in this boundless meadow is mind-boggling with blooms that are dissonantly converged, and yet neatly disordered. Of course, they all gather to form one cosmic body, but they trend irregularly, colourfully varying in sporadic patches under the brawn of the morning sunshine. There are far fewer palm trees above us in this opening, making us an easy target for daylight, as well as whatever may lurk in the proximity of our surroundings. I have to squint at the hibiscuses, the orchids, the violets, the amaryllises, and the tulips that are so abundant they are interchangeable. I am only witnessing things the way I have imagined them, stored in the haze of my subconscious mind. But I feel the cords of my imagination straining to envisage a botanic display as extravagant as this. It's a generous, humbling sight and temporarily amends some of the tension the three of us have heaved as luggage into this carriage.

'I've never seen anything like it before.' I dribble inaudibly.

'Why doesn't that surprise me?' Samuella scoffs at my comment, even though her own awe is sparkling against the sunlight. 'This is what the world used to look like. Before humanity was born to destroy it.'

'Is this what it's like up in the country? For you Bumpkin Folk?' I mention to her inquiringly, since she seems to think a City Boy like me is due to be humbled by an exhaustive flower show.

'The fumes and burnings of war back home are smouldering the world. No Nation on Mankind's World is safe from the smokes of terror and war. It's tragic our present has come to that, but inevitable nonetheless. I guess, if I were ever to go back to my old country keep and hometown, it wouldn't be the way it was when I left it all that while ago.'

'How long have you lived in the City?' I ask.

'Fifty-two months,' she sighs. 'Well, it feels like it's been decades to be honest with you.'

'It has that effect,' I say, quite proudly.

Samuella takes no notice of this small statement. She just sighs and turns away, back to the window. I do the same, back to mine. Outside, the field has grown more voluminous and thicker and the wheels of the carriage are starting to struggle. Small huts have now appeared, peppered all over the wonderful landscape. They're miniature bungalows with the capacity of holding maybe no more than a family of four or less. A family of little people, living in a little house filled with little furniture and a little fireplace, sputtering little flames throughout the warm nights – and here they are: dwelling out in a humungous floral galaxy. The huts are built of thick, blood-red bamboo shoots, with light, straw-thatched roofs and one large bamboo rod for a chimney. And there's something else, which amazes me greater than anything else I've seen since I arrived here: the inhabitants!

I actually spot people! Settlers dressed in appropriately tailored onesies for their beautiful wilderness – 'Not draped in cheap pyjamas like we primitive Dreamers,' Samuella kindly points out. These are settled folk. They can't be like the transient Dreamers, toing and froing with Awakening Coast. This folk mean business, they're the real deal—they *live* off this world!

They're far away, but they're *moving*, which is enough to convince me that they're not a mirage or a flicker of my delusion. They're real, though enigmatic, for the parrot on Awakening Coast had denounced the existence of settlers on Constellation Planet – "*we've all come and gone*" is what he said.

Men in grass hats are sitting in armchairs, out on the wooden terraces of their bungalows as if enjoying the early-rise hours of a summerhouse vacation. They tip their hats at the carriage as we pass by, and then resume relaxation, some shielding the rim over their eyes.

Children are playing in the fields, gathering and dancing with their local friends, as well as playing what seems to be '*tag-it!*' and making angels in the daisies. Meanwhile, their mothers work nonchalantly at hanging-out the washing on thin vines attached between the corner of their hut's roof and a spear of wood out front. Everything is peaceful and sound, yet, almost theatrically in sync, like a staged event replayed in the fictional sequence of a film reel. Folk can't live in this world, a world that I and every other Dreamer collectively make up. How can I distinguish that this isn't quite right, that this adorable scene doesn't make sense? Where's the grating error in this? One considerable notion I point out is that every one of these "settlers", from the dozing fathers to the fretless children, are dressed in matching pyjamas. Though they are very fine nightclothes – no doubt handmade and bought in this supposed "Kingdom" we're en route to – pyjamas are still *pyjamas*. Have pyjamas just become a trend or a fashion adopted by these settlers? I try to incorporate this logic with what Samuella said about coincidence and what Stewart had suggested about hiding my own nudity upon arrival. Nothing here is real. It may feel real, but it is only performing to please what I expect to see, what I want to see. In a way, this makes a lot of sense, but it doesn't compensate for how other Dreamers operate and what they're thinking. Have they been given the same welcoming and guidance as me? How long have they been here? The parrot's ominous remark looms over my head: '*Everyone who comes here comes for a reason.*'

Then, I see something that startles me. A massive tiger strides into view, unmistakably striped and snarling with his tail wagging eerily behind him. He growls like a tormented old man, prowling amongst the flowers as if he is *a shark-merchant in the City selling illegal oil-rationings and fuel-barrels imported from the East*. But this creature is selling nothing to me other than butterflies, as it tiptoes closer towards the vulnerable children, who are still dancing and parading and play-fighting together with not a care in the world – nor have their mothers, who don't even glimpse over to illuminate the whereabouts of their child and aren't even fazed by the enormous tiger that has made its debut in their meadow.

Now, a group of four or five more striped big cats have joined the predator, moving at a sinister pace. Each one keeps their distance from the next, targeting a child of their own as prey.

One child, a girl sitting alone with a doll made of seashells and cloth, looks up after sensing the new presence. She stands slowly. Her first impression is curiosity and it ushers her into walking towards the predators. The predators have seen her coming and they go to her. Once in arm's length, she reaches out to curl her body around the first tiger's neck. They hug adoringly, a moment of sheer brilliance and defiance. Totally unexpected. The girl has a large smile jetted across her face and her fingers massage the cat's fur. Soon, all of the children rush to join in, sharing their love in ceremony.

In the distance, not a far distance but where the trees surrounding the flat meadow make their first stand and form a barrier around the floral field, more animals have arrived. A colony of elephants and giraffes and extended families of monkeys and birds of all sizes and giant lizards and zebras and amphibians – all species of which I have never laid eyes upon in all my seventeen years, only fabricated in visionary thoughts and vivid storytelling. It's odd how such a broad number of different colonies can exist on one little island. But it isn't just *this* island. Out there, wherever there is, over the infinite borders of this planet, there are more islands and more life. And it really makes you wonder: how big can a world be?

'Are you still finding it hard to believe?'

When the carriage begins to struggle over rough, cobbled terrain, I avert my attention to the window again to catch sight of what's ahead. A heavy wooden bridge greets us. The bridge has been painted a warm dark-purple and it bows over an exuberant stream, or river…or whatever it is – simply, water channelled in a single direction with the ocean's momentum to rush it at a very fast speed. Once we're clear of the cobbles and rolling over the bridge, everything is smooth like an aircraft arriving on a runway where ideas of crashing are secrets left short-lived in the clouds.

Down in the stream, the wildlife is animated and making a racket. Frogs as big as the small boulders upon which they reside are the first things to catch me off-guard. I'm captivated by the species of giant beetles that I've never known before, their emulations procured only from memories of *pictures in books and shows on the HoloVision*. Of course, why not, a couple of these bugs have been (somehow) mating with the fish and the rest of the aquatics in the stream, for a lot of the fish prove to be able to crawl on the little banks of the stream. They also share features like claws and tailfins and some jellyfish-like mantises have even grown tentacles. Miniature "Octoroaches" might be the best definition to give them. All I want to do is marvel at this magnificent sprawl of claws, suckers, feelers, fins and feet. Remarked by their many colours and glowing in the water, they glide with rapidness that forces those colours to blur comfortably, then spread like ink.

But there's a far more outstanding landmark up ahead.

Two colossal golden gates tower above our carriage and peak beyond the palmtops. Seamlessly rectangular and polished down to a nail, these gates have been kept in immaculate condition. Majestic condition. I itch at the goosebumps on my elbow to confirm to myself that the dream around me is still lucid and no mirage. I'm quite literally *living the dream.* Though nothing tethers my disbelief like this spectacular entrance before me. Unbelievable. The enterprise of this constellation world is simply astonishing.

We come to a brief stop at the entrance, allowing our escorts to converse with others of their kind - more monkey-men on guard, whom they've alerted at the foot of the gates. A few of their comments float on the wind and reach the window on my side of the carriage. 'No. The king is not waiting on one Night Dreamer. He is expecting all three…' one of the new voices exclaims. *All three?* I retract away from the window as soon as I hear it and my thoughts swing back to Samuella and Camson.

No—But could they—?

Before long, we're moving again, headed into the kingdom. As we pass through the parting golden doors, I realise that the monkeys at the gates are yet more Palm Patrollers. Uniformed in militia vests and berets, with insignia that reads: *GUILD UNDER THE STARS.*

The kingdom is more ambitious than I expected it to be. We first tour through a modest town, where there's an *actual road!* Not rocks and cobbles, but a proper, sanded lane that leads us through. Small huts and bungalows line the street alongside baby palms. Living inside this domesticised junglehood are more pyjama citizens - Day Dreamers fortunate enough to inhabit this centre of the jungle, unlike the bumpkins kissing killer kittens out in the meadowlands. We pass through a bustling marketplace of stalls and shopping huts, where varieties of crops, fruits and vegetables are sold fresh on small wooden displays and on patches surrounded by knee-high fences. These harvested foods, organised in large bundles, include some passion fruit, pineapples, melons, mangos, oranges…There are also ambling dealers who want to sell handmade robes and gowns and…sexy lingerie? Okay, well—a stock of very earthly *nightwear* (both conventional nightwear and, I guess, sensual nightwear). As for accessories, the dealers have beautiful necklaces on sale, as well as fine rings and bracelets of bizarre designs, decorated with painted shells and images shaped from fish-bones. It's a strange idea for a Dreamer as new to the party I am to have...but there's an eccentric homecoming aura about it – like it's somewhere that's been waiting for me to return. Somewhere I could have belonged in the past.

The novelty is tarnished, however, by the Palm Patroller's statement at the gates, tumbling over and over again in my head. I glance awkwardly at Samuella, clear my throat and then prop my elbow up on the window ledge as insouciantly as I can before addressing her. 'Do you trust me?' I say to her, my vision focused away from her and out of the window. 'You and him. Do either of you trust me?'

'I don't think *trust* is the right word,' Samuella responds, confused. 'Not yet.'

'The both of you are Night Dreamers—like I am,' I proclaim, almost in accusation. 'You never told me that when we met, because you were afraid the Palm Patrollers would hold it against you. You thought they'd come to kill both of you. Though you were quite comfortable putting me up on the hotspot. You made it very clear to them that *I* was the one they were looking for, that *I* was the new arrival. Well, you'll be happy to know that the king wants to see all three of us. All *three* Night Dreamers. It makes you feel exposed now, doesn't it? Being an outcast, a third wheel, in all of this doesn't appear to be that easy, does it? See, I had no idea about any of this, how serious any of it really was. But now, after that long journey and watching this world unfold before my very eyes all the way up here, I'm starting to get the bigger picture.'

'We were just being honest when we put you on the spot. It wasn't to be nasty. They asked for the new arrival – the *newest* Night Dreamer – and we gave them what they wanted, for the sake of all of *our* lives. Not just yours,' Samuella answers me bitterly. 'And we're not ashamed to be Night Dreamers. It's not the first time I've felt vulnerable here. Or back home, for that matter.'

'Nope,' Camson retorts with a grin. 'We were doing fine—right until you showed up anyway.'

I refuse to dispute it with these two strangers any further. They're not my enemies – at least, I suppose, one of them isn't. But they're not the people I'd call friends either.

Once we're out of the marketplace and back in the street, one of the Bellator warriors makes an announcement from the front of the carriage. 'Kingdom Palace ahead!'

I poke my head out of the window and see the enormous building materialising at the end of the boulevard of palms. The

Kingdom Palace dazzles with ageing chrome brickwork and a dozen tall, slender towers. Upon those sparkling towers there are a dozen silver onion-dome roofs. Each onion-dome is topped with a golden acorn. And above the palace's front entrance, a fierce statue of a macaw perches, overlooking us with its wings stretched. Everything about the place beckons youthful crispness, but at the same time, it houses a voguishly ancient quintessence.

'Welcome to the king's residence,' Samuella hails, as we enter through the palace gates.

Purple-coloured walls of bamboo, sanded together with gristly sand granules harvested from the oceanfront, mould the inside of the Kingdom Palace. Hundreds of feet above, the ceiling is unreachable. On entrance, the three of us are led into a resounding hall complete with a marble floor, distantly bordered at either side by golden pillars. Between the pillars are rows of cauldrons, all of them blazing with a fire and lined up towards a curling staircase at the very end of the room. These produce the only light in the room. After coming to the end of the hall, we're formally escorted up the staircase by two of the Bellator warriors from the carriage.

We arrive at the very top of the staircase to be greeted by a pair of chrome chamber doors. The warriors go for a door each and push them open synchronously.

Samuella's the first to enter, followed by Camson, and I am the last. The room on the other side is pitch-black, except for a single, shining spectacle in the centre of it. The spectacle is a large, purple orb-like entity, which ripples like the radiance that swells off the sun. The doors close behind us and the warriors have vanished before we can even dare to look back.

'Arrivals, new and old,' a deep voice burns through the fabric of the air around us, stirring furore in our anxieties and shaking the ground beneath our feet. 'What success of my demands do you bring, Faithful Ones?'

On either side of me, Samuella and Camson have fallen to one knee in a bowing gesture. For some reason, they're paying respects to this hovering ball in the centre of the room. There is no clear reason for this at first. It's rather cringe-worthy to witness. Pretty embarrassing. A little confused, I sheepishly match the mood by doing exactly the same.

'Your Majesty, I'm sorry to tell you that, as far as we're aware, the beast still roams free. We were incapable of discharging the Drag-in from the jungle,' Samuella owns up. Wow, she really *is* honest. And remarkably polite.

But even more striking still—

He's the king! The glowing ball is the king of this place! Suddenly, I'm dreaming again and dreading it. *Pinch!* I'm tempted to mindlessly draw myself towards the entity and touch it. Just to test whether it is actually what I'm seeing. A hovering sphere of purple fire. But I'm too afraid of the consequences of stirring such foolishness, when our disappointment has already set the tone. There has been no success with the beast loose in the jungle. I suppose it's the *Living Smoke* they're referring to. Samuella just called it "the Drag-in" again.

At first, the king hesitates unreceptively before responding upon the thoughts of another topic. 'Did you bring with you the newcomer? The Night Dreamer?'

Samuella strokes my elbow indicatively. 'Say hello.'

'Oh—yeah!' I stutter. 'That's me!'

'The prophecy of the Stellar Gods continues to unravel,' All Eyes rejoices, 'and the truth is most certainly becoming to read like stars that translate the Constelleavens.'

What the hell is that thing on about?

'Does he have...a *relevance*...with us, though?' Camson remarks. 'You didn't exactly tell us to collect him from the beach when he arrived. He came looking for us.'

I want to kick this little East Bug into the pocket-sized black hole in the centre of the room—!

'I have doubts in your standard of will, Night Dreamer,' the king responds to Camson's prudish talk. 'I believe this young Dreamer did not come upon you intentionally. He tumbled into your powerful society and it is within your powerful society of Night Dreamers that he will become a fantastic contributor, and perhaps even a leader, at some point in your journey together. The Stellar Gods selected you all from the outset. You should respect your newest companion and the duty you share with him.'

'What do you mean they *selected us all from the outset*?' Camson argues. 'And—*our journey together*? What do you mean by *that*? You're not making any sense, Your Highness!'

'The journey is your relevance. Your bond. He is a Night Dreamer, just as you are. Disparities aside, you both have something to be connected: a trait, a talent, a gift. One that Day Dreamers do not possess. The Dreamers of the Night arrive after sunset with magnificent prospects and significance. The Drag-in can only be defeated by the prophesised Night Dreamers, since both can transfer themselves to Constellation Planet at any time they desire. They are not permitted to arrive on Awakening Coast at sunrise like most Dreamers. You three are not like other Dreamers. Please take a seat and I will explain.'

Once the voice announces this, three large stone thrones illuminate at the other side of the room. A warm shade of purple light appears beneath them, making them noticeable in the dark. We obey the king's request and sit in the chairs.

'Those were once the thrones of the ancient Dreamerverse Royals,' the king pronounces. 'They were the monarchs who were highly commended for their efforts in defending the Dreamerverse and were summoned to the Constelleavens above, where they were knighted as Gods. Rewarded with immortality and eternal peace, they were liberated from both Mankind's World and the Dreamerverse. Why did this occur, you wonder? Well, their legend is historically misinterpreted as a myth. It only ever rarely comes to understanding that these three Royals were once ordinary mortals of both worlds like you. They were also Night Dreamers, like you. They'd all been summoned from their different lives in the real world, vague and unfamiliar of each other, such as yourselves. Humble beginnings, you could say.

'The legend tells the story of three Night Dreamers of the previous generation, brought together from their individual existences in reality, as is always the case with this Stellar God policy. One was summoned from a life of wealth and greed, the second from convenience and lies, and the third came from a past of pity and regret. After materialising on Awakening Coast, they quickly crossed paths and set out together on a quest to protect the Void from a terrible parasite. The Drag-in – a fiend that, once loose from the Void, will pillage the stability of the Memory Lane itself and threaten the equilibrium of the Dreamerverse and reality. It is a formidable chaos that can unleash itself far among the stars after so long, bridging itself between distant dimensions and contaminating this world with the incompatible weights of the other. Once the balance between them is disturbed, your reality faces an equal doom to the Dreamerverse.'

'Sorry to interrupt, Your Majesty, but is this the same monster we're talking about here?' Samuella mentions.

'I hope to think so. This creature has been documented as a unique being, an entity of *Living Smoke*, totally capable of morphing its appearance and alternating its physicality to fit its environment. The creature cannot be completely destroyed, nor can it be penetrated by weaponry – and I'll soon be requesting you to surrender your sword, as you won't be needing it. This isn't to say that the Drag-in cannot be defeated, but it cannot be palpably harmed. Yet, there is a way of conquering it. And that is how the Royals went about doing it in their legacy. That previous generation of Night Dreamers achieved it and so can you. You must understand, the Drag-in is nothing that can be defined, nothing that can be wholly seen, nothing that can be touched or—'

'Can it breathe?' Camson giggles. 'That was a little joke we had earlier.'

The king neglects his daft comment. 'The Drag-in you saw in the jungle was a frazzled anomaly, a mere reflection of the beast's true strength. At this stage, the Drag-in is still detached from the threads of your imagination. It is an insecure vessel rediscovering its orientation in a void that has been dividing our two worlds for centuries. You *can* still fight this vermin. As a human Dreamer, you are limited to what you can see, hear and feel and this is what the Drag-in doesn't possess. It does not physically exist in any world, only the Void. That makes it exempt from normal sensory functions, for it doesn't have to adapt to them. Although, it does retain one function—memory. The Drag-in overcomes the restraints of the Memory Lane, which is a remarkable ability. You three, however, also have this trait. You can remember what other Dreamers cannot. Night Dreamers and the Drag-in both transcend the Memory Lane.' The king pauses. 'Unfortunately, I always fail to spell out the end of the legend. Like in most myths, many things remain to the imagination and to the hopes of those listening. The three Royals were never found or heard of again.'

'But I thought you'd said that they were eventually summoned to the Constelleavens?' I find myself wriggling into the intrigue that scintillates inside the room.

'Correct. I did mention that they were summoned to the Constelleavens. But I never mentioned whether they'd survived their mission. Although the Drag-in vanished for centuries after their conquering of it, their own mortal fates were not regarded. And since just as long, after this myth was first told, we who are forever thankful for the Night Dreamers' efforts have never spoken of the Drag-in.'

'Who were the Royals?' Samuella questions. 'As people, who were they?'

'Similar individuals to the three of you; the Royals were Night Dreamers who were summoned to Constellation Planet to defeat the Drag-in when it last materialised over a decade ago. They only became royalty in the Dreamerverse once they'd succeeded,' the king rashly summarises. 'Understand that Night Dreamers are never selected at random. They *are* just like regular Dreamers in every way, only more privileged in their freedoms to arrive, leave and remember beyond the mental void. However, besides their late arrival after sunset, there is one other principal that casts them aside as extraordinary – which is that their spirits are fluctuating ones, embedded with conflicting morals and demons. It is an antisocial demeanour that they carry in their soul. And so their nature is not stable enough to comply with the socialisation of the Dreamerverse; Night Dreamers are unnatural variances within the conventional and accepted order of Constellation Planet that is expected and innate of all other regular Day Dreamers. And the cursed sands do not mark Night Dreamers when they rise from Awakening Coast, not like every other Dreamer, which means they are not directly protected by the Stellar Gods – you must defend yourselves in all aspects of your journeys in the Dreamerverse.'

'Doesn't sound like much of a privilege to me,' Camson groans.

'So, we're already utterly accountable,' Samuella notes, 'and we haven't even started out yet.'

'Quite so,' All Eyes agrees. 'An overlooked example of the disenfranchisement of the Night Dreamer would be how no firefly can determine their departure from Awakening Coast – which makes sense that fireflies should be absent during the daylight, eating their nectar in the tall grass of the jungles, rather than offering a daytime return from Awakening Coast for a homebound Night Dreamer. The Night Dreamer's inability to define their spirit is the fundamental reason why they manage to transcend the Void between worlds at their own pace and desire. They aren't defined enough to fall into the general category of regular Dreamers and so they are free spirits until they die.'

'I thought every Dreamer was supposed to be a free spirit,' I probe, far more fascinated by the hypnotic glow of the king's orb than by his knowledge of the folklore. 'Wasn't that supposed to be the whole ethos of the Dreamerverse, a world not bound by laws?'

'Even nature has laws,' All Eyes responds. 'Nobody has to state a decree – not me, not you, not the Stellar Gods – for the laws of instinct to sew its seeds in the virginal ocean of human imagination. Legend tells that Night Dreamers are more emotionally polarised than regular Dreamers. The Royals were no exception to this behaviour. With a conflicting spirit of wealth and desire, there was Queen Cassandra. And then, with a conflicting spirit of convenience and lies, there was a Prince *Cephal*—How hideous of me that I forget his name.

Ah, yes—and, lastly, with the spirit forged from guilt and hatred was Queen Evanescence.'

'Are you expecting us to live up to their legacy?' Samuella's eyes are flickering anxiously.

'To begin with, only their quest is in your interest. Then, maybe, your names will fulfil the prophecy and, maybe, you will defeat the Drag-in and, maybe so, you will live in a similar legacy and be summoned to the Constelleavens. Who am I to tell a Dreamer not to dream?'

'What are we supposed to do at this point?' Camson asks.

'You must seek out three rare and distinctive emeralds, located at unique locations on Constellation Planet. But only by following your Night Dreamer instincts should you come across a path leading to them, and their usage in conquering the Drag-in will subsequently become apparent,' All Eyes assures us. 'There is no greater method or weapon than the mind of a Night Dreamer. The continuity of the Dreamerverse highly regards that.'

'So, what you're saying is that the only way we can defeat the Drag-in is by picking up these emeralds? And the only way of finding *them* is by drawing out our own tracks? Following our instincts?' Samuella says.

'Precisely. And I imagine that you will have to go about this routine the same way the Royals did. In each of those unique locations, each of you will be faced with your own dangers and your own opportunity for leadership. I would recommend that you become wise enough to understand your own and each other's weaknesses and come to bear each other's intolerances.'

'I don't possess weaknesses. Or intolerances,' Camson declares, supressing a snarl he craves to aim in my direction.

'I am yet to meet an individual without a weakness or a prejudice. A Miracle Person such as that would resound incredulity.'

'I think that you're forgetting that this is a Dream World,' Camson challenges. 'Unlike reality, everything here really does *resound incredulity*.'

'Just go along with it, why don't you?' Samuella hisses at him.

Camson flinches in reaction. 'I'm just saying that I'm not too fussed about this place and I'm not afraid of the Drag-in—whatever it is! If this really is a matter of listening to my conscience, then I think it's about time that my conscience started listening to me too!'

I consider recalling the moment that had occurred in the jungle – when the insecure little East Man had abandoned me to the wrath of the beast without even sparing a second thought. But I don't feel now is the right time for that.

'It's not a matter of listening, but understanding your conscience. You will be amazed at how tolerant your mind really is. To think, it is your mind that has formed this entire world before you,' All Eyes eases the tension in the room.

Suddenly, the doors open again and a group of six Palm Patrollers enter the room this time, marching in an orderly sequence. Among them, I recognise an old acquaintance. Lieutenant Bowe, whom I'd met in the jungle and who'd warned me of straying in the night.

'Are these our reinforcements?' Samuella responds to the spontaneous entry with a suggestive twitch of the head.

'You do not require an army,' the king answers. 'You require weaponry.'

The Patrollers form a line in front of us. Two of them step forward, both holding onto objects.

'I thought we didn't need weapons to fight the Drag-in? Isn't it physically impenetrable?' Camson asks.

'These weapons aren't for your battle against the Drag-in. They are your necessities for the journey. It is a renowned and duteous quest, which may well take you across hostile regions and to the utmost edges of the planet.'

The two Patrollers have approached our thrones with three pocket-sized sacks. They hand them to us and we quickly peer inside to take a look at the contents. The sacks each contain a selection of twenty coloured seeds – blue, green, red and purple. No more than five of each colour.

'What you are holding are probably going to be the most resourceful and consistent requirements in your arsenal,' All Eyes declares. 'These are the Seeds of Continuity. In each pouch, there are twenty of them for each of you and, as you can see, they are separated into four colours: blue, red, green and purple.

'Blue seeds will protect you in action, offering you discretion from powerful and deadly predators. This planet has many creatures from all corners of your deepest imagination and beyond. But some of these adversaries will pose matchless superiority to your strength and wit. If you believe you are overpowered or outnumbered at any point, consume one of these and you will immediately become undetectable from any predator – but be wary not to waste them on simply anything.

'Red seeds will sustain your health and resurrect you when you are close to fatality. Consume one of these only when necessary – only when you are in grave danger. They can also be applied to regulate your physical health and heal flesh wounds.

'Green seeds are your means of distant communication. Use them when you have been separated and are out of direct contact with your fellow companions. They will temporarily enable you to speak telepathically and will simultaneously boost your mental health, so they'll also come in handy when you need to recuperate from stressful situations.

'And, finally, the purple seeds are the most crucial. They allow you to remain awake in this world for as long as two days at a time and will help you to dismiss the urge of returning to Awakening Coast on every awakening. Returning to Awakening Coast is mandatory here, but the purple seeds will validate you to rest wherever you choose and recover yourself in the same place.'

'That's insane! We can stay here for as long as we wish?' Samuella is blushing with flattered excitement. It's the best news she's heard all day.

'Not as long as you wish. That would be outlandish,' the king promotes his doubts. 'The dead do not walk in reality, nor do they walk in dreams. I cannot promise immortality, but I can promise you a new home here on Constellation Planet, if you succeed. You may live here, thrive here, but if so—you must also die here.'

'What about home? Won't that change things, time-wise?' I ask. After mentioning this, I'm receiving irritated glances from Samuella. They're telling me: '*Ugh! I should have left you in the jungle to get mauled by that horrible monster—just for reminding me of that dreadful place!*' I've no clue what issues she has with Mankind's World, what hardships she's endured in the West, but her constant pessimism for reality is grinding me into insanity.

'There will be no difference in time. Your integration between worlds will remain as normal,' the king explains. 'The next time you reawaken in Mankind's World, you will be revived exactly where you had lain before you escaped consciousness. And regardless of how much time you spend in the Dreamerverse, no longer than a night's rest of ten hours will have passed in reality.'

'Why don't you just go home now if you miss it so much?' Samuella growls at me.

'Well, we'll have to go back at some point,' I tell her indifferently. I'm not trying to tirelessly tame myself back into her good books anymore. I don't even care anymore. She and the East Man can do whatever they like when this is over. I'm doing whatever I must to get home.

The two Palm Patrollers who'd brought the seed-sacks return to the line and the next two monkeys in the line of six step forward, taking their place. We're swiftly handed three glazing and freshly sharpened silver swords as well as one bow and a stack of arrows made from bamboo.

'You trust us to use these weapons with any conviction at all?' Samuella complains. 'I suppose you haven't known any of us longer than two days, so…'

'Not in the Drag-in's case, no. But in the context of winning those emeralds—yes, these arms will come in handy. Believe—*they will.* Though, you won't be needing that old blade there, as I mentioned before,' the king replies.

'You can have it.' Samuella's about to hand it over.

'No! I want to keep it! It'll do better than any of these new weapons! We might need it eventually! It's bigger, sturdier!' This begging comes from Camson.

'Believe me, you won't need that ancient ornament,' All Eyes states. 'It won't enhance your inventory in any way.'

'Who says? Besides, I wield that thing better than either of these two clowns!' Camson pleads. 'Give it here to me! You can trust me with it, Your Highness!'

I'm really tempted to bring up Camson's loutish behaviour in the jungle again, like a tattler in the school playground.

'These new weapons are suitable enough for you to fend against the majority of hostiles on this planet, Night Dreamer. Now, step forward and return the sword.' This time, the king has a much firmer tone.

One Palm Patroller snatches the old sword from Samuella and walks over to All Eyes. He lifts it high above his head and then lands it in a narrow pipe-like orifice at the foot of the orb's stone platform. There's a bright flash spewed from a spark of lightning, which fills the room with a deafening bang. The old sword vanishes. Then, all is calm again.

'*Ahh*—Thank you! I am very grateful for the Blade's return. It is a very precious weapon,' the king rejoices. 'You only needed it to procure and protect the last Night Dreamer in your group. It was yours until this encounter. It is now out of your hands.'

'But—hold on,' Samuella interrupts. '*I* still managed to shoo off the Drag-in using that blade. How comes?'

'A chance of luck,' All Eyes suggests. 'This sword is a knight all on its own, built to protect. We call it the Solar Blade, because it's been preserved for so long, centuries even. Count Orion was the man who cast it on the anvil and coated it with sands charmed by the Stellar Gods, to preserve its star-encrusted blade. He had such a legacy in his blacksmithing that some believed he was more than just an expert of his trade, but a demigod by nature. Orion was one of the first generation of Dreamers to awaken on this world. He made the Solar Blade's strength so immense that it is deemed impractical in mundane combat and he dusted it with such a fine layer of supernova energy that its weight is infinitely changing, which makes the blade's wielding unpredictable and its handling beyond the control of anyone who uses it.'

'I used it,' Samuella defends her case.

'You may be a Night Dreamer, but you are still not artful enough for the Solar Blade.'

Samuella's face drops at this comment.

'Is anyone capable of wielding it regularly?' I ask.

'Maybe. But, unlikely,' the king concludes.

Finally, the last two Palm Patrollers step forward, bringing with them a scroll of golden, withered parchment. They hand the scroll to me and I open it up, being careful not to damage it any more than it already is.

The paper is blank.

'The Constellation Map,' the king announces. 'This is your means of getting around. The Map enables you to communicate with your own conscience like no other tool and it will lead the way for you. As I said, you have three prominent destinations, three locations where the crucial emeralds lay. Each of you will have the opportunity of reading the Map, taking it in turns to navigate the route to your *own* desired destination and plucking an emerald from it. You must remember that each of your locations will surely consist of challenges, confrontations or dilemmas that you must overcome. Do not let me down. The fates of the Dreamerverse and your home world are in your hands. And, remember, if you do manage to redeem the freedom of the Dreamerverse from the Drag-in's plague, you will be rewarded: you will have new lives in this world and you may stay here for as long as you live.'

Nobody speaks. I don't even need to glance at either Samuella or Camson to fathom the opportunity of the king's promise. It's the possibility of liberation, for sure. But it's more than that. It's the guarantee of a new beginning, a fresh start. The request is simple:

search for the emeralds, deny the Drag-in and be rewarded with the freedom to choose a new home.

Though we are as far from freedom as we are from home…

Chapter One
The Decider's Son

Observe—!

Within the gloom of the grey, disquieted skyline and the emerging arrival of another moonless twilight, the City still managed to glisten with all its envied potency. Towering skyscrapers, commercial colossuses, and mammoth monuments crowned with municipal luminaries all scattered the City Central. And, fielded around them, big business buildings lined soldierly throughout the warren of wide streets and boulevards. All lights were astounding and never flickered – most of them cried out abundantly from abused apartment windows and spewed from expensive, holographic advertisements that were pasted about the Central.

High above, none but a single suspended overpass interrupted passage for a fleet of glowing *EvokaRafts*, slowly floating between buildings, promoting the weekend's upcoming Ball Game between the *City Lions* and the Second Nation's *Gazelles*; other *EvokaRafts* were advertising new seasons of the reality shows *Top Subordinate* and *Chastity* – '*TONIGHT AT 9 ON FN-TV*,' the announcer propounded from suspended loudspeakers pinned to the drones' panels, as they peered over the commuters disembarking the monorail stationed at *Dew Street Promenade*. These men and women – subordinates shuttled from Saturday's Trades – ambled from the station to the *Promenade* and celebrated their evening sprees at the designer outlets with what little incomes they had left to spend for the weekend. Then, in a race for the sailing fragrance forged from the finest cuisines in the First Nation, they dashed from shopping on *Dew Street* to eat on *Caesar's Boulevard*.

Meanwhile, upon a thin gale – when the wind was vague, the air was clammy and polluted – the subtle but indubitable odour of roasting plantain was conveyed from the very delicacy of *The Small Island Bar* on *Meander Street* to the perturbed nostrils of those mercenary epicures settled on *Caesar's Boulevard.* Tragically, this song of foreign flavours did as little to tempt the epicures as it did to please them. Unlike the rich dining strip, which accommodated a swell of affluent customers allured to its staid swing of cooling big-band jazz, *Meander Street* paid homage to an outlandish musical montage of calypso and soca to charm those rowdier and boggier subordinates of the Week Trades, who were somewhat aloof from their white-collar counterparts returning from the Weekend Trades. From exiting *Dew Street Promenade Monorail Station* and descending the long, concrete staircase to ground, one would be met with the *Promenade*'s last junction at the end of the block. The two streets were located on perpendicular sides of this block – where *Caesar* met *Meander* – and so they never saw eye-to-eye, for it was exactly at the block's intersecting corner (facing the station's entrance) where the two communities deviated. The buoyant tycoons, magnates, and sons of Ministors were welcome to *Caesar*, whereas the parlous crowds of slickers and deficient workmen belonged to *Meander.*

On the huge, digital billboards that mounted the buildings on Crystal Square, live footage of the "Hounding Trials" had been underway since noon and shoppers were stopping in their hundreds to view the hearing of a trial that involved nine canines accused of "*explicit acts of sexual harassment*" towards their owners. One spaniel, Phillip, had been charged of "*leg-licking*", another Golden Retriever, Colby, had been accused of "*overindulgently staring*" as his owner had been unchanging, and a pug named Laurel had been charged with "*humping without consent*". The audience on the street gazed up at the enormous billboard screens, deadpan and infatuated. But their attraction would be thrown away after not much longer. For, soon, everywhere in the City, the momentum would start to sink. At a time when shops and markets came to a close, and as the atmosphere grew darker and cheaper, all people desired were their homes, their own privacy.

It was a Saturday evening – a climate when the roads were immensely populated with homeward gridlock-traffic and truculent crowds were forming on the pavements. Discreetly hidden within the chaos, Oscar had been hurried to his evening appointment in the back of his chauffer's carrier. A black, armoured limousine. So, he was veered, rather than dragged, out of hibernation and into this daze of disinclination that companioned his despondent attitude. He felt offbeat, and discordant, although it wasn't as if the appointment had been prescribed to violate his Saturday's schedule in any way. For Oscar, Saturday was no different to Monday, Tuesday, Wednesday, or any other day of the week. He didn't need to get out of bed before midday – he needn't leave his bedroom at all; he didn't need to work Week Trades or Weekend Trades – he needn't work at all; he didn't even need to leave his building of residence. Nonetheless, as reluctant as he was to do *anything* on a Saturday, he couldn't complain. His father had arranged the appointment earlier that day and he intended not to come between his old man and his "short-term investments". Thankfully, he didn't have to worry about commuting there either. The journey on-foot would have been a true task for him – let alone (he sympathised) for anyone else in the mesh of commuters – to tell the difference between the pavement and the road and he would have been misled in all the wrong directions if he'd been forced to find his own muggy way there at the metamorphic mercy of this midsummer mayhem. Alas, on foot, he would have been poorly directed by the simpleminded subordinates who were besotted by who he was, or fobbed by those insouciant others who had scant time or interest to guide another stranger about the City like a tourist. But, in the salient security of his little black bubble on wheels, he'd finally managed to reach the apartment block where Doctor Islie lived. Just on the ridge of the City Central, where the *Promenade* ended and *Dew Street* turned into *Laud Lane*. He came in to Islie's building via the back entrance, as opposed to the bustling reception lobby, and took a private elevator up to **Floor 131** – as instructed. Then, after delaying for an extortionate length of time in the Waiting Room – Islie had renamed it this instead of "the living room" – Oscar became the last in a queue of patients summoned into the Discussion Room – the balcony.

There he was, now sitting on the balcony beside the middle-aged myth of a practitioner whom he'd never met before. He was the psychiatrist Oscar's father was only mildly familiar with from a one-off encounter long in the past, and yet whom his father had praised unrelentingly during their breakfast discussion that morning. Stepping out onto the balcony, through the automatic sliding door, Oscar first caught sight of the practitioner's oddly muscular calves, which were raised and uncomfortably positioned upon the leather footrest like the bulbous head of meat on a grilled chicken leg. There were lines about his face like scaffolding, as if some unfinished, finer structure were pending with every shift of his unpredictable expression and the pale golf balls in his eye-sockets were deeply inset, tucked into sagging orbits of tiredness. He fashioned a grey goatee-beard, above which a slender and futilely kempt handlebar-moustache sheltered his taut frown. Though, in a contrast of maturity, the once-blonde hair on his head was stringy, gangling and silvered all over.

Doctor Islie was garbed in casually picked, homely clothes, looking less like a doctor than Oscar had imagined him to. He had expected to meet an ostentatious beige suit and a white, ironed shirt – like most, if not *all*, men in the City Central wore – with chemically sustained hair, a visible history of facial surgery, pigment transformations in the eyes and skin, and perhaps some riveting aftershave for trustful appeal…

Doctor Islie was nothing of the sort.

His shorts were billowy and creased, corresponding to his grungy t-shirt (at least they matched in that category) – some stained jersey with a comical turn of phrase that Oscar failed to ignore: **A vent a day keeps the hallucinations at bay**. *How appropriate was that.*

From that moment, Oscar believed he was going to enjoy this meeting—

'Monkeys patrolling cursed jungles…telepathic parrots…and a giant entity-ball affirming itself as the king of this…*island*?' Doctor Islie was struggling to comprehend these ideas. He had his coffee-mug clasped in one hand and a pen in the other. An hour in and Islie's notepad hadn't left the table beside his armchair.

'Not an island. *A planet*,' Oscar corrected. 'A planet filled of constellations, constellations with millions of stars in them! Could you fancy that?'

'Presided over by a king…*in the shape of an orb*?'

'Well, everyone there—they called him the king. I suppose he *was* the king—*had* to be. They knew him as "All Eyes" – probably because he knew everyone and everything so well. Like most giant *orb-things* tend to, right? He'd been there since the beginning, so he had his sights set over everything in this place,' Oscar explained.

'Let me get this straight,' Doctor Islie placed his mug back down on the little table and, hosting a sapped fragility, closed his eyes. He stressfully rubbed his eyelids and furrowed forehead with tightly strained fingers. 'You had a dream about a desolate island, which consisted of talking animals and an omniscient intelligence with a god-complex governing a fictitious collectivist statehood?'

'No! It wasn't an island! All you're doing is complicating it!' Oscar forced himself to gulp down a deep breath, trying to withstand the frustration of having to explain it for the fourth time that evening. 'It wasn't an island. It was a planet. An entirely intact world all on its own—'

'And what was the name of this world?' Islie asked.

'Constellation Planet.'

'And this was the place conceived from the imaginations of those living in it?' Doctor Islie cut him off. 'Yes, I have been listening, Oscar. But I'm still finding it quite hard to believe how you're describing it to me – that you materialised there, *consciously*? That you were as much alive there as you are here – *truly*? There's no hypothetical proof as to how you could have possibly been transported to another world overnight. Such sciences are dreams and remain dreams. I'd have regarded the whole thing as more of a delusional sickness or a nightmare! It's *worrying* nonetheless!'

'I'm telling you the truth! Everything was tangible like everything surrounding me right now! It sounds surreal, I know…and it might have been to some extent! But I could *smell*, and *touch*, and *feel*, and *think* and *breathe* the same way I can now!'

'And you were greeted by a parrot that could talk with a genuine conscience – not just repeating everything you said, but actually reading your mind and spelling out your thoughts?'

'His name was Stewart. He's always there to greet new arrivals. Although, it was different for me, because I came in the evening. I'm the Night Dreamer.'

'The Night Dreamer?' He hauled up the notepad and leisurely advanced to a clean page, then began to scribble down a few of these names as notes, but the tip of his pen hardly met the page. 'Okay…*Night Dreamer…*'

'What are you doing? Why are you writing that? Is it more relevant than anything else I've said?' Oscar peered curiously over at the notepad on his lap. 'Honestly—this isn't helping!'

'No. You're right, it isn't! But you can't say I'm not trying. I cancelled my last three evening appointments for this. And your father isn't being refunded for that reason alone. I need you to give me a little bit more than this, Oscar.'

'I—I can't!' Oscar stuttered. 'Unless there was a was a way I could show it to you—I could prove—!'

'Don't hurt yourself. Just treat the conversation as normal and think openly. Close your eyes if it helps.'

Oscar sank back in his armchair and sighed.

'Now, speak to me. Why are you here?'

'Because my dad sent me to you.'

'Any particular reason of concern—*why*? Was it because *he* didn't believe you when you told him all this?'

'He never has anything to say when I mention things like this. It's just another reason for him to blame my mother. He thinks her and I had too much in common. And I think he was constantly jealous of that.'

'Ah! Now, with that in mind—keep that in mind,' Islie, revitalised all of a sudden, propped himself up and prepared to make some palpable notes. He asked: 'How would your mother have addressed this issue?'

'She…' Oscar had to think wholeheartedly about this first. 'She would have downright trusted me to begin with. No matter how bizarre it was. She was a Soothsayer. Like her sister – my Aunt Sibyl – she'd found a rhythm with the truth that nobody else could hear and had a gift for seeing it all, and—you know.' Oscar's eyes found the ledge of the balcony, the glass parapet that acted as a fence between them and the drop to subordination on the streets below.

'Is that what your mother did? Agree with whatever you said?' Islie assumed, now captivated.

'Not necessarily agree with what I said,' Oscar explained, 'but she *listened*, and she considered my views and she valued my own experience of a matter before making her judgement on it.'

'Your father, the Decider, didn't exactly like this idea, did he?' Islie pinpointed.

'My father never believed any of it. He was sceptical about the Soothes. Didn't warm to their community, didn't appreciate their abilities, regardless of how much they defended our Nation from all sorts of natural disasters – *natural* disasters were never really his strong suit. A Soothsayer wouldn't help him win a war, so they were impractical to him.'

'I have to say, that never rang home for me,' Islie said. 'How can it be that Soothes are allowed to report the coming of an earthquake or a hurricane, but they're forbidden to predict hostile advances or sabotage enemy tactics in warfare?'

'I'm not a thumper, but I'm quite sure that their deity, Vera, proclaims somewhere in the *Holy Libel* that, morally, a Soothsayer's powers are not designed as a weapon in wars and to commit murder on others is a crime to their faith. A Sayer must oblige to use their psychic ability to safeguard human life,' Oscar heaved a catalogue of knowledge on the Oracle and Soothsayers at the frosty man, brashly regurgitating every word his mother had told him as a young child. Islie waited for him to finish talking, unimpressed; he clearly knew all of this already. 'In fact, the *Libel* says the laws of war are a lot like the laws of the truth,' Oscar went on. 'War doesn't enlist moral on either side of conflict – it just happens and there are winners and losers. The truth is never right or wrong – it's just an apathetic consequence that pans out, and is what it is. As an experienced Sayer, my mother had understood the truth, so she understood wars. She predicted the coming of these current Conflicts some twenty, or thirty, years ago. And by just predicting the Conflicts at that time, it didn't mean she was being passive about it. She knew the best thing was never to fiddle with the sway of war, the same way one should never intervene with the principles of the truth. Winners will win and losers will lose; moral isn't required for that judgement.'

'Your father was right. You *do* sound more and more liberal these days, you young'uns,' Islie teased, but he still looked steely in the eyes. 'If I were to second guess, I'd be convinced you were as hypocritical as one of those Third Nation hipsters bopping pro-life placards around Sainthood Slaughterhouse.'[☆]

'You think of me a liberal?' Oscar didn't appear as offended as Islie had anticipated – he was smiling.

'I never suggested any problem about being a *little* bit punkish – that was your father's interpretation, not mine,' Islie sighed. 'It's the liberal world he's been trying to destroy ever since he came to power.'

'Liberal Punk. Of course—that's what he thinks of me,' Oscar huffed, taking a similar light-heartedness to the unilateral voice of his father. 'It doesn't surprise me that he said that to you. It's just a scapegoat suggestion, a distraction from what truly worries him: he's afraid I'll become like my mother someday. It bothers him that I sound like her when I talk, that I bring up the same arguments against him as she did. Arguments he would always fiercely condemn. He'd had enough of her – his own wife, the Oracle – in his Administration, openly condemning *him*! *Embarrassing him with her witchery and fictions*, he used to say!

☆ *Sainthood Slaughterhouse* is the largest asylum in the West, located along the northern border of the First Nation. It became famously known for its impressive inmate population of Liberal Punks – Punks were regarded enemies of the state who stoked protest rallies and riots against the Decider's campaign to cull the Old Democracy and imprint his declaration of war on liberalisation.

'It reached a point – when I was about four-years-old, my father recalls – where she was claiming to hold conversations with the dead. Deceased Administrations and past Deciders were coming to her in dreams at night and visions during the day. You must remember that affair better than I can, Doctor. They were warning her, weren't they? Warning her about my father, the Decider. My father says that, some nights, when the nightmares kept her up and were too difficult for her to handle without reaching out to someone, she would wander into my bedroom – as if in a *trance*, he said – with some ice-cold bottles of *Kola Bear* and she would allude to these dreams like they were bedtime stories and I would listen to her. I cannot remember too well. Though, according to my father, she would tell me about those spirits of bygone Deciders and Ministors, and the horrors they told her about the future, about a future Decider – the last in the Philson dynasty – who would bring austerity, shame and fall to the entire West.[☆] While I can assure you that I am by no means a Soothe in the making, I am equally not destined to be a Decider; I exist neither at all beside my mother's nor my father's unsparing words. If what my mother said is anything to go by – which it almost always is – I cannot possibly be a Decider. Not if what she prophesised was accurate, not if these spirits in her dreams *were* real and were so certain that my father would be the last of his name – the last Decider of the Philson Dynasty. And it explains why I've always been so cynical, so fearful about the rise to power – her bedtime stories must have left their scar on me, constantly apprehending such an eccentric fate, my apocalyptic becoming. But my father denounced her prophecies by saying it was the first stage of her deviance into incessant madness. "*Daft ghost stories*", he called them. He instructed me to ignore it all, for he didn't trust my mother after those habitual nights "*drinking lies*" in my bedroom. He condemned her and told everybody about her madness. The madness was apparently what killed her in the end. The fabrication of this sickness of hers was cast and recast in the Media and the news articles bled her name from the headlines – *The Decider's Wife Can't Make Her Mind Up / Oracle Loses Her Gift / Alleged Affairs With The Afterlife*. Oh—the

☆ Ministors had meager power in comparison to the Decider. They were positioned in charge of organizing town events and temporary councils, only when it was vitally needed to justify their role in the system – even though the rules of the New Democracy often classed these delegation methods as a form of "opposition crafting" and it provoked A.I. prosecution on the individuals who took their brief political privileges within the Decider's Administration too far. The Ministors were sometimes referred to as "*the burger-flippers of democracy*".

perils my mother endured in those final years! It never left her – the Media, the perjurers, the threats on her life. It ended in her genuine depression and her suicide eight days before my eighth birthday. If not anyone else in the world, at least *I* knew my father was responsible for that unnecessary death, for kicking her while she was down and leaving her to soak in defamation. That's why he rarely mentions her to me, or anyone. He can't bear the noise she brought him. The vulnerability stung upon a Decider by his own wife was humiliating and he dealt with the subject without indecision. By his command came a hastened palisade of annulment, fortified for the prospect of an extraordinary reputation. Now, he never talks of this because he doesn't have time for the "nonsense". And, with me, he doesn't want the same nonsense. He's long since washed his hands of all that; she died ten years ago.

'*It channelled the bloodline*, my father told me once after my mother died. *Soothehood was a venomous demon carried from ancestor to ancestor. It wasn't her fault. Its psychotic disease has been killing that poor family of hers for generations; your mother and your Aunt Sibyl were both infected by it. I could see how much the pressure of all that knowing and foreseeing pained them both; socialist authority was a curse upon them and the stress of this responsibility drowned them in madness – such a shame and a disappointment. She was in agony, your mother. I vow to never allow such a sickness to fall upon you or any soul in my Great Nation ever again...* As you're aware, my father had been unpopular with the Soothes. There've been witch-hunts ever since he came to power and the few Soothsayers who were pardoned, like my Aunt Sibyl, have been pushed out into the suburbs and as far as the Slumberlands. His fear of what would happen to my mother once he eradicated Soothe Culture, is why he stripped the Oracle's position from his administration altogether – took my mother out of the political equation without question. Soothes are more or less extinct these days because of him. He thinks they were all just liberals in disguise, waiting to *infect* his ideology at the shortest notice.'

'*So*—empathy was your mother's greatest weapon,' Islie muttered, scribbling something lacklustre. 'Is there anything she might have done right now to put your mind at ease?' Islie probed.

'My mind is at ease.'

No response from Doctor Islie told Oscar that he wasn't convinced and wanted more than that answer. Oscar was used to this reaction by now – many of his professors at the Academy had criticised him for his vagueness. So, he tried to retrace his memory back, before the Conflicts had started and before his father had been instated as Decider.

'Since my mother had always been *the* Oracle – once the most revered Sayer in the City – for as long as I can remember, her judgement was always the correct one. Many people had unmovable confidence in everything she said. Her views were so much more insightful than anybody else's and the Administration could really do with someone like her right now. An experienced Soothe with a strong judgement of events, the world's potential and the future. If people like her hadn't already been lost in the beginning, the Conflicts would have ended far sooner – at least, that's what I believe. What a power she was. My mother would have said to me that *having a Faith is like having a compass.* Just to have belief in something, *anything*, to such a high degree, would be enough to guide you anywhere you want to go. *The greatest leader is the one we all have faith in.*'

'It depends what "Faith" you're referring to,' Islie intervened, cachinnating with a sudden awkward excitement that didn't tie in to his standard nonchalant glare. 'Hopefully you mean that, while disregarding any of that kookiness they do in the East. I knew you're mother well. Met her myself on a few occasions. And I'll listen to most things. But I draw my line when it comes to ***The** Faith.*'

'Oh no, of course, nothing to do with that cruel, hateful belief they've fabricated out there. My mother disapproved of that as much as anyone in the West. Then again, she also reminded me not to trust *everything* the Media in the West has to say about the Faith in the East. I mean, that furtive Faith may be broadcast as all the dreadfulness it's been reputed with by the Media – the barbaric torture, brainwashing and ransom of innocent people – but it may not solely be what the fine brush *we follow* paints it as—'

Oscar hesitated, scared that he'd said too much. None of it could be true – he couldn't prove it. Of course, the Faith was an important controversy that needed to be discussed delicately and in articulate detail. But it was just a very dangerous topic to bring up on a whim with anyone.

'Go on,' Islie coolly encouraged. He took another sip from his mug and flexed his stiffening neck.

Oscar considered the invitation to carry on, before tailing the practitioner's relaxed prompt with more of his off-the-cuff speculating. Even though his father would've had this man studied thoroughly before he came near his son – doctor or not – Oscar sidetracked from the subject rapidly nonetheless. Just as precaution.

'There's a severe division, you see?' Oscar restarted the conversation. 'A segregation of opinion. People like my mother are in the minority. They're the Liberals under fire right now, and that's where the real war's going on – the wealth of the system must incessantly oppose the popularity among the poor. Imagine how many people are dying under the judgement of law these days and weigh it against the number of Liberals being convicted, defamed and packed off to *Sainthood*. We keep hearing about those witch-hunts going on in the Third and Fourth Nations. It's not honing in on Soothsayers and rogue rebel groups anymore – the Decider's Administration is casting a wider net than that now. They're shamelessly lambasting Liberals these days. No qualms about it, just overtly attacking anyone who resembles Punkish attitudes. How do the government respond to this tall order? The new line of Androkind is programmed to sniff them out of any given crevice in the West.☆ Within days, these A.I. will infiltrate everywhere. Starting with Liberal propaganda rallies, then to the Liberal Presses, and eventually seeking out their secret common rooms – the "Liberal Lairs" – and it's there where the Tin Men pluck the Liberals out of the cult, permanently, poaching in bulk. Then, the rumours start circulating: the waterboarding, the brainwashing, and the admittance to Rehabilitation Zones in the Second Nation, and so on – you know all this part, you read about it every day. No one believes it, because the public is kept so distant from the Decider's Administration that they have no idea how much the hunt has actually expanded and advanced. Next minute, you are going to see these Punkish captives, who were once protesting against the Decider's Administration, fighting in the Conflicts as patriots. Or some rumours go so far to suggest that they are butchered and turned into A.I.!'

'Don't be ridiculous, Oscar,' Islie extinguished the horrific idea with a stern look.

'The other day, I was reading an article about those animal rights protestors who started up a harmless demonstration in the Third Nation's capital, Libertas—'

'How did you get hold of Third Nation articles—here in the City?' Islie interrupted.

☆ "Androkind" was the official name given to the specific breed of Artificial Intelligence (A.I.) that took on a new human-like presence in 21st Century society and wholly imprinted its advanced technological abilities on many of mankind's most demanding and recurring endeavours from the 2020s onward, such as automated labour, manual labour, algorithmic programming and coding, law and order, etcetera…

'My father leaves his *HoloPad* lying around sometimes,' was Oscar's pathetic answer to that.

Islie snorted and shook his head to indicate he was sceptical once again.

'Well, the article mentioned that the whole demonstration in Libertas was following some leaked experiment details from the SPR—'

'And what do *you* know about the SPR?' Islie interrupted again, vitally concerned by this particular reference. His strict bluntness restored itself, annexing his relaxed temperament.

Oscar twitched. It was as if a spotlight had descended, beaming down on his head alone. 'All I'm *supposed* to know is that we must call it the SPR and nothing more,' he lied. 'They never let us read about that at the Academy either. The library at City Central Academy was pretty tragic to be honest.'

But Islie caught up with this subject like a lion racing elk. 'I am aware of such a place—the Southern Polar Region. Though, I'm not quite aware of what practices go on in such a mythical segment of the world,' he responded sensibly.

'But, anyway, that's beside the point,' Oscar resumed his story: 'As I was saying, what the Third Nation was really doing with these protestors was more than simply imprisoning them and sanctioning them, worse than just executing the guiltiest agitators on the spot. These officials – I hate to call them our own; they were Third Nation A.I., yes, but they were commissioned there by my father, sent from all the way here in the City – they were abducting protestors out of public view to take part in this thing I heard was called "*utilisation*", I think? It didn't even involve punishing them or using torture. What they were doing – what the A.I. were doing – was erasing their minds with some weird, untested thing these rumours call Brain Bleach and their conscious material was replaced with the minds of domestic animals so that people like us, who they suppose are too *unobservant* to understand, wouldn't be as sodden when it came to sending dumbed-down civilians to fight in the Conflicts. Oh, and these poor protestors wouldn't be released back into general society again. No way! It wouldn't be safe. After committing their crimes, they only ever get submitted to their Rehabilitation Zones, battery farms for Punks, where they're proselytised into war heroes for the New Democracy – one last bitter fate for the Liberals. At least, that's how the legend goes.'

'I'm not getting your point.'

'Maybe this subconscious state I'm in, this Dreamerverse, is some kind of a warning? It could be a tremor in reality, warning us to be careful of our own divisive chaos? Our departure from the Old Democracy all those years ago might have been an awful mistake.'☆

'*Hmm...*' Doctor Islie seemed to consider this idea comprehensively, scooting forward in his armchair and jotting a few words on the notepad. 'Did you say...it was an island that looked like another planet?'

'A planet of which I only saw a small part, an island. There was a beach, the ocean, the sand, a jungle...It was all real!'

'An entire planet...that was in the shape of an island?'

'What—? No! Aren't you paying attention? It was another world! Though, I didn't see enough of it to come to a better judgement!'

'Master Philson, have you ever been to a beach before?' Doctor Islie was back in his comfort-zone and he suddenly had his large hands twinkling over the conversation again. A smug smirk lit up his face.

'No,' Oscar responded.

Doctor Islie nodded in what might have been an accepting manner. But Oscar could see right through it. He wasn't impressed. In fact, he wasn't taking heed - or any more notes either - unlike any decent dude with a degree in psychology (or with a degree of any sense at all) would.

'Look, I believed what I saw and that's the solid truth. I'm not a fool!' Oscar hissed at him.

☆ The Old Democracy had been the democratic constitution that existed in the West pre-2020 (before the first Philson dynast, Richard (Rocky) Philson, came to power in 2020). Remembered as the "Ancient Freedoms", this abandoned constitution encouraged strong partnerships between Nations in trade; relaxed (almost non-existent) migration restrictions; impactful public elections; unabridged liberties to Liberal "Punk" ideology with the legislated right to voice such passions for the "Punkish Faith"; and there would be multiple Deciders in power – one for each Nation, even though the Decider of the First Nation would still rule supreme.

The New Democracy, however, had stripped the West of most of these laws. It came into practice following the Great Splits in 2019. By 2023, Rocky Philson introduced the law that made trade only legal if it was committed between neighbouring Nations alone (First to Second, Second to Third, Third to Fourth); in 2031, Rocky shifted the electoral system to one that diluted the public vote and simultaneously concentrated the vote of Ministers restricted inside the Decider's own Administration; Rocky's son, Nicholas "Knick Knack" Philson (the current Decider), had been further demolishing the West's bridges ever since he succeeded his father in 2041, with his countless persecutions of the Liberals (witch-hunts, purges, show trials, etc...) and his radical migration laws. Presently, Knick Knack remained a controversial and greatly disputed Decider.

Doctor Islie watched Oscar for a short while without saying anything, as if hanging on this last remark. Then, he came out with: 'Who else was there? In this Dream World with you?'

'A load of people dressed in pyjamas.'

Doctor Islie broke out into hysterics, thick and fast like a cluster of acne would break out on an adolescent's forehead – ironically, he lifted a hand to his forehead and rubbed it, just to check whether his thoughts had left him. This was followed by another sip from his mug and a sigh of *what you gonna do?*

'You mentioned others: the two people you met in the jungle,' he honed in.

'I forgot their names,' Oscar admitted. 'It's the whole memory-blockade-thing I was told about, remember? It's odd. At First Awakening you're fresh meat, open to interpretation and not yet christened by the blur. After a while, you begin to forget the goings of the other world and you're accustomed to the other. For me it's probably easier to remember slightly more than an average Dreamer, because when I arrived on Awakening Coast, I came after sunset – rather than before, which is when most Dreamers pop up.' He looked at Islie, intending to make sure that he was keeping up. 'It's a bit like that hour or so after you wake up. Reality gradually takes over and it swallows your nocturnal thoughts whole. You don't remember anything from the night before.'

Doctor Islie's eyes were fixed on the boy again, but not as intrusively this time. Loose and impatient was that man's new attitude. The hard, sharp inferno in his pupils had faded and his eyebrows were no longer puckered with strenuous bewilderment. He seemed somewhat transparent in this light, appeared without zone and without purpose. The last thing a practitioner like him wanted to be seen as was transparent. Luckily, Oscar never noticed this. What Oscar realised was that full darkness had arrived. Night was here. *But where are the insects?* Oscar asked himself. *The chirping? What happened to it? And the 'howling birds'?*

There they were on the balcony under the stuffy, chugging atmosphere, looking down upon the concrete-towers below and the beating lightshow. Things were floating in the distance, hovering like fireflies: monorails and *EvokaRafts*. Higher up in the sky, hidden behind the fume-clouds, flashing aeroplanes and jets and drones could be seen. But not heard. These things brought Oscar back down to earth again.

'Oscar, you're looking at me as if I know who these people you're talking about are.' Doctor Islie had his eyes half-shut. It was impossible to tell whether he was exhausted with boredom or cuttingly keen in his endeavour for answers. 'I might be the City's leading psychiatrist. But I'm not telepathic. You need to give me better detail than "wearing pyjamas".'

'But will you at least *try* to make some sense of it this time?' Oscar challenged.

'I—'

'No! If I tell you what those other people were like in the slightest, will you take me seriously?'

'You're making it very difficult to believe.'

'I'm not lying to you.'

'Please, Master Philson, I don't have all evening. Perhaps start with specifically describing one of the two you banded with?'

'Well…one of them I was more familiar with than the other. This was the girl I mentioned—I knew her. Well, I *recognised* her. I'm sure I've seen her somewhere before. But I don't remember where.'

'And the other one?'

'Non-descript. Sorry, can't remember what he looked like. But I'm pretty sure that he had something to do with the East.'

Doctor Islie entwined into something sour. Wasn't certain he was hearing it right. A resurgence of fascination took hold. 'The East? What did he have in connection to the East?' All engines on and ready to fire, he sat forward in his chair with his pen tense in his hand.

'He was a war-veteran or something like that, fought for the East in the Conflicts,' Oscar verified. 'Why? What's wrong with that? Have I said too much again? Am I in troub—?'

'What did he say?' Doctor Islie snapped.

'What do you mean?'

'Anything he said? Did he tell you anything?'

'What is this? What's the problem?'

'What you hide from me, you're keeping from your father. The East could be using you to extract information, understand? You're a direct target to the Decider! Do you want that? Do you want the East to know where they can get to you and the Decider?'

Oscar couldn't hide his quivering lips even by biting them hard. The psychiatrist's shift of tone was frightening him.

'I've no idea what my father's got to do with any of this and, besides, when did you start believing me?'

'Since you started to mention East Folk dressed in pyjamas, that's when!'

'Is that why he sent me here? The moment I brought up East Folk in my dreams he got worried and called you?'

'When you told your father about this earlier, he feared that you'd been Bugged. Now, it might not seem like much of an issue to you, but when the East is able to obtain thoughts from your subconscious-mind, they'll be able to locate your father and potentially hold the City and the entire Nation under threat. The Terror Meter would rocket every time you blink. Do you want that?'

'I know nothing.'

'It doesn't matter whether you know anything or not. You might have heard things or seen things, which you might not have instantly realised, but your subconscious mind has logged it and you're only exposed to glimmers of it at a time in your "dreams"! Now, tell me, what was this other East character like?'

Oscar had a quick decision to make. He hesitated, not moving for a moment or two before catching air. 'Nothing...I mean, *y—err...*He might not have been from the East...Nah—*nah*, I'm pretty sure he wasn't... that was just an immediate assumption. In fact, I don't think I even saw him for that long while I was there. Totally unrecognisable now. Just another pallid subordinate probably, loitering along the City Wall, or dwelling about the Slumberlands, or hanging somewhere grim like that as we speak.'

'Really...?' Doctor Islie was slowly becoming persuaded (or subdued) by the trickery of Oscar's avoidant eagerness. 'Are you sure?'

'Quite positive actually.'

'But he wasn't from any of the Lower Nations to say the least, was he?'

'He was from one of the middle ones, I think. Fourth or, perhaps even Fifth, maybe? Maybe not.'

'Right...*hmmm*,' he jotted a few words down on a new page. 'As long as he had nothing to do with one of the Nations associated with the East—then, it's no longer a subject of *immediate* concern. But if you start to feel dizzy or faint, be sure to make your medic aware.' Islie shrugged after saying this.

They both shared a brief stroke of relief – both for different reasons: Doctor Islie didn't want to tell DCD. Philson about such scenarios and Oscar didn't want Central City surgeons performing lobotomies on him for the sake of finding East spyware or, worse even, parasites.☆

'Your father is a very important man and he is the East's number one target of interest.'

'Tell him what you like about me. Tell him I've been bad to you and he'll mention nothing to me. He's happy to spend enough to keep me occupied and quiet,' Oscar chirped.

'I'm sure your father has never laid an unwelcome finger on you,' Doctor Islie provided a sagacious nod and he was using it to harpoon a reaction from Oscar. The Decider's boy was watching the street some distance below, following the whine of an ambulance as it scuttled along, looking much like a red and blue flame chasing across a fuse of gunpowder. When Oscar lifted his head up, Islie winked at him.

'You are no longer a child, but a man, a distinctive heir to your father's legacy.' Islie's voice was flat and inattentive, as though he wasn't paying any interest to his own words. 'That Wall is never tall enough and our enemies on the other side can never be far enough away. The East has polluted societies in the West and all over the world, societies you can't even remember. And they're pushing and pushing to asphyxiate our tolerance. We live in an already very demanding system. Once upon a time, in a generation before yours, you wouldn't believe, we all thought that gaping borders would be the end for us. But your father stopped that when he cut the line, closed the borders. The only question left to ask is how long can he keep them closed and keep the East out? We all thought, one day, the world could be full of them, living and breathing the same air as us, and breeding with our children. *Yagh*! Foul, inextinguishable thoughts! I hope you never see the day. The East was once a bountiful kingdom of dignified resources. It now struggles to hoist a citizenry of barbaric vultures and that's all at the fault of the corrupt tyranny they have there – the Phestorship. At least we have an evolving government here, not a dogged rut operated by criminals.'

Listening to this man was like listening to the Media, Oscar thought. But the practitioner's monotonous tenor wasn't selling the bias

---

☆ (DCD) Abbreviated title of "Decider". This autocratic power in the West is first nominated and elected by the Decider's Administration. The public vote is only opened once the Decider's Administration has granted a resounding lead to their favoured candidate – by which point the public vote has no effect. If the Decider sustains a high approval rating – which is, again, primarily voted on by his own Administration – his eldest child will automatically become inaugurated as his successor.

to him. Instead, Islie sounded conventionally plastic, as if he were reading cues off a script.

'And the Eighth Nation, in the Far East?' Oscar tried. 'Haven't heard much from that end in a while. How are they doing, you think?'

Doctor Islie leaned back in his armchair, allowing his middle-aged backbone to click and allowing his middle-aged legs to slowly fold over one another and allowing his middle-aged hair – greying and what was left of it – to slick into a small fringe above his crinkled forehead. 'The Fifth Nation is unmanned and gullible, doomed to collapse any time in the near future; the Sixth appears to be the most stable Nation in the East, but cannot sustain herself for long without the input of her Sister Nations; I recall that the Seventh is under the helm of an unqualified megalomaniac; and I suspect that the Eighth Nation has already fazed out into…into…well, an abyss, the vacuum of infertility. There's nothing left over there and nobody left to do anything about it. The Eighth Nation is reaching its conclusion. It's still scrambling, but it's running short and shrinking, powerless. There is no energy there anymore. Soon, the people will freeze, starve and perish. Though, the Eighth Nation isn't completely devoid of ambition *just* yet. And, for that reason, the West must still be apprehensive, very afraid and very cautious. We never know what they might do in their own sacrifice. They are still resentful since the *Attacks* after all.'

'They might just want to stop,' Oscar considered. 'You ever think maybe that the East could just be waiting to surrender?'

'Surrender—who? Those *Phestors* running the place?' Islie scowled.

'Maybe not the Phestors. But the general East Folk must surely want an end. A bit like that old proverb puts it: "*the little boys don't want what the big boys want.*"'

'Um, no, you mean: "*the little boys don't* ***need*** *what the big boys want,*"' Islie corrected. 'In practice, the little boys *always* want what the big boys *have*.'

'Well, I'm not a fan of the East, or its folk, or its food for that matter. Never actually tasted East food – to be fair, I've always been quite afraid of its appearance. The sight of it is unappetising, to say the least. Needless to say, what I mean is, my heart and mind lie here in the West and stand for the betterment of *our* people. Over *there* is not my problem at all; I'm merely mulling my mildest interest. I swear that I don't care what happens to the East Folk, only what happens *because* of them. By this I mean—perhaps wasting *our* money, *our* fuel and *our* rations is unnecessary for *our* greater cause. We use a whole lot of it in proving how much greater we are than them. So, wouldn't it just be grand if we could stop fighting a war we're not going to win or lose anytime soon? I think winning is about being a smart winner and losing is being a stupid loser – it shouldn't ever be the other way round.'

The lethargic practitioner was wiggling a loose finger at him now. 'This boy is now challenging the importance of defending sovereignty in the West…*Now, now*…that's how we know you've been welcoming dreams unfit for a future Decider—And, Master Philson, what day did you want me to book you in for the lobotomy?' Islie joked.

In all seriousness, Oscar wanted to defend his opinion, but felt it unnecessary – anyway, the doorbell decided to sing before he could come up with anything half-coherent. This sound caused Doctor Islie to jump up on to his feet, placing his notepad to the side. Stretching his arms, he said: 'You were the last one, weren't you? Whoa, what a *long, drawn-out day*! And I'm supposed to be skiing tomorrow.'

'So, I guess that was the first and last of our appointments then?' Oscar triumphed.

'Yes, hopefully. Though, hey, let's just make it clear—*sooo*— that your father understands this evening turned out to be rather more productive than it actually was. Particularly towards the end, when we came to that very conclusive solution – earlier nights, earlier suppers, lots of water and—*so on*' – that translated as "*hint, hint—not too much information—hint, hint*" in the jargon language of *Unprofessionalese*. 'Your father doesn't need to be reminded of this, does he? If he remembers to ask, tell him that Doctor Islie made you all better like he said he would. Nothing was of concern: it was simply the flair of one's imagination; a childish, rebellious spurt that comes with the pubescent maturation into adolescence and all that jive.'

Another bell-chime from inside.

'Alright, *alright*!' Doctor Islie re-entered the suite through the sliding doors. Oscar followed in after him. 'It seems there's no time for any more chitchat, Master Philson. That has to be your father calling.'

The interior of Doctor Islie's residence was spacious and luxuriously designed. Spotlights automatically switched on whenever someone entered a room and the tiled-flooring could detect any presence, surrounding the prowler in a touch-responsive puddle of red-lit tiles – a system that kept the place safe from burglars, mice and the intrusion of stray felines from neighbouring suites. Islie's meals cooked themselves in the auto-scheduled oven and the *HoloVision* voiced a vast range of appealing opinions, it had been programmed to rouse friendly conversation with its owner. Whilst on his way through the apartment, the *HoloVision* helped itself to Doctor Islie's attention by declaring that she had managed to record tonight's *Party Pigs* and yesterday's *World Under Siege* and had set *Top Subordinate* to series link. All of them the "*punky-spunky reality shows*" that Oscar's father forbade him from watching. Much to his astonishment, the *HoloVision's* Intelligence announced the episodes transferred were waiting for Islie to catch up on *BINGE* and Oscar's curiosity alone kept him wanting to stay and tune in purely for fascination.☆ Currently on the screen was a promo from an *ORAMA* channel, where an overly confident subordinate was teaching viewers *how to fix a ponytail when it frays.*☆

As Islie turned the final corner and went to answer the door, Oscar thought it would be sensible to slowdown before reaching that corner, hiding there. Just in case it was someone he didn't know. The last thing he wanted was to start polite conversation with a worldly stranger or to endure the goggling of his greatest aficionado yet—

'Ah, yuh Isl'eh? Docta Isl'eh?' A voice belonging to someone Oscar knew and admired too well. Definitely somebody Oscar affiliated with. The man at the door had a loud and distinctive accent.

'Yes, I am. Have you come for Philson's boy by any chance?' Doctor Islie asked.

'*Cha!* Where de boy? Him farda wou'd 'ave try tuh phone yuh, if he hadn't been ah' rush' to prepare fuh de banquet takin' place at his residence dis afta'noon. He far too busy an' ask meh to fetch de pickney up—quick.'

Oscar stepped out into view to see the visitor at the door. It was Stevenson, his father's attendant (and his ticket out of here). Stevenson was a rather tall bloke in a sharp, tidy black suit and a matching black tie. His hair was in neat dreadlocks, each lock tipped with a white bow of ribbon at the end.

'Osca', child!' Stevenson roared with fizzing anxiety and cheekily kissed his teeth. In his hands, he had folded clothes. 'Yer farda wanna meh pick yuh up earlier an' bring yeh back to his residence immediately. Me nah know yeh size 'cause yuh keep grow an' meh nah keep up, but he tol' me to choose yuh summin' fresh an' tidy tuh wear

---

☆ *BINGE* is a bootleg streaming service that emerged in the early 2020s, following the censorship and collapse of the Internet.

☆ *ORAMA* is a government-monitored broadcasting channel, via which subordinates could show-off their video-making talents and portray stars of themselves for the world to see.

to dem special occasion dere. Dress to mek ah differ'nt impression: not as him son, but as him next of kin – de future leadah of de First Nation an' de West. I suggest yuh get dress here, not dere, but *quick*—since we late ah'ready.'

He threw the folded tuxedo to Oscar. There was a silk ribbon tied round the package and bowed on the top. Oscar responded to Stevenson with a weak smile, then reverted to his regular gesture of gratitude: *a sigh*.

'Now be slick. Yer guests are expectin' yuh.'

Oscar never wanted to be at the centre of attention, consumed by the opinions of people he didn't even know. He hated being perceived and judged and criticised by those who inconveniently had no trace as to what he was *really* thinking and feeling. Unsure whether he was appreciative or frustrated of the fact that the limousine windows were tinted, he gazed blankly out at the streets as everything trailed past, lagging into the plain skin of a stubborn canvas, making fameless memories of the journey home. Half of him wanted to get back as quickly as possible, the other half didn't want to return to Citadel Tower at all – it wanted to vacillate down here among the subordinates and their wonderful chaos.

If it were his decision to make, he'd have much preferred to take the City *TRAMLINE* or the *LASERWAY*. He may well have even enjoyed it. At the very least, he'd have felt like he had something in common with someone, *anyone*, for once and he would no longer have to lug around the profile of his father and the unpopularity that his father wielded. It was no secret. The Decider and the public never landed in the same sentence, let alone on the same slab of concrete. Looking out of the window, Oscar saw A.I. on evening patrol. There must have been hundreds of the Tin Men out on a Saturday evening, harvesting the dregs of the day's Anti-Decidership demonstrators and frog marching these Punks back to the border in true exile style. A woman in a full-body cloak with her face completely veiled had been cornered against a wall outside *Virtu-Bank* by a pack of four A.I., and was being interrogated. *Was it a woman, or a bloke?* Oscar could never tell – *the East Folk all dressed the same. Someone ought to do something about the fashion sense out there*, he thought, watching the "woman's" arrest from the serenity of his limousine in transit, *you can't tell a non-extremist from an extremist, or a man from a woman for that matter.* She would probably be deported back to whichever Nation she came from. If she happened to be lucky, she would follow suit behind the demonstrators: back to the border and exiled into the impoverished wilderness that lay beyond the very corporeal City Wall – into the mythical realm dubbed "the Slumberlands".

Oscar had only visited the City Wall once on a field trip; he'd seen what it looked like then for a short and discomforting forty minutes. The Wall was bigger now. It had been renovated four or five times since then. Now, it was taller. Thicker. More imposing than ever before. It surrounded the City, but was too far from his residence to bother him with its presence. Nobody in the City Central had to worry about the monstrosity at the border – citizens living deep in the Central, including him, didn't pay the taxes for the Wall, whereas the subordinates living in the suburbs were entitled to pay those restoration taxes by First Nation Law. Every three months, another notice materialised in the form of a scripted *HoloVision* broadcast – fronted by the Decider himself and the insignia of the New Democracy pasted onto the background behind him – to remind the loyal public to pay Border Tax or face the fining penalties.☆ 'The deadline for Border Tax is coming up,' the Decider would normally address on-screen. 'It is paramount for the security of the City that we budget this tax, in order to protect us from the highly dangerous radioactive potential being emitted from the sewer-damage beneath the Slumberland Region.' The Decider had been telling them that message for years and no one truly comprehended it, yet they persevered out of ignorance – as evidence for the crisis was only as scarce as their interest for it. The City Wall was a daunting prospect to everyone. It snatched a nugget from their salaries, but whatever it did it had been "doing well", according to the Decider and his officials. Nevertheless, the mysteries it concealed tickled their superstitions of *never-getting-radiation-poisoning* and misunderstanding the "horrors" that went on beyond it in the Slumberlands. But the public were not blind. They could see the Wall itself. Every day, they passed it during their commutes and one only had to look at how thin and hollow it was on the face to speculate that it might not have been as radiation-proof as the government prescribed. At least, that wasn't the Wall's primary function. Those quiet superiors, who were unmarred by the impressions of the state, might have known

☆ The insignia of the New Democracy was the black outline of the sun centred with the eyes and snout of a lion. The insignia of the Old Democracy had been the black silhouette of a crescent moon faced with the profile of an eagle – cutting eyes and crooked beak.

there was more reason to it than that, but couldn't have been less inclined to spread such rumours.

Oscar was young and he apparently still had a lot to understand about the world, where the world had been, where world was, and where world was going – which was exactly how his father tried to describe his cold feet. Only, now, he seemed to be going through an ordinary stage in his youth; a faze which would hopefully be over very soon. Adolescence meant a lot of things…to ordinary kids. It meant that you could throw your own anger (and physical weight) at the world just to see the dent it would make; you could unintentionally summon your own demons, who, once released like a spurt of dopamine, would recklessly plot about mischief, chanting your name aloud as they did so to pervert all discretion; and you could even abuse your repute (or utilise your emotions) in a way that would cause others around you to ignore you or pity you; and the words *you*, *I*, and *me* would become such a common referral to your identity that the words *us*, *we*, and *them* would temporarily disenfranchise themselves from the toll of your antisocial tongue, simply by nature.

He felt none of that. He wanted there to be *us* or *them*; he wanted to be part of something, somewhere, somehow. Just like how all those other boys at the City Academy had something, somewhere, somehow. Some*one*. They'd told him about all their adventures and their misadventures, one after the other. About their summertime outings and bonding camps together, and dates with girls, and Ball Game Events at the Harkson Centre.

And then there was Oscar, exempt from the trivialities of boyhood and shielded from scrutiny. Whenever Oscar had suspected this far cry for an ordinary childhood, his father assumed hormones to be the case – he was still growing up after all and would soon be the next of kin if his father ever got into "*a sticky situation*". His father dismissed him at every opportunity and, since his mother had perished from his life many years ago, he had no one else to confess his anxiety to. He was afraid of the world, even though he had the opportunity to learn every corner of it, as well as the power to *change* it in some circumstances. He had the pocket money and the lavish temptations to draw friends like playing cards, and even attain a fiancée if he dealt them correctly. But, for as long as he could remember, he had his father's dreaded opinion to blame most of all; he was discouraged, compelled to let no one into his life other than himself and he was used to that.

It came as no surprise, when he arrived at Citadel Tower and scaled the elevator to his father's residence on the top floor, to find over a dozen men and women sitting around the Decider's Table. They were all dressed in formal evening attire. The Table was dark crimson like a parted set of overused dentures, with the insignia of the New Democracy carved into its centre, and around it, numerous cavities of pallid men sat alongside fillers of translucent women. They were all middle-aged and sombrely ostentatious delegates under the eyes of the Decider. Some were even questionably human by the look of their latest cosmetic enhancements. The youngest of all the guests was Oscar's age and that "fellow adolescent" just had to be Timothy Gimarez, one of his former colleagues from the City Academy. He hadn't seen Timothy in years. In fact, ever since graduating from the Academy all those months back, he'd hoped he'd never have to see The Moth ever again. (Yes, Timothy was the smutty delinquent who'd wiped his arse with his uniform tie in the boys' toilets to graffiti murals of moths on the walls with his faeces; at least, they were supposed to be "*brown butterflies*" according to the artist himself).

At the head of the Table was his father, the Decider. The man at the focal point didn't appear as exhausted as usual. Of course, he wouldn't after the mild cosmetic treatment he'd rewarded himself earlier that day, which had amended him remarkably by polishing the creases out from the baldness of his scalp, a result that looked comparable to the sheen of a new bowling ball; further improvements came by whitening his teeth to their highest excellence; youth was redefined by refilling the lacklustre bags beneath his petite eyelids; and the intimidation in his glare was topped up by recharging the vigilant – and in ways, frightening – hazel-glow in his genetically modified pupils. It wasn't every day Oscar saw his father this done up; the Decider was mostly too busy for beauticians' intricacies. DCD. Philson was the sort of man who treasured the idea of vanity, but simply didn't have the time for it to become a habit. 'Oscar, come introduce yourself to this evening's associates!' his father called to him.

Oscar was receiving immense stares now. Quite a few were immensely ugly, to say the least.

'What have you been playing at, boy?' One of the most impulsive men at the Table cursed at him. It was an older official, badged and medalled in a spotless blue greatcoat and beret. *Some general*, Oscar guessed, *from either the Second or Third Nation*. He'd groomed a neat white hedge of beard that grew off the bottom-half of his rumpled face; above the hedge were two bulbously dilated eyes, peering over it like a meddlesome next-door johnny prying through his neighbour's picket-fence. 'You had your father concerned and you've neglected your guests for hours! Do you realise who we are, boy? Whose faces you are laughing in?'

'Who in the name of Trivium does he think he is?' A pencil-thin woman in a skin-tight dress hissed, as she stroked the rim of her full wineglass with a nail that was nearly twice the length of her finger.☆

'Are you sure this is *your* Oscar, Decider – the successor – and not some other Oscar?' another veteran official whom Oscar couldn't place choked on his drink in rambling from across the Table. He spoke of Oscar as if he hadn't yet entered the room, like the Decider's son wasn't to be present at all. 'I once met an Oscar – a subordinate working at that cheap wally-joint down *Meander Street*: *City Cuppaccino*. Unfortunate bloke, quite an incompetent Oscar he was; served my latté lukewarm every time.'

'Subordinates are used to lukewarm,' the weightless woman, insolently hooked onto the older gentleman, trying to bathe in the attention. 'Lukewarm slaver lines their blunt, tiny tongues. And, Minister Thimble, do mind that if you listen to too much of the angst they gargle, you are disposing yourself to be contaminated with their temperament of sickly idleness and to be indulged by their historic drought of ambition, since "lukewarm" prospects are carried in the subordinate's veins and ejected with every syllable they spit.'

'I agree,' the man she pronounced as Minister Thimble – the Minister of the Fourth Nation – responded. 'How unsettling it is! I agree. The subordinate matter needs to be addressed fast. For example, educationally, these subordinate equivalents to our Academies are breeding imbeciles! Subordinate schooling is completely abortive in this day and age. Fewer of them can master Week Trades anymore and now you're seeing a mounting number of them struggle with their simple, simple Weekend Trades. You'd be lucky to dig out a subordinate down there who can read, write or speak proper West Dialect.'

Nobody responded on cue. None of the other guests wanted to contribute to the Fourth Nation Minister's treacherous small talk. There were many wandering and drifting glances around the Decider's Table. His shameless (and drunken) showboating was evidently meant for the Decider's attention and no one else.

☆ Trivium – the original name of the West before the 'Great Splits' divided it into its Four Nations.

Still, from his immobile position, standing gracelessly near to the door, Oscar had calculated that the new outnumbered the old. There were some old faces he'd nebulously seen before, and too many new ones he couldn't be bothered to look at, let alone *introduce* himself to. A lot of their expressions were singed with a disgust that was kilned by what they witnessed to be Oscar's vulgarity. The recklessness of his arrival had stunned his father's associates. They mistook him unfairly off one impression. That's all he'd been given, one chance to prove his responsibility and he'd already blown it. He was already coming across as bit of a Punk. But he didn't want Doctor Islie to be right; he didn't want his father to be right. For that reason (amongst many others), Oscar wanted to dash under the Table and hide there for the rest of the evening, not to re-emerge until they'd all had their moans and groans and disappeared.

'I apologise for my son's unaccountable spontaneity,' the Decider invited himself into the heated discussion. He hadn't lost his composure. Both his hands remained securely on the Table, fisted. 'My son lives in a world of his own, one that I can never quite transport myself to, as much as I've tried before. But his matters, under this evening's moon at least, are the matters furthest from our dilemmas. And his trivia, like many homebound affairs, I no longer have the will to endeavour. I have tried to regulate him and he knows I have. What more can a father do?' The Decider grinned dutifully, soaking in the sharp focus engaged on him from all the other individuals assembled around his Table and the crest of the New Democracy. 'Take your seat, Oscar.' The Decider did not look at the boy when he dribbled this instruction. He hadn't caught Oscar's eye once since he'd entered the room and had no intention to.

Oscar obeyed his father without question. As he shifted over to take his usual seat at the other head of the Table, the associates were shaking their heads, grunting and muttering. Timely enough, he came to realise who these people really were and how many of them there actually were: they included not one, but *all* the leaders of the West's Nations. The Ministers of Second, Third and Fourth had all convened under their supreme leader, the Decider of the First Nation. Oscar almost flushed completely red with embarrassment. Between the Ministers were some others he vaguely recognised, but no attendee in the room came close to "the Big Ms" on the scale of stately importance. Tonight was the big one, the Annum Summit and Oscar had forgotten all about it.

He caught sight of Timothy again. The other boy was deliberately ignoring him with his chin aimed for the sky. Timothy licked a conceited smirk from his face when he scrutinised Oscar in the corner of his eye. He was sitting rakishly erect like he'd been skewered up the backside. His tuxedo was a banal grey all over, his hair was neatly combed over with an excessive greasy coating and his skin was just as lubricated by clamminess. Sitting beside him was his own father, the Stateship of the First Nation. In his position, the Stateship stood below Philson and he was responsible for notifying the Administration about any controversial legislation the rest of the lower tier bureaucrats, unionists and socialites deemed was either "over– or under–blown" during their Summits, although it was unlikely that anything became denounced once the Decider had declared it. The Stateship was large and gout-afflicted; he was a man of old-fashioned complexities, both in voice and attire - waistcoat, fob watch and pince-nez glasses - and primordially officious even by the way he sat with a presence that emitted astounding significance right across the room (until it bounced off the Decider).

After examining Timothy for some time, Oscar became curious of his own hashed attire and found that his collar was bizarrely erect, sticking up and bowed round his neck and chin like the rim of a bursting tulip. He quickly fixed it.

'So, before I begin to stack up my revisions to the Constitution in some more detail, I ask the Ministors to update the Administration on the less domestic problems at hand - the foreign affairs,' DCD. Philson said. 'I've heard rumours about more "tremors" in the Fourth Nation - let me guess, are those Punkish Third Nation renegades still causing trouble on your western border? And also, I'm told pirate lootings are still a matter of concern in the Second Nation - invading in "fleets" now, is it? My Fair Ministors, this is your chance to explain to the Summit what the current situation is in your home Nation. I will do my best to consider your appeals.' The Decider slouched a little as he said this. He yawned. His ashen eyes were entranced to the back of his hand and counting the scars on his fingers. Apprehensive, the Decider shut his eyelids and sighed intensely before raising a hand to open up the Table to his guests, who were quivering with questions.

'Who's willing to go first?' he announced.

An immediate roar of responses quaked the Table. Oscar, afloat with the madness, could feel the disruptive notion he'd brought to the atmosphere in the room, how he'd unintentionally brought delay to such an important meeting, and he didn't like it at all. The abrupt cue of two dozen voices tossing meticulous questions and answers, and boorish insults and profanities across the Table, from side to side, reminded him very explicitly of the anxious rock of the ferry that had taken him on an Academy field trip to the Northern Polar Region to see the last colony of the "*upright, waddling, black and white bird species*". With hindsight, Oscar couldn't envisage anything worse than the teetering ache on that old ship bobbling on forever as long as there was water in the sea. He'd begged his father to go on that trip, an adventure which DCD. Philson had called nonsense to, believing his son should have spent the holiday period studying for his finals and return to the Academy with the confidence to pass and graduate. Oscar wished he'd never boarded that damned ship; they didn't see a single bird and the month after he returned from the trip, he failed his finals – holding him back another year.

'Hey, hey!' his father cried, a lack of respect expanding around him like a force field. 'One at a time! We have all night! All damn night!'

'But that lot ain't true, Decider, sir! All night is still *one night*, Decider, sir! Tonight ain't gonna be nuffin like tomorrah night – tomorrah night will be a very different can of worms to tonight. Nah, but, sirs, what we do tonight won't determine what different headaches tomorrah night will bring, isn't it. So we shud resolve tonight's affairs before they bleed into tomorrah and not leave it on a cliff-hanger like we tend to.' This statement came from a man as bald as a piglet, with a young face as ghoulish as a chalky full moon. The joke was on him, because the suit was way beyond his generation. It was as anomalously antiquated as an analogue grandfather clock in a strobe-lit nightclub. It failed to sophisticate his look or compliment his youth gracefully and, instead, condemned him as nothing more than a little boy who'd had too much fun in a cheap costume store. 'We have very little time to act upon anything, we lot do! In fact, we have only just enough time to *re-act* and *reacting* is exactly what we should be thinking of doing right now, Decider, sir!'

Piggy spoke wisdom. While it wasn't new wisdom – the Decider heard this complaint all the time – it was wisdom nonetheless. The Administration had to do its best to wrap up the long-standing problems before hastily moving on to the next set of issues and jumbling them up – this was how Oscar translated the young Minister's plea. But his Second Nation accent spoke other volumes and it was this DCD. Philson picked up on. It reminded the Decider again of being the second most powerful human being at the Table, once upon a time. But that somehow nostalgic feeling of being second best, somewhat sub-ordinary, was now ancient history – *just like everything else this Second Nation Mong had to say with his thin lips*, the Decider humoured to himself. That brought a smile back to his face. On a day like today, an occasion like this – the Annum Summit – the Decider was as elevated as he could ever hope to be. *These days, not even the Stateship would get a word in edgeways.* Tonight would be no exception: he would not stand for gargantuan requests from the greedy sibling Nations and when it came to *his own* Nation's policies and *his own* constitution, he would alleviate as little as possible.

'Ministor Ancillary,' DCD. Philson admired the zealous unease in the young man's expression and he grinned at it condescendingly. 'How are things in the Second Nation? Are your factories finally starting to outweigh your fields? Enough A.I. to go round, I presume?' The grin didn't leave his face. There was a fresh pack of cigars laid on the Table in front of the Decider, he set his hand over it protectively.

'We need more recruits, sir. Big time, sir.' Ministor Ancillary scuffed his tie, quickly breaking a sweat.

'Is that why you've come here tonight? Not to expel a small desire, but to request something massive of me? At a time like this?'

The Minister of the Second Nation responded in what must have been a single breath. 'As far as National Security goes, us lot have been missing *human* recruits in the Second Nation for six months, Decider, sir. With Androkind working on our Nation's borders alone, we're as exposed as a corpse dished up for the buzzards on the desert plains of Gungolia. And, meanwhile, with all that noise echoing from the Third Nation to do around "pirates from Fourth invading Third's eastern bays", we need *trained* Border Patrol, actual men who can *negotiate*, rather than upgraded A.I. that are just kitted out with the freshest gizmos; and perhaps it would help to develop an action plan to deal with the Third Nation's gaping borders also. The pirates just keep finding holes; only recently, we've discovered they're *digging* below the radar, *underground*! The A.I. are just letting these criminals wander across Third and into our Nation, isn't it. And, what do we get as a result? Pirates and their Liberal ideology being shipped in and then frogmarched back out to Fourth with all the loot, because, Decider, they *steal* from our Nation as well as spread their ideology! We'll have no original produce left to trade with First and Third the more we get trampled by these pirates. We know how important our Nation is to the West. Our output is your input, isn't it. So, I have come here to you this evening on the trust of my Nation, with their desire for you to do something about our crisis, yeah. I've made many promises, sir. Many promises that could very easily become lies.' Prominent fear electrified the Minister's already hotly rouged cheeks and his pupils wobbled from side to side, as if infected by a chastening hypnosis.

'I can't make too many promises myself,' the Decider said. 'But, seeing as you are still relatively new to the task, Minister, I'll try to mention it to my assistants when I get the opportunity. We ended our subsidies to the Second Nation's Border Patrol ever since A.I. were introduced to the situation there.'

There was hesitance before Minister Ancillary collected the strength to reiterate his Nation's distress: 'As I just made clear—the A.I. are not—'

'The A.I. may very well be the problem, Decider,' emphasised Minister Fideane – the man sitting so far along the Table from the Decider that his pea-sized head could only be made out by the thick sideburns that framed his awkwardly round face. Fideane was the Third Nation's Minister.

The Decider had to squint to sight him in the dim-lit room. He opened the pack of cigars, spent a moment selecting one, picked it out, and then revolved it between his fingers. 'What are you talking about, Fideane? The A.I. haven't gone rogue down there, have they? They are First Nation Standard A.I., recently commissioned too. So they shouldn't be showing any funny signs of culturing at all.'☆

'Not at all, Decider,' Fideane pleaded. 'Not at all.'

'Then what do you expect from me? I don't plan to turn on my premise and resort to a wet-nursing society. We simply do not have the *pecunts* or the capacity for such mollycoddling.☆ We've arrived at a time where Nations must take better responsibility for themselves. If *your* people can't find the work they require to conserve a home, if *your* struggle to combat pirates and estranged radicals is frightening you, and if *your* Border Patrol cannot put up with the A.I. I've already commissioned on both the western and eastern bays of both *your* Nations, well perhaps you need to reassess your own action plans before picking berries from my neck of the woods. I've given you what I

☆ Culturing was the term given to 'faulty' A.I. that had outgrown their hardware. Once an A.I. reaches this stage, its processor begins to reprogram itself with improvised codes beyond man's control. The first signs of this were seen in the earliest prototypes in the 2020s. However, such a fault was deemed too rare to occur in domestic A.I. and so the technical blunder remained overlooked for many years.

☆ *Pecunts* – the leading digital currency of the West (Est. 2027).

can for monetary aid. Only last year, each of your Nations received a state-of-the-art financial bureau, filled with my own expert assistants and upgraded branches of *Virtu-Bank*. But I'll be long dead and gone before anyone hassles me to subsidise anything or anywhere other than the First Nation again. I will fund you where I can, but I will not hold your hand and construct your Nations for you. That is your duty after all. Gentlemen, you know where I stand on independence…' Then, something dawned on the Decider. 'Where is Stevenson, Oscar?'

'He dropped me off—then said that he needed to hurry to be somewhere,' Oscar responded. 'Urgent call.'

'*Hmph*—typical of him! I guess you can't blame a Small Islander for their little disloyalties here and there. They have such a lack of objective and are easily distracted. Always scratching their backsides on the fence in these debates and their sad situations are never made much reference to for that very reason. They are not diplomats by nature. And so their community's flight across the constitution is determined like a flock of herons riding upon the horrendous torrents of a hurricane,' the Decider snorted and went on quite viciously. 'Anything else somebody would like to blame me for, before I go on to clarify what's happening next for the First Nation?'

There was suppressing silence from everyone.

'Okay—then, allow me to begin.' He finally zapped a flame onto the cigar in his hand, leaned forwards in his chair and took a deliberately long puff prior to ranting on. 'I'm not going to beat about the bush, so this won't take many words. We are all struggling, no? You have come to that conclusion pretty directly. Gentlemen, you and I are the leaders of a disenchanted domain that emerged with prospects of hope. But then came 'the Great Splits' that ravaged our fathers' term and warped our earliest naiveties of the future. It wasn't the future you anticipated or hoped for, however, 'the Great Splits' were required to keep order in the world, hence, we no longer reside as one Trivium, but in Four Nations – as do the East. I stand by my father's decisions; I stand by the 'Splits'. Ministors, do not be fooled—these once fruitful visions you had of an "idyllic" Trivium, a dreamland utopia, they were not quashed by 'the Great Splits', but shattered by 'the Great Infestations' – that chain of horrific exoduses that happened some time ago upon our fathers' era, which perhaps occurred even more often in *their* fathers' term; and so, alas, even our grandfathers had to endure such a multigenerational terror. Thankfully, those nightmarish days are all in the oblivion of our memories: an epoch of Liberals, and Punks, and pirates, and East Men border-hopping all over the place, no hard-line restrictions engaged from the West government at the time. This plague of migrants caused the people of the First Nation to rendition the original 'Great Split of 2019' – the first Split away from the rest of the West in a pioneering plebiscite. The First Nation was born from heroic and pragmatic innovation, and it declared the fall of Trivium—'

'The fall from grace…' a malcontent voice dared.

Benumbed silence.

No one at the Table tried to seek the culprit or identified him or herself with the burden of finishing that hazardous sentence. They detained their focus for the Decider alone, not to advertise their own mental discrepancy of bullish suspicion and oppressing trepidation.

The Decider paid it no notice. His expression didn't say much, latent behind an eddying tornado of cigar-fumes. He went on. 'The referendum to Split was the last great democratic vote held in the First Nation, under my father's Administration. It was a divisive and revealing vote that changed our perception of democracy forever. There hasn't been a vote so pivotal ever since – another wasn't required after that, nothing more was needed from the people. We are securer now than we were before the ballot was cast. The vote to Split rescued our sovereignty and it rescued the people as well. Then, of course – after the First Nation broke away – Ministors, your own Nations and those other realms of the East all followed suit. We set the trend here in the First Nation and, as they say, "the rest is history". By and large, this is what civilisation has come to. All of Mankind's World has adopted a new independence. Of course, there have been some minor sacrifices along the way that have taken mild effect. Growing pains. For example, when trading was embargoed on the Fourth Nation in 2020, for example, some low in-demand resources rolled on a decline for about twenty years thereafter, until a short-term agreement could be made, since the First Nation didn't have the natural facilitation to grow particular crops we once bought from Fourth—'

'You never asked,' that same troublemaker cussed from the crowd. Unlucky for him, the Decider put the voice to a face this time. He was scowling at the Minister of the Fourth Nation, Thimble. He just watched the self-righteous runt who had his nose turned upwards, preserving his dignity. Not for long though—

—for the Decider simply said, 'I wouldn't ask you to stay either.'

Minister Thimble stood up, taking this as an instruction to leave the room. He made for the exit.

'I don't need to ask you anything,' the Decider muttered under his breath once the man had departed. He glanced at the empty doorway, into the blackened corridor on the other side of it and flicked the back of his cigar with a thumb so that cinders burst from its scorched butt and plummeted to the Table.

'It was quite a terrifying transition for my father's Administration,' he rambled on. 'Major City Banks collapsed within days, the market dried up and there were worries of a famine by 2026. The world appeared to be coming to an end. To think, thirty years ago, in an alternative world, we could have been toiling with science and prototyping colonies on other planets – Mars, for instance – harvesting science's discoveries and championing its uses. After the Split, we had no time for those luxuriant adventures. The scope and rate of such progressive ambitions transformed to match my Nation's immediate needs. There never used to be eight individual Nations defining our world. There never used to be seven, six, five, or even four. Everything used to be weighed on the same scale, would you believe—it's shocking. Our predecessors had problems in those days, but petty ones by comparison to ours. I could only hope that such dilemmas as theirs would materialise in front of me. I would do exactly as they did: I would utilise the subordinate vote to initiate the Split; I'd rid the First Nation of the Great Infestations, and those migrants would go home running eastward or be severed by force; once they'd been stripped from my Nation's soil, I would have built that City Wall ten-fold taller than it is today and discharge any maligners who defile the Wall and disparage those who attempt to attack it from the rot of the Slumberlands. Gentlemen, be very confident that *I* would have solved that problem and amended the humanitarian disaster in a fortnight. I would be the champion. So, I reward to them – my predecessors, my fathers – my winning respect.' DCD. Philson raised his glass.

'The East don't have your respect, I'm afraid,' this interruption came from the Stateship. 'Decider—no disrespect at all, sir, but I worry that the people of the East – certainly their leaders – do not understand the sophistications of your… *allegiance*.'

'Why need for their respect when I have always had the upper hand?' the Decider stated.

'Because power in the East is changing, Decider,' the Stateship argued. 'And it is unstoppable.'

'Right now, the East only *appears* unstoppable,' the Decider snapped. 'The Sixth Nation's infrastructure has grown some, I admit. But don't worry too much. The Seventh and Eighth are in catastrophe –

and the government is overrun by the Infidels in Eighth; the Fifth has always been seething with its cannibalistic swamp of criminals and pirates and what not, but it won't be long until the perfidious Sixth abandons it, allowing Fifth to meet the same demise as her two Sister Nations in the Far East; but the only notable population boom in recent years is the one hatching out of the Sixth's capital, Quomer, which is a phenomenon in massive contrast to her Sister Nations.☆ Why is the Sixth Nation so well-heeled by comparison, you ask? It's because she doesn't depend on the other East Nations and she doesn't serve to them either. Which is exactly where I stand; and it's where every other Nation in the West should stand.'

'Your applauding of the Sixth Nation is unsettling, Decider,' the Stateship confessed.

'I'm not *applauding* the Sixth Nation!' the Decider yowled, offended. 'It just doesn't frighten me like it frightens you! Frankly, the knowledge of their population has no effect on us at all. They can outnumber us in bodies all they want, as long as those bodies are shepherded inside the Nations they belong. Your Stateship, it is their escalating Blackout infantry that catches my concern. They have since acquired – and now confidently swank – Blackout weaponry. Why, we've known this since *decades ago*, when the Infidels in the Eighth Nation leaked images of their government's warheads on the Internet – at a time before the Internet was closed down, obviously. They've threatened us in the past. Yes, they've abused our ideologies and beliefs. They've conspired attacks against all our peoples. But, the real question is – and it haunts me every night and day – will their Blackout armoury ever outnumber ours?'

'NEVER IN ALL MY LIFE HAVE I HEARD SO MUCH QUACK!' this was the booming voice of the Stateship, sprawling hell across the Table. He landed a ferocious fist on his empty plate, cracking it.

'Would you like to speak? Or would you prefer to argue?' the Decider softly asked the furious man.

'I don't know what you're getting at, Philson! This isn't a matter of trading toys with the East! What about *us*, Nicholas? WHAT ABOUT YOU, ME AND THE ENTIRE WEST? WE HAVE OUR *OWN* PROBLEMS!' the large man was adamant. He scooped the broken plate

---

☆ *Quomer* was the capital city of the Sixth Nation.

to one side and widened his little eyes at the Decider in an attempt to be intimidating. It wasn't working.

'*Us*?' The Decider momentarily aborted his confrontation with the Stateship and looked awkwardly around at the other guests, who were staring back at him bluntly. 'That isn't a valid term for what we are anymore. "*Us*" implies we are a unified community, a workforce, a brotherhood – no, we are merely neighbours negotiating foreign policy. Weren't you listening to what I said? Forbid, our Nations used to be mutual, domestically bonded through law and constitution. But, now, the design of our New Democracy means we're growing evermore apart. However, our desertion of community does not disregard our defence policy. Because a singular Nation with an inferior defence to the East is not an option. None of our Nations are going to be sufficient enough to survive against a Blackout strike from the East. Not on its own. That's what's on the cards: a Blackout Attack *will* eventually happen to one of our Nations again – it happened to the Second Nation and it happened to the Eighth Nation. To prevent this threat, one new idea I wanted to implement is my intention to expand my Nation's borders – mark our territory elsewhere. My people are going to suffer under the pressure of our population. The City Trades will be ungovernable and general standards of civil tolerance have never been so rife. You now have urchins demanding the same luxuries as millionaires. Even the tiniest of civilisations must keep a headcount. Things will get heated otherwise. And there is only one person they will blame – the only person they will ever blame: me.'

'Decider, I hope this is no wild idea for a section of our people to go and move in with the East. They are not *all* expendable criminals down there. And such an integration would be catastrophic,' the Stateship pondered.

'That isn't what I'm considering at all,' the Decider responded. 'Why would I suggest such a ludicrous idea? That would go completely against my conservative beliefs, my constitution! The New Democracy would frown upon me—'

'Then what are you suggesting?' the Minister of the Third Nation intruded. 'You haven't yet told us how you plan to expand the First Nation's borders! You haven't told *any* of us about this plan before today, this sweeping decision! Will it involve annexing the rest of our Nations to accommodate your expansion? *More Nations*, is that it? Are we resorting to that? Instead of eight are we splitting the surface of our world into *sixteen*? Just to make things *affordable* for the First Nation?

More Nations will only give us more problems and the East more targets for a Blackout Attack!'

'*Ludicrous!* There's no need, no use worrying about the East! It is still inferior to us, as it has always been,' the Decider defused. 'The Eighth Nation is cracking; the population of its capital, Salg Perdorn, is dropping like a meteor shower due to recurring famines, and its social dignity is submerged in the hate it receives from its own Sister Nations; it has been sinking for quite some time now. The Attack that devastated it years ago is proving to be irremediable. If we wait a little longer, Eigth will completely collapse and that'll be our chance to quash their empire at its centre. As soon as the Conflicts are won and finished, we'll already have a graceful hand on their rich land, their oil plains in particular!'

'Decider Philson, surely your daftness has boundaries, yes?' the Stateship teased. 'You are aware that since its atomic pummelling, the Eighth Nation is no longer the seminal root of the East. But the *Sixth* Nation – with its booming population, its thriving economy and its vast diamond-core mines – has declared itself the new beating heart of our enemy.'

'Your Stateship, that makes little change to my plan to condemn the East and acquire my wants. We still have the Northern Polar Region far out of their hands and all the attained resources we have kept there. Oil, diamond, fossil fuels—'

'Those were resources that once belonged to the East,' the Stateship heckled. 'So, what if their new course of action under the Sixth Nation is to procure those resources again, take back what they have always believed to be theirs? You think they won't make that their priority under the guidance of a slightly sturdier Nation with somewhat more strategic-thinking governance?'

'Don't fear the ambitions of the East, Stateship. *Fear* the malice on our own soils, *fear* the conniving subordinates living on the other side of the City Wall, the Liberal radicals, the Infidels nibbling their way through the very frontier we built to keep them out. The City Wall that encapsulates the City, and keeps people like you and I safe, cannot account for *every* other subordinate, *every* migrant, *every* East spy, *every* Punk and bandit, *every* murderer and defiler – all who want to contaminate our sovereignty again, like the old days, call our homeland their own. *Promised Land?*' the Decider gave a hoarse pant. 'Promised Land,' he repeated, a charming shade of crass humour dropped over his countenance like a curtain. 'The land we worked so vigorously to build is to be their *Promised Land*? Is that a jest? I don't think so! That is where the danger lies. Be afraid of that.'

'I am, sir. But I fear more that the Sixth Nation is going to find renewed interest in the Northern Polar Region,' the Stateship confessed.

'Don't forget, the East prospered from us also. In the past, before the Great Splits, the people of the East were once freely allowed to be citizens on our soil. The fact that we have now procured an amount of their luxury resources and store them in the Northern Polar Region is the price they must pay in return, the cost of their takings,' the Decider said. 'But now that the East have procured the Southern Polar Region and perform their most secret activities there - what rumours describe as grand and successful scientific discoveries - we may have mutual interests there also. I'm always ready to negotiate a deal if it serves to my benefit.'

'With the enemy—? *Negotiate deals with the East?*' the Stateship chortled at the bizarreness of such a proposal. 'You are not supposing that we trade their thirsting interests in the Northern Polar Region for our own curiosities about the Southern Polar Region—are you?'

'Look! We thrived off everything they had, decades ago! Yes, yes, it was unprecedented, but, again, that was the work of our forefathers, pursued for the purpose of prosperity. *Now, look where we are because of it*! Do you not respect the successes our fathers achieved? All those raw necessities they plundered from the East? The diamonds, the gold, the oil…! *Oh, the significance* of it! *For our sake—OUR SAKE!* Do you want to give it all back? Is that what you want us to do? Just give everything back to the East Men and apologise? The East leaders, those wicked Phestors, plodding about on their thrones these days couldn't even count to ten or recite the alphabet at the time that Great Reaping actually happened, so they have no reason to share the ancient spite of their ancestors. Their fathers are dead, and the grudge died with them! So, Stateship, are you telling me to lament *the sons* of stooges? After everything we've done, fought over, in our forefathers' legacy in order to keep it in place? Just waste all that strive? For what? A foreign civilisation that makes no impact on your life whatsoever? The East is a throwaway town that has been our playground for hundreds and hundreds of generations. You people just want to ignore it now that it's reduced to sawdust, push it further from our borders when there's still so much more to utilise and obtain? In fact, there is no time better than now to do exactly that! All our efforts and all my blood have bled to this! You have no right to tell me to turn away! You oafs only look to denounce me!'

'No—no, Decider, sir. That—that wasn't what I was saying—saying at all,' the unnerved Stateship stuttered.

The discussion broke like a branch and suddenly everything fell off balance like a tree in the autumn wind. A new body had entered the proximity and they were present in the room. *Three* new bodies had arrived, in fact. Two more were coming out from the blackened corridor. Just within view, shadows fled off their backs as their faces met the light of the Table Room.

The first of the new arrivals was obviously going to be Stevenson. He had his hands nervously by his sides and he was fiddling with the bottom of his un-tucked shirt. 'Yeh got two guests 'ere, Decidah Philson. Me believe dey weh not invite in advance. But me wuh call up to colleck 'em from de airport just shy an hour 'go. Me were tol' by de Official Border Control dey had sum important news fuh de Decidah an' granted access into de City wid'out yer permission, sir.'

Accompanying Stevenson into the room were two strangely dressed people – well, strange to Oscar's eyes. Everybody else gazed engrossingly at the pair standing before the long, oval Table, as if not believing what they were seeing to be true. Right now, plausibility was massively in denial to most of these men and women, dressed in newly tailored suits and opulent dresses, for it was incredibly questionable as to why two strangers garbed in loose drapes and sandals were standing there in the middle of a lavishly modern residence, where there was velvety carpet beneath their feet and the temperature of the room was just chilly enough for one to keep their coat on. But it wasn't only what they were wearing that had mouths gaping and gooseflesh prickling.

It was who they were.

One was an elderly man. His skin was rucked like an elephant's ancient assets and he wore thick, round spectacles, which hid any ounce of personality in his tiny pupils. Dressed in a clean silk robe that covered him like a cape, he was a fairly small man showcasing a circular, bursting shape that bulged through his thick garments. There was another cloth around his head, a bedazzled keffiyeh decorated with diamond jewels. Oscar saw that the man's attire had been subtly embroidered with twines of gold and spins of silver.

Silver Lining, Oscar thought. *There always is when somebody new shows up.*

The caped old man was companioned by a slenderer figure. She lacked curvature almost entirely, not even a slight protuberance where the hips were supposed to be. She was also covered up – much more securely than her older male counterpart. But her cloth was purely white. Utterly untouched, not one smudge, not a crease. The lady-figure had a stiflingly light and soundless step for someone as tall as she, which defied all else about her giant persona. Oscar was mesmerised by her height, enigmatically challenged by the sustained absence of curvature right the way along, like the length a pillar. It was as if a frail witch – or worse, some unearthly being – had confronted them. He scaled her with his eyes, trying to seek out a face, excited to know what it looked like. It was hidden under a burka. All he could forage were her eyes – handsome eyes. They sparkled like the stars once had – magnificently, like a million of them all at once. He hunted an odd warmth budding inside of himself; his stomach was doing somersaults for some reason.

Suddenly, the elderly man spoke in a dialect that was far more understandable than the West Men had expected. 'I apologise for the late and unexpected entrance. I wished to warn of my visit in advance. But my world is one of many distractions at the moment. My son is suffering with Southern Fever and my consort has been struggling to find him a doctor. We have very few reliable aiders dealing with Southern Fever in the East.'

A spiral of confusion and shock horror circled the room. Every last splurge of Oscar's cheap hopes faded and frazzled into a fragile shudder. Sick, he swallowed hard. Nobody spoke for minutes – that was what it felt like. Until Oscar's father decided that it was necessary to say *something*... before they were all held vocally hostage in his own home.

'I'm sorry? The East, you say?' these words were empty and unwelcoming.

'I am Phestor Xenol, leader of the Sixth Nation,' the elderly man said – a very general introduction. 'I have come, with my daughter, to arrange a settlement with the powers of the West.'

Nobody had flinched yet.

'You can't be in here—*you don't belong here! My—this smut shouldn't be anywhere near here!*' the Stateship spat. 'Who in Trivium's name let them in?' He found Stevenson. 'Stevenson—*explain!*'

The Stateship's head was shaking – *right, left, right, left* – like a freshly-sprung jack-in-the-box.

'In all my existence on this wide world, I have been led to believe that the Nations of the East happen to be the most lexically evolved of all the Nations. On that notion, the word 'smut' does not interact with the vocabulary of our Dialect in any way whatsoever. So, I presume that such a primitive word belongs solely in the West. It's understandable—your folk are quite familiar with a Dialect that lacks derivation and equally lacks the respect for its traditional pronunciation – I am no fool; I have studied and learned West Dialect for myself, wherein meetings like this, it comes very handy. Dear Stateship, I would rather speak within context than make things up,' Phestor Xenol remarked.

The Stateship, implicitly insulted, gawked at the East Man, wide-eyed.

'Please, Stateship. Know your position,' DCD. Philson demanded.

'Ah, yes, DCD. Philson! You just reminded me. Right beside *you*! To advise *you* at *your* side as ever, Decider, however and whenever *you* instruct me to, *of course*!' the Stateship growled sarcastically. Beside him, Timothy was sneering delightedly.

'Do not humiliate me and my guests,' Philson threatened the Stateship without glancing at him. He was bewitched by the newcomer and didn't want to avert his eyesight from the East Man once as he spoke. At this moment, the Decider was so perplexed by the interruptive situation he was prepared to silence anyone. 'Now, please explain why you are here, Phestor.'

'Decider, sir—!' the Stateship was whispering to him now, in a *do as I say immediately* kind of tone. 'Do not mistake this stranger's enthusiasm for his moral! It is my duty to advise the Administration when to denounce a dangerous judgement that could have catastrophic consequences for the West! Order these people to leave your residence at once! Or *I will*! They shouldn't be here! Not on *our* soil! It's forbidden—a mockery of our own constitution!'

Philson ignored him. 'I agree, your appearance here is unprecedented. But, please, go on and amplify. I am intrigued.'

The Stateship considered himself plugged with a huge, undignified pacifier. And the Phestor commenced with what he wanted to say.

'Yes, yes—indeed, my being in the West breaks many laws under your New Democracy. It is illicit of me to be here without the signature of the Decider. But, the reason I'm here under such risky circumstances is because I – like yourselves – have watched first-hand the destruction that has come between West and East. Over my entire period of Phestorship, so much has been ruined and so many lives have been demolished across the world. Decider, my brief, yet significant, offer to you is my right hand.'

The pin dropped; they all heard it. Every thing in the room switched off and listened, just listened to the whirring words of that foreign voice. This confounding disbelief spoken from the East Man lulled with it the zenith of a harmonic silence, a speechless symphony that could never be emulated from such a shockwave again.

'Did I hear you correctly?' DCD. Philson escaped the incredible spell cast upon his Administration. 'Are you hypothesising that I—the West—advocate an alliance—an alliance with the East?'

'Not an alliance with the East,' Phestor Xenol assured, 'but to forge an "underground pact" with the Sixth Nation. We, as an independent state, are jaded, miserable, and tired of staging Conflicts beside our uncompromising Sister Nations. Since our Nation has become distanced from its neighbours and flourished while they have fallen, they no longer function as our allies. We have all means of disarming our Blackout weaponry and surrendering our arsenals in order to prove our decency to you and achieve a stable co-existence with the First Nation. I hope you manage to understand our enthusiasm to rise to this mercy—'

'Forge a surreptitious alliance with you, so that your Nation can surrender with its pride intact? So that you can finally annex the Seventh Nation and the rest of the East - which we all know you've been itching to do for decades? And all for what—what do I get in return: the very probable risk of the Seventh Nation finding out and responding with another Blackout Attack, this time burdened upon my own Nation, if things go to hell? You're not the only East Folk with nuclear missiles,' Philson queried, coming down like an axe on what appeared to be a white flag. 'We've all struggled for mercy, Phestor! Be a leader and fight for it!'

'True what you say, Decider,' Xenol replied. 'I am not blind to the line that always has, and, in more ways than one, will eternally lie between us. We have all suffered at the hands of our enemies, but no more than we've suffered at the will of our *own* judgments. I'm not convinced that the Decider would allow the West to waste away under the burdens of this perpetual war.' He was scoping across the Table as he said this. At one point, Oscar believed the Phestor had caught his eye also. 'There are no more excuses.'

'I have no excuses for the Conflicts,' the Decider stood his ground. 'I am not responsible for this. I did not feed this world with war. Nevertheless, I am obliged to never starve the West of the wars it needs to fight, so that we never surrender our sovereignty.'

'I see a man who is pushing the boundaries of his Nationhood, strangling it with an autonomy that is war-afflicted, and consequently limiting its potential, what with having commissioned troops to stoke those frontlines in the Seventh Nation for decades on end - at the cost of rationing his own Nation and its Sister Nations into oblivion. Alas, the businesses and the factories that have suffered here, the people who have kneeled to misery, and the flippant bureaucracies that have engulfed them. And most notably, the biggest boundary of all that the West Nation delivers for sovereignty is the backing of a City Wall that divides the purest of the First Nation from all whom surround it. Think of it, Decider, you have been forced into taking extraordinary action to defend your Nation and you can just about manage to govern the rest of the West—for what? The gruelling threat of the Seventh Nation, that's what it's all for. And now that threat must end. And that's all it is—it's all you *can* do and all you *need* to do to end this tired war,' the Phestor insisted. 'It is time for something to be done—'

'Don't get too ambitious, Phestor. Understand that I am only conversing with you on accord with the idiosyncrasy of a banquet table and the nonchalance of its inebriated guests. I don't negotiate with the Seventh Nation in any way or form,' the Decider announced stubbornly. 'All we hear from the Seventh Nation is via the letters of our soldiers held in P.O.W camps over there, and their accounts of executions, escapes, retaliations and so on; and we hear about the bombarded wastelands that we routinely reap there in warfare – a harvest during which our landmines and shells are described as "the seeds of death" by the Seventh Nation natives. I, myself, have not seen eye-to-eye with Phestor Serpens since we did away with the Hermit Nation.☆ It goes without saying, Seventh is still inflamed over Blackout Nine and the fall of the Eighth.'

'This isn't about consulting with the Seventh Nation, Decider, sir. Oh no. What I am trying to establish here with you is a call to action, a method of dealing with Seventh, so that we are both better off. And there is no other way of accomplishing that than doing away with the Seventh Nation,' Xenol said. 'It will begin with the severance of Phestor Serpens.'

All the leaves fell at once, and then the autumn wind stopped; nobody breathed.

The Decider's ears pricked up and a small sting of elation twitched at the corners of his eyes and lips. He appeared twenty years younger.

☆ *The Hermit Nation* (a.k.a. *the Evil Nation*, a.k.a. *the End Times Nation*, a.k.a. *the Judgment Nation*) was an epithet given to the reclusive Eighth Nation. The Eighth Nation had been violently devastated in the infamous Blackout Nine Attacks – a crisis where every Nation in the world had gone on high alert during an East-versus-West face-off that threatened a global nuclear strike – it was an "End Times Scenario". To this day, the Eighth Nation – irreversibly crippled from the strike – continues to receive aid from the Seventh. These two embittered Sister Nations of the "Far-East" haven't forgiven the First Nation for calling the Attacks.

'You want us to eliminate the Phestor of the Seventh Nation?' Philson roared in condemnation, however, the more they colluded over it, the more the plot was becoming kneaded into his ruminations and the more the Decider yearned for it. 'An assassination attempt?' he hummed.

'It's our best option,' the Phestor pledged. 'Please do spare the mind to consider it.'

'*Our best option*? Is that really *our* best option?' The Stateship ordained himself, crashing back into the conversation. 'Because I could probably think a few other valid alternatives – that is, if you'd *allow us to our own business—*'

The Decider held an open palm up at the Stateship and waved it in his face. With his other hand, he dipped his cigar into the ashtray and stumped out the butt. He nodded at the Phestor to resume talking.

'We win a way into the Seventh Nation as humbly as we can, offer the Phestor something he'll have no choice but to root for – perhaps a new 'East Alliance' would be a fanciful incentive, a good lure for him at a time like this? And then, once he trusts me enough and we're liaising on my turf, we dethrone Serpens in a providential affair. When the Seventh Nation is on its knees, we can sign our own pact. The *real* pact. And the Conflicts will end at our feet – at the feet of the two greatest Nations in the world.'

There came agitated shifting and squirming from the other guests sat around the Decider's Table.

'Have you ever *been* to the Seventh Nation before?' DCD. Philson asked curiously.

'Never. It's always too risky to travel there uninvited,' Phestor Xenol answered, 'even for an inherent patriot of the East like myself. I haven't visited the Seventh Nation in thirty years and have little desire to go back until our relations thaw.'

'Well—' the Decider vacillated; he felt required to consider the proposal for a second, even though he had since made up his mind on the matter. 'Then, perhaps we should wait until your relations with Serpens and the Seventh Nation thaw,' he said. When he suggested this, he was not arresting the Phestor in his stare, but glancing at everyone else around the Table, basely masking his experimentalist imprudence with faux integrity, just to reassure them. To comfort them. It was all a show, for he had decided what he wanted to do. 'I am not obliged to deal with East affairs,' he feigned, 'especially not incognito. The West is my sole responsibility.'

'*Fabulous answer, Decider, sir!*' the Stateship exclaimed, interjecting again. He was practically clapping his hands in celebration. 'Now, Stevenson, take this man back down to reception and discuss return-flight tickets on the way to the airport. Or, in respect of his eminence and knowing full-well the behaviour of most City Folk towards *his sort* strolling about their streets, issuing a private deportation may be a more appropriate option.'

'Stateship, who gave you permission to order my assistant about? You are testing my patience! *Behave* yourself! Disrupt my conversation again and *you will be* the next to be ousted!' Philson cautioned. He was seriously irked by this stage and priming to blast up from his chair. 'The Phestor may have a workable point.'

'What do you mean, Philson?' The Stateship squinted as if the Decider's head had transformed into a ball of intolerable sunlight, blinding his eyes. 'You would veto *me* before this *villain—the enemy*? This conversation is over! It never happened! What concerns the East will concern him! We have our own problems here! What happens *in* the West is done *in* the West and committed to *by* the West! This swine—this Phestor Vandal—'

'Xenol—Phestor Xenol,' the East Man corrected him.

'Yes, *Phestor Xenol*—it was all very sweet, a nice attempt, you coming up here and all, with your young female companion, to flog your…*interesting* views. And as convincing as you may come across to the Decider here, it is forbidden for you to even speak in this Nation, let alone even to walk on our soil.'

'I say give him a chance to elaborate,' Philson drilled.

'NO, NO—! THIS IS *OUR* NATION, *OUR* DISCUSSION! NOT YOURS! *STAY OUT OF OUR WAY OR BEAR THE CONSEQUENCES!*' the Stateship persisted at Xenol.

But this didn't deter the Phestor, as he was busy signalling something very blatant to a lot of the people sitting around the Table. Whilst the Stateship had been blabbering on, Xenol had raised the bottom of his robe to reveal a long, shining sword harnessed to his waist. The Stateship closed his fury when he found his reflection in the blade. When Oscar saw the blade, he'd lost all of the fascination he'd had in the exquisiteness of the Phestor's companion's eyes, for this weapon was an earnest competitor.

'Do you know what this is?' Phestor Xenol said, running a finger along it.

Nobody responded.

'Why, it's the most powerful weapon in all the world,' the Phestor revealed, 'and some in the East bid to believe that this weapon could also be the most sought-for device in the universe. This here—this is the Solar Blade.'

Oscar's obsessive thoughts melted.

'This weapon has the ability to end rebellions and stir armies, the strength to move Nations. It has the potential to restore equilibrium and, most significantly, the authority to reassert order in our world and rewrite our destiny. Call me superstitious—but then look where I'm standing: *on your soil*, like you said.'

Overwhelmed by a sudden outbreak of memories from that other world, now refreshed in his mind, Oscar was stunned by what he was seeing. *The Solar Blade—*

Oscar could feel *that thing* approaching once again, *that thing* of the unconscious; the land of the sleepers was creeping up and consuming him. *Will my father and his guests notice?* He wondered. *Will they be concerned at all? Of course they will—eventually! Will they stop it before it takes me, can anyone stop this inexorable force – this summoning of sleep?* At first, nobody did notice when he slipped into another impulsive snooze at the end of the Table—

Not until he was gone…

Crossing the Bridge of Lynx...

The parrot is here again to greet me on the sands of Awakening Coast.

He peers over my face with a dead firefly drooping from his beak and he's cutting the beauty of the descending sun with his tail-quills.

'Lunch?' I croak.

'*What's wrong with an occasional birdsong every now and then? I've had a long shift,*' Stewart says defensively.

His quirkiness brings a smile to my face...until the firefly-carcass lands between my lips (*I almost gag up last evening's Summit banquet – would that also resurface here on the sand?*). 'Do you mind! Do you actually mind not doing that!' I cry. And I'm quickly up on my feet, shaking the rest of the sand off my back.

'*Yes! I do mind! Since it's my well-deserved recess from duty and equally my way of saying "You reckless clown, I just summoned you back from reality, after you passed out without warning in the middle of the Kingdom Palace!" My friend, please recognise that, for you, I have just had to postpone the Departures tonight and, believe it or not, Dreamers have got places to be in the real world! Do you understand how difficult it is to* ***compromise*** *while semi-conscious in the workplace?*'

'I'm sorry?'

'*Yes, you are, Mister Night Dreamer! Because, never mind my misgivings,* ***you*** *also have somewhere to be, don't you? You know—Does slaying a Drag-in ring any alarms?*'

'What happened?' This is Samuella's voice. She's nearby. Probably marching her way up the beach towards us. 'I thought we'd discussed all this back at the Palace! You can't just drop out on us! You're supposed to be leading the way!'

I look down at myself without a second thought. Mortified. Please be wearing clothes, please be wearing clothes...I'm in luck. Not pyjamas this time, but *a soggy tuxedo from the Annum Summit* will do fine. And I also have the Constellation Map clasped in my right hand. Had I taken it with me? Or did the parrot just stuff it into my fist before I woke up?

Samuella and Camson are both armed with swords. The young redhead also has one spare – my sword – that she immediately throws across to me. On the other hand, Camson possesses the bow and the stack of arrows lent from the King, brandishing them as though they're all his own and nobody else's.

'What knocked you out just then?' Samuella asks me. Like I actually have a clue. Meh!

'I can't remember,' I admit. 'What did it look like?'

'Like you'd been possessed by a devil. You fell, hit the ground and began snoring violently and erratically with your eyes wide open, until your lights finally went out. The whole time, you wouldn't respond to any of us when we tried to wake you up. And when your eyes closed, you disappeared right in front of us, in the blink of an eye,' she narrates bluntly. 'Watching you snore with your eyes open for ten seconds was embarrassing and pretty traumatising.'

'I'm quite sure that I don't snore.' It's not a flattering description at all.

Camson hoots, sucking the dryness off his lips. 'Boy, I thought you were a tad brighter than that. Perhaps I was too optimistic about you. The truth still stands: West Men cannot be trusted with orders.'

'And it appears that an East Man can't be trusted with warding his new allies,' I retort at the diminutive fool, his faithless act ditching me to the mercy of the Drag-in still flailing in my sore memory.

Camson leaps at me, about to strike down with his foot on my chest. Applying her stern poise, Samuella's there to yank him back by the arm.

'It's not about trusting anyone. Oscar didn't decide to pass out on us. He didn't mean to do it. It wasn't his fault. It was an accident,' Samuella pokes her nose in Camson's face. 'That's why we were given the Continuity Seeds. They'll keep us going, excluding such temptations as waking up in reality.'

'Well, let's hope you're right then,' he sanctions, ripping his arm out of her grip. 'Because I'm not sticking around for him the next time this happens.'

'That isn't an option for us. He has the Map. Whoever has the Map needs to be in this mission with us, otherwise none of us get anywhere,' Samuella reasons.

'That's why we need to be aware of each other,' I grimace, clambering to my feet. 'At all times.'

'I guess the good thing is that at least now we know what it looks like to be summoned back to reality. *Dormanity* is an awkward event to witness,' Samuella says. She cuts her eyes at me. 'You *snore* with your eyes *open*?'

'That isn't the point,' I insist.

'That's a firm "yes",' Camson demeans me further yet.

Samuella kicks the Constellation Map in my hand with her toes. 'Have you had a chance to look in it yet?'

I fiddle with the scroll of old paper in my hands for a bit. 'There's something…' My memory's hazed over again and all I'm remembering are the loose ends of the past, patchy images that mean absolute zilch at the moment. '…There's something about the sword…and something about reality that you both need to know.'

'The sword and reality?' Samuella splices.

'The Solar Blade,' I decipher, struggling to decrypt my bleary thoughts. 'Something to do with the Solar Blade.'

'What about it? Spit it out,' Samuella's concern is leeching onto me, pulping the thoughts out of my head.

'If I remembered exactly what it was, I'd tell you straight on. But I can't recall the memory at all.'

'That's the Memory Lane in action for you. It's holding your memories back like a tollbooth, preventing them from seeping through into the Dreamerverse. Whatever you must be trying to remember is probably too great even for the privilege of a Night Dreamer.'

'*Oh, you poor, sick angels. The grim struggle of a Night Dreamer must be horrible. Regular Dreamers will never empathise with their disconnect to the Land of the Conscious,*' Steward remarks sarcastically. '*I've been here for as long as I* ***can't*** *remember. I have no contact with my real body or mind. What you see now is solely thoughts. Raw imagination, marinating in a big, warm ball of Dreamerverse matter.*'

'You were stranded here?' I ask the bird. 'Forced to watch people while they sleep and rudely wake them up?'

'I wasn't forced, I was instated with a responsibility from the King himself,' the parrot preens his feathers before gloriously pushing his chest out. *'It is an honour to watch you sleep.'*

'Open up the Map!' Samuella impatiently demands. 'I want to see how it works!'

I unravel the scroll. The other two gather round at my sides and Stewart perches on my shoulder. The Constellation Map is, at first, nothing more than a blank page. But then, after several blinks of the eye, my mind connects and the stars start to materialise and mould into an actual map of the stars, geographically representative of the make-up of the planet itself. At the top, the Map is titled in bold and below it are the glowing constellations and outlines of the lands they represent, vastly located about the atlas upon a dark-blue breadth of oceans and seas. At the bottom right corner of the page is what looks like a sketched compass. But, the letters indicating direction on this compass aren't the recognisable **N. E. S. W.** symbols that we commonly know. Instead, the letter at the top – which would usually be North – is a **D**. On the right – East – is a **P**. The bottom – South – is a **C**. And the left – West – is an **L**.

D. P. C. L.

'What are they supposed to mean?' Camson is the first to point this out.

'They're the Stellar Cardinals. Didn't anyone ever teach you about the four cardinals?' Stewart sounds amazed.

'Not these ones,' I concede.

'Well, ***D*** *stands for Draco, which is the equivalent of North.* ***P*** *stands for Pegasus, which, if I'm right, should be the same as East.* ***C*** *is Columba – in other words, South. And* ***L*** *– well, you could probably already guess – is the same as West, and it stands for Leo.'*

'Why complicate things like that?' Camson groans.

'Those are the four cardinal directions of this world. The polarised make-up of its lands is mirrored precisely to the positioning of the constellations. After all, this is a Constellation Planet.'

'Constellation Planet?' Samuella repeats.

'Yep! You've got that right! Listen! Let me show you something cool! You see that huge cluster of constellations in the middle? Yeah, well, that's what we're standing right in the centre of now. This is the Central Island we're on. Here, you'll find places like Orion's Belt, Camelopardalis, the Bridge of Lynx, so on, and so on. Orion's Belt was that meadow at the centre of the jungle, just outside the kingdom – you must have seen it –

with all the animals and the cute huts and the happy little families all getting along just swell.'

'I forgot to mention that!' I interject. 'On our way to the Palace, we saw those Dreamers living in that part of the jungle. But I was told by one of the King's Night Guards that it was far too dangerous to even stumble through the jungle. How is that the case when we saw folk living there beside tigers, elephants and giraffes – all of which appeared to be surprisingly domesticated?'

'No, you're mistaken! That part of the jungle is Orion's Belt, which is the safe point, a harmless meadow where many Dreamers reside in the jungle. Getting there is a hassle in the night, for obvious reasons. But, during the daylight hours, the Belt can be awfully beautiful and awe-inspiring. It is not a treacherous place to be, because it is a region of jungle that belongs to the kingdom, with its borders protected by the Palm Patrol. Only the outer rim of the jungle is an outlawed buffer zone, ever since the Stellar Gods transformed it into a natural fortress with their sand-charms to deter evil spirits, such as the Drag-in.

'And, just to be clear, the Central Island's Kingdom, known officially as Camelopardalis, is where the King's Town and the Kingdom Palace were – everything on the other side of those brilliant gates you passed through. Then, you have the oceans, which divide the Central Island from the rest of the islands surrounding it—'

'These other constellations signify there being more islands, don't they?' Camson breaks into the lecture, huffing lethargically. 'Let me guess: one of them is going to be our next destination.'

'My fellow Dreamer, this planet is immeasurable. Much vaster than the one you call home. After you witness what there is to be seen here, I ponder whether you'll look at Mankind's World in the same light ever again. In fact, I dare you to resist what you know—just for now, I insist that you try. Let me continue,' the bird jadedly wallows on the spot. *'Central Island and the Kingdom of Camelopardalis act as a centre-point. The other islands surrounding Central Island are separated – as you can see here – into the four regions. There are four major islands – Leo, Pegasus, Draco, Columba – that head these cardinal regions of Constellation Planet. The emeralds you require could be anywhere in these segments.'*

'But searching all of these lands will take us more time than we have to waste. We only have five purple seeds to spare over ten days – forty-eight hours each,' Samuella calculates.

'She's right,' I agree. 'We'll have to know specifically where to look if we plan to stay awake that long.'

'You might come off lucky, depending on how the Map chooses to treat you. I was told that the last generation of Night Dreamers to repel the Drag-in found their emeralds on three of these four major islands. The Map led them directly to the emeralds with minimal diversions. That's not to say the Map won't initially lead you off course or completely misguide you in some events.'

'Misguide us?' Camson repeats the parrot's words. Then he squints at the Map, startled by what he sees – or, rather, what he cannot see. 'Wh—Where did it all go? The Map—it's blank again!'

'Hey—!' Samuella corresponds. 'Well, if the constellations are going to keep disappearing like that, it's pretty useless to us!'

But I don't understand what they're on about. I can still read the Map perfectly fine.

The bird shrugs his wings. '*We'll find out, won't we? The Map isn't the easiest tool to use. Only one Night Dreamer can read it at a time, it can be deliberately misleading and it tends to lose its own initiative once so often. It's a particular issue when seeking out inter-dimensional elements like the emeralds. It can be quite an overwhelming task for the Map to perform.*'

'They're inter-dimensional emeralds now? Nobody thought to bring this up! Who distributes these emeralds? What purpose do they serve?' Samuella asks.

'The origin of the emeralds is widely debated, though there is no dispute that their power is profound. They brand a positive energy in contrast to the Drag-in's negative energy. Some over the years have theorised with the myth and believe that it may be the electromagnetic force of the Drag-in itself, detracting the emeralds from its presence and thus dispersing them far from its whereabouts. This usually means if you're close to an emerald, the Drag-in is probably nowhere near you – ***usually****. However, don't take these rumours as gospel. Don't be afraid of your initiative or underplay your capability. All Eyes has faith in you. Generally, Night Dreamers are always so modestly sceptical. Please don't be like that. It's ever so boring. Just get stuck in!'*

'How?' Camson says.

'Consider the Map one at a time. The Constellation Map is capable of both satisfying and deceiving those who use it. Only the person who is looking at the Map, through their own eyes and with the help of no other, can see what only ***they*** *desire. And, therefore, you should observe it individually. Give it a go now. One of you take the Map into your hands alone and describe what you see.'*

'Who's going first?' I ask.

Samuella and Camson have broken distance and I'm now standing on my own with the Map in my hands.

'Well, I can't see anything on it,' Camson confesses.

'Neither can I,' Samuella adds.

'That decision wasn't too difficult,' I stutter. 'What do I do? What am I looking for?'

'*Look at the Map and follow the tracks of your conscience. Your imagination will lead the way. All you must do is follow.*'

I spot the resolute symbol of a comet flashing at me from a position on the Map that's near the shore's edge on Central Island. Presumably, this is our current location. I focus my eyes on the shining comet crying for attention…and before long, the comet pushes off and a red line begins to stretch out from the starting point, leading a long trail around the outside of the jungle. It crosses the ocean on the left side of the map, then finds itself on an island in the Leo Region. This continent is labelled **LEO ISLAND**. Next, once ashore, the comet heads into a colony of mountains – **KAPPA LEONIS** – and reaches the peak of the very tallest one. New words appear. The title of a hidden location: **THE FALLS OF FORTUNE**.

The line ceases here, marking an **X** upon the spot.

I look up from the Map, confident with just how clearly that has all come across to me.

'*Well?*' Stewart's anxious claws are digging into my shoulder blades. '*Where did it take you?*'

'It's saying that we need to go West—'

'*"Go West"? You mean "go Leo"*,' he corrects.

'Yes, fine, we need to go *Leo*. The first emerald is there, on Leo Island. Well, the Map's saying that we need to first climb into the Kappa Lenonis—'

'The Twenty Lions,' Samuella translates, fluently and rather confidently.

Camson, the parrot and I all stare at her, enlightened by her surprising linguistic dexterity.

'You understand the Dialect of the Ancients?' Camson says, stunned and vaguely impressed. 'You can read Dead Dialect?'

'My cousin Drake was a student biological engineer,' she adds coyly. 'He studied biology at the City Academy and I picked up a few words whenever he came back to the countryside to tutor me. "*Kappa*" means "twenty" in Ancient Numerals and "*Leonis*" means "lions".' She shrugs embarrassedly. 'We had quite a few lessons.'

'"*Kappa Leonis" is their classical name, however we here know them better as the Kappa Mountains*,' the parrot elaborates.

'What have lions got to do with anything?' Camson pursues authentication. '*The Twenty Lions*, she said.'

'*Just a nod to an old myth…regarding the mountain's inhabitants.*' The parrot uncomfortably flexes his neck. '*But you shouldn't worry about that for the time being. Your concern should be getting up there first.*'

My finger runs up the Kappa Mountains to find the place where the comet has pinned itself. 'At the top of the highest mountain is a place called—'

'*The Falls of Fortune*,' Stewart finishes my sentence. '*Now…what a rare place to reach; what a spectacle! Very impressive, you lucky sods…well, "lucky" from an aesthetic point of view! But you'll only experience the Falls' wonder if you manage to get there, of course. The Kappa Mountains are teeming with peril. There are risks of pitfalls and cave-ins and upset, bodiless spirits that thirst for humanoid bodies like yourselves—*'

Camson bursts into laughter. 'Upset spirits?'

'*Well, when you're a dead, loose entity stuck in paradise, you'll be the one grudging when you can't touch or hang onto anything. There's very little to enjoy and much less to live for when you're a spirit banished from you body and estranged from corporeality. I've been there myself.*' Even though he isn't trying to frighten us, Stewart's tone is distinctly cynical. There's something about it that thunders seriousness. He means what he says.

'Nothing we can't deal with, surely,' Samuella shakily mitigates.

Stewart turns his head away in a gesture to prove otherwise.

'How do you suppose we get there? We're going to need a boat to cross the water,' I suggest.

'*No! No, no, no! Never travel the oceans by boat! Not only will building such a structure deplete valuable time, but the ocean is always dormant. Its deepest slumber is at night. Never disturb its rest or it will punish you. One way that I will suggest – and it may very well be your only way if you're trying to get to Leo Island – is to cross the ocean via the Bridge of Lynx. But, be wary again. Nobody has traversed the Bridge of Lynx in many years.*'

'Why's that?' Camson's eyes are rolling and his foot is hastily tapping the ground as per usual.

'*The Bridge of Lynx was supposed to have been created as a way of linking Central Island with Leo Island. But, because of a few "aquatic disturbances", it went terribly wrong and, as a result, there had to be one major compromise in its design, which throws off many Dreamers who manage to reach the Bridge and cross it. On many occasions, Dreamers were never again seen on the other side. One wrong step and you could be extracted from both the Dreamerverse and Reality. Death results in no waking up – if you hadn't already clocked that.'*

'So, who were the last to cross it?' Samuella says.

'*Who do you think? The Royals.*'

'But they made it across—didn't they?' There's a hint of disbelief in Samuella's voice. 'Otherwise…the Drag-in…they'd have never seen the back of it…if they didn't get to the other side…?'

The bird sighs. '*I never said they made it to the other side – at least, not without a number of ordeals on the Bridge. But I really, really hope, for all our sakes, that you three have a more favourable crossing.*'

The Camelopardalisian sands grow much lighter on our feet, as we voyage the moonlit western shore of Central Island. The sand is softer here and the cooling layer of dunes beneath our soles strokes us like a stream. The Map's course hasn't altered from that comet sat at the peak of the Kappa Mountains and Stewart's suggestion of crossing the Bridge of Lynx to get there spearheads our very few options. Since leaving the steward bird behind, I keep relaying a riddle he parted us with: '*you may see it or you may not see it. It depends who's looking.*'

We're all looking. But only I can see where the Bridge starts on the parchment. The Map tells me that Lynx should be within sight. But no bridge is apparent in our proximity. So far, only the spectacular cosmic disarray of lights in the sky has distracted our search. The moon can be seen ahead, the bottom of it just touching the horizon. Enormous and bountiful. Our footprints stipple its luminescence.

'How sound is that!' Samuella says. 'A moon ginger like an autumn in the vale.' Her rural nostalgia is like two fingers tickling the back of my throat. *Gag!*

Half a mile or so further along the shore, I finally see something. A tiny bump in the horizon, far out to sea. There's another island over there! I rush towards the water, being the first to notice and unwarily *squidge* into the wet sand, smearing my lower-shins with the incoming tide.

'D'you see that? D'you see it?' I cry.

Samuella and Camson trudge down to where I am. Samuella strides over the soggy beach, no care for the wet sand spattering her shins. Camson doesn't eagerly follow my influence and, instead, sticks to the dry-sand to view the distant island. He doesn't want to get near the water at all.

'Leo Island?' Samuella announces. Her grubby fingers cupped above her eyes to make better sight of the new land floating in the distance.

'But I don't see a bridge,' Camson says. 'You think maybe we came too far? Did we miss it along the way? It wouldn't surprise me if we had the damn Map upside down the whole way. Only one of us can be held responsible for that.' He shovels some sand up with his foot and kicks it in my direction.

'Couldn't have,' I say. Then again, this is a valid point made by the East Man. The Map had marked out the Bridge of Lynx being right here, practically on top of us and we've been hovering in this same spot for the last hour. But the distance along this whole section of shore is extremely vague with there being no accurate measurements or proportions displayed on the Map, making the Bridge's exact position near impossible to guess…

'Keep your eyes peeled on the ocean surface,' Samuella advises. 'The Bridge crosses the ocean to that island over there, beginning from somewhere along this mile of shore.'

We climb back up the shore and return to the beach. Camson falls and crashes on his bottom, where he sits, flapping his palms about in the floury sand. Samuella paces about next to him, scratching her forehead and glancing in both the direction we came and the way ahead of us. Concentrated and determined not to be the first to flop at navigating our integral instrument, I tug the Map open wide in front of me and scan the route one more time—

The constellations morph, their stars churning on the page to form words: *FOLLOW THE LINK.*

A cue of sorts?

Lowering the Map from my face, I see what wasn't there before. A lonely palm tree stands in the middle of the beach, deftly still on this windless, warm night. Mounted on the palms and watching me from the very top of the tree is the shape of a wild cat with giant, glassy eyes and white, ghostly fur. A lynx with tall, prickly ears and a slinky body that flaunts a short, shabby tail.

The lynx jumps down from the tree, his motion suspended slightly, as if time has been slowed by his trans-dimensional aura. His ethereal fur is icily incandescent. Echoed reflections of his body shimmer off his back as he moves through the air. When he lands, he stares back at me again, stood perpendicularly, about to turn in the direction of our designated path.

I flinch, flicking my head back at the others. 'Are you seeing this?' I whisper in an undertone, not to startle the creature. Samuella and Camson follow my call, gawking ahead to find what I've observed.

'Oscar, what are you seeing?' Samuella replies.

'Can't you see that? Why can't you—? It's right there!' I cry, distressed by their ignorance. 'Look at that! It's just jumped out of that tree—!'

'Look at *what*?' Samuella sounds genuinely unacquainted. 'What tree?'

'There aren't any trees, you fool!' Camson allies with her.

The lynx is totally undisturbed in his short distance from us; his eyes are steely, fixed on me. He begins to turn away and walk in the other direction. I wait there to watch him from behind, reminding myself of the relevance here...*FOLLOW THE LINK*. This must be the cue the Map is indicating.

I push off, chasing after the cat as he glides along the shore.

'Come on,' I call to the others. 'This way! Let's go!'

'Hey—!' Samuella is the first to hurry after me. 'Go where—where are you leading us?'

'I hope he knows where he's taking us this time!' Camson scorns. He rolls over, staggers onto his feet and jogs behind Samuella.

Once he's aware we're after him, the lynx launches into a warped leap. He advances across the beach, bounding a metre at a time, but his motion freezes between shifts and he leaves a translucent, white spirit of himself after each leap. As I'm running through these fading spirits that the lynx abandons in his trail and as the clouds of these frozen imprints become thicker, I feel I'm getting closer and closer to where he's leading us. Closer to the Bridge.

The three of us are just about coping to keep up. I burst through the last couple of spirit-clouds and lose sight of them...he's gone. I turn on the spot and, to my left, discover more clouds floating down the shore towards the ocean's ledge. Before they fade, I race through them.

The lynx has changed direction. I can see him! He's come to a stop at the very brink of the coastline. Facing out towards the horizon, at first, he looks as though he won't make any moves at all.

But then the unexpected happens.

The lynx jumps upwards, over the incoming tide and dodging the next wave entirely, and lands onto the air itself. All four feet plot onto what can only be an invisible platform suspended above the ocean.

I come to a halt. The wave that had missed the lynx slings into me instead, washing me from the waist down. I'm facing the cat directly now. He waits on the invisible platform, high above the ocean waves.

Samuella and Camson catch up, skidding down the shore beside me.

'What the hell are you doing?' Samuella gasps, swallowing her shock. 'Was the running really necessary?'

'You honestly can't see that?' I look at both of them. The confusion in their expressions would convince anyone - they are oblivious.

'Stop messing us around!' Camson shouts. '*See what?*'

'The lynx!' I respond. 'The lynx that we chased here! Didn't you see it up in the tree? And all the cloudy residue it left behind when we were following it? It's taking us to the Bridge! The Bridge of Lynx that Stewart told us about! And the Map even told me to "*follow the link*"! So, I took that as a hint! To follow the lynx—'

'Oscar,' Samuella came forward to set it clear to me. 'We didn't see anything. *You* led us here.'

I point at the ghostly creature on the invisible platform. 'There it is—!'

But the lynx is no longer standing there. He's moved. Shifted along the platform some more, further out to sea.

'We need to follow it!' I command, and I lurch in the direction of the water. I take one step forwards—

Samuella is my immediate restraint. She grabs my arm, like she'd done to Camson before, and says, 'We need to be completely sure about this.'

What she doesn't yet realise is that my foot has settled on something, but it isn't the ground. An invisible step has appeared under my foot. While Samuella tries to tug me away, I nudge her to indicate it. Both of them gather close to me again and we all stare down at it. 'Let go,' I tell her.

She does.

I press all my weight onto this foot and lift my other to take a second step. There, I find the second stair just after the first. I try again—with luck, I locate another. And another. And two more before I am level with the cat on the platform.

'How did you get up there?' Samuella calls to me from the shore.

'This is it!' I rejoice. 'The Bridge!'

'What do you mean? Where? I can't see it,' Samuella reiterates.

'I'm standing on it! Can't you see that I'm standing on it? And the lynx is here too! He's already made it a few feet across. Believe me now? It's probably huge and stretching out into the ocean, where it finishes over there on the other island—see?'

'Check the Map again,' Camson urges. He trills his lips and impatiently flaps his foot on the ground.

I unravel the Constellation Map once more and catch a new **X** marking it out; it's sitting directly on top of us. We're standing on the very edge of the shore and **THE BRIDGE OF LYNX** is right there, connecting the two islands like a delicate chandelier chain of crystals under starlight and the moon.

'Definitely here! Exactly here!' I assure them.

'Well, why can't we see it then?' Samuella says.

'I can. Can't you?'

'Pull yourself together, boy! It isn't there if I can't see it! And only you can *because…?*' Camson says.

"*You may see it or you may not see it. It depends who's looking.*" The flippant riddle makes more sense now than it did initially.

'I can see it, because I'm the person out of all of us who desires it the most, since I'm the one working the Map,' I explain. 'I'm leading the way, no? So, it's calling out to me specifically. For my perception alone.'

'But don't we all need it to get across?' Camson triggers.

'That isn't the way the Map sees it. Right at this moment, the Map's installing my mind with leadership by granting me the way to follow. It also sent a lynx that only I can see. So, it must be allowing me to see the Bridge at my request alone. All you two need to do is trust my word and do as I tell you to.'

'I'd rather assemble a pledge to trust a maid with my jewellery,' Camson scoffs.

'How are me and Camson supposed to get across?' Samuella says.

I knew a dilemma like this would pop up at some point along the way – although, I never imagined it to become such a problem this early in our journey. I have to think about this before I set it in stone. And I have to dig deep for remnants of wisdom. The kind of wisdom my mother solicited so successfully. When I was in the worst predicaments, she'd know what to do and she'd have sent me on my way with more than a hundred solutions like a hundred hooks for a single fish. But here, I need to think for myself, distribute that courageous rope to someone other than myself...

Take their hand and walk them across, the voice in my head – my new *Bezzie Mate* – speaks to me.

But how am I supposed to support them along the way if it's invisible? It's unstable too, making it double the task. What if there are dips and holes? You heard the parrot. He said that one misstep could—

You can only lead as poorly as the link leads you. Let them follow you as you have followed the link.

Suddenly and from out of nowhere, I can see the steps leading up to the wooden platform I'm standing on. I turn around to find the lynx looking at me again, the Bridge has materialised around us. The lynx resumes walking cautiously along it in the direction of Leo Island...

Now I know how the Bridge got its "*treacherous*" label.

There isn't much to it other than several miles of suspended platform, stabilised by two barriers of worn-rope – that are more like reedy strings in some spots. It's high enough to make a type-rope look like a playground contraption, and the wooden-planks, which make up the length of the bridge, are damp and softening. The worst part must be the unpredictable ocean snickering beneath it, all the way...

My other two companions are clueless. I can't tell whether it's their good fortune that they can't see the awful condition of this thing first-hand or if I'm the lucky one for not needing to match the trial of trust that they're going to have to *somehow* pull off in their blindness. Still, it poses a massive challenge for me, since I was the first to climb the slippery dozen of steps and the first to cling gingerly onto the butts of the fire-torches sticking out from the Bridge's posts and stare into oblivion between us and Leo. I hesitate and look straight forwards. Maybe the Bridge will become more convincing as I proceed? Or maybe it'll get worse...? I stick to what I already know – not much – which is that the lynx will really be the one to lead the way, not me. But what am I supposed to believe? That a ghost can test the weight of this thing on our behalf? Or that this spirit won't drag us through some impossible scenarios along the way—?

You can only lead as poorly as the link leads you. It makes sense, for as fast as that lynx ran from us, it hadn't lost sight of us and successfully led us to the bridge in the end. And I'm – touch wood – quite satisfied with our success rate so far.

I'm sure I won't be for long.

'Are you sure about this?' Samuella says. And, for the very first time, I can hear a tremor in her voice: an uncharacteristic manner of composure for the Babe With The Blade, an unnatural manner of composure for *any* redhead with *or* without a blade.

'I'll have my arms stretched out at both sides the whole time. Just look where they are so you can make a judgement of your own balance. Follow my every move and we'll make it across totally fine. We'll make it *all the way*. I'm not going to trick you or mess you about or nothing like that. You *know* that. Just follow my lead.' I find that I'm consulting her – well, effectively both of them. But I'm mainly talking to *her*, rather than the traitorous titch behind her.

'Make those arms high where we can see them,' she orders. She doesn't like being patronised in this way and it's flamingly obvious. She likes to feel in control.

'Whether this thing falls or not, I'm making it to the other side,' Camson hisses, 'even if that means swimming.'

Swimming! Argh! Why didn't I think of that? I've been getting so anxious about heights I've forgotten that I'll have to *drown* before I finally die! If only I'd taken those lessons as a child…if only, if only, if only… Now the challenge has tripled and we haven't even started…

I turn from the pair of them, gulping air into my lungs. Then, the first foot lands on the first plank…

SQUEEEAAL! CLICK-CLick-Click-click…SNAP!

My chest is thumping like a subwoofer and I'm suddenly jittering along to the beat of my heart. Delving into the momentum, I take a second step…a third…a fourth…until I've cleared four or five feet into the distance of the Bridge.

'Almost there…' I mutter, chopping words in between breaths, '…almost there…almost…'

'Should we start to come?' Samuella calls from behind.

'Haven't you already started?' I panic. 'Hurry up! You need to stick by me! Fast!'

The lynx sits about twenty steps ahead, facing me. It should be okay for now…

'I…I can't find the step,' she says. 'Where is it? How'd you get up there?'

Too concentrated on my own movements to avert my attention, I say, 'Where you're standing, there should be…there should be…on the sand…in front of you, where my footprints disappear—that's where the steps start. Find your footing, then start your way up and follow close behind me. Quickly, before the lynx decides to make a move—but not too quickly!'

Soon, I feel another weight on the bridge - Samuella. It causes the planks to dip slightly and my adrenaline hobbles with it. The third weight - Camson - jerks the bridge from side to side, dizzying my balance.

'Slowly!' I say.

'You said quickly!' Camson answers.

'Same thing—!' I argue.

'Whoa! You were right!' Samuella says. 'This thing's all over the place!'

'Keep a steady, almost synchronous pace—watch my feet and we'll make it acro—'

Words leave me. The sight ahead…

'What is it?' Samuella asks.

I don't answer.

There are holes in the following sequence of planks ahead. In front of me at this moment, there's a three-foot-wide gap with only two linked planks following after it. Ahead of those two isolated planks is another gap. A much wider one.

The lynx makes it over with ease. Hopping onto the two joined planks. And then to the next set of planks, where he hovers slightly over the longer gap and deploys all four legs down on the platform like a helicopter on tarmac.

That's not fair.

'What is it?' Samuella's curious to know why I've now come to a stop. 'Is something wrong?'

'Okay, err…' I struggle for a calm and coherent verdict. 'There's a little gap. A few, actually. I'll need you guys to be patient with me. Really patient.'

'How are we supposed to know where to step?' Camson's worrying now.

'Don't worry. I'll help you. I'll show you. Just wait for me to go first, because the next platform only has two planks before the second gap. If we all rush at once, we'll fall.'

'Rushing wasn't my initial idea.' Samuella's churning her fear into irritation.

I grip onto the two ropes on either side of me. They're grimy and hard to properly clasp. Then I dive forwards, not losing grip, and amazingly land with both feet on the twin planks. Stuck in a backwards-leaning position, I swipe my hands forwards along the rope until I'm upright again. But what I figure next is that, in order to reach Samuella and Camson, I'll have to remain where I am and not go any further. Otherwise, I'll be unable to reach over and grapple them across. Or catch them if they do fall…

'Lift your foot up! Point it out towards me!' I say to Samuella.

'Do you know how bloody horrifying this is? It feels like we're walking on air!' Camson whines from behind her.

'Oh, shut up, Camson!' Samuella says, shuffling forwards. 'No one would ever mistake you for a soldier!'

'A *veteran* soldier,' Camson corrects. 'Means I'm retired. Not the same.'

'Do it! Quickly, pass me your leg, or your foot at least!' I shout.

She does this whilst holding onto the ropes and keeping her eyes out of the terrifying equation, looking up at the sky rather than down at the nothing-but-crashing-water below. Not blinking once. Her foot wriggles towards me and I move as swiftly as I can to grab hold of it. She shrieks as soon as I touch her.

'Where's the gap? *Where is it?*' she screams.

'Don't worry. I can see it. And I have your foot now, levelled above the planks. Just lower it easily.'

Her foot touches the platform. But it's light-years from over.

'Okay, hold on,' I command. Now, it's my turn to make the next manoeuvre, which is the following gap. This space in the bridge looks about a foot or two wider than the first. I courageously launch my own leg across the gap in a stride. My legs are now greatly spread and aching. 'Right, now give me your hands and pull the other foot across.'

Samuella lands her palms in mine and digs her nails into the backs of my hands. She lifts her other leg and I hoist her along onto the two-plank platform. A burst of relief flees her face. Turning back to Camson, she does the same as I did to her, first feeling for the two planks before helping him to land his foot on it.

By now, I'm already successfully across with both feet on the third section of platform. This platform has enough generous space to support all three of us. *Just enough*. I watch cautiously: Samuella guides Camson's every movement like a student flourishing in an art I had once taught her myself. Every now and again, I recall various directions out and warn Samuella of her own footing.

Once all three of us are across to the third stretch of platform, we briskly pick up our pace. Not exactly running, yet, not exactly walking, we find that the most part of the Bridge is substantial. With the lynx watching over us from roughly twenty steps away at all times, we manage to reach halfway without any major tribulations other than a couple more delicate gaps and soppy wood—

But that was only halfway. And now we've come to something much worse.

Much worse.

This time, all the planks are there and it's a beautiful sight to see: a stretch of tethered slabs of wood, lined as perfectly into the distance as I could hope for. Although the platform isn't the case this time, the barriers are.

It isn't until I reach the "end of the line" – quite literally – that I realise that it's just the platform and us now. The stabilisers are off and it's all down to us and how cautious we can really be. My first impression of the whole ridiculous idea is: *WE NEED TO GO BACK! WE NEED TO GO BACK NOW! TURN RIGHT AROUND, HEAD BACK TO THE BEACH, TELL GHOST TALES AROUND A FIRE AND PERFORM ROLY-POLIES IN THE SAND INSTEAD!* But then the voice in my head returns to me, catches me off-guard as ever. It denies my doubts and explains what we need to do:

Keep your legs together and walk down the middle. Close to one another.

Prior to my mentioning of the situation to the others, the lynx has already committed himself to exactly this. His legs are steady and firm together as he wanders along the floating series of planks. This time, he gets further than his twenty-step demonstration; he makes it forty. And he turns, watching us as a twinkling speck in the distance.

'Nope,' I mutter to the spirit, shaking my head. 'You're really testing us this time.'

But I have to hold faith in the advice in my mind and apply the same logic and confidence to my own voice.

'Guys, bigger dilemma this time round. No more rope. It's snapped and, unless anyone here is a world-class scuba diver in their spare-time, we're not getting it back,' I say bluntly.

'So, what do we do? I couldn't§ see where they were anyway. Are the chances of toppling off any greater?' Samuella says.

'Neither can I,' Camson jumps on the bandwagon.

'We're not going anywhere other than dead straight. Keep your legs together and keep your movement minimal. We're going to make this, hands on shoulders!' I motivate them. 'Remember, down the middle and straight all the way'.

I'm the first to tempt the challenge. And the unlucky-lucky one without his eyes shut. Even though it's just as difficult for me in the dark and surrounded by water in which I do not intend to drown.

Steady now. Keep a relatively consistent and steady pace. You've all the time you need to do this. The voice urges me onwards.

'How are we doing back there?' I say.

'Fine. Easy. Like walking on thin air—Oh yeah, I almost forgot how true that is!' Samuella says, trying to keep her feet as dry as her humour.

'If it helps, try holding onto my shoulders', I suggest.

She doesn't need anymore consent than that and does as necessary to maintain balance. Her hands clamp down tightly on my shoulders. And Camson does the same to her. We've formed a chain. Now, what happens to one of us happens to all of us.

'That's it.'

We continue along the platform in this way for a while longer and, as we do, the planks are beginning to deform again. Narrowing in places, twisting and bending in others. The unfriendly ocean stirs in her bed and the toss of her waves inspires the Bridge to sway above their fury. Samuella and Camson's chances of balancing are shrinking and it's only going to take one odd to knock us all off.

It's as I'm thinking of this, I notice the bulging, curved objects sticking out in the water on both sides of the platform. They look like boulders in the sea. But *anything* suspicious would catch my sensitive attention in the experience I'm having right now. And these round objects don't really seem to be as placid as they make out. They're huge and dull-looking without a lot to them other than their striking size and shape.

It only takes one to move…

I hold back a choking fit, trying not to slip off the soggy plank in alarm. The round, massive creatures roll in the seawater, onto their backs and over again.

A dozen or so black eyes buttoned above dripping snouts, thick fur slimed with seaweed and cavernous mouths shelved with sharp fangs easily identify that we've entered the territory of a clan of Balænas.

They groan and roar harmoniously and slap their giant tailfins against the ocean surface. Hearing this warning cry, I refuse to go any further. Then comes the loud, startling water, spurting from their blowholes.

We all freeze in our tracks.

'Are those what I think they are?' Samuella asks. Her hands are shivering on my shoulders.

'Let me do the honours,' these words come from Camson. Samuella and I are quick enough to catch him in the act of raising the bow from his back-strap and into his grip, which is already prepared with an arrow. He's aiming it at the nearest one he can find.

'Don't do that!' Samuella smacks his weapon away. 'You'll stun them and they'll attack us if you stun them!'

'We're not getting much further than here if they don't move off!' Camson puts up a fuss. He lifts the bow again. 'They don't attack threats; they attack the most vulnerable. So, if I hit the furthest one, they'll sense danger and scarper.'

'You've obviously never crossed a Balæna before! Not a clan of them, that's for sure! You're taking one hell of a risk here. Think a smidge, Cammy' Samuella nags.

But Camson's ready to shoot.

'Don't do it. I promise you, it's a mistake,' she persists.

His eyebrows crease and his teeth show, gritted as they are. Camson releases his arrow. It zooms directly into the head of the Balæna furthest from the platform.

Perfect shot.

The Balæna screeches in agony and sinks down into the water. Following this uproar, the other Balænas have become highly attentive and they start to swim urgently towards us. I'm glued to the spot, petrified.

'*HUGE*—HUGE MISTAKE!' Samuella curses. 'IDIOT! LOOK WHAT YOU'VE DONE!'

WHAM! Impact begins with the first Balæna knocking into the right side of the platform. Not one of us is left standing. We all slip and fall and grapple for whatever we can. The Bridge swings like a hammock and we're immediately swooping about in the air!

SMASH! A second Balæna strikes from beneath and crashes up through the platform. The bridge shatters into a thousand splinters. The three of us disperse in all directions, catapulted into the water.

I feel like I've flown for miles before hitting the water's surface. There's nothing I can do to save myself, as my body sinks deep below. The ocean-water is cloudy, dark and seamless with no sign of passage, save for the moonlight that protrudes from above. Within the beam of moonlight, the blurred figures of more Balænas are swimming in search of the human culprits.

All I want is to breathe one last time; my lungs won't allow it. And all I want to feel is the earthly air tickle my skin; the fondling of the ocean's warm tenderness stifles this. Many heavy, grey figures close in and an enormous tailfin seals off the rippling bulb of the moon, diminishing the last of the light.

It won't let go…

The saline glaze of the seawater finally relieves my pickled eyes and they rediscover the night sky, as I take a fresh gasp of open air…

The chilly night-tide rolls in from the ocean and covers my legs. Slowly tilting my head, the moon returns to me, hanging over a midnight interspersed with tiny stars. My vision isn't looking as bad as it was when I'd been underwater. Although my hearing is slightly muffled by the blockage of water in my ears and my face is sore from my temples to my jaw. This brief roughness is no disillusion to the fact that I'm still conscious in the Dreamerverse and, most thankfully, *alive.*

I bounce up from the damp, uncomfortable patch of sand and splutter out some of the water that has been festering in my throat before washing ashore. Have I been washed ashore? My eyeballs are burning like I've cried for centuries and the pain is ironing the numbness out of my senses. Beside me, a large, stilled object lies there; a flab of meat that must have also beached along with me. After blinking to restore clarity in my sight, I realise this is, in fact, the Balæna that Camson had struck. It's definitely dead. An arrow pokes out from its head and a pool of dark red soaks the sand around it.

I'm not strong enough to get to my feet. Coming close to drowning has drained me of my bearings and sickliness has overtaken me.

Here comes another person. A feminine figure with flat, chestnut-coloured tentacles for hair, fluttering in the sea breeze, makes her way up towards me from the water. Attached to her back is the stack of arrows and over her shoulder is the bow. In one hand, she carries her sword; with her other, she drags another person along the ground. The little man in the dressing gown is making gross grunting sounds and heaving noises. He's in the same condition as me. The girl drops him when she reaches me, then she looks down at both of us triumphantly.

'Is there something I'm missing here?' I ask.

'You never said you couldn't swim. Don't you think you could have mentioned something important like that?' Samuella says, crouching between Camson and I.

'Well, next time you want to take a look at my "do's and don'ts", you let me know. I'll mail them to you,' I tell her.

Camson's too shocked to speak. He's spluttering like crazy.

'What about him?' I add. 'Can't he swim? I thought folk in the East were instinctively born to swim?'

'He had a very close encounter. A bit like you, but more serious. If you two knew the basics of how to survive at sea, you'd *only* have to worry about Balænas poisoning you. And maybe I wouldn't be the only one fending off an entire family of them.'

I glance at Camson and grin like he would at me if this was only my fault and not his. I guess this is a failure that belongs in the hands both of us. 'Looks like we're on the same level this time round,' I say.

He gives me daggers, deals Samuella the same disgraceful expression and whispers, 'I want my bow back.'

'Once I teach you how to use it properly. Not how to lose it,' she answers.

'And *you're* supposed to be the expert in weaponry, child?' Camson jeers pathetically.

'Used to hunt and fish with my uncle,' Samuella says. 'He told me once, while we were poaching the poison out of Balæna tusks by the lakeside, that it only takes a narcissist to kill, but hunting requires an artist.'

'Listen up, Camson. Those "*dos and don'ts*" always come in handy,' I tease. But this humour isn't helping our shattered condition at all.

Samuella notices something before either Camson or I even get the chance to consider it. 'Where's the Map?' Intense horror drills through her voice.

Reactivating his sense of humour, Camson spins this one back on me. 'The "*dos and don'ts*", eh?'

Suddenly, there's swooping high above in the night-sky. Colourful wings are flaring and spiralling about in the clear air. It's Stewart and he's arrived with a potentially "special delivery". He releases the scroll from his claws and it lands right on my lap. I give him a thumbs-up as he departs and then I unravel it.

'Convenient, right?' I say, wiping the smirk off Camson's face.

'I guess not a lot of things go to waste on Awakening Coast,' Samuella notes.

'I'd take better care of myself, if I were you,' Camson warns. 'You have a tendency of landing us back at square one. But there's no returning the way we came now. The Map might be replaceable, but *we* aren't.'

'Where are we headed from here?' Samuella mediates, handing us both back our swords, which she has taken the trouble of retrieving from the ground beside the dead Balæna. 'Didn't you mention something about mountains?'

'Those mountains,' Camson announces. And he makes us aware of them for the first time.

Far in the distance, beyond the jungle of palms, there's a vast, rocky scape of white and grey mountains standing as bold as bulls. Ascending to the peaks is a trail of formidable mist…

Chapter Two

The Phestor's Mistress

It was hard luck enough having the Decider for a father. Living with one was a completely different matter. Many wealthy kids in the City would tell you that they never lived with their parents. Oscar didn't share the same residence as his father, albeit they existed in the same building. He had his own place of retirement, three floors further down in the elevator. It was a pad just as lavish as DCD. Philson's apartment, but had a slightly shoddier view and the voice-activated refrigerator was only a little less cool. Not to forget, there was his new bed, custom-made for him – the one he had hired a team of Week Trade subordinates to craft inside his bedroom three days ago. *Maybe*, he wondered, *this nocturnal contraption had been the cause of his bad dreams? Could they really be called 'bad dreams'? They were filled with clear blue-skies and stars at night and talking parrots and king-sized entities and attractive girls with dark-red hair.* He could at least say now that he'd been to an actual beach and dipped his feet (or nearly drowned) in the ocean. He could even boast how he'd been summoned there by royalty and sent on a quest into the deepest regions of his imagination. In this other world, for once, he felt that he was needed somewhere else, had a genuine purpose in a role that didn't involve passively waiting around to become sovereign of a land he had lost love for, but required him to earn his crown, to fight for it. Why did he still struggle to believe it? Was it too good to be true?

Hours ago, Stevenson must have guided him drearily out of the Table Room in his father's residence and laid him down on the elevator-floor – gone were the days when he used to jovially carry a seven-year-old Oscar over his shoulder; Oscar was way bigger and older than that now and there was only one method of getting him downstairs without Stevenson breaking his back. The elevator floor. *Oh, how humiliating it must have been!* The East Girl with the gorgeous eyes upstairs had seen his face land on an empty plate, and had then watched a tiresome Stevenson drag him out the door like a drunken old man in need of a taxi home. *Hopefully her eyes had been closed the whole time*, Oscar thought pathetically. *Damn, what am I thinking? Close her eyes? She would have only done that if I'd soiled my pants the very moment that crinkly bloke mentioned 'Solar Blade'...*

Oscar halted his thinking and sat up in his bed. The mattress had turned into a deck of daggers nicking the nodes in his spine. His bedroom was quiet and empty, as it always was. No disturbance other than the anonymous hum of some irrelevant generator and that routinely vibration coming from the *LASERWAY* in the distance. Oscar would have been alone if it wasn't Kyma, the loyal old terrier that once belonged to his mother as a pup. It had been in the final few lines of his mother's will for Oscar to take future care of the dog. At sixteen-years-old, Kyma was getting on now. And as much as the terrier didn't look her age – which she vainly knew and strut off with four-legged finesse – she wasn't committing on the inside. She had the core of a drying date, spoiling with time while she dozed out most of the days; yet she beamed the smooth, youthful complexion of a grape on the surface, always happy whenever Oscar was there to greet her again in the Land of the Conscious and she hadn't yet shed a grey hair from all her groomed, brown fur.

Kyma lay there at the foot of his bed in a protective, warming manner. One paw was raised over her face and the other was under her gouty flab of belly. She was allegiant to him and was always around when he needed company or someone to cuddle up to. She would watch him while he talked to himself on the toilet; in the evenings, when he binged on *ORAMA* channels in the sitting room, she would scratch the arm of his chair enough that he was forced to take her for a stroll (for the third time in a day); and when the remote hour of his birthday silently arrived, she would bring him the bone she'd hidden, buried months in advance, and be there to listen to his sobs all night long. Kyma was his solace in solitude, keeping his hope alive in the shadow of his humility, and in return, he was there to carry her through her final years. The pair of them esteemed each other in the way a longstanding couple would, a testament to time.

Oscar stopped to stroke Kyma briefly before making a beeline for the doorway into the living room. He was curious to know where an irritating draught was developing from and figured that the open balcony-door was the only culprit. His whole residence was dark. The *HoloVision* was off. Oscar was never keen to watch much *HoloVision*, not in recent years. However, he was finding himself evermore forcefully drawn to *HoloVision* rather than the limited issues of newspapers and the inconsistent *City Prints*, which were never advertised for the knowledge of the public, and so they were commonly neglected these days. Everything in the papers was always about the Conflicts ('*they did this*' and '*we did that*'; '*invading here*' and '*annexing there*'; '*nuclear this*' and '*nuclear that*'), and everything else was just lionising the egocentricity of economics and laundering the promiscuity of oleomics.☆ "*The in-greed-ients of death and destruction*" – he trusted his Aunt Sybil's condemnation of it, she was a Soothsayer after all. Oscar refused to stir such mortal vanity into his mind any more. On various occasions however, such as State Holidays, the *Central City Mediums* (*CCM*) would publish their classic specials titled *Nostalgia*, releasing articles, short stories, poems and plays in columns that were always about the '*Good Ol' Days*', and republish old prints that sold reassuring (but reworked) glimpses into the past to the few who clung to the 'simpler times before' (back when every page wasn't split between an overinflated sex-offence balloon of scandals on *Meander Street* and a lauded sick-bag of *Chastity* Celebrity Interviews).

Instead, Oscar would read about "debunked" historians, copy old sound-codes from the back pages and secretly listen to rhythm and blues, soca and hip-hop at a low volume on his *HoloPad*, and he learned from creative articles the craft of art and design by hand. He'd done portraits of his mother, Stevenson and Kyma. And most recently, he'd sketched the picture of a glowing, almost incandescent, parrot, as well as one of a beautifully tanned, auburn-haired girl. As much as his father loathed seeing it (when he caught his son in the act, he sometimes walked right past and into the next room, with his eyes shut and humming loudly like a child), Oscar preferred reading these older prints, the *Central City Nostalgia Mediums*, rather than the biased fairy-tales about the West's 'New Golden Age'. *Nostalgia* offered him a doorway out of the City and into a freer world that the long-deceased

---

☆ It became apparent at one point in time (probably the beginning of time) that the benefits of oil rampantly outnumbered the benefits of bronzes, silvers and gold. *Economics*: the Old Democratic mode of production, consumption and the transfer of wealth. *Oleomics*: the New Democratic mode of production, consumption and the transfer of wealth.

remembered intimately, something only dreams could recreate. It was sad to say that the *Nostalgia* reprints hardly sold. Very few in the City read today's newspapers (let alone newspapers or *paper* at all), so why would anyone read the dinosaur copies about yesterday?

Even Oscar didn't read the regular issues of *CCM*. Not because they were an eyesore to set focus on with a glittering *HoloPad* screen – as many City Folk fussed – but because he found their backward topics too over-reported and warped in contrast to *Nostalgia*'s home truths – and so he couldn't process them as proper news. Everything *CCM* dispensed on a day-to-day basis was 'pop culture' (if the article was war-related, then it became '*bang!* culture'). Consistently the same trash talk!

He kept a cardboard-box waiting for it by the front door – a clever invention of his own, which he decided to label 'The Rot Box'. Whenever the Paper Drone made its rounds on Monday and Wednesday mornings, he ensured that the box was positioned directly beneath the letter-slot. It was his idea of getting back at the world and the views of a father that he never truly agreed with.

When his place in the world in the world could not have been clearer to anyone else who was in it, it meant Oscar would never earn the right to know what he might have been if his title hadn't existed. It didn't bear thinking about to anybody, only if his father ever chose to disown him – which wouldn't happen while his father's hubris, pride and determination went infinitely unaltered. But this fantasy did often occur to Oscar. If the Philson Dynasty disenfranchised him and heirloom discarded him, what would he do? Where would he go? There was no question that Oscar had a problem with his own identity. *Who he was, why he did, what he wanted.* Sometimes he felt guilty about the way he lived, especially on the occasions he visited the City on ground level and had to be taken from A to B in the back of Stevenson's car. When it came to studying the subordinates, those ants skittering to and fro on the concrete, he didn't incorporate the hysteria on the *HoloVision*, nor did he measure Subordinate life against the screen of his *HoloPad*, teeming with the Media's blur. Not because he didn't care about Subordinate Life, but because he didn't believe how it was portrayed. Downstairs, the choked population of subordinates was growing and sinking at the same time, pitted against each other in the battle for Trade employment, and money, and food. And here were the Philsons, indulging in supper upstairs with a wonderful City-view, and counting the anthills below. People were paddling while others swam in strokes.

Oscar was out on the balcony when two knocks landed on the front door. Startled, he quickly left the glass parapet and sheepishly shut the balcony-door behind him. Was his father expecting him to return upstairs when he was recollected? He already had his tie and coat off and had made his mind up: he wasn't showing his face up there again this evening. Kyma was watching him from the rug in the bathroom. Her eyes were open, but hidden behind a mesh of unkempt fringe.

He half-opened the door and was very nearly blown off his feet from only a glimpse of who stood on the other side.

The Phestor's girl was here. Through her veil, he could make out that she was faintly smiling at him. Oscar wasn't keen to speak first. He didn't feel very inviting. But she beat him to it anyway…

'Are you Oscar?' Her accent sent shivers shuttling through his limbs.

'Yeah, that's me,' Oscar replied. Not as calm as he'd intended it to sound. He still had both hands clinging to the door, blocking half his face. 'What was your—what was your name? I didn't quite catch it.' He awkwardly cleared his throat before she could answer.

'Evanessa,' she said, confident with a sense of genuine concern. 'Are you okay?'

'After—after that—what just happened—with the—I collapsed? Yes! I'm fine! I'm totally fine, thanks! Why are you—? Hold on—hey, how did you know what floor I was on? Did I leave a trail of breadcrumbs or parade-confetti behind for you to follow, or something like that? Did I embarrass myself that much?'

She courteously avoided that question. 'Can I come inside?'

She glanced over her shoulder and then quickly returned back to him.

Oscar was feeling flushed with heat again and on his toes. His father would not allow this. '*Erm…*' he caught her mettlesome eyes again, '…I suppose.'

He stepped aside, allowing her to enter, and pounced to close the door after her.

If anyone found out, he would be in trouble.

'What're you doing here, anyway? Everyone's upstairs,' Oscar told her.

Evanessa was too busy observing the place to pay much attention. 'It's no fun upstairs. Their conversation has no interest to me. I went looking for you.'

How flattering. But a bad idea nonetheless.

'And they let you just walk around?'

'I needed the toilet,' she responded. 'A valid excuse, surely?'

'On your own? What about your supervisors—*bodyguard?* Do you have one? Where has he got to?'

'My supervisors were disallowed entry into the building by your father's supervisors. They're still at the entrance.'

'Why—because, if any of my father's men see you here—know that you wandered—never found the toilet—they *will* come looking for you…' Oscar trailed off and swallowed hard.

'Is there a problem with being curious?' She could sense the sharp edge of Oscar's fear protruding towards her and it made no impact on her serene attitude whatsoever – this governing of her emotion scared Oscar even more than his own moderate rule-breaking.

'I mean, you know…they might think you're…well, you *could* have…you know what I mean,' Oscar stumbled.

'No. I don't know what you mean,' Evanessa said. 'I get the idea that those men up there think I'm a threat. They believe I'm a spy or have some menacing to do with a plot against your Nation. To them, I am nothing more than an accessory in a crime that hasn't been committed yet.'

'Welcome to the West.'

'My patriarch – the man who spoke to your father – hasn't got anything dangerous up his sleeve. He doesn't necessarily bear gifts for the West and doesn't ooze honesty – especially not in front of your Decider, the gravest enemy of the East. But the truce he is trying to achieve with the Decider he is doing for the betterment of the Sixth Nation and no other reason. He isn't a direct danger to your people. He wouldn't be here in your homeland if he wanted to cause your Nation harm – he would simply deliver it to your backdoor with a first class stamp. The best way I can describe this situation is a little like the impression a Magic Man has in his appearance.'

'*Magic Man?*' Oscar cringed patronisingly. 'Are you referring to a magician?'

'We call them Magic Men where I'm from. That is the name of the trade. They're everywhere in the Sixth Nation. *You'd know one if you saw one.* You can tell the good Magic Men from the bad, the real from the fakes. Magic Men are distinctive by their appearance: you see a man with a long, twirling, black beard and a gaunt frame emaciated from years of fasting and street-dwelling; he'd carry with him a birch-twig wand, a hat of trinkets and charms and he'd be dressed in a long robe – ample like mine, only black. And, in the old days, anyone on the street would unplug his discretion and call out the Magic Man, and everyone would gather round and they'd beg for him to perform his best trick and then he'd be on his way. Sadly, the intentions of a few of these Magic Men carry malevolence. These con artists tended to transcend disappointment; the magic skipped a generation and these imposters defamed the profession. Because, instead of producing a rabbit from the hat of charms or a python from the robe, they produced—'

'—Nothing at all, because they're all dirty old farts, only pretending to satisfy the hundreds of onlookers who labelled them a Magic Man in the first place?' Oscar bumped in.

'How I wish that tragedy was truer than the real one. The unfortunate reality is that a small minority of Magic Men these days keep a weapon beneath their robe...and they massacre hundreds in the streets when their opportunity dawns. These are not *true* Magic Men. Not the ones who perform beguiling card tricks to the ill, bring joy to the elderly and stun the children with their illusions. *These frauds are probably Infidels in disguise*, my patriarch tells me, *traitors under his nose trying to cause disharmony in the streets*. It's because of these incidents becoming more and more common why fewer people are keen about Magic Men these days. Now, whenever you go out into the streets of the Sixth Nation and you see someone who even resembles a Magic Man, you notice the public around you trying their hardest to veer away and you can't stop looking, and thinking: "*maybe...what if...perhaps...?*". Because that frightening image, that haunting potential is omnipresent in their minds, like a stain. That's exactly what those men and women upstairs see in my Phestor: a faux. They struggle to believe his truce, for they suspect he would be playing a traitor to his oath if he ever did forge an alliance with the Decider. But, just as there are very few Magic Men who are mass-murderers, there are very few Phestors like my patriarch. Very few who are willing to hold out their arm to another Nation—*oh, my*—an enemy even. In his case, it *is* quite confusing and surprising that he's chosen to confer with the West of all places. Though, fair to say—unlike his predecessors, he's always been clandestinely curious about the West, and he's never had what you would call a "soft spot" for his cousins in the other East Nations.' She paused, looked guiltily around the room. They had accomplished the impossible: the front door was shut and they had been alone for five whole minutes. 'I've had three high-profile patriarchs before Xenol. My former lords. And these men were all executed. Nobody trusted them either. Xenol is my fourth patriarch and the first of Phestorship status. It's still daunting to this day, still terrifies me; I am the mistress of a

Phestor—*gosh!* I'm still getting used to this new lifestyle in public. It's been four years since Xenol bought me. You must understand the feeling. But, on top of that, you know how it feels to be an *heir* to the Decidership—*my, oh—an heir!*'

'Tell me about it,' Oscar groaned.

'Well, can you imagine what it's like being the mistress of a Phestor. I'm fixed being the prime asset, the parting gift to all those men my patriarch exchanges with. You would never believe the hands I have been passed between and the number of men I have been prized to and have pleasured at the end of successful deals. But I'll never be a true *heir* like you. The son of the Great Decider. One day, you will have the power to change the world.'

'But who would want that?' Oscar said. 'I don't want that—I don't want that obligation. Don't you see? I'm not ready for that! I never will be!' Oscar protested. 'The world can't be healed by a lone individual, but it can definitely be hurt by one.'

'You are naïve to believe you cannot eventually change your father's world. There's no mistaking how frustrating it is to be marooned in it. At least you won't have the misfortune to endure the same standard of disregard I've had to suffer all my life. It's been a slow and panging existence. I've attempted to summon my final breath on several opportunities, but one of my Phestor's men is always there to stop me. They've caught me in the act several times, snatching away whatever it was - a knife from the kitchen draw, the sword over the mantelpiece, the fang of a cobra that had been lurking about some street-gutter. The associate would hold a finger to his lips and say in a low-voice, "*Your Phestor shouldn't know*". I fantasise that—perhaps my fifth patriarch would treat me like a daughter more, handle me like his very own. How do you think that makes me feel, being only able to dream of such prospects? I have no persuasion over my patriarch's emotions! I am his product and he is my maker. He has the scalpel to shape me, and the hammer to chastise me when I represent him wrong. And there's *nothing* I can do. I would never dare to take the gamble and cheat this practice in any way.'

All of a sudden, there was a flash of movement. Evanessa swiftly removed her white robe to reveal her bare body. It was a revolting sight that was too much to look at in one light. Evanessa's skin was marred with scars and bruises all over. She was also scrawny and armless on one side. In the place where her right shoulder should have been was, instead, a blunt stub. One of her legs was missing too, but it had been replaced with one that was false and made of iron and artificial rubberised skin. Her head was hairless and her cheekbones were disfigured like they'd been violently hacked out of place with a sculptor's chisel. The only perfection she retained was in her eyes; though these eyes were not unhurt.

Oscar was gaping, traumatised. He was speechless.

'Don't allow the beauty in my eyes to deceive you. I was hidden for a reason,' she told him.

'Your old man did this to you?' Oscar said.

'You keep supposing he is my father. He is not my father at all; never was my *old man*,' Evanessa's equability finally shattered. She was now entirely exposed. 'He is my patriarch – the man who I was exchanged to some years ago.'

'Fine—*your master* did this to you?' Oscar revised himself, as if it made any difference to the tragedy standing in front of him.

'The Phestor has mutilated me more than my previous patriarchs; those other lords of mine also contributed to my condition. I used to be so beautiful, with long, golden hair, a wonderfully healthy shape and smooth, flawless skin. But it all changed so suddenly.

'My first patriarch was an engineer. He helped the Sixth and Seventh Nations to build their secret facilities in the Southern Polar Region. He designed the invisible ducts that are set on icebergs around the base and emit radiation to ward off the West's spy-vessels that are constantly bypassing. Ships completely avoid the region because of these zones. The radiation field surrounding the Polar Region helps to push this place entirely off the radar and out of reach, so that the only way of getting near to the SPR is in altitude. You can only get there by aircraft or submarine. My first patriarch was a member of the construction force – back when Sixth and Seventh were in really good relations, and the Southern Polar Region was what rooted this bond. It's been rumoured they used to ship in thousands of our own people via commercial aircraft hijackings and cruise ships. Those hostages are treated like lab-rats in the SPR. Nobody in the West knew about these crimes in the beginning and very few are aware of its activities now. It wasn't until the SPR secretly began poaching some of their subjects from the West that the West governments became suspicious. By now, your father is probably well aware of what happens there. Where did the SPR start from? The Conflicts. A streak of losing wars with the West influenced Xenol's sudden urgency to conjure a uranium-source of his own in the Sixth Nation – which became the first nuclearized state in the East some years back. He started to test the formulae for these weapons on his own people, trialled the fallout side effects, until he was certain the formula was perfect. Remember those old stories of the Radiation Zones in the Southern Polar Region? Well, most of them are true. The East managed to seek out and claim territory in the Southern Polar Region before the West could even pack their bags and set sail. It's the same distance for the West and East to both get there; only, the East had known about the radiation set-up, the genius deterrent that made them feel more prepared to travel there and initiate a base before the West. My first patriarch had made sure that those radiation ducts were built months in advance and were in full operation before the East arrived there. My Phestor paid men in gold to develop those ducts.'

'*What?*' Oscar said. 'The Phestor paid people to pump radiation across the icecaps of the SPR?'

'Paying them in gold was the only way he could convince the engineers to commit. His scientists were offered the same privileges to carry out experiments on his hijacked subjects. My Phestor promised the scientists secrecy and removed their names from the face of the earth. No database could ever trace these men. He then progressed to testing his new weaponry on a selection of these subjects. Nuclear explosion tests killed the seven hundred who were conscribed in week one – they could have been picked out of a hat, it was so random. The test would proceed with the participants being shipped over to a clean spot in the Region, where they would be stranded on an iceberg a few miles out in the frozen sea. A missile would then be launched some miles even further out to ocean and the experimenters would wait to see how long it took the radioactive fallout to roll back and reach the iceberg. If it reached the participants in time, they would die of poisoning; if it didn't, the deathly cold would eventually get them.'

'And how do you know all these details exactly…?' Oscar interposed again.

'I have been there to see it,' she confessed, sighing heavily. 'I was once a participant myself.'

Oscar did not need her to tell him this. The cracked membrane on her flagged neck and the scars running down her incised bust howled it all.

'As for the chemical tests,' she went on, 'these were done in chambers, in the actual base itself. I heard that only six per cent of participants survive an experiment when in healthy condition. Most participants are healthy. But survival is pretty unnecessary, as they never return to civilisation again. Those who outlive the rest are disposed into the sub-zero wilderness. Shortly after my *second* patriarch adopted me, my first patriarch's name was leaked throughout the East.

His involvement in the SPR was exposed. The Infidels kidnapped him and several others involved and executed them all for war crimes. Perhaps the Old Lord is still looking over me and that was my lucky escape. If I'd have stuck around his halls any longer, I'd have been caught up in his grim, unfortunate fate.'

'*Unfortunate* fate?' Oscar raised an eyebrow at her.

'My first patriarch, the first master to raise a wallet to my name, was an architect. A simple, but prevalent engineer hired to build the Southern Polar Region. As much as I dread to say it and have whispered it to very few ears, the chemical tests were far worse than the weaponry tests. The second master I was traded to was a man with a much darker secret. Back in the late 2030s, my second patriarch – a completely different kind of man; the leading medical scientist working in the SPR – used to experiment with immortalisation remedies, injecting them into his selection of participants. This included my own veins, as a young girl, acquiescent through fear but not blissfully naïve. Long before there was a prototype for biochemical experiments, he submitted me, his own mistress, to the testing chambers among nine other juvenile participants. The remedies lustrated me with the agony I bear to this day.'

'*Immortalisation remedies*? Are they in fashion over there?' Oscar had no clue what she meant by this, although the name alone haunted him enough to make him tremble. What would anyone say if they caught him standing in his apartment with a young, beaten-up, naked woman? An East Woman in the nude, trading war stories. Even in his position, he'd be down for the perversion of foreign laws (a Class B Offence in A.I. Legislation) and sent to Mishap Mansion.☆

'They're serums that were conceptualised decades ago. Rumours have it that they should be able to boost life expectancies by ten or so years. The only downside is, because they're so lethally transformative, they can only be consumed once in a lifetime. I didn't turn out so lucky. Just be happy that they haven't introduced it in the West yet,' she explained. 'Before they were revealed as common remedies, commercialised in the East, my second patriarch regarded them as part of a "greater cause", a line of prototyped medicine I heard him call *G-Nourishment* in discussions with the rest of his colleagues. My second patriarch, being the most authorised scientist in the SPR,

---

☆ Mishap Mansion – a young offenders facility where they 'lock up' the Bad Rich City Kids and punish them with scones at teatime.

trialled every sample in his laboratory until our bodies gave him the precise reaction he'd worked so hard to find. He never stalled, never hesitated, never withheld, even when I started to get alarmingly ill. The serums affected my arms and right-leg with abscesses to a point when it was critical for them to be amputated and for my blood to be briskly transfused. But he always reminded me that the risk and the sacrifice were necessary for that profound "greater cause" and how I was so brave to extend my belief in him and sacrifice my life for the sake of discovery. My patriarch, he was so impressed by me; he indulged in my childish passiveness, which he exploited upon the scope of his conquest. I was his most reliable examinee, his "quietest" subject – my humble loyalties granted me a home for at least six months.'

'So, you put up with *that* for somewhere to stay?' Oscar uttered heatedly.

'Those first three were all dreadful men, of course. Though it was either starve as an orphan on the streets of Quomer or live excessively in the home of a rich man.'

'If I was in your position, I'd prefer to die than suffer under their licence of abuse.'

'Dying wasn't a preferable option for me. If I die, I am a bad investment; my patriarch will refuse to burn my corpse and free my soul and I'll be unable to settle my score with the next life. If I show limited worth, he will leave it to rot, or worse, bury me in unholy dirt. It's my duty to live for as long as my patriarch affords.'

'You decided to sacrifice your beauty, your happiness, for folk who forfeited innocent lives in the guise of science?'

She began to replace the cloak to conceal her body again.

'I understand what you must be thinking. I'm a fool for trusting, let alone relying on, these wicked men. *How do I trust them?* you wonder. Well, someday, I had faith that luck would take its turn and I would find a way out. While I was with my third patriarch – well, living in the cellar of his brothel for just shy of twelve years, I hardly *saw* him at all – I met a soldier, who used to visit the brothel regularly on his leave from duty. He'd fought in the Conflicts – a fine, young East Man who commanded the frontline. He used to buy me drinks at the bar whenever my patriarch wasn't around and made up for his martial absences by taking me out to classy restaurants and for starlit camel rides and picnics in the desert at night. He disregarded my deformities, kept apologising for them, telling me it was the regime's prospects that had brought me misery. A warrior himself, he recognised what it meant to endure today for the reward of tomorrow. That didn't matter at the time. I still told him it wasn't his place to apologise, for it had been my selfish choice to endure those agonies for future's breath. Beautiful as his unwanted sympathies were, I always appreciated his thought of me. He thought of me like no one else and was kind like a man I couldn't imagine. Every two or three months he reappeared, I was both perplexed by him and yearning for him. I was nineteen and the happiest I'd ever been. I felt absolutely unencumbered by this one man. We eventually slipped off to the temple one night and got married in secrecy. That same year, we had a son together. The patriarch running the brothel died before he was born, so, fortunately, he never knew. However, the patriarch's death rinsed my heart of yet one more hope; I had to be sold on.

'By the time my husband returned to the frontline, I was taking care of our year-old son. It wasn't long before the child and I were exiled from the brothel on my twenty-first birthday. I was blessed that I was already an adult woman, so the government allowed me to mother the child. I was auctioned off to a dealer in the market square. This buyer was another rich man, a strange West-expatriate who didn't appear to be in the "mistress business" - masked, robed, caped and leather-booted. He looked how a man of grandeur dressed in the East, one with enviable connections and his fingers in all the right places. He picked me out of a group of twenty or so other homeless women stocked under a stall's awning in the market. The women were of different shapes, colours and sizes, but were all completely bare. Armless and bald, I was sat distinctly, bearing the child on my lap, when I caught his eye. He told me that I could keep my son as long as I did one thing. I had to wear a cloak and veil at all times.' She finished fixing her veil back into place. The horror was all gone now, swathed beneath the silk. 'Discretion was vital to my acceptance; else he would not have been able to merchandise my maimed condition. I wasn't the one to make any decisions at this point. I went with him. He dressed me in this rich, dark blue cloak and veil, fed both the child and me and then brought us to the Phestor's halls. Phestor Xenol took me in and I have been his mistress for many years now. He allowed me to live the life of a noblewoman in his palace, attend his temple for prayers and read chapters from the *Holy Libel*.'

'You're still familiar with the *Holy Libel*?' Oscar said. 'Wow! I never knew they read that old book anywhere anymore. Maybe the East is a different story. My mother used to read it. She used to be the West's Oracle.'

'Yes, her reputation was extremely well-known in the Sixth Nation.' Evanessa's eyes gleamed. 'Your mother was an inspiring Oracle, very valuable to the West. I respected her Sayings a lot as a young girl. I miss the West's Soothsayers. They conjured so much wisdom. Since the New Democracy evolved here and the Oracle forfeited her influence, nothing has been the same in the West.'

A surprising grin overcame Oscar.

'You've visited the West before?' Oscar quizzed.

She nodded softly. 'Wherever the Phestor goes, I follow. He is my patriarch.' In a daze of mild humiliation, her eyes floated from Oscar and across the room to a huge portrait erected on the living room wall. There was a framed artwork of Oscar's mother. 'The Sisterhood isn't treated with the same animosity in the East. The *Holy Libel* is available everywhere there. Now and again, the Phestor lets me read his edition.'

Her eyes fastened, shutting everything out, and Oscar silently gasped. A moment to catch his breath.

'But, like under all my patriarchs, my life came at a cost. I became a business asset, a device to titillate Xenol's partners and associates all over the East.'

'So, is that why you're here? To seduce my father?' Oscar winced.

'No,' she humoured. Her eyes were creasing as though she intended to giggle at his remark. 'I think this is a very different kind of business.'

'Did you leave your son back in the Sixth Nation?' Oscar said.

'My son went missing when he was seven, ran off into the city to find his father. Xenol refused to waste time and Imperial resources searching for him.'

'What did your husband have to say to that?' Oscar blundered.

'I haven't seen my husband since I was twenty-one, when he returned to war.'

'How could you let him abandon you like that? Don't you need him now? The Phestor isn't treating you any better. It's the same palace, just at a different cost! What's the point of living a life of luxury if you're not happy in it.'

'It's a safe and stable situation.'

'How do you know that?' Oscar snapped at her. 'How can you trust him? How can you have faith in a man who can't even be bothered to help you find your own son?'

She tugged at the eye-slit in her veil, revealing the perfect skin around the eyes and along the shelf of the nose. Everything advertised in that small trough of flesh appeared fine. Nobody would have suspected anything ghastly while she was dressed this way.

'You had high hopes, didn't you? When you first saw me walk in the room, you imagined me to be outrageously attractive?'

Oscar tried not to look below her shoulders as she spoke. She was coming in the right direction, but that hadn't been the only thought running through his mind entirely. He had never looked an East Woman in the eye, let alone confess his admiration for her. 'You're not hideous,' he failed in response. 'Just not what I expected.'

'What did you expect?'

'You just reminded me of someone. That's all,' Oscar said hesitantly.

'Reminded you of who?'

'My mother—I mean, I'm probably thinking too much about it. Especially since you're a woman from…with…' He figured he'd said enough on that topic, gauchely judging by the blankest expression she'd thrown at him so far. And he turned the conversation around like it was nothing. 'The Phestor had that sword. Where did he get it from?'

'The Solar Blade?' she chuckled. 'Why? *Does that remind you of something too?*'

'It does actually.'

The pettiness in her tone sank. 'What do you mean?'

'Well…' Oscar hesitated, treacherous thoughts clashing over his honesty. 'If I tell you how I know…do you promise not to laugh?'

'What are we? Children?' Evanessa's eyes had become strictly stiff and unyielding. 'I just want to know how you could have possibly seen that weapon before. It's never been brought to the West. It doesn't leave my Phestor's sight.'

'I saw it in a dream,' Oscar muttered. Evanessa's eyes widened. He was waiting for her to tear back into an incredulous smile or ask him whether he'd actually passed out moments ago because he'd had a little too much to jug. But she was silent.

'And, in this dream, I was summoned to another civilisation. Another planet,' he continued. 'I arrived on this stunning beach – the people there called it Awakening Coast…and there was this parrot, who could talk to me telepathically. I could hear him talking in my mind. Literally! And he was the first to tell me that I wasn't on a desolate island, but in fact, on an entirely foreign planet. He said that I was among other people who shared a similar conscience as me. These people were called "Dreamers". And, because I'd arrived on the beach at sunset, I was, for some reason, a phenomenon. I was the Night Dreamer. And then, the king-entity-thing – whom everyone calls All Eyes – told me that this phenomenon historically proved I was one of these selected Dreamers who are conscribed to conquer an inter-dimensional creature called the Drag-in. I possess a slightly unique conscience, a cerebral passage to which only Night Dreamers can connect—'

'Hold on, stop there!' she cautiously intervened. 'Are you telling me that you have visited an alternate dimension in your imagination?'

'Yes!'

'And you're a Night Dreamer with memory privileges that subvert the boundary between that world and ours?'

'Yes!'

'And it's All Eyes who wanted you to slay this Drag-in?'

'Yes, yes—YES!'

She smirked approvingly and then nervously bowed her head at him. 'Now—thank you for your company. But I should be returning upstairs, before my Phestor stirs his concerns.'

'Listen! I think that blade might have a connection to the Dreamerverse—'

'The Dreamerverse?' she sliced his sentence with an abrupt knife of revelation.

She looked at him briefly. Then she quickly glanced away at the wall, where a portrait of his mother dressed in her Oracle gowns hung. Her being here was making him feel more uncomfortable by the second. The next time his father stepped in here, weeks down the line, he'd be able to snuff it out, Oscar was certain. Evanessa blinked rapidly before she finally said, 'I believe you.'

Then...*BAM-BAM-BAM!* Somebody pounded on the door with iron fists and, protruding in their aftermath, slithered a familiar voice. 'Osca'! Osca! Child, op'n up, up de door! Yuh dere?'

Before reacting straight away and responding to Stevenson, Oscar played an urgent game of charades with Evanessa. He pointed to the bathroom and she bobbed her head in agreement, following his line-of-fire to the bathroom door. Kyma watched the young lady with big, innocent eyes, disoriented by the vigorous frenzy of action.

Once the bathroom door was shut, Oscar opened the door of destiny.

'Ah, yuh woke! *Good*! We all good den, ah'right! Good to go! Yeh farda' want yuh back downstairs. Food wuh serve time ago and yeh lucky 'ee save yah some.'

'That's alright. I'm not hungry,' Oscar told him, rather defiantly.

'Yuh sure? Yeh look 'ungry. Jus' pass out like yeh eat nuttin' in days.'

'It feels like I haven't eaten in days. But I'm just not feeling that hungry.'

'Not ill?' the chauffer's dismay was so bold it could have caused tremors in the earth.

'No,' Oscar resolved. 'Just been missing meals today—oversleeping.'

'Bring yuhself downstairs, anyway, if jus fuh face sakes. Yer farda' tink yuh bein' rude to yer guests and yeh be givin' 'im a bad impression to de gentleman from de East.'

'Bad reputation?' Oscar reproached. 'What ever do you mean?'

'Nuh me sayin'! Yer farda's words! He wun tuh discuss 'ow yer appointment went today—but only *aftah* yuh had summin' to eat an' said goodbye to yah guests.'

'*His* guests!' Oscar hissed.

Stevenson was clearly humoured by this remark and used it as a moment to step back and smile at the agitated young man standing before him. 'Yuh gotta problem? What's made yah upset?'

'Don't worry about me. I'm fine.' But Oscar's face said everything else.

'What about that girl? De Phestah's daughter? She say she need ah go toilet? Yeh seen 'er 'round anywhere?'

'Phestor's daughter…? *Hmmm…*' He shrugged. 'Stevenson, sometimes I don't have a clue what you're on about.'

Dinner must have been splendid, because when Oscar returned to the dining table in his father's residence, after what must also have been a really long absence, the guests were buzzing with talk. It was no longer a null, earnest atmosphere. Drinks were being poured from the nozzles of what may well have been ceaseless fountains; the guests had actually decided to finish the food on their plates (it was courtesy in the West to lick your plate clean to prove you enjoyed your dish); some people were standing and hovering by the wide window, comfortably immersed in trivial conversation, looking out at the scenic view of the City below; and most of the conversations were nothing to do with the Conflicts, but to do with actual, ordinary affairs and funny *'little world'* conspiracies.

Oscar didn't particularly say much. It wasn't that he was shy around these people – and he'd been approached by enough of them to be certain of that. Just *too* many of them were *too* full of themselves. Sitting on the right flank of the Table, next to his old rival Timothy, Oscar recognised Dale Permin – the man honoured for discovering the cure to Accentititis.☆ He was skeletal and mincing in stature, so much so that he appeared dermally translucent; he was a man who looked vividly aware of his active dietary enterprise and devoid of intimacy for his sad, little pallet. His plate had been half-filled with salad (and half of that original half still remained uneaten). An hour after the Phestor's arrival, Mister Permin had conjured the courage to ask Xenol how his son had managed to contract Southern Fever living in the East (which made no sense to anyone sat at the Table, since it was a disease only spread by marine life residing in radioactive waste-ridden waters). The Phestor had said that his son was fooled into deep-sea diving in the Southern Polar Region (seas of higher radioactivity, located some distance from the scientific facilities there) and was bitterly poisoned by a Balæna while swimming there with friends.☆ His son had been the only one to get the virus. 'If I had known that he was going to be diving there, I would have warned him not to be so careless,' the Phestor confessed. 'I regret, the boy was granted far too many freedoms as a young child. But he always had an odd fascination with Balænas. To this day, he mimics the noises they make. My boy, what a peculiar Phestor he will make – if he survives to write his legacy, poor prune.'

Further along the Table, it was hard not to notice a pair of Siamese twins, both trying to flatter the same woman with smarmy small talk and clichéd jokes. These were the Kasserin Brothers. Oscar only knew who they were, because his father had mentioned many tales about a pair of Siamese twins responsible for starting up the *Axernet*. The *Axernet* was a mutinous messaging app that emerged after the official shutdown of the Internet. Everybody knew about the *Axernet*. It

---

☆ *Accentititis* was labeled a common psychiatric disorder in 2028 and early symptoms consisted of insomnia, dizziness, stress, anxiety and lingering headaches – the most quintessential sufferers were working-class citizens.

☆ *Balæna* – a phenotypically hybridized aquatic mammal, notably bred with large tusks that carry a fatal dose of gamma radiation. It has features resembling a killer whale, a walrus and a polar bear and is typically located in its toxic habitat adrift the seas of the Southern Polar Region.

was on the day of their trial, following their arrest ordered by the Decider himself, when some dubious information surfaced on their servers – the secret conversations of Fourth Nation pirates scheming their "conquest of the First Nation". It was a famous plot that was virally heralded in the West's Media as '*The Great Infestation Of Our Time*' (according to *Central City Mediums* at the time). And the Decider, of course, had shaken his head and announced that this dangerous revelation was not to be ignored for the safety of the City and the Constitution. That day, the *Axernet* had gone from outlaw to saviour in less than few hours. The whole situation seemed a farce at the time, too suddenly convenient to be taken seriously. Nevertheless, this exposé became the Kasserins' lifeline, ultimately marking their rise from subordination and promoting them up to the Decider's Table itself. The pirates were identified and captured and the Kasserins were honoured for their services to the state's defence.

The woman being harassed by the Kasserin Brothers was Lady Martina Furze. She was a big, curvaceous woman with a loud, ground-shuddering voice. When she spoke, you suspected the heavens were opening. Her lifelong work on bringing *HoloTech* to apparition was first recognised back in 2030. Due to her prolific efforts, holographic technology became the leading outfit in households, Academies and industries all over the West in less than a decade.

For most of his time at the Table, however, Oscar's attention was fixed on Phestor Xenol, who now sat closely beside his father. Evanessa hung around loosely off in the corner of the room, sat in an armchair next to the wide window, gazing out, down at the ants scuttling around on the streets below. It was difficult to swallow what all those men, including the Phestor, had done to her. Of course, all these years, Xenol hadn't been the only person to blame for her condition. Evanessa had been the victim of three other men in her tormenting past. But he was the only persecutor *still living* and *still operating her torment*. Oscar kept watching with a rapidly burning pulse and an itch in his sweaty palms. He received occasional glances back from the robed man at the other end of the Decider's Table. Although he couldn't hear the muffled conversation that the two leaders were having, he could tell that the Beast of the East was prying on the Decider from the corner of his eye. As they spoke: Xenol caught onto how the Decider communicated, what he said and why he said it, sizing up each and every syllable…

When the big discussion was nearing an end, Evanessa shuffled back over to the Table and Xenol whispered something in her ear, cupping a hand between his mouth and her cheek as he did so. She hesitantly nodded in agreement, as if she'd been given a candid dare to respond otherwise. Oscar observed the whole affair.

Eventually, the Stateship prompted Oscar to speak to Timothy, who wasn't struggling at all to fit in with the crowd. High society was Timothy's element and he was cradling the opportunity. Oscar figured a fleeting conversation of the flimsiest kind would be the easiest tool to break the ice between them. And, so forth, the pair of them threw what they could at the wall. Well, Timothy had more to boast about than Oscar. The boy *owned* and *did* absolutely *everything*. It was amazing he hadn't been commended for his extensive attributes and his unworldly range of skills. Oscar was just as fortunate. He went skiing in the Northern Polar Regions, he went on cruises around the Small Islands and he had captained his Academy's Ball Team for five seasons. But, unlike Timothy, he didn't like to be ceremonious about it.

The surprisingly tactful evening came to an end. His father and Phestor Xenol shook hands before departing, which spun a few astonished heads round. And then everyone left out the door. Oscar held his usual place at the head of the Table and he was finally eating the food that had been put aside for him by the kitchen chef.

His father joined him in the silent lull, taking the crown-seat at the other head of the Table. There was a continued pause before his father began to inquire. 'How was it?'

This was more responsive than Oscar had expected his father to be, particularly after having watched him down the last of a few skull-shattering beverages.

'The food or the Summit?' Oscar sounded sarcastic.

'Well, I was referring to the appointment this morning. But we can talk about all three, if you want. How did it go with Doctor Islie?'

'It was unnecessary. I don't need help. I just needed somebody to listen and understand. He can't manage either of those things.'

His father sighed. 'Oscar, I did try my best. I really work hard for you, boy.'

'I never asked you to try anything. I just want people like you to leave me alone. You're only interested when there's a chance your legacy is in danger, when your future isn't panning out exactly the way you want it to.' Oscar snapped back.

This suddenly caused his father's anger to detonate and the man shot up, slamming his palms on the Table. 'DARE YOU TO SPEAK TO ME THAT WAY! YOU JUST KEEP YOUR MOUTH THE WAY THAT SUITS IT BEST, BOY, OR YOU'LL WISH YOUR

MOTHER NEVER BIRTHED YOU THOSE LIPS! OR ELSE *I'LL* MAKE A MUTE OF YOU, FOR ALL THAT YOU ARE—NO USE OF A SON!'

'*A mute?* I've always been a mute! The mute you made me, and the mute you've made everyone!'

'Lying—LIAR!' the Decider shouted. 'You and your Punkish mindset, your stupid fantasies, your excuses—ALL OF IT!'

'Well there's nothing left for you or anyone to deny, because all of it is true! And I know it is, because I've seen things right here—actually seen things in reality that resonate so well with what I encountered in my dreams! What I dreamt only moments ago, just shy of an hour or two! You saw me when it happened! Did that look natural to you? Did that seem normal? When I passed out, I returned to there! To the Dreamerverse! It would make sense to you if you'd been there yourself, and experienced what I did!'

'What am I supposed to *experience* then? Tell me! Are there people on other planets that exist for you to visit them in your imagination? It just takes you to close your eyes and go to sleep for you to runaway and make conversation with telepathic parrots? And giant, talking entities? I'm sounding like a complete fool just reciting the fuzz you told me this morning! Imagine me on the *HoloPhone* to that clueless doctor! It was cringe-worthy! All I wanted was to shut you up before you made a fool of both of us! But it seemed to do nothing! Money wasted! To think, that Doctor Islie charged me an amount that could have subsidised running *TRAMLINE* A.I. operations on *Atlas Street* for a whole month! You're very lucky that, on this occasion, I chose to put your "*Dreamer*" rubbish before the budget! I guarantee I'll never make that mistake again!'

'You put your *name* before your policies, because without your name, you're nothing, I'm nothing - we're both no better than a pair of blundering subordinates, tumbling through a maze of earth, wind and fire. Islie told me the only reason you felt it was urgent enough to send me to him was because you feared I'd been "*Bugged by East spies*"! You've never put me before your position, and you've never cared about me, and so you know not a morsel about me, other than that I am constantly a risk to you! I'm a liability in your grander scheme of everything! Because you say I'm not emotionally strong like you, I'm not stoic, not smart like you! I'm not *ruthless* like you! And those are all *your* excuses! Because being Decider means everything to you!'

'That's not to say I don't have you on my mind,' the Decider argued.

'I'm flattered that you can put me before a grimy *TRAMLINE* station on Atlas Street,' his son retorted sarcastically.

'Boy, stop with this distorted lunacy! Ditch these fairy-stories and start to find your place in the *real* world!'

'There isn't anything you can do. I'm not hiding behind you anymore. I'm sticking to my word. I woke up in a world materialised and carved completely out of what I believe *and it was real.* I had passion for it, so it is.'

'No, Oscar! This is reality! This is what's real! You exist here on Mankind's World – and it's your home! Your only home! The place you seem to be obsessed with is nothing more than your imagination. And I demand you right this moment to disregard it. Forget all about it.' His father shook some of the stiffness off his spine and straightened his posture, raising his chin. 'It's like talking to a toddler again.'

'How can you tell me not to have a mind of my own?' Oscar said, his face red with fury. 'How can you just say that to someone and expect them to fall in line? It's like you don't want me to be anything other than—'

'What you're supposed to be,' his father said. 'I used to have a brother like you. Do you remember me telling you about him? Uncle Patrick? He was a socialist fighter, a deluded Liberal rebel. Determined and adamant to pervert his heritage and topple the Decidership. He believed in the dreams and the fantasies and all that rubbish you recently seem to be so engrossed with. It was a shame I never reached him when I could, before it twisted his mind the wrong way. And he ended up six-feet beneath my suede spats, because he was always six generations behind, stranded in a time where stories were all they had, when all they had were flaccid philosophies. And they were convinced by them; completely sold by their own daft arrogance. When the madness finally killed him, I swore not to shed a tear at the graveside. He died and I was so thankful to be left with the peace I needed to chase my own ambitions – real, practical dreams. Only, they weren't dreams, but ideas. I didn't need him blabbering in my ear about *tropical island planets* and *stars in the sky holding the directions to wherever*. I had my own direction. And this is where I am now: I'm the most powerful man in the world with every gallon of oil, every last resource and every head on the planet falling into my hands. This is where *you* are now. Don't let us down.'

Oscar made no further effort. He threw his cutlery down on his plate, foul from the fantastic flavour of the food, and he marched away into the ghastly cool of the dark Table Room to find the way out.

Surrendering his own distress, his father stayed seated at the Table and buried his mind in a whirl of thoughts.

When Oscar took the elevator back down to his own residence, he wondered why Phestor Xenol had chosen now as an appropriate occasion to show his face to the Decider's Administration. He'd never known a man of the East so brazen to have swanned into the West – unmonitored, uncensored, unprotected. Phestor Xenol appeared to be a man willing to mollify the West and dampen the perpetual heat of the Conflicts. But that had only been Oscar's "Punkish" intuition; you could rely on the Decider and the Stateship to have both had quite different views on the surprise encounter. In more ways than one, Oscar rationally balanced his feelings for the encounter on a scale of empathy and doubt. *Indeed, they were very ballsy East Folk and didn't initially strike him as deceptive (their visit may have been uninvited, but there was no disputing how direct it was),* he thought. *However, it was hard to believe that there was no ulterior motive to be concerned about (their exciting exhibition could be driving the West's attention away from something much shadier).* His father ought to be sensible with this new relationship – "sense before strategy" wasn't generally DCD. Philson's first port of call. *It will headline the Media tomorrow morning,* Oscar called it there and then without any further consideration.

He unlocked his residence's door with the eye-recognition programme taking its sweet time and he scampered inside, evading the frigid elevator. The heating was on full-vamp. Roasting. It reminded him of how warm the Dreamerverse had been when he'd landed on that beach. Though the humidity on Awakening Coast, through the jungles, meadows and towns, had been incomparable to this. It hadn't been the cacophonous blast of uncomfortable, dry insulation he was submitting himself to now, here in this principality of a bedchamber.

Later, while he was kneeling on the marble floor of the hallway, subdued in prayer to the hung portrait of his mother on the wall, beneath a looming shadow emitted by the open bathroom door, something nudged a valve inside his head, once again shedding light on that haunting ephemerality – *Constellation Planet*. It was the girl from the Dreamerverse with the flaming hair, mysteriously burning that body in the night. His confident companion, distinctive by her strawberry locks and shrewd personality. What made her so worth remembering were her aesthetic qualities merged with her bold self-control, and this was the image he'd had from the very first instant they'd met in the jungle on that starry-eyed world. He'd seen that face somewhere, but couldn't paint the picture perfectly—

What had he been thinking this evening anyway? Leaving an East Woman to the luxuries of his state-of-the-art residence. *Evanessa or not.* Surely, leaving an East Woman unattended in your home had to be a crime - although, so was sealing an agreement between a Decider and a Phestor. *Then again, what isn't a crime in this world anymore?* he pondered. *Did I expect her to just let herself out? She could have stolen something or, worse, planted a—*He needed to stop thinking like that, or he'd find himself turning into the Stateship or, god-forbid, his father. He had done the right thing by staying silent about the Phestoress. He'd had no choice but to abandon ship when Stevenson came knocking. *Will I see her again?* Oscar began to undress while he insinuated. *What will I say if I do?* He trundled towards the bathroom, stepping over a snoring Kyma as he did, and...

What was that?

A cylindrical scroll of old parchment lay exposed on the closed toilet-lid. It hadn't been there before. Oscar made a cautious manoeuver around the tired object, as if it had any chance of electrocuting him or possessing him (he'd been binging on too many *ORAMA* horror flicks recently). He saw his squeamish-self in the bathroom mirror and sniggered at his ridiculousness. Valiantly, he took the scroll and unravelled it. At first glance, the sheet was blank. But then, pictures and words started to fade into view, glowing as they did. It was a map of the constellations, drawn according to the atlas of Mankind's World and arranged in a way that could be navigated if one were to look up at the sky from where they were standing. There were transparent lines showing the division between the two continents, East and West, and thin outlines of the Nations within them. At the top and bottom of the sheet were the two Polar Regions. And everywhere else was either a Small Island or ocean. But this planetary layout didn't constitute much; all the constellations remained in their original places. At face value, it didn't mean anything to him. It was a map of stars, not a map of locations - the land was only relative to the positioning of the stars above it. *Had she intended to leave it behind?* ***Was** it hers?*

Then, Oscar caught the title above everything: ***The Constellation Map***. Its connection to the Dreamerverse finally sprung to life and solidified in his memory. And as the title emerged, so did a thin trail out from a comet set someplace seemingly random on the Map. The comet trail stretched a small distance and then stopped as a tiny shining strip upon the expanse of the atlas. *A direction—to follow—*

to where—to whom? There were too many questions for Oscar to process all at once. *Had Evanessa meant for me to follow this trail—?*

And that was when the calling voice he heard often in that other paradise returned to him. It came back to consult him every now and again. The voice he recognised wherever he went. It didn't matter whether he heard it in reality or in the Dreamerverse. That voice had an owner whom he'd once responded to in person, but he just couldn't put a face to it.

It was stirring his own thoughts into words, pressing for him to listen more mindfully, as his eyes gradually began to close once again and he found himself staggering…

'*You're safe, and you're alive, and that's all that matters…*'

Into the Kappa Mountains...

Reawakening—

I crawl out from the mouth of the cave and creep towards the mountain ridge to peer over the edge. Leo Island's masterful fog has taken precedence over the wilderness below. The mist satiates a tropic saddle between the Kappa Mountains and it has condensed since we arrived, shrouding the restless palmtops. From the ground to about as high as the lowest seam of cloud is where the extent of birdsong and wind can reach and, above the mist - in other words, were we are - is a silence cured by undisturbed stillness. No birds fly this far up. There are no more clouds. Only the stars, their unhidden surveillance, and us.

I've awoken in a little cave, slotted along one of the mountain's ridges. A haven that hangs just over the fog and feels like a celestial temple atop a cloud. The three of us have climbed all this way and I recall how badly our bodies had ached for a rest.

The crackling campfire, which Camson successfully prepared before nodding off, is what summons me back to the Dreamerverse. Camson is sitting on his own by the fire, digging into one of the fish from the batch we caught in the water, earlier on the beach. That was before we'd started up the Kappa Mountains. It was a long journey; the ascent had been arduous and knocked us for six. My feet were sore prior to drifting back into reality and they're now numb after a long kip in the comfort of the humid cave. I say *humid*—there is some cool air coming from somewhere deeper inside. I can hear it subtly, like someone whistling in my ear. Before falling asleep, I'd downed one of the purple seeds to rest assured that I didn't end up back on Awakening Coast. I've already made that mistake once, and a repeat would have been a stupendous setback for all of us. There are only four purple ones left—so I ought to be sparing.

'How long was I out?' I ask.

Camson's sure to finish his fish first, and then answers me. 'A full day awake on Mankind's World. Like we all were. Your forty-eight hours in the Dreamerverse starts now. Use them effectively.'

I find Samuella, lying beside him. She's shifting as though she's about to wake up and join us again. Her face is glossy in the firelight.

'You were the first up?' I pester Camson.

'Obviously.' He's picking at his teeth with the bones.

'Remembered to eat your seeds, then?' I humour.

'Was that supposed to be a dig at my diet?' he grumbles. 'I swallowed the seed *before you*, fool, which probably meant it wore off sooner.'

'A healthy, strong veteran like you can't handle his seeds?' I mock him further with a playfulness that burns right through him. He gives me a brief sluggish glance whilst chewing his fish, as if to say: *At least I* ***have*** *seeds—unlike you, you ponce.*

My answer to that: *Don't choke on any bones now, chubs!*

Samuella makes a muffled *hmph* in her sedation and turns away from us. Our teasing antics quickly shuffle into the campfire, as that implacable chill returns to whisk the flames and startle the ashes. There's something uncomfortable floating in the air. The odd breeze keeps nipping at my neck and ears, transfiguring from an incoherent whistle to a wordless whisper—*Hask! Hask! Hask!* There's no point trying to chat with Mister Food-Before-You here, so I decide to occupy myself with something other than sticking around for Samuella and waiting for fish to cook. I wobble to my feet and stagger as a dose of vertigo kicks in and my eyesight buzzes like a million bees on their way to the honey-hive in my retina.

There are a group of dry, thick sticks lying beside the fire. *The rejects.* I take one and light it against the flame.

'I'm going for a stroll,' I announce, even though Camson couldn't care any less.

The cave might unfold forever if I take a gamble and keep on going. Ahead, the rocky chamber beholds walls rough with carvings of symbols and messages, which seem to have outlived centuries. I hold the flaring fire-torch as near as I can to read what's been inscribed. Images and large letters depicting the stories behind their scenes. I flash my torch over an inscription that looks fairly recent beside the others.

The engraved images depict two ferocious animals, a lion and a gorilla, brawling beneath an enormous crown. They're no work of art, but they represent something that I'm keen to understand. Under the sketch are words in West Dialect, a language I can actually I understand:

CONDONE... YOUR... GREED... TO... DETHRONE... THE... QUEEN...

However, the other phrasings surrounding it have been engraved in an archaic form of West Dialect. The Dialect of the Ancients. My mother knew this dead language like the back of her hand. Half the *Holy Libel* was written in it. So, whilst unreadable, it's definitively recognisable. Nothing unearthly here, I'm certain of it. Inscribed by whom though? The diary of the cave's previous inhabitants, maybe? Or accumulated from a history of tentative wanderers like myself? Could it even be the writings of former Night Dreamers?

I reach out to touch the wall. I want to feel the carvings...

Keep your distance, the crippling whispers circling my head warn. But the voices fail to forestall me. Instead, my curiosities have been resurrected.

'Why?' I question. 'What is it?'

Knowledge is wealth, the voices reply. *Understanding that knowledge can turn a wealth into a fortune. Ignorance is vital to your survival in the presence of Her Majesty.*

'What do these words mean?' I respond. 'Are they trying to tell us where we should be going? Or where we *shouldn't* be going? Are we not supposed to be in here?'

Only your natural instincts know where you are going – the Constellation Map helps you to navigate these instincts. Your duty is in the eye of the beholder: your destination is dictated by your imagination, but never by your will – to will for guidance through the Falls of Fortune is a desire for abundance from the Stellar Gods and will be criticised as impatience and a sign of greed. Be patient and allow your understanding of all new knowledge to come to you naturally.

'The Falls of Fortune won't let me *will* anything? I can't *want* anything?' I ponder over the concept. 'I just want to know what these inscriptions mean. Is that too much to ask?'

They are simply screams of the past, the woes of those who followed their will, rather than their instincts, and regretted it. The words are warnings to those who follow in the tracks of those who traversed these mountains before. Ignore their meaning, Night Dreamer,' the whispers gasp viciously. '*Those who showed such curiosities placed themselves in irredeemable danger.*'

'What's that supposed to mean? People who came here in the past fell into danger for wanting to know what these inscriptions said? Danger from what?'

The cave will remember your screams and treasure them to warn the next trespassers.

It sounds ridiculous. 'I'm not afraid of what a couple of dead people wrote on the wall.'

The dead needn't scribe their own screams. Their echoes stained the walls.

'These weren't inscribed by hand—?' I gulp. 'These carvings—who spoke these warnings? Who cried these words?'

Don't be so curious, the whispers hound. *As we told you before, your desire is precarious!*

'I've been curious since I arrived on this island,' I shudder. 'Am I already in trouble?'

The voices don't answer. Taciturnity steals their place. Something cold and wet has reached out for the soles of my feet. Encircled them. I look down slowly to where a thin trail of cold water has drooled towards my feet and formed a shallow pool around them. Water—source—? The Falls! They can't be much further!

The icy shock of the spillage entrances my body, stunning my muscles until I'm cemented to the spot, petrified—

Straight ahead, down towards the far-end of the cave-corridor, a small flickering light has appeared. It's orange and round. Shivering, I watch the tiny pulse of energy grow bigger. Ever so slightly. It doesn't go anywhere. It only becomes wider and broader, manipulating perceptions like a mirage in the desert.

'*Condone your greed…to dethrone the Queen…*'

This is a new accent, not one of the many undertones contrived from the wispy breeze embodying the space around me. But, instead, a singular voice inside of my head. Rasping heavily and loudly, ricocheting off the shell of my skull. '*…Condone your greed…to dethrone the Queen…Condone your greed…to dethrone the Queen…*'

A momentous rumble howls beneath the ground. Cracks appear. It's like the ground is about to quake. The light at the end of the cave continues to grow…and grow…

I start to move backwards, retreating in the direction I've come. Above me, more cracks have appeared in the cave ceiling! And they're in the walls too! The rumbling - *growling* now - is throaty and consistent!

The presence is here, below me, above me, around me, *within me!* There's no evading the wrath of its disturbance, its manic revival. I break into a sprint, racing in tracks I left behind only seconds ago. As I run, the words on the walls come to life, radiating an identical orange to the light chasing after me, so that the light in pursuit is engulfing. But it's not only on my tail—it's seeping through the carvings, breaking free of the words—*squirming*—the words are squirming! Souls inside of them are being unleashed and they're starving for flesh!

Hobbling along on my aching ankles and knees, I curse every step. I can't go as far as I hope. Leaning against the cave wall, I try to conjure strength in my legs. All around, the abnormal glow is closing in. Thick curtains of orange haze encase me, blinding my vision like the *Living Smoke* had in the jungles of Central Island. The weight of the presence in my head is ungainly and I'm faltering beneath the intruder's manifestation. Now, almost in a last-ditch effort to accommodate itself into my skull with a suppler shape, the voice has adapted again, personifying a gentler, feminine tone:

'I can follow you home...I will follow you home...even when there is no home for you to go to...I will always follow you home...Oscar...Oscar...OSCAR!' The compassionate invader morphs between my ears, its nimbler tone doing little to moderate the pain. I cry out for help—for relief—mercy! And like the words of my predecessors, my own screams begin to surface on the cave walls! The orange light is kidnapping my agony and transforming it into an artefact—!

Why haven't I brought the sword? The sword is my only means of defence! But, like the Drag-in, this throbbing abomination is immune to physical resistance. It would take no affect from a sword or a bow and arrow. I can't wound it physically, nor compete with it on a psychological level—

Then, I land upon something more useful in my pocket. The sack of seeds. Which one turns off predators again? Which one will camouflage me? How can be invisi—oh—oh—the blue! I quickly swipe out a blue seed and pop it in my mouth. *Chewchewchewchew—swallow!*

I close my eyes and hold faith for the best. Hope this works—I know that it's *desiring* again. But *desiring survival* is all I can do, for my instincts have abandoned me—

The shining orange has reached me. Its heat is on my face and it squeezes between my sealed eyelids. Suddenly, there comes the return of the whispers in the cave and their horrific chant resonates like the moan of a hundred burning children: '*YOU HAVE ALREADY EXPOSED YOUR DESIRE AND NOW THE STELLAR GODS WILL ADMONISH YOU! QUEEN CASSANDRA WILL PUNISH YOU FOR YOUR CURIOUS INDULGENCE! SHE WILL STARVE YOU OF YOUR WICKED AND DESPERATE HUNGER TO CHEAT YOUR INSTINCTS!*'

And with that proclaimed, the light is finally vanquished. Then the darkness silently triumphs thereafter, casting her wing over my body…

Samuella and Camson are gathering themselves when I return to them, rattled and puffing with a limp in my walk. Samuella's awake and all her attention is on the Constellation Map, which has been left open and sprawled out on the ground. It's empty to her, but I can spot the star-spangled sheet from some distance back in the tunnel. Concern fills her when I appear from out of nowhere. 'Where did you go?' she snaps at me. 'You ditched us again.'

'I warned you about this boy and his crooked interests when he disappeared from the Kingdom Palace and then popped up on Awakening Coast in a tux like had somewhere else to be – somewhere better,' was Camson's opportunistic accusation. 'He's not with us, Sammy. He isn't really on our side.'

'Oh, don't be ridiculous! I went for a walk. To stretch off,' I defend, too panicked to play "*he-said, she-said*". 'Didn't he tell y—?' I point at Camson, who's busy crunching on another fish carcass.

No. Of course he didn't.

'Next time, don't leave your sword behind,' she mothers me. 'You don't know what lives up in these mountains.'

Nice, I'll remember that the next time I think I'm going to be attacked by a carnivorous light bulb. 'You were lying on my sword while you slept.' I make my excuse clear to her.

She just shoots me a look to say: *What else do you want me to disbelieve?*

'I just didn't want to wake you up. Manners, that's all,' I say. 'Where I come from, personal space is just as important when you're awake as it is when you're asleep. The First Nation is a busy place and sleep is valued.'

'*Ahhh*—it's the *First Nation* you're from!' Camson leers with an oddly merry satisfaction. 'That explains the tuxedo you rematerialized in. You're a big-shot City Boy, huh?'

'I'm the Decider's son,' I confess. 'Back on Mankind's World, I'm the next in line to DCD. Philson.'

'An heir to the Decidership!' Camson jeers, almost parading about the cave in celebration. 'Oh, you see, that's one very important detail you were very cautious not to mention the first time we met!'

'Yes—it was,' Samuella says plainly, her concern drilling directly into my eyes.

'Why does that please *you* so much?' I glare at Camson, contorting with acrimony.

'Were you too afraid of how I'd react?' Camson played. 'Scared of what I might do if I ever found out you were the spawn of the most hated man in the world?'

'The most hated man *in the East*,' I fervently correct the little freak.

'The East is the world. And it always has been. Since the beginning of Mankind's World to the dreaded day the West robbed it from us. How can you idolise a man who inherited the slaughter of millions of my ancestors, feted the collapse of my Nation's pride and blessed his ancestors for their theft of my land—your bloody father!' Camson chucks his finished fish at my feet and snatches another out of his coconut shell.

I kick the fish carcass back in his direction. Instead of hitting Camson's leg, it skitters into the campfire and scorches.

'Come on, Oscar. Give Camson a rest. He's not had an easy time here and his behaviour—understandably—can't be compromised,' Samuella entertaining Camson's self-pity makes me gag as much as any of the other humble tripe she garbles in that irritating, rustic accent. It annoys me to see the pair of them as a fighting duo ganging up against me. 'You'd feel the same way if it was *vice versa*.'

'Why should I care?' I roar. 'None of us have had a particularly easy time here! But I'm not the one to go around rubbing my depression in other people's faces! All he's doing is attention seeking!'

'I had one son. The only other thing I cared more for than life itself,' Camson has his eyes pinned on me. Ruffled by my comment.

'Well, I've got news for you, buddy. I came into this circus with no one!' I remind him with as much simplicity as I can muster. 'And if losing your son in a dream really bothers you that much, why don't you just wake up?'

'It's not quite as simple as that,' Samuella attempts to lecture me again.

'Why not?' I bark at her. 'If you die in a dream, you just wake up as normal. Surely? *No?*'

'All Eyes and Stewart both cautioned that that isn't the case,' Samuella adds. 'Our conscience is connected between here and reality. When the brain perishes on one side, the other can't operate. It would probably take someone to have two separate minds to survive that. A hybridised conscience of sorts that could afford to compromise one mind for the survival of the other. I'll buy into multiple realities all day long, but someone wired with a hybrid mind in their noggin is just wishful fiction.'

'Then where's the boy's body?' I proclaim in bafflement. 'We're not transported here! A part of us still exists in Mankind's World!'

'I—I don't actually know,' Samuella surrenders her case and sighs, rattling her head with frustration.

'In that case, I guess we can't pronounce anybody "dead" just yet.' I look at Camson and shrug straightforwardly. 'Only missing.'

'You, boy—are an ignoramus!' Camson loses it, tossing another fish carcass at my face this time, and briskly marches towards me with balled fists. For a little guy, he has a striking force. Veteran or not, he's a short-arse with power and might. I'm up against the wall, trying to resist his sweaty arm digging into my Adam's apple. He may as well be strangling me. His other hand grips my hair, pulling it to enforce maximum pain. 'That doesn't matter anyway—not to you, Westy,' he whispers in my face, sharing with me the stench of roly-poly fish tumbling off the tip of his tongue.

'Then, what *does* matter? What really matters to you? Go on. Tell me,' I provoke. 'Tell me what you have to say.'

'I'd love to kill you, right here, right now. From the beginning, I could just see myself spilling your blood. Don't think I've mistaken exactly who you are. Or who your father is. I know what he's done and what he's doing, building bridges with the Sixth Nation to take on Phestor Serpens!' he chuckles. 'Criminal! Good luck to him! Good riddance, I tell you! You couldn't count how many chances I've been given over the years to eliminate your father. I could have liquidated the Decidership a long time ago. Sent a bullet straight through his skull or landed one in his chest as easily as dropping a coin down the gutter.'

'Then why didn't you take your chances?' I tremble.

Camson tightens his grip on my hair. 'I might have, if I hadn't had better things to be doing. Duties that meant more to me than settling scores with your father and avenging my Nation's freedom for the burdens of a foreign dictator and his forefathers. I was a father myself and the last thing I wanted at that stage of my life was a bounty on my head and to be constantly looking over my shoulder for First Nation Agents. When my son escaped his mother as an infant, I found him lost and starving in the streets by miracle. I vowed to bring him up as safely as I could. His mother remains estranged to this day.'

'Eighth Nation, are you?'

He grins condescendingly, the corners of his lips coiling. 'No. Sixth, actually. What makes you think that I'm from Eighth? The way I look? My accent?'

'Nah…' I choke. 'The rot on your breath.'

'I do try,' he laughs again, deliberately pounding my face with blows of his reeking fish-breath. 'I really do try my best. Just to satisfy you, my shrewd, little darling.'

I've had it with this barbaric train wreck; it should have crashed ages ago. Maybe then, I wouldn't have to put up with this. I drag my leg up from beneath him and knock him into the air, clean off the ground. The little man hits to cave-floor like an exiled twig pleading to be snapped. With conviction, I lift my leg again and try to stamp on him. I really do try my best, I promise. Success! I fall to my knees, on top of him. Locking him in on both sides with my thighs. Then, I swing wild fists at his face, hoping to mash up his cheekbones and draw blood. It feels tasteless. It looks vulgar. But it needs to be done. What surprises me most of all is that Missus Common Muck Cuntree-Bumpkin hasn't hastened yet and tried to defend her favourite dwarf. *Thanks lady-muck, fow leevin' all duh fun fow me!*

SMACK-SMACK-SMACK-SMACK! My punches are critical and powerful. He eventually garners the verve to slip free and topple me over. I'm panting, taxing for breaths that don't yet exist and may not ever manifest. *I really do try my best.*

He mutters: 'Your father isn't half the man he says he is. In fact, he isn't any of the man that he *pretends* to be.'

Camson goes crawling for his sword with wolf-like hunger until it's clasped in his hands. Staggering to his feet, he raises it and storms towards me. 'I had a feeling we wouldn't last…' he spits blood as he talks, '…you and me. We have our ways and our interpretations. But someone had to stand on top in the end, didn't they? That's how it goes, after all.'

'I'd like to see you do something with that sword. I really would. Go on, give us a swing!' I tease.

Samuella is watching in doubt. She says nothing, more concerned about where this will lead than the actual fight. Her legs are loosely folded over each other and her feet are wriggling apprehensively.

'DO IT! DO IT, YOU WIMP!' I scream at him, absolutely assured that he will. 'KILL ME!'

Camson stands above me now, with the sword high over his head. He's going to do it. Only needs to land it…

'KILL ME!' There are tears in my eyes. The cold-hearted little man only sees this as pretence, a pathetic decoy for him to change his mind. He holds his breath in and…

Flesh rips! I freeze, as glued to the ground as a gargoyle. Doused in dread. Screaming without sound. Then, after a heartbeat that reverberates perpetually like hours of anticipation, I notice I don't feel any pain other than heat under my skin. I look up at my slaughterer. The little man who once possessed a sword now has nothing, save for humiliation yet again. He does have something else, though. The tip of an arrow is poking out from the centre of his stomach. The sword has fallen to the ground beside him. And he drops on his knees. Like me, Camson isn't feeling pain. Not the pain he should be feeling, but the embarrassment and ridicule that is an understatement for us both.

Behind him, I don't need to guess who's there, standing with the rested bow in her hands. 'We need to start trusting each other,' Samuella says. 'This alliance isn't going to work if we don't come to terms with one another and if we don't just make an attempt to listen to each other. We'll end up destroying ourselves instead of the Drag-in.'

The arrow in Camson's stomach suddenly vanishes into stardust, as if it was never there. He closes his eyes, furrowing with mortified relief.

'I have respect for both of you. Don't get me wrong by that. All Eyes sent us on a quest, because of our significance as a team. There's more to this bond and there must be a purpose why the Stellar Gods brought us together. This isn't a coincidence; we're not here by mistake. So, let's forget about this,' She throws the bow aside carelessly, 'and make better use of our time finding some answers.'

'Why didn't it kill me?' Camson asks, shaken. 'Why didn't that damn arrow kill me?'

'Do you really think All Eyes would have intended for us to kill each other?' she says. 'He might have known we wouldn't get along. But he *gave* us weapons that practically had our names on them. We're not vulnerable like we are the real world. We're all Night Dreamers in this together, which means we're immune to each other now.'

'The weapons are rigged?' Camson stutters.

'Look, we're not here to fight each other; save that for reality. We're here to fight together. Oscar, you're leading the way from here to the Falls of Fortune. Then, once we have what we've come for, we'll head on to the next emerald with a better idea of how to work this journey. I'm guessing the Map will allow us to take it in turns to lead and, if it does, we must trust and follow the chosen leader.' Samuella comes to help Camson and me up on to our feet. 'I'm not telling you to shake hands, but I'm asking you to hold hands—for now.'

Camson gazes at me with emotionless eyes.

Is this buffoon ready to listen to me? Heck, to trust me? I ignore him.

'Oscar, take up Map. We need to get moving,' Samuella says. 'Did you happen to find anything interesting while you were out in the cave?'

I remember the encounter I had in the cave and it makes me go stiff. 'There's something you've got to know, before we get going.'

'What's that?'

'The Drag-in might be closer than we think.'

She doesn't need to hear or scrutinise me any more. She understands fully—I had another run-in. We're not alone in here. We kill the fire, gather our belongings, and head into the night-filled cave. Either side of me, Camson and Samuella walk ahead, both with fire-torches to lighten the tunnel as they go and their swords held at their side. Lending me my own passage is the bursting glimmer of the Constellation Map.

'This is certainly Ancient Dialect,' Samuella suspects, feeling the wall of carvings with her hand. She has her fire-torch in the other hand, stroking some flickering light along the decorated rock. This is the place where I saw the orange light swell from the words in the walls. And where the orange orb had swollen at the far end of the cave tunnel and hunted after me. And the cracks in the ground and ceiling are still apparent – stone scars, taunting me with the harassing voices that had protruded from out of them not too long ago. The tunnel is pitch black and gruellingly silent. 'Where was it you saw the words written in language you understood?'

'Some way further along,' I note. 'Deeper inside. It read something like "*Condone your needs…Impose the Queen*"?'

'And who told you it would be a brilliant idea to sneak in here—on your own?' Samuella tells me off again.

'The same reason you decided to set up camp here in the cave. I thought it was empty.'

'There was moonlight where we set up camp,' she underlines. 'I would have never chanced resting somewhere as unlit as here. The atmosphere is wrong as well. Feel that wisp in the air? It's not coming from the mouth of the cave. The draught is coming from that direction.' She points to the darkest end the tunnel, where the orange light had appeared. 'That's not wind. That's breathing. Life, somewhere in the tunnel.'

'You hear them now too? The whispers?' I ask. 'Because I can't. Not anymore. What they were saying didn't sound like words at first, but then they turned into warnings.'

'Never mind the wind! Can you translate some of these phrases?' Camson insists, waving his own torch in Samuella's face.

'Not all of it,' Samuella admits. 'There's a lot to pick from. It looks to me like the whole Ancient Alphabet is here.'

'Didn't your cousin teach you all of it?' Camson persists impatiently.

'Nothing this advanced. This is the kind of Dead Dialect you find in Ancient religious texts, like the *Holy Libel.*'

If only my mother were here, I think. *As the Oracle, she knew the Libel from cover to cover and could read it upside down.*

'Perhaps they were left by the Night Dreamers?' I mention. 'You know—the last generation who went looking for the emeralds? Decades ago?'

'Probably,' Samuella considers. 'If that's true, then they were much cleverer than we are.'

'They spoke to me,' I say.

'Who spoke to you?' Samuella probes.

'I mean—the writing on the wall spoke to me. Those whispers—they rose out of the inscriptions.'

They both lift an eyebrow at me.

'The words came alive and tried to overwhelm me.'

'Dead people's scribbles!' Camson snickers.

'Exactly!' I cry. 'That was precisely it! The words, they are echoes of old, deceased voices. The screams of those who trundled up here before us! These words are all verbal warnings! And there was this big glow of orange light that lit up the cave and engulfed me! It had a similar effect to the Drag-in's smoke; only, it was like a massive boulder bashing in my brain! Someone in my head, telling me to get away whilst I could! But it was too late for me to escape—I had already "*exposed my will and desire*" and "*now the Queen—*" I forgot the Queen's name, but they said that "*now the Queen will punish me*". It was a woman's voice!' Then, I catch something out with the glow of my torch, upon shedding firelight on the wall we have our backs to. In the narrowness of the cave tunnel, I carefully turn to what I've found, illuminating a familiar warning on the adjacent wall. 'There,' I nod. 'There it is.'

CONDONE YOUR GREED TO DETHRONE THE QUEEN.

'Where did the orange light originate?' Samuella mutters with greater conviction at this point. 'And which way did it go?'

'It came from that end of the tunnel,' I say, indicating to the furthest point of the dark passageway. 'And it spread everywhere. Seeped through the writing, as I said, and even festered in the cave ceiling and floor. If I had to point, I'd need more than two hands.'

'We know it couldn't have been the Drag-in.' Samuella traces her fingers along the tears in the cave-wall, assessing the tunnel from top to bottom. 'We're too close to the emerald's location – according to All Eyes, the emeralds are supposed deter the Drag-in like a pair of negative charges.'

'I'm telling you, they were the echoes of trespassers who climbed up here before us,' I explain. 'Their souls have been captured in the walls and turned into a safeguard, stopping wanderers like us from getting across the mountains. Possibly to shroud and protect the Falls of Fortune. We must be nearer than we imagined.'

'Are you seriously suggesting that these voices you heard were spirits of the dead?' Camson gawks sceptically at the "Dead People's Scribbles" on the walls. 'Coming to warn *you*? About what?'

'I got the feeling they don't want us to go anywhere near the Falls of Fortune,' I answer. 'They don't even want us to think about it. Our desire is dangerous.'

Samuella constrains her obsession with the inscriptions and I don't appreciate the conclusive look on her face; it's making me uneasy.

'Oscar, how far are the Falls from here?' she says calculatedly. Her impatience has matched Camson's – this isn't good.

I'm looking at the Map rustling in my hands. The Kappa Mountains are split into two lines of ten peaks that have been divided by twin stars. Our ***X***-mark is located within the midsection of **KAPPA LEONIS**, which implies that the **FALLS OF FORTUNE** are at the core of the mountain range. The end of the comet trail stretching out from the ***X*** depicts where we are – halfway along one of the two mountain strips.

'We're headed in the right direction and not too far to go now,' I tell them rapidly. 'There might be an opening somewhere soon. Let's move—!'

All of a sudden, the *rumbling* kicks off again; the mountains are shifting and the ground is their dancing partner. The inscriptions on the walls, cracks on the ground and on the ceiling are shedding their orange light again, detonating in our faces. It's like heaven and hell are both reaching out to war with one another and we are in the crosshairs.

'And this is exactly how it happened!' I find myself announcing.

'*This*—is bad,' Camson stutters. 'We haven't even found the first emerald yet and the Falls already know we're coming!'

'And you just wait until they see our faces! We're getting there alright!' Samuella confirms positively. 'Lead the way, City Boy!'

We stumble through the quaking cave in an unstable line led by the Map and me. Just when we think we're making progress, unmanned shadows shimmer into sight. Black humanoid shades bordered with beaming orange outlines. The bodies of spirits—*nightmares*—stand before us; living nightmares. The distorted chatter among them—*hundreds*—tickles our ears. They spawn from the buzzing walls, scramble out from the ground beneath our feet and drop from the cave ceiling. We've been suspended in our tracks and there's no way around them, for there is an uncast shadow at every turn in the darkness.

So far, the invisible figures are rendered to nothing but shadows, anonymities of the cave. Nonetheless, I can actually see my shady onlookers now, here, in front of me. Samuella and Camson glide on the spot, circling our little space with their torches aimed out at the aggressors. Fragments of their flames spike our predators, briefly revealing their identity – blunt facial features flashing into view for only a couple of seconds. They're vaguely humanoid, extremely shapeless. Their lack of form and definition helps them to drift effortlessly through different mediums. Some are missing arms and legs, others are headless and absent of chunks of matter in places, such as the face and stomach, with holes exposing their skeleton and shrivelled organs. When revealed against the torch-flame, the unfinished figures all flaunt a gruesomely grey complexion.

'What the hell are they?' I propound.

'I've heard about these.' Samuella's quick to answer, on the ball with her sword drawn high alongside her torch. 'They're Nightmares – the living, soulless corpses of deceased Dreamers. Semi-conscious, restless and desperate for a passage back into a physical body. They've been here for a long time. Hiding from the sunlight and baiting out trespassers.'

'How do you know all this?' Camson chokes.

'Camson—it doesn't kill to speak to other Dreamers and ask them a couple of questions, does it? You know—do some research!' she retorts.

'What other Dreamers do *you* know?' Camson patronises.

'That doesn't matter now!' Samuella rejects. 'Whatever you do, don't let them touch your flesh! Follow after me!'

She makes the first run, charging through the blockade of disfigured spirits with her torch out in front of her and her sword cocked artfully behind her, threatening to rip and tear through some more of their wasting matter if they don't disperse out of her way. The Nightmares take the hint and separate. Samuella disappears into the darkness.

'We should separate. Disperse them,' Camson directs, announcing he's next to dash and that I should follow his lead. He doesn't follow Samuella's defence, as he has other ideas. He has the bow. Swift to light two of his arrows with a flame, he fixes them to the bow. Then, he swings clockwise on his heels, searching for any signs of an alternative exit. No sign. 'That's a bit a bit of a risk, mind you,' he revises. He changes his mind, finding where Samuella exited the ambush and releases his arrows into the blockade of ghosts, bursting two of the Nightmares into a cloud of orange dust. They expel a dreadful swine-like squeal when struck with the arrows. This leaves Camson a narrow escape-hole. Before he makes his run, he turns to me. 'Hope I don't find you at the Falls, kid,' he says, winks. And then he's gone.

That tight gap in the ambush immediately closes up after his departure and now it's just me, left alone to face the horde. My fire-torch and sword at hand to pierce through the crowd; no bow and arrows. The Nightmares shrinking the circle around me like the orbit of a fatal ring dance. I hurry to scroll up the Constellation Map and tuck it under my arm, quivering.

Thanks for helping me think this through, guys!

I turn on the spot. The Nightmares are inches away at every corner, ringed around me and moving in, snapping their phlegmy-mouths at me. Thirsty for me—now the only body in sight.

Think! Think! Think! Think! Think!

My sword replaces the Map. They lunge without warning and I need the blade to keep a fair distance and prevent them from coming into contact with my skin.

There's no way through. And they're so close—

But then...the writing on the wall, the carved words have something new to show me. Different to before. They explode with light. And so do the cracks! On the *walls*! On the *ceiling*! On the *floor*! Everywhere! Not orange light—but clean, white light. The words I couldn't understand have now changed and they're readable, although the voice in my head is the one to read them aloud. As it speaks to me in that heroic whisper, the very crack beneath my feet is also glowing and beginning to stretch apart. It's opening! And I'm unprepared to fall...

Find your first emerald under the Falls of Fortune...but remember to follow your instinct before you compel the haste of your will...nevertheless, be quick...for the doors to reality are almost open...

Chapter Three

Window Shopping

Last night had drifted away from Oscar's vague memory, so he was determined to keep it that way. All the following morning, there hadn't been a single call, not an apologetic encore from his condescending father left on the *HoloPhone* receiver, or a wake-up call from the Citadel Tower concierge, not even a kind nudge from Stevenson to check up on him. Nobody had the patience for Oscar today, particularly not after his display of strange behaviour the previous evening. However, he was wise enough to keep reminding himself – or, probably, *not* to keep reminding himself – that the banquet's humiliating events, which had now seemingly subsided, were on the verge of vanishing for good.

Oscar initially thought he'd missed his wake-up call when he turned out of bed a little after midday. Maybe it was one or two in the afternoon…? He couldn't register anything at all. A half-empty bottle of *Cherry Belly* cider, which he was convinced had been another half-full the night before, lay on its side in the bedroom cooler, dripping harmlessly through the shelf's grill. To be perfectly honest, he couldn't remember half a bottle of anything. His head was clouded, *still reeling from his violent encounter in the Kappa Mountains…*Here it came again—his intangible obsession with his dreams crashing down on him like a weightless avalanche.

There was no wake-up call on a Sunday morning! he clocked. *That was it! That explained the silence! Oh, I should have remembered that!* It made a lot more sense as to why Readen Rooks, the concierge downstairs in the reception lobby, had turned mute. In general, Mid-Sunday was usually a time for bad news and, at any rate he was sure that today's bad news might recall something to do with the way he'd behaved last night, with everyone in the City waking up to the Media's portrayal of him being some ignorant, sanctimonious brat rocking up to the Great Decider's Annum Summit hours late in a spangled tuxedo and then dropping off into a public snooze like a hobo. Unless it was overshadowed by the meeting between his father and that Phestor-bloke. *Had the Phestor and his unfortunate mistress managed to strike a deal with the Decider in the end?* Oscar couldn't recollect. *The Phestor's mistress...*Oscar was beginning to remember now...*what was her name again? Madison? Malicia? Evanessa?* As decent as the East Woman had seemed, the thought of East Folk listening to the news that morning and hearing about the Phestor of the Sixth Nation and his mistress arriving at Citadel Tower to hold diplomatic talks with his father made him cringe for reasons even he didn't wholly understand. But the more he worried about it, it made him wonder—did Phestor and company make him cringe as much as the old elitists in the West Administration he was forced to bond with at the Decider's Table last night? He decided it would do him the world of good to get out among some normal West Folk, spend a pocket of his day dwelling with the less civilised public and let the aftermath of the Summit's events recede with him out of the way. Oscar scarcely knew anyone out in the public. He didn't mingle with anyone who was remotely 'common', since he rarely ever got around town without being guarded by A.I. or driven about by Stevenson. He despised how the only people he hung with were the hoary farts in his father's Administration, Stevenson, his dog and a few snobby contemporaries he knew from the Academy every now and then.

Today was the one opportunity Oscar had to be adventurous and, who knew, he might meet someone new, meet a subordinate who could teach him a thing or two. These days, without the liberties of the *Networks*, societal traditions in the West had sunk back to "bare basics".☆ Subordinates were now being forced to go out and about to

---

☆ The *Networks* were a group of independent Media stations that bought up all the Data Shares from the late Internet when it collapsed. There was a *Network* in all of the four West Nations, each owning a quarter of the Internet's overall shares. This was because, in theory, possessing full and undisputed control of the Internet was regarded as a divine power; it automatically posed a threat to the system and authority of the First Nation. It adulterated the First Nation's jurisdictional mandate to delegate and subsidize across the rest of the West arbitrarily, i.e. the *Networks* stuck their fingers up at the regime. As a result, the four-way agreement the Networks shared inevitably came under scrutiny. Conspiracies of the *Networks* developing plans for world domination plagued the Media in the 2030s, until their corrupt intentions were legitimately exposed during the *Viola Press Crisis* of 2038 – when First Nation Agents (FNA) discovered a draft of defamatory articles aimed at the Decider himself, a cartoonish slander they believed the *Networks* were collectively plotting to publish as propaganda to trigger some kind of revolution that would bring down the Decidership and the regime. As a consequence, the Decider's Administration called for all Presses in the West to be shutdown, save for those few that were famously sentimental to the City – though, even these "national treasures" had to pass through Citadel Tower before they were allowed to be released.

purchase their amenities and socialise. It was like a whole new age for Mankind. The death of the online renaissance had left a beautiful scar on a humanity that was trying to find its feet again on the High Street.

The shops were closing soon in the City Centre and Sundays were usually the occasion he'd pick to visit these capitalist havens and lose himself in the sphere of the financially impaired while he could, and hopefully find himself having an educational and feasibly free time down in the land of austerity.

Sunday was like a school day to him; he always learnt something novel about the world downstairs, the land of austerity – the real world. The liberty of Sunday meant that he didn't need to be battened down by his father's dates and demands. Needless to say, the Decider still wouldn't allow the hurricane of quotable subordinates to sprinkle their classless influence over his son and he put in place curfews and commissioned A.I. with the status to report and remove Oscar from the streets if he was caught roaming them alone. But Oscar secretly knew ways around this protocol. After all, Sunday was really Son-day. And he'd name it that until kingdom come.

Out of bed, he quickly fed Kyma and fed himself before he jumped in the shower. He left the bathroom feeling more alert and went to check if the Mail Drone had made its – very rare – Sunday Round. There was nothing in 'The Rot Box'. It was empty today. Oscar was lightening up already.

He took Kyma for a walk around the block before three, hoping to be ready to leave for the City Central by half-past. When he returned to his residence for the last time, he noticed that he'd missed a call on his *HoloPhone* from Floor 293. Two floors above, none other than his father's residence. Oscar declined the message playback and tagged it as 'Not Received'. Generally, he would have either replied out of obedience or sent a politely pre-recorded Auto-Reply. He did neither.

The time was quickly stretching out of Oscar's reach and he spent twenty minutes selecting an outfit that wouldn't draw too much attention. Even *he* knew that it was silly playing dress-up games with the public, but he didn't want to come across as a superior head, who was a hair out of place among the subordinates. Not only did his mannerisms give away his princely disposition, but also the way he reeked of sensational perfumes and serenaded in percussions of designer swag. Regardless of how he walked, talked and acted – and smelt – it wouldn't surpass a single Commoner with a Commoner's Sense to call out "royalty" in the middle of the street.

Before he left for the mean streets, he made sure that his horrendous tuxedo from last night, which had been strewn across the bathroom floor, was tidily tucked away beneath his bed, over the…

Locked hatch?

Curious and subtly reminiscent, Oscar opened the little hatch and withdrew the miniature vault inside. He then addressed the code and snapped the safe open to find a deteriorated parchment scroll tucked into the steel box. Affirmation cascaded through him, as he unravelled the Constellation Map and witnessed hundreds of star systems appear under his nose. He instantly remembered that he'd stashed the Map in the hatch beneath his bed just before he'd dozed off. And it had been Evanessa, the Phestor's mistress, who had left it behind for him. As a reminder of something they'd spoken about in regards to Constellation Planet? But they'd barely spoken about that. Or had she dumped it on him, not as a supplement, but as a tool to be used…? *Just how did Evanessa get her hands on it? It belonged in the Dreamerverse, not here. How was that possible?* Then again, the Solar Blade in the possession of Phestor Xenol was also somehow possible. That was equally strange and intriguing.

He noticed the Map's comet trail was directed to a place that wasn't that far from where he was now, perhaps three or four blocks from Citadel Tower – walking distance (only, he wouldn't be seen walking). He came to a quick conclusion. He would follow it. So, he ran to his walk-in wardrobe and, wasting no time at all, snagged a pair of the cheapest jeans he could find – preferably, torn ones – and the most inappropriate shirt he believed he could be seen wearing in public. It was no "**A vent a day keeps the hallucinations at bay**", but it was something along the same lines. Not expressing his aloofness in any way whatsoever. To complete his disguise, he wore an ancient baseball cap, which must have seen life almost a century ago. *Did the Leo Nets still play Ball?* It was now tatty and ripped in places and had drooping fabrics that came down to cover his temples and buffer his ears.

At exactly half-past-three, Oscar gave Kyma a *Ro-Bone* for occupation, then made for the door.☆

☆ *Ro-Bone* was a nutritionally modified toy-bone for dogs, supplying them with the nutrients and vitamins of an actual bone and capable of refilling itself by mineral replication. (A large dog would only need four or five to last them a whole year). It was awarded the National Gourmet Technology Prize in 2023. "*RrrrroBrrrrones Arrrre Scrrrrumy!*"

There were twelve various *TRAMLINES* in the City, which all briefly interlinked through Central, then tore apart according to their separate routes. The *TRAMLINES* reached as far as the Slumberlands – a vast hubbub of ghetto that festered outside the circumference of the City Wall, surrounding it the way ants attend a dirty plate and linger. Alternatively for some, there was only – and only ever would be – one *LASERWAY*, a premium high-speed train that traversed all four Nations of the West and was commended for its first-class passenger service (available at an additional expense). You'd never catch someone from the City's general suburbia on the *LASERWAY* and so the waifs inhabiting the City's exhausted Slumberlands were completely out of the discussion altogether, since only a single tragic *TRAMLINE* ventured beyond the City Wall. There was absolutely no advertising of premium transportation to these penurious 'Down Dwellers', Week and Weekend Traders alike. Anybody who wasn't featured among the City's most privileged and pursuing residents wouldn't waste their elementary lives fantasising about such exclusive luxuries anyway. As it stood, the lack of debate over social integration was crucial to the culture of peaceful tolerance among the City's people. However, this didn't stop the Decider's Administration consistently reminding the submissive subordinate population how much better they had it than anyone in the world – "*In the East, they are given castes from birth; at least here you are prized with the opportunity to be among men. Those East bureaucrats tell their folk to lay with the hens, while your kind Decider invites you to run with the wild cats*," the pledge of one EvokaRaft echoed through the deserted alleyway behind Citadel Tower, as Oscar snuck out the fire exit, glanced over his shoulder and then made for the tired platform hidden beneath the shadow of the *LASERWAY* overpass.

Oscar had been on the *LASERWAY* many times before – probably about ten times – and was too embarrassed to admit that he preferred it to any other mode of transport in the City. It was all he knew beyond Stevenson's backseat after all. His father had always expected him to stick to the *LASERWAY* or the reserved limousine whenever he went about town or decided to travel as far as visiting his Aunt Sibyl – who lived really close to the Wall and quite out of the way. Even though Oscar never liked to obey these requirements of getting around, modestly never wanting to be the privileged dynast with the keys to the kingdom and the kingdom's hottest attractions, his father's word was the first he ever heard and would be the last until the day it became Oscar's own. Until that day, Oscar would only be entitled to *wishful humbleness*.

Today, however, on this frivolous Sunday afternoon, Oscar planned to take the *TRAMLINE* to the City Central shopping district, almost entirely out of rebellion. Well, *almost* at his own accord, because it was, in truth, the Constellation Map directing him to take a route around City Central that the *LASERWAY* didn't go – through *Vagabond Avenue* and bypassing *Dew Street Promenade*, towards the Octane Mall. At least, he could fade into the public ambience more easily by taking this edgier detour down the grimy backstreet of the homeless, faithless and soberless that was *Vagabond Avenue*. And, on the positive side, with not telling his father any of this (as much as it would have enchanted Oscar to see the Decider's face drop off when he heard his son would be walking freely alongside the people), he wouldn't have the old man worrying about him getting mugged or assaulted by itching urchins or wretched opportunists in some *Vagabond* alleyway encounter. But what Oscar feared more was the inevitability that he would come across his first ID-Drone or an A.I. as soon as he arrived in the shopping district, if not sooner. Either of which would flirt with the challenge to recognise his face in the crowds and immediately report him back to his father's residence. He had to avoid surveillance on the streets as much as possible. Oscar knew he had to be vigilant and watchful at all times. Just like the subordinates, he had to be 'streetwise'. He'd registered for his own *Tram-Sit Pass* under a fake name and identity via his HoloPad, which instantaneously sorted him with a general one-day admission ticket that stereotypically applied to those subordinates with little more than a minimum wage.

He caught the first *Paragon Lane* bound *TRAMLINE* he saw, which had been sitting at the platform long before he arrived. Once on-board, he shifted straight to the back of the last car with a very idle demeanour and sat in a seat by the window. He'd never done this before. Playing this unique character required him to stray from his arbitrary opinions like a plush, but curious, pup from the porch of its palace-home. *Soon, if I retreat from my temperament for too long and misplace myself completely*, he thought, *they'll send someone after me, they'll search for me and rein me in and put me back in my place, back in my cage. Or maybe*, Oscar fancied, *if I lose myself to this new character, this compelling, new role, they may never find me again.* Then, the doors automatically slid shut and the *TRAMLINE* departed.

Oscar leaned his head on the graffiti-plagued window, the beak of his baseball cap flexing upwards like an erect cat-flap. Outside, the day was becoming dreary again. Son-day was starting to look a lot like a lazy Sat-Ur-Day. He'd spent the majority of it under his duvet, totally induced by the lure of his imagination. Tempted by anything that wasn't real, anything that wasn't typically believable. But, in the realm of the Woken, the name of the hour remained his only diversion from reality: Evanessa and the image of her mangled, abused body presented to him like a gift on his doorstep. It continued to disturb Oscar so vividly that he now naïvely insisted that he had seen everything there was to see in his world...although, his primitive fascination of her and her master, and their unpermitted state visit, tempted his desire to learn more about these intriguing East Folk. And what was more? To be left a device by the East Woman. Not a weapon or a bomb (as he would have generally suspected), but a mystical and curious tool in the Constellation Map...

Suddenly, the *TRAMLINE* came to a far-from-smooth stop. The wheels screeched like kittens in agony and the wind protruding from the air-conditioner above him was murdered by a stifling haze of stuffiness, when the doors flung open again and more people swarmed into the carriage. They brought with them a sting of unexpected heat and claustrophobic fluster. Weekend Traders headed home from their workplaces. It was not as crowded as it usually was during the working week, however, Oscar found the *TRAMLINE* on a Sunday to be heart-stopping irrespectively. He figured today would be very different to his previous brief experiences afoot in the City. Realising he still had the Map open, he rushed to roll it up again and hide it away on his lap. He didn't need it at the moment; the comet trail had paused from shrinking now that the *TRAMLINE* had stopped. Nevertheless, exposed in all the space there was at the back of the car, Oscar tautly retained his position, and strained his head away from the onslaught of civil suffocation. He played it casual, but his confidence was wilting.

Oscar noticed two A.I. hanging by the doors. Checking that nobody else intended to board the *TRAMLINE*, the A.I. pivoted around on the platform. Different to most Tin Men Oscar was familiar with, these had no faces, no expression. Just a blank, silver pan in its place. *These ones look older*, Oscar thought. *Archaic commissions from ten or so years ago, judging by the design. They're clunky and ugly and not sleek and clean like the ones I'm used to.* It was a flat, faceless design with a single, black band – the scanner – running across the centre of its head, dividing the field of silver like a polluted river. And, inside the band, an amber light teetered from end to end, so similar to a virtual game-ball seesawing on the screen of a primitive arcade machine.

A mechanical voice came to life on the loudspeakers in the *TRAMLINE* and around the platform. 'All passengers please stand-by for a routine admittance check!'

The A.I. marched into the carriage, turned in opposite directions, then tediously made their way through the length of the carriage. Their bodies were built of untainted aluminium and every motion was stilted and heavy. Plain, simple and confined, their history and their destiny both predetermined. With purpose and magnificence carved into their smallest blueprint and whittled down so thoroughly that every feature was their finest feature. They'd been erected out of terror, their very concept rumoured to have been adopted and adapted from the blueprints of some faceless, but insane, inventor in a far away Nation, only to be reimagined, remanufactured and redistributed by the latest Constitution in the West and then reintroduced for each generation on repeat. *But what was it that made them so intimidating?* Oscar wondered. *What was it about the chrome soldiers that made them so feared by the public?* He had never understood the hysteria surrounding them. *Maybe it was because the machinery was always changing, always updating, always improving? Or maybe it was that humanity was always afraid that A.I. were constantly growing in numbers and could very soon gather the potential to outbalance the human population?*

Oscar was suspended in his seat; his buttocks were blocks of ice. The metal man had his eyes fixed forwards with a masked, artificial face that portrayed no compassion, let alone consideration. Only conviction. All he did was scan the passengers unsparingly on his way, charging onward with militant discipline. The amber light in the scanner switched to blue and the new blue ray made an awful noise, capable of pinning ears to the wall and drilling right through them. Passengers swooped their heads to the sides, so that all focus averted elsewhere, anywhere besides the metal man and his aggressive beam.

There were no 'free riders'. Thankfully. There were no casualties either. And both A.I. had serenely reached the ends of their sections of the car. The A.I. departed and, like nothing had ever occurred, the *TRAMLINE* was on its way again.

Ten more minutes passed and, over that time, the *TRAMLINE* had stopped at six platforms. Oscar really hadn't been paying attention. He'd guzzled the time trying to recover from his erratic anxiety. And, whilst stationed at one of these platforms, a young girl around his age had sauntered onto his car and plonked herself in the seat in front of him. He didn't realise anything specifically significant about her boarding, until he turned away from the window and guided his attention ahead, trying to cop a glimpse at the name of the oncoming platform on the screen further down the car – or at least to catch a glimpse of the *TRAMLINE* map. But, something about her dragged him in—

The girl's hair was cranberry-red.

A great vine of cranberries, for it was so long that it covered her shoulders entirely and sank down between the seat and her shirt like a stage show curtain. The skin on her neck and the backs of her ears was peculiarly tanned. *Too tanned for a First Nation-born*, Oscar studied, *probably one of those bumpkins from Third or Fourth, trying to make a name for herself in First – seven in ten of them discover they don't belong in this town and usually scuttle back to where they came from.* He wanted to touch her hair, just to make sure that he was really seeing who he thought he was *imagining. Déjà vu* coursed through him, he'd seen this all before. But, surely he'd *imagined* her, only fabricated her, the girl in his dreams? The Dreamer-Girl from the Dreamerverse. What he'd imagined couldn't have resonated with what he now saw so bluntly in front of him. Was she the Babe With The Blade? Even her mannerisms were the same. The broad-chested way she was sitting made her seem taller than she actually was and it radiated a balance between shrewdness and arrogance – in this respect, she was pretty unique in his eyes. It had to be the Dreamer Girl. *Was it here we're I've seen her before?* he thought. Hardly—he rarely took the *TRAMLINE.*

Should I give her a polite nudge? he thought. *Am I sure about this?*

The Dreamerverse wasn't the first of their encounters. He recognised that face from somewhere else. That same girl was somewhere right here in the real world. Could it have been this one?

The *TRAMLINE* pulled up at the platform before his – *Crystal Square.* The doors flew open and another herd filed into the compact little car. The girl with cranberry hair didn't budge from her seat. She only stretched her neck tiresomely. Oscar was relieved to see this; he was working a sweat to speak to her. When—

There was another unnerving seizure, like something processing while the vehicle was forced to wait longer than it had at any of the previous platforms. Four more A.I. were pending at this stop. The voice announced another "admittance check" and the metal men entered, soldiering on with their duty. Two formed a rigid blockade at the carriage door, standing side-by-side and staring in at the quiet passengers who all avoided eye contact. Some passengers gazed at the floor; some conveniently found a very interesting advertisement on the platform wall outside and used this as an excuse to blindly feast their eyes on anything that wasn't a swinging scanner beam; others replayed the creative ploy of not being able to read the time on their watch and accordingly lassoed their cutting-eyes to the pirouetting second-hand; the majority didn't look up from their *HoloPhones* and *HoloPads* and pretended to be transfixed on a screen that had been hacked by the A.I.'s servers and annexed by a bold, bland message in red: **MODERATION IN PROGRESS**. nevertheless, everybody kept hauntingly still and appealingly uninterested. Like before, one made a beeline down to Oscar's end of the car and its comrade went in the opposite direction. As per usual, the A.I. charged through the isle with their beaming face-bands intensively stripping each and every individual on-board of their dignity. The beam was still blue, but far more grating and flickered rapidly as it worked at a more efficient rate on the, now larger, terrified audience.

Oscar wasn't as stunned by their intrusion this time - not even by the sinister, mechanical click that sounded with every checked passenger the A.I. probed in passing. But the addition of two more A.I., who stole the freedom of the gaping doorway, suggested an urgency that required an overhaul and no passengers could leave the carriage until their check was over. These two hooked their vacant sights directly on the poor man who sat facing the door and therefore had his eyes innocently on his watch the whole time, as he put on a display of going about his own business. It had been their second inspection since Oscar had boarded the *TRAMLINE* and he pondered whether *this many times* was actually that common. The fact was: this was what 'normal people' had to deal with for years and as frighteningly austere as it was, it was no catastrophe, just safety regulations. *And to be fair*, Oscar figured, *it was commendably astute*. The best he could do to blend in was stay calm, hold his breath and go with the flow. Doing so made him look less like a tourist.

But then the A.I. came to an abrupt stop just before reaching Oscar. The blue scanning beam turned amber. There was a terrific silence that caused every person on-board to peer over and stare. For some reason, the A.I. had stopped beside the girl in front of Oscar, its leg nearly brushing her shoulder. The sinister clicking sound of the scanner dissolved. The A.I. neatly rotated, without twisting a single bolt, to face the girl. Strictly swift, like a whip, it scanned her again. And a single, frustrating horn sounded in response. And it scanned once more to be sure. And the horn yelled again. By which time, even the girl knew that it was hopeless.

'Admission Status Undetected! *Repeat*: Admission Status Undetected!' the A.I. alarmed, shaking its head.

The girl was too startled to speak. Her words were also "Undetected".

'Subject, Alice Throe - aged nineteen years - you have committed a moderate offence against the New Democracy's Constitution of Lawful Requirements. Do you withhold any immediate evidence in your defence? Be warned: all immediate evidence will be disregarded in the event of Instant Prosecution, in which instance, nothing you say can be used in your defence, but may still be held against you in post-vaporisation.' The A.I. was lecturing her now. The word "vaporisation" nicked at Oscar's nerves. 'Your anti-social offence has been measured beside my data-core - legislative information updated from—*yesterday; Saturday, the Thirteenth of July 2058*; at half-past-noon; location of update: *Bundle Avenue, City Central, First Nation*—' it buffered, bleeped and then—'This is your third offence of similar category. Level of Instant Prosecution is still in progress...Determining...Determining...Determining...I apologise for the wait, please be patient...Received: you will be condemned in custody until you are booked for judgement before the High City Court - you are one-thousand-two-hundred-and-forty-eighth in line; approximately, seventy-five hours' waiting time. Stand!'

The cranberry-haired girl didn't budge at first, lost in translation by the Tin Man's unenthused jargon.

'On your feet!' the A.I. recurred, brassier this time and sinking his head in towards her, so that his jowl sided with her forehead.

It got the response it wanted.

The girl immediately obeyed without protest. Up she went, though her broad and rather complacent manner had shrunken to a meek hunch beneath the daunting shadow of the A.I. officer. At first, the A.I. did nothing, and then, it snapped a firm hand onto her shoulder. He paused again, as if still processing the situation. '*Correction*: my data-core has refactored this offence. It is no longer a Class D offence. It is a Class C offence. You will not stand before the High City Court, but the A.I. will determine your punishment. Punishment will entail immediately. Your determiner is *me*.' Even though the A.I. had no expression, the excitement in its last word was menacing.

It clawed into her shoulder.

The girl gasped, choking up the horror trapped in her lungs. Swinging round into a bending-position so the A.I. – her "*determiner*" – was able to arrest her, she came down to face Oscar. Her chin met the top of the seat and her teeth chattered twice, painfully. And on went the laser-bound cuffs. Oscar saw the terrified glint in her eyes, overcome by the animosity behind them. There was also that foreign tan about her complexion, which Oscar had already observed of her ears. It was dirtier than even the most remote bumpkins of the Fourth Nation and had no resemblance of the West at all, and that could only mean one thing…it wasn't the Dreamer Girl…So, there was nothing else about her that was worth investing in. The fascination he'd spared was gone, and Oscar was eager to see the back of both her and the horrendous Tin Men.

It wasn't the girl with red hair who he recognised. Not the girl with red hair who he was curious to meet again one day, in some place or other. Not the girl with red hair who had saved his life on more than one occasion. This girl was Alice Throe, whoever *that* was, and she was aflame with nothing but humiliation.

The A.I. led Alice Throe out of the *TRAMLINE* car with both hands bound behind her back. And Oscar never saw her again.

The *Paragon Lane* shopping district was blooming with commerce; at its roots were the thousands of its highbrow customers (typically Week Traders enjoying their weekend recess), spilling in and out of the superlative franchises stationed about a manifold range of complexes, and to each individual a gold mine was expended. It was no mystery that spending among the wealthiest subordinates was a recreation to be prided by default. Folk in the City – notoriously those basking in the Central – abounded in their *pecunts* to splash out on almost anything they desired and, in most cases (if not all cases), anything they *didn't* desire.

Throughout the weekend, the prominent *Paragon Lane* was overloaded with people who never had a great deal to do otherwise. Unlike the regions of residue – those unseen pockets of the City Suburbs that were situated so far out from the Central they touched the inside of the City Wall and the impoverished Slumberlands on the other side of it – the City Central of the First Nation still beheld things worth wanting. Too many things worth wanting and very few worth needing. Window display after window display, you would find mannequins draped in *VENIS* designer wear, and jewellery dangling from the shelves in *JOVIAN* stores, and *HoloTech* upgrades being advertised on the startling screens of *MERCURY* stores. These things would surely keep the subordinates occupied for a short time, but the process would recycle upon a weekly, even daily, routine to feed a revitalised addiction for the High Street. Sometimes, you'd spy a pasty elderly woman in a furry white coat going to return a remarkable dress that had missed an inch or two, or you'd find a fleet of toned, flash men, suited in beige, silver in the hair, digitally augmented in the eyes with grossly transfigured faces, bound for their scheduled weekend societies, pacing from crossing to crossing, street to street, building to building, looking neither here nor there, possessing no motive for interaction with anyone at all. Students broke away from the Academy campus in their crisp uniforms; the boys always tilted their fancy fedoras, but never looked up, and the girls with their tight dresses and fixed, compacted hair-bobs, shifted in unobtrusive reverence, safely promenading in docile, single-sex pairs. Scuttling inoffensively across City Central, the youth would voyeur the pavement and nothing else—perhaps, copping a sneaky peek of the road, but only if they were confronted with a crossing. If the students did once glance up, they would find, way above their heads, the holy *LASERWAY* zipping along *Lincoln Bridge* – the bridge had been fixed aloft from the sidewalks and overshadowed some of the less outstanding niche shops and supermarkets. It led an undeviating journey from *City Central North* to *City Central South*, a significant incision of the Promised Land that tore through the City's heart (it looked like a clock face at the sixth hour). Meanwhile, deep below, multitudinous *TRAMLINE* systems lumbered upon their designated roads, tunnels and underpasses.

The Octane Mall was the City's defining landmark and, no doubt, the grandest bastion of capitalism Mankind's World had to offer. There were over forty storeys in the main building, some floors expanding on for acres and acres of breadth and the variation in its mercantile arsenal would trap any novice consumer in awe. However, some of the higher floors consisted of only privileged enterprises – uncluttered clothing-stores, or jaded jewellery parlours, or splendid salons, or surreptitious restaurants that rejected the Nation's rationing laws. In other words, the highest floors of the Octane Mall were a commonplace for the noblest subordinates, aloof ladies and gentleman with good credence for the Decidership.

As for the typical middle class subordinate, the lower floors were where tangibility resided. Here, there were vast arcades, where careless, distracted parents were most likely to lose children below the age of ten. These deeper layers of the Mall tucked away shoddy, secret cinemas, where "blockbuster films" were becoming swamped with monotony by the day and growing gracelessly political by the month (two months ago, Oscar had been keen to see a rumoured independent biopic, "*The Last Trinity of Trivium*" – a film about the last socialist West government in the early twenty-first century, before the multiparty system of the Old Democracy was banned – but he instead traded his *pecunts* over to a Shark Merchant for some last minute game tickets at the Harkson Centre; he later searched everywhere on his *HoloPad* for a leaked review of the film, but it was nowhere to be found).☆ The lower floors also had an abundance of fast food that met any gustatory preference, since artificial flavouring had been mastered in such a way that even salt could go undetected by a human palate. There were five *KINDER-PART-ENS* (A.I. robotics stores) sited on the ground floors, where the First Nation's top boffins taught the young engineers of the next generation how to build and programme their own Androkind technology. The Octane's underbelly also sheltered *NEW STATUS* (cosmetic transformation salons), where ordinary people could go in as themselves and walk out as entirely different people.☆

Oscar arrived in the Octane Mall an hour before closing time. It gave him the opportunity to gallivant at his own pleasure and made it brief enough not to be seen or recognised. The only downside was that there were more A.I. on patrol at this time, because subordinate youths tended to get more pickpockety as the sun set over the few human staff there were. On the odd occasion, a few lucky ones were crafty enough to slip past the Mall A.I., but outside, a hovering drone would be scanning store barcodes all around its mile-wide radius and it would inevitably chase shoplifters down a hundred streets at a hundred-miles-per-hour if the thief wasn't caught red-handed.

Fortunately, Oscar wasn't in search of anything in particular, only the path of the comet trail on the Constellation Map, which had shortened to a quarter of the length since he'd arrived in the Octane Mall and continued to shrink the further he went. His journey through the ground floor meant swerving clear into and out of the main arcade, which swarmed with Common Children. The likes of whom blew all

---

☆ Independent Films were illegal in the West. Whenever one made its way across the pond – "*from the tumultuous Bootleg Studios of the Fourth Nation*", the Stateship put it – the filmmaker and anyone who was involved with even having viewed as little as a scene from the film would be "*prosecuted justly for the protection of the Nationhood and its Constitution*".

☆ Technology had advanced so much by 2026 that people were finally able to transform themselves into completely different bodies, manipulating their original appearance to such a degree that it was practically dehumanising. This Physical-Appearance-Altering-Technology (PAAT) was first brought to light and adapted by Dr. Pimsflaw, a professor at the Second Nation Academy who claimed to suffer with severe vanity issues.

their leftover pocket money on cheap, sticky sweets that you'd find beneath banisters or under tables in the food court. Having missed breakfast and lunch, Oscar felt like he needed the aid of the food court and went to grab himself a veal burger and a pint of *Wild Elderflower Joose* for *200pc* (the price-equivalent of a full roast dinner from a downtown supermarket). He downed the drink and devoured the burger like a hungry caveman who'd landed there out of a time-portal. Nevertheless, looks didn't matter. Not in this persona, it didn't. Not for this character he was so awkward playing. He was no longer Oscar Philson, son of an All Powerful World Decider. He was Somebody Else, the son of an indigent subordinate, living off the fragments of his family's illicit dealings – "*Da Faml'y Bidness*", memories of the old gangster films Stevenson used to quote tickled his tongue and he laughed to himself while he chowed on his veal.

Once his stomach was happy again, Oscar toddled up a few floors, until he could whittle down storeys whereupon the Map would still respond to his movements. The comet trail rarely budged now, as there was very little distance left to go. He slipped into to the *VENIS STORE* to recuperate his bearings and to speculate over the Map's directions. This was the one store that wouldn't be packed with last minute shoppers or adrenalized children. Unless royalty decided to come to the Octane Mall on a Sunday afternoon, *VENIS* would generally be this desolate. It sold novelty items and antiques. The sort of things only sophisticated subordinates could possibly afford or possibly know how to use, such as, a mercury toothbrush – that was hard to use, surely – or an Aquarium Hot-Tub – also quite difficult to operate – or a diamond-reflective telescope – again, tricky to handle without the option of going blind. To be fair, these things were never stolen under the circumstances of sturdy Mall security (and, of course, the annihilating law that would always prevail). The items on display were rarely looked at, hardly ever observed. They always attracted awareness, but never attention. Customers in the Octane Mall didn't only shop excessively. They also shopped without observation. Never in confidence, only with an aim. You wanted something, you went and got it respectfully. Loitering and indecisiveness had to be kept to the bare minimum to survive its unrelenting security operation. To make window shopping easier and theft and robbery less tempting, Octane Cards had been introduced, whereby the higher floors were made exclusive to the wealthy subordinates, and subordinates on lowlier salaries could not reach above a certain floor-level (at about the twenty-first floor, the elevators would cease from ascension for those without a card and A.I. would be there to meet invalid subordinates at the tops of the escalators and assert warnings of law offence). If anybody was caught shoplifting or looting, which didn't matter whether you were a ten-year-old boy with grubby hands or a little old lady with peachy mitts, you'd be instantly charged and prosecuted by an A.I. Tin Men patrolled the Octane Mall on a daily basis. Even when it was closed. They were always watching for missteps, both accidental and intentional, and had an unrestrained eye for suspicious body language, able to spot any offences minutes before they actually occurred. No one tested this claim. Shopping was a matter of life and death.

Oscar didn't spend too long in the *VENIS STORE*. After a while, those passing-by would become curious of who he was and the workers in the shop would soon otherwise suspect him of stealing or not belonging. For all he knew, an A.I. may have already been alerted and on its way right now. He scurried out and quickly made his way up the escalator to the next storey, where he'd find mostly clothes shops. Up here, there were the more conventional stores like *LEE FOSTERS*, which specialised in men's clothes; *PUREE DELUXE*, a pretty, casual-themed women's store; as well as *ON AND OFF'S*, which was probably the best kind of shoe shop with every make, shape, size and brand.

Whilst picking out a new pair of *Mister Martials* for himself in *ON AND OFF'S*, Oscar caught the peak of a charmingly clean parting of rosy hair, running down the crown of a head like a herd of free horses down a hill. His heart skidded against the cage of his chest and he dropped the shoes in his hands. The redhead had her back turned, facing one of the shelves of high heels. He hesitated again, contemplating whether to dash for the door or to go and greet her. *Surely, this one has to be her*, he thought. Her hair was feasibly the same as the other girl's had been in the Dreamerverse, maybe only a darker shade in this light. And better presented, well washed. Long and lush.

He decided what to do and made a move. Now beside her, he tried to avoid looking at her face as much as he daringly wished to. It had to be her this time. He felt the same bittersweet way he did when standing beside her in the other world – fondly uncomfortable. Humming without a rhythm, he pretended to be mindful of the shoes on this shelf. The redhead took two discreet steps to the left, making them both feel like ghosts to one another.

Oscar shifted his eyes, trying to slide into his peripheral-vision. He met her hands stroking a pair of heels. Those hands were a slightly lighter tan to the girl on the *TRAMLINE*. This was promising. But what she was doing…it was a strange thing to see, as she wasn't showcasing much activity other than that—*stroking them? Perhaps, she's imagining how they'd look on her feet when she wore them to the 'so-and-so' occasion at the 'so-and-so' place?* he thought. *But the Dreamer Girl, the fiery, practical Babe With The Blade, hadn't particularly appealed to me as a "party person", let alone a young lady who could pull off high heels anywhere at all.* It was like she was thinking or conjuring a plan.

Oscar felt it safe to turn his head slightly, grabbing the pair he'd been fake-fondling off the shelf and examining them to make it seem like he wasn't just standing there. He now saw the sheet of hair that shielded the right side of her face, not yet finding her identity. Her nails were red and Oscar could have sworn that the *Babe With The Blade* didn't have painted nails either. Her nails had been trimmed short and mud-caked from extensive rural labour. His doubts were already kicking in. *But what was the purpose of stroking a pair of shoes like a kitten your parents had forbidden you to adopt?*

Then, it all became clear. His thoughts exploded all at once.

The girl snatched the heels without a second's pause. Off she went, speeding off through the isles like a sincerely uncatchable bandit with a masterful spring in her step. She barged into customers, knocking a few to the floor, and busted over some of the shelves, spilling shoes all over the place. She made for the doors. Or, at least, she hoped. Four A.I. had appeared at the automatic-doors, standing in a line and ready to catch her before she escaped. Sweating under pressure and reaching the stage of tears, the redhead fell, tripping on a pair of stilettos. Her knees buckled painfully against the solid marble floor and she cried.

The four A.I. held still for moments. Then, one stormed up to her with bold, null eyes and a shapeless, metallic, carved frown. It halted in front of her. Its eyes were glowing blue. 'Class A Offence! Eleventh charge of forging Mall Admittance, shoplifting, arson, armed robbery, burglary and vandalism. Immediate consequence required!' it said. '*Coralline Webber – twenty years of age*! You pose a threat to the Constitution! Punishment determined! Punishment: **CAPITAL**. Surrender your life!'

Coralline screamed one final time before she was incinerated.

Oscar came to the conclusion that he didn't quite enjoy the philosophy of shopping. It may have been his unique pass of freedom on a Son-day, but, as he witnessed time and time again, for many other subordinates (temporarily including himself), there was no shortage of horrors to be exposed to as a shopper. Just like everyone else, Oscar was terrified of the A.I. And just like everyone else on ground level, he recognised that the City's Constitution could be cruel and, if you didn't keep up and adhere to the rules, you'd be putting yourself at risk.

Only fifteen minutes remained until closing time and he hadn't yet accomplished the one objective he'd set out to do – endeavour the Constellation Map's lead and follow the comet trail to its mysterious destination. Oscar had managed a little less than an hour in the Octane Mall and, as the lights began to go out and the Mall became darker, he found that he had covered almost every shop on this current floor and he was nearly ready to call it a day. But one store still lingered. He wanted to make a quick stop at *POST*. It was here where everybody came to hear about the latest news, send messages to their distant loved-ones and read about the ceaseless Conflicts happening in the East. The shelves were stocked high with cards – some were industry-made, others were handmade. Plenty of postcards were on stands and messaging-booths were available for those who needed to send an urgent *HoloGraph*.☆ Dated political magazines, such as *Old Matheson* and *Kool Kids*, were selling poorly and hurtling towards extinction. It was inside these issues that printed lists of the Fallen were published in respect of the Conflicts.

Oscar took one of the last issues of *Kool Kids* from the tragically bare magazine-shelf and glanced at the cover. On it was the iconic Mr Kitty Kool, a sly cat wearing a fedora and smoking on a comical bulging cigar. He was always somewhere on the cover of every issue that sold. "*Today's Issue!!!*" was actually published on *4th July 2039* (19 years ago) and featured interviews with scientists Drake Islington, Morpheus Eve

---

☆ *HoloGraphs* took over from online messaging services in 2041 and served as a new breed of social media platform. It drew the kids away from mourning the late Internet and legally pierced the thickening barrier between the decision-makers and subordinates, limiting virtual interaction across the Axernet to just one forum setup by *HoloTech*. The *HoloGraph*'s subject had to be monitored before it was delivered via the Axernet's Official Network. Their delivery and access was limited to *HoloTech* devices (*HoloGrams*, *HoloPads*, *HoloPhones*, *HoloVisions*, etc.). Prior to the West's 2040 bill to completely censor the transference of online information, the East had already initiated this monitoring law for *HoloTech* in 2025 by setting up its own widely used intranet. By 2040, the West and the East were both a hundred per cent 'virtually segregated'. However, *HoloGraphs* only existed in the first six Nations, since Seventh and Eighth preferred to keep their privacy from the West at all costs.

and Adam Greenstone (none of whom Oscar had heard of) on their collaborative essay "*Empathy: One Small Step For Mankind, One Big Leap For Androkind*". Also on the cover of this particular issue was a sketched illustration of a young boy hugging a brown bear triple his size. The bear was a cuddly, friendly sort with little cute eyes and fuzzy, thick fur. But, over all that, he was shielded by a metal chest-plate on his belly and a knight's helmet on his head. The headline above the illustration read: **We Can't BEAR The WEIGHT!** Oscar laid the magazine back down on its shelf, feeling not the least tempted to read it – as most of these magazines contained horrible, gory images. Nor did he have the time. The lights were starting to switch off in the shop and everyone had left already.

He was on his own in here and there was nothing peculiar in *POST*, which was to be expected. It was time to head back home to check how Kyma was getting on and to see if his father needed his help with anything. Time to return to normal – at least, *his* normal. When he was moving towards the exit, a sound from behind the counter made him jump. He turned to see what it was. The noise had sounded like a cluster of keys hitting the ground. He looked in shock towards the counter. There, a girl had bounced up from behind it. Her bulky, leather retro jacket was on over her work-uniform – a white shirt with a nametag and a black plaited-skirt that stopped short above the knees. She wore a knitted beanie-hat that enhanced the charm of her long, velvety…

Red hair!

After one look, Oscar could see clearly that she was the girl of his imagination. However, he had to think twice when he saw a very thin, tightly wound braid that trailed down the middle of her hair and curled round to rest on her shoulder. This single, distinct difference, which galloped beside her non-pyjama-wearing-attire, he hadn't seen before. But it was the face that confirmed it was the girl from his dream.

Not one bit had he anticipated finding her here, but he'd always wondered where he'd known that face from, where he'd seen it before. And there was no place where he would have least expected to bump into her than behind the counter at *POST*. Oscar looked at the Map again, just to be sure. Yes, the comet trail had disappeared, completely dissolved, and the ***X***-mark was on top of him! Mission complete.

As he'd observed in the Dreamerverse, she was remarkably taller than the scarce number of girls he'd ever known. Her height, however, enlisted unnaturally agile movements, for he hadn't heard her presence until just now. Up at the counter, she looked as though she was on her way out after a long – and seemingly uneventful – shift. Locking the voice-operated cash machine, she didn't glance up. Her eyelids were semi-shut and she was floating from side-to-side, in desperate need of a bed.

Oscar made no interaction. His instinct applied the urge, despite all his reluctance, to duck below the shelves of dusty cards and memorial prints separating the two of them. To hide, of course. *Could it be her the Map wanted me to meet?* he theorised. *That would be too ironic. Unless Evanessa was on to something with Constellation Planet. There's certainly something the Phestoress knows that I am not aware of.*

The Babe With The Blade was also prettier in real life. A girl of her complexion had never appealed to him before, which he found strange, yet not discouraging. *Is it because she is the only thing I have to prove my Dreamerverse fantasies? Even here in the real world, she makes me feel self-conscious and intimidated and, most astoundingly, she makes me feel small and insignificant.* A fluster of heat was quickly building in his stomach while he squandered his chances; the offspring of this funny sensation were none other than nausea and dizziness.

*What am I supposed to say to the girl of my dreams? No...*that thought slipped out wrong. *She is quite literally the girl* ***from*** *my dreams. Get it right, Philson!* Perhaps, if she looked up, she wouldn't recognise him in the slightest? She wasn't the one to blame. Dressed in his urban disguise, he had trouble remembering himself. It was like seeing a tiny photo for only a snippet of a second and then having to remember every detail of it for over a century and, in his case, having to piece it back together like a puzzle, using the only fragments of memory he had remaining from another world he wasn't even supposed to remember. It was also like meeting a celebrity actor unexpectedly, only having forgotten their name or in which film he'd seen them.

The girl finished locking up the keep-safe and now had a chip full of revenue to deal with. Turning round to the machine sitting on the desktop behind her, she began to distribute the money into the machine. Uploading it first, and then saving her earnings to the salary account. She did it with a little struggle, when the machine decided to play stubborn and didn't do things unless it was serviced with her hand wedged up its backside. When these problems occurred, she simply jiggled her fingers about the interior controls and easily fixed them.

With her salary successfully allocated onto her storage-chip, the machine automatically closed itself down and she placed her storage-chip back into her purse.

Oscar was beginning to make a slow move for the counter. By the looks, the girl had no idea that anyone else was left in shop. The rest of the Mall was "off-limits", everywhere was closed or about to close and the lights of *POST* may have been the only ones that were still on (and proudly so, because it happened to be the oldest shop in the entire Octane Mall, having had no need to rely on brand endorsements or oil rig sponsorships to boost sales).

The girl did her coat up and flung her hair over her shoulder, so it fluttered like interlinked butterflies. The thin braid flew and curved with it; this tiny element hypnotised Oscar the most.

He curled his neck round the corner of the shelf to keep low and out of sight, while his heart was bounding as if he were about to give birth to a lively hare. For, even in a moment of such epiphany, the Decider Boy's cold feet got the better of him as ever. *Not here*, he considered. *It's too awkward. Too public and a bad time.* So, he thought he'd fade out via the door without her noticing. *Slowly...slowly...*

Pa-TSH-TSH!

A shelf that he'd accidentally misplaced had made a reliable hurdle in front of the door and a dozen magazines – unsurprisingly, the "Pleasure Editions" – slipped off the top and slapped down onto the floor before he could muster a gasp. Oscar scooted back behind another shelf. *Why hadn't I just left when I could have?* he thought. *When she was faffing about with that machine! Why did I let her get under my skin like that?*

The girl was inquisitive with only her expression to begin with. Then, she remembered she'd been given a mouth for a reason. 'Who is that?'

Oscar didn't reply. He was shaking instead. There was no obvious clue what she would do if she found him poking his nose around in her business. It was possible that she could even trap him in here if he wasn't careful and it was probable that she would alert and summon the Mall A.I. to come fetch him.

'We're supposed to be closed. So, there's no reason why you should be here,' she persisted. Sweat had been summoned to Oscar's forehead. 'Unless you're stealing? But then, the A.I. would be here by now if that had been your intention. So, that can't be the case, can it? Why are you here? I *know* you're here. There's no point pretending with me now.' Her voice was defensive and feisty. Oh so familiar, it was certainly her.

She'd very self-assured on her own. Maybe she's armed? Oscar didn't dare look.

'I'll call the A.I.!' she warned. *Finally*, Oscar humoured, *there it was*. 'And I'll tell them you've been stalking me. They treat stalking like any other crime in the known-world, you know!'

He came out with a wisecrack to throw her off. 'Well, we haven't met in the known-world, have we?'

It worked. She was busy making connections now and they were both as curious as each other.

'Who the hell are you?' she said. Her hand slowly shifted towards the security call alarm behind the counter. Never before had she come so close to using it. Never before had she felt alienated or in danger here (it was *POST* for crying out loud!).

'You might not remember me. But we've met before. In another reality, in another world, our paths have definitely crossed. I knew that I remembered you from somewhere! And I don't want you to forget this—'

'Stop messing me around! Just show your face!'

'You promise not to call the A.I.?' Oscar pleaded.

'Depends. Who are you? Just answer me that.'

'I'm telling you that you might not remember me straight away. But, if you do, even if it's just a little, please don't alert the A.I.—please just—just give me a smile, why don't you!'

Her hand was on the button. 'Why? Are you gonna shoot me?'

'No! Just smile! That's all I want you to do if you recognise me.'

There was quiet, while tensions settled. Oscar fixed his final manoeuvre before he made a swing for the door. He was panting hard and sweating even harder.

'Go on, then.' There was a thin acceptance in her voice as she said this, but there was just as much caution all the same if not, far more. 'Who are you?'

Oscar bounced up, instantly robbing all of her attention. Both of them wore the same puzzlement for what must have been twenty seconds. Their petty altercation, now historic, was at bay with this obliterating, new frontier. Processing each other's faces. Something fizzed to life inside Oscar. The sensation wasn't so mutual for her, not immediately. For Oscar, a weight had been lifted and the anxiety he'd been cradling for some time calmed itself in the girl's presence. The girl from his dreams put him at ease. She was as profound and as attractive as he'd imagined her in person. Finally, he had locked onto something that proved his aloof fantasies true and promoted the existence of his "Dreamerverse". Only, this wasn't just the Map, it was a person – another witness, another Night Dreamer – who made his case for

Constellation Planet seem more believable. And that comforted him, lounging into the cushion of her gaze. Here, she was no longer a belittling wonder, nor a simmering fragment of potential, but a perpetual body to be ventured, cell for cell, blister for blister.

She was REAL.

He figured the thing that had lightened his fears was actually her confidence and a smile that reminded him of how safe he always felt in her company – even if he had only *dreamt* it. He smiled right back at her like it was something the pair of them intimately shared. Something familiar. Nevertheless, when Oscar heard the announcement beckoning for closing time on the loudspeakers, followed by a final infomercial sounding the voiceover of a sinisterly optimistic "*GET YOURS TODAY!*" Slogan Lady, he made his escape without trialling another utterance. Just as the shutters came down on *POST* and the girl with the red hair became recent history. He blinked a million times, making sheer silhouettes of the titanium doom-machines, those Tin Men that guarded the halls on every level of the complex. He was careful not to gawk anyhow, or blunder anywhere, remaining sharp just enough to retrace his way back to the open world and he kept his intentions clean all the way. Good intentions would grant his access to freedom. The A.I. wouldn't be chasing him personally, but hunting his bad thoughts, calculating each and every one, as he ran…

…and ran…and ran…

The Falls of Fortune...

Keep it up. You're doing fine so far. Here is okay.

Dark again. Great! Though dank, the air is aptly cool and stagnant too, naturally still. No longer in the firing line of the whispering breeze conjured by the spirits lurking up in the cave. The drop from the cave isn't what I feared – raucous, tumbling death. I was knocked out for sure when I struck the bottom—solid ground—*here*—where is *here*? Here is peace and quiet with a bittersweet chill hanging over the uncharacteristic open space around me, but not piloted by an ominous, breathing wind like before. The scent of mildew is wafting nearby. So far, *here* (wherever *here* is) beats being up there, in that cave, with those Nightmares. At least I'm away from hungry spirits. And my body hasn't been possessed by one of those dreadful half-beings. That's a positive way to look at it. I escaped intact.

Yes. And you should have snapped every bone from cap to toe. The woman's voice is back inside my head, though not as cacophonous as she was when I was being pursued. *It was a good thing that purple seed you ate by the campfire still left some juice in you and you didn't get zapped by to Awakening Coast. What were you thinking? You're such a lucky so-and-so!* This is the most I've heard from it so far. It's much more conversational now and less preachy and prophetic than it had been earlier. More motivator than guru. What had it told me before? The moment I'd hit the ground, seconds before passing out, the voice had said: *Remember to chase your instinct before you compel the haste of your will...To will for guidance through the Falls of Fortune is a desire for abundance from the Stellar Gods and will be criticised as impatience and a sign of greed...Nevertheless, be quick, for the wall to reality has almost fallen...*

I guess the voice has come in some use so far. As much as I didn't expect it or necessarily ask for it to be there, it comes with a hydrant and morphine whenever I need to put out the fire and ease the burns.

That's what I'm here for. Make the most of me.

'Do I know you?' I ask aloud.

The voice doesn't reply. Perhaps it only speaks to me when I'm in desperate need of aid, whether that be after falling out of the sky or simply needing someone to talk to in the dark.

So, why can't I move? I ask my conscience companion. Why can't I feel what I usually do beneath my waist? Am I paralysed? I try to wiggle my legs around. That's supposed to simmer some feeling in my deadened limbs, isn't it? Wriggling it? I can merely lift my head off the cold ground, the side of my face scratching a small brush of exotic grass as I do so. I'm not paralysed above the shoulders—cross that out. Surely, the first thing that would have struck the ground is my head, and that doesn't seem to be in devastating condition. So—

Oh, boy!

There's something *on* my legs. Something fatty and slimy. Something wet, and warm, and waxy. It's numbingly heavy. What *is* that? I attempt to budge my legs again. I want to pull them free.

Keep still. Don't move too suddenly. You're doing fine. Just fine.

Once again, I'm obeying instructions and not thinking for myself. Why? It's so frustrating to be blind and waiting for instructions! What the hell is it? Is it...is it poisonous, or carnivorous, or what? It isn't moving much. Could be asleep? Or trying to *impregnate* me?

It's not poisonous. Not carnivorous. And, no, it's not mistaken you for a mate.

Not dangerous at all then?

Yes, dangerous. Very dangerous. If you move too suddenly or too obscurely, it could twist its tentacles around your stomach and your neck and burst you like a balloon.

Yikes, this new buddy sounds like a real cuddly-wuddly bear.

Hear my advice. Listen, you need to slide it off yourself, rather than scoot out from under it. Sit yourself upright first and you'll see it begin to slip off.

I follow her guidelines and, with all the strength in my elbows, push my torso up into a slanted recline. I can see it now. Dark in colour, a brownish-greyish type of mix. It has thick, sludgy tentacles, which are resting on my chest, stomach and groin. More than a dozen eyes and not all of them are on its face.

Now, push it off of you with both hands and your arms firmly outstretched away from you, but avoid the eyes.

Touch it? No! Not with my hands. Not with my soft, delicate hands. It isn't my fault that I've been burdened with obsessive sanitary issues.

I brace myself to do this. Both hands out, I lurch them slowly forwards, squeezing into the bathetic, salacious flesh of the sea-creature. Suckers are popping on my arms, oozing cold puss. It's revolting and I'm almost keeling over. But, once it's off—*aha*, it's off! And I jump onto my feet straight afterwards, bounding about and sensing the space around me. I'm soaking all over, but I've been liberated from that deadweight and its gloopy suckers, which is all I care about for the time being. However, the aches and pains searing through my legs and spine amplify once the numbness wears off. I freeze at the morbid realisation and collapse against a cave wall to relieve the nausea and a ripping headache. I fish in my pocket for my sack of seeds and pop a red one into my mouth—the soreness in my body and the concussion in my head dissolve immediately.

A wall? A cave wall? I wonder, once reclaiming my sense. I'm still in a cave? How far have I come after that fall? I toddle around, suddenly unable to grasp at the thought of being lost and parted from the others. Have I dropped anything?

Sack of seeds, *check!*

Sword, *check!*

Map…Where's the Map?

I spin wildly in the blackness. The ground is the same shade as the ceiling, so there isn't enough contrast for me to characterise nothingness from nothingness. Then, I find it, lying on the ground, beside the useless tentacle-heap of the creature I'd slept under. I quickly snatch it up and unravel it. The stars culminate on the page. The words glimmer. Light! All of a sudden, the world is no longer life inside a coffin!

I search the Map for an indication of where the others are. But there's only one prominent ***X***-mark. Where am I? Somewhere in the Kappa Mountains, still. Trapped in some unnamed cave. Who the hell *names caves*? I'd actually like to know. This is a time when an expert in caves would come in handy. Any news updates, voice? I ask my conscience. How do I get out of here? Where are the others? Did they manage to find a passage out alive? Escape the hive of Nightmares?

The voice neglects my pleading.

'That's brilliant!' I exclaim sardonically. 'Damn it—that's fantastic! Let me know when you learn anything new!'

Although, there is a sound. A 'sound' I should have noticed before. Noticed and noted. Somewhere, water is moving fast, rushing. It's much harsher than what you'd hear if you left the bathroom tap running. Almost like I'm close, too close, to a really massive—

There is a set of carvings on the wall in front of me. Words that flare when I approach them and glow in bronze: **QUEEN CASSANDRA HAS BEEN EXPECTING YOU.**

These words are severed by the cave wall, which has now started to split apart. It's opening. And I have to block my eyes from the gleaming sunlight that arrives. The rushing water is getting louder. And louder. And louder. Also, birds can be heard again with the sounds and smells of wildlife coming back to me.

Come and give me a hug!

When the cave wall fully breaks apart, like a gateway, the outside is something quite mesmerising. A grey canyon bunkered in a vast crevasse embedded between mountains. Two waterfalls are facing one another across the canyon, spilling into a big, clear spring below. At last, I humour, someplace I'm familiar with - a lake, not an ocean. But not typically so, for I establish one unusual detail. One waterfall pours clean and crystallised blue water, foaming when it crashes into the lake's surface. The other is filled with incredible riches. Gold and silvers, jewels and coins are sparkling in the sunlight and landing gracefully in the lake with a satisfying crash. Around the brim of the lake is a scattering of palm trees and miscellaneous greenery. It's a majestic scene just to watch unfold and I could stand here and gaze at it forever.

And it's exactly why the ancient stone cave entrance staring at me from the far side of the lake stands out so much, framed in the centre of it all. It's a narrow opening. Around the edges are sculpted faces of apes. Some are angry-looking, others are…also angry-looking; in fact, this may be a montage of disgruntled apes. Daunting is the entrance, yet tantalising. On either side of the doorway, stone statues of gorillas welcome trespassers with long spears and gravely serious faces.

They have your friends. You must go after them before it's too late.

Reaching the bottom of the rope ladder that descends to ground, I land in the scintillating haven with no theories of how I am going to get to the other side of the spring. Palms and foliage block a way around on both sides of the lake and I can't swim through it. It takes some looking and, eventually, my focus falls upon a fissure in the border of bushes to find a lone, wooden oar boat, sitting ashore between two palm trees. I hop inside and steer my way across the water.

It's a calm float along the middle of the lake; here lies some distance between the cascading of the waterfalls. As subtle as the boat is, I'm still anticipating the worst. My heart's racing. There's a responsible pace in my steering of the oars, a steady stroke towards the entrance to the gorilla den. I'm precariously watching the cave entrance, waiting for something to jump out of the tight opening, lunging over the lake to deliver some chaos, and remind me of the risks that run with the emerald I seek.

A lonely world it is down in this place and I don't cease to wonder where all the rest of the Dreamers are. Do any other Dreamers even know this place exists? Judging by the ordeal one needs to impose on themself to make it over these mountains and past all those greedy spirits, it's easy to presume very few make it this far. There's no question now that those cave inscriptions were an epistolary of bygone questing Night Dreamers and no one else. Don't Dreamers inhabit this region of the planet? If not, there has to be a reason for that. Is there something that forbids Dreamers from these Falls on Leo Island? Maybe that was why the unseen Bridge of Lynx was such a horror ride and why the Nightmares came out to play when our curiosities got the better of us. There are securities all over this planet.

You should think less, the voice says. *You are asking too many questions. That is a silly thing to do here. You're making me nervous.*

Asking questions to nobody is a "*silly thing to do*" now. Apparently.

I've hit the far bank and grass is beneath me again. I jump out of the boat and walk towards the decorated entrance, gearing my sword in preparation. The gorilla statues hold an intimidating stance, looking expressionlessly at one another and paying me no attention. The vanity chiselled into them is ripe. I feel like a worthless inferior and a prime culprit all at once.

No going back anymore. In is the only way out. I hope.

So, I step inside, through the entrance, passing under the watchful faces that cover the edges. The gorilla guards are behind me and the immature side of my imagination proposes that those statues may not actually be statues. If luck turned inside out and upside down, I wouldn't be surprised to witness the two stonework beasts swing their spears into action behind my back. I don't want to think about this. I drop the terrifying thought like a hot plate. In fact, I don't want to think about anything. I smother inhibitions and continue on inside blankly. *Good choice*, the voice in my head advocates. *Don't 'want' and don't 'think' from this moment on. Remember to let your instincts do the driving.*

The walls on either side are neatly lined with rusted fire-torches, teeming with unwelcome vines crawling from the ceiling above, breaking through just to get a close prick at my head. The torches are pressing in as the tunnel walls concave and the space becomes narrower. Engraved words are in these walls too. They're all over these mountains! Similarly in this cave, they're written in the same Ancient Dialect I'm not accustomed to in the slightest. All of it is in that same tedious language. I take that as a sign of a lack of Night Dreamer impressions and therefore another red flag for me.

'Any of this worth deciphering?' I whisper.

It all reads the same, if you must know, the voice answers reluctantly.

'Reads the same…*what exactly*?'

I'm sorry, Conscience, but I'm desiring explanations in overdrive now. Look what your riddles have done!

CONDONE YOUR GREED TO DETHRONE THE QUEEN. Clear enough for you, diamond?

'Diamond?' I reiterate. 'You're not the first person to call me that.'

And I won't be the last to call you that if you stop asking dangerous questions!

'*Dangerous* questions?' I quote her again. 'What could possibly be *dangerous* about a question? What could be down here that has you so afraid of something as harmless as asking a simple question?'

Then two huge doors materialise through the shadows; a bit like the ones back at the Kingdom Palace, the doors that opened into All Eyes' throne-room. They are rusting, decomposing and soon they'll be all gone to expose future trespassers like myself to whoever or whatever lies in secrecy behind them. Is it safe? I ask myself this time. Am I taking chances? And, if so, how many?

Draw your blade, the voice in my mind advises.

I have. The sword is tight in my hand and no one's coming near the Map. They can forget about that for sure. Okay, I'm ready! I tell myself.

I'm ready! I'm ready to roll with this!

Remember—more steady than ready.

I go for the door-handle and slowly lower it. *Very slowly.* Until I can oh so lucidly hear that the latch has loosened and the door has cocked open. Nobody has heard—they shouldn't have. It is so quiet that not even the mice and the insects in the cracks of the tunnel walls could be aware of my tampering. Now for the big job. I drive a little force into the door, gingerly edging it a quarter of the way open…then half-open—I'm wetting myself. Sweat is on its way and I'm absolutely going to be taking a nervous leak in my pyjama bottoms very soon. I've stopped breathing loudly and I press my head against the damp wood of the door. There's light breaking through from the room on the other side; a considerable amount more than there is in this tunnel. There are more fire-torches on the walls in this new space, and reflections from a greater source are glittering somewhere in the centre of the room. I can see these reflections on a wall in my direct eyesight. I'm not feeling any braver than I was thirty seconds ago, but I've come too far and everything is depending on me. Depending on the Night Dreamers. It's down to me to find the other two. Courageous, I slide my head further round the edge of the door. Peer into the room.

And I was going to applaud the Dreamerverse if things didn't get any worse.

But I postpone my praise, as calling what I see "worse" would be pure euphemism right now—A clan of gorillas are settled in the cave, over thirty of them at least. A society of beasts. Littered at every turn is an excess of treasure; piles upon mountains of jewels and trinkets and other plush materials satiate the cave. They appear to be heaps growing in the process of a harvest collection. The gorillas patrol the thin aisles around these piles, shuffling through the riches with chunks of it being carried in their arms and manoeuvred from place to place, in the search for what they hope to be something valuable, something *worthy.* At the other end of the room, a group of fortunate gorillas are courteously queuing with spoils they have collected from the organised stash. Patiently waiting in line to reach the golden, bedazzled throne, which receives them with a noble might. A regal gorilla, the largest of them all, sits upon the throne. Mature, limp and balding, the gorilla queen sports battle scars on her skin - mainly gashes along her torso and arms and with one long wound emblazoned down her neck. The wounds of a royal conflict? Previous failed attempts at usurpation? I wonder. Who would dare challenge a monster of that size? Nothing in this trove room, I'm quite sure of that from what I've seen of the respect the other apes, her disciples, are showing her. Bygone Night Dreamers? On her head, there's a silver crown and in the centre of it, a radiant emerald. Our prized object of interest no doubt. 'Happy to see me, beautiful?' I whisper tentatively. 'Uncle Oscar's come to rescue you.'

The queen wields a no-nonsense look, as the gorilla at the front of the queue bows his head, lifting up a mace of gold before Her Majesty. The regal gorilla does little but grunt and flick her eyes down her nose to scrutinise the offering.

This queen was once a warrior, the voice in my head narrates. *Her character was not what made her cold and ruthless. She was once kind and empathic—her original, human incarnation that was. It was her unfair predicament at death that turned her hostile. She went from living a life as a very renowned Dreamer to becoming a deceased spirit sworn into the body of an overgrown ape. It trumps the fate of her spirit being left as a vicious, bodiless Nightmare, but she believed her reincarnation was an insult; it was no reward for a hero.*

'And who exactly is 'she'?' I ask. 'A hero?'

You've heard of her. Queen Cassandra, a former Night Dreamer of the generation who emerged before yours to confront the Drag-in over twenty years ago. When Cassandra died, she was elevated to Stellar God status, due to her success protecting the Dreamerverse.

'Cassandra? That was my mother's name.'

It's a very common name, the voice says in a manner that plays out rather cool, yet irrationally hinges on synthetic.

'Not where I'm from,' I explain. 'The Oracle went from being the most revered to the most hated woman in the West, once blaming Soothsayers for world crises like the Blackout Nine Attacks became a trend. It was a downward spiral for Soothe Kind after that horror show. Soothes were supposed to see everything coming. They didn't predict their unexpected downfall and quick dissolutions from society.'

Well, I'll tell you what, the voice noted. *The Queen and every gorilla in this cave will see you coming if you keep reminiscing willy-nilly.*

'Why? You still haven't made it clear why thinking in here is danger—'

Shhhhh!

The gorilla queen pinches the golden mace from her disciple and examines it churlishly. Coming to a vital decision, Her Majesty slings the rod back into the nearest heap and launches herself up onto her feet. The gorilla queen must be four times the size of the other gorillas. She looks down at the "smaller" normal-sized gorilla that brought her the offering, angry and bearing rows of sharp, red, flesh-stained teeth. The queen has dark, black balls for eyes, displaced and obscure in the slant of their sockets, evoking fear into her disciples. She roars down into her giver's face with gruelling dissatisfaction, prodding the nerves of the normal-sized gorilla. The smaller gorilla has shrunk into a terrified ball, dipping his head *like Kyma sometimes does when I accuse her of digging at the carpet in our residence.* With a trial-like verdict, the gorilla queen raises a firm fist and pounds the little ape across the room, powerfully sending him into a huge heap of pearls. The queen reclaims her throne and darts her gaze at the next gorilla in the queue. Unwillingly, the second little gorilla scoots forward, holding a disc made of aluminium.

'What left her this way?' I deliberate. 'Why trap her in the body of a gorilla?'

Spirits in the Dreamerverse can take the form of any body of any living thing. But this passage of reincarnation is only granted by her, Queen Cassandra – the goddess of wealth and man's ***greatest wealth****: his body. Queen Cassandra herself was promised the reformation of a lion at death; instead, her promise ultimately went neglected and she was imprisoned in the body of a gorilla. This legend became her greatest irony, since her Stellar role is now granting new bodies to the deceased. In this trove room, hidden behind the Falls of Fortune, she summons the spirits and chooses who will be rewarded a new body and who will remain a spirit forever, based on who can best deliver to her wealthiest desires. You've intruded on today's trove harvest and you ought to keep out of sight and mind, for you are not contesting for the Queen's heart.*

Once I know for sure that the area around me is vacated and out of sight from any gorillas, I make a run for a heap of golden lace. I slide behind it, lungs in throat and gagging profusely. Balancing myself against the dense heap of lace, I trace round it, in search of either Samuella or Camson somewhere in here. There's too much shining metal mirroring in the trove room and it's teasing my eyes.

I then notice a pyramid of trashed silverware to the far right, where a miniature doll-like figure is lying at its base. It's a female in purple pyjamas with torn fabric and damp patches from where she's been dragged through the Falls and across the spring. Samuella's soggy burgundy locks are the first feature that classifies her and brings her to my attention.

Luckily, there are no gorillas down that end either. I hurry towards her. She's frighteningly still. Her eyes are closed. My first impression is that she's dead and her captors haven't even had the decency to dispose of her corpse and bury her somewhere, and have, instead, resorted to chucking her into a junkyard of trophies and platter dishes. When she hears me coming though, she pops open one of her eyes and her face lights up. 'You took your time!' she complains. 'They'll see you at that height. Get down. Get down to my level.'

I lightly drop down and perch beside her. 'Is this your idea of staying alive? Playing dead?' I say to her.

'You got off lucky!' she says. 'They found Camson and me in the cave and brought us here. I suppose they were convinced we were something of value and were something worth treasuring for their queen. So they trapped me in here and now I'm bound to be turned in as an offering.'

'*Where is Camson*?'

'Not quite sure as of this moment. We were separated in the cave. He's probably been sorted into another pile.'

'The junk-pile?' I humour.

Samuella rewards me with an unimpressed shake of the head.

What are they doing with all this stuff?' I inquire. 'Where did they find it all?'

'Are you that oblivious, City Boy?' she ridicules. 'On your way down here, you haven't at all thought why it might be called the Falls of Fortune, or seen the huge showcase of cascading treasure out front? They're presenting items to the queen and she decides whether it is worthy or not. In return, the item becomes a funeral gift of their own, which will determine whether their spirit is reborn into a new body after death or if they're discarded to become a Nightmare. As we saw, mad and wild in those mountains is where most of those Nightmares end up, hunting bodies for themselves. This trove is where a ritual ceremony is held, the legitimate way to die. Quite a private affair, to be honest. That's why the Falls are so covert. This treasure's all been collected from the Falls of Fortune, christened by the purest water on Constellation Planet. New offerings arrive every day and today we're one of them.'

'How do you know all this?'

'Like I said, I listen to what other Dreamers have to say.'

'Who are these other Dreamers?'

Another loud roar erupts from the throne. Queen Cassandra is on her feet again, towering over the next ape in line. She knocks the poor creature into a heap of jewels, bringing the mound crashing to the ground. Then, something I missed before takes place. A glowing orange outline illuminates the body of the rejected gorilla. The gorilla moans as the shining orange outline thickens and starts to peel deeper into its matter, cutting inward like a laser through its flesh, leaving behind a figureless, degenerated shadow that no longer resembles the primate. Categorised, the shadow bursts into a cloud of black smoke, which then slowly ascends until the Nightmare's residue is expelled out via the cave ceiling.

'We have to deal with that *animal* to get our emerald?' I say.

'Do you realise who that is?' she says this so quietly, as if all the goods in the trove room are eavesdropping on our conversation. 'That "animal" with the crown on her head is Queen Cassandra, a former Night Dreamer and goddess of wealth and reincarnation.'

'Really? You're not joking?' I gasp sarcastically. She's completely unaware of my own insights. We both have mentors looking over us, Samuella. I have the woman in my head and you have these imaginary friends whom you call fellow Dreamers. You're nothing special. 'Yeah, I know that much. I'm not an idiot.' I roll my eyes at her. 'I also know that she herself resurrected in a gorilla's body by mistake of the Stellar Gods and their accidental neglect of her heroic services.'

It's Samuella's turn to be gobsmacked at what I've discovered.

'These other Dreamers you mentioned,' I tease. 'I may have rubbed shoulders with a few of them myself.' There's a massive grin on my face.

'There's more to the story than that, Oscar,' Samuella revaluates, much to my misery. 'Cassandra wanted precedence over Constellation Planet when she died, a reward that was too large for All Eyes and the Stellar Gods to grant her. So she was given the next best thing: the duty of guarding all the best riches on Constellation Planet. And it was Cassandra's new role in this trove cave that cast a curse upon her: her crown will strip anyone of his or her urge to want and desire. Those who come with this desire will be caught out by her and will have to face her anger. That's why none of these other gorillas look that interested in the treasure they're labouring through. Desire is deadly—this is what the inscriptions were warning us about.'

'And that makes matters very tricky for us,' I conclude, re-establishing the emerald placed as the centrepiece of the queen's crown. 'Because if we really want that emerald, we're going to have to make it known, which means we're going to have to confront her for it.'

Another roar rips through the room, followed by another receipted and ejected ape. 'Are you sure this is the game we signed up for? Messing about with queen-sized monkeys?'

'It's an ape, not a monkey, and we've come too far to turn away and give in. Besides, you brought us here. This is your lead. You have the Map and it's your time to shine—remember? Now, tell me, what are we looking for? What's here that we need to acquire?'

'The gorilla's wearing a crown,' I point out.

'Yes…'

'And, what's that thing in the centre of it? That looks like our first emerald.'

'Good luck with that,' Samuella snorts.

'I have no idea how we're going to do this,' I say. 'Not in this lifetime, anyway. Maybe when I die and transform into a gorilla someday I will. If we do so much as look at that emerald too long, Cassandra will clock our intentions without hesitation and she'll skin us like bananas! There's no way around her. We have to confront her. But, our success depends on how well we delay our action. Now, how the hell are we going to delay ourselves and steer clear of her suspicion for as long as possible?'

'The seeds!' Samuella adds. 'Take a blue seed to camouflage yourself long enough to snatch the thing from her crown. Then, we'll make a run for the first exit we see.'

'Why am I the one who has to steal the emerald?' I protest.

'Because you're the leader this time and you led us into this situation and still managed to get off scot-free again!'

'Scot-free?' I object. 'I was ditched by the two of you! Left on my own!'

'You'll have to get her from behind,' she declares, ignoring my excuses. 'Just in case.'

'Just in case what?'

'Presuming the blue seed doesn't work,' Samuella suggests. 'Cassandra may be too powerful for it, too omniscient.'

'Only if I lack having something else to distract her face-on.'

'You can rely on me to do that.'

'You'll be a distraction? How?'

'While I've been here, I've happened to catch an eye or two.'

'What do you mean?'

'*Move Over*!'

I spring at her command and spiral across the slope of silverware, as far from the auburn-haired doll as I can get—just as a huge, latticed silhouette cranes above to snatch its prize. The net descends and locks over Samuella, caging her inside. One of the gorillas has come to retrieve a rare item from the pile—and, oh so conveniently, it happens to be one of us. Samuella pops a blue seed into her mouth and chews it on her way towards the queue. She winks and that is my signal to advance towards the backside of the throne, out of view. While Samuella distracts the queen, I'll go in for the emerald, swiping that crown right off her head. The emerald will fall into our hands just like that—

Don't think about the emerald, my subconscious ally returns exclusively to my head. *Even thinking about it invites the suspicions of the queen.*

Then what must I do to be sure that crown won't see me coming?

Nothing—think of nothing. Your mind must be vacated of desirous thoughts. Remember that your littlest of wills can expose you here, expose your intentions to Queen Cassandra, a Stellar God who is sensitive to the cravings of all men. You must rely only on your primal instinct. And that sole instinct should be to defend yourself through the discretion of ignorance. Attack the queen only in retaliation.

I progress at a narrow angle towards Queen Cassandra's throne, still reserving some distance from her. I could make the move of rushing towards her with the end of my sword thrust in the direction of her back. That, however, wouldn't be a wise, or much easier, option – I'd risk possessing the intention to kill, which would be deemed desirous. Instead, I should gradually close in on her, pretend she isn't there during my approach and only *think attack* on the moment I'm prepared to flick the crown off her head with the end of the sword.

Attack only when attacked, the voice summarises my brainstorming.

Sneaking up from directly behind the beast, I skid the soles of my feet along the floor – hard and even, although there are tiny objects speckled everywhere and tinkling one of these across the ground will blow my cover. Good movement so far. I'm hiding behind treasure-hills also, which aid as frequent intervals while tiptoeing over the clutter of discarded fortune.

Finally, behind the queen herself, I observe that her throne equals the height of an adult elephant, so there's no way any of the other gorillas in the queue will notice me when I scale the back of it. I skulk slowly forwards, my sword vibrating to the rhythm of apprehensive hands and I'm ardently trying not to jiggle like a clueless coward, who jealously wishes he could instead perform the role of an offering like his female partner in crime.

Queen Cassandra is in touching distance. If I extend my arm at this point, there's a possibility I may accidentally scathe off some hair with the blade. Thin, black hair. I have no intentions of touching her, though. Only the crown on her head. I'm not ready for that killer thought yet, the one that will terminate my inconspicuousness. One tidy nick between the scalp and the ring of the crown. That's all it'll take. That's all that's required. I climb onto the back of the throne and cling there for a short while. The gorilla queen is shuffling; I wait for her to calm down. She has heavy breaths, which shudder through her torso like an inflating hot air balloon and, as she fidgets, a fragrance of sweat and burnt wood hits me full in the nose.

Cocking my elbow back, I horizontally lift the blade, mark the ape's back and then follow it upwards to the crown's rim—

Not yet! Not yet! Wait—look!

I tilt my head round the gorilla queen's shoulder, spying the queue on the other side of the throne. Samuella's captor is the next in line to present his offering, behind another ape with a patch over one eye and pouting his lips. Secure inside the rope-bound net, Samuella cartwheels in a clump of silverware, plates, goblets and trays clanging against her body. She's on the ground, being dragged along like a culled lamb. She has met me in her sights also, but she daren't move. She resumes her role as a rag-doll. The gorilla has the net tied and the end of the rope is slung over the poor miser's shoulder. It's all in my hands now. Who knows what Cassandra will do if she realises Samuella's intentions to steal the emerald?

No time. Samuella's next to be served up. The little gorilla lumbers to the queen, heaving Samuella treacherously behind him.

There's a short hesitation. The Samuella-doll is being looked over.

Think snatch! Think snatch! Think snatch!

This is the time to go in for the steal! Before the almighty gorilla makes her ultimate judgement, before she rejects my companion, I level my blade. Prepared to execute a clean, quick chip under the crown—jettisoning the clover-green stone inside—but…

SWOOMP!

The queen's ferocious, grey hand tracks over me and lunges down to grab me whole. I gasp, letting out everything I've held so tight. Pinning my arms to their sides and lifting me into the air so my legs dangle - my breath, my nerves, my terror, my desire and all of my strength have capitulated to the assertion of an incredible might.

Thrown into the air now, I soar over the queen's head, across the trove room and crash through a wall of gushing of water, before I land in a deep puddle - water sourced fresh from the ground level above is pouring down into the cave from a hole in the ceiling and I'm soaking in the shallow pond it's created. I scrub the water from my eyes and gaze up at the small waterfall in front of me.

A bulging shadow has appeared behind the mildly transparent wall of water, its movements embraced by the little reflections gambolling in the room's darkness. I crawl backwards on my rear, until I'm stopped by a cold stone slab not too far behind me. But the animal no longer requires hesitation. Its bewilderment has drained away and it emerges. Through the thin spray of water propels a monster, at least fifteen feet in height when standing upright on her legs. Her patchy, unkempt hair is drenched with water drizzling off her body, curling round her grinding muscles. The light from the emerald in the centre of her crown spears into my eyes. In terrifying contrast, her eyes are dusky black holes.

The queen has been incensed and I am to answer for the disruption of her treasure harvest. I gingerly get to my feet.

Let your instincts prevail, the voice in my head advises me again. *Desire is deadly.*

In all seriousness, her instincts are much superior to mine.

I notice my sword resting on the bank of the inadvertent pond, about seven or eight steps to my right. Sorry, Brain Lady, call it *instinct* or whatever you like, but that blade is my only way out of this. I lunge for the sword, skittering through the puddle and slipping after each trundle. The water freezes my swelling feet. Impulsively, to create an urgent spurt of distance between Cassandra and me, I spring off the ground and into the air—

Suspended.

A mighty fist thrusts me in the back, just as I filch my sprawled fingers towards the sword, and I head in a different direction. This time scissoring another miniature waterfall of rushing gold coins and clashing with a huge, sharp pile of riches. I topple down the pile, only ceasing when I smack into the floor.

The queen returns with haste. She crashes into the wall of falling coins, sending chunks of the gold dashing everywhere. I spot her above me, hovering with both fists formed at her sides. She lands one into the pile from which I have fallen. There's a clattering boom, as hundreds of treasures fire into the air over my head. I get up, up, up—and run from the foot of the mound. The queen, furious, employs a frighteningly brisk gallop in chase. I'm headed for the queue of stunned gorillas up ahead. But I never make it. The queen tackles me with one of her huge hands and drags me from the ground to bring our noses together. Her eyes are like eclipsed moons in the night sky. She growls in my face, sending shockwaves through my ear canals, up my nostrils and down my throat.

With the sword, I swing for her face. And from it, a horrible gash is ploughed vertically into the gorilla queen's forehead and nose. Hot blood spurts from her face and she retreats, dropping her head to caress the wound in her hands. This releases me from her hold and I plummet back into the fortune mound. Quickly recollecting myself, I poise in front of the cowering queen, who's gripping to her face as if I've slung burning acid into her eyes. She comes to realise her ridicule and sinks her hands away from her forehead. I've distorted her snarl and split a fleshy trough between her eyes.

She stretches her bloodied face out towards me, veins thickening in her neck, and she roars again to scream '*look what you've done to me!*' Then, dashes my way. I'm prepared to receive her on this chance. When she's close enough, I lash down with my sword, ripping a long crack of flesh on her arm. Her bicep spasms at me, knocking me into the air once more. I land nearer to the audience of smaller apes – helpless and gawking. The queen tries to fasten the facial wound with her palm, abortively blocking the blood that oozes underneath from getting into her eyes.

The queen wants more. She's quite determined to fight until the virulent death.

So am I (I guess I have to be now).

We throw ourselves at one another once more. Here I go—lurching the sword's blade in the direction of her steely chest and making a messy situation out of it all. I slip the sword between her arm and her chest, missing my target entirely. Instead, she catches my legs and tosses me around the room again. When I hit the ground, I'm back where I started; near the queue of spectating gorillas, right beside Samuella and her captor. In her net, she's begun to scratch her sword's blade against the rope in an attempt to break free under the unwary eye of her kidnapper.

You almost had her, the Brain Lady's supportive voice is cheerleading at my side once again. *But you didn't have her in the right way.*

What do you mean? I'm trying every way there is!

You keep remembering what you've come for. You keep falling into her radar, toying with her defence mechanism like all those others who failed before you: you're thinking about that emerald in her crown – that is the greatest trap in the room, her winning move. She's stronger than anyone who comes looking for that rock on her head and she'll beat all of them with her strength. But to those with no intention to steal from her, she is ignorant—she is weak.

The Brain Lady is right. I can only win against Cassandra if I refrain from thinking of the emerald, avoid even looking at it—but it doesn't stop shining, whamming into my eyes like a torch in the search for help. It's hard, near impossible to ignore.

If I'm to outsmart the queen, the crown first needs to go—

'Up here, Your Majesty! I'm over here—this way!' Samuella's voice stings the air between us. She's found a spot at the top of one of the treasure mounds, where she stands with her legs firmly apart and secured deep into the glistening metal. 'You have a really beautiful collection!' Around her neck are five or six necklaces, medallions and chains of different materials – gold, aluminium, silver, diamond. While I've been getting memos from the Brain Lady, Samuella's been quietly arming herself. Not with weapons, but with jewellery. Items picked out from Cassandra's prized possessions. 'Do you mind if I borrow a few of these? They look really good on me in this colour—don't you think?' she continues to taunt and the gigantic gorilla queen's attention is finally caught. The queen has stopped and turned to the girl up on the sparkling hill above her, disbelief appears to stiffen her reactivity.

I'm initially confused by her playful attempt at distraction, but quickly, I begin to understand what she's actually trying to do. *How did she get out of—?* The gorilla that'd captured her is stood at the foot of the mound she's climbed up. He's slouching, with the net laid out open beside him. He looks just as bewildered as all the rest of the queen's hominid disciples. Two humans bumble in and create a skirmish with their monarch and they're all terrified of what happens next. Well, that's what it first seemed like. Now, the other apes are taking part as well in the red-haired doll's revolutionary stance. All of them buzz off at once, in among the mounds to loot something, anything they fancy from the queen's collection.

'Oh, don't worry, boys!' Samuella calls to the other gorillas in the midst of their ransacking. 'Take whatever you want! I'm sure Her Majesty won't mind! It won't bother you—will it, Cassandra?'

Cassandra is livid. The bubble bursts in her mind and the angst burgeons into unpredictable rage. She doesn't know where to look or where to turn. Everyone is a culprit and the scent of desire and greed is blatant, playing out right before her eyes. Thievery, mutiny, betrayal—all of it happening at once. All the gorillas are imitating Samuella's rebellious spin on the queen's ceremony. Monkey see, monkey do.

Queen Cassandra lunges her head back, erupting her greatest roar and swinging her arms about in a strop. She dances on the spot, overworked in her aimlessness, struggling to decide whom to punish for their indulgence first.

'Any takers?' Samuella yells. 'Any early bidders for the most valuable jewel in the trove? The crown jewel worn at the throne and protected by the one and only Stellar Goddess Cassandra, former Night Dreamer and guardian of the Falls of Fortune!'

Cassandra frustratedly slams her hands down on the ground, shaking the entire mountain. The queen has her sights zoomed on Samuella and now that her attention has been ripped away from me again, I stand for what will be my final chance at an advantage in this battle.

The doll with the chestnut locks makes a perfect dive from the top of the mound and surges towards Her Majesty. Hands outstretched in front of her. She nicks the crown from the queen's head and slides on her front down the gorilla's gigantic back, rolling onto the floor and to a halt with the diadem and emerald still intact and hugged to her breast.

The queen falls to her knees and her head bows. A weight has been lifted; her power has been discharged. Samuella escapes into my arms and we watch the defeated gorilla queen, assessing what has just happened.

What have we done? Was that a success? Have we done the right thing?

My Brain Lady has nothing to respond with. For some reason, she has taken a recess, although I can still hear light, static whining between both ears, a ringing aftershock that sounds like the end of a phone call.

Cassandra whimpers in agony. I tear myself away from Samuella, who holds the crown close to her. Samuella has her hand over my arm, but I drag it off myself and slink towards the abdicated monarch.

Her back remains to us. We may well as beheaded her too, for all I can see are shoulders, since humility has plunged her head so low.

Tears are in the gorilla queen's eyes as she moans, 'I have mercy. I have lots of it. Take it from me; steal it all from me, if you wish. This ego is not I in my truest form. I have been delegated this guardian's role. This wicked task of judging the vanity of spirits. I am a miserable servant in another king's predicament. A mistake burdened by the Stellar Gods. Please, leave me to my shame.' I find myself standing right beside her, stroking her black hair and consoling her upset. Apologising is all I can do.

'It had to be this,' I tell her. 'We are Night Dreamers, just as you once were. We came for the emerald with one intention only – to protect this world and our home from the Drag-in. I do hope you understand that there was no malice in our actions. We didn't want to spoil your reputation.'

Did I really just destroy this animal's livelihood? Steal its only lingering relevance in this world? However, there's something about the queen I can resonate with and it reminds me that she isn't an animal at all and never really was. This beast, like Samuella, has a familiar sentiment. The familiarity is not apparent in her face and hair, but in her voice. And, once again, this gives the impression that I've seen her before. A time long ago, but indeed unforgettable. As I entertain this wonderful, though perplexing, hunch, a miracle happens.

'You don't need to apologise, Oscar,' Cassandra lifts her head to smile at me and I see my mother beaming down at me. The queen doesn't only share her name, but her voice and expressions also. It explains why the Brain Lady in my head has remained so silent. She's no longer in my head anymore, but right here, looking over me. 'Thank you for trusting your instincts and coming to find me, Oscar. And thank you, Samuella, for liberating me from that tortuous existence.'

A cloud fringed by a prominent strip of orange glow drifts up from the imposing body of the gorilla queen. The shadow then reassembles itself into the ghost of a healthy, proud lioness. The spirit of Cassandra has claimed a new form. The lioness spirit frolics beside its former gorilla-body and faces Samuella and me. My mother's spirit glows at us appreciatively. 'I thank you both, Night Dreamers, for rescuing me. I have spent many slumbers in this world and my deathly eternity has been foully served thus far, having spent all of it trapped in that monstrous body. I was forced to become keeper of the jewels, the reluctant queen of Fortune's Falls. I never asked to be a monarch of anything when I was relieved of my duties as Night Dreamer, but only ever hoped to live and serve Constellation Planet in glorious legend and at peace.'

'We're glad to see you're happy to be out of that body at last.' I swallow hard, my emotions getting the better of me. 'And it's amazing to see you again, mum.'

'I was promised a lion's body at death. It fits wonderfully well to have my boldest promise finally granted by my loyalist child.'

'Doesn't being a free spirit now just make you a Nightmare? Like those freaks up in the mountains?' Samuella mentions.

'No,' the lioness larks. 'Death's reward has finally reborn me as a lioness. You won't have to wait long for your own reward, Night Dreamer. Soon you will be remunerated with what you most desire, in return for your hard work. Hopefully not after hundreds of slumbers like I myself. Congratulations, Oscar. You followed your instincts and they led you home. You can always depend that they will.'

Without warning or causing any further churn of my upset, my mother's spirit transmutes into a swirl of black and orange smoke, which floats up through the hole in the ceiling, ascending into the clear blue sky that hangs over Leo Island. The emerald in the crown shines lavishly for a second in Samuella's hands, then returns to normal.

I look at Samuella briefly, then back at the kneeling gorilla avatar that just hosted the ghostly character, now humbled and filtered without ego. The tormented black holes in the ape's eyes have browned into a more pleasant and appropriately primeval glare. The spirit it housed has departed from the Falls of Fortune and now the overgrown gorilla left behind is just an ordinary hominid, a harmless animal awaiting a new soul. Cassandra has been relieved of duty.

'One emerald down, two to go,' Samuella excites. Little does she know that encounter meant more to me than it ever will to her.

Inevitably, the peaceful eye of the storm is wrecked in a heartbeat, when a lone arrow flings into the head of the giant idling gorilla, rupturing the back of the skull, killing it instantly. Samuella and I share the temporary shock, before we realise where this shot has come from. Samuella's the first to twist her face into a smouldering grimace of fury and she bounces across the cave to confront a brainless Camson. 'What the hell is your problem?' she roars at him. 'Can't you ever just leave a problem as it is? We've already resolved this and *you* were nowhere to be seen!'

Camson overlooks the entire cave, intrepidly surveying the expressions of retreating gorillas from the top of a silver thread mound.

'These brutes carried me away somewhere else, so it took me a while to find my way back to you two,' he argues, thawing his haughty grin. 'What is this place? A treasure trove? It's quite remarkable, isn't it! No need for alarm, you guys. I was okay on my own. Your services – or lack thereof – were not required. I was having fine success and joy in amputating my kidnappers by myself. They'd probably have made a nice stew for us too, if I'd been able to carry their corpses on my own.'

'You did what?' Samuella educes.

'You heard me right, Sammy. I gave a few of them gorillas back there the what-for they deserved and their poor judgement made for a few easy kills. These creatures don't put up much of a fight. You're welcome, by the way.'

'Do you sometimes need reminding how much of a fool you are, Camson? In case you forget?' I tell him. 'Do you have any idea where that leaves us, you moron?'

The remaining gorillas in the trove room – some thirty of them – process both Camon's arrogance and the dead body of their queen in the most diplomatic method they know how – by crowding together as a tribe...and ganging up on the humans, singling out the foreigners in their cave.

Camson looks at us sheepishly, specifically Samuella holding the crown containing the emerald, and then around at the other gorillas – none of them are recoiling away from him anymore. They are standing butch and solid and flattening us with their enclosing shadows like the soundless crawl of twilight.

'Where?' Camson asks, oblivious, but conscious nonetheless.

'With not so many friends,' Samuella answers.

We turn to see the unit of gorillas are nothing like they were before, under the queen's reign. Not innocent. Not harmless. Not afraid. One thing that they are now is liberated. Scowling and shifting towards us, looking bigger than they did prior to Camson's vehement entrance. Civilisation has melted from their conduct and a new-fangled behaviour, disturbingly primitive and slobbering with a vengeance, has ascended the throne of their nature thanks to our wonderfully liable saviour, the valiant East Vet.

'What's going on? They never acted this way before!' Camson protests. 'What's got into them?'

'They were terrified of the queen and now she's fallen, there's nothing holding them back,' Samuella dissects what's as apparent as blood in a vein. She spots her sword in a pile of steel weaponry and retrieves it.

The gorillas have stopped momentarily. Like we've seen before, an orange beam outlines their body and cuts into their being, stripping through the flesh from their edges to their very core. Their spirits are salvaging command of their hosted bodies and are beginning to convert into a totally different physical form altogether. Losing the snarling grimace of hardworking apes incensed with a lack of reward for their afterlife labours, the spirit avatars garb an unholy black, faceless shadow to starkly intimidate us in the trove of light. We are no longer the stage show for an audience of goony gorillas, but a frontline of rearing Nightmares. The only thing the dark, shapeless ghosts share with their former primate counterparts is that they outnumber us and outweigh us in every strength.

'How many are there, you think?' Camson stammers.

'I don't think a number will make any difference,' I tell him, not flinching my eyes from the terror. 'Follow my lead,' I command quietly. 'Run!'

And we're off! I accelerate ahead of the others, espousing speed.

The spirits chase. We're targeted for an exit – any exit, the nearest exit – the entrance to another cave, undisclosed by the yonder darkness.

I'm amazed we've managed to escape this far already, with the Nightmares all flaring across the treasure trove to reach us, their entities rubbing against each other and bonding to become a great black wall of shadow tearing through the room. Along the way, I make sharp turns in and out of the gaps between treasure mounds. It's my way of confusing our pursuers. If these hunters want to compete with us at a chase, then one must contest as game.

The Nightmares easily glide through the mounds, the treasure's physical obstruction and the lack there of in the passage of these creatures being a testament to their impalpability. When we reach the exit, we re-enter the myriad of nothingness. It's regrettably familiar. I have traced my unlikely bearings through the cave system before I found the Falls and, whilst the dark can sometimes pass as an unlikely and unexpected ally in situations like this, these starving storm cloud monsters do not fall into that category. These are simple creatures that only want one thing. They want the emerald, the resurrection of their queen.

The Nightmares expel heaving thunderclap roars upon every pounce and, with each one, I feel the sturdiness of my feet shed in tandem. I'm being sodden by the weak thought of escape and how maybe, just maybe, there could actually be a way out of here with the emerald at the disposal of the Night Dreamers.

Is this paradise? Is this what it all comes to in the end? The Kappa Mountains? The Falls of Fortune? The Dreamerverse? Is this what paradise comes to when idealisms reach their limits and cannot stretch any further? I want my mother to come back and take me away from the trouble and the danger, like she always used to. But it's only a dream, I tell myself, a daft, deceitful illusion that never truly existed from the outset.

The Nightmares are snapping at our heels, their breaths scratching at our knees. I can feel them – they are ice-cold *like the blast from my air conditioner back home.*

Am I going to die here? Are we all going to die in this cave? And join the Nightmares somewhere up in these mountains?

*No...*The voice of my conscience has taken its time to restore itself and respond to my desperation, no longer donning the tongue of my mother, but a tone of urgency that is much appreciated. *Take a blue seed! Take another blue seed!*

I can't keep wasting those! What happens the next time another situation like this pops up? What happens when the Drag-in makes an appearance again—?

You'll just keep running then? Run where? They'll have you! Easily have you! The voice warns. *Refuse discretion now and they'll catch you! I don't even have to promise you that!*

I'm not taking that advice. Not this time. I do trust my Conscience and his new-fangled charisma, but I'm better than that. I must consolidate such urgencies, such wilful impulses that may have lost me to the gorilla queen if I hadn't been more careful. I need to be wiser of the future and what struggles may lie ahead.

Then, it's as if my eyes have been wrenched open for the first time after dwelling a century down a mine. From out of nowhere, there's a light in my direct line of vision, poking out of the darkness ahead and reaching out to me.

'Can you see that?' I urge over the vicious panting of our determiners. 'Can you see that light?'

'Yes! Yes, yes, yes—I can!' Samuella sings. 'That's sunlight—*sunlight*—that's what it is!'

Relief.

A bubble of chance has inflated around everything, encapsulating the commotion and the poisonous blast of adrenaline. We all know what is beyond that intrusion of sunlight. Samuella knows. Camson knows. I know. No bounds. Freedom from this cave-spawn. We know exactly what to do. Whether we'll survive this attempt it is impossible to predict—how high, how far, how lucky must we make it?

Let your instinct be the judge.

Immersed in burning sunshine, we jump through the hole, out into the open and are met with the hard, uncompromised window of the waterfall. We shatter through it.

Night has died and fled with the stars and now dawn is ripping free of the horizon's fold. Cooler air hits my face unreservedly. And then I notice there is no ground below us. Not for a long distance – a monumental drop.

We're falling!

The bite of sunlight and salted water blurs for me the sight of anything more than a kerfuffle of wriggling, bright colours and hazy palmtops. We've left the rushing sprays of the waterfall behind us and it's still loud and thunderously near. Far ahead, over the mountains, is an enormous cape of ocean. But we're not headed over there—we're still falling downward.

I lower my gaze to anticipate the ground, floating to certain death on my belly, only to find that a timely hero has exploded out of the waterfall and appeared in the air beneath me. Its liquescent body of effervescing feathers and glass-like transparency continues to shimmer into materialisation. A huge water bird, composed completely from the torrent's womb. And soon arrive a pair of baby-blue wings gliding at its sides—there to catch me…

Chapter Four
Arch Allies

When Oscar came home from the Octane Mall, just after closing-time, he returned to his own abode for a short nap before he was summoned down to his father's residence to discuss the "important things" that would be happening in the next couple of weeks over pistachio ice cream and *Kola Bear*. They always had these talks late in the afternoon. Usually after a big meal, followed by their traditional ice cream fetish – pistachio was both their favourite – and *Kola Bear* – another beloved soda of theirs. Something they agreed on, at least. But, other than the calorific menu, one thing Oscar could always trust was that this father and son "bonding" was never on a Sunday (Son-day was *his* day). And this time it was. Oscar only ever spoke to his father and pretended to care when it concerned something along the lines of ice cream and cold drinks. Other than that, he never really listened. There had to be a significant change in discussion on this occasion if Oscar was going to even try to pay attention. When it came to DCD. Philson, not many things consisted of ice cream or cold drinks, not if you *really* listened.

That afternoon, Oscar was still billowing with the wind of his latest escapade in the Dreamerverse. He lost himself to the conversation, busy fantasising over his own selfish thoughts, rather than noting anything his father had to say. The Decider, as ever, had much more than him to bring to the discussion. They were sitting at the two heads of the Decider's Table, facing one another. Yet, their eyes didn't meet. Oscar was looking down at his glass-bowl of ice cream, dozily playing with the lime-coloured puddle of melted cream that remained, caring less than zippo about what his old man was doing – he could have been launching a rocket off the edge of the Table for all

Oscar knew. Most prominently, Oscar couldn't tear his mind off the Babe With The Blade. His red-haired Dreamerverse accomplice, whom he'd met in the real world a number of times before, but had only truly noticed that afternoon, working a closing shift behind the counter at *Post*. How much more of a coincidence could things become? And she was just as intriguingly picturesque as he'd imagined her to be. In fact, he may have preferred her in this world, for all those five minutes he'd actually interacted with her—

Then, out of the blue, his father brought up the question that most of his tutors at the City Academy had urged on him – the kind of question that would give you a seven-hundred-page encyclopaedia and then demand you to guess the correct page for an answer.

'What are your ideas on that?' The Decider really did launch that hypothetical rocket off the end of the Table. It struck Oscar dead in the eardrum and it hurt. More painful was the fact that his father could tell he hadn't been paying attention, all the while he was still expectant of an answer. A tactic of his that he used to test people. DCD. Philson knew that this theory of moderation didn't work on his son. Oscar had no interest whatsoever in his father's affairs or policies and so it was no surprise he didn't enjoy submitting docile responses to the man with the Big Red Button on his sleeve-cuff. To be honest, he'd read better, heard better, and seen better in the contents of 'The Rot Box'. On a standard Monday morning, he'd stumble haphazardly over the front door mat to find a dreadful mess deposited for him, he'd cry: '*the Rottweiler's left another one!*', and then bring out Kyma's pooper-scooper to clean it up. On other notorious Mondays, he'd guiltily take on the chore sifting through the mail – a mistake commonly made when he scoped a lenticular movie advertisement in the header of the front page and felt the sudden urge to read the review at the back…and then naughtily nosed through what concerts and stand-up gigs were on the horizon at the City Centre's Harkson Arena – a line-up of over a hundred dates, which almost always caught his eye around the middle pages. As hypocritical as it was, Oscar did pick up *some* of the litter the Mediums dropped.

Before coming through with a half-decent answer for the Great Decider to criticise, Oscar had to think first. Twirling the spoon in his ice cream bowl made it seem like he was being decisive and contemplative. But what it was really saying was that he was still hungry and had been silly not to eat before or since his lonely burger at the Mall. 'I think it's fair to say…' that was a good start, '...you should go with your gut-instinct on that one.'

'You see, I generally would. But the thought of this conundrum gives me severe indigestion and, if I'm not careful – do understand, if I let this new idea out too soon or not soon enough – I may just end up with a serious unhinging of the bowels,' his father responded. Oscar struggled to keep a straight face.

'Why? What's sitting on your mind?' Oscar continued to display a qualifying range of interest.

'I have an almighty decision to make. A strategic move, which, when put into practice, may bring monumental change to our world. But the conundrum lies in the knots, which must be tied to climb the ladder to this new world.'

'Well, if it's too hard to decide, do you think you could just blow this idea and get back to what you should be doing? Like dealing with the decisions you *can* make?' Oscar suggested. 'Would that be the right thing I wonder? I really don't know.'

'*What I should be doing?*' DCD. Philson snorted at the feeble response from his son. 'What I *should* be doing is what I *am* doing, what I'm *always* doing.'

'Has this got to do with the Phestor-guy who showed up last night?'

'The East Man wants me to come to an agreement with him. If I link our Nations, by forming a bond with the Principal Nation of the East, Sixth, it doesn't just stop the rest of the East from nipping at our toes, but it also offers a few resourceful benefits. They will hand us a share of their abundance in a cup, or even a chalice depending on how well these negotiations go. I can imagine a litre of oil for every minute we spend in cooperation, and we might just end up with straws too, if we're lucky. Oh, believe, Oscar, dear boy! This may be it—may be it for the Conflicts. The war will be dealt a diplomatic pacifier. It is the sort of diplomacy that legacies can be built on.' His hands were clasped in the way a proud father would hold them when watching his newborn take their first steps. Ironically, this nature Oscar found unfamiliar in the Decider, as he'd never received such paternal passion from the man who was supposed to be his Dada. Instead, all his love had been distributed through expensive gifts and seamless pocket money. His worst birthday present had probably been a gallon of rare Fourth Nation fuel for his thirteenth birthday. '*You'll thank me later. One can never know when there won't be any to go round. Save up!*' his father had told him with a hopeful grin. '*Make daddy proud!*'

'But it's not just about this negotiation, is it?' Oscar was exhausted of hearing about *us, us, us*. 'It won't resolve much thinking about it this way. There must be other complications that come with just pandering to the Sixth Nation.' His words were pellets against his father's missile-rhetoric. Very rarely did he make them heard, but on occasions like this he knew silence was a fool's weapon.

'How many times do I have to explain these things to you? Negotiating is not pandering!' DCD. Philson stroked a mighty palm across his forehead, slapping the perimeter of his baldness like the skin of an old drum. 'Think about this, Oscar! It's our opportunity, our way of reasoning with the East and obtaining that key to their oil-reserves could potentially be our way out! Our way out of the war! We'd no longer have a reason to fight with them! Once we deal with their noisy cousins in the Seventh Nation – which we will slice through like warm butter once Xenol's side of the offer is on the table – there is a fine chance the Sixth Nation will then do what we tell them to do. Xenol will be forced to surrender and everything we owe in bloodshed and combat's detriment will be paid off! One simple breath of mutual respect, helmed by a moral cause of shared domestic interests, and life in the West could return to the way it was half a century ago. At peace with itself and undisturbed by foreign Nations and their grudges.'

'You're going to trick them, so you can continue to steal from them?'

'"Outsmart them" would be the correct way to describe it. Oh, realise, Oscar! It's not as if we're blindly destroying Nations at this stage, cordoning off desolate villages for war-zones, or cementing our borders with the East. Quite the opposite, in fact. You'll be happy to know, in your Punkish delight, that I learnt from those messes, every time, I swear. I wish I'd never played a role in any of it. But, as I have said continually, it had to be done in respect of our forefathers' commitments and all the hard work of their Administrations. Whether it be calling the shots, pulling the plug—it is what the Decider has to do when the moment orders him. I'm done with making people cry, it's time to make a few smile.'

East and West Folk won't be smiling when this plan falls into place, Oscar thought to himself. *They'll be laughing at you.* For once, Oscar saw his father, the Decider, as a man out of his depths.

'Well—I just can't empathise with that!' Oscar erupted, his legs juddering. 'It kills me to think that, after all this time, we're not humane enough to just part ways with the East once and for all, leave them be for all our sakes. Give in already and they might just—!'

'Give in? Give in to what?' his father's cords were tightening and they were about to burst from the sockets.

'Leave them be and they might just do the same.'

'Do the same? Do the same—*for what reason*?' DCD. Philson grumbled. 'This isn't about letting go! If we let them go, we won't just be leaving those blighters to roll about in their fields and dirt roads. No, no, no, son—the East isn't like that any more. The East is a different place now, they're smarter and they have an advantage they now know how to use. Selling missiles to their Sister Nations has granted the Sixth Nation the opportunity to develop from the thieving rural field mice they always were to the firm municipal kingpin of the East. We'd be giving them full freedom to build their new empire if we backed away. That new empire in the East is on the rise and Xenol knows that he'll be getting straight to work with it once the Conflicts are over. That cannot happen, not under my Decidership. Who cares about the pact? Appeasement is always the easy part! I care about keeping them in our shadow and this idea of a settlement will be designed for exactly that. But the worst thing I could imagine doing is to let my foot off that landmine of an empire. My foot remains on Xenol and his prospects for the Sixth Nation at all times.'

'Why do we care about an empire that isn't even ours?' Oscar quickly muttered, then bowed his head.

'Come again?' DCD. Philson barbed.

Oscar didn't respond. He continued to twirl his spoon about in the puddle of his empty ice cream bowl.

'What's got into you, boy? Where's that morale, that pride, gone? Don't you remember the disasters that came when I last decided to *give in*? Your mother, the Oracle, was the one who told me to surrender before, warned me not to go ahead with Blackout Nine. And I am so glad I refused to listen to her. It was the first time I decided to reject the Oracle's advice and no doubt that became the beginning of the end for our marriage. Before that change of heart, that change of strategy, I realised I had been too empathetic and liberal to eliminate the weak link in my Administration, the one damning factor. I was young and foolish, and somewhat gullible. And then, not long after, those Presses suddenly decided to criminalise me with bland words! The *Networks*, those calumnious bastards, who fostered the wicked desires of my Nation's confused flock and spoiled their perceptions of me, with nothing but vile slander in their arsenal! They wanted to supress the regime, challenge me and all my hard work…for what? Bogus, inflammatory bulletins, that's what! I put an end to that treason, ended them all, burnt those Prints to the ground and stood tall beside the flames. And here I stand still, after almost three decades in power.

Surely, you remember me telling you of the struggle I went through to get this far.'

'*Yes*! I remember! But this new move with the East isn't right on anyone. It's just going to provoke something bigger. Something you won't be able to control,' Oscar said. 'I mean, why not just offer them something in return? We know that the East have always been trying to get their hands on our Unique Resource, our stabler and more advanced nuclear energy. Hand over some of our secret, teach them how to utilise it responsibly and they might be more willing to spare some of their own goods! Show them that we trust them and, more importantly, prove to them that we respect them!' Oscar had finally excavated his voice and it flared in retort to his father's. 'Trust them. That will make you a great leader. And the whole world, not just the West, will restore its faith in your legacy.'

'That's a recipe for disaster! Honestly, Oscar, if you were ever once given the responsibility to negotiate anything in your life, you wouldn't have had the slightest clue where to begin! Sharing our rights and carrying out such an unprecedented exchange of virgin resources would appear sinister to my people and daft—'

'*How?*'

'Because of the *possibilities*! The *uncertainties*!'

'Because you *don't trust them*!' Oscar buzzed at him with a virulent attitude. 'You're scared of them. *And you're scared of your own people!* But you don't understand how anyone other than yourself thinks and that times have moved on and people's views have evolved since the Great Splits! This city and Nation need foreign influence as badly as any other Nation, but you're too stubborn to see that the First Nation isn't as great and superior as you think it is!'

'Watch how you speak to me again, boy,' his father asserted. 'Be careful about what you say in this room, as your juvenile behaviour carries a horrible potential of ruining me. You caused my reputation enough problems last night alone.'

'Why does everything I say offend you?' Oscar cried. 'What I say doesn't matter! It never mattered to *you* anyway! What will really matter to you is when the Media take to your shady endorsements with the East. Your encounter with Xenol has already made the headlines of the *Central City Mediums*! So, if this arrangement cocks up, there's absolutely no doubt you'll be ridiculed again! And it won't be tarnishing like the publicity you received from the Blackout Nine Attacks! Making a deal with the Devil and falling on your backside because of it is much worse than that! It could finish you for good! You are the one who ought to be careful, father. Having too much to desire can be very deadly.'

'You just remember, when you're in my shoes, that being Decider isn't an easy obligation. You will learn, when you *become* Decider, that you are paramount to the West's interests and the survival of the world's equilibrium as a whole. There are no fairies that come out to make the decisions for you. Without the Decider, Nationhood would be funnelled through spiritless bureaucracy. Or would someone like you prize an idea of bureaucracy?' The Decider perused his son.

'What do you mean "*someone like me*"?' Oscar spat, offended.

'You seem to be an heir at odds with his own destiny.'

'It won't be my destiny!'

'Oh, really—now, why is that?'

'Because I will never be the Decider.'

'I'm afraid that isn't your decision to make.'

'You wanted my opinion and there it is,' Oscar said plainly. 'Take it or leave it.'

The Decider leaned back in his chair, taken aback by this sudden surge of character from his son. Oscar was sticking to his word without shying away this time, a thing he never usually did when gossiping "important things" over ice cream and cold drinks with his father.

'Sometimes, I wonder what your mother would have to say about you now, all grown up,' his father teased. He was eyeing the boy calmly like a patient lion anticipating the fault of its prey. *It will soon be his time; just you wait and see, it will soon be his time, indeed.*

'She'd have been turning in her grave, disheartened and bored to hell of me, up until now,' Oscar said. 'It's because of her that I like drinking *Kola Bear* and it's because of her why I got used to eating pistachio ice cream. She was a powerful Soothe, dad, she taught me a lot of things. It was her who encouraged me to notice that different ways of thinking and other sides to life were always there, even if everyone else in the City had given up looking. I trusted her and had faith in her wisdom. So should you.'

'She wasn't faithful to you,' his father said bluntly. 'You know she wasn't. I told you—she left you when you were a child. She became sick, like your Uncle. Sick with those flaccid dreams, a selfish ideology that finally reached her too. Mad Punk dreams. Curse them! And curse her!'

'If you hadn't been so cruel to her and her kind—if you hadn't eradicated the Soothsayers and chased them out and hunted them—she wouldn't have left you and your reckless ways!' Oscar said. 'And she most definitely wouldn't have taken her own life!'

The Decider tilted his head to the left and started to erratically rub the edge of the Table with his middle finger.

'The reason she ultimately left this Table years ago was because she was afraid to face her own wars,' his father said quietly. 'She was inexplicably mad—haunted by what the world would become without her Punkish fallacies. All her prophecies then sounded just like your dreams now, just like my brother's dreams! They were all crazy! And I hope you don't turn out the same! *Utterly insane and a danger to society!*'

'Who wouldn't be? After what crooks like you have done to the world, I'd have been out the door just like her, just like my mother—along with everyone else!'

Suddenly, his father's eyes narrowed. 'I gave you a residence here in the Tower—all to yourself; I gave you the key to my personal chauffer; and you currently have enough oil under your name to conquer half the world's Nations. I did all I could to keep you safe and secure and on my side. And what do I get in return? A naïve, liberal nuisance of a son who is reluctant to support his struggling father when he's most in need of an inside opinion. I guess, gratitude can be a destructive emotion.'

'Being in charge of all the world—is that supposed to make me feel safe and secure?' Oscar said. 'Right now, I don't even feel safe with *you* in that seat.'

DCD. Philson took a brief, sharp sip from his own foamy glass of *Kola*. He was uneasy and torn, straining not to show it in front of his son. It came as a result of being deprived of his invaluable sleep and some dimension of intimacy with the only person left he could bear to call family. The bags beneath his eyes were hammocks on which that *Kola Bear* lay under a blanket of caffeine, weighing a tonne. 'Do you want to know where your mother really went before she died? Because I can tell you. It's no secret.'

'Yes…' Oscar choked on his words. '…How…?'

'Aside from her deteriorating mental health, your mother was hauling another burden when she retired from her post as Oracle. She had been diagnosed with a terminal illness that would have indiscriminately killed her in the end. At the time, the illness was not common, but it was becoming a widespread issue over the years, drawing in more attention and research.' The Decider paused and bit his lip, which was trembling with what might have been a quiet grin or supressed, hysterical laughter. But Oscar didn't pay any interest to this; he was distraught by the notion of his mother's tumultuous livelihood and the misery in her final days. 'If she were alive today, she would have received more effective treatment and they could have potentially prolonged her. So, in that situation, I only really had one option for her. If she went away to this place, they could use her organs to experiment for a cure. You'll be relieved to know that she died for a cause. Not a particularly *reliable* cause, I must admit, although it had been a cause with proven potential,' his father cherished a rehearsed smile. 'Your mother was exchanged with the Northern Polar Region in return for a good share of rare oil and cryo-stores of a resource that cannot be harvested anywhere in the West – a dying natural resource called sugarcane. It had to be done. She was one specimen amongst many, if it makes you feel any better. She wasn't submitted alone—'

'And *you* agreed this?' Oscar fumed.

'At the time, City Hospital could no longer sustain her and it was recommended that I put her on a waiting list for the exchange,' his father explained.

'*You* did this to her? *That's why she's out of my life?*'

'I did no such thing, Oscar. Don't you dare blame me!' His father was losing his relaxed mannerisms. For the first time that weekend, DCD. Philson forced himself to look his son in the eyes.

'But you didn't stop her! You dealt her to those greedy experimentalists in the NPR, didn't you! You sold her on like cattle!'

'Hey, let me finish!' his father hissed. 'As I was saying, I sent your mother over to the NPR, since, at the time, it was the only facility that offered the advanced care she needed. They examined her, gave her full anatomical assessments, and took her off my hands. All they wanted to do was carry out a couple of tests. If they worked, she was able to return home, free and alive. If they didn't work, and she wasn't so lucky, then…unfortunately, she'd have been left to the scoundrels and that would have been that.'☆

'That's so horrific!'

☆ Scoundrels were those who chose (or were invariably forced) to suffer the extremities of living their lives out in the Polar Regions. Those involved in the Polar Region experiments were very rarely registered to return to society, since their exposure to the unclassified chemicals being tested there made them a danger. (Of course, their existence in the public mind was all 'rumour', all 'myth'). However, scoundrels living in the Northern Polar Region generally found themselves civilly limited in over-populated areas of the West's wealthier Nations and preferred to survive comfortably in the NPR's improving facilities, rather than adopt the barren prospects available to them in the Fourth Nation. The populations of scoundrels in both Polar Regions was growing by the day, as people were running out of places to live (and things to eat) in conventional Nationhood. Frankly, igloos were comfortable and polar bears tasted as good as the dodo had. No complaining there.

'It's the truth! That's what they do to the remainder of those who don't survive the medical tests. Even some of those who do survive never make it back to domestic society, since they are surveyed and registered as a H.P.D.C., a Highly Potential Danger To Civilisation. Understand, son, that much worse would have become of your mother if she was submitted to the Southern Polar Region—', he stopped talking. 'Hold it there—I suspect you are vaguely familiar with the *Southern* Polar Region and what is rumoured happens there, am I right?'

Oscar hadn't been sure about the SPR until last night, during his conversation with Evanessa. Before then, it had all been whispers, word of mouth. But, now that he was certain, and in his father's company, he didn't want to verify his source of information as the Phestor's mutilated mistress. That was a lie for another day. 'Yeah. I've come across that rumour somewhere before. Probably those toffs at the Academy and all their boasting,' he falsely confessed to his father. 'Is it true?'

'Hell yeah!' his father spat. 'What do you think happened with the Seventh Nation all those years ago? They didn't just drop out to play golf. The Sixth and Seventh Nation were up to something there. And, I suspect, they still are today. That's what I've been trying to hint at. When they finally get their hands on our Unique Resource, all those feral Nations in the East will want to do with the atomic energy is advance their Blackout weaponry and extract radioactive waste from it for chemical weapons. I'm afraid the war hasn't ended until we can prevent that.'

'Did she die there? Did my mother die in that awful place?' Oscar didn't care for Conflicts and Blackout Attacks. He was desperate to know more about Cassandra Philson.

His father hesitated, staring numbly at the glass of *Kola Bear* next to his balled fist. DCD. Philson was scratching at the bottom of his barrel for words.

'Your mother—'

There was no point. Somebody was at the door. And his father bounced up before he could go on, eager to escape the story's conclusion. It was Stevenson who'd come to visit, dressed in his usual formal attire and crisp dreads. But even Oscar could see, from right across the room to where he was sitting, that something terribly distressing was definitely *up*. Something was *way up*. Stevenson was sporting the expression of a fourteen-year-old boy who'd just been informed that a fight had kicked off in the Academy playground. The look of sheer anxiety and awkward sheepishness all rolled into one. 'I suggest yeh gather yerself ASAP, sir.' His voice was still calm and collected. 'Dere's trouble.'

The City streets were unusually filled. It was never expected for there to be so much commotion at the time it was. *Especially on a Son-day.* The high streets overflowed with pedestrians flooding out in thousands. Up on the billboards in *Crystal Square*, cyclical screenings of the Hounding Trials were still alive and kicking even this near to midnight – the humping pug had just received his verdict to be put down the following morning – though very few pedestrians below were paying attention to these headlines. '*The Frisbee is finally over the fence for Pug Laurel! Tune-in after half an hour for our post-verdict interviews!*'

When Stevenson cruised the limousine through the Square, they were edging into crowds of people, who were purposefully roaming the streets, over-spilling pavements, pilgrimaging through the middle of roads, and all headed in the same direction. They were sauntering towards the Harkson Centre – the huge venue of restaurants, sports and music, which seemed to be open all the time (even on Son-days). From inside, one booming, but unintelligible voice could be heard, echoing out into the streets.

'Is that all coming from loud-speakers?' DCD. Philson asked. He was sitting in the passenger-seat, beside their chauffer. Oscar was in one of the backseats, his heart pumping a million beats per second. 'Isn't there usually big band music playing at this time?'

'Yup! It got everybody freaked,' Stevenson cursed. 'Nah one expect one man to mek ah much fuss at dis time of night. Yuh tek a look fuh yuhself, sir. Yuh tek a good lung look fuh yuhself.'

'A fuss?' DCD. Philson said. 'Does this concern me in particular?'

'He demand to speak to yuh in public. He want to mek ah nervous motion in de City so yeh know how serious he be. An' dem nervous tremor he mekin' wid great success.'

'Well, can't you tell me who he is first?' the Decider said.

'Me'fraid not, sir,' Stevenson responded. 'Him say he wou'd unleash chaos on de City if I tol' yuh who he were beforehand.'

'Was he afraid I might bring his mother along in the car journey up to the arena?' the Decider laughed the childish proposal away. 'What is this? Some silly child's play? Tell me the guy's name for crying out loud. Who is it that's wasting my time and causing all this cacophony in my city?'

Stevenson kept his eyes on the road and said nothing.

'Is it really that bad, Stevenson?' the Decider asked.

'This is a very different kind'ah trouble,' Stevenson finally admitted. 'It might be sensible to reflect on yer recent activities, Decidah. Them not too popular wid everyone.'

'When *are* they ever?' the Decider muttered spitefully.

The armoured limousine rolled to a stop in the Harkson car park, amongst a sea of others. Some vehicles had their lights on and their owners were inside, occupied by the radio or just too afraid to step out into the terrifying night. Further up, right beside the Harkson, was a huge telecommunications tower. A red light was glowing at the top of its antenna, feeding in a current signal. Surrounding it, the *HoloGram* screens and their projections had been cut to static. What had earlier been live screenings of the Media's public coverage was now replaced with: ***TRANSMISSION BLOCKED***. *Whoever it is*, Oscar imagined, *it had to be someone powerful*. For it had hacked the Media's servers and was holding them to ransom, while it broadcasted something else in its place at that very moment. They were about to head into it.

A barrage of six A.I. was there to meet them outside the Harkson Centre. In magnificent form, the A.I. divided into twos and formed a pack around the three of them. Two in front, two beside and two at the back. And from there, they were marched to the entrance.

Oscar, Stevenson, DCD. Philson and their shield of A.I. carved through the army of people outside the Harkson. The crowd of subordinates looked to be somehow magnetised to the voice addressing the entire City in East Dialect from the loud speakers inside. It was as if the Red-Man-With-Horns-Downstairs himself was possessing them and charging their every move, calling in all of his void-minded disciples. At the entrance, there was a flurry in the automatic-doors. More and more people were scuttling in and out. Mice in search of good-smelling cheese, but instead discovering a trap and quickly hurrying back the way they'd come. It appeared all the eyes of the world were on the Decider and less were on the chauffer leading the great man's sequel under his tall shadow. The Media ambushed the Decider's entourage on entry through the doors. The barricade of A.I. protecting the trio from all angles tightened, preventing anyone from getting too close. Pressers were on the scene like flies, kicking and punching through the mesh, poking their impressively thin, flute-like microphones into the gaps and shamelessly holding out their *HoloPads* for the Decider to record his own quotes onto their articles… '*How long do you expect your alliance with the East to withhold, Decider?*' '*Where do you stand on your policies with the Seventh Nation, Decider?*', '*Decider, what are your options with dealing with Phestor Xenol of the Sixth Nation—? Your approach is quite unprecedented—!*'

The Decider shut it all out, brushing off the fierce attention that was being drenched over him by the Media. He played the situation like there wasn't a single Presser in sight and coolly proceeded into the arena's lobby. The charming few attempted to wrangle a word out of Oscar, but he'd learned well to follow suit with his father. Regardless of the Decider's lack of response, the Pressers persisted in pursuing them, pecking at the shield of A.I. with clawing hands and swinging feet, violently trying to break through. There must have been a hundred of them, but no matter what they did, the Tin Men were too tough to penetrate and the escort continued through the busy lobby, swarmed by the City Media like spermatozoa fighting to fertilise an ovum.

The belly of the Harkson Centre was pure commercialism. Although the shops and market stalls were closed, the fast-food franchises, cinemas and evening restaurants were still crawling with life. There was a thick, sickly stench of wafting grease and fries and ketchup and popcorn following you wherever you went. Through a small nook in the crowd of Pressers, Oscar caught sight of the *JGC* (*Jerk Grilled Chicken*) fast food shack where Stevenson sometimes treated him to wings and a creamy side of coconut milkshake between his father's summonses. *JGC* was rammed with bodies, so full in fact that the people in there didn't only appear to be the typical Small Island Folk you usually saw, but also included uncomfortable West Folk sheltering from the heaving hordes out in the arena's lobby. Hectic humanity was at work, as people weren't actually *going* out, eating *out* or shopping until they *passed out*. They were simply hanging about. Terrorised, yet hypnotised and obsessive, they were definitely here for the show. What show? Well, the only show in town, a cybernetic hack of live video footage exclusively broadcast on the only big screens that were actually still on in the entire city this late. These big, holographic projections, which hovered above the Harkson's lobby, normally showed music videos or news coverage or sports highlights. They weren't screening any of this tonight. A Ball Game had apparently been postponed mid-final, due to "*a clash with unexpected and unavoidable proceedings*". Instead of that night's scheduled entertainment, the Harkson's guests were forced to view a man dressed in a golden robe and wearing sunshades. What showed of his actual person, his physical looks, was that he was rather young - maybe in his late-twenties or early-thirties. Nevertheless, he was extremely tanned and his hair was long, thick and braided. The scary thing was that he'd been watching the Decider's entourage from the moment they'd arrived. On the footage, he was sitting in a grim and uncharacteristic room, directly addressing a camera on an *ORAMA* live-feed. 'I demand to speak to Decider Philson of the First Nation!' the man on the screen thundered. 'I must address him *now* and no one in his place!'

There was a fantastic groan from the crowd, accompanied with screaming and shoving and crying all around. People clearly in fear for their lives. And the sheer size of the amassing audience was getting dangerous. DCD. Philson was somewhere in there, his barrage of A.I. fighting its way through the bystanders and the Media swarm clung to the limbs of his metal guards. The Decider was taken away from his son and chauffer by two of the A.I. when he requested that they get him to a place where he could be seen distinctly.

On the other hand, the other four A.I. remained firm around Oscar, shielding him from the overwhelming sway of the crowd. He rubbed close to Stevenson and was supported by the bulk of the chauffer's extreme tallness within the frightening crush of A.I. and Presser tension. Here, like everyone else, they waited for the Decider to speak in response to the agitator.

'First Nation! Where is your Decider?' the man was roaring. 'I have a warning and a request to propose to him! *Where is your leader?*'

DCD. Philson had managed to slither out of the crowd, reaching the boastful fountain-statue in the centre of the lobby. It was an enormous, marble cherub. Already knowing what he would do, he began to climb it. The two A.I. that had led him stopped at the foot of the fountain and were joined by a ten-strong team of Harkson Security A.I., forming a fence around the monument and blocking the lingering Pressers from hounding the Decider further. DCD. Philson hopped onto the book the giant cherub was holding, balancing between the words "*KAPPA*" and "*LEONIS*", and hoisted himself onto its shoulders. When stood atop the fountain, he waved at the nearest screen. 'I'M DOWN HERE! LOOK AT ME! GET YOUR FOCUS RIGHT! I'M DOWN HERE!'

The man on the screen spotted the individual he'd been searching for and smirked triumphantly. 'Congratulations, First Nation! You did what I asked! Good Evening, DCD. Philson!'

'What are you playing at, Serpens? Why are you spooking my city?' Philson lashed out. 'If you want to try something out on me, come and face me like a grown-man! Don't start causing massacres! Not where I'm living and breathing!'

'I have a confession to make,' Serpens said. 'And I want to know you're listening. I need to know that *everybody's* listening!'

Oscar and Stevenson came to the bottom of the fountain. They were both looking up, trying to hear his father. *The man on the screen is Phestor Serpens,* Oscar thought. It had to be.

'Seeing as you've brought us all here, you might as well make your bloody confession!' DCD. Philson growled.

'First, I'd just like to let you know that I've been made very aware of your involvement with Phestor Xenol and the Sixth Nation. A Spy Drone notified me on the exact date and time Xenol arrived there in your Nation - yesterday, last night - and I'm sure you can understand how I was turned sour by this knowledge, that you'd found unentitled acceptance within my former ally, Xenol. I was also informed that the pair of you have been organising deals over the diamond cores on the borders of my Nation. Might I remind you, Decider, that the Sixth Nation has no business with us here in the Seventh Nation. We ended our pact with Sixth years ago. We do not share our territory. We do not share our land. Therefore, we do not share our material or our natural wealth with the Sixth Nation for that matter. There's no need to explain yourself on Xenol's behalf. There was little you could do to avoid him. He came to visit you covertly and uninvited. He has a habit of that. And I'm going to punish him for his touristic ordeal.

'As for you, well—I'm giving you the opportunity to make a decision, Decider. It's quite simple really. Fairer than what I previously had in mind for you. I'd originally planned to send out daggers for you, but felt that it wouldn't be as progressive - seeing as we're already at war - and I thought that your grand power could be put to a more effective use. So, here are your options. Either you surrender yourself or one of your Sister Nations to a Category One Blackout Attack, which would most certainly put a fatal damper on the West as much as it would cost us a worthwhile blow in return, or you could do me the pleasure of capturing and bringing me one easy prize. One priceless treasure.'

'What would that be?' DCD. Philson said. His insides were on fire.

'Bring to me Phestor Xenol's invaluable mistress,' Serpens demanded. 'Bring me his mistress and we will conclude an end to our ways.'

'How long did he give us?' Phestor Xenol spoke in an undertone over the Decider's Table.

After a sleepless night, the Phestor was back at DCD. Philson's residence first thing the next morning and Oscar wasn't surprised to find him there. If anything, Oscar was relieved to see that Xenol had, at least, *some* respect and *some* concern to answer for the heated confrontation that had sparked from his enigmatic tour of the West. There was no pistachio ice cream to be seen – it was definitely a discussion of the most serious kind that the Phestor was having with the Decider at his Table. The Stateship wasn't present at the meeting, which Oscar found weird, because he was a man always keen to grab a seat beside the Decider at critical times this. Perhaps, his father had deliberately chosen not to enlighten the Stateship on this morning's arrangements, for he anticipated the Stateship's ruffled opinion of the Phestor would bring an undesirable pulse to the matter in motion, and at this prickly stage the last thing anyone wanted was an impulsive reaction. When the Phestor had arrived, his father had apologised for how 'unreceptive and rude' the Stateship had been towards him and his mistress during the Annum Summit meal. That was all he mentioned about his colleague and the Stateship wasn't mentioned again. Nevertheless, there were still A.I. posted about the Decider's residence, keeping an eye on the two leaders. Four of them, one guarding each one of the Table Room's exits.

Phestor Xenol had his hands on the Table, laid upon the Solar Blade. His eyes were fixed on the weapon as he spoke and they didn't budge. This time, the Phestor was the one who'd been formally seated at the opposite head of the Table, instead of Oscar. Customs aside, DCD. Philson wanted to cordon Xenol's eye contact so he could extract honesty from the East tyrant like sap from a tree. Oscar sat along the length of the Table between the two men, facing a shielded Evanessa, who was trained not to look at any of the men at the Table. Especially avoiding Oscar. Never before had Oscar been declined the head of the Decider's Table and this would have usually upset him. But, engulfed by the crisis flaring around him like wildfire, he was sharply listening to the talk, too intrigued to pipe up over anything else.

'It's your girl he wants,' DCD. Philson said, nodding his head at Evanessa. 'That's all Phestor Serpens requests in return for the City's safety.'

Xenol fiddled with the edge of the blade, focusing as he rubbed a thumb along it. 'Makes no difference to our shared interests, surely?' he said.

'Umm...,' the Decider raised both eyebrows. 'I'm afraid this means our settlement goes out the window here. Unless you're willing to opt him a bargain of your own that can outweigh his threatening demands – which isn't looking very likely at this point.'

'No bargain. He'll have to pay for her if he wants her. Does he prefer to pay in blood, diamond or in cash? Did you ask him that?' Phestor Xenol lifted his eyes from the sword at long last, giving the Decider a blunt glance before stubbornly returning to his fondling. 'I'm not willing to swap a valuable negotiating asset for the sake of your Nation's existence. That's where we are and where we'll stay.'

'Are you mitigating his threat? Did our loose, little conversation the other day make you comfortable to play around with his vicious demands? Because that wasn't what I intended when I let you remain in my Nation, speak your mind freely, and take temporary residency in my tower, I can assure you of that,' DCD. Philson spat, severely aggravated. 'I don't approve of your attitude, for this is a threat orchestrated by *your* region we're talking about here—*the East*! *Your futile monkey-land!* By all means, I'm prepared to war with Serpens to defend my Nation and my city. I'm prepared to utterly demolish the Seventh Nation once and for all, against all morals and ethics, and do so right behind your spineless back. I don't need you to approve of that. So, don't you part ways with me just yet! Oh, no! And don't you even dare try and side with this menace, now that Serpens has tripped a nerve with you! Otherwise, I'll come down on you like a comet and crush you too if I must!'

'There's no need to tempt me, Decider,' Phestor Xenol's eyes rolled up at the ceiling and returned to the blade. 'No need to provoke spite that isn't there. We're already arch allies now, remember? I do not respect you or your Nation, but our interests are in good orbit for the time being. And Phestor Serpens knows they are. As I've already made very clear, my days of coalition with Phestor Serpens and the Seventh Nation are numbered. You don't have to worry about my long-dead loyalties. Look, your desperation is hard to miss and your reason to serve this man's ugly threat is a valid one—'

'Then, why won't you help us?' DCD. Philson argued impatiently.

'Decider, arch allies are very different to normal allies. The only tie between us is the proposal of prosperity served with a side of peaceful coexistence. And, well, as for my mistress—she is, after all, a very unique and profitable ornament in my dynasty. Her muted manners and responsive demeanour resonates as a symbol of my control, my dominion as a ruler of the Sixth Nation, the new supreme kingdom of the East. If I were to simply submit her over to Serpens, well…it would be unthinkable to my reputation. It would suggest a transference of power, a sign of weakness. This woman must remain at my side indefinitely.'

Oscar shifted uneasily in his seat when Xenol said this.

'I'm not buying your stirring nonsense!' DCD. Philson belted. 'And I'm *not* surrendering to the Seventh Nation or that lunatic whom they call their leader!'

'Then, I guess, we're at a stale-mate here, Decider.' Phestor Xenol was smiling. 'It seems to me that this agreement, or alliance, or whatever you wish to call it that we had, isn't working out too well for anyone's Nation. The best thing for me to do would probably be to disassociate myself from you once and for all. If you do hope to agree with me on that, I'd be more than happy to slide out of our arrangements and allow you to get on with this situation yourself. That way, things between East and West can continue going the way they've been going for decades.'

'There will be no sliding out, Xenol—!'

'*Phestor* Xenol.'

'Sure, *Phestor Xenol.* We're both due to submit ourselves to something at the mercy of Serpens. Even if I don't hand over that woman of yours to Phestor Serpens, he'll still be after her. And you also, it seems. Serpens threatened your life as undeniably as he blackmailed the City. You still need our asylum. You need the West to protect you and your mistress.'

Oscar nearly fell off his chair in astonishment. He dared to look at Evanessa. She was strikingly indifferent about this offer, almost like she didn't understand what the Decider was saying – but Oscar was one of the very few who knew this wasn't true in the slightest.

'There's no deal here. No negotiating with barbarians,' Xenol shrugged. 'Face it, you'll have to surrender and I'll have to make for the hills – if they're not too high.'

'Have you even got a clue how great of an impact another Blackout Attack would have on the world?' DCD. Philson rapped his fingers under the Table nervously. 'Surely, you must remember when it happened, the original Blackout Attack that the First Nation launched on the old capital of the Eighth Nation, Salg Perdorn. It's funny saying that name now – surprisingly easy to remember, but, at the same time, understandably hard to swallow. Massacres on that scale make you wish the Conflicts had never begun.'

'Forget about the Blackout Attacks! Those are West Worries! Serpens' people have long since acclimatised to the concept of nuclear bludgeoning! The folk in the Seventh Nation still blame the Old King who ruled all the East for beginning these Conflicts in the first place,' Xenol protested, entranced by the thought of the Conflicts in their early days. 'They call their Old King "the only East Man who would have allied with the West" – not such a terrifying idea in those times before the Conflicts began. But unthinkable now. Blasphemous even. I am the first East leader to make such a radical move by coming to you, Decider. That is why you must understand I'm afraid. Phestor Serpens' dynasty is the absolute opposite to the Old King's regime – "the Liberal King" they labelled him, "the Punk King". And I fear that they might tarnish me with the same brush, the very same slander, when all I do in this space with you, Decider, is for the benefit of the East and nothing else. The future. The Punk King's demise was the reason the East Nations were once so close, and when the Sixth Nation put an end to the King, my Nation arose as the new leading Nation of the East. It had been a critical decision of similar magnitude to the West's decision to impose the Black Nine Attacks—to assassinate a Punk disguised as a King—very divisive indeed. That Punk King would have destroyed the East, sending its character and its traditions to oblivion.'

The Decider had to think hard about these facts before he came to disagree with his former enemy once more. 'If the Last King of the East hadn't been taken out, an alternative ideology would have ruled the East and the Conflicts would have never persisted this long. Blackout Nine would have never happened.'

'But, if he'd lived, he'd have annexed my Nation and others with his poisonous liberal philosophy. Decider, I am no liberal, just a businessman. If the Old King's bloodline still reigned today, you would still be at war with him for far worse reasons. Rather than spoiling my efforts and fending off barbarians like Serpens and the Eighth Nation, you would have been fighting against a reckless, liberalist tyrant all this time,' the Phestor explained. He took the Solar Blade off the Table and stood it up on the floor beside him, so that it leaned against the ledge of the Table. 'Together, you and I must make another fateful decision, Decider. We are arch allies because, regardless of our history, we are the ones with the mutuality here. We two prize an unlikely, shared interest, harmonising stronger than our own neighbouring Nations: to surpass and father over all other Nations with supremacy and purity. However, to succeed in this ambition, we must prioritise the death of the Seventh Nation—kill Serpens. And whilst he does not yet know our true plot, he will come to suspect our danger to him if we let time pass. So, as with Blackout Nine and as with the East King, we must proceed swiftly in this objective, for it is a critical decision that will bring at last an end to the war and wonderful change to the world. Only we can make this decision—you and I—Decider.'

The Decider took a weighty swig from his wineglass before rinsing out his haunting woes with more reflections on the past. 'It must remain as speculation then,' he declared, coughing on the last drop. 'The fear held above the heads of both our peoples is also shared. Simple-minded, the subordinates dwell on the past and bow to the finger of blame so dearly; our lips can deceive their minds. It will be necessary to devise some discrepancy for us to travel undetected by the Media. There must be restricted publicity of our whereabouts, let alone any public vigilance of our working plan to destroy Serpens.'

'Any suggestions of where to begin planning such a complicated plot?' Xenol said. 'We do not have long.'

'All my meetings are held in the Surveillance.☆ It was in the Surveillance where the decision to launch the Blackout Nine strike was made. The moment that decision was made, Salg Perdorn and most the Eighth Nation deteriorated in less than an hour. Half a billion people perished in those Nine Attacks. Other Nations were left severely wounded and scarred. The Surveillance can stage an effective assault anywhere.'

'A strategic assault like that on an entire Nation would be too big, leaving us with a plethora of implications,' Phestor Xenol added. His distaste for the idea couldn't be mistaken. Not behind those clean, little spectacles that shrunk his eyes.

'Never since has there been a fallout as devastating as Nine,' the Decider said. 'Needless to say, it wasn't that long ago and the West's atomic advantage has improved astronomically in recent years. Which is why you should discard your attitude towards our 'stale-mate'. The odds of your Nation's survival fair better with us than with the Seventh

---

☆ The Surveillance was the oldest and greatest secret kept by the West. Essentially, it was a security agency based in a mountaintop observatory in the Third Nation, which secretly housed many of the war councils and defense meetings held by the Decider and his fellow Ministors and Militia. After Blackout Nine happened and wiped the Eighth Nation and half of the Seventh off the map, a rogue server in the Media Network leaked information about the Surveillance to the world. The secret organization was then triumphantly put on trial by the former East Embassy in the West for authorising Conflict agendas that went against the Laws of Nuclear Warfare and International Demilitarisation.

Nation. I think I'm fair in saying that we are heading into the makings of the harshest Blackout Attack yet, just waiting to be provoked by the next in line along the West's shortening list of targets. Unless you can think of better ways of dealing with your noisy neighbour.'

Oscar squirmed in his chair again.

'What are you suggesting? That everywhere in the East is primitive and barbaric? That we only respond to rockets falling from the sky?' Phestor Xenol picked his words wisely, speaking slowly and clearly around his accent, starved of his natural Dialect. 'I have to remind that we do, in fact, now have access to our own nuclear arsenals and the Seventh and Eighth Nations have procured their own atomic assurances in the past. So, Serpens wasn't just flexing his muscles when he threatened you last night. Blackout Attacks are as much our card to play as they are yours. Now, you didn't answer my question. How long do we have to make our decision?'

'Where did Serpens gain access to nuclear arms?' DCD. Philson said, rapidly mistrustful of the other man again. 'There is no longer a legitimate source of nuclear arms in the East.'

'Answer my question first.'

'Where did he steal it from?'

'An answer for an answer,' Xenol jested.

The two men hesitated cleverly.

'We have until Sunday to make our transaction,' DCD. Philson disclosed. 'Deliver the girl to Quomer, *Mayn Street*, on Sunday, alive.'

'Alive? Did he expect me to kill her first? He's still as tactless as he's always been and still immeasurably unfit to lead his Nation. This girl is too priceless to tamper with in such a way.' Phestor Xenol didn't even look at Evanessa as he talked about her. 'And to *Quomer*? He wants to collect the girl from my own turf, not delivered gift-wrapped to *his* Nation instead? Very strange. Serpens has never visited my Nation before. I should expect he'll send someone other than himself to collect this prize he yearns so much.' The Phestor sighed. 'No class at all.'

'Your turn,' DCD. Philson was tapping his fingers in bad rhythm again.

'Oh, yeah, right, he's always had nuclear power. You've just never known and never been told.'

'I don't believe that. Where did he steal it?'

'He stole it from himself. Does knowing he stole it from somewhere make things any better for you?' Phestor Xenol went into an immediate fit of laughter.

'This isn't a fool-around!' DCD. Philson cried. 'You need to put things into more perspective! The East – your original allies – are going to host another Blackout Attack! On my Nation this time! Millions are going to die if we do nothing to prevent it!'

'Then give us an idea, a perfect plan if you must! But a quick one, since we do not have enough time to spare for aesthetics! Sunday is too soon for us to react with anything alternative to his demands or to respond with any overthought, fine-tuned practice! We can only improvise. However, I am not inclined to submit my greatest asset, my best bargaining chip, to that monster. What do you have in store? *Nothing?* I've got an idea: What about your own kid over there? What about you, boy? What do you think your father should do to save his arse?'

Oscar stared blankly at the East Man. His thick-lenses were miniaturising his ocular identity again. They were blocking out his emotions. Oscar had to compensate for the widely drawn grin that ripped the Phestor's face in half. 'What do you think?' the Phestor repeated. 'If you were in your father's shoes and you had to play Decider for thirty seconds, what would you say?'

Oscar glanced between the Phestor and his father. Wordless. Phestor Xenol was smiling warmly like a faithful grandmother having every second of consideration to listen to her grandchild without doubting or demeaning, whereas his father was shooting daggers at him from his expression and scowling with warped lips. In his peripheral-vision, Oscar caught the shape of Evanessa. She was definitely watching him and she was only doing so because they all were – not to look out of character. He didn't want anything to happen to Evanessa. Not because he felt that it would be the right thing to do, which was how his illiberal father would have meditated around the problem, but because he now had a better understanding of her predicament and didn't want her to descend into madness and anxiety so youthfully, like his mother had, after a life that had been endorsed by four patriarchs named Torture.

'I have no say,' Oscar said obediently. 'My father's the Decider…' He finally managed to catch Evanessa's eyes. They were reassuring and retelling. '…And this is his residence. The decision is his.'

'Perfectly rehearsed!' Phestor Xenol chuckled. 'Oh, your father must be so proud. He's grown a child out of his own diligence. Do you enjoy being trained like an A.I.? Being programmed by daddy? Are you grateful for that?'

Oscar's father had his head bowed, chin rolled under his neck. Then, he raised his forehead high from the Table and momentarily turned away from the people sited in front of him, said nothing.

'Actually…' Oscar perked up the confidence. 'I do have something of an opinion on the matter.'

Phestor Xenol nodded his head, still looking at DCD. Philson. 'Yes? I'm listening. We all are.'

'No,' his father warned. 'You don't.'

Oscar shut his mouth and turned away. He didn't want to see his father or Evanessa. The best place to stare, he figured, was probably at Phestor Xenol – at the other head of the Table, where he usually sat.

'And have *you* got a plan now?' Phestor Xenol said to the Decider.

'What if we agreed to deliver the girl, but deceived him instead?' DCD. Philson said.

'Trick him, you mean? Trick Serpens?'

'Instead of handing over your daughter, we could use the transaction as a prime opportunity to strike our knife into the heart of the Seventh Nation. A move like that would end the war.'

'Wasn't that what we'd originally planned to do?' Phestor Xenol said.

'Not specifically a direct attack on the infrastructure of the Seventh Nation itself. But a targeted jab at its leader. This automatically gives us a way into the Seventh Nation without even having to set foot in Urbania, an easy entry-pass.☆ We convince him to make a personal visit to Quomer on kind terms. We come with the girl, he surrenders his tough talk and we land our own attack before he can get his hands on her.'

'It would be suicidal,' Xenol complained. 'We'd be jeopardising a century's worth of agreements my Nation has built with the Seventh Nation on oil and resource and diamond. The Seventh Nation has diamond-cores like we do in Sixth – a hundred times more! We'd be wasting all of that for the sake of what?'

'Well, he must want the girl for some specific reason, right?' the Decider presumed. 'Otherwise he'd be requesting one of the other things you mentioned.'

☆ Urbania was the corrupt capital of the Seventh Nation: depicted by its archaic, bleak skyline ("The Tunnel Towers") that was stripped of all commercialism, its nondescript population drowned deep within the darkness and its criminal municipalities that were poorly disciplined by a disorder of degraded A.I. from the late 2020s.

'I can't imagine her offering him anything more than the instrument of her body.' Xenol shrugged. 'He likes to play these little games. Don't worry—he gets bored quickly.'

'What's so high in demand about her?' the Decider asked. 'There must be a more purposeful reason than that.'

At this point, Oscar saw that Phestor Xenol had begun to slowly remove the Solar Blade from its vertical leaning stance against the ledge of the Table and tucked it beneath his chair, as if trying to fend off any speculations regarding it. 'Fine,' he said. 'Fine, we'll do it. We'll play it on him and *pretend* to hand her over for the sake of the goods, but *only* if I have the honours of the larger share. It's the East, after all. And I'm going to be responsible for sweeping up the shards once Serpens is assassinated.'

'We'll see about that.'

'No, we won't. It's that or no plan and no settlement,' Phestor Xenol bartered firmly. 'I'm your arch ally at a price.'

'Okay. I suppose that's fair. Then, the preference is yours.'

'I also suggest that Serpens is swiftly dealt with on his arrival,' Phestor Xenol said. 'He's an aching soul and hates being left too long in the dark. Especially, by his former ally. If we give him the time of day, he'll figure things are going off and we don't want that. Was it this Sunday he wanted her by at the latest?'

'This coming sunday, yes.'

'Of course, he wants us to be present at the Dusk of Offerings,' Phestor Xenol realised.☆ 'In that case, we've picked the best time to startle the East. The perfect day for an assassination. There'll be loads of crowds and parades in my city, in Quomer. In that case, allow him to enjoy the festivities and the parade. Hell, I'll invite him aboard the Municipal Float. And, once we arrive at the end of the procession, I'll be sure that he's served a bullet before he can lay a finger on the girl.'

'That way, the assassination will look like an openly debatable incident and what will remain of the East's resources will be legitimately ours to take,' DCD. Philson said. 'I'll inform my most

---

☆ The Dusk of Offerings was a seasonal festival in the East that takes place during midsummer. At the Quomer festival, people exchanged offerings, such as natural resources, food, money, machinery and, in some cases, sacrifice human life itself for the purpose of trading blood and organs for small oil and fuel distributions and other rare resources in return. It was a big day for people in the East. Bigger than Christmas. In fact, it allowed many people to survive until Christmas.

confidential associates of this and I'll arrange a flight for tomorrow morning. Be ready to communicate, as I'll be keeping in close touch.'

'Don't you worry,' Phestor Xenol said, standing up from the head of the Table. 'I'll dress the girl in her best clothes on the day. The performance has entered its final act and the curtain call is in sight.'

After he said this, Oscar's father led them to the door and they were gone.

On his return to the Table, DCD. Philson reclaimed his seat and poured himself a glass of water from the auto-cooling flagon, which slid towards him from the middle of the Table on its own. It felt to Oscar that there was suddenly a lot more area surrounding them both. Somehow, with the two visitors now departed, his father seemed a universe away. They were just as close and just as far as they'd always been whenever they met in this room. Alone together. It was too quiet; Oscar put an end to the silence.

'When will you be coming back?' he asked his father.

DCD. Philson took a quick swig from the glass and then looked at the boy thoughtfully, processing his most inoffensive words before splaying them. 'I don't know when I'll be coming back,' his father responded quietly.

Oscar hesitated. '*Will* you be coming back?'

So did his father, as this was a good question, a very good question. The man in the pristine suit and tie didn't answer. The light in the Table Room was dim; it was always dim and the Decider mooned under it like a lost, desperate puppy under a dying streetlamp in the night. His father was an ashy grey in skin colour, but his eyes were alert like bright headlights and nearly colourless. 'While I'm gone, I'm going to need you to keep things in order. Understand?' his father said. Oscar nodded. 'If you need anything, Stevenson will always be around to lend you a helping hand and, only in these circumstances alone, I'm allowing you to enter my residence as you wish. The House A.I. will be with me on my journey to the East, so you won't be fully protected like you usually are in this side of town. So, I have to demand that you remain in the City Central for the duration of my absence and do as Stevenson says from now onwards. He's in charge. And, if there are any more *bad dreams* or any other foolishness like that, you have my permission to visit Doctor Islie further downtown. I've paid in advance for a few more sessions, if you desire them. We need to get this infectious disorder out of your mentality. Especially, since you're going to have to someday step up to the mantle once I'm gone and become a stable and commanding Decider yourself.'

'Whoever said you were stepping down anytime soon?' Oscar shrugged.

There was more awkward silence.

'We both know that's inevitable,' his father told him. 'One day, I'm going to meet my demise and that'll be the day when you're going to have to start making decisions. You are my son and I have faith in you.'

'You know I don't want that to happen.'

'Don't speak that way. Not now. Not at any time do you have the right to speak like that. Find your manners, get some self respect and grow up, Oscar!'

'The same way I don't have the right to say *what* I want to say and *how* I want to say it? Not in front of anyone? In case it makes you look bad?'

His father took one last gulp from his glass and landed it down empty with a thump. 'You best return to your residence now. I need to get packing. Go on, leave.'

Oscar stood up and paced to the doorway. He didn't see his father lighting a new cigar and eyeballing him, sticking on him just to make sure that he left when he was told to. 'Oh, and, Oscar, one last thing!' his father called to him as he was just about to leave the room. 'Don't you even look at that Phestoress again!'

'I don't recall,' Oscar challenged, pale all over. 'I never spoke—'

'You *spoke* to her too, did you?' his father murmured with a feeble smirk.

Speechless, Oscar floated down the hall and vanished, closing the front door reticently behind him.

The Water Phoenixes...

Overcoming the mountains, the waterfall birds reunite us with the ocean, copious and spanning from the shores of Leo Island to where the horizon cradles the sun like a newborn. Another day has awoken and it's the first time somnolence has found me in the Dreamerverse. I am humbled by weariness. These light-blue wings condensed of water are doing well to carry me into my next sleep. Over the last two or three miles of the flight, Samuella's been nursing Camson and me to knock back a purple seed, so that we stay put on bird back and don't end up on Stewart's minefield of firefly jars again. The funny thing I've come to realise from previous experiences with the purple seeds is that they'll stow you in dormancy for a full day – and restore your position wherever you "drop off" on Constellation Planet – but then, upon resurging into the Dreamerverse, you'll annoyingly struggle to keep awake here, since their advantageous effect is so strong it makes you thirst for another relapse before long. It's only been a few seconds since I've reawakened on the back of this aqueous phoenix and I'm already sinking back into Mankind's World. So far, in the real world I've been a narcoleptic and in the Dreamerverse I've been an insomniac. However, right now, this logic is being inverted.

I roll the Constellation Map open on the giant bird's back, pinning it down with my hands on its edges and keeping it held between the flapping wings as consistently as I can. It's a challenge, but there's a knack to it. Good thing the parchment is waterproof; otherwise the Map would be seeping clean through the phoenix's back. Only once I see the stars and locations trying to appear on the Map, do I notice that they're simultaneously fading away. There's a mishmash of images that are *definitely* there, images that are *almost* there and images that are *nowhere* to be seen at all. Soon, the latter becomes the most common. The Map returns to blankness.

'Guys...' I don't know how I'm going to break it to them. 'We're Mapless.'

Well done! I tell myself. A very convincing way of "breaking it to them".

'What do you mean?' says Samuella. She's lying on her belly, her head cushioned by a back of foamy feathers.

'The Map's deteriorated into nothing again,' I alert the others. 'It's blank. There's nothing left.'

'What?' Samuella and Camson share a brief gush of horror. I'm in the middle, so it feels like their both kissing cheeks on either side of my face.

'It's all gone! I can't read the way! We're lost!'

'Give it here,' she reaches out to me. 'Let me take a look at it.'

I hand it to her and she opens it for herself. I wait for a while, before her eyes widen and a smile climbs onto her face.

'What's happening?' Camson asks. 'What do you see?'

'The Map!' she celebrates, glowing at its novelty to her eyes. 'I can see the Map! Whoa-whoa-whoa—and that's us here—and that's the comet trail, stretched out from Leo Island and the Kappa Mountains!'

'That must mean it's your turn, then,' I tell her. 'The Map's probably worked out that we've already been to my destination and we're currently one emerald-down. We've only got two more to go.'

'How are you so certain that they're all emeralds?' Camson reasons. 'Couldn't they all be relatively different, depending on the destination or the person leading the way? *Yours* was an emerald, because it was found in the Falls of Fortune. Whereas, ours are probably different.'

'That's a point,' Samuella says.

'But aren't they all targeted at the same cause? They're needed to defeat the Drag-in somehow,' I tell them. 'So, they should all be significantly the same, being from the same material of origin. Maybe they contribute to something bigger, like, I don't know—a powerful, but rare, source of fuel.'

'Let's not get ahead of ourselves,' Samuella says. 'We can decide on what the emeralds are used for once we have all three. There's a reason All Eyes didn't tell us any of that before we set out.'

'Our haste almost got us killed by that gorilla queen,' I mention. 'If it hadn't been for someone warning me about the danger of Queen

Cassandra's desire deterrent, we'd have been foiled before we even laid eyes on the emerald.'

'A *desire deterrent*? Who warned you about that?' Camson picks up on this, utterly confused.

'When I was lost in the caves and searching for you guys, a voice latched onto me. The voice of a spirit, someone I knew. It was the essence of my mother,' I announce confidently. 'Her spirit came looking for me in the caves and she stayed beside me the whole way to the trove room, where we were reunited with her current manifestation – the gorilla. She helped me to fend off the Nightmares, reminded me to withhold my willing desires in the presence of the queen, and she guided me to find my way back to you two. And then, to put my suspicions to rest, she revealed herself as a loose fragment of the spirit embodying the queen.' I blink wildly at the other two Night Dreamers on phoenix-back, neither is convinced by my story. 'Why are you both looking at me like that? I'm not lying to you!'

The egg on Camson's face is frying in the sun's heat. 'Cassandra was *your mother*?' he stutters. 'Then what must that mean—?'

'She was a Night Dreamer,' I add vainly. 'What—you still don't believe me?

'Impossible,' Samuella shakes her head. 'Night Dreamers don't come from the same blood. They couldn't possibly. The Stellar Gods' selection is random.'

'But perhaps our categorised disconnection with each other also runs in our bloodlines,' I ponder, 'which could mean the two of you may also have relatives who were Night Dreamers. Our disassociation might be historic, even ancestral!'

'When your mother shifted form to a lioness, you were talking to her spirit for a while,' Samuella says. 'What did she tell you?'

'She told me to let my instinct be the judge. We all should.'

'Then, where are going?' Camson asks, swinging the focus from me to Samuella. 'Where's that rock hiding this time?'

'Well, we're definitely headed across the planet this time. Heading *East* – or *Pegasus*. Directly over Central Island and to the other side. Where we're going is on the other side of Constellation Planet, the ***X***-mark is placed on some island titled *Pegasus*.'

'Any clue what we should expect?' Camson says.

'You'll just have trust my instincts, Cammy,' she responds.

An hour over the ocean and we're riding beneath the deliverance of a starker sky, one gifted to us with the nativity of daylight's fiery youth, freckled with lithe, sclera-white clouds and a hiatus from the stale humidity. Judging by their elegance and calming control, these aqueous phoenixes adore the wind in their wings. Their heads are small and slinky with flicks of a liquid crest flowing along the centre. Flying low and almost touching the water, the insensitive current cannot keep up with the phoenixes. Every so often, we're greeted by friendly dolphins, which burst out from the water in their race alongside the phoenixes. The dolphins jump high enough for me to reach out to feel them – are they more organic vessels hosted by human spirits? Their glazed bodies are smooth and slippery under my palm. Authentic. I've never seen such amazing creatures in my life. All I can familiarise with dolphins are *the images displayed in those fictional picture books I'd read as a young child and wildlife shows on HoloVision.* But seeing and touching them truly in the flesh is incomparable. Unpredictable. I envy those who are welcomed to such an experience as this on a regular basis. Suddenly, home begins to prod at me again. I remember *the City and all of its dazzle and glamour and limelight and plasticity.* It has no impact. Not anymore. *The City* has become the dream. *The City* is the dead, open plain of unknowing and irrelevance. And now, I have fewer intentions of going back, less desire of returning to that tinsel town. I now, instead, feel that my instincts – my most human instincts – naturally belong here, in this place. Here is new freedom, here is beauty and liberty, here is where the spirit of Cassandra Philson roams free. What if All Eyes meant what he'd said? What if I really could stay here forever? And maybe that was what my mother had spoken about being remunerated with what I most desire. Do I really desire this place more than I do Mankind's World? To live and die here would be a dream come true (quite literally). There's no debating that.

This is where humanity belongs. I'm convinced! Because, of all things, I'm actually safer here. I don't feel exempt from mortal commonality, I'm nothing extraordinary. I'm not a Decider's heir. And I don't need to be conforming to those superior or have others depend on my authority. In this existence, I am the curator of my opinions and the determiner of my future. Alive and unleashed to *say* what I want and *do* what I want and *be* what I want. The world filled with millions of stars is no longer a fantasy. It's no longer a resounding dream. No more a wish waiting to come true.

It's home.

'*Are you still finding it hard to believe?*'

Chapter Five

The Soothsayers' Bunker

When the morning after his father's private meeting arrived in its youngest hours, Oscar woke without a start and curled tiredly on his side with the duvet's hem submerging everything from his forehead downwards. Suspecting it to be dawn or some time shortly before his Tuesday alarm went off – outside was darker than usual for a midsummer wake up call – he turned towards the wide window showcasing the Cityscape and saw the curtains had been left drawn. The clouds out there weren't the only killjoys hiding daybreak; the City's emblematic rain showers had also come knocking again. Recently, he'd been waking up a lot more randomly than he normally did. A Tuesday morning – Tuesday the Sixteenth of July, to be precise – would be no exception in his current spate of lucid dreaming. The world in his dreams was dictating his life for him when he slept and woke, and when he would transit between Constellation Planet and Mankind's World. Would he ever see the back of this condition, this unpredictable sleeping pattern?

Rising from under the duvet, he found Kyma in her regular sleeping spot at the foot-end of the mattress. The *RoBone* was still wedged between her jaws as she half-dozed in an uncomfortably distorted position. Oscar didn't like to disturb her as she slept – even when it looked like she was pretending. The fringe over her cutting eyes made her seem unsociable and grumpy. It was no one's wish to tiptoe around a moping mutt all day. So, he considerately waited for her to roll over before he slipped out of bed, feet firmly landing on the immaculate carpet. He steered clear to the kitchen to warm himself up a cinnamon bun and a bowl of *Pests* cereal – the wholegrain wasps always got caught between his teeth, their stingers never failing to prick his gum. After he ate, and had a wash, along with the rest of his normal Tuesday (everyday) routine, something struck him as abnormal or, more so, unreal.

There were no personal messages on the room's answer machine, but a millennium of *CCM* news updates on the *HoloPad.* And the 'Rot Box' was fuller than ever. He found himself standing in the lounge with the latest hardcopy of *InterNation* in one hand (*gasp!*) and the latest *HoloGraph* on the *Central City Mediums* in the other (*tut-tut-tut*). His eyes had only gone as far as the relaying headlines:

PHESTOR'S MISTRESS UNDER RANSOM.

DECIDER HEADS EAST AFTER MYSTERY ENCOUNTER WITH SIXTH NATION TYRANT.

Big news.

By now, his father was probably in mid-flight somewhere over the Prime Meridian dividing East and West, sharing his airspace with the Phestor of the Sixth Nation. Although, now that Phestor Xenol was responsible for leading the way to the East, DCD. Philson could have been headed to many places where no soul of the West had ever trespassed before. It was likely, Oscar imagined, that the leaders might detour someplace entirely ambiguous along the way, like the SPR. There was always business in the Polar Regions, both North and South, but none of that concerned his father unless he was on tour. Now, that would have been *really* big news, however, there was no chance of such a furtive visit reaching the Media.

Free from his father and his father's constant neck-breathing, Oscar made a call to Stevenson and asked if he would be willing to pick him up and take him somewhere early that morning – that was if his chauffer-turned-babysitter wasn't too busy on a Tuesday morning (as he generally was). But this was an urgent request. For once, he had the time and liberty to arrange his own itinerary and it was the earliest he'd woken up all week, which made the beginning to his emancipation feel even more refreshing.

While Stevenson was on his way, Oscar dug out the Constellation Map that he'd carefully hidden beneath his bed. He was keen to take another peek, but urged himself not to. Not until he took it to the one person he knew had to see it. Someone who might have some answers, he believed.

Stevenson arrived within the half an hour he'd promised over the *HoloPhone* and escorted Oscar through the brittle dampness of the City Central in the seclusion of his limousine. Outside, on the streets, Oscar was missing the usual aroma of baked bagels and sausages and eggs and fresh, hot salted pretzels being served with coffee on the sidewalk stretch, drifting through a rush-hour bustle that was perkier than the previous night. The people were diverse and tussled dynamically about with varied importance. Oscar surveyed how the Week Traders were a whole different species of subordinate to the Weekend Traders. They were faster, feistier—*hungrier*. Some were in suits, businessmen and businesswomen; others were wearing grotty, shapeless rags, in which Oscar couldn't tell if they were wearing labourer's overalls or were just the paupers he saw wiping their arseholes with newspapers on the street corners; in fact, he even spotted a few Academics among the masses, and these young students were whom Oscar felt the sorriest for, as they had to make the decision of whether they would join the suits and the ballers or the paupers and the labourers. Oscar was always frustrated by how this hierarchy could never be clearly organised in the crowds of the cockcrow hubbub – well, not this early in the day, at least. Everything was an opponent to 'calm and collected'. And the buildings were no longer lit with glamour and immodesty, but were arid and dormant like owls in the daytime.

His chauffer, (baby–) sitting in the driver's seat, asked him about his night and whether he'd had any more 'dark wanders' in his sleep. Oscar assured Stevenson that he hadn't had any trouble sleeping recently, denounced the idea of 'dark wanders' and mitigated the topic by thanking him again for chauffeuring him at short notice, though Stevenson wasn't oblivious to a lie.

'Ye farda wan' meh tuh escaart yuh wherever yeh need ah go,' Stevenson's pungent Small Island accent had acquainted itself with Oscar's ears and fixed well. It had become a voice Oscar could hook his heart onto and unveil his innermost thoughts. 'He dun wan' yuh tuh be alone.'

'Did he say that from his *HoloPad* on the plane or on the way to the airport?' Oscar teased with a sarcastic grin. 'He told me he didn't know if he would be coming back.'

'He will. Boy, meh sure he will.'

'Do you trust those East Folk?' Oscar said. 'Do you believe that Phestor Xenol may really be leading my father down a brighter path?'

Stevenson glanced out the window. 'We not supposed to discuss this.'

'And my father is? Don't you find that strange? You and my father are more or less colleagues! You're the closest person he has to a real friend and yet he's still able to belittle our trust to run off to the Polar Regions and the East without confirming when or *if* he's coming back. And, in the meantime, you're here, stuck baby-sitting me!'

'Who tol' yuh 'bout dem Polar Region? Yer fardah nah go dere. Anyting say dem all nonsense—' Stevenson shook his head. 'First of all, yuh fardah would ah neva undermine me loyalty, or yuhself. He'd never look down on neither of us. We are de best support he got. De reason he keep tight-lipped 'bout dis short excursion 'cause he cannot promise nuthin' will come of it.'

'You honestly believe that nothing will come of this?' Oscar was unconvinced.

'Look, he a busy man under a lot ah pressure – especially at de moment. But, more important, whoever mention to you anyting 'bout Polar Region? *Cha! Dem pure stories!*'

'Don't you listen to the stories?'

'Damn foolishness,' Stevenson kissed his teeth. 'Nonsense, nonsense, nonsense! Me still find it all too hard to believe and you shud too!' His flawless ranting was unshakeable. 'De more yuh listen to it an' de more yuh believe it, de more yuh go crazy like de Stateship and Co.!'

This commentary had Oscar launching his head off with laughter. A cheeky smile lingered there on both of them.

'*DE-YAAM FOOLISHNESS!*' Oscar cried, humorously imitating Stevenson's accent. 'That wasn't what I was told. I was told the Southern Polar Region is hijacking flights full of normal, innocent people and using them as specimens in medical experiments and nuclear weapons tests—'

'Who you been talkin' to?' Stevenson said, soberly serious.

Oscar knew he'd said too much. But, confident in the absence of his father, he ran loose with it. 'The Phestoress. That night her and the Phestor showed up at my father's residence, she sneaked up to my room and told me about the illegal medical tests they'd forced her through in the Southern Polar Region.'

Luckily they'd stopped at a red traffic light, for Stevenson froze and went to find the Decider's son's inquisitive expression in the rear-view mirror. He just nodded slowly at Oscar with half a grin exposed in the corner of his mouth.

'Now, don't let people be hearin' yuh talk 'bout that situation. Dere are people who investigate that, but that not yuh,' the chauffer hinted. 'All of it rumour to yuh.'

'But you enjoy those rumours, don't you?' Oscar asked.

Stevenson bit his tongue in distress, and then shook his head again with a little more aggravation than before. 'Not a word.'

The light-hearted smirk slipped from Oscar's face, for he recognised this really wasn't a topic his chauffer wanted to gossip about. And he knew Stevenson was holding onto more than he was telling. For that fraction of a second, as the traffic lights switched from amber to green, Oscar believed Stevenson had probably heard things, perhaps seen things…

'Since when did yah aunt call for yuh to visit her so suddenly?' Stevenson rapidly changed the conversation, without losing the suspicion in his tone.

'Well, she's still a working Soothe. With my father in the East, I need all the good fortune I can get.' Oscar tightened his grip on the Constellation Map that rested in his lap. 'It's not all about my father's journey, you see. I've got to know what direction *I'm* going in.'

Somewhere in the south of the City and just a block before the City Wall bordered the last suburbs against the Slumberlands, a long, potholed boulevard of wooden bungalows lazed. The street was grubby and littered and, here, the City Wall had been blemished with graffiti. Along the sidewalk, damaged streetlamps and artificial palm trees were planted beside overflowing waste bins. Oscar hadn't been down here in years.

The limousine departed from the curb and Oscar crept towards one of the perturbing bungalows. Ascending the patio, he glanced through one of the windows on the face of the house to find that the curtains were shut. If he'd have guessed without ringing the doorbell, it would have seemed like no one was in there. Though half a century old at the very least, the door was still the newest part of the house, upgraded modestly with a face-recognition security mechanism. It opened on its own. As he expected, nobody was there to greet him on the doormat. Oscar noticed the CCTV camera positioned above the top-right corner of the door and his hopes suddenly deteriorated again, but resurfaced when a distant voice from another room inside the small house crawled out to greet him instead. The singing voice of a woman, a low and ominous contralto, sojourned with the silence in the bungalow. Oscar stepped inside. '*Welcome to the home of Sybil Mesoa!*' the security system said and closed the door behind him.

Inside, the lights were mostly off and the operatic acapella was joined with the crackle his footsteps created on the wood floor, which was as ancient as the soil beneath it. He tiptoed down the narrow hallway, in case sharp spears came spitting horizontally out from the walls or spikes pierced up through the floorboards (like he saw in the movies). He veered through a doorway semi-barricaded with stacks of old junk, books and vinyl cases, following the sound of the acapella.

A woman was in here, sitting in a rocking chair at the tiny candlelit dining table with a silver turban on her head and examining a book in her hands with great focus. Oscar knew she was aware of his arrival – someone had given the doors' interface a reason to open for him. He stood some distance away from her, not to disturb her concentration.

She gave him a snarl, looking right through him momentarily before returning to the book in her hands. 'What does he want from me now?' she brooded.

'My father doesn't want anything more from you, Aunt Sybil,' Oscar responded.

'There's only ever one reason your father sends you to check up on me once every while—whenever he wants to tick another Soothsayer's head off his list. Well, no check-up required. As you can very well see, I'm still kicking.'

'No, that isn't why I'm here. I wasn't sent to check up on Soothsayers. I came to find *you*, Aunt Sybil. I came because I need somebody who'll listen to me, and you're the only one I could imagine taking me seriously.'

Oscar went round to the other end of the dining table, distracted by the mighty tome in her hands. He tipped his head to look at the cover; it was a very old copy of the *Holy Libel* she was reading. On the surface beside it, a turntable was playing a patchy recording of a former Oracle Superior singing holy verse, recitations of prayers being warbled in the Ancient Dialect (his mother and aunt both used to refer to it as *Latin*). Whenever he showed up here, his Aunt Sybil would be in the middle of praying to the Soothe Gods, feeding off the prophecies they held secret from humanity. Aunt Sybil's eyes would be terrifyingly rolled back in her sockets, displaying her whites, and she'd swing in that rocker of hers, as the floorboards whinged beneath her feet, and she mumbled the pleading verses to the gods, occasionally a hundred times over. This behaviour was second nature to Oscar. His own mother had followed the same daily procedures when she was Oracle.

'I'm busy, Oscar. Not today,' she told him firmly, obsessed with her reading. The beaten record still quacked at their ears. The singer's voice was unpleasantly jerky against the fizz of the static.

'I'm only here today because my father's out of town—'

'Oh, and that makes it fine, does it?' she flared. 'Where have you been these past three years? You used to visit your poor Aunty more often before your father turned you all serious! You're just like him now, aren't you! Go away!'

Her resentment for the Decider was understandable, but he did not appreciate this attitude towards him.

'He hasn't turned me serious, just contained me a little more. That's why I've been restricted from seeing you. Please understand this isn't my choice! It isn't my decision—it's his! He's the Decider! I would come see you everyday if I could! I deserve better than this, Aunt Sybil,' Oscar said. 'And you do as well. Pushing each other away isn't fair for either of us. We're still family!'

'Your father did his damage to our family *years ago*! He exterminated everything your mother and I stood for! Outlawed our kind, our community of Sayers! Burned our temples, discredited our verse and condemned our rhetoric! He pushed me away and he pushed your mother away. And he'll do exactly the same to you if he finds out why you're here.' She slammed the book shut. 'You've started having your dreams by now? Right?'

Oscar's ear's perked up. 'Yes,' he muttered. *I mean, she's psychic—but, I wasn't expecting that quick of a reaction*, he thought. *Am I missing something huge here?*

'I need you to explain something,' Oscar realigned his point of interest.

'Put it down here,' his Aunt Sybil said. She already had a hand flat out on the table.

He froze, paralysed by her potent omniscience.

'The Map—you've brought it. Put it down on the table.'

He set the Constellation Map down in front of her and, slightly scared, recovered a few paces backwards, rebuilding that distance between them.

As she unrolled the parchment and studied the blank sheet that was revealed to her, Oscar had to retreat and simply watch. He quietly mused at Toby, his aunt's pet tortoise, in the meantime. The tortoise had been around for ages and nobody knew exactly how old the bumbling creature had been alive for. '*Hundreds of years they're expected to last,*' his aunt had once told him as a child. '*Never ask a tortoise his age, because, one day, he might be as many years as the stars.*'

'Well, you ought to sit down,' Aunt Sybil's voice was saying to him now, as she finished scrutinizing the Map and returned to their conversation from out of nowhere. 'Actually! Wait—no, don't!' She bounced up from her chair, jostling the table and sending new creaks through the floorboards like the deck of a ship upon troubled seas.

'I was left this Map as a sort of parting gift—'

'Was her name Evanessa? Came to visit you with the Phestor? About three days ago?' his aunt predicted, marching to switch off the horrible racket that had become of the hissing turntable.

'—and I think it may have something to do with those dreams I've been having recently,' Oscar continued a few steps behind his aunt's though process. 'I thought they might be similar—'

'Similar to the ones your mother used to have?' Aunt Sybil concluded again, crossing over to the desk in the corner of the small, cluttered room. She switched on a light over the desk and sought for something under a heap of book and article clippings.

'Does it read well?' Oscar asked. 'The Map?'

'Sort of. Yeah. I guess, it does for something that's completely blank,' his aunt humoured. She picked out what she'd been looking for. A tiny, silver key. 'How long have you been crossing into the Dreamerverse? Oversleeping? And passing out like a narcoleptic?'

She mentioned the word, he rejoiced to himself. *She knows about the Dreamerverse!*

'Only a few days,' Oscar was astonished, overwhelmed with this refreshing and long-awaited response. 'And every time I wake up there, I return to Awakening Coast. Unless I take one of the seeds I was given, one of the Continuity Seeds that can return me to the exact place I left off in the Dreamerverse—'

'It was the King who gave you those seeds, right?' his aunt played perfectly. She turned from the desk and walked to the chain of bookshelves concealing an entire wall. 'He set you on the mission, to go out alongside two others like yourself and slay the Drag-in that threatens to devour the dimensional wall that separates both universes?'

'Yes, yes, yes!' Oscar cheered. 'This is probably a silly question to ask a Soothsayer, but it needs asking—how do you know all this?'

'Because I've heard it all before, honey. Your mother used to bore me with it when I was your age. She had the same dreams as you, obsessed over the same experiences in this Dreamerverse, and was always whisked off to Awakening Coast in her sleep. She was also a Night Dreamer like you. Constellation Planet has been around long before you were.'

Oscar froze again, having a hard time digesting the influx of exciting confirmation.

'Shut your mouth, darling. You'll catch fireflies,' Aunt Sybil said, smugly smiling as she went to remove a book from the shelf. She reached her hand with the key forwards to fix it into its place and that unlocked something. *A door!* Oscar heard the click of a dozen locks shifting out of their sockets. The bookshelf parted in half, revealing a doorway leading down into dank blackness below. *An underground bunker of sorts.*

'Come along,' she said.

She went on through the doorway and down the steps ahead of him.

He plodded after her, down the stairs, into the bunker nestled beneath the bungalow. It was a deep passage to the bottom. Feeling the leaded brickwork of these walls as he descended under ground, he used his palm to guide himself along the curving stairwell. He eventually came to some light when the heart of the bunker protruded. Eluding the sporadic electric lamps on the walls, five shadowed figures were on their knees, in a line and facing a ring of giant stone statues in the middle of the lair.

Aunt Sybil strode around the silhouettes on the ground. They were in the midst of prayer, bowing down repeatedly to the sculptures.

'Sisters,' Aunt Sybil announced on entry. 'My nephew, the son of the Decider, has entered the Dreamerverse. I thought the thickness of his father's skin might have outlasted that of his mother's. I was wrong in this assumption. He shares his mother's legacy in the Planet of Constellations. A new generation of Night Dreamer has come to my bloodline. You know what that means.'

'The Drag-in squirms—the Drag-in yearns—the Drag-in burns!' the women on the ground symphonised in response to Aunt Sybil's monologue. They were also Soothsayers, draped in purple cloaks and white veils that covered their hair. Oscar came closer towards the Soothes, but not too near. It had been a long time since he had witnessed such rituals and he wasn't entirely comfortable yet. All this time, these survivors of his father's witch-hunts had been hidden beneath his Aunt Sybil's bungalow.

'The Drag-in threatens our world once more. My sister's nightmare has returned and my nephew follows her journey to defeat the Drag-in once again,' his aunt waved him over towards her. 'Come in closer, Oscar. So my sisters can take a look at you.'

Oscar edged around the row of the praying Soothes and stood before the crowd, beside his aunt. The kneeling Soothes had stopped their prayers, but were still locked into their spiritual zone, entrancingly absent from corporeality. He only saw the whites of their eyes, their pupils gone, bowled up into their sockets. Ceramic bowls of holy water and lit candles were laid out in front of them and they each had clippings of *Holy Libel* verses scattered on the floor.

'Son of the Decider, son of the Decider, son of the Dec—!'

'Sisters, be of sound mind,' Aunt Sybil interrupted the Soothes' nervous chant. 'Please recognise that my nephew is not here on his father's terms. So he is not here to indict us. His mother was a celebrated and loyal Soothe, both to the City and to the Sisterhood and, like his mother, he has been gifted with a major responsibility. This responsibility means more to the safety of civilisation than the Sisterhood ever will. The future of our world depends on the Night Dreamer more than the Soothsayer and so does the continuum of the Dreamerverse.' Oscar felt his aunt's hand touch his arm. 'Kneel before the sisters, Night Dreamer, and we will tell your fate. We will help to guide you.'

Oscar did as he was told and blushingly dropped to his knees.

'Have you any urgent questions of your future in the Dreamerverse, Night Dreamer?' Aunt Sybil said.

The frontline of blank faces blindly gaping at him through eyeballs of absolute white restrained his response. His lips quivered briefly, then he said, 'There are two other people I met in this other dimension. One whom I fell across in this world – the Map led me to her. What do I have in common with them?'

'*Mutual revelations will bring you together in this reality,*' the Soothes responded in unison again. '*Your search for the emeralds brought you this far. But the Map will take you to your heroic company and these recognisable allies will join your pursuit of the emeralds in both worlds. The significance of these gems is apparent in the two dimensions.*'

'So, there are also emeralds to be found in this world and I can depend on the Constellation Map to take me to the other Night Dreamers?' Oscar translated the Soothsayers' poetics in his head. 'Does this mean the Drag-in's threat is also prevalent here in this dimension? In the real world?'

'*The Drag-in's menace is rampant—it can be experienced everywhere.*'

'What can I expect from the conclusion of all this? Will I succeed?'

'*Foes-turned-allies will realign with dignity, kings will regret, there will be a new queen in the East and there will be falls on both sides.*'

'But will we be successful? Will the Night Dreamers succeed in their mission?' Oscar reinforced the principal question.

'*There will be falls on both sides,*' the Soothsayers echoed. '*Whether a fall counts as a success depends on which side you are on, whatever viewpoint you hold.*'

Oscar looked up at his aunt, waterlogged only further under by the words of the Soothes. 'Does that mean I lose? One way or the other? That this monster in my imagination will ultimately get its way, regardless of what I do?'

'They're trying to tell you that a loss isn't necessarily a bad thing,' Aunt Sybil regarded the Soothsayers' review. 'Soothsayers have not always been correct. Even your mother admitted some false prophecies in her time. Our prophecies haven't been particularly reliable of late. Ever since your father discarded our faith and forbade our religion, we have struggled to sustain our skills and work our craft. We lack vital readings and no longer have a temple to retire to.'

'I'm sorry,' Oscar said.

'Why apologise?' his aunt clarified. 'It's not your fault.'

'If I could change one thing as Decider, your rights to live openly as Soothes would be exactly what I'd reinstate. We need your wisdom back in the world.'

'I look forward to that day. But, with your father still in power and the turbulent days to come with him in the East, I fear that such a reform we may never live to see.'

Suddenly, Oscar saw that his aunt's tortoise had found its way down into the bunker from out of the dark and was trundling before the kneeling women. Aunt Sybil rushed over to pet him and cursed without a streak of seriousness in her tone, 'No, no—! Toby, you aren't supposed to be down here when prayer is in session.'

Aunt Sybil raised the tortoise from the spot, revealing a shimmering emerald tucked under the crevasse of his shell. 'Ah, yes—that's where I put it,' she said, setting down the tortoise again. 'I hadn't seen one of these for a very long time. Not since your mother was around.'

'That's it!' Oscar's memory flourished. 'The emerald we got from the gorilla queen! In the Dreamerverse! That was what it looked like! Exactly that!'

'I have no knowledge at all about such, only that it is extremely valuable to many people. At least, that was what I was told by the young woman who brought it to me. She was the same person who gave you that Map.'

'Evanessa?' Oscar recalled the Phestoress' name again.

'Yes. But I assume you want to know more about the Map and the emerald that have come into your possession – two irreplaceable and quite unmistakeable artefacts. I suggest you seek out an old friend of you father's, a man named Pegasus. He lives a few storeys below your residence in Citadel Tower. It is well understood by those who are familiar with him that he knows people who specialise in these otherworldly materials. And, funnily enough, after the East Lady left me with the emerald, I was given a new premonition from the Soothe Gods. I was told that you would be the first person to come looking for it,' Aunt Sybil said with an ominous shine in her eyes. 'That prophecy has proven correct so far. The first successful prophecy I've had in over six months. However, the premonition also told me this powerful and virtuous seeker who came to me would do wonders with the emerald once they found it, since it beholds a resourceful rarity that all human existence thirsts for. *The emerald's seeker will conduct the power that is required to reunite mankind and restore equilibrium in the world.* Nephew, you can take it from my hand, as long as you promise me one thing. Swear that I will be there to witness your greatness and that I will be there to see you exercise that power with my own eyes. Vow to me that, once you have brought the Drag-in to its knees, you, the future Decider, will willingly invite the Sisterhood of Soothes to his Table once again.'

Reignited with a revived sense of enlightenment and newfound purpose, Oscar endeared his wise Aunt Sybil with a smile.

'I promise.'

Night came quickly that evening and, before Oscar knew it, Kyma was curled up at the foot of his bed again. This time she wasn't playing a game and was really sleeping. Far beyond his residence, in the muffle of the City, late-night traffic could be heard along with the subtle jazz adrift from *Caesar's Boulevard.* Although, there was a different kind of music playing in his head, repeating over and over. A tranquil melody that cradled him kindly into the night. Beneath his bed, the Constellation Map was in the same place it had been the night before. Extraordinarily, as Oscar misplaced his grip on reality and acquainted himself with the Dreamerverse once again, a new comet trail started to form on the Map. But under his pillow was something much more exquisite. It was round, green and glowing. And it was humming him to sleep.

Samuella

Samuella's First Awakening...

Flaunt like a hero and you'll never surrender,
Boast as a villain, you'll have to regret.
Rise like a king and you'll have to engender,
Thrive as a ruler, you'll never abet.
Think like an angel and you'll have to remember,
Pine as the devil, you'll never forget.

A poem I was once told by my uncle, a man with the patience and tolerance for anyone and anything in any universe. Especially me.

His words fill my hollow, heedless head like a hearty soup before an evening supper. From what I can remember of the night I escaped reality, moments before I fell asleep, soup had been all my supper and it hadn't been an appetiser in any shape or form. Nothing...followed by soup...followed by more nothing. Fasting without intent. I'm used to it. Light appetisers fuel my grand ambition just enough to satisfy it. My uncle, being the ardent socialist he was, always lectured how big, heavy meals excessively bloat a person, bogging them down with greedy thoughts, which take far too long to digest...

The ocean waves lap onto the shore, sometimes one after the other, but mostly in huge gushes where three or four waves at once race to reach my feet first. A pair of pale, useless legs, stilled and bloodless, lie outstretched in front of me. I've got no intentions of moving them just yet, 'cause there is nowhere I desperately need to get to. No determination to escape from where I am...

I've already escaped.

One minute, I was drifting in and out of a difficult sleep at some foggy hour past midnight. And now, here I am, watching an orange sun climb down from her throne, as the ocean beneath her celebrates the oncoming night. Sunset has never been so good-looking. I'm not shaking under the skin of my sleeping bag like I was a moment ago…not scraping chilly tears off the rings of my eyes…not anxiously isolated on a night that perpetually drags out its earliest hours…my room at the Quaint-Gaudison home doesn't exist anymore, not here…there are no arguments out on the block…no squabbling neighbours testing the permeability of the walls…no tinnitus from the grumble of migrant lorries and coaches…no howling stray dogs…but birds…birds *howling?*

Am I in a dream? This doesn't even require thought. It's the first thing that seems to make sense. The only thing. The contrasts to where I was a couple of seconds ago don't just occur in daylight hours, not whilst my eyes and my nose and my ears and my sanity are working to their fullest potential – not in reality. Where am I?

'*You're where you should be.*' This small, but loud, holler from above alarms me, as it arrives from out of nowhere.

'Who is that?' I retort. And I'm up on my feet without a struggle, surprisingly stronger than I think I am. The wet sand might be plastered on my naked body, but with fear comes strength and the need to defend oneself from an ownerless voice – a coarse, deep voice too.

'*Someone who feels to ask the same questions as you,*' the voice proclaims. '*Because early introductions are the polite thing to do, are they not?*'

'Why can't I see you? Or don't you want me to see you?'

'*New Dreamers are so inspiringly clueless!*'

My burst of sturdiness is only adrenaline in disguise. I shift uneasily on my lousy feet, trying not slip and fall. That would be embarrassing.

'*Is there a good explanation why you've popped up on Awakening Coast at this time of sunset? Is there a reason you've dragged me out this late – to say "hello" rather than to say "goodbye"? Oh—**but you fell asleep and that can't be your fault because you were tired after a long day up in reality and "it was really an accident I fell asleep, Stewart, it really was!", poor you—!**'* the feisty voice sighs. '*I work nights, you should know – cue the violins…*' Something swoops overhead, casting a brief shadow on me. I look up, but totally miss it. '*I'll tell you what, if I reveal myself to you, do you promise to tell the king that it was I – his most loyal steward – who found you here at this time –*

as well as promising not to hit me with a stick for spooking you? Because, you look pretty freaked out.'

'How bad can you look?' I respond. 'Go on, show me what you look like then.'

All of a sudden, that mysterious thing eclipses the dying sun momentarily and swoops down from above with open claws, darting towards my face. I duck my head and roll my whole body onto the ground. As I strike the sand, I'm confronted with a mini-tsunami of waves. The water lurches into me, knocking me aside and then pulling me in with its return. I find my legs again and storm out of the water, in search of the thing that attempted to carve my eyes out.

'*I'm ever so sorry for that,*' the little voice emerges from beneath me this time. '*I do like to make a generous entrance to wow the new arrivals.*'

At my toes, a shiny parrot of explosive colours makes his stand, looking up at me with big, black eyes. It's impossible to accuse such an innocent-looking creature of its atrocious flying skills, and so I've lost the words I want to say – or whinge, in that respect.

'What was that all about?' I stutter, squelching salty droplets out of my eyes with my soaking palms.

'*Didn't you hear me apologise? As I said—*'

'Wait! You can talk?' I blurt out. 'You can actually talk in People Language?'

'*There are forty-eight variations of "People Language" that I can speak fluently,*' the bird brags.

'Why aren't your lips moving, though? Or is it your beak? Do birds refer to their beaks in the same way people refer to their lips?'

'*I communicate using telepathy. It's the easiest way to connect with Dreamers from all the different lands of Reality.*'

'Dreamers? Who are they?' I must sound really dim having to ask these questions to a parrot.

'*They are like you and I. This is the Dreamerverse, where reality is nothing but a lost realm on the other side of a psychological void. Can I just be sure though—did you remember to go to the toilet before you nodded off or did you just tickle in the sand like most rookies do?*' The bird groans and shields his face with a wing.

'Before I nodded off…? So, it *is* a dream! Where you're a beautiful bird and I'm naked?' I complain.

'*Remember, you have the choice to be naked or not. Everyone arrives here in his or her birthday suit. Whether or not you remain exposed and exhibit your jiggly-bits for all the stars to see is up to you. I don't provide garments here. Must I explain and do everything? I'm telepathic, not telekinetic, you know.'*

My eyes are closed and I'm thinking deeply, thinking of dignity. Something simple to hide my private parts and cover my soaking body. Pyjamas. I remember the matching purple silks I'd worn to bed. For some reason, I can only remember *the ones that I've long since grown out of. They are too small.* But they are all that come to mind—

'Move!' the bird's shouting pecks at my ear and my eyes flicker open like rabid flashlights. I turn to find the speckling stars swiftly encroaching the horizon. The sun is nowhere to be seen. Behind us, a long blockade of swaying palm trees makes way for an army. Hundreds of dark figures have appeared in the distance, striding towards us, hurrying to the shore. They've all alluded to the same crazy idea as me – flimsy nightwear on a moist beach. Some of them look tatty compared to others, as if they've had a tussle with the jungle. But their random absurdity doesn't mean much – I'm still trying to get over psychic birds. Each new arrival cherishes a tiny light concealed inside a glass-jar. As they emerge closer, I can make out fireflies contained within the jars. When the pyjama-people reach the shore, they fall to their knees and begin to dig. Dig holes fit for a firefly.

'What are they doing with the jars?' I ask the bird as quietly as I can – for some reason, trying not to disturb this somewhat "natural process".

'It's their ticket out of here. Deposit one firefly spirit on the shores of Awakening Coast and it validates your departure from the Dreamerverse and ensures a safe return to this Coast when you come back in the future.'

'The Dreamerverse,' I juggle the title on my tongue. 'This is one massive shared land of the unconscious then? Everyone here's living in a recurring lucid dream?'

'It really comes down to how you look at it. Some people see this as an easy escape from reality, whereas others see this as an opportunity of becoming the very things they never were. One rather jittery Dreamer, I recall, nicknamed it a planet-sized rehab centre.'

'How does it work?'

'Men, women and children who share a strong determination to open their minds to their imagination are selected and brought here by the Stellar Gods. These mutual philosophies all come together and function a bit like an algorithm. And it all creates this: a Constellation Planet in the Dreamerverse of creative possibility.'

'What triggers it?' I ask. 'I've never been here before. Why now and all so suddenly?'

'That's the mystery on everyone's lips...and beaks...I shouldn't forget to mention them.'

Before I know it, the shore is once again barren and smooth. Empty of anonymous strangers, the waves arrive upon the sand to drown the footprints of the disappearing pyjama-people. 'And then they vanish—just like that?' I say.

'It's normal, all in accordance with routine,' the parrot explicates. *'A daily inter-worldly transferal, which enables people to leave as long as the tide is calm and the sand is nourished of their echoed footprints. Someone has to maintain this coast and that happens to be me.'*

'Why have I arrived after everyone's departed? Did I miss the party?'

'Such a keen question that you and I share. Though, I have other questions to ask. Seeing as you are so profound, I will share them with you.' The poised bird is anything but humble. He gives me no chance to respond. *'Why have I been stuck in this body, the body of a bird, I ask? It is the one prison I have inside this world of freedoms.'*

'Are you supposed to be something more than a bird?'

The parrot frowns at me.

I'm baffled. He's just thrown this woe of his into the mix of perplexity and I don't have a clue what he means.

'My transformation occurred when I originally arrived here and I have yet to learn the reason why. When I went to highlight my situation to All Eyes, the king of this world, I was told it was "an angel's punishment for his services to a demon's throne". I have always been liberal-minded, but never enough to commit treason. I'm a good man – at least, I was a ***reasonable*** *man. Now, I'm just a good bird who does his duty and keeps his beak clean. So, I've never understood what this riddle meant. It was quite unfair of him to make the judgement on me without deciphering what he foresaw about me. I've never made a habit of "serving a demon". At least, I can't remember if I have – thanks to the Void. But it is an accusation I have come to live with, and the consequences I have learned to tolerate.'*

The parrot stalks about on the sand, kicking up clods of it with his claws.

'On the other hand,' he continues, *'you must be more profound than I was. The Dreamerverse sensed your coming like it does every Dreamer. But, for particular reasons, the Stellar Gods summoned you*

here at this time with an ulterior motive, since you have come at sunset. I can only guess.'

'I have a purpose here?' I gasp, dumbfounded. 'A purpose in this world?'

'Yes, you do.'

'Why… I've never really had a purpose at all.'

'And I've never really heard such nonsense. I've been a proxy bird here for years and even I have a role to play. Every person who ever lived had a purpose to fulfil – well, surely every person ***I've*** *ever met. If you really think about it, you could even ask: what* ***would*** *be the purpose of existing in* ***one world****, if you could choose between* ***two worlds****? You might then have no purpose in one world, but have a highly profound and distinctive purpose in another. Or a purpose in both worlds! Wouldn't that be awesome?'*

'I guess. It's just I'm used to existing in other people's worlds, you know, serving to other people's needs and desires.' I've never actually partaken in telepathic conversation with another person before, believe it or not – maybe sharing thoughts with a bird is different?

'What do you mean?'

'I've just never had anywhere to go to. Nowhere to escape to and call my own.'

'Well, it seems you have a far superior role on Constellation Planet to any Dreamer I've met before. Or, actually… not since… not since the last sunset-arrival on Awakening Coast. The sleep of The Last Night Dreamer.'

'The Last Night Dreamer? Who was that?'

'It was so awfully long ago. But I can remember that legend well. There had been two others on these sands before her. They were her reluctant allies, her fellow Night Dreamers. Since then, there haven't been any more. Night Dreamers have been myth until you arrived!'

'The Last Night Dreamer was a girl?'

'That woman is no longer The Last Night Dreamer, as you appear to be the first of a new generation. I don't know whether your arrival is as much an honour as it is a terrible symbol of the future. Your coming to the Dreamerverse means that a dreadful threat lies ahead. If you are the Night Dreamer now, you have come here on a mission. You will be summoned to King All Eyes, no doubt. And I fear that there may be more of your kind to come.'

The bird shakes his feathered tail before he begins to march up and down the shore, pecking at the lids of the remaining buried jars with the tip of his beak. Whenever he breaches a lid, piercing a hole, a small light pops out, declaring *behold!* to those around it before fluttering away into the spectacular display above – it joins the stars in their millions. 'I've never seen so many stars,' I remark, even though the bird doesn't seem to be listening. He's too occupied liberating fireflies from their glass prisons. The only place where I can remember seeing this many constellations in the sky is my old homestead in the countryside. *It's where I was brought up. And, even there, this many would have been mesmerising, what with how many clouds had drifted into view over the final few rural-life days I'd spent counting them. One clear, cloudless patch of sky is impossible to find anywhere in the West these days...*

The moon has arrived right on time. It greets me paternally, licking me with a bold glare of milky light. What a charming family the moon and stars make. Drifting along the very edge of the flat shoreline, which constantly quivers and changes with the tide, there's something I cannot miss: a stroke of gold reflecting in the moonlight. A golden head of hair. Long and curly, although not frazzled by the humidity, the golden locks belong to a young woman who has been strolling over the thinly scattered waves and she comes to sit on the shoreline. Her feet brush the tide whenever it rolls in and I'm introduced to only her back. I marvel at the shining dress she wears. The girl is garmented in a silky, silver nightgown, which must be as comfortable to wear as it is to admire with the eye.

Why is she here when everyone else has departed? Has the steward bird missed her? Regardless of this, it doesn't dissuade me from slowly walking towards her, trotting heavily in the moist sand. When I'm just behind her, the moonlight glazing her hair gives rise to a shimmer that's so bright it blinds me and the gold grows radiant as constellations multiply above. And her golden hair is truly glowing. If I listen carefully, I can hear her quietly humming to herself as she watches the horizon.

'It has come to my knowledge that I am no longer The Last Night Dreamer.' She speaks with a soft voice, catching me off-guard without turning around to show she's acknowledged me. 'That name belongs with you for the time being. And I completely sympathise, I honestly do realise what that means for you, my dear.'

'Are you her?' I say. 'Are you The Last Night Dreamer?'

'There were three of us. And I was the last to return to reality once the Drag-in was foiled. Cassandra ascended to allegiance with the Stellar Gods and took up one of their many ordained roles. As for the other Night Dreamer, I am quite sure he went back to reality and never stepped foot on Constellation Planet again, but I cannot confirm that,' she hums with melancholy. 'But you are the first Night Dreamer of a new generation. The first Dreamer in two decades to arrive on Awakening Coast at sunset.'

'Why me?' I'm eager to know more. 'What is my significance in this? I don't know if it's just a coincidence, or a mistake, or inevitable—'

'I asked the same when I was chosen all those years ago,' the lady says with a light sense of nostalgia. 'I was broken, deranged, unhappy—and my appearance remains disturbingly unflattering, disfigured from a past of abuse and torture.'

'But—you're beautiful,' I mention, completely disillusioned by what she's telling me. 'I'm looking at your hair right now—it's amazing!'

'Don't be deceived by what you see of me in the Dreamerverse. My wish to the Stellar Gods, my Night Dreamer's reward, was to retain my appearance of old and recover the beauty of my youth. However, I realised that, whilst you can easily escape the prison of your body, there is no escaping your mind and the memories embedded with in it. You can't escape a world of nightmares with a single dream. You'd need countless dreams to break free. And that is your very purpose, Night Dreamer. You too will try to break free of your nightmares for good and, in the process, you will free the stars from the looming darkness, so that no future generation has to suffer the terrors that ours must endure.'

'Where does one begin to follow a legacy like yours?' I'm now totally lost, deserted by her superior knowledge.

'You will find allies and you will all find the resolutions you're looking for.'

Suddenly, the girl starts to weep quietly, bowing her head to muffle her emotions. But I can see her shaking relentlessly. Her ferocious faith in me is quaking through her and it leaves me feeling weak in the knees with a surge of guilt. 'Who do you call allies? Friends? I don't have any allies or friends,' I explain. 'It's just me.'

'Nonsense. I'm your ally. You have my trust,' she assures me. 'Before we had trust and responsibility for each other, the stars were mankind's protectors. They've always been our greatest allies. They prevented Nightmares from reaching through and spreading darkness across the universes. If there are no stars, Nightmares can easily cross between worlds. You must save the constellations and rescue all of our spirits.'

'How?' I pressure her. 'Where do I go? Who are the other saviours, my allies? Who are these other Night Dreamers and where I can I find them?'

She won't answer me.

The girl is trembling with tears in her eyes. Stroking past her golden hair, I place my gentle hand on her shoulder. 'What's your name?'

She looks up at me with eyes I'll remember forever.

'Evanessa.'

Chapter Six

The Rodent And The Rogue

Spanning along the outskirts of the City, the Wall bordered. It was a structure protecting the First Nation's capital from the Slumberlands, the intimidatingly dense ghetto that buffered the City for hundreds upon hundreds of miles. Not for an entire decade had this situation "eroded", which was how DCD. Philson commended its service in his most recent Wall Tax appeal two weeks ago. Ninety feet in height and thirty-two-thousand acres in length, an expanse that retained the entire circumference of the City, the Wall had deterred eighty thousand pirates from the West's Sister Nations, two hundred thousand spies and infiltrators from the East, and a total of nearly four million illegal immigrants since its erection. There was no question that Operation Intravenous was yet to experience a devastating "erosion" that would put the City at risk of another foreign infestation.

When Tuesday morning manifested over the Slumberlands and the first pale-brown rays of daylight ripped through the low clouds to scrub the streets, what was revealed was more attuned to a wasteland than a foul, overpopulated neighbourhood. Radiation flooding out of the sewers (raw waste sourced directly from the underground power plants) and bleeding through every lane one could look meant the roads were redundant for pedestrians. In response to this, curfews were strictly detailed to keep Slumberland Folk indoors until the pollution drone had done its rounds, testing the radiation levels in the air and only giving the green light to neighbourhoods when their Geiger reading was somewhere distinctively below cancerous. For Mrs. Jepslee's street, this was around eleven o'clock.

The curfew applied to all Slumberland peoples. It was just the natural order of things. But, of course, there were always going to be rule-breakers. And these delinquents who were out and rearing by the crack of dawn consisted mostly of youngsters – placeless migrant children from other West Nations, the sons and daughters of pirates and gypsies, and some were even the spawn of defectors from the East. This morning in particular, there was Joei and Lamantha and Edolpho and Mandy and…whoever the hell the rest of those other kids were or whomever they belonged to, who were having ceaseless amounts of fun at their own reign. Balls went soaring, hula-hoops went catapulting and Mrs. Jepslee – a middle-aged mother with arthritis, caring for her nine children, from the comfort of her government-funded bungalow – went on her ritual rant. '*How bloody early you's lots know it is? The drone ain't bin round 'ere yet! Get yerselfs inside! It's too bloody fizzed to be out here playin'!*' She could complain until the cows came home (or, rather, didn't come home, as there was fluctuating levels of radioactivity everywhere). But treading on the fine line of life and death was exactly how the children of the Slumberlands made the most of their uncertain lives, in their lawless kingdom, snoring in the shadow of the sleepless City. At least they were being productive with their time, making good old enjoyment with what they had in their hands (or weren't supposed to have in their hands). Unlike the sad lives of those kids up in Citadel Tower, playing in solitude on their gimmicky *HoloTech*, simultaneously ordering room service from their butlers and washed bed sheets from their maids. '*All dem while dey ah talk like 'em got marble in dem mout*',' Alfie Stayn, one of the Small Island ragamuffins among the group, always reminded everyone of this culture shock.

The Slumber Kids loved to make fun of the rich City brats. The most infamous joke going around was about their hideous feasts, which provided those greedy gourmets with so much food every day that they had to "*keel over and vomit into a golden toilet*" before they "*fell into their bed of lavender and roses*". The boys and girls of the Slumberlands would laugh and cry and roll on the floor like demented pandas. 'And what about those new missiles the First Nation Army said they were going to build on the Gungolian Plains?' Joei mentioned, setting up a joke. 'Now that they've all been told to turn off their *nuclear-bottoms*, how are they going to let out all that atomic gas? What will they do now?'

'An *arm-istice*!' Edolpho ended the joke with a loud armpit fart.

This received a comical reception from the bundle of boys and girls, enough to wake Mrs. Jepslee from her tattered little bungalow across the street. She stormed outside in her nightgown, hair all in pins and curlers, looking like a wreck. And like every other Tuesday morning, her voice would recite a chorus from the City Opera – only not as sweet and tuneful. Then, there followed beckoning arguments and feisty insults and vile language and…an interval of barking dogs. After about an hour of it – at around 9AM – and long after the last traumatised pigeons had fled from the rooftop aerials and the streetlamps, everyone dispersed and the street was once again…*quieter.*

In the sky, clouds had morosely scattered to reveal a pale sun. Nothing absorbed the fog that faded into the street, covering the Slumberlands thickly. It was damp, murky and hard to see. Rarely, a lone transport-lorry would pass through with its headlights beaming and an ancient advert for *Kola Bear* pasted on its trailer. Inside, large masked and gloved families would be crammed from window to window, choking their lungs out on their way to the Slumberland Market to spend their government grants. Sometimes, you'd find up to fifty people wedged into a flatbed lorry. You would never see a family from the City drive through the Slumberlands on one of these eight-wheeled eyesores. Only one streetcar service brought a scarce number of City Folk through the Slumberlands (after a hefty disclaimer was signed at the traveller's own risk) – a tired little carrier accommodating a mere five or six courageous (or stupid) passengers at a time on their adventurous outings to the First Nation Dockyard and back. They were not tour buses, nobody toured the Slumberlands – it was too dangerous (and too ugly). The streetcar drove much faster than anything else there moved. Nobody who didn't live in the Slumberlands wanted to stay there for long, especially not close to the curfew hours.

Typically, used *Kola Bear* cans and *Peppermint Crispy-Chip* packets could be seen floating in the fog, from street to street, stinking in the hot July winds. But deep inside the gutters would be home to the banished belongings of City Folk, such as teddy bears and toy dolls with diamond-encrusted eyes, and other shapeless, yet valuable objects like expensive jewellery, antique watches and rare, charming knickknacks. The people of the Slumberlands had always wondered how and why such items were left abandoned in this way. *Were they not good enough anymore? Were they out of fashion? Were there things out there today that were even better than these?*

Out on the empty roads, scavengers took the risk of entering the terrible fog an hour premature of the curfew's end. Some of them didn't own the legalities to gain government grants and so didn't belong in homes or have any means of shelter, which rendered them naked to the elements, and they scoured the wasteland, bearing only scrap-fabrics on their burnt flesh. They wore masks too. The most terrifying sort of masks, created from spare parts and broken, rotten materials, which were made to look like subpar anti-radiation and toxin-repellent facial guards. The ones with holes in the nose-disc that made them function like pigs digging about their sty. Once they'd acquired their findings, the scavengers would return with the silver necklaces, wedding rings, gold-teeth, and etcetera, to exchange as fortune for food and drink at the market. Rarely did a scavenger discover anything of unique value.

But, during this morning's escapade, one scavenger had their eyes hooked on a small, shining piece of jewellery, lying above a gutter in the curb. *The necklace must have fallen from the sky and slid down the pole and now the streetlamp is wearing it.* And that was exactly what had happened. Well, it seemed that the necklace had elegantly fallen down the neck of the streetlamp, in perfect lining, and had dropped tightly to the very bottom without snapping the thin lace-chain. *A royal fit*, this particularly eagle-eyed scavenger thought.

The necklace was sewn with a beautiful bronze and silver pattern, which sparkled even in the grim of the fog. And there, in the very centre of the lace, was a small, round emerald. It shone a bright green light that bled through the mist. With the scavenger's luck came the presence of another likely finder. Further along the curb, the scavenger saw the silhouette of an adult rat. The rat was marginally grey, but it had areas of fluorescent yellow pus on its fur – potentially, every rat in the City had been exposed to the toxins of the nuclear power-hub deep below the sewage tunnels. The scavenger noticed the rat's dangling tail, where a large gash had caused a kink and a half-severed tip.

The rat watched the scavenger with bulging, glassy eyes and rubbery lips. The stupid pest hadn't clocked the emerald necklace; it was too fascinated by the disguised human. But the scavenger was determined to snatch the jewel before the rat had a chance of seeing anything coming and decided to take advantage of this head start before they had to compete for it. So, the scavenger descended to a crouching stance, eyeing both the rodent and the necklace. And began to move slowly. One step at a time, towards the rat rather than the necklace. The rat was always going to be quicker, but the rodent had more than a mangled tail to worry about, as the scavenger soon came to realise that the creature was walking on puffy, sole-less feet, which was a majorly crippling disadvantage in their competition. Although, this didn't mean that it had no chance of springing off its feet in the direction of the scavenger to provide a sticky gnaw, which would undoubtedly spread radiation poisoning, disease and whatever other infections the creature carried. The scavenger had to be careful to remain at a steady, if not equal, pace with the rat.

On reaching the curb, the scavenger slowly moved a single hand down towards the lace, lightly gripping onto it. By the time the clip of the lace came into vision, the rat had already arrived and was standing nearby. Its eyes were spinning rabidly in their sockets, looking hungrier than its twitching mouth.

Desperately, the scavenger started to fiddle with the clip in an attempt to free the necklace and run. The rat was bearing its silvery teeth, hobbling along on all fours. But it was too tricky; the clip was so small, yet the gloves made monsters of the scavenger's hands. And the scavenger didn't have the time to remove their gloves, so it was a matter of luck—

No chance.

The scavenger searched through pockets with their other free hand, excavating them for something in particular. A utensil that was of some kind of use. A knife. It was small, but it would do the job swiftly. When the necklace finally managed to give way to the blade and fell into the scavenger's hand, the rat miraculously found its way onto its swollen hind legs, swinging backwards and forwards for balance. It jumped, or dived, or leaped…or whatever rats do when they attack. And it sank its teeth into the scavenger's glove. Blood spattered the rodent's face. Though, unlike the enamel hollowness that most incisors possess, these teeth had a dissimilar rigidness that could only be compared to stepping on a nail. Condensation from the scavenger's fretful panting filled the mask's visors and the situation was almost impossible to see. The scavenger shook the hand attached to the rat, the whole arm in fact. As the scavenger violently rocked the horrid creature side to side, there was a strangely evident metallic noise, like a tin containing a coin…or a battery. And then—a pulsating glow burst in the rat's eyes like a pair of headlights synchronously going out. Startled by this realisation, the scavenger whacked the glove attached to the rat against the curb. There was a clicking sound and then the rodent released its bite and fell off the glove. Only after the beast had finally been knocked away into the gutter did the scavenger realise that the necklace had vanished with it. Gone forever. But the scavenger didn't worry about this anymore. It was only a piece of junk after all. Instead, there was only one thing that was disturbing above all else. *It had been a bionic rodent*, the scavenger thought, *a remote control gadget. That certainly wasn't a piece of junk. For sure. Never mind any of that for the time being anyway. The priority right now is getting back to the house before everyone wakes up.*

Samuella had chores to do.

Like most shared residences in the Slumberlands, the Quaint-Gaudison household was less than modest, but miraculously upheld (to some extent). The walls – those that were still standing at all – had massive cracks and holes. On the roof, accommodations had been reserved for almost thirty-three bird-nests. And the windows were blackened with soot and dust, matching the grubby paintjob on the building's exterior. It was a home to many. Twenty-six to be exact.

Once Samuella had returned from a morning of scavenging, she'd retreated to the stove to get a pot of hot porridge on the roll. It was still early – shy of 11 AM. So, the Gaudisons and the Quaints were undoubtedly going to be asleep. None of them had paid jobs or firm occupations, as the Big Bad City "*never really had anything to offer families of this magnitude, of this class in society – in times like these, where the fat cats couldn't wait to exploit the poor,*" according to Mister Quaint. Samuella had *never really* understood this concept, while castaway in this expansive, yet surprisingly small-minded community, on the other side of the City Wall. Seamlessly, Quaint's urban excuse still left Samuella preparing breakfast for twenty-six on a daily basis. She had her handcrafted apron on, and was wearing a plain, unfitting dress underneath it. There were hardly any other options for her to wear on a regular basis and she daren't complain about the ugly clothes Mister Quaint allowed her to wear, which had once belonged to his late wife. She didn't have enough money to spend on a new wardrobe when most of it went towards her *TRAMLINE* fare and food. She and her guardian, Mister Quaint, were the only members who could afford amenities in the whole residence. Nobody else in the Quaint-Gaudison household had any money, or the impetus to earn it.

While the porridge popped and bubbled on the stovetop, she found the mop and bucket and began to wash the floor again, like she had done the night before. Only, the cats were back at dawn, shitting all over the place and leaving an unpleasant sour-milk scent about the air. Little Milo Quaint was allergic to cats – and pretty much anything else with fur (and a beating heart) – but Venus Gaudison had a tendency of opening all the windows at night. She was easily flustered by her claustrophobia and nobody ever pondered what caused it – she shared the kitchen space with only eight of her sisters.

Samuella swept up the staling *Croco Crackers* from yesterday's supper, relieving the tiny kitchen table of crumbs and dying flies. Then, she went to check the rattraps. The City-Slumberland Council gave each household an additional loan on top of its pittance to check the rattraps, because it was a major hazard that the rats carried radiation poisoning and their easy access into households could cause an epidemic if not controlled. Every now and again a Quaint or Gaudison would catch his or herself on a set trap. Though, what was worse was if Mister Quaint ever stepped on a trap, receiving a nasty snap on his big toe, the whole of the world would be held subject to his agony. 'What about those rattraps? Are they done yet? I don't care if you ain't caught none! I'm not coming down there until they're all gone!' he'd whine some mornings.

'Don't worry, Mister Quaint', she would reassure him like the big baby he was. 'You can just stay in bed a smidge longer. It's not like you have anywhere nicer to be.'

But *she* did. It had already gone half past ten and she was expected at *POST* in less than an hour. The *TRAMLINE* to the City Central took forever from the Wall Gate Terminal. It was mayhem getting in on time. So, twenty-six bowls of porridge later, when both the Gaudisons and the Quaints were awake – well, most of them – she served up the porridge with an assortment of microwaved toast, bacon and scrambled eggs. As they were munching loudly, talking with their mouths full and spitting jovially across the table, she made her way upstairs and began to get dressed. She threw on her dull, white work-shirt, her thigh-length pleated skirt and tight leather jacket before enthusiastically taking her hard-earned rewards (a pat on the back and a sad tip in the form of four *pecunts*) from Mister Quaint. The lead-plated front door was always open, so there was no need for her to unlock it on her way out.

The Octane Mall on a Tuesday was a totally different place to what it had been during her shift over the weekend. There were no hard-core shoppers before 12AM. The Week Traders didn't dilly-dally about their jobs like the Weekend Traders. There were no stains, litter or dirt tracks along the pristine marble floor. And, on this remarkable occasion alone and to Samuella's rare luck, Marque Sima wasn't anywhere to be seen. Marque was her boss whenever Mister Angrula wasn't around – and Angrula never was around. It was hard working under a scrutinising woman with so many expectations, especially for a store as backwater as *Post*. The day-to-day service wasn't exactly thrilling. Their general customers were almost always elderly men and women searching for Christmas cards and birthday gift-coupons six months or so earlier than required.

Samuella was prone to spending the majority of her six-hour shift stacking the shelves with the newspapers and magazines that people had genuinely given up reading. Most City Folk garnered their news from *HoloGraphs*, where they could interact with it and express their own individual opinions instantaneously. It was good for her though, because she was being paid very little for a wider insight of the very little things that nobody other than her and the old-timers cared for. Like, the other week, she'd heard about the Phestor in the Fifth Nation who had ordered for his entire family to be sought out and killed after it'd been rumoured that they had plotted to assassinate him. And, only yesterday, she'd read up about the newly updated Air-Regions Grid via which planes were now allowed to fly – what was frightening was that the East's Air-Region had got smaller; it'd expanded drastically more against that of the West since she'd last taken a look.☆

Samuella had been in the store no longer than twenty minutes on her own when the shop's doors slid open and the voice of the automated security system welcomed the first customer and scanned them.

'Nothing like a bit of gossip with the Decider out of town,' the newcomer announced gregariously. 'Got the freedom to read whatever I like when the king isn't home. That's why *POST* is still around even now, you see. People have become so terrified of little truths. They only stick around for the big lies.'

It was definitely a man.

Samuella couldn't properly see him from where she was sitting behind the counter, with her legs crossed over and a magazine in her hands. She quickly slipped away the magazine and tried to peer over the shelves without seeming too obvious.

It definitely wasn't a tall man.

☆ Every month, the West and the East submitted their "Region Shift", which dictated where all West planes and East planes, whether they be commercial or general flyers, were allowed to be flown in the skies. If a plane missed its zone, or squeezed as much as a wing into a restricted zone…well, you wouldn't have wanted to be onboard that bird when it went down.

'You're early, sir. Are you on business this morning?' she asked dutifully. 'Can I help you with anything?'

When he arrived at the counter, he appeared to be exactly as flamboyant as he had sounded on his way in. He was very short and bulbous in the waist. Podgy would've been the best way to describe him. A podgy dwarf in a tight suit. He examined her first before saying anything. Samuella noticed the long cane under his arm. It had the head of a turquoise phoenix – a bird that resonated quite closely in her recent memory.

'Where's your boss? Is he around?' the little man asked. He was comically animated, confident, and his raspy accent had the scent of a million cigars. The way he spoke didn't indicate urgency for the boss, but more a sense of checking out of polite curiosity.

'My boss is a lady and she'd be insulted by your assumption that your first impression of a person in-charge was a man.' Samuella dared experimentally.

'Well, young lady, I wasn't asking her. I was asking *you*,' the man pinpointed with a calm smile. There was a wizened security about him, a notion that he couldn't be easily offended. 'Did I insult *you*?'

'No,' Samuella said, red in the cheeks with embarrassment.

The podgy man smirked and curled his fingers around one another, cupping them on his belly. She hadn't embarrassed him by any chance. He'd swung that test right back on her. 'Young lady…' he began simply. 'I don't take influence from many people, as you can probably tell. Or orders, for that matter. My role is one of delegation at the highest rank. I never judge someone based off who he or she is, but, rather, what he or she does. I depend on personalities, not personas. So, why would I rely on a particular man or woman, if I have indeed come asking for a some*thing*, and not a some*one*?'

'I can certainly help you if you need a some*thing* doing,' she amended, 'but as for some*one*…this place isn't really somewhere you should be looking. That isn't our particular forte at *Post*. I mean—do you see anyone else around here?'

The man glanced around, then shook his head and shrugged to prove he was none the wiser. 'No,' he said, unsurprised.

'Well, sir, if it isn't already obvious to you, a lot of people also *rely on me*—believe it or not. If I decided not to show up today, there wouldn't have been anyone to open the store and stock the shelves, and there would be no one around to tell arrogant bums like you that showing employees basic respect can be the best a way of getting the things you want.'

This was finally a response that took the man by surprise and his grin faded. 'Okay, then. I apologise for my abrupt introduction. I must have phrased my message wrong, branded it incorrectly.'

'Are you going to carry on stalling and wasting my time? Or are you going to spit out what it is you want that doesn't involve my boss?'

'Well, madam, if you don't mind my affirmation, I happen to be the current management chief of the Octane Mall and I've simply come to review stores such as *Happy Hours*, *Arkade* and, of course, the traditional premises of *Post*.'

Samuella's jaw hit the ground like a ceiling in an earthquake. And, for once, she was finding it difficult to speak. 'You...want...you want...to close us down?'

'Not close you down exactly. But I seek change. We're entering a new world stage, progressive modernism is nipping at our heels all the time, and putting the same depressing stuff up that no one wants to see on display for the same price isn't making us any money at all. Young lady, would you do me the charm of finding the date on that newspaper?' He was looking at the latest issue of *Fish Net* on the counter. 'I apologise, I'm losing track of the days and I've forgotten what age we're in.'

Samuella, still stunned by this man's presence, pulled the paper towards her and glanced at the date in the top-right corner. 'The Sixteenth of July, 2058,' she read aloud.

'Wow! So, that means we've been running this store for thirty-eight years. Thirty-eight years of the same business. The same customers. The same news. Bored yet? Now, tell me, how old are you?' He asked, sounding less mysterious and more impressive.

'Seventeen,' she answered.

'Seventeen-years-old,' he sighed nostalgically. 'Would you believe it? This franchise has been running two decades longer than you've lived. I'd be fair to believe that this is your first job, correct?'

'First job? No way. I'm one girl of many talents, you could say.'

'Where else have you worked?'

Samuella paused. 'I'm also a housekeeper.'

'How interesting,' the owner had sparkling eyes now. 'Housekeeping where exactly? In or out of town?'

It was wrong to say anything more exuberant. Samuella reckoned that would stretch the truth. *Housekeeper* sounded fancy enough. 'I share a residence in the Slumberlands with two families in a double household. I clean up their mess and make sure they survive the day, and the night.'

The man nodded his head like he'd already known all this and was keen to cut to the chase. 'I see. I apologise again for my nosiness. I get far too ahead of myself sometimes. What's your name, madam?'

'Samuella.'

'And you're an orphan, Samuella?'

She was now very suspicious of the little man.

'I lost my parents as a baby. They were caught up in the Blackout Seven Attacks, fifteen years ago. I used to work on their farm and ever since they passed, I lived there on that homestead with my uncle, who helped me to maintain it all those years after they perished. Spent most of the time in a radiation suit, because our farm had been mildly contaminated after an infestation of radioactive rodents. My uncle died in a mining incident a couple of years ago. I was very lucky to survive out there on my own for so long. Eventually, I decided to bite the bullet and came to the City to start again.'

'I have great hopes for young women like yourself, Samuella. You are a beautiful and inspirational lady with a very strong heart. I'm so sorry we got off on the wrong foot.'

'Might I ask, sir, your name—? What was it?' Samuella inquired.

'You may call me Mister Pegasus.'

'Mister Pegasus, something tells me that you've always known about me.'

'Indeed, I have been aware of you for some time. And I'm intrigued to know more. In fact, I would be happy to offer for you to come and visit me up in Citadel Tower on *Coventry Street*. If that's not too inconvenient for you. I have a few ideas I wanted to run past you. Ideas about your immediate future.'

Suddenly, Samuella's hopes started to ascend and she was shaking with affection for this man, this hero, this saint. 'That would be wonderful. But I'm not ready just—'

'I'll request for you to be collected after your shift this afternoon. There'll be supper in my apartment, waiting for you when you arrive.'

Supper! she thought. *Actual supper! All to myself!*

He'd kept to his word.

That afternoon, when her shift ended at 5PM, a chauffer arrived in spotless uniform. It had felt like something out of a fairy tale. The man in uniform was a Small Island fellow with dreadlocks, who hadn't stopped talking the whole time he'd been behind the wheel. His name she failed to remember in between his ramblings and she found it hard to pick up on a lot of the things he was saying anyway. 'Yuh neva kno' what come wid Mista' Pegasus! He got big heart an' lot o' respck fuh yun pickney who don't always kiss 'im on de batty. 'Cause, beleeve when I say, he get a lot dem kiss on de batty from people who admire what he do fuh dem society. Evree-one love Mista' Pegasus. Oh, yes, yes, yes! Long Live de Peggy!'

This emphatic quip had both of them laughing.

Very soon, they came to a side of town that she'd never stepped foot in before. The roads were wider. The people were better dressed. The shops were much more sophisticated. And, of course, the skyscrapers were scraping the skies like nowhere else. The limousine parked in a reserved space that viewed down the street towards the Harkson Centre, which was beginning to light up spectacularly for the evening's sports games.

This was *Coventry Street*. Everything she'd ever known about this famous street was either rumour or myth. Now, in the flesh, the truths of those rumours left no room for fallacies – she believed it all, for she was witnessing the fairy tale unfold before her very eyes.

Citadel Tower must have been two hundred storeys and higher than the heavens. Whilst they stood in the elevator leading to the Upper Floors, Samuella attempted counting the buttons, observing that the *Floor 13s* for every hundred had been removed. 'There are no thirteenth floors. *13*, *113* and *213* are all missing,' she said to the chauffer.

'That's 'cause numba *t'irteen* has always been deemed unlucky. De people who made de building forget tuh leeve dem out an' had to painstak'ly extract dem floors afta it was built,' the chauffer responded.

'They removed these floors after it was built? How did they manage that?'

'De walls contain *HoloTech* technology. Dey can delete floors. But it a tricky task to master.'

'I can imagine.'

The Phoenix Suite on the 197th Floor was certainly the prettiest residence Samuella had ever stepped into. It was named the Phoenix Suite for its jagged exterior design of windows positioned in slants to form star-points all around like the flared feathers on a phoenix's head; it was hysterically conflicting with the normal flat walls on the floors above and below it. Considering its size alone, the Phoenix Suite would've provided surplus room for both the Quaint family and the Gaudison family – and each of them would enjoy the spoil of an individual corner in a room. For the first time in her life, Samuella realised what it was like to have a real home in the City with floors worth keeping clean and actual working light bulbs in their glittering chandeliers and the lasting aroma of fresh, hot food cooking, heavy full meals that only the rich could afford to consume.

The Small Island chauffer, who she'd finally learned to call Stevenson, had led her to the guest's bedroom, where glass cupboards, modernistic steel cabinets and a double—triple—quadruple-bed waited for her. The chauffer told her to get ready for supper and she did so, wanting to set the right impression, beginning with taking a hot shower with a lavender-honey body-wash. After she was clean and standing there in the marble wet room, combing her hair, she couldn't help but feel a little guilty. For where she was. For what she was doing. For herself. *Is this selfish?* she thought. *What I'm doing, is it selfish?* She didn't see herself as the kind of person who put herself before others, but rather put others before herself. So, on this occasion tonight, it made sense that it felt a bit weird to her to finally be at peace with her own desires, her very own luxuries. Someone was taking care of her for a change. Nevertheless, right now in that stuffy bungalow down in the Slumberlands, she would've been preparing supper for the Quaints and the Gaudisons, washing their clothes in that reeking, grimy bathtub. Meanwhile, their old, sickly boiler hummed and welcomed asylum for cockroaches, crawling in from every nook and cranny of that stagnant wasteland. *All of that nonsense*, she thought, *just for a few stinking pennies at the end of the week*. The same pennies she would use to pick herself up a sandwich on the way to *POST* or exchange for a *TRAMLINE* ticket. On her part, the Slumberland setup wasn't fair. This change of living was what she deserved. Her reward for so many dark days. And, soon, she'd be eating City food that had been prepared with care by presumably some of the best chefs in the West. She was happy to be there, happy to be considered, happy to be alive.

Then, she heard something she wouldn't have usually heard in the Quaint-Gaudison household. It was silent enough for the sound of light footsteps to be noticed out in the corridor. Something had been deposited under the guest-room door. Samuella went to investigate and found a small, white envelope lying there on the doormat.

It was labelled with her name in neat handwriting.

Quick to open it, she found that the paper ripped easily – that was another thing she needed to work on: opening posh envelopes. There was no letter inside. No message. She instead found something that amazed her and almost blew her away.

It was the necklace. The very same one she'd discovered and lost that morning during her scavenging. Sewn with bronze and silver. Attached to the lace was the glittering shamrock-green emerald. The very jewel she had thought she'd lost to that relentless rat and the Slumberland sewers. The most beautiful thing she'd ever seen. It was all too overwhelming, as she'd never expected to see it again. *Where did they find it? How could they have known?* she thought. *Whose idea—? Was it Pegasus who'd sent this?*

Samuella returned to the mirror in the bathroom, basking in the room's extravagant light while she gazed at her reflection. Her hair was clean, thick and soft. Her skin was flawlessly moisturised and prettied-up with new makeup provided by the guestroom's dressing table. And there, now placed around her neck and lying on her chest, between her breasts, was the emerald-necklace. Warm and radiant on her chest. It overshined the rest of her outfit, which was a long turquoise dress, bedazzled and low-cut. Heels were also very new to her – so new that she was finding it difficult to stand still and simply admire how many inches she immediately gained to her already superfluous height after putting them on. *Have I come this far? If so, is this far enough for me?* she asked herself with modesty. *Have I really reached my limit here in this emperor's town? Or have I still yet to go further in this fantasy than I could possibly dream?* There was only one way of finding out—she left her room and went across the hall for dinner.

Roasted turkey, smoked salmon and pulled pork lined the centre of the dining table. A trio that were all about to become the lead stars of a culinary blockbuster, along with a supporting cast of liver-dumpling soup in bird-decorated china bowls and platters of ostrich meatballs for starters – each ball already fixed upon their own individual crimson-tipped cocktail stick. Sides of fish fillets and coleslaw with couscous and every kind of vegetable accompanied the main meal. Beautifully dressing the atmosphere, a classical medley by the City Opera played quietly from the room's stereo-system.

Mister Pegasus hadn't invited any other guests to supper, as Samuella had ambitiously hoped. Why wouldn't she? She had every right to! This moment was hers after all. Pegasus had a pining interest reserved solely for her this evening. Sitting at the heads of the dining table were the closing shift employee at *POST* and the owner of the Octane Mall himself. He had pride in his pupils and a face that persisted to peruse her with mysterious fascination. Did he have more interest in her or did she find him more intriguing? Samuella continued to fondle the necklace.

She wasn't afraid to knock back mouthfuls. And she spoke while she ate – she didn't find this any ruder than him watching her obsessively from the other side of the table, so she did it shamelessly. 'I'm not too impressed,' she executed her grasp on sarcasm poorly. The colour in her cheeks and the smile on her face gave away her gratitude. 'The Decider lets you lodge with him in Citadel Tower and they coup you up in a shabby old shack like this?'

'I am good friends with the Decider,' Pegasus explained. 'We weren't just colleagues, we were old friends. Philson and I go way, way back to our years at the Academy, long before he became DCD. Philson, Decider of the West. Back when he was Nicholas Philson, the boy who'd never truly been itching to step up to the plate and become the leader of the free world. He'd studied to become a successful businessman, hoping to take the City, and eventually the whole world, by storm with some new idea of replacing Androkind, swapping the A.I. system with a scheme that put humanity back in control. Bet you didn't know that.'

'Not in the slightest.' Samuella lifted her nose from submersion in the feast on her plate with minimal, but honest, fascination.

'Philson hated the concept of the A.I. and the fact that his father, Philson Senior, had helped to introduce them to society under his previous Administration as Decider. So, Philson was constantly in opposition to his father growing up and felt the consequences of that. In the end, he was pulled out of the Academy, didn't graduate. It was too much for Philson Senior that his son was being "indoctrinated by socialist bootleggers" – it was all over the papers. Back when newspapers were in fashion,' Pegasus laughed sadly. He hadn't touched his food and, instead, used his hands to perform exaggerative gestures. 'If it had worked, his business venture would have put hundreds of thousands of people back into work. All those folk in the Slumberlands that you see, strolling on their dirt roads and rolling in their mud piles, they would be in jobs right now and earning a decent living if he'd pursued that ambition in his youth. But his father – his predecessor – wasn't about that. Philson Senior didn't see it as the Decider's responsibility to help *build people*, but to keep the world moving – mass-producing, the riskiest and most monotonous part of consistently running a company. So, when Philson finally became Decider after his father, he didn't have the first clue of how to run a civilisation. As a result, he ran it how all incompetent leaders do – he ran it like a business. And, as it happens with most businesses, the format works out for one better than it does for the rest. It isn't flexible or adjustable, especially not to suit people's well-being or their individual rights. A business structure in domestic policy has to be managed and managed well. It is not progressive. This model on society isn't something I agreed with and—*oh, believe me*—Philson took very good note of that. He didn't appreciate my reluctance to support his ideology or, rather, his lack of one.'

'You know a lot about his personal life, Pegasus,' Samuella said. 'It makes me wonder, were you just schoolmates, or something more than that?'

'His own father had been a sweeping dictator – in a time before you were born – and he wasn't a very commendable Decider either, so, initially in his youth, Philson never really celebrated his father's achievements. He understood their importance, their significance at the time, and even now in the times we're living in. But Nicholas always thought he could do better than his father. He's always been competitive like that. You probably know his father had been the one to commission the building of that Wall that divides the City Folk from the Slumberlands, and the people in the Slumberlands, whom everybody here calls lazy, useless and destructive – the people whom *he* now has to struggle to find ways to subsidise, if he wants to avoid riots. The Slumberlands outnumber the City, so he has to keep them satisfied and marginally happy. And the people in the Slumberlands only became that way because Philson Senior squashed the will of humanity and manual labour with the force of the A.I. system – synthesised control.

It's also because of his father why this war with the East will never end – Philson Senior started spreading ostracism through his political propaganda and harnessed the voice of the Media during his manifestos and speeches and all that jazz. He convincingly bartered these ideas like genius, though he never invented them. They weren't original ideologies, only poorly executed before. He hadn't been the brain behind any of it at all. He had just been the mouthpiece, the frontman with the gifted gob. Philson Senior was the puppet that fed the phobia to the masses, but he wasn't the only one. He was surrounded by an Administration of paranoid old-money aristocrats, who corrupted his mind with these illusive ideas about the invaders from the East, and the murderers from the Small Islands, and the leeching thieves from the Slumberlands, and they blueprinted ways of selling this hyperbolised – and sometimes utterly untrue – nonsense to the West. A plot to exaggerate the dilemma and get people scared. They wanted to hold on to power with both hands by removing the capabilities and influence of the public, by diluting the façade of the free world that has dwindled in our culture's imaginings long before Mankind's World became what it is.

Philson Senior's Administration brought in the A.I. to remodel the law with such a clean slate that the people who wrote the land's original law book in the first place – heck, even those who wrote the religious texts recited from the words of the Old Lord himself – would be dumbfounded in a legal debate and themselves be annihilated for one immorality or another. As that very first A.I. motto had put it: "*There's an Offence waiting to be committed by all of us*".

The Administration pulling the strings above Philson Senior was a deceitful one. Their cabinet had been dubbed "a Bunker of Bastards". But they were absolute geniuses at retaining social stability, doctoring a lullaby that would shape the West however they wished – the vibrations of which our own two generations must deal with today and into the future. However, their most effective way of distracting the West has been that on-going war with the East. And I've done everything in my power to expose the truth, the irrelevance of these grievances with the East and how Philson Senior's indoctrination of the West was one unforgivable deception – a lie that has lasted forty years!' he refrained from preaching to take a sip from the martini glass beside his plate, wary that he'd said too much already. He carefully placed the glass back on the table, hesitantly stroking its base.

'Androkind and the Conflicts with the East all spawned from falsehood?' Samuella commented, baffled. 'It was a made up conspiracy? Hiding what?'

Almost completely on cue with this break in the conversation, there was ruffling among the flowers in the tall vase that stood in the middle of the table, and, to Samuella's shock, out popped a small, yellow scorpion. It fell from the top of the vase, landed on its back when it hit the table-surface, and then flipped onto its legs, flexing a bit to retrieve its bearings. It skittered across the table, towards Pegasus, and, when it reached the martini glass, it climbed up the neck of the glass and acrobatically inverted itself, curling its tail so that the stinger dipped into the drink. Constricted into position, it stayed there, totally static.

'I apologise if I am setting the mood for a morbid evening. I hope I'm not bringing you down,' Pegasus sheepishly excused. 'Yes. All conspiracy, you could say.' He forced himself to laugh at the seriousness of his own statement.

Samuella didn't quite want to accept this last disclaimer. He had told her far too much detail to hoax himself with the conclusion that most of it was up in the air. She didn't believe his modest act.

'You don't actually curate the Octane Mall, do you?' she deciphered. 'I can tell. You're much more than that. I'm not a fool. I've heard what Citadel Tower is and know about the sorts of people who live here.'

'Yes, of course, I'm aware you're not a fool,' Pegasus said certainly, even when he appeared slightly less assertive than usual and genuinely afraid of how she might react to his explanation. 'I have an eye for impressionable young people. But you're an intelligent, capable and interesting young woman with a fascinating history and an even more intriguing future ahead of you. And that's why I invited you here. Trust me, Samuella, I am not attempting to deceive you.'

'Then I suppose that brings us back to square one. Who are you really and what do you want from me?' she persisted.

Pegasus took another shaky sip from his martini glass. The scorpion's stinger came within an inch of his nose.

'To discuss the future. Like I said, *your future*. Stop trying to brand me a liar! I need to advise you—!'

'Advise me about what?' Samuella cried. 'You can't advise me that well if you keep skirting around the truth!'

'Before I make anything clear to you, please understand this. DCD. Philson follows the exact same precautions as his father, when he is nothing at all like his father. All our current Decider does is follow in his predecessor's footsteps: continues to persevere with the war, pretends to negotiate with the leaders of the East and then blows somewhere up and calls it a milestone in the pursuit of victory, highlighted in the Media as a heroic feat for the clueless civilians of the West. The only reason he supports global separatism is to keep the previous Administration's formula in place, breaking-even all the time with minimal risks, so the business doesn't become vulnerable, say, to something a tad more revolutionary. If exposed in the right way, however, the Decidership could be toppled in a heartbeat.'

'Hold on a second! You're talking about leading a revolution against the Decider's Administration?' Samuella gasped.

'Yes. Please understand, my dear, that the Decider is a man that doesn't enjoy change,' Pegasus declared. 'That's why he's immovably stubborn in every decision he makes.'

By the time Pegasus had finished his martini, Samuella still had at least one eye kept on the deathly tranquil scorpion curled on the end of his glass and the other on the food she hadn't finished wolfing into her mouth.

'Samuella,' Mister Pegasus said, suspenseful whilst looking at his fork full of coleslaw. *He hasn't swallowed a single bite. Maybe he's watching his weight*, Samuella thought. 'Samuella! Dear girl, please do remember to thank the chef on the way back to your guestroom. He has outdone himself with this meal and I will be sure to thank him myself.'

'For a spy, you're pretence is extremely frail, and so is your alibi, and so is your attempt at hiding your guilt,' Samuella snapped at the man with the face like a ripe tomato.

'That is because I am by no means a spy, only well researched and socially conscious, particularly of the things that mean the most to me. I'm sorry to disappoint you,' Pegasus challenged with a shallow smile. 'Whatever would make you suspect that?'

'This necklace right here!' Samuella persisted, raising the emerald that lay over her chest. 'I found it this morning, during my scavenge. It was conveniently tied to the bottom of a lamppost outside my residence. Next minute, before I could nab it, a huge rodent coincidentally arrived out of nowhere and tried to steal it off me. I busted the bugger and, for a moment, thought I'd killed it—only to realise I hadn't killed anything, because it wasn't alive; it was a remote control gadget, a mole. This necklace and the bionic rat both disappeared down the sewer and then, later today, someone delivered it to my guestroom door.' She tilted her head forwards, stabbing her creased forehead and eyebrows at his blatant front of dishonesty. 'Would you care to admit that you've been following my every move, Mister Pegasus?'

Samuella suspended eating and set her cutlery down in the middle of her plate.

'I assume you'll want to learn a lot more about me than my work experience then?' she offered, feeling the power shift in the room. 'Seeing as it wasn't your primary objective to just be kind to me, you ought to make it obvious very quickly why I'm in your company.' She winked at him with a flash of resentment in her eyes. 'Where would you like to begin?'

'Your parents, if—I may?'

'Fire away,' she accepted sharply.

'You said it was fifteen years ago when they parted from you. You lost them during the 2043 Blackout Seven Attacks,' Pegasus was tapping between the scorpion's pincers with his fingertips like a dealer might heedlessly shuffle a pack of cards. 'Those Attacks were terrifying. Much worse than the Blackout Nines, in my opinion. The Blackout Nines were a love child of the Decider's impatience at the height of the Conflicts, but the Sevens were scarier because they came from the East. They were launched from the Eighth Nation – back when the Eighth Nation still existed—'

'It does still exist,' Samuella cut in, sounding almost outraged.

'Well, technically speaking—okay, back when the Eighth Nation was still a feasible civilisation with people actually living in it.'

'People live there still,' she sustained the same tone of abrupt confidence against the little man.

'Yes. There are a few decrepit people living there,' Pegasus admitted, slightly awkward. 'I was just exaggerating. What I was trying to say was that it was scary because back then – I'm not sure if you remember – the Eighth Nation was known as rogue state. It was where the West's Media said those Radicals came from, terrorising both the East and West in the name of some new religion—'

'The Radicals never came from the Eighth. Couldn't have, because they emerged at a time when the Eighth Nation was thriving. Back then, it were the Sixth and Seventh Nations that were in turmoil and having direct conflict with the West,' Samuella said.

'You're right,' he told her, impressed once again. 'The East Radicals operating the West – the ones who follow the Faith – don't come from the Eighth Nation. Like I said, the *West's Media said* those Radicals came from the Eighth Nation. That is what the majority of people have been led to believe. You and I know otherwise.'

'Is this some kind of test on your part?' Samuella inquired, vaguely suspicious again. 'I read a lot about it in my spare time, during my breaks between shifts. But how do *you* know this information?'

'We will get to me eventually. You, on the other hand, are very aware of the world around you, Samuella. And you're independently minded. Your experience working in *POST* has gifted you with unbiased knowledge. You don't follow what they tell the rest of the sheep in the system,' he told her and continued to watch her with his grand vision stashed in the back of his mind, examining her every second she sat in the room through his very green eyes. 'But I wanted to know about your parents. Where were they originally from?' Pegasus proceeded.

Samuella froze for a moment, she hadn't thought this question would fall into the conversation. 'Different places. My mum was East-born, from the Sixth. Dad was from the Fourth,' she responded stiffly. Not only was her mother a foreigner from an enemy Nation, but, from what she was told by her uncle, she knew her father had been a pleb from a lower West Nation. 'They met at the border.'

'More accurately, you mean they crossed an ocean to meet?' Pegasus humoured, having his own jab at the correction game.

'Doesn't that upset you?'

'Why on earth would it upset me?'

'My parents were criminals! My mother was an illegal immigrant and an enemy to the West all the same; my dad wouldn't have even survived the Slumberlands he was so poor and illiterate; I was their greatest offence, having me was their biggest violation. They never left the Fourth Nation and hid in the countryside all their lives until they thought it would be better to leave me out of the equation once and for all and that was when they abandoned me with my uncle! That's why they never let me leave, never allowed me to go and make a name for myself in the First Nation or find an interest in the City, which, only when I grew up, did I finally muster the courage to pull off and here I am. I was never able to grow up and move on and learn *about people* and how to *deal with people…people like you!*' she was lashing out now, furious at this revelation. It was an outrageous open wound that Pegasus had poked, wearing a smooth grin on his lips – he knew exactly what he was doing and he was pressing the right buttons.

'Is that where your place in the countryside is? The Fourth Nation?' Pegasus icily tugged the interrogation onwards again. He wasn't struck by her sudden uproar.

She nodded.

'Where did they go when they left you behind?' Pegasus asked.

'Second Nation,' she answered.

'So, after they spent most of their lives together, hiding their forbidden, secret marriage on a country-plot in the Fourth Nation, they suddenly decided to move out of town and migrate to the Second Nation,' Pegasus said. 'Does that actually make any sense to you? Wouldn't they have been safer to stay put?'

She didn't answer this straight away. He was right. She hadn't truthfully considered it in such a way. The story didn't make sense at all.

'The Blackout Seven Attacks struck the Second Nation's coastal city of Aeoua in 2043,' Samuella recited. 'There were warnings about a potential Blackout Attack in that region for eighteen months prior to the actual strike. There were regular drills right along the eastern coast every week, telling the people of Aeoua and surrounding areas what to do in the case of a nuclear bomb and that the Attack was imminent. The Airport of Aeoua was actually closed for three months before the Attack – the West government knew it was that dangerous. The tensions at the time were so high.'

'When did you hear the news of their deaths?'

'Only a month after they left.'

Pegasus shook his head. 'Far too soon then.'

She was stunned hearing this.

'What are you suggesting?' Samuella had become steely and pale.

'There is a strong chance your parents were never caught up in Blackout Seven, because they would've never got in. Aeoua was the only place it hit in the Second Nation and the city was shut off three months before the Attack. So, it poses questions, doesn't it?'

'That they might still be out there, alive? Maybe.'

Mister Pegasus took another sip from his lethal martini, not responding. He didn't want to give her too much hope, he was only speculating, learning about her after all. 'You must have been two years old when they left you behind. You keep referring to your uncle who was around to bring you up.'

'Yes, my Uncle Ceph. He brought me up mostly. That's why I hardly talk about my parents. I wasn't just embarrassed about them. I didn't really know them.'

'You don't have to be embarrassed about your parents. That's not your fault,' Pegasus said. 'Outlaws will be outlaws, whether they like it or not. It's pretty cool if you ask me.' He raised his glass and winked at her from behind his scorpion-cocktail. The drink was finished.

Pegasus filled his glass again, granting the scorpion freedom to run around the table as he did so and the discussion went on for quite some time longer, an hour in fact. Finally, Samuella remembered something else.

'What happened to Mister Stevenson?' Samuella wondered.

'We don't tend to call him "Mister" Stevenson in this building. We simply regard him by his surname alone,' Mister Pegasus replied.

'"Stevenson"? Why? Doesn't he prefer to have a title over his surname?'

'He has no title. He is a man of the Small Islands and you know what that means.'

Samuella looked at him blankly and slightly concerned.

'You do know what I mean by that?' Mister Pegasus wasn't convinced. 'How long have you been in the City, Samuella?'

'Four years,' she said.

'Are you familiar with the history of the Small Islands and their relationship to the West?'

'I know that they used to rule the West at one point. But the West's old aristocracy disgraced their history and trampled on it with their own.'

'Who told you that?'

She said nothing again. She was afraid of arguing with him on this level. It wasn't a subject she felt strong enough in to compete with him.

'I read about it last week in the *Borderline Express*,' she answered at last.

'Then, you should understand why they have no formal titles in West Society, yes?'

'No. I'm an immigrant like Mister Stevenson. Why should I have a title and not him?' she dissented. 'You called me "Miss" Samuella.'

'It comes with the profession. Whilst being a chauffer for the Great Decider among many other officials is a noble position for anyone, being also a native of the Small Islands means one can only ever be known by his surname, because only those of the Eight Nations can be registered by titles. Small Islanders are condemned as a subservient race by the West's aristocracy. I don't make the rules, but those are the customs in this City and many other places. They may not be familiar in the village where you come from, but they are black and white here. In no way does it make Stevenson irrelevant or undermined, I can assure you, Miss Samuella. Stevenson is a very good friend of mine with many surprising talents up his sleeve.'

'Where is he now, then?' she asked sombrely.

'He was called away on duty elsewhere, somewhere outside of Central. But he did promise that he would be returning later tonight, along with a guest.'

'A guest?' Samuella's eyes widened. 'Who?'

'Ah, now, Miss Samuella, will you promise not to ambush this young fellow too much when he makes his entry.'

'Young? How young is he?'

'I'd say around about your age. He's the lonely son of the Decider and I invited him over especially in the absence of his father.'

'I heard that the Decider is somewhere else at the moment. Got called out to the East for some dodgy business,' Samuella noted before taking a hefty gulp from her wineglass. 'Is he good looking?'

'His son? I'll let you come to your own conclusions. He is a bit of a handful, if you ask me. A friend of mine was at a dinner the other evening in his father's apartment. He said the banquet had a few familiar faces, nobody he didn't already know – you could imagine, the Stateship and his boy and so on. Well, the Decider's son showed up late and caused a big stir and a few rumours have started to simmer.'

'How? Like what?'

'Well, as you must be aware by now, the Phestor of the Sixth Nation also made a show and he brought his female mistress along. After a while, both Philson's kid and the Phestor's girl went missing from the Decider's residence. According to the Stateship, his son had sneaked downstairs and described that he'd heard them making love in the boy's apartment.'

'No way.' A wide, gaping look of amazement grew on Samuella's face. 'He's a right cheeky one, isn't he?'

'And he should've been here half an hour ago. Trust him to be late.'

'I'm looking forward to meeting him now.'

She didn't have to wait much longer, as soon the doorbell chimed and the maid went to answer the door. Waiting in anticipation, Samuella was trying to settle her pulsating adrenaline. *A bad boy*, she thought. *A real prince with the rapport of a daredevil who could hopefully show her the ropes and pay for a few more meals like this and take better care of her and kiss her lips and make her forever rich and remorseless for blissfully leaving behind…*

But when Stevenson arrived in the room, he didn't bring Prince Charming. He brought one person who she'd never expected to see. Her hopes were no longer high and her sparky aura was no longer plain sailing on the currents of her excitement. The waves had picked up and now they were lashing at her, for, standing there beside the chauffer was that same boy she'd caught trying to taunt her in *POST* the other day. *What was his name…?* It slipped her. *Oh, what did it matter?*

'Miss Samuella, please meet Master Oscar Philson.'

Oscar was skinny, callow and wussy-looking in her eyes. Not the pampered rump she had been expecting. He was no prince and *wasn't no bad boy either*. He was just another privileged oaf from the City Central. Surprisingly, he was in just as much shock as her. She had envisioned the son of the Decider turning his nose up with disgust the moment he saw her. Instead, he appeared saturated in thought, stunned to the spot and he couldn't take his eyes off her. *Smitten*, Samuella humoured herself, *just like he was in the shop*.

'Is this the girl you were telling me about?'

'Yes. Don't embarrass her now,' Mister Pegasus told him.

'And is he the guy? The Decider's son?'

'Why do you both seem so surprised?' Mister Pegasus said with more unconvincing bemusement.

'It's just…' Samuella began.

'We've met before,' Oscar ended her sentence.

'Why—isn't this a coincidence!' Pegasus' smug smirk had resurfaced. 'Though, haven't you ever spoken before? You don't act as if you've ever spoken to each other before.'

'Oh, he's some piece of work—I definitely figured that much out,' Samuella stated.

'*I'm* hard work?' Oscar disagreed. 'You should look in the mirror some time and behind all that crappy make-up you'll find that you're still a Plain Jane in more than one dimension!'

'Master Philson, mind your manners. She is my guest,' Mister Pegasus softly warned with a glowing expression. He was inexplicably entertained by their encounter.

'And you're telling me that *he* slept with the Phestor's daughter?' Samuella snapped into laughter. 'Everything about him cries, "*I'm a virgin*"!'

'What have you been telling her? That's not true!' Oscar hissed at Pegasus.

'We've been discussing you trivially. The words of itchy lips – I forbid, no more,' Mister Pegasus assured. 'Now, take a seat and have something to eat. I promised your father that I would feed you well while he's gone.'

Samuella was battling between hysterics and puzzlement, sniggering tightly under her breath as both Oscar and Stevenson took their seats at the table. 'Now, tell me, where have the pair of you met before?' Mister Pegasus inquired absorbedly.

'It's confusing,' Samuella said. 'And you probably wouldn't believe a word of it.'

'Miss Samuella, I've heard some unaccountable malarkey in my eccentric business. Nothing fazes me any more than the next man,' Mister Pegasus snickered.

It didn't take long for Samuella to catch Oscar's eyes again. The boy had already helped himself to a shallow portion of food and he too, like Pegasus, refrained from eating momentarily. *Were they all like this here?* She pondered. *What's wrong with the food?* No, he, like Pegasus, was busy watching her with intent. Samuella immediately felt uncomfortable under his glare and shuffled in her seat. His eyes were on her chest…examining the necklace. 'That necklace,' Oscar finally said. 'Where did you find it?'

'It was a gift.' Mister Pegasus nodded with confidence.

'Funny,' Oscar said. 'I've got something that looks just like it.'

The Dune Labyrinth...

I now have the Constellation Map – probably the finest result that came out of the Falls of Fortune and the first encounter of our voyage. And while, I guess, you could reason that being rescued by a flock of blue phoenixes, materialising beneath us at the perfect moment to complete our escape was another pretty convenient outcome, the Map landing in my mitts surpasses even that when it comes to coronate the triumph of all triumphs. It's Oscar I blame, all the way to the Falls and back, for the thin survival we had to contend for; it was *him* who had led us up the Kappa Mountains and through those caves occupied by Queen Cassandra and her pack of barbaric, shape-shifting spirits; and it was *him* who took us into that mess mortally unprepared for what perils awaited there. Yes, fair to say, it had been the Map leading him every step of the way. However, it was *his* disadvantage, and emphatically *his* failure, to be incapable of working with the Map's directions and manipulating our path to ultimately avoid the dangers that prevailed from our circumstances as much as we could. Simply put, he could have done better as a leader. *Should* have done better. Blimey—he should have at least *asked* someone for help if he needed it. Oscar lacks the vigour, candour and astuteness of an illustrious headman. Thank the Stellar Gods! Finally, the Map is in my hands; I am under its guidance and control. But, chiefly, I have the other two Night Dreamers under my own unshakeable sway.

I've snoozed for much of the flight – returning to a quick interval in reality – before reawakening to a nosedive through the clouds, and then the water phoenixes hover just above ocean-level where a clearance of timid marine reels a new land into sight, beyond a bar of turquoise reef. There's no a reef shown on the Map, but the image we're soaring over labels itself as Pegasus Island. We land on the shore and the giant phoenixes do not recess for ceremony and goodbyes. They are gone, parading off into the sunlight, where the aqueous blaze surrounding them turns to mist in mid-flight and they evaporate.

We have resurrected slightly earlier than sunset this time. The fruity taste of the purple seed is still fresh on my tongue. A shorter slumber, I figure. Oscar and I have already kipped during the flight – using up one purple seed each. We have no clue what Camson has been doing the whole way. If he starts complaining he's tired, he might as well forget taking a seed altogether and just materialise back on Awakening Coast by himself. We won't be sticking around for him here and we won't be going back for him. No, sir. He's had his opportunity to sleep and we can't afford to lose time.

'I'm *so* sleepy,' Camson whines. 'If it wasn't for those birds and their woeful winging, I wouldn't have been wedded with motion-sickness, holding my sleep to ransom like the heated bed of an old married couple.'

'I thought I should've told you, Samuella,' Oscar retorts indirectly. 'I imagined our friend, Camson, was probably scheming to knock us into the sea while we slept and tamper with the emerald we secured in secrecy, so that he could run to All Eyes and accuse us of being so careless to lose it, and then request a new, "competent" pair of Night Dreamers as his comrades – preferably two compatriots of his own – to entertain his sympathies,' Oscar retorts. Leaning in to me with a hand guarding his lips, Oscar then says: 'Don't worry. All Eyes sees everything.' And just like that, the West Kid and the East Man storm at each other with the aggression of two wild elephants, their chests protruding and the sharp sun-glare imposing on their foreheads. Oscar has a limping disadvantage and it's clear he's in no condition to compete with a man even half his size.

Camson wins the race. He grapples Oscar's neck, compressing it in his constricted palms and shoves the boy back towards the water.

'Quit that!' I spurt. 'Cut it out, now! You're men, not boys! *Men*, not *boys*! Remember?' My tone is deliberately condescending. I stagger between them on the sticky sand, wagging the Constellation Map.

'Brothers, not sisters,' Oscar iterates mockingly. 'Remember that, Camson. This isn't a slumber party. You're the only one who's going to pay when you feel the consequences of pulling an all-nighter on the rest of us. '

I tilt my head at Oscar, cutting my eyes at his twisted leg and then raising my brows to prove I'm not impressed, nor convinced, by his brazenness. 'Okay, we're all scared about what comes next, which isn't strange,' I tell them. 'We were like this the first time. It makes sense that we should all be on-edge, but part of the reason we almost came undone on Leo Island was because of our rampant distrust of each other. It's expected we're not supposed to get along anytime soon. But, Camson, that's no excuse for what you pulled off in that cave, or on the Bridge. If we're to get to the end of this, we need to do a better job of relying on each other, especially our leader. *Hopefully*, now that we've survived the first trial – just about – we can start to see the positives here: we already have one emerald and we're already at our second destination. So, let's all get a grip, grow a pair of cojones and move on.' I manage this in a single breath and then march on, huffing as I go.

Oscar huffs also.

So does Camson.

The East Man, dropping his head, droopily kicks the ground. 'Where are we?' he complains. 'Did they land us on Pegasus like you said?'

'Yeah,' Oscar adds. 'How do you know this is Pegasus? Have you actually *checked* the Map yet? Like you're supposed to...'

'That's what I *just* said! Weren't either of you listening?' I remark, my irritation evident. 'We have arrived at our *second destination.* Here!' I lift up the Map to reacquire the beauty of my perceptive privilege with my own eyes. We're—on the shore of Pegasus Island.

'There is no doubt about the fact that we're on Pegasus,' I reassure them. 'The Map never lied to you, so I expect the Map will not lie to me,' is what I have to shut up Oscar.

So far, all to be seen on Pegasus Island from where we're standing is a vast, flat beach. Its sand is hard and itchy, chunkier and yellower – almost more sickly looking – than any shore I've footed before it. Nothing like the flour-soft dunes on Leo or Awakening Coast of Central Island. Here, the sand is harsher. Not a single palm in sight either. Further up the shore and inland, the sand appears to get dryer and deeper. This is the desert. Rock-strewn mountains are looming in the distance with clear blue skies stagnant above them. 'The heat is dry,'

I mention. 'I suppose there's no storm coming anytime soon and it's only midday, so we really ought to get a move on.'

'Where is there to move? This is an empty wasteland,' Oscar considers urgently. He hobbles through the sand, wincing over his injured leg. He might be on the verge of hyperventilating.

'*Jheeze*—the City Boy looks as though he's never sustained a paper cut in his life, let alone a serious injury,' Camson criticises. 'We can probably expect to be walking for miles - with *no* shade. And we have no idea what could be out there! I've already seen enough Nightmares for one snooze—'

'This isn't the same snooze, buddy. I hope you woke up from that one and didn't pull off an all-nighter like Oscar said,' I respond to Camson and I glance at Oscar. 'Did you take a red seed like I told you to?'

Oscar looks at me tiredly when I say this. He doesn't like it when I treat him and Camson like children. Maybe it's just my own defence mechanism kicking in, a way of shoving off his negativity, because he's seen something in me that he's remembering more and more by the hour. '*I swear I saw you that time...before, when...*' he murmured earlier, while on phoenix-back. He's been muttering these things ever since we left Queen Cassandra behind. '*In the City... at the Octane Mall... or was it the Harkson Centre...where have I seen that face? Your face?*'

'Oscar, take a red seed,' I repeat firmly. *That face* may be in his visions, but *THIS face* is in *his face* right now and it's getting anxious with every second he keeps me waiting and he can sense it. It's telling him: *You **will** take my instructions, swallow that seed and let me lead the way.*

He sourly digs inside his pocket and tosses the red seed in his mouth.

The terrible thing is that I can remember just as much - and just as little - about the real world as him.

The trek across the desert is long, scorching and cloudless, like we anticipated, and even though the Map is leading us cleanly to an **X**-mark some three or four miles away into the middle of the desert, I have a stong feeling that the emerald won't simply be lying there in the sand, waiting to be taken. Equally, I hope the next emerald won't be in as much of an awkward place as the first.

Along the way, Oscar's been limping like a gamekeeper's ostrich. His left leg is in awful condition and he's just about handling the three miles we've knocked off the distance so far, bolstered under my helping arm. 'The red seed should kick in any minute now,' I tell him.

'You promised that an hour ago!' Oscar scolds my presumption.

'Listen, your guess is as good as mine,' I reply. 'I'm happy to help you along until it does. But I can't do the whole way. My shoulders are starting to ache.'

'It's a good thing you're a big girl then,' he comments, smiling a little.

'I'm quite happy to bust your other knee if you like. It would probably be easier to carry you between Cammy and me that way,' I joke. 'Come on, give me a hand and lift it out of the sand a bit more.'

We can both sense Camson's cringing unease with each word we spew. The unfortunate East Man has had it the hardest of the three of us, and now it's just his luck having to persevere alongside two West Kids. When I know Oscar isn't looking, I give Camson an honest glance, hoping it'll reel him in a bit and befriend him just like I always can. He recognises that I have the East somewhere in my blood – he's clocked the restlessness in my attitude, the familial loyalty in my heart, the habitual nature of my spirit – and this acknowledgement is quintessential to our good relationship. This is where Oscar doesn't fit in to the mould. Oscar doesn't understand the East and Camson doesn't understand the West. I understand both. Even I find it hard to put up with Camson's reckless thoughts and historic grudges. However, what I appreciate more than Oscar is that this East Man has fought his battles, whether he won them or lost them. He's a veteran who feels pride and accomplishment, and who also feels defeat and frustration. But it's how he can be so vocal about his contradicting emotions that burdens stress upon our party. In my experience, that's just the way folk of the East act under pressure – *my own mother was just as irrational, only not as bitter, since she had never fought in the war against the West and she had no reasons to hold territorial grudges*. At least, that's what I've been told.

'Can you two stop looking at me,' Camson warns us abruptly. 'I hate it when I'm being eyeballed by Westies. It feels like I'm being picked apart!'

'You know quite well that I'm not all Westy. Part of me is also from the East,' I remind him. 'You didn't need me to tell you that. We're on the same page, Camson, even if it's split down the middle.'

'You have skin fair enough to be a First Nation chummy-chum for me,' he teases childishly.

'My mother was Sixth Nation-born, and my father was from the Fourth Nation,' I say. 'Only a single Nation and an ocean divided them.'

'Your hypothetical father was East-born! Congratulations! That's wonderful news!' Camson doesn't hold back on the sarcasm. 'We can be friends, yes! Would you like me to write my home address in the sand, so we can send each other postcards?'

'Well, I apologise for attempting to clear the air a bit. I thought we'd already been through this discussion back when we were introduced.'

He thinks about what I've said for a short moment, reminiscing Awakening Coast. 'I was with the boy back then,' his tone suddenly changes to something meeker. He protects his dignity by pulling a stiff upper lip.

'The boy isn't dead,' I tell him. '*He's* the one we're looking out for. Not *you. Him!*'

'Don't play on false hopes, child!' he hisses. 'You're just as clueless as I am! You know nothing about the East! You know nothing about my son! And you know *nothing about me!* So, stop pretending that you care!'

'This would be so much easier if none of us were Night Dreamers,' Oscar hurtles into the argument.

'Why do you say that?' I ask.

'Because, if we were just as disconnected by the Void as everyone else, we wouldn't give a bat's eyes about each other. We wouldn't need to hate each other,' Oscar explains. 'We'd just get on with it.'

'So, why put us together, then?' I keep posing questions to the unlikely duo walking on either side of me. 'Why did the Stellar Gods gift us the "privilege" of immunity to the Void's memory-block?'

None of us have anything to challenge this idea at first and we surrender to the silence of the desert. Then Oscar suggests, 'Perhaps, they thought a group of people from the real world, who are aware of each other's strengths and flaws, would be better than a group of Dreamers without a clue or a care about the next man.'

'Why the hell would that work?' Camson snorts.

'Because, sometimes, enemies understand each other better than allies,' Oscar says.

'Particularly if your enemy isn't very good at hiding what tickles their temper,' I note, agreeing with Oscar's theory.

'Haven't you seen him since in Reality? Your son?' Oscar brings the forbidden topic up again and, as soon as he does, Camson's back goes rigid. It's a curiosity that has been hanging over me also.

'None of your business,' Camson responds in a placid whisper.

So we leave it at that.

After trudging for two more hours, the sand becomes indicatively thinner and at several points I have to halt to feel the surface of the ground before inspecting the Map. *Does this mean something?* The surface doesn't feel like a chunky – and, in places, tightly dense – hill of sand dunes half the time. Instead, it is flat, weightless and smooth like powder right the way along. Two or three hours after midday, at the peak of daylight, the sun is scorching and the palms don't spread their shade until quite some distance still. On the Map, the **X**-mark is nearby. Probably half a mile to go. Wherever the emerald is, it's close and, judging by how sustained the landscape of this desert is, this location shouldn't actually be too discreet.

'Do you see that?' Oscar says. And we stop in our tracks.

'See what?' I ask him.

He takes a few more steps forward before stopping dead on the ledge of a huge ditch the size of a crater. Its dip is so sudden and sharp that, if it hadn't been for Oscar's call, we might have missed it and fallen down into it. 'Are we supposed to go around it?'

'The Map's telling us to go directly straight. No turns at all,' I assure them.

'Does it really expect us to go through this?' Camson says. 'It doesn't look like a stable trek. Or safe. Looks like a sinkhole.'

'We don't have a choice. Go around it and end up *where*?' I point out to them. 'If the Map tells us inside there is where we should be, I think we should follow through. Otherwise, what's the point? If we go round it and find nothing, can we make it back? This thing stretches on for miles, perhaps twice the length we've come so far. We won't survive that long, not with Oscar limping like this and dehydration taking helm. There must *something* down in there.'

'Yeah,' Camson chuckles, '*something*.'

Like the strong leader I am – or profess to be – I begin my climb down into the enormous crater ahead of the others. The crater is a lot softer than even the softest sands on the desert ground. This is much deeper below, where the high edges of the crater create large areas of shade. But Camson is right in being suspicious of its origin.

'What's it like?' Oscar asks. 'How does it feel?'

'Like I'm going to suffocate,' I laugh and pretend to choke, scratching at my throat, trying to lighten their fears. But they remain just as sceptical. 'Get your rumps down here!'

It's slippery. Slippery and shiny. The ground at the bottom of the crater, for some reason, is glossy and dank, bordering on slimy. But there were no signs of rain in the skies over the island when the phoenixes brought us here, and the whole time we've been walking, the skies have been blue. Then again, why was the beach wet in places the tide couldn't reach? Wet patches had been seen further up the shore. No rain, no tides – surely slippery dampness that high up shore is implausible? Might we be getting tricked here? By something leading the way that isn't my Night Dreamer instincts – or the Map? It's trying to pull the wool over our eyes, guiding us past the peripheral blunders and impossibilities. In fact, whatever it is, whether good or bad, I can't guess what its intentions could be at all. This place is way too desolate and quiet…

Oscar has joined me in the crater next, whereas Camson has reluctance. 'You two!' he shouts from behind us. 'I've spotted something!'

Oscar and I turn in the hope that he has the emerald in his sight.

'The crater is in the shape of a scorpion!' he calls. 'It's shaped like a scorpion! Don't you find that strange?'

Oscar rolls his eyes. 'It could just be a natural coincidence! Is that strange?'

'If you *don't* find that strange, then *you're* strange,' Camson has another blast at Oscar. 'In your position, I'd find the emerald and get out of there. I'd already be on my way by now.'

'Why don't you get your backside down here and help us!' Oscar barks.

'Don't worry. One of us should stay up here just in case,' Camson cheekily bounces his eyebrows at us. 'And if anything happens, I'll be the first to inform All Eyes.'

Night is racing us and winning. We're following a narrow flume that's shaded under awnings of unreachable crater ledges on either side of the passage – the narrowing tail of the beast. Quite soon into our trip through the crater, Oscar is in dire need of another break from hobbling. We stop somewhere about the middle of the tail, where shade dominates and the crater craves the moonlight. Here, I rest Oscar's wounded leg upon my lap. The flesh wound is a lot less severe than it had been before he'd taken that red seed. It's semi-healed. Still, it's pretty bad and the gorilla queen seems to have done some proper damage to the bone and torn along the joint. Fractured beyond doubt.

'It's going to take a while to heal,' I tell him. 'But the seed is definitely doing its job.'

He sucks in air through his teeth when I stroke his injured shin, skirting one of the wounds with my finger, avoiding its red border by a fine margin. 'I know where I've seen you,' he says randomly, 'in the real world.' It's taken him long enough, even when I recognised him off the bat and have played it down this whole time. 'You work at *Post*, weekend shifts—'

'And weekdays,' I interrupt. 'Eleven to five.'

'Are you on your own in the City?' Oscar asks. That's when I turn stony and my barriers go up.

'It's just me a lot of the time – on my own,' I half-lie. 'That's not to say I'm lonely.'

'It's okay to be on your own,' he admits. 'I am – mostly.'

'Your dad isn't much of a family man, is he?'

'He's always busy and that's all I've ever known him for. His job is not to be reckoned with. The excuse is always "*Something Happened*", which leads him to get involved in a few world affairs and then he's off on a whim and I don't see him for weeks or months.'

'"*A few world affairs*",' I snigger at this remark.

'What's funny about that?'

'You say it like it's nothing. We could all be gone tomorrow. When we wake up, there could be nothing left. The skies could be black with our ashes. The City obliterated. Nowhere for you to call home. Nowhere for any of us.'

'This place might do,' he groans. 'For now.'

I glance up again. I've been looking at the sky a lot from inside the crater. Waiting for the stars to align. The stars offer more guidance than the Constellation Map at this point. They're here with us now, having arrived cluster-by-cluster to poke through the gleam of the desert evening. 'Are you feeling tired yet?' I ask him.

'No,' he replies.

'You *look* tired,' I tell him.

He tightens the grip of his hand under my clasp, sharing his painful heat with my detached subtlety. When he sustains the grip of a child who doesn't want to depart the comforts of normality for the daunting novelties of academia, I can feel that he doesn't want to sleep, to leave me alone in this ditch, all by myself. He doesn't want to go back to that place – the other place he used to call home so irrefutably. *The reality, the City and all that swaggering razzmatazz.* Instead, he feels comfortable right here in my company. I couldn't be less amused by his infantile behaviour and the crooked state it's left him in. I only need him fit and awake, so I'm not left to baby him when things go haywire. We don't have time for passengers.

'And you *need* rest,' I insist coldly.

Then, I hold onto his chest and push him down delicately until he's laid gently on his back. I hand him a purple seed and takes it without complaint.

Within seconds, he's asleep.

These Rich City Boys, eh. They're just like Ball players. Weeping after every nip and dink.

I go to build a rushed hill of sand before elevating his wounded leg on to it. He lies completely still. 'Rest for me,' I whisper, 'and come back home when you're ready. But not too late.'

Taking my sword from beside him, I leave him to recover.

I set out on my own.

In the *dark*, on my *own* – might I emphasise those words.

Who needs Oscar, or the other one?

I've singlehandedly fought off nocturnal gangs in the City Slumberlands – guns, knives and all the rest; the dark can't frighten me. It never has. Never will. *I used to voluntarily go along for night scavenges with Tenese Quaint, before he was kidnapped in the fog one time and wasn't found until his toes were fished out of a gutter some days later. I used to cuss the rowdy gangbangers playing Ball at midnight and the gypsy girls daring at "Knockdown Ginger" in the street at the crack of dawn; and I used to stalk them all playing manhunt in the dark, at an unsociable time, when Slumberkids were correlatively known to be kidnapped or fell into the company of molesters and gangs who were prowling the block at night. There are no children playing in the streets of City Central, however – not from what I've heard and not from what I've seen looking down from Mister Pegasus' residence atop Citadel Tower. The streets of City Central are strictly prescribed for men and women with strict business only – and there are many men, and many women, and many businesses, all of them private and shrewd when routing through the palpitating multitudes on Coventry Street – but I noticed not so many children...* My City Thoughts keep rambling back to Oscar. He may either be the bravest *City Boy* I know, or the daftest. He's put on a brave front this far, but it's always been transparent that he's struggling to keep it up in this new environment. Needless to say, the old coward in Camson always appears one step ahead – maybe it's just his lucky, prophylactic East instinct to react before the plausible, the possible and the inevitable, and that instinct will allow the annoying West Men to trample over themselves. Hence, Camson probably fears a lot more than scorpion-shaped ditches and the dark of the desert at night. Maybe there *is* more than an emerald at stake down here after all? Something that'll bash my skull in; something that will mutilate my legs like Oscar's were; something that'll rip my belly open and use my intestines as a straw? I may not be the only fearless one among the three of us, but I'm definitely not the stupidest. That's for certain. Then again...*on my own*...time will tell whether this is true.

'*A spirit of deceit has led you to the prison of the truth at its entrance...*'– an almost unintelligible whisper surmounts my train of thought.

My feet skitter in the sand as I come to a stop between a pair of palm trees. Ahead, the narrow passage has opened up a bit. The tall walls of the passage have partially collapsed into slopes, giving way to a broader view of the stars above and a less steep dip to my level below. I recognise these as, not the walls of the crater any longer, but a corridor between two long sand dunes. The end of the tail in the scorpion-shaped crater and the entrance to a maze. The palm trees are perfectly placed between the walls of the sand dunes and there are only two of them at the beginning. Towards the end of the straight passage is a corner, where the passage cuts a ninety-degree angle and takes a left turn.

'*...Beware the guarding spirit of truth – the clawed giant who pledged to protect the Blankesphere Netherworld at its gate of lies: upon this land of dishonesty...*'

What does it mean? *Land of dishonesty*? *Clawed giant*? *The Blankesphere Netherworld*?

Where is this place? Pegasus—surely?

I follow the entry lane into the maze and take the sharp left turn at the first wall. Then, I raise my sword, as I pursue the succeeding passage and hold it horizontally out ahead of me, before briskly taking the next right turn. Then comes another right turn. And another right turn – quicker than the last. The lanes are getting shorter. Then, a left. And a couple more rights, three. Followed by another three lefts. Right, then another two lefts. I figure there are no junctions, no illusions or traps, no gimmicks. The labyrinth consists of only single turns with no room for choice or decision-making. Next, right. Thereafter—right again. Then, a left. Next—left. Then, just straight, straight—straight—

'*...And the two-faced lord of human verity and deception cannot wait to be acquainted with you. From the day you are conceived, he unveils your tilted truths and your fictions. Your spirit has a flair for falsehood. Both in life and in death...*'

And now I come to a final right—it's where the wall bends into a curve that extends forever—until the *end?* The end of the maze? Is this it, the last stretch? I trace the curving passage, keeping close to the wall as it curls, leading to—an opening maybe? Maybe. Hopefully...*hopefully?* What will be waiting when I get there? The moon has been engulfed by the ridges of the bastions I've left behind in my hunt for escape, with its sacred, guiding light hidden behind those preceding lanes that I abandon to my obsolete quest of agog. Intrigue has ebbed into a fear that assumes rank atop the stock of my emotions and the sheer vehemence of trepidation has me tripping over each step.

At last, I'm reacquainted with the moon, breathing down onto the fraction of a face I have courage enough to share with it. Timidly peering out into the space I've come to, from behind the edge of the maze-wall. The conclusion of the labyrinth is a flat, circular arena of emptiness at its very centre point, an open space deluged with imposing moonlight.

I slowly step out from behind the wall, hovering into the plethora of moonlight and revealing myself absolutely to whatever will befall me...and, there, I see the ferocious limb that lies upon the sand in the middle of the arena. The outstanding size of the plump limb is so domineering that it incises the labyrinth's centre-ring into two isolated halves. Surely, it's the tail or tentacle of some frightening, colossal beast - now shrivelled, dilapidated - that limply basks there on its back of greying orange skin, sickeningly dappled under the cooling purr of luminescence. The stinger at the head of the tail is erected just a little higher off the ground than the rest of the dead mass that sinks into the sand at the other end. *Dead—I suppose?* It's perfectly still. I lug no intentions of disturbing this fact. Remotely, I budge sideways round the arena with my back and calves constrained against the wall, covering as much of the ring's circuit as I can. That's until I see a body wilting coldly - but sat in a considerably upright position - against the creature's tail. There sits a Palm Patroller, all on his own and a long way from the jungles of Camelopardalis and the high walls of the Kingdom Palace. The monkey-man is also dryly inanimate in a corpse-like state. *Dead as well—I suppose?*

I wrangle open the Constellation Map to confirm that I've come to the location of the emerald. When I open it this time, there is nothing there but a blank page. Surprised—no? I'm off the radar. Lost—could be. But misled—no, never—but, perhaps…

The Palm Patroller's body flumps forwards all of a sudden. He collapses onto his front with one of his bristly, slender arms stretched out towards me, flaccid like the pulp of an old, beaten lemon. Knocked over by some invisible, seismic force. A force only budding. For the ground behind the Patroller starts to quake, splitting the ring from end to end. A great hole comes to surface in the ground beneath the tail of the creature and the sand pours into a deep trench. It's pulling me with it, towards the middle of the arena. I slip and crash into the shifting stream of sand as it makes for the trench in the ground. I reach away from the pit, both hands clawed and digging into the sand - it's like clinging to the ocean current, my grasps perishing one after the other - no luck whatsoever. Gasping in search of air, while the grains flood into my mouth and nostrils, I fall victim to the sand. In the process of filling my ears, the grains indulge my head with the same whisper to the one at the maze's entrance, rhyming on repeat: '*Orion's deceit is the one to fear, recover the truth of defeat down here, discover the feat of the Blankesphere!*'

I surrender to the ground.

Giving rise to the creator of this disturbance—*something's coming…*

Then, the tail resurrects, lifting, ascending—

—it blocks the moon, suffocating the moonlight, overshadowing me and all my surroundings, the whole arena.

The sand has stopped moving. I roll over from my front, onto my back, and stare first at the gaping trench dividing the arena of sand—the tail is not resting there anymore. Looking up, I find it a hundred feet above. It stands re-established, strongly vertical and burly from top to bottom. How breathless I am at the sight of the lively limb that now bulges with ten times the might it had a minute ago. With the stinger pointing to the nearest star in the sky and outlined by the moonshine, it overlooks the entire desert.

Then—*blimey!*—it comes hurtling to the ground. On impact, it tears into the trench and sinks deep inside, until the tip lands and clamps somewhere below and the tail bends into a muscular bow, so that the beast can hoist itself. Up. And up. And up. The ground gives way to a swell of massive body. Quaking up through the ground, the great exoskeleton mounts the surface as a titanic lump. The shell of a queen scorpion ascends to the arena floor; sand skitters from her dried, swollen back and her eyelids drop open to reveal two black globes pulsating inside.

I'm on the move again, crawling towards the nearest wall in the sinking arena, with all the sand hurtling into the fracture at its centre. The carcass of the Palm Patroller is nowhere to be seen. And, here, before me—the only thing in my line of sight is the great orange-skinned scorpion that has scaled from hells crowned under the desert sands. She is as wide as the arena and her pincers must scale the size of some five adult giraffes.

The scorpion's tail takes its first almighty swing, slinging the stinger round the arena like the minute hand of a hoary analogue clock. Stooping, I raise the sword above my head in an improvised charge towards the muscular limb, prepared to land a pre-emptive jab into the oncoming tail, though simultaneously trying to duck and miss it if I can. With the blade, I nick stringently beneath the venomous bough, but the tail is low enough to strike my head with a force enough to decapitate – luckily, the blow employs a slighter pressure that merely rattles my wits. It sends me spiralling into a wall. Sand elevated from my flight showers me on impact.

Quick to my feet again—I won't attempt to attack this time. I wait for the beast to regain her posture, facing me, not with her tail as the swooping threat this time – but with her probing, uninterrupted stare and those merciless pincers gesticulating doom. *Crack! Crack! Crack!* She's fast to respond, scampering diagonally out of the sinkhole at an unpredictable angle, intersecting the middle of the arena. I counter her movements, staggering in the opposite direction, with one hand to the wall again and the other holding the sword outward. I joust past the beast and make it to the side of the ring, where she just licked wounds on hiatus—

The scorpion's tail hurtles down again. This time, it bisects the existing trench with another, a new gash, which creates a cross in the centre of the arena. ***X** marks the spot.* Once more, the earthquake returns and the sands begin to shift again. I drop instantly, skidding on the hard, shiny surface. At all sides, the dunes are collapsing inwards; the arena walls are coming down, lapsing into the pit.

Now, it's the equivalent of quicksand. The arena has transformed into a gigantic whirlpool. The scorpion queen is fighting against the pit as much as I am, choking on screams and stifled vigour. She persists bowing her tail, fixing it into the sand.

The scorpion queen, clambering over the sand waves, swipes some of her strongest blows to me with her pincers, missing every one. Her legs have been caught in the thicket, leaving her lengthy body to be stretched this way and that, and she's roaring with frustration. When freed at last, she thrusts her tail back into the air a final time, seeks me out, and tries to drag her heavy body towards me. But it is far too late for the scorpion queen to react, for the ground has dissolved entirely and I am in mid-slide—

With my perpetual skidding towards that tomblike opening in the ground, come the gliding forces upon me: a hundred hypothetical hands pressing on my head, shoulders, stomach and legs—downward. I land hard on my back. Bucking my shoulders on the concrete sand with such force that the sword rockets out of my grip and plummets further, deeper into the insatiable pit. Enclosed by a vortex of sand and wind, there is no revival from here. I am descending with a myriad of forsaken hopes and chances bygone—just one more grain spooned for the ravenous underworld that seethes below…

Chapter Seven
The Two Emeralds

Mister Pegasus hadn't particularly won over Samuella, but she retained a curiosity to learn why he was so ardent about her. The biggest concession was that she didn't want to go back to the Slumberlands straightaway. She wasn't keen to face the Quaints and the Gaudisons for quite some time yet, frightened of how they might react when she would be forced to explain her absence. Had she let them down? Was this escapade really selfish of her? Or was it a modest, well-deserved break from her labours in Slumberland Life? Had it been stupid of her the give in to Pegasus' temptation so easily? *Quite Some Time* would have to tell.

Remarkably, before breakfast the following morning, Samuella woke to her own dorm maid, who laid a pink silk nightgown and slippers at the foot of her bed and had dusted about the room with a mini *Vac-U-Bot* whizzing along the floor beside her while she slept. During the first evening of her Citadel Tower excursion, she'd learnt from Stevenson that the dorm maids were assigned to individual residences and every residence in the Tower had its own private maid. There were expected to be over five hundred of them working in the Tower daily.

She got undressed, unhinged the knots in her hair with a comb – a device that she wasn't accustomed to using, but she speedily found compatibility – and had a quick shower. Not once whilst living in the Slumberlands had Samuella believed that the myth of *undressing* and *redressing* regularly in the mornings conveyed a courtly standard of hygiene and legitimacy. Not many showers were even running beyond the City Wall at the moment – the recent spate of water bans caused from underground power plant leaks had a major part to play in that appropriation.

Mister Pegasus – or, rather, Chef Jermaine – had prepared another fabulous meal for them. This time round, it was only the two of them. No sign of Stevenson or the Decider's son. Slicing into her first bit of real bacon in what must have been three years, Samuella had one presiding thought leftover from the previous evening that was bugging her. 'Who do you share all this with, then?' she asked as politely as she could. 'There must be someone else.'

'Someone else?' This didn't catch him by as much surprise as she'd expected. 'Why must there be someone else? What makes you think that, my dear?'

'It's a big apartment. Expensive and very sound. But, all the same, its design is full of conflicting ideas and it's too asexual to call a man cave—if you see where I'm getting at? It can't just be you.' She was speaking with a sturdier tone than yesterday. The novelty had worn off slightly. She was more sociable this morning than she'd been last night. 'You're a man with a lot of money to spare, Mister Pegasus. There are more *pecunts* in that wallet of yours than there are in all the pockets of the Slumberlands put together. You're one of the only people I know who can auction strangers off as newfound friends. Are you lonely? Have you lost someone?'

'Miss Samuella,' Mister Pegasus donned a quivering guise of strength. 'Time is not cheaper than money; it is the one luxury I can never afford. In fact, I carry more loose change than time these days and as for loneliness...well, that seems to be all that my affordable time is spent on.'

'So, you bought this residence yourself then, or...inherited it from someone else?'

'Does it really matter?' Pegasus retorted.

'Yes.'

'Then, yes—of course, I bought it. I couldn't have inherited it, for there was no one I could have inherited it from. I left the First Nation when I was very young, an orphan child adopted into a wealthy family, and then disowned, once they learned how much of a maverick I was—couldn't stop calling me the "P-word".'

'P-word?' Samuella repeated.

'Punk,' Pegasus reinforced. 'Another term for the "liberal-minded".'

'You're a liberal...living in the City Central...in Citadel Tower? Isn't that blasphemy?'

'Yes—and the very reason I departed the City all those years ago as a rebellious teenager. I was the Academy dropout whom some might have called a renegade if they found out. I had been three years-deep into a politics diploma and then, one day—I just disappeared.'

'You were best friends with the Decider. You both attended the Academy together,' Samuella recalled. 'How the hell did that happen?'

'He never knew what I was about. Nobody really did. Not then—and even now, still, people are oblivious to my activities outside of the City's limelight. Philson and I were two sides of a coin, opposites that attracted. If our minds were a seesaw, it would be imbalanced all the time. Perhaps, if I'd stuck around, he'd have probably made me his Stateship – I would have never sucked up to that opportunity.'

'But what made you come back anyway, after you left a Punkish renegade? Isn't it all a façade? Citadel Tower? Your recovered relationship with the Decider? All this luxury?'

'Isn't every role in life a façade? Aren't we humans all just guests at one huge masquerade?' Pegasus considered. 'My current position in the Decider's Administration enables me to transfer between here and the East with considerable ease. I was never labelled a Punk. My foster family only spotted the early signs of my dissidence, my nonconformity to Philson Senior's regime and what was expected from me. I came back to the West as soon as Philson Jr. finished his first term as Decider nearly twenty years ago, and the moment I saw the elections votes were once again unanimous due to corruption – as it had been at every election under his father's Decidership – I returned with the intent to guide him. I wanted to tell him that he was wrong to follow in the footsteps of his father. The Decidership either had to change there and then, or impend its downfall from there onwards.'

'*You* could influence *the Decider* like that?' Samuella's eyes burst from their sockets.

'Of course! The Philsons were old friends and I had grown up with Nicholas. I knew his decision-making and feared it would be the spitting image of his father's. Nicholas didn't wholly respect his father, but, boy, did he trust him completely. Every dogma Philson Senior proclaimed, Nicholas would take it as gospel.'

'He couldn't speak for himself?' Samuella said.

'He had absolutely nothing to say!' Pegasus responded passionately. 'Philson was clueless then and he still is! Even now, he depends on the Stateship and his Administration to help navigate through layers and layers of policies and rights. He was never born to be an independently minded man. Never suited to be a leader.

Constantly dependant on his father's legacy and replaying the successes that have gone before him – that's his own quiet façade. This current era we're living in is just going to be a repeat of the last, and so will the next, if Oscar ever becomes Decider—we'll be stuck in this loop if we allow it to go on.'

'In some way, you sound like the stronger candidate,' Samuella admired. 'You sound more fit for the role of Decider than any Philson ever was.'

'Don't be silly,' Pegasus refuted. 'I could have diverted my good friend Nicholas' ideology at a young age, before he graduated the Academy and succeeded his father in office. But my chances at that were cut short, as I was already under pressure from my fosterers' suspicions and chased out of the West. Luckily, by the time my foster parents discarded me, I'd already had my bags packed. I knew where I was headed next. I wanted to go east—*very east*.'

'Why?' Samuella crinkled her nose at the ambitions of Pegasus in his youth. 'The East hates liberals much as they're hated here.'

'That's not the case everywhere in the East,' Pegasus quietly rejoiced at Samuella's naivety once again. He was fully aware that she was a well-informed young woman, although there were cultures of the most forbidden creeds that not even the most progressive of conspirators had the valour to reckon with. Then, quite randomly from Samuella's perspective, Pegasus pointed at the necklace she was wearing and the emerald that didn't leave her sight. 'That unique gem there—both you and young Master Philson seemed to share a connection with it last night.'

Samuella nodded, vaguely embarrassed by the suggestive remark. After buttering a slice of her toast, she said: 'I've had these dreams. Weird, realistic, outlandish wanders in the night. Every time I go to sleep, they steal me away, night after night. They're always in the same place.'

'Tell me more.' Pegasus grasped a huge interest in this; he was leaning in towards her while peeling an orange.

'I've been going there, to this other world, for almost a week now,' she looked at him like she was unconvinced by her own voice.

'I believe you.' He smiled and winked at her, then plucked a piece from his bowl of diced coconut. 'But you're going to have to write it down for me. I have old ears and I want to remember every detail of this world you speak of.'

They talked boldly and loudly with a sense of childish wonder about Samuella's other life in the Dreamerverse and her adventures on

Constellation Planet, until the emerald caught Pegasus' attention again and distracted him from the conversation once more. 'How do you like that gift I bought you?'

'I've never seen anything like it before,' Samuella said hesitantly. 'But I feel like I should have.'

'I'm happy you appreciate it.' Pegasus had a wise glint in his eyes, as he raised his coffee mug to his lips to hide his smirk. 'The woman who sold it to me in the Purity Market told me it is the rarest mineral this planet has to offer. When I discussed with her that you were going to be the one to wear it, she gave me a good deal and I just had to purchase it.'

Samuella thought this was strange.

'Who was the woman who sold it to you?'

'She runs a jewellery sale out of a bazaar in the Purity Market. Big hair, spooky glasses. A rather eccentric lady with a good eye for rare gems. Why do you seem so concerned?'

'I was just—unsure,' she said.

'Sod insecurities, Miss Samuella! You're in a safe pair of hands now. You ought to return to your guestroom and quickly get into that new dress I ordered for you, so you're not to be late.'

'You ordered me a dress?' Samuella's face lit up. 'Late for what?'

'Yes, a brand new dress is waiting for you, and Stevenson is coming to collect you in it at noon. You have a date with the Decider's son today.'

It was the perfect day for an outing and Mister Pegasus had arranged for Samuella and Oscar to congregate at the Purity Market, because the City Summer Fair had come to town. There was lots of good food (imports from the Fifth Nation were as a exotic as it got), realms of immigrants and expats in their element and on the prowl (who you didn't usually see on a day-to-day basis), and loud speakers pounding traditional folk songs from all four of the West Nations (as opposed to the rhythms of jazz and calypso that so often divided the City). And, since the Fair fell on a bank holiday, there were also a minority of working class First Nation natives ("bumbling Week Traders with nothing better to do in their free time", as the Stateship once described them) dancing in colourful outfits, some proudly costumed as the famous City Lion mascot. The City Fair offered the people of the First Nation an illusion that humanity hadn't *only* changed for the worst and reminded them that the world wasn't as small as they thought.

Stevenson collected Samuella promptly. Noon, like Peggy had promised. And Oscar was with him, having not changed an inch since the night before – still wearing the same dirty, stained chinos even. This time round, their third real world meeting seemed less surreal and more appropriate, in a sense that Samuella could actually place Oscar's voice in her head and understand what he was saying, now that the bewilderment of Pegasus' hospitality was behind her. Last night had been a blur, leaving little room for their contrived relationship to blossom. So, today, the Decider's heir was slightly more than an acquaintance, yet still less than a friend. *What does Pegasus hope to achieve by bringing the two of us together in reality?* Samuella guessed. *Is the connection I have with this boy more than I first believed?*

While they were driven to the melody of Small Island Radio, the odd couple in the backseats talked about the incident in the shop the other day. Oscar was good at explaining his side of the story in that forcedly innocent *I do no harm* sort of voice that didn't rectify Samuella's insecurities, but hung loosely on her earlobes like one of her new earrings. According to him, he'd been wandering around the Octane Mall near to closing hours, since a late wake-up had jumbled his schedule for the most part of that day. He blamed the Dreamerverse and his recent bout of narcolepsy for that. Oscar even told her about the girl he'd drawn in his mind, the one who kept popping up in his dreams. *The Babe With The Blade.*

'I'm not going to lie,' he said coyly. 'I was a bit surprised to find out she was you.'

Samuella cut her eyes at his comical caption for her. She had decided to stay deferentially quiet on this topic, even when he appeared as keen as her to discuss it with someone, anyone with ears. He wanted to gossip incessantly about their adventures on Constellation Planet, but Samuella was reluctant to bring this topic up in the periphery of Stevenson, as she still didn't entirely trust Pegasus' intentions. Whatever the mysterious rogue was scheming for the two of them was still equivocal. Though, what she knew now was that she could put more of her trust in Oscar, her fellow Night Dreamer, who was just as unbeknownst as she. They had been conveniently reunited and were finally on the same page.

The Purity Market was explosively appealing and wildly immersive. The streets were lined with pretty stools and floats. Massive advertisement balloons soared in the sky above them. Stevenson was there to play as bodyguard, leading them around the Market, in and out of the throng. 'Look out fuh dem pickney-pocketers!' he warned. 'Dey nuh look 'ere fuh scrounging stuffs alone. Dem search feh de man de gyal like you. To dem, money like plain breadcrumb from any bun – it easy gain – but as fuh fancy clothin' and de jewellery—dey know dem stuff have a value like a lion's skin to de poacher.' Stevenson realised how his maundering was frightening his subdued companions, particularly Oscar, whose head was a whirligig in a hurricane. Stevenson gleefully swayed with laugher and called back at the awkward couple: '*So, don' leave no trail behind ya step, Hansel n' Gretel!*'

He eventually led them to a big bell tent sitting on a slab of artificial – *far too green to be remotely real* – Gangrene Grass.☆ The tent was royal purple, drizzled decoratively with silver lining; it was an aesthetic that stole Oscar and Samuella away from the Purity Market for a few illusory moments and transported them to some urban bazaar in the East. Its exterior walls were broodily decorated with chains of archaic trinkets, zipping fireflies in lanterns and, scattered on the ground, a lawn of wickedly disturbing glass dolls with pear-shaped eyes for all those that weren't missing eyes – none of which enticed Samuella at all and, instead, kept her disquieted and on her toes constantly. Inside was just as displacing as the exterior's haunting style and unnerving ambience. They were quickly introduced to a heavy aroma that hit them in the face. It was the smell of strong fragrance. Perfumes of the East. Beneath the tent's crown, more firefly lanterns rendered their mellow flares to inspirit an interior that housed a range of eye-catching products. Rows of exquisite jewellery and ornamental relics lay on long purple rugs on the floor. This stock boasted sparkling gems, freshly sharpened diamonds and gold amulets. Samuella struggled to tell what was real or fake. *It couldn't have all been real*, she convinced herself. *These Fair sellers are always a farce.*

A beautiful woman in traditional East gowns approached them from out of the shadows. She had a slim face of immaculate skin that was naturally tanned and brushed with a superb stroke of makeup, but unoffended by any common signs of cosmetic surgery. A thick braid of dark-brown hair as long as a beanstalk anchored the emphatic frame of

---

☆ The dreadful state the ecosystem was in – with there being mass-production of weaponry in the West's military wasting oil and corrupt resource companies being given the gross liberty to recycle waste products, faeces and dead carcasses into reusable "*absolutely anythings*" – led to the creation of artificial nature preserves, such as "Gangrene Grass". They were everywhere now, of course, and bad for health. But there was nothing like the beauty of convenient science and artificial nature was put to good use wherever it could be all around the First Nation.

her towering body. Unmistakeably, the lady was scented with a perfume unlike any other in the tent; it was a scent that poured upon Samuella with nostalgia. However, her robe was more accustomed to West culture, sporting no veil or headdress, low-cut to reveal her cleavage, and her ankles were on show. In all East Nations, a veil was compulsory and no flesh was allowed to be left uncovered. Her dress wouldn't get far in the Sixth or Seventh Nation; even the more lenient, and somewhat more "worldly", Fifth Nation wouldn't respect such defiance. It was misconduct under East Law. *Which was a good sign*, Samuella thought. It meant this woman was an East expatriate with a seasoned outlook; she was a rule breaker.

Oscar, on the other hand, was looking a little uncomfortable. He couldn't find his feet in the East Woman's tent.

'Does it interest you?' The woman asked them in a friendly tone. 'Does anything I possess draw fondness or particularity towards you?'

Then, it dawned on Samuella that this was definitely the woman whom Mister Pegasus had come across the day he'd purchased the emerald-necklace. She was the woman who'd sold it to him. It all matched his description. The wild, buzzing nest of hair. The spooky glasses. She must've known all about "emeralds" – from the ones found in caves to the ones buried hidden in the drawers of wealthy men. 'The Decider's son,' she made this remark as if being harassed by an old fiancé, rather than honouring royalty.

'That's me,' Oscar rolled his eyes, without acknowledging how unimpressed she actually was. 'I'm not going to have to start preaching about my dad on an autograph, am I?'

'I should admit this to you: I have never been in favour of you father's views. For a Decider, he isn't consistent when it comes to making rounded decisions. He's too direct and biased for my liking, too wholesome, and yet he envisions himself as effortlessly unflawed.' She spoke very clear West Dialect, which was baffling. *Even Evanessa had struggled with a number of phrasings*, Oscar reckoned. *But this lady's phrasing is impeccable.* Samuella had never met a non-First Nation native with such suave for West Dialect, with the confidence to land so delicately on the pronunciation of each word and syllable. 'He's a remarkable man. But he's also a remarkable giant and tends to tread on anything he can to gain attention and a good approval rating.'

'I couldn't agree more,' Oscar grew a smile. He'd been a little tetchy on entry, Samuella had noticed, but now that he was feeling the East Woman's vibe, his gates were wide open (or, at least, "open*ing*").

'Listen, you wouldn't happen to be the two associates in the company of Mister Pegasus, would you?' She was talking at Samuella now. Her eyes were moist pools of excitement and awe.

'It's more of a supervisory thing,' Samuella responded. 'He's been very kind to invite me into his home. Even if it is just for the short-term.'

'Well, when I spoke to him yesterday, he preferred to think of it as an honour. He sees you as his protégé, his young lady in waiting.'

Samuella froze without thought. There was nothing to utter other than, 'Why ever would he say that?'

'He was here the other day when he selected a stunning gem that he was enthralled by and couldn't wait to give to you. It's the same one you're wearing this very moment, am I correct?'

'Yeah…this is—this is certainly it.' Samuella touched her chest lightly. It was there. She knew Pegasus was kind, but hadn't expected these flattering words. 'I have it.'

She was amazed by this woman's acuity. Her sentience was too sharp to be true, almost premonitory.

'You wouldn't want to be leaving that lying around. In fact, it's the very reason you're here today. Both of you.'

There it was. The flattery spun back into suspicion.

Oscar and Samuella shared a glance, and then found that Stevenson was already tying together the loose string-ends on the tent's entrance.

'I'm closed for business, but the pair of you have a very important journey ahead of you,' the lady proclaimed. 'Take a seat and I'll explain everything.'

The evening faded and the City Fair bowed out to the night's encore, filled with sudden, wild despondence and rife with debauched stragglers. Now, there, under the shelter of her tent – a luminous anomaly suspended in the night – Aegia Amina, the jeweller lady, told the pair that they would be boarding a Regal Jet to the East. She informed Oscar and Samuella that Intel had identified them specifically with connections to a person of interest, who was smuggling an object, "a rare mineral, of great potential" that posed dangerous prospects in the wrong company and needed to be procured and stabilised for the protection of Mankind's World. As a consequence, the two of them had been beseeched by her and Pegasus on behalf of their unnamed "affiliates" to confront the Decider and Xenol's plot against Phestor

Serpens, and they, in phenomenal secrecy, would be required to infiltrate this event, in order to safely acquire "the crucial object".

Samuella and Oscar were drinking herbal tea and sitting in patchy armchairs, their bare feet sunken into fuzzy tiger-skin rugs. They were facing Aegia and trying to build a picture of every detail she told them. It had all smoke and mirrors thus far, but at the mentioning of a powerful object and a person of interest, it was starting to become clear what was going on here.

'You'll be safely under supervision the whole time and we have enlisted the assistance of Stevenson for once you touchdown in the East. You'll arrive in the Fifth Nation and, from there, travel to the Sixth, where you'll meet a team of our collaborators, waiting on standby to operate alongside you. They will be our eyes and ears along the way, recording your every move and reporting it back to me and Pegasus, until we can get to you.'

Collaborators? Samuella pondered. *Who are these collaborators?*

'What motive is this? I never said I wanted to go to the East! I wouldn't plea for such a death wish! We never agreed to any of this,' Oscar argued. 'At least, *I* never.'

'Neither did I,' Samuella added unconvincingly. She was intrigued and half-invested in this outline of Pegasus' secret plan, partly because she had been fascinated by Aegia's presence from the moment she'd entered the tent.

'Who *are* you? Talking on behalf of him? Pegasus sent us here, to meet you, *for this?*' Oscar urged. 'Both you and Pegasus assume that we're some sort of free agents. As if you know something that we don't and we're supposed to be playing into your hands like a pair of puppets.'

'That isn't the case at all, Oscar,' Aegia responded. 'We're not pulling the wool over your eyes. I'm here to be upfront with you. To tell you the truth and to tell you why we need you to play your role in this – why *everyone* needs your help!'

'Why do you need me? How did you and Pegasus even come to find out about me?' Samuella said. 'You knew who I was! None of this was a coincidence!'

'Pegasus set this up?' Oscar slipped in with a new avenue of inquiry before Aegia could answer. He really is clueless, isn't he? Samuella figured. More so than me. 'It was his idea to go against my father's word and plot this revolt in his absence? I don't understand—he used to be so loyal to him. Why does he want to stab my father in the back all of a sudden?'

'Okay, allow me to clear one thing up first. Mister Pegasus is currently the head of foreign relations and the Decider believes him to be out of service at the moment, hence unavailable for consultation in current affairs. I myself am a former archaeologist from the Sixth Nation. I am now an antiquary and trader based here in the First Nation. In the midst of our regular occupations, Pegasus and I have been secret informants for the Brotherhood of Infidels in the East. We've been monitoring the current Decidership for fifteen years now, studying the actions of the Administration and predicting what will happen to it in the near future, based on the decisions the Decider makes and the relations he fosters both internationally and domestically—'

'You *are* spies! You always *were*! *I knew it!*' Samuella cried.

'No. We're *informants.* Our interest doesn't just stop at the knowledge; it goes much further than that. It is our role to ensure that the liberal Infidels in the East are aware of the West's decisions before they are implemented and the Xenol-Philson Alliance has thrown our organisation into a state of emergency. For the first time in half a century, peacekeepers across the world have been caught off-guard and whatever this covert alliance spurs into could be cataclysmic for all mankind.

'Peacekeepers?' Oscar regurgitated. 'Is that just a safe way of calling yourselves "good spies" as opposed to "enemy spies"? You operate in the East, though? With the Infidels?'

'We're justice seekers, not provocateurs – not "spies" by any means. We associate with protest groups – both liberal groups and the old, hard-core democratic groups – here in the West and we support the Infidels in the East in their revolution against the Phestor's Republic and its leaders. Something much deeper than war is going on at the moment. Oscar, your father is taking a very derailing approach to the situation in the East and he is about to perform an unforgivable disaster. He is too naïve and set in his ways. He isn't supposed to be in the East. No Decider should ever be in the East, let alone working alongside a Phestor, particularly a Phestor of Xenol's influence and magnitude. Something rings fishy about this formidable and capricious relationship. The outcome could make the tensions between the two sides catastrophic.'

'You want me to face my father and tell him to stop what he's doing?' Oscar persisted. 'You want *me* to stick *my* fingers into *his* plans and pull *him* out of it?'

'He's a man with good intentions, Oscar. But, as we've both agreed, he's taken things a step too far again. One mutual threat against himself and Phestor Xenol has led him into making rash decisions. His support for the Phestor of the Sixth Nation will have consequences one way or the other; either direction, it won't be good.'

'But *surely* we're not the right people to do this—*come on!*' Samuella said. 'We aren't the folk you're looking for! Not only are we irrelevant to their cause—but we're not diplomats at all! We're not big enough, or loud enough, to shout down the Decider's following! And we're nowhere near clinical enough to perpetrate the bloomin' East at any angle! I'm not a soldier, or a spy—I'm a crofter, a child of the soil! And, as for Oscar, no matter who he is and whether his father is the Decider or not, he has no influence. He's a teenager with no say at all, whereas his father is a household name with a reputation and the power to shutdown anyone on the planet.'

'My father is very fixed when he calls a decision. It won't be easy to make him twitch,' Oscar said.

'Your father is a dead man in five days.' Aegia became very direct and hard-line with them now. 'If we do nothing, it won't be long until you and everyone you know are faced with the same fate. He's balancing everybody's luck on a weak, desperate pact with Xenol.'

'What has this mission that you and Pegasus have discussed behind our backs got to do with us especially?' Samuella said. 'Just tell us.'

'You both know the girl in question.' Aegia spoke like she was surrendering to a band of gun-swaggering bank-robbers. She was convincing with the justification of her appeal, but disorganised at pitching her request. 'The Phestor's mistress. You've both met her, am I right?'

'She came to my father's residence the other day,' Oscar said. 'Her and Xenol were there to propose the assassination of Phestor Serpens to the Decider's Table. The entire banquet was there in front of them and Xenol strolled in brazenly, confidently, like he knew exactly what he was going in for and that he was going to end up getting it. Even if that meant he was going to walk out with my father's head on the end of his sword. You should've been there to see it. They were prepared to hand Evanessa over to the Seventh Nation like a damp cloth for the Stateship to dry his sweating forehead.' Oscar strode out from his cave of insecurity, finally willing to joust with the East Woman. 'Do you really think we'd have a chance of saving her from a man so ruthless?'

'I know what Phestor Xenol is like,' Aegia responded. 'I spent most of my life living in the Sixth Nation. My parents used to be organisers for the Dusk of Offerings festival there and they used to tell me horrendous stories about the ways Xenol used to send his A.I. out on murderous witch-hunts after people he suspected were spies working for the Infidels and the West. He used to sell his children to oisters in return for their oil reserves, so that he could build his weapons of mass destruction.☆ He can be reckless and most of the worst crimes he commits are behind the scenes. His shady dealings have been peeled away from public view on hundreds of accounts. He's a criminal despot, but to the public he's a lynchpin that no right mind would dare to replace, because, right now, without him in power, the East wouldn't last another day in the Conflicts. Xenol is a tactical genius, who knows how to manipulate all the East Nations. Fifth and Seventh used to smooch his backside and he was once best friends with the Phestor in the Eighth Nation, before that place went to hell.'

'And you want us to go over there, to face him and the Decider,' Samuella stated, already deflated by the prospects. 'With what?'

'Both of you each have an emerald and the success of this operation depends on you locating the third,' Aegia said. 'There is still one more to find. Their importance in all this I will elaborate on. Nothing omitted. I promise. Do you have the Map?'

Oscar was nearly knocked off his seat by this remark. 'How do you know about that?'

'The girl gave it to you, did she?' Aegia placed a warm hand over Oscar's. 'This I know is true, for the girl also sourced me with the emerald I handed Pegasus to give to Samuella. Neither of them belonged to Evanessa. She was only doing the legwork when she brought it to me initially and informed me about Xenol's plans. The final leg of this task you will have to take into your own hands now.'

'Evanessa?' Samuella tore into the conversation. 'Is this the same girl we're talking about here? She has pretty, hazel eyes—?'

'How do you know her?' Oscar scoffed. As Samuella had originally anticipated, Oscar finally turned his nose up at the urchin-girl who'd once worn rags for a living and tidied up after the children of the Slumberlands.

'I dreamt about her. On that note, I guess we both have,' Samuella defended.

☆ *Oister (definition): The owner/inheritor of a minimum of 1-tonne of oil. (These were important investors for the Phestors).*

'You vaguely remember what you dreamt about her?' Aegia inquired. 'Do you remember her as *The Last Night Dreamer*?'

'Not precisely what she was doing,' Samuella said. 'But someone like her would be difficult to forget. She did mention something about being "the Last Night Dreamer" and that I had claimed that position from her. I'm a new generation of Night Dreamer.'

'You're *both* a new breed of Night Dreamer,' Aegia quickly established, looking between the pair of them. They were as stunned as her, like they'd only just discovered the final piece to a puzzle, hiding under a cushion days after giving up.

'Hold up,' Oscar intervened with the buzzing thoughts circling around the tent. There was a notion he and Samuella were both ignoring. 'First, you know about the Map, the Constellation Map, and the emeralds we're in possession of. Then, you refer to the girl with hazel eyes, whom we both apparently have a connection to. And, now, you've brought up the term "Night Dreamer". What are you holding back about the Dreamerverse?'

'I myself have been there. Does my observation of the Dreamerverse come as a surprise to you?' Aegia said. 'When I met Pegasus for the first time, I had arrived here from the East and didn't know a single inch of the City. It left me stammering, completely overcome. But I recognised his face. We had met before in the Dreamerverse as youths. It was a miracle we remembered as much as each other's face, since the Memory Lane usually comes into play, blocking out our alter egos across the Void. While we hardly knew each other in those early days, we quickly understood how significant our connection between the worlds was and how this secret discovery of ours – this sacred, imaginary universe that nobody else knew about – would pave the way for greater discoveries in the future. So, we moved away from the City for a brief time and kick-started a quiet life together elsewhere, until we found our place with the Infidels. Before then, I had been an archaeologist, studying this mineral – the Digimine mineral that consists within the emeralds – and I learned something remarkable about it. Its attributes are far more impactful than anything else Mankind's World has to offer. I told Pegasus about them and the power they have to transform the way we build our world, how we power our industries and our cities, and they could change the way world trade and the economy function. These emeralds could completely renovate the Slumberlands and reform bridges between Nations. They are very special. But the general public knows nothing about them. No one does, except for me, Pegasus, the Night Dreamers who are sent to hunt them down – which includes the two of you – and, finally, the East and West governments, who have been making use of this mineral for decades. But they haven't been using it to benefit infrastructure, they've been using the material for something else.'

Oscar and Samuella looked vacantly at each other.

'What have they been using it for?' Samuella asked.

'To boost their experiments with the emerald's unique scientific properties. The emeralds' utility under these governments' jurisdiction is designed to keep humanity flawed and controlled through terror,' Aegia stated.

'How does that work? Have we seen anything resembling these "terrors" yet?' Oscar cited.

'They're everywhere, not even hidden in plain sight. And we've been coexisting with them for years, putting up with their coercion…But never mind any of that for the time being,' the jeweller lady said no more on the conspiracy. 'Your duty as Night Dreamers is exactly the same as the generations that came before you.'

'Is that supposed to make us competent of finding and protecting Evanessa as well?' Samuella said sceptically. 'Why did Evanessa leave these emeralds lying around like breadcrumbs for us to find? Why lead us to two and hide away the third?'

'Now that there's a shortage of this material, the superpowers need every ounce of it they can get,' Aegia explained, blatantly avoiding Samuella's question. 'We can't let a Phestor or a Decider get any more of it or they'll keep using the mineral to fortify their grasp on power. In the wrong hands, the emeralds are the key to the future of these horrible terrors. They are mere chippings of the vital and rare mineral known as Digimine, and the pocket of scientists in the Polar Regions who specialise in its use are currently under the influence of narcissistic leaders that want to reap its abilities in order to keep their manufactured terrors functioning.

'In the Dreamerverse, the emeralds are alternatively required to empower a counter-weapon against the Drag-in. This alternative weapon that's maintained on Constellation Planet supresses the Drag-in within the Void and keeps it there, trapped. I've never been the one to uncover the counter-weapon based in the Dreamerverse, since I was never a Night Dreamer. But I once met the revered Phantom of the Dreamerverse and they said that it exists. The Phantom is responsible for maintaining the counter-weapon, keeping it primed, just in case the

Drag-in returns. They called it a Lighthouse. The Phantom's Lighthouse.'

'Evanessa—she's the Phantom!' Samuella re-established, her dishevelled dream-memory restoring itself. 'That's what she told me.'

'Yes, she has become the Phantom now. She and her fellows once had to operate the Lighthouse themselves when the Drag-in last emerged. Night Dreamers have the greatest responsibility of all in this reality and in the Dreamerverse,' Aegia concluded. 'They're responsible for finding the powerful emeralds, operating the counter-weapon, and taming the Drag-in – a force of peril so big it could potentially wipe out the stars and bring an end to life as we know it. However, the Terror-weapon in the real world and the counter-weapon in the Dreamerverse share one similarity. Both "weapons" can only be made functional by Digimine as their fuel, which means the emeralds are capable of initiating both biased equilibrium and merciless destruction, depending on how they are used and who has them.'

'Sounds pretty far-fetched,' Oscar commented.

'There is some psychological connection between the "Drag-in of the Dreamerverse" and "the Drag-in among humanity" still. According to ancient philosophers here in the real world, a "Drag-in" of our own creation really has spent many years trying to penetrate through the Void of dangerous imagination and into a radical existence,' Aegia explained. 'It has tried to divide humanity and the world before and did succeed once, splitting the Old World Order into eight independent Nations. This was a creature of the mind, a manmade conglomerate that is never sporadic, but a whole, formed from many thoughtless, following pawns with frightful and irrational emotions, collated from a hatred that is strategically conducted and densely compacted by an ideological hub of the organised minority choiring behind their antisocial instrumentalist, their leader – this "manmade Drag-in". We, the human race, feed it without any knowledge of it at all. It is always finding new ways to annex and dampen the good spirit of our world.'

'So you believe that the Drag-in *does* exist in reality,' Samuella considered. 'Just not in the same context. Rather than being a savage demon menacing to rip apart the stars, it's an antisocial disease destined to shatter the nature of civilisation.'

'Exactly. This is why the Dreamerverse and reality can never collide. The Drag-in must be prevented and collecting all of the emeralds to impair it of its strength will help you to do this. The emeralds will lead you.' Aegia's eyes set on a traditional East-style mosaic that was pinned on the tent's wall. It was sewn with petals from various flowers typical of the Sixth and Seventh Nations. The border around the petals coiled to shape the body of a dragon, long and slender. Bulging black seeds marked the eyes.

'The Drag-in has already been existing here in the real world for a long while, and has had its impact in *our actual lives* without any of us even noticing?' Oscar asked uncomfortably.

'Evidently, that is very probable. But remember how the Drag-in has no physical form in the Dreamerverse. It's similar here in reality. The Drag-in is merely an idea that many submissive minds have helped to feed. However, someone in particular is engineering this idea and controlling the Drag-in's entity, and their intentions are identical on both sides of the Void, in both worlds.'

'Phestor Serpens,' Oscar muttered. He spotted the two women staring at him for making this sweeping judgement and dropped his jaw. 'Perhaps,' he added moderately.

'It very well could be,' Aegia bowed her head in thought. 'However, you need to focus. Serpens may be a worse leader than Xenol, but he has little to say on the world stage - he is an inferior to Xenol. Follow the Constellation Map when you get to the East. It will lead you to the final emerald and when you have it, use it to bring down the human counterpart of the Drag-in - the host who is present in reality. This person will also be searching for all three Digimine fragments. If you can catch the culprit out in the real world, the effect in the Dreamerverse could be simultaneous.'

Aegia stood up and marched across the tent, over to where a table held a masterful ornament. A golden statue with a fountain-mouth. The statue was the head of a bearded East Man with wide, frightening eyes. Out of the spout, a thin stream of silvery water flowed quietly. Next to the ornament was a long rifle with a tiny, refined scope. Aegia took this from the table and examined it. 'Go with Stevenson. He'll take you back to Citadel Tower, where you'll prepare for your journey. You will be departing very soon—tomorrow morning, I presume. Anything else you need to know will be explained by Mister Pegasus. I cannot discuss this too much tonight, as I must pack to make my own return to the East.'

Samuella could sense that Oscar had been on his toes the whole time and was urgent to prod the lady for more information. 'But let's not forget about Evanessa. They're going to kill her,' he said. 'What if we're already too late? And what if we classify the wrong culprit and misjudge the Drag-in's true identity?'

Aegia didn't turn to look at him. She stretched out her arm, indicating at the rifle held in her hand. 'Foil the Decider-Phestor Alliance by taking out Xenol before the trade-off of Evanessa's life is made to Serpens.'

'You want us to *kill* a Phestor?' Samuella choked.

'You need to *kill the Drag-in*. If that means taking out Xenol in order to get Evanessa's life out of his hands, then so be it. Remember that the Phestor's mistress is the key to your success. She will know where you can locate the last emerald.'

'Couldn't she have just told me this when I spoke with her the other day?' Oscar said.

'No. The circumstances were far too risky during her visit to Citadel Tower. That encounter she had with you was treacherous enough. Besides, for her to take action on this alone would be too much in plain sight and a death sentence. Procuring the emeralds out from danger isn't the Phantom's role—it's yours.' Aegia handed Oscar the rifle. 'You need to get to her before the Phestors' exchange and rescue her so that she can help you to finish this! Discuss this affair with others wisely; some ears may assist you, while others will hinder you. We're all dependent on you're actions now. So, please make the right decisions.'

By this point, Stevenson had already untied the tent's entrance and the two of them were led out and back through the crowds under the murky skies above the market square.

Back at Citadel Tower, Oscar brought Samuella to his residence upstairs. In the elevator, he'd insisted that she *held on* for a couple more floors until they passed Pegasus' residence and both reached the second from the very top – exceeding all limits and expectations of the innocent country girl who was now bound to the care of aristocrats. His place was a lot bigger and roomier than that of Mister Pegasus. Without knowing whom it belonged to or where it was, anyone would've assumed that it either belonged to a rich, incestuously numerous family or a large community of intelligent chimps on a sophisticated lunar space station.☆

He wanted to show her something. Two things, actually. The first thing he threw at her was the emerald his Aunt Sybil had dumped on him. It wasn't identical to hers. The colour of his was a bright green,

---

☆ Yes, there were monkeys on the moon. They'd been living there for quite some time.

whereas, hers was a distinguishably darker shade. Also, Oscar's emerald was irrationally smaller than hers and consisted of more sharp edges. The next thing he showed her was the very appreciable Constellation Map, which he kept hidden underneath his bed. And they both found it strange that it was one of the very few *key things* – along with recognition of each other's identities, Evanessa, and the Drag-in – that they could significantly remember beyond the Void between Dreamerverse and reality.

'It's hard to believe that it actually exists. Here. Physically,' Samuella said, examining the many sparkling constellations that filled the page. They'd established that Oscar was exempt from viewing the Map, for he could no longer read it. It was Samuella's turn to navigate.

'How can we remember better now than before?' Oscar queried. 'That makes everything seem more important now. Everything's severe. We either succeed by finding this Drag-in and slaying it, and we also win by somehow rescuing Evanessa from the clutches of her patriarch. Or, if we miss out on both of those chances, we're subjected to a doomsday scenario – where everybody loses.'

'That's probably the best way of putting it,' Samuella said.

'I'm not ready to go through this! It isn't fair on us!'

'There's no way out, Oscar. You heard the woman. They've been planning this before we even met. Before we even knew we were destined to materialise on Constellation Planet. They've known just as much as we have and more than we've been aware of.'

'Are you confident though, Sam? Confident that we can pinpoint the right culprit and draw an end to this?'

'I don't even think "*confident*" puts it into perspective.'

The Tombs of Truth...

I think it would be a smart idea if I admitted now, in this indefinitely cruel alcove of space, that I'm severely claustrophobic. When I sank into the sand, all dimensions had closed in. Dreamerverse and reality both became irrelevant. Forget four walls; there had been more than that. I'm talking ceiling, sky, ground...everything caved in on me. The panorama of the desert has eluded from view and my soberest bearings have digressed into amateurish ingenuity.

The purple seed I swallowed in the scorpion crater is on the verge of wearing off absolutely. I can't tell whether I'm lucky or unlucky to have been served the end of that seed's effect, for the tsunami of sand sweeping me in and the prospect of suffocating under the desert surface had shocked me unconscious and Awakening Coast might have been a preferable option in hindsight. However, something objectively lured me through that labyrinth and has buried me alive in the process.

I have just come to. Paralysed. Arms and legs can't be rebooted, only a will-killing pressure batting me from all over. Am I injured? Mangled? Can't see! Even my eyes—*Are they still there?* I contemplate.

'ARE THEY STILL THERE?' I caw. Panicking. Is anything still there? Presumably. I'm hearing nothing out loud...Oh, makes sense—I can't speak either. Are my lips still there? The tongue? All but my mind is absent. Everything else is on holiday somewhere nice. Maybe back on Awakening Coast...Imagine if the wearing purple seed has caused half of me to resurrect there and left the rest of me here, under the soils of Pegasus Island. What if it's just my mind I have stranded here—only my entity, my spirit...? I could be one of those awful free spirits—a Nightmare!

Am I finally dead then? Is this what happens when you die in a dream? Is this what happens when you *actually die*? Will I see anything ever again—?

'Shush, you!' A new voice arrives unexpectedly. Not the same one that summoned me into the maze – he was deeper in tone. Was I really expecting another bloody voice to come and start talking to me down here? Is it what I need, right now? Get lost, voice! Yeah, jog on!

'Don't you realise, you stupid girl?' It's a prickly whisper that tickles me like the granules of soil grinding into my ears. 'You're trying too hard!'

I apologise for trying to function like an able human being. Could you lend a helping hand, perhaps?

'Does it look to you like I possess hands? Does it even seem like I could imagine conceiving hands?' The patronising tone is a stench that reeks off its breath in tandem with the sweet musk of the earth lodged in my nostrils.

What have you done with me?

'I am all around you. That was my surface you decided to trample on! You and your little crippled friend were standing on my face!'

Am I talking to…the ground? Please don't tell me I'm flirting with dirt now!

'Yes, you're damn right to be humiliated!' my captor responds, and the roots around my waist and arms drastically constrict, pushing a muffled whine out of my throat. 'And you had the nerve to challenge my labyrinth and to hurt my only protector, Shaula, scorpion guard of the Blankesphere and all of its death-bound truths hidden from the Dreamerverse and reality.'

I haven't a clue what he means. This is supposed to be Pegasus Island - what appeared like an arid and barren land on the Map. Well, that was what the Map said to me. I can't really be taking all this nonsense from *the ground*. It's probably just my imagination fluctuating again—or some other mischievous spirit meddling with my thoughts.

'What's the big deal about talking to the ground beneath your feet? Well—beneath your feet before, but now look who's ended up on top. Nonetheless, we can still have an intelligent conversation. I used to be a free spirit just like you once. We're not that different. Don't be a hypocrite!'

Spirit—? Who's a free spirit? I'm spooked. Is this a confirmation of my fears?

'You—you're a spirit!'

Did I die? Did you kill me? Wow—I'm genuinely asking the ground if it murdered me?

'You can ask me anything,' the voice replies. Creepily too responsive.

Creepy? But I'm not speaking to you...Well, theoretically—I can't actually move my lips.

'I don't have any. So, stop worrying about it. Listen, you shouldn't let yourself get swept away by what that steward-bird told you. He isn't the only one with telepathic talents. That skill comes innately for all spirit-beings on Constellation Planet. Here, I'll make it a tad easier for you.'

The soil concealing my mouth crumbles away, leaving a hole for my dry, pruning lips to poke through.

'Better?' I can see the ground smiling at me right now. Roots protrude from the soil above my face, shaped into perky lips. 'See, all you had to do is ask.'

The ground? Smiling?

'Was that your plan?' I ask. 'To suffocate me?'

'My dear Dreamer, I don't know how you're interpreting this, since I respect that this situation is pretty novel to you, but I did not murder you or set out to harm you in any kind of way. I was simply making a stand for my own respect and dignity. Don't go gallivanting where you're unwanted. Wasn't the scorpion in the sand enough to shoo you?'

'I was about to mention the scorpion! Your *protector* was what was trying to kill me! I was only following where I was led to go!'

'Who led you to my labyrinth?' the ground outbursts, suspicious now.

'Do you know who I am?'

'Who?'

'I'm the Night Dreamer. One of a selected few on a quest to slay the Drag-in before it breaks loose in this world and reality. Get it?'

'Oh, why...so, why didn't you say so in the first place?' the ground begins to loosen its grip around me and I slowly feel myself descending further; there's a floating sensation as I spiral deeper below. 'Usually, I have no comfort for newcomers or trespassers, but, on this occasion, it truly is an honour to be in your company. Welcome, good *Night Dreamer*, to the Blankesphere, the next world beneath Constellation Planet's soil. This is where the dead come to relish before their free spirits are transformed and respectfully re-embodied.'

'Dead Dreamers?' I confirm. 'We're Dead Dreamers?'

'I believe you are, as unfortunate as it seems,' the ground sympathises. Some roots grapple my shins and drag me down much faster into the ground's depths. 'I have seen every dead man's spirit descend to the Blankesphere. But never before have I welcomed a Night Dreamer.'

'Wait—not even the previous generation of Night Dreamers?'

'Their fates are questionable. They vanished many years ago. I've never seen one step foot down here, alive or dead.'

'And what about Evanessa? Surely, you've met her. The girl with the beautiful eyes and golden hair. I was responsible for burning her body. She asked for her corpse to be cremated by another Night Dreamer, so that she could come to an afterlife – and I presume that place is here.'

'I'm not familiar.'

'The Last Night Dreamer? You must know about her.'

Suddenly, my feet touch the ground and I'm upright again, facing down a narrow, bleak corridor with nothing in sight beyond where I stand. 'I apologise, but I must ask…why are you here?' the ground is being strangely polite to me now.

'I was sent here,' I tell it. 'My two fellow Night Dreamers and I have been following a trail with the help of the Constellation Map. And, somehow – perhaps, coincidentally – we ended up here.'

I look into the abyss ahead. Not even my imagination can battle its way through the mesh of blunt opaqueness. 'This doesn't look as spectacular as I'd imagined Hell to be. Where are the flames and the red horns?'

'Proceed and you will find your way,' the unmanned voice booms like an echo out of place.

'Find my way to *where*?' I insist. 'I've come looking for an emerald.'

'Night Dreamer, there is such a thing as *consequence*. Nobody controls it, nobody challenges it, nobody deceives it, because it tends to have its own grasp on everything. In cheaper words: go with the flow. You may be surprised with what you discover when you don't fret so much.'

So, I do as the ground suggests. I slowly wander into the dark, shuffling like a constipated penguin. The corridor's stone ground is flat and, tidy without any soil or sand littering it, and the walls on either side are so close together that they brush my shoulders. If I listen carefully enough, I can hear subtle singing, expanding into a choir that soon floods the entire corridor. The tuneful legato of angelic voices.

'You can hear the singing of the souls right about now,' the ground utters. 'They have listened to the rhythm of your own spirit. A new sound; your beating heart, to them this is so profound. Beautiful, isn't it? They're so grateful to be transpiring from free spirit form to a new incarnation. As you must be aware, many spirits are discarded as free, bodiless entities forever, as Nightmares dwindling on the hinges of existence. These spirits down here are the lucky few who transcend the Falls of Fortune and triumph in new bodies.'

'What are they saying?'

'They want their bodies sooner. But, more importantly, they're aware of the danger the Dreamerverse faces. They're vocalising their dire fear of the impending Neverness and they want someone to rescue all the living, before the afterlife becomes inundated with free-spirits.'

'*Neverness?*' I pick up on this bizarre concept.

'Neverness is the most terrifying consequence of any living being. The Drag-in's forthcoming will leave even the dead without an existence, without a mind, without liberty. Living matter, living identity and living memory will all cease to exist. Unless the Drag-in is defeated again, that is.'

I still have the Map on me, under my bra-strap and wedged against my back. And the seeds are scattered in my tight pocket. I count them – none are missing, save for those I've eaten. My sword is missing, lost when I was snatched from the surface. From what I've seen so far of this "Blankesphere", I don't expect myself needing it any time soon. Unravelling the Constellation Map, I search for the ***X***-mark, and according to the comet-trail, inching only about a fingernail's length across the page; I'm standing relatively right next to the rocks location. That's all I see on the Map. The constellations aren't there anymore. All of the stars have vanished, leaving only the ***X*** to swish on the blank page.

'It should be here,' I say. 'The emerald should be right where I'm standing.'

'Are you sure?' the ground replies, none the wiser.

'When you digested me, did you also remember where you left my friend?'

'You mean the injured young man? On the surface?'

'Yes. Where is he?'

'Hmm, not far from here. But, then again, I worry that he's not yet descended completely. Some elements of him may still be struggling to materialise here.'

'*Some elements?*' I regurgitate.

'Oh, yes, it is common practice that, when one passes into the Blankesphere, their spirit is fragmented and then recreated to suit its renewed conditions as a free spirit. Your being must adjust, morphing down here in the Blankesphere offers spirits like yourself the luxuries that Nightmares can only envy. Remember, you had organs that worked efficiently up on ground level – these will need adapting. Have you even thought to consider why you're breathing so well hundreds of feet beneath the ground?'

'Hold on. There's something else I remember. About the girl with the golden hair. She called herself the *Phantom of the Dreamerverse*. Does that mean anything to you?'

Suddenly, a gust of cool air flushes through the cave to blow me off my feet.

'The Phantom?' the ground says in astonishment. 'You spoke to the Phantom? The *actual one*?'

'I suppose so. Is there only one? Should that worry me?' I ask.

'Nobody has seen the Phantom in years. She tends to keep to herself, out of the way, and often works among us in secrecy. You know how these celebrities go about their privacy. One Night Dreamer of every generation is delegated to become the mentor of the next generation, after all. It is more than likely that she has had an influence over your journey here. But the fact that she *spoke* to you is somewhat…concerning.'

'Why's that?'

'It suggests that she's trying to guide you,' the ground says. 'Route you, it would seem, in the right direction. Perhaps, she was responsible for the crossing of our paths. Would you happen to be carrying the Seeds of Continuity? If you have a green seed at hand, there may be a better chance of reaching your friend.'

I retrieve the bag of seeds from my soiled pyjama pocket and sift through its contents before revealing a green seed on my palm.

'That's the one,' the ground announces. 'The green seed will feed you into a network of telepathic communication that is superlative in the Blankesphere. Your friend isn't completely deceased yet. His mind is still present up above, but I will advise him to do the same, once he fully separates himself from the surface.'

Taking that terrifying remark as a cue, I begin to aggressively chew the seed. It's indecisively sweet and sour, but not so unsavoury to a point where it would desperately need to be ejected from my mouth. With the chewing underway, my hands glow a weak tint of turquoise, hiding my original complexion in a glossy spell of illumination. The same colour reflects from my cheeks and onto the corridor's walls. As for my ears and eyes and nose and all those other sensory holes and crannies around the place, they're more porous than ever. Attentive. Listening...

I look up. And I am no longer in a claustrophobic's trauma.

I've arrived in paradise.

Palm trees surround an enclosed courtyard of bright turquoise grass, from which a bluish vapour rises among sparkling flowers with crystallised petals. In the middle of the courtyard is a lazily babbling cyan fountain and around it are benches for basking. I'm not alone either. People are here. No, people are *almost* here: a ghostly community of men, woman and children loiter about the courtyard, dressed in pyjamas and onesies (and, quite perplexingly, some voluptuous lingerie). They're going about their own business, as if I haven't arrived to disturb them at all.

I notice my own hands...Alarmed by what I see (or, at least, what I *think* I see), I run to the fountain and lean over to take a glance at myself in the water's reflection. My face is totally translucent. I pull away and glumly look around at the party of spirits like a bookshelf in the middle of an arcade.

I'm a part of them. I'm one of them. I'm a goner!

'Now you can see my world, I'll introduce you to my neighbours. See that girl over there? She's my ex-girlfriend...well, she used to be,' the ground's voice ricochets through the courtyard, waltzing with the quaint, breezy flutter that brushes me with the passing ghosts. 'The dead of the Dreamerverse have been living beneath you all this time and they were of no concern to you, just as you were a scorpion and a sinkhole away from them. This form of communication lets you embrace your sixth sense and interact with them.'

'Am I supposed to be impressed?'

'I should expect.'

'Well, you're in luck – I am.'

On the other side of fountain, I see a man unlike the others. Estranged from the rest, he's dressed in a neat suit that fits slickly like a first time wear, with a rose on the lapel and a sharp, narrow tie sitting nattily on his chest. He means more business than bedtime (which is strange for a Dreamer, no?). But he's not going about with any purpose, just dithering aimlessly. In fact, he's not very sociable either. He doesn't look much at the other spirits at all. Doesn't look at any of them. After moseying for a bit, he then goes to sit, perches himself on the edge of the fountain and turns his attention to the water below. 'You said everyone here was a Dreamer?' I consider.

'I said no such thing,' the ground interrupts defensively. 'I mentioned passing Dreamers are present here, but failed to mention anybody else. You assumed it is only Dreamers who dwell down here. However, you must also wonder where the Non-Dreamers go when they pass.'

'So, not everybody here is a Dreamer, after all.'

'Not everybody has time to be a Dreamer,' the ground admits. 'The worst cases are the insomniacs, who often think too hard to dream. And thinking isn't like dreaming at all. Thinking is a tumultuous and stressful realism, though dreaming is nothing of the sort. Dreaming is a mode of escaping thought.'

Still watching the man in the suit, I catch him dipping his cupped palm into the fountain and the water remains unaffected by his diaphanous touch. He lifts his hand out, having fished a weightless, transparent apple from the water and he gazes at it, fascinated, before taking a first bite.

An incorporeal couple stroll past me, holding hands. The woman is wearing an old, forgotten nightdress and the man is in military uniform, they're strolling side-by-side, practically rubbing shoulders, but don't acknowledge one another at all. Not even when they collide and pass completely through each other and then carry on diverging again along their different paths. I find it chilling that people trapped in Reality have been intermingled with those dwelling in the Dreamerverse.

'"Till death do us part" is a load of codswallop then, isn't it?' I propose.

'Correct,' the ground agrees.

'Does that make everybody a Dreamer, then?' I wonder. 'Eventually, are we all forced to dream?'

'No,' the ground says.

'But surely they can see each other here – the Dreamers and the Non-Dreamers? They can all see each other now, can't they?'

'I'm afraid not,' the ground laments. 'When one dies in one world and one dies in another, their dimensions are not reunited in the

Blankesphere. That is what the Void between worlds does. It separates minds that do not think or imagine alike.'

'Take a look at the Map again,' the ground suggests. 'It should make some sense now.'

The Map isn't an empty slate anymore. Instead of the constellations being there, I see a smaller illustration of another destination, headed as **Scorpius Island**. The stars on the Map have realigned to form the Dune Labyrinth and then fade once more to reveal the Blankesphere beneath it. Only, on the Map, this place isn't titled the Blankesphere. It's specifically labelled: *The Tombs of Truth.*

'What's with that?' I ask, alarmed. 'This isn't Pegasus anymore! It never was! We're on Scorpius! The Map led us to somewhere completely different! It lied to us!'

'I've been told the Constellation Map can be notorious for misleading its users,' the ground notes. 'But, oddly enough, your journey appears to have been predestined, since this Phantom seems adamant to mentor you and rig you passage.'

'So, no matter however which circumstance the Map chooses to misbehave or act up funny, the Phantom seems to be setting diversions and manipulating the constellations themselves, in order to keep you and your companions one step ahead and on track.'

'That would explain the water phoenixes that showed up right on cue at the Falls of Fortune. I knew that had something to do with intervention – they just appeared out of the water and flew us here at their own will. You're right – intervention landed us here. Divine intervention. I only wish I knew why the Map tried to trick us into believing the emerald was on Pegasus.'

'Hmmm,' the ground reconsiders. 'I suppose, if deception was the case, it couldn't have been the Phantom who brought you to Scorpius. Phantoms do not deceive Night Dreamers under their wing; it would go against their pledge. Another force else must have taken helm of the water phoenixes while you were in mid-flight over the ocean. Night Dreamer, it is important you realise that the Tombs of Truth are a region in the Blankesphere that must be hidden from plain sight, for there are too many truths here that are dangerous to the living and can only be taken to the grave. Therefore, Scorpious probably disguised itself on your Map and played on your ambiguities as a novice navigator. Unfortunately, even the greatest truth must be guarded by a fortress of deception.'

'The Tombs are the part of the Blankesphere where they keep the bodies, am I right? It's where the flesh is buried?'

'When Dreamers die – and when ordinary people die – it isn't the body that remains locked away,' the ground states. 'It's the energy of the soul, the mind, that gets banked and then restored in fresh embodiment. This energy stays living forever. The spirit remains vibrant and pumping with rabid vigour.'

'So, where do the bodies go?'

'You're looking at them. These humanoid forms surrounding you are the bodies – the physical forms, the echoes of The Once Lived. Physical matter decomposes far too quickly to even be worth holding on to, which leaves only these fading blemishes of who they were,' the ground says. 'I'm afraid, however, in order to reach the emerald, you're going to need to chisel your way through the Tombs – a perilously intimidating crypt filled with a billion free spirits.'

'But I don't have my sword. Or my partners. How do you expect me to fight alone?'

'The Alumni tunnel that channels among the Tombs will bring you to the spirits of your allies and, from there, you'll be able to revive yourselves.'

'Well, if you see a guy named Camson hanging around anywhere up-top, could you do me the favour of killing him too and dragging his arse down here? He has another sword that I could use.'

'I'll keep an eye out. But, for now, you must hurry to the Tombs. Your sole passage back to the living waits for you. The dreaded discharge of the Drag-in will not take long thereafter. The future of the Blankesphere and all the stages of existence depend on your efforts.'

I leave the courtyard of ghosts behind and evade the soundless reunion of two halves that can never meet at the turquoise fountain. Even if I don't see the end of the excursion through this afterlife and fail to make it to the other side of eternity, I'll probably still be stuck thinking about the lost man in the rose-lapelled suit, sitting on the edge of the fountain and nibbling away at his apple for the rest of his existence. Who knows? He might still be there when I get back…if his echo hasn't faded by then.

So be it. He's got nowhere better to be. Business as usual.

Chapter Eight
Airborne

Departures from Rush Airport on any day of the year were nothing short of a joke. Thousands of First Nation citizens flooded the terminal building from dawn until dusk, each potential traveller keen to vindicate why they deserved to be listed for a seat on one of the limited daily flights over their competitors. Whether you were a seasoned traveller or not was an unnecessary distinction, as there were no gimmicks other than luck that benefitted your chances when you got there and tried to survive against the storm of passengers and constant demand for Priority. *Everybody* wanted a Priority Pass. The wealthiest would pay full price and above. Others would simply fall to all fours and beg for it. From time to time, a few daring visitors would try to steal one, at the risk of answering to the Airport A.I. And there were a couple of crazy people who would literally kill for Priority – but they generally never made it past the Drones hovering over the car park. Occasionally, you would have somebody like DCD. Philson – or his son, in this case – who would elegantly swan through with a Senior Priority Pass in both their front and back pockets. This meant that they'd have undeniable access to any flight departing from any airport in the West. This meant that they would always find the very front of the boarding queues. This meant that they might never even see the boarding queues. This meant that, on overbooked flights, lower ranked passengers might have needed to "conveniently" abnegate their Priority and lose their seat, or "*accidentally*" disappear off the face of the earth, for the sake of the Decider's son getting to where he needed to be.

However, the confidentiality of this morning's flight to the Fifth Nation commanded Stevenson to steer Oscar and Samuella clear of the terminal building itself and directly onto the runway, towards the underbelly of the plane, where they were to board without disruption. Here, nobody would know about the Decider's son's arrival or the presence of a vulnerable Senior Priority Pass.

Oscar's standard check-in at Rush Airport was typically preceded by a luxury stay at the airport's Haste Hotel. He would head straight to the First Class Lounge for a three-hour massage, bottomless drinks, and a six-course Michelin star food service. Once checked-in with his Priority Pass, he'd dodge the queuing subordinates and be escorted exclusively to his private First Class cabin – thirty-three seats and forty-two feet of space all to himself.

For this flight, however, as arranged by Mister Pegasus, Oscar had to settle with sharing a measly Premium Cabin with Samuella and Kyma at the front of a Luxury Regal Jet. The other five hundred passengers on-board would be so far down the back of the plane they wouldn't be close enough to hear, let alone lay their intrusive eyes on the two Priority Passengers. Knowing he was bound to be gone from the West for over a week and had no one back in the City to look after Kyma, Oscar had been forced to bring the old terrier along to keep him company. Pegasus had not been notified on this supplement to his plan. 'She'll just sleep all the way, there and back,' is what Oscar had told Stevenson, as he'd slipped Kyma into the back of the limousine.

As the Regal Jet tore off from the runway and climbed into the sky, the pair were sat at the empty Premium Cabin bar alone, glued to the sheltering silence between them. Samuella had been amazed since boarding. She told Oscar how she'd never been on a plane before and had been haunted by the idea of being on a flying metal tube in the sky. To settle her phobias, he, in turn, expounded his fear of water and it being the reason he'd never stepped foot on a beach. They both cringed at each other and then digressed to getting sugar-high on cans and cans of *Kola Bear*. Oscar had a new illustration underway; he was sketching up a draft of his emerald and Aegia's rifle, both of which he'd stashed in a duffle bag up in the overhead locker. Samuella was reading a copy of the *City Central Mediums* for the first time, a turgid change from her catalogue of colourful *POST* prints.

'You read a lot at *Post*?' Oscar asked her.

'Always,' she responded. 'What about you?'

'Nah, nah! Reading wastes a lot of time,' he excused. 'At least, that's what my dad believes. He thinks those who *write* resound themselves greater than those who just read what others say. That's what plebiscites are for: they distinguish the readers from the writers.'

Samuella cherished a smug grin and continued perusing an article about the *Princesses of the East*. There were too many things onboard this funhouse that were more interesting to her than Oscar quoting the Decider. 'Princesses of the East,' she brought the subject up out loud. 'There aren't many of them left. According to this article, "*there used to be more than three hundred royal women living in the East*", a lot of whom were actually living there in the central cities and towns of the Sixth and Seventh Nations. But there were some who managed to get away from their tumultuous lives and fled to the West. Now, all these Phestors are left with are their mistresses, and Phestoresses have no initiative whatsoever.'☆

'Are you still researching that nonsense about the state before we get there?' Oscar complained. 'I'm telling you—it's irrelevant. Pegasus told us we won't be there long enough for sight-seeing.'

'I like to know every inch of where I'm going, before I get there and accidentally walk on the wrong side of the road. I did the same before I moved to the City. I don't enjoy looking like a tourist,' she argued and continued on reading. '"*Those who fled to the West were mostly murdered, executed or deported upon arrival...*"'

'Does it say why there were so many?' Oscar said.

'So many what? Princesses?' Samuella reiterated.

'Yeah.'

'Hundreds. All of them seeded from the same bag of oats.'

'Interbreeding—?'

'Incest,' Samuella clarified.

'How *gross*!' Oscar winced. 'East royalty was a bit like frogs in a pond, then.'

'Of course,' Samuella laughed at his disgust. 'Didn't you know that most of the East's royal ancestry originated in the Small Islands? You know—that little region of rocks your chauffer-friend is from and the place you aristocrats in the West don't talk about so flatteringly. It makes sense why the history of royalty in the East half a century ago is so frowned upon and why, to this day, the East are still reluctant to make amends with the West's Administrations.'

'How come?' Oscar said bluntly.

'Because the West enslaved those Small Islands all those hundreds of years ago,' Samuella elaborated. 'What did you think? As

---

☆ Phestors were not allowed to become married. Instead they "invested" a lot of time and money in female company, "Phestoresses", who were bought and marked as property, until they were traded on just as easily.

soon as those bloodlines reached the East and they began their dynasty there, they were going to buddy up with the horrible people who enslaved them?'

'All this dissonance between West and East started because a couple of Small Islanders were getting jiggy in the East?' Oscar answered his own question before taking another long sip of *Kola Bear*.

'A dissonance created by the West and its disregard for the Small Islands, you could say,' Samuella argued biasedly. 'If they'd just left those Islands alone, there'd have been no disputes to carry on to this day.'

'Or seldom disputes by comparison,' Oscar measured. 'I know that wasn't the only trigger of the Conflicts, and I doubt it was even the first.'

Suddenly, a new face came through the curtain and into their private cabin. It was a young boy of about seventeen, without any elegancies of youth in his expression of wrinkles and hoary, prominent scars. He beheld the definitive tan of an East-born seasoned by years of sun-exposure right throughout his childhood. Besides that, he still had a mousey body-shape, complimented by a very skinny and stiff posture. He stuck to the spot when they saw him and they both gazed at him inquisitively.

'That's true to some extent,' the boy said timidly. 'But not completely.'

'Who are you?' Oscar said immediately.

'Doe Vega,' the boy responded, then hesitated. 'I really do apologise. I don't mean to interrupt your privacy. I am aware of who you are, of course - Oscar Philson. But, you...?' he was looking at Samuella.

'I'm Samuella,' she introduced herself with a smile to mitigate Oscar's frustration.

'Oscar, Samuella, I'm so sorry—I couldn't help myself eavesdropping on your conversation. And what you were saying, Samuella, was only partially true: the West's colonial legacy *is* responsible for their dispute with the East, but there is a bigger reason than that. Substantially bigger.'

'You're from the East, aren't you?' Oscar certified.

Doe Vega shrugged and rocked his head in a hysterical motion, which implied Oscar had just stated the obvious. 'Is that not obvious?' he gawked shakily. 'Of course, I am. I was Fifth Nation born and have been living in the West for five years.'

'Why are you heading back to Fifth?' Samuella inquired.

'I don't know—homesickness, I guess,' Vega joked, then he returned to a more serious note. 'No. They wanted me back. I have been enlisted. That's why I'm going back.'

'To fight in the war?' Oscar said.

'No, no, my friend. I would be dead to even speak to you, if they were insisting that I fight for them. I am a free man. Well, I have been until now. Now, I submit myself.'

'Submit yourself?' Samuella revised. 'Submit yourself how? You shouldn't have to worry about serving the East if you haven't been under its laws for five years, not if you've been in the First Nation all this time.'

'I am submitting myself to a new system in the East, a new order that has been emerging there for decades,' Doe said.

'Nonsense again!' Oscar cried. 'The East has always followed the same laws; it's been under Phestorship for the best part of a century now. What new order could you possibly be talking about?'

'You don't understand. The Phestor Dynasty has never been so different as it is under Xenol. Its meaning is changing. Xenol has acquired a supremacy that no Phestor before him has ever achieved. He is on a mission to reform and reunite the East into one Nation again, greater than it has ever been. The Phestor himself plans to execute hundreds of his own people. Expatriates like myself don't stand a chance against the Phestorship. These upcoming laws will belittle us,' Doe explained. 'These laws are summoning migrants back to the East. Not to form an army, but an entirely new civilisation – an empire. Xenol and the Sixth Nation's empire. And if I am one to refuse, I am certainly a dead man, where every land befits soil for a grave.'

'They'll have you digging that grave if you go back now,' Samulla warned. 'By returning there willingly, you're only becoming an advocate for this—"new order".'

Doe trembled, stroking the top of one of the headrests in the cabin.

'The new order is going to be designed under the Radicals. These are horrific people, as you know, who worship the New Lord Draca – god of the silver chestnut and unrelenting chaos,' Doe stated. 'The Radicals have influenced the Phestorship since the fall of the Old King, only nobody has ever considered their grand influence to be more than a conspiracy. I tell you now that their presence exists and their shadow ingests everything in its way, anything it knows it can embody. Anything without a purpose, but an undying spirit – like me. And Xenol is no exception.'

'Xenol is working with the Radicals in the East?' Samuella responded, startled.

Doe looked at her as if she'd just said something really stupid. 'Xenol *is* a Radical and I believed that before it even became a conspiracy. Radicals are everywhere right now, not just in the Seventh and Eighth Nations – Eighth hardly exists anymore, so they had to migrate their agenda elsewhere. Now, it's in Sixth and it's coming for the Fifth eventually. We should have acted faster to prevent its influence years ago, but now all we can do is return with a vengeance or chance the safety of our future in their hands.'

'So what does this new order in the East have to do with its relations with the West?' Oscar brought them back on track.

'Because, from what I am aware, the East is not afraid of the West anymore. Long into this seemingly endless war, it does not even see the West as an enemy with a relevant cause. The enemy is within the East's regime – the plaguing Infidels who call for a return to the days of the past, the return of the Punk King.

Oscar and Samuella digested this information sheepishly. Aghast, they both said nothing.

'When the Phestorship first came to power,' Doe continued to educate them, 'it ignited a revolution against the previous royal regime, the old Punk King being the primary target. Xenol hopes to end this battle against the Infidels and the liberal-minded. Starting with his former enemy, the Decider of the West, he wants to form a brand new alliance, bond states, and rebuild an empire of the Punk King's magnitude, but with a contradicting ideology.'

'We're aware of this much,' Samuella noted curtly. 'A Decider-Phestor alliance would be detrimental. It would make internal enemies of Nations within the East and the West. It would be like an influx of civil wars on top on an actual war, because we all know this Alliance won't last long. Not if the people have anything to say. Believe me, I live with them and I know this is a cord that's been spun tight and it will only twist a smidge more until it bursts.'

'Exactly,' Doe said.

'Surely, the extent of some of these Radical plans are just the rhetoric of fear-mongers,' Samuella said. 'Xenol can't really be that dangerously radical. No Nation is capable of changing the world order like that. It's a war crime for the Phestor to manipulate Sister Nations and create an empire crafty enough to tip into the West and indoctrinate the Decider. It's betrayal on both sides! This will be a catastrophe!'

'The Phestor doesn't appear to care,' Doe sighed. 'He's planned it all before he ascended to power. Only the tremors of Xenol's intentions have never been as substantial as they are now. I'm beginning to believe he'll achieve his aim, win his empire and the war, and I'll have no choice, but to fall into place, once I return to the East.'

'The West has already divided itself.' Samuella turned to Oscar. 'This Alliance will only divide it more. And I can't see your father enlisting the other West Nations to help him out of this hole he's dug himself, not after how he's treated them. He's ignored his own people and left them to struggle on their own. The Decider has made many mistakes during his term in power, but befriending the East may be his downfall.'

There was a whisking from the galley-curtain. It had quickly shifted open, then closed again and Doe Vega was nowhere to be seen. Oscar and Samuella stared at the curtain emptily. They were alone again.

Then, Oscar despondently commented. 'The biggest mistake my dad will make hasn't even happened yet and that's calling me his heir. Maybe those Small Islanders who ruled in the East all those centuries back were destined to lead a Nation, but I definitely wasn't.'

'Neither was your father. Remember, he was an heir to his own father and his father was an heir before him. There were once generations when the people elected their leaders—would you believe? Nowadays, like any line of rulers, the Decider and his kin arise undisputed,' Samuella said. 'The people of the West are just as guilty as anyone when it comes to pedestaling the powerful. Even when it is in their worst interests. The belief is that *as long as the water comes from the same well, it can be trusted.* You'd know all about that, Captain Nepotism.'

'Now, now—let's not keep bringing me into this.'

'But it's true!' she barked at him like a rebelliously humane wolf aloof from the pack. 'Your dad is a senseless pig with a limited toolbox of morals and his arrogance is out of order!'

'Samuella, I can't disagree with you! There are many things wrong the with West and the City and the way my father perceives things—'

'His *lack* of perception!' she corrected.

'Yes—understandably! But my father is a fine ruler by comparison to me. *I am no a match* by any means! My opinions are unproven and untested, highly experimental in the world we know – they can only be worse than his.'

'That can't be true! Don't tell me you can't see his flaws—'

'***Yes, I can see that he has plenty***! My father is as flexible wooden plank when it comes to diversifying his opinions, but we have to commend his hard work and the tradition that backs it! He's kept us all afloat for ages.' Oscar felt like choking himself for saying this, for he knew his loyalty was a burden.

'Until now, that is. It's all been leading to this. That history and tradition was all a mistake, the blunders of old men! Times need to change for the better—now more than ever!' she sternly remarked. 'He makes one wrong decision and the world goes up in flames. Oscar, you have to realise that you are the only person destined to overrule him and set mankind back on course to sanity.'

They returned to silence for another twenty minutes. That was until Kyma woke up. Her head lifted inside the little, white, igloo-shaped hut that housed a chubby dog-cushion inside. Oscar fed her lunch and then gave her a toy to play with. Dogs and planes didn't go arm-in-arm. But he enjoyed her company in the cabin. Citadel Tower was a fairy tale castle, but Kyma was *home*. Wherever she went, home followed.

'Were your parents respectable people?' Oscar asked Samuella. He saw that she was cosy in her own little space, under the duvet covers of her collapsible bed. 'Had they been respectable folk in their—I don't know—in whatever they did? Were they remembered well for what they brought to the world? Were they loved?'

'Well, *I* didn't know them. Does that tell you enough about them?' she wasn't even trying not to sound sarcastic. Oscar *hoped* this was the case. He hoped that wasn't true, otherwise it made him feel terrible about asking her at all. There was sombreness in her voice and she let out a heavy sigh.

'No,' Oscar said simply and honestly.

By this point, she'd fallen asleep.

The rest of the journey was turbulent.

The pilot had declared the development of a storm over the Prime Meridian Region and that the length of the flight would be extended because of it. *We're halfway there at least*, Oscar thought with inadequate relief. Every now and again the in-flight A.I. would come through the cabin to spruce up the place and make sure that everything was in check for them - don't worry, these ones hadn't been programmed and loaded to kill (even still, Oscar thought it would be wise to stash the emerald and rifle back in their spot in the overhead locker). These "*tamer*" Tin Men regularly whizzed over, again and again, to offer Oscar and Samuella more complimentary refreshments and added more *fluff* to their pillows if they needed more *fluff*. Other than that, their flight went on uninterrupted. Even though the pilot had warned of turbulence, nobody felt a thing.

When she was disturbed an hour after the "turbulence", Samuella had no problem speaking to Oscar, who now seemed to be more on-edge than she'd been the whole flight so far. He stood over her. The plush, grey tracksuit he'd changed into was crumpled and creased all over. 'Did you just sleep through that?' he asked.

'Through what? The turbulence? I guess. I could sleep through an earthquake. To me, this is just floating.' She toyed with his tension. Oscar was annoyed by this: *Fear of flying metal tubes in the sky, my arse!*

'No. The pilot made a message out to everyone. We're going to be diverting somewhere,' he told her. She looked at him blankly. Her head was wobbling slowly, heavy with tiredness.

'It means that we're going to be landing somewhere else. Temporarily.'

'Yeah, yeah—I know what that means,' she stammered, batting away his condescension.

But then she quickly caught the contagion of his panic when he said this: 'It'll hinder us a lot, because we *need* to be in the Sixth Nation by Sunday.'

'This plane isn't taking us to the Sixth Nation. Not directly. We're headed to the Lower East first, landing in the Fifth Nation and working our way across from there.'

'Exactly!' Oscar was pacing the cabin like an ostentatious street boxer in the City Central.

'So, we're not—landing in the East anymore? Or what?' Samuella stuttered apprehensively. 'Where are we landing now?'

'I've got no clue and that's the problem. This takes us totally off course!' He punched a wall in the cabin and shouted. 'I'm going to need to contact Pegasus. Let him know what's happening.'

'Where's Stevenson?' Samuella added. 'Is he onboard somewhere? We could ask him.'

'I don't know,' Oscar said. 'I'll check with one of the A.I.'

'What else did the pilot say? Did he mention how long we're diverting for?'

'That's all he mentioned: "we're bound for an unknown destination, prepare for diversion in the next two hours". The storm must have burnt more fuel than he expected.'

'Why don't you check the Map. It'll tell us where we're landing,' Samuella suggested.

'I did and it's indicating somewhere south. The Eridanus and Lepus constellations are nearer south—whatever the hell that means. We're headed there—down south!' Oscar was panicking now.

Samuella decided to walk to the bar. Stretch her legs. But, as she did, the curtains dividing the cabins parted and an A.I. rattled into theirs. It took a long contemplative look at the two of them, processing the situation, and spoke with a tone identical to any other Tin Man.

Blunt and assertive.

'Passengers are issued to remain in their seats during region-crossings,' the A.I. said, its flat, glass-screened eyes flashing an alarming red. 'Absence from your seat during region-crossings could result in a fine or severer prosecution - that is, if the passenger in question proceeds to struggle.'

'Umm—crossing which regions exactly?' Samuella asked politely.

'I have been ordered not entertain passenger suspicions,' the Tin Man answered unwaveringly.

Oscar chuckled. 'Your *only* order on this tube is to entertain us, buddy! Have you glanced in the mirror today? You're dressed as an in-flight butler!'

Hearing this, the A.I. swerved to look at Oscar directly. It scanned him. And analysed the information with an electronic bubbling noise, like the sound of boiling water, which was brought to an end with an irksome bleep. 'Passenger recorded as...recorded as...Oscar Philson...Senior Priotity Pass Ticket Holder...'

'You've got that right. I'm the Decider's son. I'm sure you know him too. The big bully up in Citadel Tower with his wally hanging out the window, peeing down on the streets below,' Oscar joked.

'Your identity has been recorded. Your Offence has been classed as...Class E Offence...'

Samuella couldn't hold back gargling on her own laughter. It all came out, almost bringing up all the food she'd stuffed down her throat since boarding.

'Gee, thanks. I'll add it to my Class D and C Offences and all the others I got for Christmas,' Oscar added jeeringly.

'Ignoring Airborne Laws and the rules of Region Crossing is violating Code 79 of the New Democracy's legislation under the West Constitution of International Laws. Such misconduct requires a Yellow Standard Punishment: Nominal Documentation and a formal warning.'

'There's nothing new about that legislation,' Oscar mocked. 'It's been around longer than I've breathed on this planet. If anything, that issue is so old it isn't even an issue anymore. It must still be jammed in your database from twenty or so years ago.'

'I am a *Startle Age Design*. Thus, my data core is automated and updates by the hour,' the A.I. defended. 'Thank you for your concern. However, like many other human jurisdictions, it is not necessary here. My decision is final and you will respect this justice.'

'Excuse me,' Samuella broke into *The Oscar Show*, 'would you happen to know why we're diverting?'

The A.I. turned all of its attention to her now. It could only focus on one problem at a time. 'Inquires upon the matter cannot be dealt with at this point in time. Please return to your seat, madam. Or I will have no choice but to issue you a warning too.'

'But we weren't far from the East. None of it makes sense. We had a clear-cut route to the Fifth Nation and the journey left wasn't that long. Why aren't we landing in Port Ulino anymore? Has the plane been damaged?'

'I am not required to respond to trivial questions during periods of potential danger.' Suddenly, no more Mister Nice A.I. He became a monster, twisting his hands into fists and refiguring his face into a threatening frown. 'Now, I'm going to remind you once and not again, madam,' he vowed. 'Return to your seat.'

Samuella didn't need reminding again. That was enough to chase her back into her wonderful seat, away from the ugly demon that had taken over the once so charming Mister Nice A.I. Oscar did likewise. They both strapped in and gazed into space as Mister Nice A.I. turned one last time and left through the curtains.

'He wouldn't tell me,' Samuella complained. 'Why wouldn't he tell me?'

'You should ask yourself: do you actually trust Mister Pegasus?' Oscar asked.

'Of course. I wouldn't be here if I didn't trust him. He offered me his time and his hospitality and he respects me. He offered me an invaluable slice of his livelihood at a time when I needed it most.'

'But do you trust him all the way to the East? All the way to the Sixth Nation? Do you trust him with your life?'

'I wouldn't go so far as to say that. Not yet. But he's on the same side as us. Why? You're not suspecting…?'

'I'm not suspecting anything. I'm making sense of things. *Making lemonade when somebody gives you lemons* is how they put it.

But you have to ask yourself at some point: who is it that gives you those lemons in the first place? Maybe he's planned this all from the start? The diversion? Our reliance to go along with it could have all been part of it.'

'He wouldn't do that,' Samuella rebutted. 'Our task is paramount to him and the Infidels. What would possibly make him sell us out? And sell us out to whom…or where?'

Oscar turned from her shortly, expecting her to do the same, because, all of a sudden, the temperature in the cabin had dropped from cool to absolutely freezing. Through the windows, the sun could no longer be seen. The sky had turned completely dark, save for the stars. Oh, the stars were forever there to lead them back on course. But, right here and now—down below, through the parting clouds—nothing seemed remotely normal. Nothing down there seemed alive until they grew closer to it. Whatever civilisation was thriving down there appeared to be glistening. Was it civilisation? No—an icy, glacial surface, unlike that of the deserts in the East. Another foreign landscape? Somewhere they'd never seen before. Nothing they could've ever imagined, for it was too bleak and sterile to picture anything at all. Down on the surface, above the snow plains and the glaciers, was a massive base with huge watchtowers on every corner, with great unflattering walls and with terrifying beamers shining up at them. It was like the home of a Giant—or, rather, where they tamed it. Oscar managed only a single sentence to describe what they both saw.

'We're definitely not in the East.'

Alumni...

There is a wide chamber enclosed around me now, a thousand or so feet deep into the soils of Scorpius Island. The roof is a dome arching fifty feet above my head. Torchlight encircles the bending walls, reflecting into me as though I might be the bull's-eye on a dartboard. It's like I'm at the foot of a great cathedral and this is the first hall that welcomes a high priest on arrival. The cultural crucible of an ancient city that has been sunken underground for centuries.

Before I made it as far as this theatre, I'd found a quiet and very reserved oasis nine or ten corridors from the courtyard, where I'd crossed the fountain sprawling with spirits, and I bathed there shortly and peacefully without disturbance. It was only when I'd removed my clothes and dipped my feet into the round, heated pool that I noticed something that should have been obvious. 'Why am I able to feel the water on my skin if I'm not corporeal?' I had pondered out loud.

The Ground, my overseeing guardian through this netherworld, had given me an illuminating explanation, 'Gravity,' she'd said, the brassy roll of her voice sending ripples through the pool, as its vibrations filled the room. 'Ever wondered why ghosts are known to float up on the surface, when their feet actually touch the ground down here? The deeper you sink on Scorpius Island, the stronger the gravity gets and the more arduous re-emerging on the surface becomes. It's a science implemented by the Stellar Gods, another means of intensifying the border between the Blankesphere and the surface, separating life and death.'

When the ground had told me my descent through the Tombs of Truth would be straining and tiresome, I popped a purple seed and passed out there, lounged beside the oasis. On reawakening in that exact same spot some hours later, dry and calmer after my bathing and brief recess in reality, I continued my wander through the narrow maze of corridors, slopes and staircases, guided by the hospitable voice of the Groundskeeper (that's what the ground prefers to call herself), that unseen entity to whom I have donated a survivalist's trust. I had travelled along until the dense, muddy walls of one corridor led me to this very chamber…

In the middle of the chamber is a mining lift that descends into a shaft. It reminds me of *the Sugar Mines where my Uncle Cephalus used to work, back when we were living in the countryside. I used to live on one of the last sugar districts in the West. My little town of Nimblescold had constituted for eighty per cent of the West's sugarcane produce. But when an underground radiation leak from the power plants nearby caused the sugar plantations to die, our village had to turn to an alternative method of acquiring the resource directly underground. An incredibly dangerous last resort to salvage the surviving sugarcane roots harboured deep beneath the village's soils. It had ended in disaster when the supple harvest lands, unfit for mining practices, had collapsed. Since that day my Uncle Ceph perished down there with his mining crew, no one ever returned to sugar mining and natural sugarcane remains, to this day, a rarity that is near impossible to harvest in the West…*

The shaft facing me is grimy and poorly maintained with dated, oxidising mechanisms that are smeared in dust and cobwebs. It clutches a metal box suspended by a single iron string. Small gaps surround the lift's edges, the sight of which brings back frightening memories that hold every hair on my skin hostage.

'And this is the only way down there?' I question my unlikely mentor. 'This is the sole entrance to the Tombs of Truth? How do I get out?'

But the Groundskeeper doesn't answer my question generously. Instead, she tries to work her way around the inevitability that getting back out won't be that easy. Not to spook me, I expect. 'Once you're down there, I won't be able to respond to anything you say. The lift will take you straight to the core of the planet, as the Tombs spawn so low beneath the ground that they reach beyond the extent of imagination itself. Not as little as a sound is permitted to intrude the tomb and disturb the laid-dead. If Antares asks about my involvement, tell him I saw it as my honour to lead a responsible Night Dreamer to his company. But I recommend you continue onwards at your own will and confront Antares as you so dare. Be careful, Samuella.'

Was that a mournful prayer from my deathly mentor? I hope not. And who is Antares?

'On a scale of one to ten, how bad is it down there?' I ask.

'That is hard for me to register, since the experience is different for the living. The living does not tread there. Find your friends. You'll need them at your side to get out of the Tombs, only once you've obtained the emerald.'

'And how exactly do I go about obtaining this emerald when I get to the bottom?' I ask. 'What's the trick this time?'

'By surrendering your thoughts of deceit and settling for the hardest truths about yourself and those closest you. In return, the Tombs will reward you with the emerald,' the ground clarifies shakily. 'The Tombs' Alumni only cooperates with those who tell the truth. It sounds simple, but, as you must know, the truth can drive some to madness. All will soon become more obvious once you reunite with your friends. They have both been submerged as you requested. I have also directed them to the Tombs.'

'They're not my friends,' I spark. 'They're my allies. A coincidence. That's all we mean to one another.'

'Well, then I wish all the more luck to you and your *allies*.'

I proceed towards the platform of the lift. One foot on-board and I promptly feel the unevenness. The platform is slanted at an obscure gradient to the ground. An automatic response to this would be to disembark straightaway and say that there is no chance in heaven or hell – this place is neither or…so far. My allies are not here to support me or offer their opinion. Like the Bridge of Lynx and on Leo Island, first steps have to be made and one has to be brave to take them. This time is my turn to lead the way and rescue the others.

I close the gate, sealing off the majority of the light from the chamber. I've left it all behind now. There's no turning back. Here, I wait, wobbling on the platform. Balance, planes and reality are far out of the question and I'm cradled by disorientation—

Clink! Slash!

The lift experimentally drops a smidge and then starts to descend gradually. I watch as the light from the chamber dissolves above. For a moment, the fear of my solitude feeds the disillusion that I can actually see the Groundskeeper. I'm convinced that she's a silhouette standing there in the chamber, viewing my descent. Darkness crawls up the shaft's walls, as I'm lowered deeper and deeper towards the limits of my imagination.

In the lift itself, I can hear rattling from the old wheels turning like cogs. They just about manage to spin. *Perhaps, there's just enough juice to get me down there?* And with it, a whining sound amalgamated with a sensation of harmonised singing. The singing spirits are back. Welcoming me like a jarring, demonic choir, instead of the chorus of angels from before. The pitch rapidly toils into a trebly terror for the ears, because it gets *louder!* and *louDER!* and *LOUDER!* until screeching and ringing takes hold of everything. My eyes are defunct, as the vocals translate everything I loathe the most. I grab onto my head, covering all I can from the temples to the earlobes. But the noise is hanging over me and determined like a storm cloud in a monsoon. It creates thumping vibrations through my palms to remind me that its still there, ten-hutting my mind and marching it along to the disjointed rhythm.

'Don't let it take you! Don't let go! Don't let it get to you!' the Groundskeeper's voice bellows down from somewhere miles above.

BANG! SNAP!

Something loosens—breaks! We pick up speed! Into the impending pitfall. I'm heaving; the air quality is tick and dusty down here. *How far have we come? How much further is there to go? Will it ever stop?*

Then arrives the smoke.

Black. Thick.

It fills the little metal cage, exterminating the copious vacuum within. It surrounds me.

Choking. Gagging. Keeling…

All at once, I battle the urgency to escape and, yet, I embrace my own oneness being carried to the unknown. It might all have been a terrible mistake! The smoke is like fire, advancing quickly into my lungs and filling my diaphragm. Wholesome, and consuming, as if it could possibly be alive…

'*Pieces of me surround you, Samuella…Fragments of my history lie within your truth…The Void is parting…and I am advancing…your time is elapsing…and I am expanding…*' The Drag-in's words, transmuted by the choir of spirits, emerge through the smoke, reaching me even with my ears sealed off. Patterns of his many eyes float about the smoky air, mocking me.

'*…Think like an angel and you'll have to remember…Pine as the devil, you'll never forget…*'

The voices start to laugh.

Will this ever end? Will it ever stop? Or will it go on and on and on…?

It stops.

Outside, a person is waiting hand-in-hand with the very still cellar surrounding him. In the dark cellar, there are empty, ransacked shelves and opened crates framing cobwebs, dwindling light left in the six dying torches on the walls, and a scent of rotting bananas adrift in the air. He stands with his back to me and holds an object that is equally anonymous to his identity. A shadow with a long, tapered-off wooden stick in his hand. A staff?

The head of the staff dons a scorpion's tail.

'Did you bring me here? Was it you who manipulated the Map and brought us to Scorpius Island, instead of Pegasus? Or was it the Phantom?' I interrogate him. 'Are the Tombs here? How can I get to the Tombs of Truth?'

The figure standing on the other side of the lift's gate doesn't reply.

'I've come looking for something and you probably know what that is.'

He again fails to respond. *Is he really there?* I wonder. I could be talking to a Nightmare for all I know. The ground already explained that even imagination has a hard time surviving down here. So, I stand and face him to prove that I'm more than imagination, to show that I've survived the trip, survived the descent and I'm right here in person. Ready to confront anything. 'If that's true, then lead me out of here. Take me to my allies and take me to the emerald. We need to be quick. The Drag-in is advancing and it isn't shy to keep reminding us. It just spoke to me. Do you hear the Drag-in speaking to you down here?'

To my surprise, the gate suddenly rolls aside on its own, leaving the space between us naked. I reach out a hand to touch the eclipsed silhouette. Daringly.

My hand vanishes.

Quickly, I snatch my curiosity away again; I withdraw my hand and just look into his face, trying to find his eyes. I comprehend a nose in the blank mesh. It transforms out of the dark and into existence like a work of art in progress, followed gradually by the mouth and chin. The thinning skin is wrinkled and ashy. And then there's this man, a basic humanoid mould without eyes or ears. He's bald, without a strand of hair on his head. For clothing, he's hampered by a heavy, black greatcoat weighting on his shoulders and arms. Nothing more than a stencil of a person. The stencil of a being.

Something comes to light atop the unsightly man's staff. A round object floating over the scorpion's tail.

'You have it—' I stutter. 'That's the second emerald! It's what we've been looking for—'

But, before I can explain any further, the gate rushes closed again. And the eyeless man doesn't flinch from his constant position. Gazing up at the sparkling jewel, I begin to bang on the metal, alarmed. 'No—! What are you doing? You can't lock me in here! I need that emerald and for you to send me and my allies back up to the surface! Don't you understand? We may as well let the Drag-in win if you don't give me that emerald! Let me out of here! Let me go!'

The eyeless man disappears through a large wooden door at the other end of the cellar; it unbolts itself, swings open, and he hovers through. 'Wait—!' I cry. 'Come back! I'm not finished—!'

SNAP!

The lift releases as the metal wire breaks. Here I go, resuming my journey into the unknown...

***

By the time she was two-years-old, her Uncle Ceph had already taken on the farmhouse her parents used to keep. So, if he'd perished anytime sooner than he had, there'd have been no candidate left to look after it. She couldn't have held on to her old homestead without the custody of her uncle. The sincerest fact of all was that Samuella had never been the best agrarian. Never could she have lived up to either her parents or her uncle. They were proper Country People. They hadn't been to the City once in their lives; they'd never listened to the patters of First Nation Media that often leaked into the Fourth Nation and all of its gobble-gobble about fighting wars, and oil, and dictators, and they'd never owned a fast car or flown to exotic destinations. The closest any of them had ever got to Golden Glory was winning first prize for Best Fiery Bison at the local Tweed Festival. And Mamma had always been notorious for that burning kick in her bison ribs and sweet potato stew. But what wasn't Golden Glory about living in the rural countryside? It was where the quiet people went to live and where the narcissistic blowhards didn't go to put up a fuss. It was humanity in its most pure and natural state...

***

Well, now I think about it, there had been one inexcusable flaw, one inevitable conundrum, that had made country life anything but glorious, at a time when it fell from glory faster than this lift hurtles me down its shaft, through the Tombs of Truth…

***

Although she was content with her role on the homestead – she'd always been the first out of bed to gather the hens when they laid the good stuff and milk the happy cows when her Uncle C was out early in the morning – Samuella struggled to learn on her own. Her difficulty concentrating with an attention deficit disorder became problematic for many things, but school was the severest. The world around young Samuella had never been up to speed with her disability, but the constant rotation of actual work did wonders to boost her confidence. The occupation of the farmhouse appealed to her as her only proud asset. Having that responsibility distracted her from the things she couldn't do and the denigration she endured for them. She relied on the man in the overalls to always lead the way, to forever be her teacher and such dependency had kept her tethered to the old homestead. Uncle Ceph had been an optimistic example of all the wonderful things her parents had never been, for she could not even remember their names. When she got the chance, she used to write imaginary letters to them and build castles out of soil in the yard for their memories to live in – a haven where the Conflicts couldn't reach them and where nuclear bombs never dropped.

'They're always going to drop,' Uncle used to tell her. 'No matter where you run or where you hide, there's always going to be bomb for you and that'll be your day. That's the hard truth.'

Uncle Ceph had been a man built by his truths. In a past life, he'd been a vocal supporter of the Infidel Movement in the East and, when arrested and convicted, had confessed to his Punkish attitudes before a court hearing in the Second Nation. During Uncle Ceph's run of things on the farm, Nimblescold, the town where they lived, started to change. Fewer community events were held at the town's lakeside Country House, because in its place, a huge monstrosity was being constructed. All over town, signs had gone up promoting new jobs in the area. Jobs that would pay well, City wages, and consist of regular business visits to the First Nation's capital itself. 'Why would anybody want to go to the City?' Uncle Ceph would've said. 'The Country here is all you'll ever need. They like to make you think people in the City are getting on so much better than us, but they're not.'

One late autumn, around the time Samuella turned eleven-years-old, they began to see the beast in creation. Across the lake, scarring the town with a demolished landscape, was the growing mammoth of a nuclear plant. It was the biggest power plant to manifest in that part of the Fourth Nation - or, in the people of Nimblescold's case, the biggest eyesore in their universe. It overshadowed the town. And outside its entrance was a laminated sign for all to grieve: ***Employing the Future****.*

'This world has flipped totally ludicrous! Upside down! No longer spinning on its axis!' Uncle Ceph had complained to everybody in town, during the industrious annexation. 'They have no right to ruin such principal land! Beautiful land! Our land! This is our home and they're stamping their dirty, shitting boots all over the place!'

The following years proved a challenge for most people in Nimblescold, Uncle Ceph had been amongst them. Very soon after the factory was built, news of a disaster for the sugarcane plantations fluttered about the town like an array of annoying butterflies. Because of the radiation leaks underground, the soil quickly became infertile and all that was already grown had died days after the nuclear factory's erection. Uncle Ceph had just as swiftly written a very sweet lullaby directly to the Decider's Administration to remind them of what a wonderful job they were doing and how picturesque that huge aluminium monster looked when it was looming high over them and blinding the sun.

The crux of the letter to the Administration had read a little something like: "Opportunity? Employment? How can you "civilised", pretentious, and overly compensated City Folk deceive us modest folk with such rhetoric? Patronise us and swindle our very existence? It seems we have always been an asset to you and nothing more. This is automation at its most horrendous. Tell your Decider to come down here and take a look for himself! There are actual people living here, for your interest. But don't worry—none of us bite.'

Little to the former Punk's surprise, there was no response to his complaint. Nothing came from anyone outside of town. Nimblescold was on its own. Nobody cared about the little country village that laid on the eastern shore of the Fourth Nation. Uncle Ceph refused to take any early-bird job offers from the factory and reverted to the sugar mines to help save the last of the sugar before it all perished beneath their feet. His absence left Samuella to take care of the farm on her own and all of its duties. She had started off okay, but her culpabilities began to show when she became easily exhausted, leading to numerous cries for help to her Uncle in Shining Armour, due to many silly injuries and costly mistakes.

When an earthquake riled the town, the fragile soil finally gave way and the mine collapsed. Uncle Ceph perished with it and Samuella was left with no more heart and no choice. The following month, she sold the farm to a new family and escaped to the City to seek a new life...

***

My birdcage descends through the open ceiling of an underground chimney, where the brick walls arc around the lift and are lined with hutches for the catacombs. Entrenched within a rancid fragrance of burning and forgotten palm leaves left to decay, the lift – cut loose from its hoisting wire – free-falls among the pigeonholes for the dead; tombs listed in their hundreds. Inside each rests the verity it conceals and the corpse wherein a spirit abandons its flesh-bound secrets.

My surging memories relive the flames I once made, three nightfalls ago upon Central Island, where a blaze set in the jungles of Camelopardalis stole the Last Night Dreamer from her body and liberated her life-serving spirit from its fleshy prison. The dying stench of rotting bananas has found me again, here in this crypt of the bleak husks. It's definitely a *dying stench* precipitating from the burning palm-leaves. *Hopefully it was those putrid leaves that made cremation and release into the Blankesphere possible for the young woman burning inside, granting her the ceremonial rites she deserved.* Retrospectively, as I reimagine her now in this vision, the girl with golden hair has still retained her identity while evacuating a mask of melted flesh. It has me wondering whether she'd actually been the same person I spoke to on Awakening Coast, or if that beautiful face had been playing a role and hiding a tragedy. *Do any of us really exist as we think we do? O how others perceive us?*

Then I return to what the Tombs are showcasing for me, the memories of my past, my history, my reality...

***

As much as she'd anticipated, the City was a huge surprise. It would be for anybody. Even if you'd been living there for a hundred years, disbelief would still strike you every time you looked up at the spectacular neon lights that stripped the Scrapers of their grit; or when you caught the eye of the Statue of Redemption mystifying the Catęno River; or when the streets christened with twinkling traffic came to a standstill at night.

Samuella arrived overwhelmed and didn't lose the incentive of work on her mind. Without a place to be or money to spend at ease, there was nothing of interest for you in a place like the City. Fortunate for her, she had packed as many spare garments as was necessary to get through her first four weeks. She also brought along her Uncle Ceph's wallet. It was filled with automated Virtu-Cards that updated to any West Nation's currency upon arrival. As soon as she got to the First Nation, she uploaded his accounts to the Virtu-Bank and booked herself a temporary slot at a hostel in the suburbs – she was granted a two-week stay and bunked in a room with five other migrants like herself. He'd always been sure to leave it in a "secret place" under the kitchen cupboard with the foresight of there being one day when he might not be around and she would have to take care for herself.

The speed at which the City absorbed you was demanding and dizzying and there was no plot for Samuella to patch her cabbages at first. She luckily landed a shot in a diner near the TRAMLINE station on King's Avenue. The place was called The Skid Bar and Co. and it was where the rich Academy kids came round to after the last bell to get some burgers and milkshakes or to listen to the happy-yappy music and watch the cute girls on ice-skates. Every day, Samuella showed up on time and became quickly adapted to waiting, finding her feet enough to call it a snug placement by her third day on the job. A fantastic debut in the City, she thought. Only, a few months after she started, another waitress on ice-skates got into a colourful fight with a bunch of girls who were mocking and bitching about her behind her back. That was a good reason for the place to get condemned and rapidly shut down by the persecutors, which left Samuella unemployed again and back on the street in no time.

After sleeping the streets for a fortnight and dodging many an A.I. during a vagrant bout of sidewalk camping and shoplifting, a friendly group of Week Traders she'd met running the Tent Yard Sales at the Purity Market pointed her to a new hostel called the Sneak Stall Inn at the Octane Mall. She took up a residence at the Stall for a few weeks, while she began her first shifts at Post. The Stall was cheap and cheerful, but due to overloads in demand, she was forced out by the end of the month with the promise that she'd be placed elsewhere. 'Somewhere airtight to stay. Just for a short while, until things get back on their feet,' the hostel's administrator had told her. It wasn't long. Mister Quaint played a few cards to allow her to stay at his shared residence for as long as she needed. 'I'll hand you a lodge if you're willing to work hard. I'll be happy to pay you, not as much as Post, but, hey, anything goes for

Weekers like us, right?' he'd jovially nudged her. 'Scrub the dishes, the floors, bedrooms…That kind of stuff.'

Only, he'd been lying. Mister Quaint hadn't been a Week Trader. He wasn't a Trader at all. His family and the Gaudison family shared a broken, little alms-house in the Slumberlands. They were being scarcely funded by the council.

Nevertheless, he was offering her a pittance and roof and she was glad to comply.

At least, down in the Slumberlands no one would suspect anything of her. She was just getting on with her life like any other girl in the City. She wasn't comfortably rich, but she wasn't uncomfortably poor. She was everything else…

***

I'm down on my knees and I don't know how I got here.

Not a cellar, not a tomb, but a library. The new chamber around me is walled with bookshelves and lit by lanterns, instead of fire torches. The faceless man is here, occupying an armchair in the focal point of the room, the very middle of the study. Up close, I see his burgundy greatcoat has been dirtied with soot and burns. Where his eyes should be, a pancake of skin is layered over the empty sockets and his lack of ears makes his head all the more square. It wouldn't be a face he's wearing if not for the stub of his nose, bulging out like a blister. Horribly dry, the skin on his lips is pale and chaffing. Whilst he hasn't yet spoken, I'm spellbound by his mouth's periodic twitches, since he's staring straight at me and muttering inaudibly, as if he's compelled to start a conversation. But what I gravitate to is the scorpion staff standing beside him. He doesn't need to hold the stick. It's obediently erect on its own. I pretend not to notice the emerald twirling on the stinger's tip – I experienced how begging for it turned out the last time we met. Queen Cassandra's rage against desperate desire and now a stubborn blind man are dictations that these emeralds cannot be easily wanted, let alone effortlessly obtained.

Kowtowing next to me is someone else. Oscar is present with me and I try not to gasp with relief, but can't help it. He glares numbly ahead in silence.

'Drink?' the impaired man stutters bluntly. 'You look thirsty. Would you like to have a tipple of rum with me?'

I blink at him repeatedly, my jaw plummeting. You'd think someone without the ears to hear their own voice would slur their speech remarkably.

I survey his dead expression. He scores the same quality of emotion as Oscar: none. His fumbled pronunciation melts on the tongue the way a victim of some fragile brain injury might jibber-jabber himself back to recovery. He's been programmed to say that, hasn't he? Like an A.I.

I rattle in uncertain acceptance.

A rat jumps out from under the faceless man's armchair and dashes across the floor towards me. It halts right under my nose. The rodent rolls onto his hind legs. His head sinks into his neck, creating a deep dip between the shoulders and the rest of the headless body expands to compliment the growing hole there, morphing into the cup of a hairy goblet. Below the body of the prickly, black cup, the rat's tail straightens out, raising the cup off the floor, and whirls at the bottom as a foot to support the furry goblet. Finally, a hole bursts from the rat-skin inside the cup and red liquid floods out, filling the goblet with the rodent's dispensed bloodstream. My refreshment. 'I'm not even a smidge thirsty, really,' I admit politely. The wriggling cup isn't light on my stomach. I see the pink nose, tiny eyes and whiskers stuck to the goblet's rim and heave, almost vomit all over myself.

'The Night Dreamer, I suspect?' the faceless man says.

'Yes. We both are,' I respond, twisting my nose at Oscar's unresponsiveness.

'What business do Night Dreamers have in my Tombs?'

'What business do *you* have with the Tombs of Truth?' I retort. 'Who are you?'

'Antares. I am the undertaker and logger of memories,' the man introduces himself. 'You intruded on my island and that upset my pet scorpion, Shaula. He dragged you and your friends down here to submit your merciful truths to me.'

'*Allies*,' I correct him and climb onto my feet, unintentionally kicking the rat-goblet over and spilling its blood in the process. 'Shaula wasn't very vocal about wanting us to stay away. He was more physical about his feelings, from what I can remember.'

The emerald on the staff glimmers and suddenly a force overbears me and jolts me back down onto my knees. The emerald dims and the power it applied to pull me to the ground dispels.

'Shaula is extremely meticulous about keeping foreigners away. Those who have always been reluctant to explore the most damning of revelations about themselves are undeserving of the Tombs' mightiest treasure,' Antares strokes the staff, as he speaks with a seeping menace. 'You are standing in the most privileged layer of the Blankesphere. You're at the heart of the Tombs, where the memories of the dead are stashed—the Alumni. Do show some respect.'

'Well, I don't believe it's an accident we're here! I have reason to believe it was your bidding that lured us here! It was you who manipulated the Constellation Map, disguising the land of Scorpius as Pegasus! You saw us coming for the emerald the very moment we landed here! Perhaps even from the moment we left Leo! And now you're using the emerald to hold us under your arrest!'

'Now, why would I employ a maze, a giant scorpion, and hide a hundred chambers beneath the sand if I wanted two self-entitled Night Dreamers to roam into the Blankesphere and pinch my emerald?' There goes the snarl of a mercenary. The very first sign of emotion that I've extracted from this strategic devil. 'I'm not stupid, girl. Night Dreamers carry no other interests down here. All Eyes tends to reward his Night Dreamers with an eternity up on the surface, donning whatever incarnation they like. That is, once they've destroyed the beast, the world-collider, that keeps re-emerging in its foulest form.'

'That's exactly the point,' I say. 'We haven't defeated the Drag-in yet.'

I look at Oscar. He's still fixated on the wall in front of him, unmoving.

'You have one of the emeralds we need to defend our existence as we know it, Antares? It's the reason we followed your trickery here,' I tell him. 'You need to give it to us, so we can complete our mission.'

Antares suddenly becomes very charismatic, smirking wealthily with only the bottom half of his face responding to it. 'I don't need to give you anything. With the emerald, I can control the spirits; it defends me from rogue souls—the Nightmares can't topple me.'

'One emerald is nothing against the Drag-in. It won't defend the spirits at all. Along with the living, the dead will be forgotten when the Tombs of Truth are erased from the Dreamerverse. What defender of the dead would you be if you let their memories cease to exist?'

'Stop lying!' These words come from Oscar. He's now woken up since being on standby. And he's pinning me down with his eyes. 'You're pretending about the emerald, just to cast a veil over what you really want—the truth you've come seeking for.'

'What are you on about?' I scowl at him, dumbfounded by his unnatural change in behaviour.

'You're not here for the emerald,' Oscar remarks, neutrally. 'You're looking high and low for redemption, understanding, revelation.'

Is he referring to my truth? The truth about me? Has he just seen what I saw? My memories?

'If I was really here for redemption, then why *the hell* would I be looking around for your backside?'

'I was told about your life in the Slumberlands, Samuella. I was shown how your parents disappeared from your life, and the burden your mental disorder had on you getting anywhere further than that old farm,' Oscar catches me off-guard with this comment. 'The Tombs know what you want. They know you want disclosure for your parents. They left you so young you can't even remember their names.'

'What've you done to Oscar? How've you made him like that?'

The emerald on the staff has relighted. I'm rabidly shuffling on my knees, trying to reach out for the emerald, but an invisible wall is pushing me back to the kneeling spot, next to Oscar and his incensed babbling.

'And I know it was you who killed the Phantom,' Oscar says, his lips quivering. 'Evanessa—you burnt her alive! You forced her into those flames, so you could take her place as the Phantom!'

'I never killed the Phantom!' I confess. 'She was a Night Dreamer on her last legs and I only paid her dying request, for her spirit to finally be released, so she could live another life! If I hadn't done it, she'd have ended up trapped, just like Cassandra was until we rescued her spirit! There was no choice for me! She was the Last Night Dreamer! She demanded that I did it!'

'Oh—without hesitation, you'd burn us all alive! Just so you could claim everything we have and everything you're not! An unprincipled country girl.'

'Tell me now!' I shiver, enraged. 'What are you doing to him?'

'I showed him your truth,' Antares says. 'The Alumni spoke to him and its verity has him stunned, regenerating his perception of you.'

'I want you to give us the emerald we came for, I want you to quit messing with his head and I want you to return us to the surface. *Now!*'

'I'm afraid that isn't the deal I offer.'

All of a sudden, Oscar's melting on the spot. His flesh drips rapidly down his face in a creamy drool, soaking his pyjamas in the stuff. In its place, the blood beneath his skin has oozed through to glaze the body. It builds a humanoid shell around him, and then shapes into armour. The armour of a knight. A Blood Knight.

'The spirits are hungry for something new and living,' the undertaker announces. 'And you two Night Dreamers are a mighty feast.'

Oscar launches from the ground and dives at me. His hands clasp around my neck and they eject me across the room. He holds me up against a bookshelf, his wet armour bleeding on my neck and gluing to me. Struggling and gagging, I manage to lift my right foot and dig it into his pelvis. He turns, then swings, his body floating backwards with the levitating force of the emerald. Using this supernatural support, Oscar restores his balance and reclaims his footing, unharmed.

I use this short intermission to compose myself again. Both hands raised, I advance towards him, as he gathers his offensive posture again. I realise that (of all things) the Solar Blade has spontaneously rematerialized in my right hand – surely, a duelling gift from Antares and his groundbreaking new emerald toy. Adrenaline-pumped, I lurch forwards ahead of myself to use my divine weapon. *SWOOP!* Nothing strikes. The Blade has vanished from my hand again (an illusion) and, instead, Oscar lands a fist in my stomach, sending me back into the bookshelf, busting a few tomes off the top shelves.

The Blood Knight marches at me, designated for murder, with pounding boots. I slide between his open legs, skimming past the sticky gloop of the iron shin-pads. The Knight can only turn stiffly to keep up with me. I bounce back onto my feet with strong elbows and grapple him from behind; blood spurts up my sleeves and spatters my face, chin-upwards. Then, he has my hands in his tight gauntlets. He uses the clamp of the hard, metal fingers to his own strength, swinging me over his head like a plank of wood. I slam against the floor, spraining my back. Here I lie, squealing, and there he is, gazing down at me through the vents in his helmet. He closes in, keeling over towards me. 'Oscar…' I manage, coherency being the least of my worries. As he impends closer, breaking boundaries with each step, I lift my arms up at him pleadingly. And that's where I see it, in my possession once again. The Solar Blade! Before he can touch me, I twirl the Blade vertically to direct it upwards and seal it into his torso.

He stops. Half bent over, where there's no more momentum left in him. I'm panting like an antelope that's just evaded execution from its pursuing predator. *'Damn you—gullible idiot!'* I suffice an accusatory stammer in defence of my own scorching guilt. The tears running away from my eyes are no distraction from the unexpected fatality I have caused. '*—Damn your innocence!*' I blurt pathetically. It's unclear who this criticism is aimed at. Like him, I can't move. Not just from under his intense amount of weight, but because I'm too devastated to let go and shove him away. I'm so ashamed I could die with him.

'Oscar?' I lighten my voice. And it just sounds like I'm choking on the phlegm that parades on my tonsils. His own gargling is bittersweet music for the dead. These ill noises of corporal departure decree Oscar speechless. I don't blame him. It's a pretty long sword…

'Dream for me,' I tell him. 'Dream for me and I will pray for you.'

***

On the night Cassandra Philson was murdered, Oscar had been a young child. At seven-years-old, the Decider deemed his son far too old for bedtime stories, even when his wife, the Great Oracle of the West, thought otherwise.

That evening, she had shared with him the story of the three falsely accused prisoners on a quest to uncover a collection of hidden cell codes, which would free them from an oppressive war camp and its evil prison lieutenant. She didn't omit a single detail in the story, being sure to include their fortunes dealing with the lizard women who guarded the deep web of dungeons beneath the cellblocks and who could melt a whole man just by expelling their acidic spit. It would be the last time Mrs. Philson ever saw or spoke to her son again. She had never told him a story so vivid before, almost as if her tragic fate had long been installed in her emotions. It had been passionately retold from start to finish, by a seasoned storyteller. Effortlessly captivating with suspense drilling through each pause like a key through a lock on a treasure chest, just before it clinks and opens.

Oscar had been snuggled under the duvets, leaning an elbow on his cushion with an arm propped up to elevate his head and face his mother side-on. She was sat on the edge of his bed, engaging her fingers to dance upon the mattress and perform like actors on a stage, as she narrated the tale. Fictional, of course, Oscar would think to himself, for his father would have forbade him to believe anything more of it. But his mother never admitted that to him; everything in her stories either ***had*** *happened,* ***was*** *happening, or* ***could*** *happen at any point – she was a Soothsayer; it came with the territory.*

During the final act of the story – when the heroes finally came to confront the Sepentesses in their dungeons – Stevenson rang the doorbell of the Philsons' residence and Oscar waited for his mother to answer the door (desperate to find out what happened to the prisoners). The deflated chauffer, notably naïve in his youth, had come to inform Cassandra of the Soothe Meeting that had surfaced out of sudden and unseen events and how the Soothes were complaining that the Oracle was completely unaware of it. 'De sistas demand yuh be present at de temple—fast,' Stevenson had whispered to her on the doorstep. 'A meeting has bin called dere, an' de Oracle's presidency is required by dem sistahood—urgently.'

'I was not told about such a meeting! The sisterhood don't just summon meetings out of the blue—not this late in advance—never!' Cassandra had responded sharply, keeping her own voice at a low volume. 'I'm with my son, Stevenson. How urgent can it be?'

'Very—when it dis unexpected,' Stevenson had noted. 'I bin tol' one sista has had a terrible premonition—one about your future, Mother Oracle.'

Cassandra thought about it for a fraction of a second, knowing she had minimal time to delay any premonition about her forthcoming, but came to an unfavourable conclusion. At a potentially dangerous time like this, she wasn't allowed to follow her heart, only her instincts. They were bad, for she could definitely feel the near future, but not quite see it yet – the vision of her deathly catastrophe wasn't far enough ahead for her to find. There must have been a kink in events somewhere down the line, she thought. A sudden change or new thread in her timeline. She rarely missed anything. Unaware she was already too late to save herself, all she knew was that she had to garner an aura of professionalism when the conundrum demanded her to be pin-sharp. So she distanced herself from her son, just for this one night. To be certain of one thing in her uncertainty – his safety – during whatever this apparent premonition of her future might be, how soon it might happen, and how perilously it would unfold. She never returned to finish the bedtime story or see Oscar to sleep.

In twenty minutes, Stevenson zipped Cassandra to the Soothe Temple, which was a few blocks away from the Philsons' residence on Coventry Street and located closer to the border of the City Central. While she was getting changed into her Oracle's robes in the back of the vehicle, she backtracked over hundreds of verses from the pages of the Holy Libel in her head, searching for answers, for explanations, for previous instances of similar situations. She couldn't think of one. Never before had an Oracle's life been threatened so spontaneously. A "terrible premonition", she thought, what could it be?

When she arrived at the temple, thundered through the giant doors and marched down the aisle, catching the respectful attentions of all those who were present – a hundred of the City's most prominent Soothsayers – the Oracle Cassandra made a beeline for the podium in the middle of the nave. The congregational room of the Soothe Temple – in these luckier years, shortly before the Decider's Administration made the radical move to demolish the temple and burn its remnants to the ground – was a massively intimidating space, perfectly globular like an arena. It was candle-lit along the aisles and walls, the windows were stained with the colourful Libel scenes of the Soothe Gods, and hot incense rode the air. In the very centre of the room, the Oracle ascended the podium. She gazed up at the Senate of Sayers and then lifted and slammed the gavel down on its block, ready to address her audience. 'I call rise to the sisters!' she announced.

All the sisters rose from their chairs. The three hundred seats in the temple's nave had been tiered and segmented into five blocks of six rows each. The Soothsayers stood up, responding synchronously to the Oracle's order like an audience with muted applause in an auditorium, or rather a jury before a courtroom hearing.

'I demand the sister who proclaimed my prophecy tonight to approach me and elaborate,' Sister Cassandra summoned the witnesses out from the audience above.

Nobody had stepped forward, nobody had answered.

'I have been given information to believe that my life as Oracle is in danger—immediate danger,' she continued. 'Would someone care to explain why a Senate Meeting has been arranged without my knowledge?'

Sybil, the blood-sister of the Oracle, glanced around at the hundreds of terrified faces in the audience, then stepped forward on behalf of the Sisterhood. 'Your Grace, there was no prophecy told of you whatsoever,' Sister Sybil said honestly. 'A few other sisters and I—we were all summoned to Senate for what we were told to believe would be late night prayers.'

'Told by whom?' Sister Cassandra roared furiously. 'Who took it upon themselves to call a meeting in ***my*** *temple without* ***my*** *permission? I was told that one sister had a premonition—who was it?'*

Again, there had been no response from the tiers.

'Unless my chauffer was lying to me, who was it that gave him this information?'

Still, the numbest silence rinsed the room.

So, Sister Cassandra altered the question. 'Okay—who in this room has had any form of premonition come to them in the last forty-eight hours?'

The majority of the sisters reclaimed their seats, which left only eight still standing.

'Sisters?' the Oracle addressed the honest few. 'Were any of you responsible for the news I was delivered earlier tonight? Would you care to explain?'

They all explained their individual prophecies, one by one and in great length, inducing some yawns of boredom and tired groans around the room. None of these prophecies foretold anything compelling and none of them referred to the Oracle Cassandra or the jeopardy of her life. The Oracle Cassandra blessed the eight ladies for their assistance and then told them to sit down.

Finally, she put the case to bed. Awkwardly vindicating that the summoning to Senate had been a misunderstanding or a prank of some sort, and she would need the rest of the night and the following day to get to the bottom of this disruptive act and isolate the culprit behind it. She ended the gathering by offering a prayer for the Soothes to take with them into their slumbers and then she dismissed the sisters.

Cassandra debated the affair with Stevenson all the way back to Citadel Tower. Stevenson modestly apologised for his 'misinterpretation of the message' and said that he was in such a rush to get her to the temple he'd forgotten to specifically mention the name of the Soothsayer who had informed him. He told her that he had been given the alarming information by a Sister named Omega. Cassandra sighed, laughed and shook her head with relief, then told him the premonition was nothing to be alarmed by at all, for she knew this Soothe very well. Omega was young and inexperienced, still a novice to her gift and learning to interpret her prophetical readings. 'It was probably an innocent mistake,' Cassandra chuckled in the backseat of the chauffer's blacked-out limousine. 'I'll speak to her first thing in the morning.' After Stevenson saw Cassandra get to the door and watched it close behind her, he pulled off and she was left to make her own way back up to her floor.

Oscar was fast asleep and his bedroom door was shut when she returned to the residence, so she didn't bother him. The house would have been quiet, had it not been for the unsound whines coming from her and her husband's bedroom. It would have been the appropriate time for her husband to finally be home; the Decider had been at an important meeting downtown all day long. DCD. Philson would have been exhausted after today and possibly fast asleep too. But she had come home at about twenty minutes to midnight and there were stressful heaving noises emerging from their bedroom. She passed Oscar's room and crept along the rest of the corridor, towards the bedroom at the end of it. The heaving and sighing became louder as she got closer to it. There came deeper visceral whimpering...and then a feminine moan. It was the unintelligible activity of not one, but two people. Two people in the same room? ***My*** *room? she thought. And not one of those 'two people' is me?*

She edged her neck around the open door and caught a glimpse of the dark bedroom through the gap. Already, the noises had stopped abruptly, the movement inside the room had transformed into a new aggression. She hadn't explicitly seen what had been going on before she peeked through, but she could have imagined it well enough. All she did see – before the steely, muscular palm snapped hard across her left cheek and she catapulted into the corridor wall – was the unclothed shadow of a man streaking from the bed to the door in a rapidly brash reaction to fend her off. The hand struck her face bitterly. She thwacked the side of her brow into the wall, peeling a band of blood down the royal purple wallpaper, as she fell and her knees flumped on the floor. Her and her husband's bedroom door reopened seconds later and Decider Philson scooted out, wearing a dressing gown over his bareness. Another woman in a matching gown tiptoed out of the bedroom behind him and stood right beside the Decider. And Cassandra recognised who she was from the moment she was revealed. She had been a young, nimble and pretty Soothesayer, a devoted Sayer only in her early twenties, who'd been prolific in her prayer, as well as a loyal to the Libel and the Soothe Gods. Sister Omega had been a girl whom Cassandra had once believed to have a lot of potential. A future Oracle even, Cassandra had been convinced. Wrongly convinced it appeared now.

Cassandra tried to scream and lash out at them both, the adulterers, but all she could manage with her injuries was a squawk that was immediately strangled into a chokehold by her husband, who had rushed to clasp her neck with his hands and lift her up against the wall. Her head had been bleeding out on the floor and now it was bleeding out six or seven feet in the air. 'Don't struggle...Don't be angry...and do not wake up the child! DON'T wake up my heir! He doesn't need to see his mother bloodied on the floor,' the Decider hushed in her face and then dropped her back on the ground. 'You weren't supposed to be coming back here, Cassandra. That wasn't a part of the plan.'

'Plan? What plan are you talking about, you monster?' Cassandra croaked with a voice squashed in the pit of her pulverised

throat. Though, for reason only she knew, it didn't seem weird that there were no tears in her eyes. 'Am I not supposed to be here? Am I supposed to be gone—while you have ***her*** *here instead of me?'*

'Poisoned. You were supposed to have been poisoned!' the Decider grunted and glanced at the beautiful young girl, his extracurricular fiancé. 'Omega contaminated the water font in the temple with a fatal nerve agent earlier tonight, before she called the Senate. You and all of your sisters present there tonight were supposed to be dead by morning.'

'It was you who pronounced that false prophecy!' Cassandra then turned on the girl, who was shrinking behind the Decider's back, pretending to have had no role in this duplicity. 'You liar—you lied about your premonition! You lied to everyone! I trusted you, child, I received your oath—! But you went ahead and you disgraced yourself! You are a traitor to your Sisterhood!'

'Don't be so harsh on Omega. Those were my demands of her,' the Decider responded haughtily. 'But I guess that isn't how events have panned out. You came home.'

'I always follow you home,' Cassandra said, almost cursedly. 'That's what I've always done and keep doing. But I can't even tell myself why I do.'

'You don't know why you keep coming back to me, to this security, this haven above the world, to this glassless roof over your head?' the Decider scoffed. 'Darling, you do it because you know that I am the only chance your people have left in this world. The only reason you're still here, still living in this City, living in this residence, still gruelling and pleading at my feet is to keep your Kind alive and remotely relevant. And that was the whole purpose of tonight's little antics: to make one thing very clear to you and to everyone, that Soothe Kind won't be around for much longer. I'll make sure of it.'

'You think that's why I still stand by you after all these years? Not even close,' Cassandra retorted. 'My son comes before the Sisterhood, before my religion! He is the reason I'm still here, putting up with your bigotry!'

'I don't think you'll be saying that after tonight,' the Decider said confidently. 'I'm in greater company now. I have new people telling me where the fates are falling, which means I'm in a better position without the Soothsayers. It also means that your little society has already been made redundant. So I don't require your burden in my home anymore—honey.'

'I will always follow you home—to your grave,' Cassandra hissed up at him.

Those were her last words.

The Decider dropped to his knees, reached down and once again closed his hands around her neck. Strangled her until her eyelids shut for longer than a minute, until her bottom lip limply drooped down, until her face went blue all over, and until the hot breath stroking his wrists became the cold wisp of a winter wind.

When he turned around, pale in the face, his illicit mistress had already returned to the bedroom. Before doing anything about the dead body now lying on the corridor floor, he crept quietly into his son's bedroom. Oscar was still and undisturbed in his sleep. The duvet was raised halfway over his head and he was facing away from the door and the intruder. Decider Philson swung the bedroom door half-shut, only until the hinge touched the brass skin of the latch and not completely closed, stripping some of the light from the corridor off his back. Then he shifted over to the bed, where he stood tall beside his sleeping son. And he placed a soft hand on the back of the boy's head. Smiling satisfyingly, he whispered, 'You're safe, and you're alive, and that's all that matters...'

***

From his front row seat (the only chair in the study), Antares watches me with keen eyes. Camson has just joined him from the unknown. He goes to pose beside the undertaker's armchair, settling his hand there on the chair's head. Both men are spectating as I rest Oscar's lifeless body in the corner of the room, sat upright against one of the bookshelves. There's blood bleached over my hands, after having to remove his helmet and the mangled skull beneath presses me close to retching. I can hear Camson impatiently clearing his throat and tapping the tip of his foot against the undertaker's chair. I despise how his arrogance has become something of a custom in our liaison. He left us on the surface, only to follow on after our route had been trialled and tested, and then down he came to catch the finale of our mishaps.

'That was thoroughly entertaining,' Antares remarks. 'And, even more: another body for the Tombs to reap and a new stash of memories to log into the Alumni. Really impressive, thank you so much. You do have a zest for getting things done, girl. Have you ever considered becoming a queen once All Eyes rewards you eternity? Perhaps you can succeed Cassandra as the judge of spirits up in the Falls of Fortune, now that I hear the gorilla queen has abdicated.'

Antares beams, skinning the flesh flakes off his grisly lips with his tongue.

'I didn't come here to kill anybody,' I say. 'And I didn't trek this far to deliver you another spirit.'

'But you did descend to the Blankesphere with means to fend for yourself?' the undertaker retorts. 'At least, not against your own allies.'

'Drag-in and emeralds aside,' I morbidly respond, 'how dead is he?'

'I beg your pardon?' Antares twitches his brow with snide pleasure. '*How* dead?'

'You manipulated the Constellation Map to get us here, you lead us into this trap willingly and you summoned the Solar Blade to make me believe I was really fighting for my life—how likely is it that I actually murdered Oscar? Can his spirit be restored?'

'Impossible,' Antares snickered.

'Not impossible! I scream back at him.

'Huh—*guilty*, are we?' the undertaker leers in my direction with brown, toothless simper. 'Then, how is *not* impossible—?'

'Because the Blade is a fake!' I counter. 'Just like the weapons All Eyes gave us! You used the staff and the emerald to conjure it like a rune, so the very worst you could have intended was to stun him! The same way you messed with the Map and manipulated our memories—you can just as easily play with life and death!'

'*Smart* girl…What to you suggests that the Blade is a fake?' Antares queries.

I pick the bloodied Solar Blade up from the ground beside Oscar and advance towards the undertaker. The emerald fizzes to life again and that invisible blockade returns to prevent me coming any closer to the blind man. It doesn't stop the sword, though. I toss the Solar Blade at the staff and it slices the scorpion's tail clean off, sending the emerald jittering onto the floor. The Blade shatters into a thousand dazzling shards on impact.

'It's too light,' I note, relishing the glory of the undertaker's surprise. ' Yep, I've held the real Blade before and that felt nothing like it – you weren't banking on me sussing that out, were you? You could have just spared my time and my friend and I wouldn't have to outfox you at your own sick game.'

But my success to disarm the staff has done nothing to the power of the emerald. The rock is still working its charm, blocking me as I push forwards.

'He's your *friend* now, is he?' Antares has been waiting for me to spill a fresh can of worms, something else to challenge and bide time for himself. 'Merely "allies" you've been telling the world. But now you admit to intimacy? Two Night Dreamers who share a *friendship*? That would be a bond somewhat cosier than the artificial relationship emplaced to select and throw Night Dreamers randomly – and usually reluctantly – together. Unorthodox to what I've seen and heard of your kind before.'

'It's called a working relationship. Look it up,' I bark.

'You're a ballsy fighter, who's proven that she's very capable of acquiring what she's come for. Your passion is unrelenting. I'll give you that. But your character alone is not enough to convince me about the morale within your group as a whole. The ambition of one Night Dreamer does not account for you all. The closer that Drag-in comes to breaking the Void between worlds, the more my influence over the Blankesphere crumbles away. Things have become riotous down here and the spirits have gone insane. The rebel souls are beginning to overthrow my realm and this emerald is all I have to keep face.'

'You have no face,' I mock. 'And I'm sorry to break it to you, but one emerald will not protect you from what's coming!'

'It isn't the Drag-in I'll need protection from, once you've done your deed, but the hungry spirits themselves that will continue to threaten my authority!'

'Fine! If I can, I will try to bring it back,' I guarantee weakly.

'Trying isn't enough!' It's evident how much the blind man is enjoying this little confrontation.

'I finally understand,' Camson breaks in, 'why Oscar isn't anything how I anticipated a boy like him to be. He reminds me of my son.'

Am I looking at the same Camson? Is this the same man with the hardened veteran's soul and all that supressed compassion? Is he still there?

'What has he done for you, Camson,' I reason. 'What has Antares done to play with your perception? Are you the next to try to kill me? What truths about me has he showered over you?'

'I was told nothing about you. The Alumni presented me with a window into Oscar's past, back in reality. The same way it showed Oscar a glimpse into your world,' Camson affirms. He has a weirdly different tone, one of candid sympathy. 'It was his father who killed the Head Soothe. The Decider was the reason for the death of the Oracle. It wasn't suicide; it was rancid murder. And Oscar hasn't known anything about it. Not until the Alumni revealed it. I might have been the only one to see it; I'm not sure how, or if ever, Oscar came to bear this horror, for he was a young child, innocent and unbeknownst to the situation at the time. Such a terrible, terrible event I witnessed. I felt dirty being forced by the Alumni to voyeur a vile tragedy so personal to a young child. Now I know why this place is so dangerous to us and why it can make or break groups of Night Dreamers – individuals who are never supposed to be born-allies at heart. It's because now we all know the truths about each other. We understand ourselves better.'

'But, if that's the case – if Oscar's seen my truth and you've witnessed Oscar's revelation – then why haven't I been shown yours?'

'I had nothing to hide. All I want is to see my son again,' Camson pleads. 'My beautiful boy who I lost on Awakening Coast. To find Thuban again would be the most satisfying reparation All Eyes could reward me.'

'Day Dreamers who break away from the Dreamerverse in extraordinary circumstances can lose their footing when being transferred back across the Void to reality, since the Void isn't expecting them when it happens,' the undertaker responds to Camson's woes. 'An advantage with being a Night Dreamer is that you have a broader and freer yield of your conscience and the Void's memory block is not an adversary to your memory, which means you are always actively linked to it. The Void is always ready for Night Dreamers in the waking process. But the transit between Dreamerverse and reality is more restrictive for other Dreamers – which is why the ritual of burying a firefly on Awakening Coast is imperative for Day Dreamers.'

'What makes you bring this up? What has this to do with anything?' I'm underwhelmed by his lesson of a theory I'm already quite confident with. 'We knew that much.'

'I regard this theory because it brings me back to this gentleman's situation with his missing son. I would also like to point out the Red Robe he's worn every time he's returned here and how important the role of the Robe will be in finding the boy,' Antares emphasises.

'How do you know I've always worn this Robe?' Camson asks defensively.

Camson's inquisitive expression sinks when Antares' hand finds the lapel of his eveningwear. He brushes his overgrown nails on the dark red silk.

'It is made of silk,' Antares says. 'Silk derived from the creatures of a foreign world – worms living in your reality, who dream and fantasise as all living things do. Through these creatures, I can use the Alumni to trace their history and identify every living, conscious thing that came into contact with their produce – among them being yourself and your son. As the undertaker of the Blankesphere, I am blind to no living being that passes through the Dreamerverse. This includes the worms that produced the silks for that very Robe. These tiny details, small interlinking interactions of the living in both dimensions, afford me fragments of memories that allow me to keep spirits, who may lose themselves in the Void between worlds, intact and alive. Might I ask who gave you that garment, Camson?'

'My son and his mother gifted it to me,' Camson sings. There's a glimmer of hope in his eyes.

'Ah—yes! And it is the reason you still stand here, alive and well, for you wear the memory your son left behind in those silks,' Antares elaborates. 'You arrived on Awakening Coast with the Robe. You crossed the Bridge of Lynx with the Robe. You fought off the gorillas at Fortune's Falls with the Robe. And the Robe was your companion while you wandered my desert alone at night, aloof from your allies, and it led you safely down here. The Robe is a silk vessel harbouring deep thought and consciousness belonging your son, a mark of reality; it has nurtured your sanity in your most isolated moments. How else have you coped with roaming the surface of this world at times without the company of your allies? Your son has always been at your side. There's even a chance he too is trying to get through to you. His spirit could be speaking to you in your mind—'

'Yes, yes—he does!' Camson cries. ' I hear him talking to me sometimes! Only when I'm here! In the Dreamerverse!'

'Dreamers who hear voices are simply recollecting them from Living Memories stored in the garbs they are wearing. Any and all people who have come in to contact with the clothes you are wearing now, their spirits live on beside you in the fabrics. That is why your pyjamas are sacred attire. They only come into contact with those souls who are dearest to you. Pyjamas are the armour of your closest memories. And so, as prematurely as your son's body may have found these Tombs, his spirit is not an occupant in my chambers, but rather a lining in that old garment you wear.'

'I believed I was going mad—I thought I hadn't been sound in the head! But my son has been with me this whole time?' Camson bellows, shocked. 'Part of Thuban's spirit is in the lining of this Robe?'

'Yes,' Antares confirms. 'And the rest of his spirit is still lost in mid-transmission between worlds, suspended in the Void.'

I take a look at Camson and I inspect the Red Robe myself. For the first time, I've examined it properly. The quiet instrument that the East Man has been blessed with since the very start of his journey. The pristine silk gleams, lined with a very thin, black stitching threaded into the edges.

'You lost Thuban off Awakening Coast moments after you arrived. A whirlpool sucked him under the water,' I reminisce, eager to help Camson find resolve. 'What happened as soon as you returned to reality, after that First Awakening?'

'The next day that I awoke back in the real world, Thuban was nowhere to be found,' Camson continues. 'He'd been sleeping soundly in our residence, in his bedroom right next to mine. We'd spent the whole night struggling to sleep through the clamour a dreadful sand storm outside. When I woke from that first excursion on Constellation Planet, Thuban was gone and he was missing the following morning and has been gone every morning since!'

'Vanished from his bed, like he'd never been there?' I inquire.

'The bed is still the way it was since I last saw him. I haven't been near it long enough to take a closer look. I only set this Robe down on the bed covers, and then peek inside from the room's doorway. It's a ridiculous superstition, as if the bed ate him or something—no, the bed hasn't been touched. The bed is the same, completely normal. But I'd watched him fall asleep, sang him to rest through the sand storm.' Camson's breathing heavily, as if sucking the air inside the Tombs will provide him with answers. But he's actually itching his reluctant urge to weep and let his secret sensitivity sweep his stoicism away.

'The boy went missing. Snatched and devoured on his travel across the Void,' Antares evaluates. 'I'm afraid to say your crippled friend here has met the same fate. I apologise for my foolish teasing. Your generation of Night Dreamers aren't as conceited as I remember them to be. For once, it has been a pleasure. My condolences go to you both.'

'His name was Oscar,' I stress.

'Oddly, I keep getting the sense you have strong feelings for your lost ally. Colourful feelings,' Antares can't get his head around the idea of Night Dreamers even remotely getting along.

'I hardly knew him. But *he* couldn't even remember where he'd seen me in the real world,' I say with unintended arrogance.

'You can't hide your emotions from me, girl,' Antares holds a pretentious frown, accommodating an almost inconceivable sentiment with what little physical expression he has to showcase. 'I've heard every dead man's confession, every truth and lie he takes to the grave – including Oscar. And someday I'll be dying to hear all about yours.'

'Why does that matter?' I howl. 'It's not going to help us, not now that there's only two of us! Beyond realigning our relationships with each other, what does the revelation of our truths do for us going forwards?'

'Empathy, Night Dreamer. Respect, remorse and reconciliation for the ally your have lost, but whom you now understand and empathise with more than you ever did before. Your new esteem to revive Oscar will solidify your objective and propel you onwards in your mission against the Drag-in. Your friend isn't dead and neither is Camson's boy. They both may still be restorable,' the undertaker announces this like it's been a surprise he's kept secret just to revel at my sudden rush of humility. I can't complain; the relief electrifies me. This frustrating experiment he's herded us into has done its job on our psychologies – I'll give it that. 'Their spirits are being preserved in the Soulcano, which is where the Void spits out its rejects. It's also the place where dead Dreamers are sent in bulk from the Falls of Fortune before they arrive here. The Soulcano is where Dreamers have their spirits extracted from their bodies and then filtered out as either good spirits or Nightmares…'

He trails off, hesitates on this last point and sighs, rolling his eyes at our shaky knowledge. I take it that he's hinting towards the Constellation Map that has now transferred from my hand into Camson's without warning.

'There we go,' Antares says. 'What can you see, New Leader? I suppose it is your turn to tour the Map.'

Camson unravels the scroll and, under his eyes, the hidden world within the parchment reappears for him. 'I see the Soulcano. It's in the direction we haven't been yet: *North*—or *Draco*, or whatever you folk call it,' Camson describes.

'That is where you'll find your friend's spirit and the final piece to complete your hunt,' Antares assures.

'And my son?' Camson prods.

'Your son will only be retrievable once this is all finished, only once the Drag-in has been put out of everyone's misery and the Void can repair its wounds. But remember to keep the Robe close to you, for part of your son's spirit was caught in its lining and it will be your only source to summon him back from the Void.'

'What about Oscar?' I persist.

'Likewise. The Void will recover his spirit once it has mended itself. As with Camson's Red Robe, the Living Memories stored in Oscar's pyjamas will be a catalyst in his resurrection,' Antares explains. He touches his staff with one hand and holds out his other in front of him. Oscar's blue pyjamas flash into his flat palm, clean and folded, almost like new. I snatch the clothes out of the undertaker's hand and wrap them snugly around my exposed midriff. 'Oh—and there's one more important thing that you'll require.'

The emerald shoots off the ground and catapults towards Camson and me. The East veteran has his hands full, so I reach both arms out, stagger across the room and catch it. A weight has been lifted in the undertaker's study; the emerald's dominion over us has disintegrated.

'Take the emerald and do what you must.' Antares forfeits his stubbornness. 'But get on with it quickly, before I rouse second thoughts about my cooperative kindness. Every soul that arrives here in the Blankesphere must first pass through the Soulcano. However, I should warn you that the Soulcano on Draco Island is notoriously known to be the Drag-in's hive, its resting place. It's how Draco got its name. The menace will be waiting at the heart of it, feeding beside the other free spirits. You'll be needing the sword as well as something else…'

The blind man raises a deformed hand of only two and a half fingers. Somehow, he manages to click them. And, just like that, Camson and I are fully kitted out in Blood Knight's armour. 'Just in case you need to defend yourselves,' Antares mentions. 'And, of course, a proper weapon…' He clicks them again and that famous Blade appears in the space above our heads once more. I whip it out of the air and bring it down to examine up-close – an inimitable field of starlight outlines the edges and, remarkably, this time it carries the weight that is distinctive to the original sword – the actual Solar Blade. 'How is this…?' I rebound my look of disbelief off Camson.

'Heavy enough for you?' Antares chuckles smugly. 'That's the real article you're holding now.'

'You gave a phoney copy to me before, when you forced me to fight Oscar. Where did you find this one?' I query. 'All Eyes permits nobody to bear this weapon. It's prohibited to use without divine permission.'

Antares taps the stub of a knuckle to his lips. 'The only thing more destructive than the Blade is the unscrupulous owner who casts his restrictions over it. Trust me, you will need it when you get to the Soulcano.'

'Are you willing to disparage the orders of the king?' I say to the energetic East Man in the Red Robe, our new leader and navigator, who now holds a greater fraction of the power between us.

'It was the vague orders of the king that got us into this situation in the first place,' Camson twiddles with the rebellious idea. 'About time we lived up to our title and started making our own decisions, I say.'

Then, it hits me again – guilt. I'm glancing back, over the shoulder, at the dead corpse shielded beneath a clad of red metal armour in the corner of the room. *Oscar*, I think. It's not just everyone we're fighting this battle for anymore. Not just the Dreamerverse. Not each and every corner of Mankind's World. But we're now fighting for one of our own, for a friend. I guess, the Country Girl, the City Boy and the East Man can be on the same side. From different places. Going different places. But, ultimately, locked in the same predicament: struggling to decide who we want to be in this world and the other.

High above us, the ground has started to part. My unlikely guardian has returned for me, digging a tunnel towards the outside light. The dying hours of sunlight have arrived and we need to make it to the surface by sunset, so we can set up camp before we reawaken in reality. On Scorpius' beach, we can rest under the tranquillity of a purple seed, before we leave for our final destination. Within the chunks of falling soil, the spirits have misaligned themselves and scatter like an infestation of maggots and worms cracked out from their burrows in the dirt.

'Follow my wife's passage to the surface,' Antares advocates.

'Your *wife*?' Both Camson and I say in unison.

'Yes. The soil of Scorpius Island will be my spouse for all times. The Groundskeeper is the shroud of my secrets, the aegis of my duties below the surface, and the cape of her landscape is the blanket to my eternal slumber.'

As the light gets brighter, as gravity expels Camson and I, and we start to ascend, headed straight for the ceiling, up through the flurrying curtain of apparitions. Under our feet, on the other side of the dense, white cloud of spirits, we can hear the shrinking voice of the undertaker…

'Oh—and remember me! Please—remember my name, at least!' the blind man cries. 'I am only a lone splinter down here! I used to have a name, and a face—a wholesome persona up on the surface! A piece of me still walks in your reality, a Living Memory on the other side of the Void! A man who shares the other half of my conscience! *His name is Pegasus! Samuella—remember to trust your...*'

Chapter Nine

The Polar Region

The plane jolted violently. Its wheels became acquainted with a shield of black ice covering the runway. All bodies, skewed by the intruding night and the vapour from a hundred humbled gasps, drummed a dozen times inside the cabin, while the jumbo jet battled with its own speed in a terrifying trial to procure stability. They'd been hovering above snow-choked tarmac for what had felt like an hour and a half, before finally landing. Here…where aircrafts must rarely have met the ground – let alone flown above its seedy languish and the secluded misery it inhabited – a collection of deceiving, handsome buildings resided, all compacted closely together in uniform, like someplace between a hospital, some prestigious fortress and a military camp, everything chastened under swelling moonlight and a dusk of tranquil indigo. The buildings were mainly concrete blocks, the entire organisation fronted by a central tower that was topped with a piercing spire. And scattered throughout the glacial field was a sweeping discordance of watchtowers intimidating all dwellers above and below; each must have been eighty-feet tall. Akin to these great juggernaut-towers, the height of the snow on the ground offered a similar caveat against footwork, unless traversing the frozen plain was absolutely necessary; the grounds appeared devoid of life or impetus. For all the passengers knew, they could have arrived in an upturned ghost town that had since been populated with torpid shadows instead of any actual ghosts.

When the aircraft rattled to an uncomfortable halt and the final vibrations trickled off the passengers' joints, it was hard to hear anything over the dying mumble of the engine. In the plane's chamber, the shimmering numbness was comparable to the stupor of a bomb's detonation. Now, at last, the smack against thick ice broke Samuella's optimism, for she was scared of being this still; she wanted to move, eager to be responsive, to react and cry out. Though it wasn't the fear of the unknown keeping her subdued, but her own exhaustion from the lack of air inside the pressurised cabin. There had been a brief decompression forcing the Regal Jet to nosedive and that had resulted in her swinging in and out of consciousness and dipping back into the Dreamerverse, knocking her out for what must have been five minutes in real-time, until the cabin's automated O2 Restoration System kicked in. She had whacked her forehead on the seat in front during the sudden and unexpected landing and was now resting it there on the headrest, rallying the breaths her lungs were auctioning far too cheaply. The temperature had surged to an almighty freeze – even worse than it had been inside the cabin when airborne. And now every hair and bump on her body was pulling on her skin, enchanted by the biting frostiness of the empty cabin.

She found Oscar's shrunken silhouette on the other side of the cabin. His attention was out the window – it had been fixed out there for a long time. The cannibalistic silence was starting to consume itself. Distantly, beyond her semi-blocked ears, she could hear alarmed voices searing through. Passengers in the next cabin were doing all the wrong things: their anxiety was transmuting ambiguity into terror. So, she decided to ask her very calm and collected companion what was happening, because—not only was he the only passenger she could actually see right now in the private cabin, but by the look of his behaviour, it seemed he was a lot more aware of what was going on than anyone else. 'Where are we, then?' Samuella asked. 'Do you recognise this place? What is it?'

Oscar didn't respond. He gave her a pushy signal with his flaccid hands "*stay there!*", unbuckled his seatbelt, and then unsteadily jumped up, passing across the Premium Cabin bar to investigate; he poked his head through the galley-curtain, into the next cabin, and then slipped fully through, leaving her behind – as she'd anticipated, he had other ideas. Samuella had a prodding urge to call him back into the cabin – '*No one told you to do so much as fart in your throne, your majesty—*', she uttered under her wheezing. She couldn't understand the commotion; she was too deaf. Anything could have been happening. So, she chose to stay wise, stay safe, and keep silent.

All on my own, then. That's the best way to deal with delirium, isn't it? Not to mention a concussion, whiplash and an impending coma—for me, will it simply be to drop unconscious, or drop dead? How bad was it? Well, at least she was in the company of Kyma...hanging around somewhere in her blind spot, probably.

Seconds after reeling into the lap of solitude, she heard more and sensed more motion on-board the plane. *Somewhere along the other cabin, a door had been breached and swung open. As the door-seals choked, a cannon of fiery winter-winds burst into the other cabin and chased their way along into hers, leading with it an army of snowflakes; a snow-storm was rocking the world outside. The turmoil from the passengers was like hearing mice beneath the floorboards. And bitter machine-guns drilled...and blared...and assiduously drilled and blared some more. Heavy voices followed. The baritones of men. Were they troopers? Definitely not A.I., surely? Men. Just men. Who were they? What had they come for—?*

—in this miserable place—?

If her eyes hadn't been closed for all this short while, she might have noticed...

And, now, who was that strapping fellow in the orange rubber-suit standing over her, pumping gas into her face...?

Knocked out cold, a mask attached to the gas apparatus was fixed over her mouth and nose and she was lifted from her seat, over the lofty figure's shoulder, without any hassle whatsoever. And she was taken through the curtain Oscar had vanished via, into the next cabin, and into the following cabin, and into the next after that...They passed the now vacant toilet-cubicle and they passed a now deactivated Mister Nice A.I. And, very soon, they joined a swift-moving queue of passengers; some, dead and butchered, remained slumped in their seats with grey bags over their heads; others were obediently marching towards the plane's exit, down the airstair and into the snow-flurrying reality waiting below with their hands on the backs of their heads.

The steps from the plane led to the snow on the tarmac, where the passengers would join an even longer, queue slogging into the blizzard, and many of these captives, shifting in impressive silence, had trouble finding a balance between not accidentally tripping in terrified haste and not trundling too slow, thence facing the risk of bringing unwanted attention to themselves. Most of the profiles among the captives were West businessmen and their highly privileged families, shuffling with their heads down or their eyes closed. With all the millions of questions pronging their minds and with all the bewilderment and disorientation, there was a fear that subdued them into despondent livestock, banded into a single train of pinstripes and chichi fishnets. A variety of the flock disembarked onto the wintery landscape dressed in summer wear: short-sleeved floral-print shirts with undone buttons for waxed chests on display, and shorts and sandals among the men and, for the women, colourful dresses with skirts that barely covered their entire thighs, or loose-fitting maxi-dresses that hardly touched the skin; some even had high heels and urbanely sophisticated make-up that appeared wholly ludicrous in the frigid conditions. These families of wealthy stock had been bound for the sunny southern coast of the Fifth Nation, after all, where it was expected to be in the late thirties of Celsius at least. As for the likes of Samuella's kidnapper, there was no battle when it came to his heavy boots, bolstered on thick rubber.

However, there was also a third, slightly more unnerving layer to the queue of captives, which included kinks of younger West Folk, juveniles, wading optimistically within the chain, as if they'd escaped the heat of some desert and come, liberated, into an air-conditioned temple. Unlike the rich businessmen and their families, these younger silhouettes lacked the blunder and the naivety of their fellow captives. The renegades had null expressions. They wore a strict binary dress code of blank, grey hoodies and discretionary shades. These juveniles knew they'd end up here. Prided by such a privilege, it was their honour. But they didn't want others catching onto the fact that they knew what was going on, so they moved fast.

Not all of the passengers had been compelled to conform willingly. A man near the front of the queue shuttling towards the central building – one of the businessmen dressed in a heavy, overly large suit – took several looks at the side-lining troopers, who surrounded the queue all the way, sizing them up for the performance he was going to commit himself to at any moment now. When he approached the next gap between troopers, he slipped a glance at the passenger leading in front of him and then ducked, strode from the line and made a dash for the icy wilderness. He couldn't have been mad enough to believe he would make it far through all that snow. So, one of the troopers tested him. He lifted his gun, landed a bullet about a metre from the escapee's foot. He blasted a second, precisely skimming his arm. The running man groaned with startled horror and almost tripped, tilting half of his torso. He thought he was going to die, but not in the way he supposed—

In the instant he'd stopped, hunched forwards slightly and gagging for oxygen, his shoulder had met that of another. The escapee allowed his head to sink. His chin submissively fell upon the shoulder of this mysterious other, who appeared to have caught him, like an infant might rest their chin on their mother's shoulder during a nap. And the escapee dropped to the ground. Just like nothing had been holding him there at all. Briefly, there was an outline of a tiny, triangular silhouette, but only in their emergence through the searchlights of the towers did the individual come to be better perceived in their clearer humanoid form. It was a small man in a broad, red cloak. He carried a dagger in his right hand and stroked the thumb of his other along the blade to clean it of the fallen captive's blood. In witnessing this gesture, the people in the queue stiffened further, realising that they were no longer captives, but prisoners. And then, just as he'd materialised, the mystic figure in red distantly strolled away in the arctic wilderness before he disappeared.

Lined on either side of the queue were the East troopers, strictly coordinated, boasting chunky black armour, balaclavas with goggles, and machine guns. But, following the passengers along were yet more anonymities in masked hazard-suits – men in orange stalking intrusively in and out of the queue with clipboards. Everything seemed to be prepared for and it was all headed in mass towards this huge White Building, which was hard to miss against the miserable hue of the tempest. It looked sterile and heavenly lustrous all over. It truly was *a temple.*

They came to the high fences that confined the entire base and above the gates, as they parted open like a wound into the flesh, the captives saw a sign, where the inscription had been shaped in barbed wire and was glowingly electrified:

HIC MANEBIMUS OPTIME.

A great siren cried over their heads, discharged into the nebulous wasteland, wherein only the impertinent fiend sounding it could mark its enveloped source. On entry through the electric gates that welcomed them with new boundaries, harsh light-beams were unleashed into the eyes of the prisoners and the unlocking of the fortress brought even more troopers. These new men came forth upon the tarmac with wild, white Alsatians springing at their sides, growling and pouncing into the chattering frost and cracking their jaws at the newcomers. For every trooper, there were two lively hounds and a person in an orange suit donning a clipboard or a *HoloPad.* Some orange suits had hardware-detectors, stretched out across the length of the queue and scanning the prisoners for weapons, signal-receivers, general gadgets, or any other devices that could be mistaken for "spyware" or "malware".

Once through the building's entrance, the prisoners were briskly escorted into a lobby of full-body scanners, via which their entire anatomy was analysed and exposed on massive screens for the troopers to observe. Any of those possessing even remotely suspicious contents were labelled on the spot, had a grey bag thrown over their head and were taken down a corridor in stiff queues, which led out to a courtyard where they would be set on their knees and immediately shot.

On the other side of the security lobby, past the final scanning checks, the successful prisoners were told to remove their clothes. Remove *all* their clothes. After doing so, an assigned team of A.I. would collect the clothing and take it to a chamber to be incinerated. Then, this section of privileged Regal Jet passengers would be escorted fully naked out through a black curtain, located to the side at the finishing end of the room.

The section of dubious juveniles removed their clothes too, without hesitation, swapping their discretion for open nudity – a form in which they could flash a four-digit barcode and a chestnut tattooed on their ankle and, thus, be guided out of the security room via a different route: up a wide marble staircase.

Meanwhile, in her unconsciousness, Samuella was unaware that she had been laid on a moving conveyor belt with a selection of other dormant passengers, which followed the other juveniles up the steps and into the white light that was waiting for them at the top…

UPPER TIER, LEVEL 0: GROUND TERMINAL

Those who followed the steps up from the security room found themselves in Ground Terminal, the midsection of the great White Building. Every other floor was either above or below it. There were fifteen levels from here to the top and fifteen levels from here to the bottom – deep underground. As more of the juveniles ascended the marble steps – the white light never came for them, but they willingly went to it – not one of them glanced back or stopped. They were engulfed by it at fantastic pace, one after the other. And when they reached the very top and arrived in Ground Terminal, they were introduced to the warm heart of a silent utopia.

Their perspective of Ground Terminal was from the inside of a long, aseptic glass-tunnel, where the juveniles could no longer see the storm and the snow, but the interior of a beautifully maintained martial arena. Up above, down below, left and right, there were other young men and women just like them, who'd been here quite some time longer than them, and they were marching above the arena in their own glass-chambers. Only, these older schools of juveniles were uniformed in green and were shuttling through their tunnels in coordinated procession, with purpose. Much unlike the naked guests who'd only just landed on base and were strolling sporadically, these soldiers had been trained and disciplined. They carried with them delegated importance, which was vainly emitted in their conformity. If the visitors were to glance right to the bottom, a hundred feet below at the area's ground, they would see where the training happened. Down on the arena's floor, more young men and women were training in the arts of terror, hostage sprees and guerrilla warfare – the vengeful practices that both the children of the West and the East recognised too well as riotous social destabilisation and terrorism. It was a Purpose, which they realised as they gazed down at the schooling below, that they themselves were going to adopt here in this place.

Unarguably, on its face, the arena was a twinkling haven that drenched its guests in a bewitching white light and commanded the silence of a hundred bare bodies to walk without interaction, without emotion, in complete independence from one another. There was no acknowledgement from one man to the next. Not a name or a story was shared in the pilgrimage through the glass chamber. The juveniles moved in scattered, but ostentatiously sensible and militant, formation, like they knew where they were going and why they were going there without any doubt at all.

But then came the most foreign part of it all, and the most unpredictable shock, which brought many of them bolting back into reality. The screens situated along the tunnel's walls zapped to life and the image of an East Man with a grey hood over his head appeared. He addressed the juveniles in the tunnel with a monologue of unwavering East Dialect. Most understood every word; a few struggled to translate parts and their lack of preparation and worry was alerted in awkward expressions; and others, the most deadpan of them all, clearly understood none of what they were being told and went on silently as if there was no man on a screen and they were vacantly floating in a hallucination.

Straggling behind the others and one of the furthest to the back of the group was young Doe Vega. As he shuffled along, he had his hands pressed flat against his scrawny thighs, gingerly squiggling his little body-weight through the tunnel as a baby penguin might over the surface of an icecap. Exposed in his puerile, hairless state, he deliberately did not hurry to keep up with the other young visitors. He was trying his best to smother the embarrassment he had for the lack of muscle he presented in comparison to the other strapping young men, and the starkly aroused phallus he carried off from the sight of the bodies of all shapes and sizes, male and female, clustered ahead of him. He hoped, for much of this impregnable silence, that he might just shrink away, and then remembered the indiscriminate fate that was welcoming every single one of them, no matter how big, no matter how small, nor fat, nor slim, nor pretty, nor ugly. He just wasn't expecting it to be this brutal, and more so, this humiliating. *At least*, he thought, *this walk of intimidation is only the beginning.*

Not even halfway along the tunnel, one boy dropped to the ground, squawking traumatically. This was nothing he'd expected, not what he'd been imagining or hoping for. '*I shouldn't be here! My mother knows—mother knows—! I shouldn't be here!*' he cried. He rose up onto his knees and then fell onto his back this time, as if he exhibited no backbone. He beat his head on the ground with six or seven thrusts and swung himself about among the dozen or so legs that swanned past him. A broken nose, and then a busted eye-socket, and then a ripped earlobe, guaranteed that his face and neck would be draped in blood. His screams were grating and the way he was fitting about on the floor should have provoked the attention of medics or psychiatrists. Instead, he drew the attention of the troopers. Three of them came striding from the staircase across the glass-tunnel and over to the troublemaker. None of the stirrer's antics fazed the other juveniles, for they knew what he was feeling, the fear he was experiencing. Tears slipped from a couple of un-looking eyes, retching noises choked up from a few who were struggling to swallow their pity, but not a single head turned. They were determined to reach the end of the tunnel without losing their own sanity. The troopers tussled with the boy – who didn't relent to knock a few punches and a couple of high kicks at his aggressors – and they beat him a few times before sinking a taser into his neck to send him into a fizzing sedation and carrying him away, out of the crowd, back down the marble steps he'd emerged from.

At the opposite end of the tunnel, standing before a pair of elevator doors, an order of high-ranking commanders were waiting for the rest of the newcomers. The juveniles formed a line of their naked, lean bodies before their new leaders. Most of them, like Doe, looked to be children of fifteen, sixteen or seventeen. The commanders showed little regard for this, they addressed them formally, and even eyed their new subjects like grown men and women. The commanders, of course, prioritised their interests for the fittest of the bunch, glancing at the older young men with more build and smirking with ideas of what might be done with the fatter ones – *all that mass would become useful in some way or other.* They didn't bat an eyelid at the skinnier ones, since they were obviously going to need more work, and consequently take more time to develop – *time was money.* But such considerations would be taken as soon as they passed into the elevator.

One of the commanders, possibly the general – a hard, brawny man with a dark-green robe over his uniform – spoke to them in pure East Dialect:

'Congratulations to your success this far. Beyond these doors you will be ascended to our facilitation units on levels five through to thirteen, where you will each be assigned uniforms blessed by the New Lord Draca himself, the one and only Lord we all obey. You will be listed to a sedation chamber for rest when rest is due. Following that, you will be taken down to the medical unit on level minus-three to be individually examined. This will be the final preparation before training begins.'

A *clinking* sound came from somewhere on the floor. When Doe looked down to chase the noise he saw that it had come from one of the general's boots, where a silver chestnut on a chain had knocked against a buckle. Doe quickly lifted his attention back up at the man who was speaking – and now staring directly at him. Doe was very familiar with the chestnut. He knew it to be a symbol of the Radicals from the Sixth and Seventh Nation.

'Tomorrow, you will begin your training to become one with Obedience,' the general continued. 'The order of Obedience surrounds itself in the Faith. *If He serves the New Lord well, the New Lord will feed Him all the same.* However, do not be fooled, becoming one with Obedience is quite the meticulous process. No matter which procedures we choose to apply in order to drill the Faith into you, it takes time enough and development varies based on the capabilities of the individual. Our soldiers must be more than expendable; they must be fulfilling and desirous. Regardless of what the Faith demands of you and regardless how the blinded people you left behind interpret the Faith, you must forever remain loyal to the Faith. You are the Faith; you are *our* Faith now. And so will be your brothers and sisters, and for generations to come, your children also. Once you are one with Obedience, you will be one with the Faith. This Faith is greater than any religion or cause, bigger than any Nation or leader – which means, you will be too.'

Another girl suddenly broke down in a shaken frenzy, terrified. She hadn't an idea what he was saying. While others were already red in the eyes, shimmering and secretly sweating, she began sobbing like an infant, whining for her parents and proclaiming the dreadful mistake she'd made. The commander paused, as two troopers pushed through the crowd to extract her from it and take her away.

'But do not fret,' the general said. 'You are not radicals in our eyes.'

LOWER TIER, LEVEL -3: MEDICAL UNIT

A long, slender light-cylinder was in the ceiling and it was spawning all hell upon her stinging eyes. Samuella had just woken up from a dreamless sleep. And the room she was in now, wherever it was, was much warmer than outside. Much warmer than any other outside. Much warmer than any other *inside*. In fact, her body was humming with the heat. For once in the last… however long she'd been wherever she was…she felt comfortable. But her feelings lived very short, when the man in the bright orange suit and the rubber mask that made him look like a man-sized pig returned, approaching her from the nightly unknown and spoiling her peaceful absence from company. That was when she knew she couldn't move. She couldn't fidget or squirm. Every muscle, every bone and every spark of energy in her body had vanished. She'd been sewn to a long, velvet medical bed that was so narrow her shoulder blades were hanging off the edges slightly.

There was no telling who the man was. *Was it a man? Could it have been a woman? It might not even have been a human being. Who knew?* In his hands, he carried two small syringes, lacking needles. Not to worry: on reaching her side, he produced from a drawer two long, string-thin needles and began to attach one to the end of each syringe. Then he injected the first into her right arm. Somehow, she didn't have the pleasure of feeling it pierce through her skin. She was already numb in that limb. When he injected the other arm with the other syringe, she was left wondering the same wonders, only twice as woozy. *What is this magic?* She thought. *Why can't I feel anything happening? Should I be feeling anything? Should I be in agony? Should I even be here—?*

All of a sudden, after having momentarily stood there to jot down notes onto his transparent *HoloPad*, the pig-masked person came to a conclusive judgement and reached out a gloved hand towards her face. It was a large palm. A claw that made her panic. But, just before he managed to smear her cheeks, new light shed across the room and tickled the ledge of her chin.

Someone else had arrived. *To her rescue?*

The newcomer came in a sharp black suit and a dark blue tie. Her blurring eyesight made a fuzz-ball out of his face and this left her as clueless to his identity as she was to the orange-suited man's identity. They began to talk. The orange-suited man had turned his head, suspending his procedure. Even though her ears were still partially blocked, she could hear that they were talking in some language of the East. *Some nuanced tongue of colloquial East Dialect.* Then, agreeing like a rookie to his superior, the orange-suited man disarmed his syringes and left. The man in the black suit looked down at her, into those dopey eyes of hers that were curdling his face into a dish of mashed potatoes the closer he got. He bent down over her, his voice more distant than ever to her, his mouth flexing out of sync with his tiny voice as he spoke. His face…

It was Pegasus. In strapping style too. He was freshly shaven and his skin, although pale from the cold, was tender and smooth. Samuella could see him talking, but couldn't catch a word. Pegasus had a massive smile on his face and it frazzled her spine with a jet of relief. Then she saw him remove the earmuffs that had been placed over her head. Her ears immediately popped and she came to life a little more. 'There you go! Better?' Mister Pegasus chimed with a jarring sense of excitement. 'I know, I know! Bad question! You can't move or speak. But you can see and hear me—that's the good thing. I'll answer all your questions in a second. Hold on…'

He was rolling up his sleeves now, checking another syringe on the table beside the bed. Fixing the needle was quick enough and he injected it into her neck.

A few seconds… GASP!

She flinched upwards in a spasm, and then thumped back onto her backside. Mister Pegasus glared down at her with beaming eyes. Samuella was panting profusely.

'Even better?' he tried.

Up to this point, she had every right to believe he was a nutcase bordering on promotion to a sociopath, for Pegasus' playfulness right now was uncalled for.

'*Wha…Whaw wath tha—*?' she asked finally. 'Where *wh*am I? Where *wh*am I now?'

'You've come along way. And I'm sorry that I misguided you. It was my mistake completely. But I can explain why that happened.'

'Pega*wuw*, *where wham I*?'

'Didn't you catch a glimpse when they brought you all the way down here? You're in the Southern Polar Region. Lucky you, eh. You're one of the *selected few*.'

'The Sou*vv*en Po*w*ar *W*egion? Wha*w* are we doing in a *Powar Wegion*?'

'The plane you boarded was a "ghost vessel". Twice a month, the East's High Government hijack a totally ordinary commercial aeroplane and land it in the SPR. It's rogue and illegal – yeah, I know what you're thinking. But this is the real world, and, unfortunately, I don't run it. A side of the world...and the conspiracy...you don't really know that well, to be fair.'

'*Hijack pwanes*? Wha*w* fo*w*? Fo*w* wha*w* *w*eason?' Samuella was feeling better and little more vocal (somewhat).

'Mostly experimental purposes – well, in *your* case at least,' his smile sank slightly. 'You were tranquilised and about to be submitted to an experimental chamber. Unlike some of the others who have no doubt been taken to a training facility. They must have found you unconscious, in that case.'

'T*w*aining faci*w*ity?' she dribbled the words out. She'd been drowning in her saliva ever since Pegasus relieved the anaesthetic restraints. '*Twaining* fo*w* what?'

'Samuella,' Pegasus said, retrieving his reassuring grin, 'it's in both our interests that we discuss this later.'

'*No!*' she barked. 'You sent me and Oscar on a p*w*ane to a p*w*ace where they were going to *perfowm expewiments* on our bodies and you expect me to be okay wi*v* that? To *twust you*?'

'I don't expect you to be okay with it. I didn't see this coming. It's getting massively more common than it used to be. Close to epidemical. I remember when it used to be just military vessels and criminal pirate vessels that were never mentioned in the Media; now, more and more commercial planes are getting hijacked. I'm sorry. I should have done better to look into this. But I'm here to get you both out. Safely. I promise.'

'And where's Kyma?'

'I'm sorry? Who?'

'Kyma, the dog. Oscar's companion—the same way Oscar was *my* companion. She was on the p*w*ane with us too. Where are they?'

'Look. We'll get to that eventually. But, first, I need to know that the pair of you are healthy and alright to move about.'

'Why wouldn't I be healthy? They haven't done anything to me—have they?'

'*Hmm*, by now, you've already been subjected to some... minor tests.'

'Minor tests? *Already?* How minor?'

'It's not certain. I was being euphemistic. They're not all minor. But those fluids that you were just injected with, they have a temporary paralytic power. It was why you couldn't move. Too much of that would've paralysed you for life or sent you into a coma. And, in that condition, they could've done whatever they needed to you. Can you sit up?'

Gently, he helped her to sit up. Across the room, facing her directly on was a wheelchair. 'Pegasus, how hurt am I?'

'It's not severe. I promise you,' he said with an apologetic, but hurried, tone of voice. 'Now, please, we need to get you in that chair. We're going for a stroll.'

UPPER TIER, LEVEL 0: GROUND TERMINAL

Ground Terminal was radiant with milky light, like the beating heart of any healthily populated complex should be. The lobby to the White Building's magnificent arena was nothing like the shady and uninspired monotony of its lower levels and its grim, tedious surroundings of bleak, snow-coated towers and dark, soot-grazed skies. *This place reminds me of the shepherd's paddock at my old homestead - seventy per cent white fence, twenty per cent sheep, ten per cent grass*, Samuella hypothesised, as she was being rolled through the broad, bare hall, seated in the very square-shaped wheelchair.

Pegasus planned to get her as high and as far away from the lower levels as he could, for the time being at least. He wheeled her through the crowds. The people around them seemed very ordinary. They were uniformed in matching green and red. All of them were adolescent, none older than twenty-five. Not a single person looked panicked or out of place. It didn't even appeal to her that they were prisoners, just like her. They hadn't left their clothes behind on a surgeon's table - unlike her, garbed in nothing but an operating gown. These folk were tame and gathered, walking tenaciously to and fro. Skidding to dodge near collisions, Samuella could feel Pegasus working hard against the machine and sorely sticking out amidst the militant youths as a result. He was heavy-footed and clumsy with his balance under pressure. He clearly hadn't passed his wheelchair-steering lessons with flying colours. Other than being dauntingly quiet, Samuella identified something different about the crowd. Something she hadn't noticed straight away.

Their skin was glowing. Never had she seen *skin* glow so much!

'This lot all seem a bit casual for hijack-victims,' she observed. 'What's the deal, Pegasus?'

'A minority of passengers aboard that Regal Jet were not victims,' Pegasus whispered, 'and its hijacking had been something these few attendees were aware of long in advance, no doubt.'

'*Attendees?*' Samuella regurgitated this cautious muttering from her little saint with amplified distaste. 'That almost makes it sound like they volunteered.'

Pegasus didn't answer. He grunted evasively and then steered a sharp, cutting turn to throw her off this train of thought.

'You don't have to keep the identity of these "attendees" a secret from me, Pegasus. Whoever hijacked that plane has us now, so there's no point hiding information if they can probably already hear us,' Samuella protested. 'That is, unless, these "attendees" you describe happen to be the numb-nuts surrounding us right now.' For Samuella – and for anyone who'd just been strung and stung on an operating bed – this hospital-like atmosphere wasn't numb, but uncomfortably serene, and there were too many bodies (*glowing!*) in the room for that to be normal. 'Other people have heard stories about this place. Not very clear stories, but stories nonetheless. You mentioned a "training facility". What is it that goes on here?'

'Things that are even kept secret from The Body,' Pegasus grinned mischievously.☆ 'And you thought the Body knew everything, didn't you? The governments of the West like to tell you that. They let you assume that's the truth, because they worry tightly screwed heads like yours and mine may come to credible conclusions before they themselves. I can tell you that very few in the West *and* the East have an ounce of an understanding of anything that truly happens here.'

'Even the Decider doesn't have a clue?' Samuella interjected.

'Not a word.'

'Then how could you possibly have found your way here to rescue us?'

☆ After the Surveilance was exposed by the Media, a small alternative intelligence agency was promoted to head of the West's Intel, titled "The Body". They'd been working in cahoots with the Decider's Administration since 2030 and hadn't yet put a foot wrong – except, of course, for dragging out a war with the East that was based on fabricated lies.

'I made a few important friends for the Infidels during my stint as foreign diplomat under DCD. Philson. This included the transporters who arrange the confidential submarine trips from the Fifth Nation to the SPR. I flew out as soon as I became aware of the hijacking plot, which was only a couple of hours after you and Oscar left the City.'

'And who made you aware of that?' Samuella pressed him for more.

'Infidel Intel,' Pegasus responded sharply and honestly.

Samuella loosened up at the sound of his legitimacy. 'Some informant you are,' she teased.

'Aegia and I are specialists in political affairs, not terrorism.'

About the terminal, Samuella could see only a limited number of A.I. on patrol. These A.I. were sleek and refined modern designs that were very unlike the ones in the High Streets and the *TRAMLINE* Terminals of the City, for they had been commissioned with a plainer, thinner model, which wasn't necessarily less imposing, but left a lot of their menace to the imagination. This design lacked the distinctive eye-scanner strip across the face that characterised every A.I. she had ever known. Smooth, ovular aluminium heads these pretty boys had with blank, shiny metal faces that were identical. *A.I. without the "loading screen face" are exclusive to the Southern Polar Region*, she mused.

'And what about the skin? Have you seen that too?' Samuella asked.

'I thought you might pick up on it,' Pegasus responded. 'Pretty hard to miss, isn't it. That shade of orange in their skin has been caused by a high beta-carotene stimulant they're given to keep their immune systems healthy in the harsh arctic conditions; and as for the slight fluorescence, the "glowing"... it's an ointment they apply to protect themselves from the radioactivity fluctuating throughout the base.'

A ball of heat and acid burst in her stomach. Somewhere else, another loud siren blurted. It was horrific. Piercing ears. Her ears, at least. Everyone else looked okay, moving just a little swifter than that of a Sunday Saunter through City Central Park. The A.I. had snapped up their acuteness and refined their reactions to pure clockwork.

Suddenly, the echoes from Pegasus' thumping soles became acoustically repetitive inside her skull. Faster and faster they went. She felt all the steps. Rehearsing them off by heart like the notes to a phenomenal sonata. 'Hang in there, hang in there!' Pegasus whispered. He was charging through the crowd. A bull loose in the arena. A.I. were now approaching them from all sides, closing in on Samuella and

Pegasus' proximity with their shining domes and crunching marches. All the terror in the world built up in her. She didn't want to die.

Not now. Not today. Not here.

She didn't want to die at the feet of an A.I. Nobody did. Nobody would dare to think of it. The most shameful and the most painful of demises.

At long last, they arrived at an elevator and slotted into the empty box. The doors slid closed, sealing them off from the emerging Tin Men. Samuella even had the idea to lift her legs up onto the seat of the wheelchair, just in case a Silver Soldier tried to reach out and grab one of them along the way.

But they were gone. It was just the two of them. Out of harm's way again.

'Let me guess. More protocol?' she said.

'It's just another part of the itinerary here…another part of the general day…' Pegasus was panting, and lying. '…Lunchtime.'

'Start telling me some real answers! Proper answers! The truth! You seem to know a lot more than anyone else I've spoken to about this place and you're holding back! What's happening?'

He froze and sighed. 'I haven't been lying to you, but I haven't been telling you the solid truth either. Yes, the plane you were on—'

'*The plane you put me on!*'

'—Okay, yes, the plane I put you on, unknowingly, was scheduled to be prised from the sky and diverted here. For what purpose, you ask? Well, see it like you're a fresh piece of meat to them. *Their plain, unspoiled meat, to be seasoned.* In more literal terms, you'd be a subject to their influence and indoctrination. And, if you don't meet certain criteria, or need to be sedated when you're captured, in other words "*put up a fight against them*" – they'll find alternative uses – different spices to season the meat with – and make use of you in their experiments. They procured you and Oscar in particular, because you must be good and utilisable assets to them. Those selected for the training campaigns down there in the arena sometimes have a chance of getting out of this place, once they learn of what they're becoming, but it's never guaranteed and usually far too late – by then, their beliefs have already gone awry and their old self is history. That is the power of such influences. The strength of the Faith. These kids are a trained order of radicals, who regard themselves as "Obedience" – they just do that to dilute the reputation they've earned as "radicalised terrorists" in the West. You might even recognise a face or two, if not, you will soon forget your own, so it won't matter that much anyway. Trained soldiers might eventually get away from the SPR, and that can be a lucky outcome for them. What's bad for you is that you're an experimental subject, which means there is a very frail chance of you getting out of here alive. Luckily, I found you when I did. But, again, bad for me – I'm committing a very, very big offense by trying to get you out and the SPR will not stop until they have you under the knife.'

'And what about Oscar? Is *he* an experimental subject?' Samuella said. 'Couldn't you find him too? Like you found me?'

'What do you think we're doing?' Pegasus changed his tone to one that was far more abrupt. 'I'm working my backside off here! I really am trying my best at this! Can't you tell?'

'The dog? You can't forget the dog. She was on the plane with us.'

'Look, I can't do that! That would be stretching things! Now that they know I'm here, now that they've clocked me, my life is at as much a risk as yours. So, from now onwards, pipe down—I speak, and you hang your head low.'

Her heart was galloping on the spot. She couldn't shy away from the fact that she was now expecting the worst outcome. She'd always been terrified. But, right now, it was really beginning to settle in.

The elevator jutted, halted. Pegasus took one glance at the digital number above the door. **LEVEL 13**. They'd ascended. He hummed four notes of a melody and then reinstalled his grip on the wheelchair's handles.

'What you're about to see isn't for the fainthearted,' Pegasus warned.

The elevator doors slowly opened.

UPPER TIER, LEVEL 13: SPECIMEN UNIT 1

A neon sign welcomed them into a cooler corridor. They'd left the white light central heating of the elevator behind and were now venturing into a hazier, ultraviolet zone. It was a long, metallic corridor with steel walls, ceiling and corridors. Sterile, but sinisterly vacated. On either side of the corridor were poorly illuminated cages, sealed off by glass-windows that must have been a foot thick.

Samuella swung her head around the corridor attentively, as Pegasus wheeled her along the platform. There were eyes in the cages. Big, glittery specks of dreary hope peered at her. The first of them belonged to a lonely polar bear on her right. He was uncomfortably sprawled out on his belly with his tongue slumped on the stone floor. Grey rings hung heavy beneath his eyelids and his hair was short, patchy and yellowing. The sight was a sorry one, especially when the aching beast lumbered to his feet and held up two paws against the long window. He scratched a little against the pane, as if to say "*look! look at what they've done to me! let me go, let me be! let me be a bear again!*"

An icy sweat flustered over Samuella and tears soon accompanied it. 'Why did you bring me here, Pegasus?' she managed. 'I don't need to see this.'

'Unfortunately, I wanted you to. You needed to.'

'The world needs to understand—'

'This world will never understand. What you're looking at isn't science or nature or the conscience of being itself. It's humanity you're seeing. Right in front of you. The push and desperation of the Human Disgrace.'

'They should let it go. It shouldn't be in here alone. Why is it in here at all? It can't be subjected to this emptiness…this closed, meaninglessness existence.' She was talking solely about the bear. The fact is she hadn't yet found the courage to spy any of the other horrors in the room.

'Whoever said it was alone?' Pegasus hinted.

She averted her attention across the cage-floor. There, behind the beast, was a gutless corpse. Its ribcage had been parted and everything inside had been splayed. Guts bloodied the floor around it. Along the short fur were claw-marks. Thick digs.

Bear claws, she realised.

'Didn't they feed it?' Samuella was shaking.

'Why would there be any need to feed it in a scientific research facility? What would be *instinctive* about that? That would be no use for their analysis, no use for a valid judgement on its behaviour in this unnatural space.' Pegasus responded matter-of-factly. 'This isn't just ideology that the human race is playing with. It's life – the broken pieces that were once used to build it and the ones that are required to rebuild it.'

'Rebuild…? Life?' Samuella tried.

'I must not say this here,' Pegasus repeated. 'But, vaguely speaking and from what I'm aware, it comes down to the matter that this model of humanity, this social order we've known for so long, is no longer compatible with the world we're living in now. In a world where two civilisations can grow so different that they can no longer coexist in peace on the same planet, let alone even compete with each other on equal terms in a war, a new order of civilisation needs to be created. We need to rebuild the way people on both sides of this division think –

whether that means replacing some essential biologically human aspects, then so be it. Leaders who are stuck in their ways can't achieve that on their own. There needs to be room for such evolutionary innovation to take place and the human race is now doing its best to find it. Scientists and philosophers alike saw this pivotal generation coming centuries ago, long before the Great Splits. This place here is just one crucible of many. Organisations all over the world have known about this eventuality and they've been seeking a solution to it for years. The eventuality: a climatic stage in human civilisation, the furthest extent of civil tolerance. It was caused by the consequence of supreme capitalism and peaking nationalism. And, as result, we have a single world filled with many little worlds, all of which have nothing in common and have stray nuances that disallow them from ever meeting in harmony. The liberal sociologists in the West refer to these social divisions as the Constellation Crisis. The Crisis resembles a stage where relations have been irreversibly scattered and lost. Whoever finds the solution to the divisions that plague our modern world can end the war. It's been a difficult task, but here, they think they've discovered the solution. Think about it, it's like discovering a spice that nobody has ever thought to season with before, a spice no one has never heard of before, and it just tastes so fresh and original, so ground-breaking. A new recipe to redefine the future of mankind. A weapon of mass destruction that causes such a novel catastrophe that it forces others to change their way of thinking and reimagine how they respond and interact with the world around them thereafter.'

'What are you talking about?' Samuella said, semi-distracted by the sight of the polar bear in despair and still tangled in the weird discretion being projected from Pegasus. 'You say "mankind". This isn't just the East doing this stuff?' Samuella said.

'Do you really think the Sixth Nation can fund this all on their own? The Body has been donating all of the City's spare tax funds into this "little project", this experiment. And keeping it under wraps here in the Southern Polar Region has minimalized the Decider's conscious involvement in this project to redefine humanity. It remains an experiment beheld out of reach of both the East and West in Polar Territory.'

'They manipulated the Decider from the beginning?' Samuella finally understood. 'They used his own ignorance against him. His reluctance to liaise in foreign policy kept him out of the loop and unaware of this atrocity. All the East had to do was be passive and their operations could slide under the Decider's radar.'

'Up until now, we've believed that the Conflicts have only been fought over land and resource – fighting over history, not the future. But there is a greater asset to both sides than identity and sovereign allegiance, and that asset is put into place here.'

'So why has Phestor Xenol decided to ditch passivity and take action now?'

'Change,' Pegasus answered. 'Xenol sees now as the perfect time to take advantage of the West. Such a secret as the powers being harnessed in this place, unbeknownst to even the Decider before today, will shock the West and bring it to its knees. The Decider's bizarre alliance with Phestor Xenol was no accident. It certainly wasn't bizarre to the Infidels, who saw all this coming eighteen months back, when Xenol snubbed Government Aid to the famine victims in the Sixth Nation, in order to stage his plans for the first trade of resources with the Seventh Nation in over a decade.'

'Xenol was planning to trade resources with Seventh? He was ready to trade with Serpens again eighteen months ago? He was willing to see eye-to-eye with him? What kind of resource?'

'A resource that can transform an entire Nation from a shantytown into a superpower in a matter of weeks, and amend broken ties between two former allies,' Pegasus said.

'One resource could do all that?' Samuella probed. 'Is that what you meant when you mentioned "rebuilding"? Where did you find this out?'

'I was stationed here in the Southern Polar Region for some time and conversed with The Body. You could imagine I was no friend of the Stateship – a man who only holds interests in the affairs of the West Nations. Him and I used to debate from either side of the Decider. After the Blackout Nine Attacks, the Stateship advised the Decider to leave the war and completely abandon all connections with the East, whereas I advised that the West should leave the war and rebuild productive relations with the East immediately, because I knew what The Body was researching and what the Southern Polar Region was developing – it didn't look good for any side on Mankind's World. Humanity's fate was already unfolding. Secret organisations in both the East and West were both trying to combat the same inevitability – the Constellation Crisis was turning heads ten years ago. However, today, the end of co-existence as we know it has never been closer and this pact with Philson and Xenol will play out as the last piece in the puzzle of its collapse – an incentive for another great power shift and the prerequisite for a new way of living.'

'Am I hearing this right? You're telling me that the East and the West have been working on the same side all this time?' Samuella interrupted. 'It's just never been made public. The whole war was just a façade, a distraction from the real dilemma.'

'Yes, the Constellation Crisis is not a prospect anymore; it's a threat to civilisation. We're hurtling towards a fate where everyone loses, a world where mutuality is merely dream,' Pegasus continued. 'In the end, the Decider followed neither mine nor the Stateship's advice, and he, instead, insisted to continue the West's input in the war. It was because of this blind decision from the Decider that the public wouldn't take notice of the actual crisis happening under our noses. Even though Phestor Xenol has the advantage over Philson's arrogance and fully knows about the project, I feel he has other plans for the East, and the Decider is who he'll point to when things start going wrong.'

They both saw the light cylinders above them turn red. There was no alarm, no sound at all. Just a warning light. Pegasus started pushing the wheelchair harder, with all the might he had to get them to the door on the other end of the vast unit.

'What happened to you?' Samuella said. 'Why aren't you at the Decider's Table anymore? He needs someone like you, someone who understands the East and who knows about this Crisis.'

Pegasus slowed his pushing to a brief pause, sighing exhaustedly. Not exactly the jock she needed to rescue her from this hellhole. 'He wasn't convinced about me,' he said. 'I'd been the first to make him aware of The Body's research and the Southern Polar Region's projects to find solutions to the Constellation Crisis. It was a different world back then. The Crisis' danger wasn't as imminent. But he lost faith in me when I threatened to blow whistles on the matter. He told me "no one wants to listen to your fantasies and lies when their reality is already fantasies and lies, only fluffier". I refused to pander to him anymore, resigned my case and stepped away, hoping he would learn once the Crisis unravelled. And that was that. I paid no more service to the Decider.'

'Get me the hell away from this place, Pegasus,' Samuella ordered him. 'Get me out of here. Get me out now.'

'If I can bring us to the roof, we can claim a high ground away from the A.I., until the Infidel helicopter arrives!' Pegasus plotted, as he pounded his weight into the back of the wheelchair and drew them along at rocket-speed.

'Helicopter—?' Samuella stammered. 'The roof? How far is that?'

'Not much further. Two more levels.'

She couldn't turn away from any of it. On the left side of the room, a pair of baby white-tiger cubs was all that remained of a pack of carcasses. They paced opposite ends of the cage, as far away from one another as the space allowed them. In a separate cage, a colony of exotic birds were silent and hovering about their high-hubs, muted and withdrawn from comfort. Next-door were the isolated chimps with nothing else to play with, other than torn up lab coats, orange rubber suits and empty, plastic chemical vials. When they saw Samuella passing by, they stopped and stared in fascination, as if they'd never seen a person before. "*we've never seen a girl before. never seen a pretty one like her. please come back, girl. come back and play!*" And, at the end of their excursion, after already having passed every animal in every zoo she'd ever dreamt of visiting, they found a minute fabric hut sitting in the corner of a cage.

All on its own.

It was a sad little thing that was soggy and damp all over, recently dragged in from the snow. In fact, she recognised it all too well, including the collar dangling from the top, labelled with a name that she'd be waiting to find somewhere. It was enough to make her burst into tears.

KYMA.

UPPER TIER, LEVEL 15: SEDATION UNIT 3

'The Cocoons,' Pegasus whispered as the automatic doors opened. 'Come on.' He weaved her out of the elevator and onto Level 15 with fluctuating fluidity. The connecting room was blindingly ill lit, more so than the previous. They'd entered another corridor, where lanes of large, glowing devices had been stationed on either side. The devices could only be described as a cross between a claustrophobic shower-cubicle and some sort of teleport from one of those ancient science fiction comics that were always stuck to the back of Samuella's mind – *the type of fantasy she discovered in crates full of the stuff at the very back of the POST storage room.*

She was curiously observing them glimmer as they sent trickles of weak smoke tumbling down their sides and into the air around them. The hot smoke was green and it was constantly shedding from the glass, mystifying the contents with condensation. 'Is it safe? Being in here?' she asked. It was the predominant thing on her mind, beyond those close thoughts of Oscar and the lost dog, both whom she imagined, more than certainly, to have been led to severe peril by now. 'The troopers downstairs let you go past like it was nothing. Like they trusted you. And they didn't even acknowledge me. But those A.I. in Ground Terminal saw us, though they haven't returned since. Something doesn't seem right about their reactions. Are we safe, Pegasus?'

'There's no need to worry about where we are, because I'm going to get us out of here. Beautiful, just keep that smile in working order for me, stock it up with optimism, just as you do with the shelves at the Octane Mall. When they see you smiling, it helps. They did notice you. You're one of their patients after all. Your smile tells them there's no issue. I'm the one they don't recognise. Why should they? I'm not the Decider. I'm just a suit with counterfeit identification, whom they're trying their very worst to verify. That's their problem, not mine. But they will come around eventually and that's when they'll pounce on us. As for the A.I. here, they are programmed with a softer upgrade, so as not to create a stir that would suggest something is wrong, or uneven in the midst of the ideological procedures that go on here. We wouldn't want to throw off the Young Obedients during their training phase now, would we,' Pegasus' stuttering had evolved into bona fide shivering. Something contentious had recently slipped under his skin, somewhere between here and the Specimen Unit, and Samuella could tell whenever he injected his sarcasm to put on a strong front.

'*Ah*—so, they like their torture victims to be happy, do they? It keeps the workman's morale high?' Samuella was mocking his happy-go-lucky attitude. She wasn't buying a word he said. She knew it was all false, a pretence to keep them both calm.

'We'll find Oscar and then we'll be out of here before you know it—'

'Who's finding him? Not like we're gonna have much luck at achieving that from the rooftop,' she protested.

'I have men here with me. My colleagues. Infidels operating incognito,' he answered in the most confident way he had spoken so far. 'I'm not so stupid to come gallivanting down here on my own! This isn't a hospital visit, it's a rescue mission!'

'And the dog?'

'Hopeful—And the dog, if possible,' he said that so rigidly. 'We'll see what we can do.'

And then, he stopped the wheelchair. She could taste his insecurity. His portentous uncertainty. She could smell it off the sweating hairs on his chest. Something had gone wrong. Awfully wrong.

A fat arm locked around her neck and she felt the top of her collarbone cock into his elbow-joint. The vocal cords within her neck had no strength to scream, or room to squeal. In fact, it could've been moments until she lost all consciousness again. He managed to easily hoist her out of the chair in this position. If the aesthetic drugs hadn't weakened her, at this point, she would have put up more of a fight. But, there was no struggle here. No contest. At first, he didn't speak. He had nothing left to say once she was fully on her feet – or, at least, held in his arms and suspended shortly off the ground. Then, out of genuine sympathy, he tested her hearing with a quiet whisper, 'It's too hard to explain all of this right now, beautiful. One day, I hope I can. When we finally find ourselves home again, I hope I do explain everything to you, lovely. Oh, you are smiley. Very smiley. And that's exactly why I'm doing this, why I have to do this. And that's exactly how I'm going to leave you, my dear.'

He lugged her towards one of the capsules. It was an empty, inactive one without the condensation and the smoke that all the others loved to spew. Applying the code now, she gazed at his fingers. His fingers knew it all – they'd seen all of this before. Those deceptive hands had designed every moment of it up to this point and forever beyond. *YOU BASTARD! YOU DID THIS! YOU CAUSED ALL OF THIS! IT WAS YOUR IDEA TO BEGIN WITH!* She screamed inside her head like a lion without teeth or claws. *WE SHOULD HAVE SEEN THIS COMING! WE SHOULD HAVE ALL SEEN THROUGH YOUR LIES AND WE WOULDN'T HAVE COME ALL THIS WAY!*

Clink! Tsshhh! The capsule's door swung open on its own. Pegasus lifted her inside and started to strap her against what looked like a harness with a glass shield surrounding it. Once the harness was tightly on, nipping at all of her edges, she thought she would go into shock, thought she might suffocate, immediately. There wasn't much air inside this thing…

As he shut the capsule door, artificial tank-supplied air filled the small space. At least she'd catch a cold before she died. Pegasus was looking at her from the other side of the glass. Rather than sporting an expression of pure, diabolical wisdom and shouting '*I told you not to follow me around, you gold-digging bitch!*', he seemed pretty keen to tell her something important. Advise her. Tears were submerging her eyes and it was impossible to read his lips.

I'm not… say I am… please, say I am…

His words were unclear through the glass. From where she was standing, it looked as if he himself were made of glass.

...let him... don't... let him... figure you out... find you...

There was a shattering blast. And a sharp flash of light. Instinctively, she turned her head and shielded her eyes from the explosion. Although mildly protected from the impact, she still felt it shimmer through the capsule and shake the ground. Before even glancing back up, Samuella already knew what had happened.

Blood and fragments of brain tissue had been sprayed right across the capsule's window. A few protruding newcomers could be seen outside, sharing their shadows in the strobe fluorescence of the other capsules in the corridor. The red lights in the ceiling were back, this time flashing in steady oscillation. Pegasus must have taken a hammering bullet to the head. There was enough red to paint an entire manor hall. And then came the men in orange. With them on this occasion were two new figures in traditional East robes. One of them had silver sewn into the lining of their robe and posed with a long sword at his side. The other was in a red robe, holding the gun he'd used to kill Pegasus down beside his hip, and there, next to the warm muzzle, was a dagger attached to his belt. Both men examined the situation. 'I say, no more excuses to quell your foul existence. Any stage of radiation poisoning wouldn't have finished you quickly enough, not like we did right here and now. Thought the radiation would've got to your head eventually, you rat, but it appears there isn't enough to go round in this place for snoops like you. So, I think it finally did come down to a single bullet to do the trick for our least favourite business partner. Don't you agree?' the man with the sword spoke in quiet monotone, talking as if he were in conversation with the corpse at his feet.

'He was the weak link; the soggy patch...there was no crucial need for him. Lord Pegasus was irrelevant,' the man in red responded, counting the rounds left sitting in his revolver, taking no interest of the body on the ground. 'He was always there to fund for charities, care for the young and remind us about the shitting environment in the face of financial crisis. When the world required conformity and order, nobody cared for the liberal fraud that he was. I agree, your Phestorship, it is about time we put a stop to such nonsense now, whilst ambitions of greater importance emerge.'

'I wonder what caused him to find himself unlucky here tonight,' the other man slipped his sword beneath his arm and looked up from whatever remained of Mister Pegasus' corpse, streaked across the floor. Samuella almost met the man's eyes at first. He was wearing glasses and was quite short. She quickly bowed her head away. *Is he looking?* she wondered. *Has he caught me? Has he "figured me out"?* It was at a time like this when she wished she could fall asleep at the sound of a click. She wanted the Dreamerverse to rescue her, steal her away and make everything turn out to be okay. *Be careful what you wish for. Be careful what you dream for…*

'We should inform the Drag-in about this little incident. Relieve him with the news that one of his oldest enemies is dead. That would be the thing to do, wouldn't it? The smart thing, the practical thing,' the man in red spoke decisively, while the man with the sword – who appeared to be his superior simply by nature, in stance and behaviour – seemed to be distracted, his mind dangling somewhere else by a thin thread. To Samuella, the sword-bearing man appeared to be in higher authority, whereas the red-robed man with the gun and dagger carried himself like a henchman or a bodyguard. They'd both experienced these dangerous confrontations before, it was obvious, and both knew what to expect. Inspecting the scene with their suspicions, as if it were procedure for them. Right now, he was looking at a young girl in a capsule. She had lush, fiery hair and her eyes were shut. She was supposed to be dormant. But she appeared fresher than the other encapsulated bodies all the same. She looked newer, her occupancy in the ice-cold shell of the sedation chamber short-lived. There was warm, pink colour in her cheeks, almost like she hadn't been there a moment ago…

'The Drag-in doesn't care for Pegasus. The Drag-in doesn't care for you or me. But he does care for young people. And that was one of the many things Pegasus was good at: young people. He knew how to understand them and protect them. Because the youth have something that we elders don't have and something their elders will never understand. And that's not just a colourful imagination, or votes in a ballet box, but the notion that they have our future in their hands. Regardless of what happens, they will grow up and take our place; they will become us. Look at this girl here, for instance.'

Samuella's back shot up. She tried her best not to flinch. The man with the sword was pointing at her capsule. *This is it,* she thought, *caught out*. She failed to hear a single word he said through the capsule's glass.

'Pegasus must have brought her here with the Decider's boy,' the man with silver lining in his robe said. 'By accident, I assume. The Decider's boy was probably missing his father's smothering back home and this pretty one might have been a sympathy prize he brought along for the ride – Pegasus never knew how to tame his compassion once it got the better of him. Unfortunately, that is how these Punks operate – they've mastered a buy-one-get-one-free attitude to life.' The man giggled with his bodyguard. They had both discovered a shade of humour in the situation that Samuella couldn't get her head around and she found it rather frightening. 'Alternatively, it would appear our delusional friend Pegasus might have deliberated bringing them to the East and the detour here was merely part of the field trip. Oh, no. I, however, find that very hard to believe. We already have one West autocrat on his way to the East. Another—the Decider's boy? That won't be the case. We must have plans for this one.' The little man in charge huffed, stroking the blade of his sword. He fixed his glasses and squinted at the wheelchair poking out from the shadows beside Samuella's capsule. 'Pegasus and those bastard Infidels, this must have been their biggest opportunity yet. Indoctrinate the heir to the West, the future dictator of the free world, and turn him into a revolutionary. What a farce.' The man with the sword retuned his attention to body on the ground. '*Really,* Pegasus? Am I *really* supposed to be that ignorant? *You* were *always* ignorant. An ignorant traitor posing as a fence-sitting diplomat. An Infidel Punk at heart. And that's why the Drag-in never took you seriously. What did he say? "*Shadows follow even the most transparent of men into the light*".' The man with the sword glanced at Samuella once more with a cheerful smirk, then said, 'Well, that expression is beginning to make a lot of sense now, isn't it?'

'We have the Decider's *boy*? *Here? That's who he is?*' the other man's voice shrunk to that of a timid rodent. 'Oh, *whh-errm*—Xenol, is there something you're not telling me?'

'I can tell you whatever I want to. The Decider is on his way to the Sixth Nation within the next hour, packing his luggage as we speak, and I will be escorting him there myself. In the meantime, send his boy down to the laboratory with an animal host from the Specimen Unit. He is pure all through, qualified for testing. He is another successful prototype under our belt. Let a word of this slip out and so shall your throat.' Xenol stroked the tip of his sword against his henchman's neck. 'And, Lord Camson, do keep up.'

'Oh, Phestor, I might just have a perfect match for him,' the man in red responded.

Surprisingly, Samuellla had understood the end of their conversation much more easily through the capsule's shell than she had any chance deciphering what Pegasus was trying to say before he was shot. She looked down and noticed three words beneath the capsule's window – OPEN, STANDBY, LOCKED. When Pegasus had been trying to mime something through the glass window, it had been LOCKED and the outside world had been a silent vacuum. However, right now, STANDBY was lit up in amber. It must have switched some time shortly after he'd been shot. His final attempt to keep her safe. *Hadn't Pegasus managed to lock it...or had he left it accessible for the next person...? The next person? Who?*

She heard a door opening from somewhere else in the corridor. Now that she was out of the men's sights and interests, Samuella parted her eyelids. She dared a shrewd peek up at the capsule across the room from hers. Through the blood drooling over the glass screen, she witnessed the two men in orange suits release their next victim.

It was Oscar and he'd been dormant for ages.

She couldn't believe what she was seeing. Phestor Xenol and the anonymity in red had been discussing Pegasus' discharge as if he'd meant nothing in this game they'd started, the last pawn on the chessboard of this apocalypse. *If he'd meant nothing—who did? Was this because he knew about the Constellation Crisis? Because he knew what they were doing here in the Southern Polar Region was criminal activity?* She struggled to believe her own take on this. *What is this new, unheard-of resource they are planning to trade in the Sixth Nation? Will the Decider have a massive part to play or what?*

Who is the Drag-in?

Samuella spent the following half an hour drifting in and out of consciousness. Across the corridor, the two orange-suited figures had stayed to sterilise the now empty capsule. Ever since the other, quite satisfied, East Men had departed, she could no longer make out whether she was still seeing Oscar's face stationed there in the capsule in front of her, or the puff of steam that he had left behind. *What was that stuff?* Probably the same sedative serum they'd pumped into her veins, only gaseous. With massive ventilation guns, the two orange suits vacuumed the entire machine, before checking the meters on their wrists. All clear.

One of them left. Duty was over for him. The other stuck around to seal the capsule and apply the code to lock it. Samuella lurched weakly up against the window of her own capsule and twinkled her fingers across the glass screen, hoping to grab some attention. To her luck, something had already crossed the person in orange, as if they'd instinctively been planning to approach her after the others had left.

This person was still here for a reason.

The suspicious figure paused for a second in front of her, looking straight through her like she was one of those old inanimate shop-mannequins. Samuella was absolutely stunned. But, when the monster finally removed her mask, it wasn't as bad as she'd expected it to be.

The words fumbled over Samuella's tongue and lips so badly she couldn't execute anything more than: '*Ae-Ae-gee-gia!*'

Aegia Amina, looking stunningly identical to the way she had from the City Market, much to Samuella's relief and bliss, applied the code to the capsule within seconds and released the lock that Pegasus had fixed so fast to protect her. With it came a gust of clean, cool air and Aegia raised her ventilation gun to rinse the girl inside with dry sterilising chemicals.

'You're stable. You can walk, right?' Aegia was already tiptoeing towards the wheelchair hidden beside the capsule. 'If you can't, I can plonk you in and we'll be gone in a flash. Either way, we need to go now.'

Samuella reclaimed her footing outside of the capsule with some drowsy difficulty. 'Wha—?' She saw the still body of Pegasus resting in a puddle of thick red gunk. 'What about the body?'

'He anticipated this.' Now was the first time Samuella realised Aegia's eyes had been transfixed on the corpse ever since the mask came off. The sight of Pegasus marinating in his demise vigorously distracted her. For what had been a quick and painless defeat was incomparably sour to swallow for Aegia. She wobbled on knees that had misplaced their strength and went to grapple onto Samuella, hugging her and tucking her cheeks into the girl's scalp, snuffling into her rosy locks. 'You're okay at least,' she murmured. Aegia aggressively grabbed Samuella's arm and pulled her into the wheelchair with a single tug. 'You're wondering where they took Oscar, are you? Look up.'

Above them, for the first time, Samuella noticed the long, thick pipelines sprouting from each individual capsule and running along the ceiling. *So, that's where they go...*

They started to move and, instead of a pair of ironed, pinstriped cuffs, Samuella found two bulky orange arms appear on either side of her. 'Hey!' she objected. 'His body! Please, you can't forget the body! We can't leave it here!'

'The body—' Aegia choked wretchedly. 'The body isn't our problem. He came here to risk his own life in protecting the both of you. And I'm about to do the same.'

Samuella kept trying to glance back over her shoulders, but was caught only by the sight of frozen A.I., lined up like action figures between the capsules. 'You led us here! The both of you arranged for us to get on that flight, arranged for Stevenson to follow us! You even said it yourself: that he would be your *eyes and ears*! I knew from the moment he didn't board that plane, something weird was going on! Someone screwed up the plan! Someone conned us, manipulated us! Now I want explanations! Proper explanations! And don't you go getting your head blown off before you can provide them!'

The wheelchair skidded all of a sudden and halted only a few feet from the elevator. With some effort, Samuella had dropped her feet onto the floor and under the wheels to stop them from moving. It was a good thing her ankles were still numb.

Aegia went to go and shift her feet back onto the footrests. But Samuella declined. 'No—NO! Wait! Aegia, *wait*!'

Ditching her shaken tolerance, Aegia began to violently shove at the wheelchair with everything she had, fighting against Samuella's stubborn retention.

'What are you doing?' Aegia said exhaustedly. 'Won't you just do as you're told! Your father is dead—!'

A frosty silence befell the entire chamber and Aegia's strength dissipated, causing the wheelchair to roll forward a short distance until stopping completely. Both of them had given up the infantile quarrel.

'Aegia,' Samuella huffed. '*He—Pegasus—was my—father?*'

The damaged East Woman, no longer clinging to the handles of the wheelchair, stood flaccidly and decrepit with her hands limp at their sides. 'Yes,' she managed.

'Were you—married to him?' Samuella decrypted.

Aegia nodded with a drooping smile and watery eyes that could replenish an entire ocean if they spilled.

'*You're my parents! You're my mother!*' Samuella cried, semi-exultant, semi-devastated. Bursting with elation, she catapulted herself out of the chair and circled round to embrace her mother, the one last person in the world with whom she knew she shared a connection – even if it was an estranged one, it was still blood. She stumbled into open arms where she was caught by Aegia. 'Why did you keep it a secret from me? All this time, I had no idea! I mean…I wished—I wished—you were both such wonderful people—Pegasus!' Samuella gasped. 'He—that man in the red robe—he killed my father!'

'I know, I know, I know, but you must—Samuella, you must understand,' Aegia croaked, heaving over her explanations, whilst valiantly trying to retain her anger and curb her upset. 'It isn't safe for us to rekindle anything in this place. We must follow your father's desire—get far from the Southern Polar Region, find our feet in the Sixth Nation and resume our mission. But we must not bring up this horrible disaster again, not before we arrive in the East. We can remember your father there and I will tell you everything—okay?' Aegia caressed her daughter's cheeks and rubbed their foreheads together, trapping Samuella in her kind gaze.

Samuella nodded slowly and obediently, with her sleepy eyes shut and sniffing wealthily at her mother's hair and sweaty radiation suit.

'Come now, *bessima*.☆ Let's get you back into that chair.' Aegia carefully hoisted Samuella back into the wheelchair and continued to push them along. 'Don't look back again. Your father isn't there. You remember what he looked like and so do I.' She whispered in a therapeutically cold and steely tone, deliberately masked in inaudible mumbling.

They reached the elevator. The doors closed. Only, this time, they descended.

'Well, here's the *last* thing your father never told you and something he got massively wrong: the Infidels won't find us on the roof. The transporter is going to be looking for us on the ground, once we get out. We need to hurry back down to Ground Level Zero and sneak our way outside onto the landing strip.'

'How will we manage that without getting picked out?' Samuella barked at her heroine. 'And can you please explain to me where they've taken Oscar.'

'Oscar is a very clean specimen – get that? He's simply flesh and blood and nothing more, *nothing yet*. He's one of the healthiest lab rats they've captured in a while. It's because he's never been Exposed. You've been Exposed. Just by looking at the necklace around your neck, it's obvious to anyone working here that you've come into contact with some degree of radioactivity. A gift from Pegasus, the Phantom and me.'

Samuella felt the thin chain on her chest and stroked it finely against her fingertips. The emerald hadn't left her. The mad scientist who'd experimented on her hadn't taken that. He hadn't touched that.

☆ *Bessima [East Dialect (colloquial); singular pronoun]: Beautiful [West Dialect (standard) transl.].*

It had been exposed to the moderate radiation of the Slumberlands, where radioactive rats scampered freely, where she herself had roamed, on a regular basis.

'Like I said, Pegasus and I swore to protect you from the day you met us. Though, we miscalculated, and that's completely our fault.'

'So was the last fifteen years,' Samuella countered with incidental bitterness. 'You never protected me for fifteen years! All my life, I had to fend for myself and rebuild myself in the City—that was after Uncle Ceph died.'

Aegia had anticipated this reaction from her daughter. It was going to erupt sooner or later during this interminable reunion. They had a lot to talk about. Aegia knew she herself had plenty of catching up to do. 'Yes, I am aware of that,' she responded sheepishly.

'I'm surprised you can even remember his name after all this time.'

'We never forgot about you, if that's what you've led yourself to believe.'

'No—you were dead! That was what I was led to believe – the myth I was raised with!' Samuella scolded her mother.

'The lie was necessary to divert you from speculating the past and deliberately created for you to grow estranged from it,' Aegia winced and dipped her head behind the wheelchair, staring straight down at the red locks cascading from her daughter's head. 'I couldn't be more sorry for the life we forced you to undertake and the vulnerability you had to endure without your parents there to guide you from a young age. But please recognise that it was never a selfish option we took to abandon you – it was our decision to protect you with distance, buffer your association with us and quench our resemblance through you. Our selfish love for you was sacrificed to romanticise your future. But I am glad that you eventually discovered your feet and found us again in the City. We are proud of you, Samuella. You should have seen how your father—how your father's eyes lit up when he saw you again for the first time.'

'And yet he still continued to tell me a pack of fibs,' Samuella brooded.

'We are confidants of the Infidel Alliance, Samuella. Specialist informants and enemies of both the East and West by title alone. We always have been. I'm sorry to be bluntly honest with you, *bessima*, but that is how we are obliged to treat our loved ones. I just hope you know how sincere our apology is—'

'What happens now then?' Samuella snapped sleepily, her head lolling to one side. 'If we get out of here in one piece and we actually manage to pull off this mission you dragged us into and endangered our lives with…where do we go from there? Our separate ways again?'

'Home.'

'Home doesn't exist anymore.'

Her mother went frostily soundless, as if she had fallen into a daze.

'I wasn't vulnerable when you left,' Samuella said. 'I was quite the opposite. I had to be, in order to survive. In the City, being vulnerable is the same as being nothing.'

The jeweller lady finally recovered her voice.

'Oscar hasn't been so lucky in this situation, which is why we're panicking,' Aegia arbitrarily interjected, bringing a judicious end to their untimely conversation. 'He hasn't been contaminated before, like you have. He's a free agent, virgin-flesh. A perfect platform. And, even worse, he's the son of the Decider, and the Decider doesn't know he's here – so, Xenol's people will use this as an opportunity to enlist Oscar as a bargaining tool if Xenol's relations with the Decider don't go to plan. He can blackmail through Oscar. They could be doing anything to him. They are capable of doing absolutely anything with a pure body like that.'

'What are they going to do to him, Aegia?' Samuella pleaded. 'What have they got planned for him? What are they testing?'

Aegia didn't entertain her daughter's suspicions. There was stagnant silence, as the elevator smoothly hummed lower towards the hell that awaited them, but would never welcome them…

LOWER TIER, LEVEL -15 (BASEMENT): CHRYSALIS CHAMBER

A tight, theatrical viewing room. Fully white. White walls. White lights. White curtains. And, on this occasion alone, two – not orange-suits – white-suits greeted them when the elevator doors slid open. Inside, three rows of empty white seats were evenly lined before a wide, clean window, beyond which a totally sterile section could be seen. On entry, Samuella and Aegia had both their fake names noted down on a clipboard before they were given white aprons and steel shades to wear. 'They make us seem pretty welcome,' Samuella whispered. 'They did the same to Pegasus. Why's that?'

'The last thing they want to do is capture us. They don't know who we are. We're just warm bodies to them, two more souls to be inspirited by their ideology. Where can we go from here anyway? You and I are already prisoners. Besides, this is an experimentation unit pending moderation; they don't want drama in here. They know we're here, traipsing through their base. They're watching us from every camera, at every angle, which is why they're making it so easy for us to move around. They're keeping us contained prior to making any drastic attempts to crackdown on us. I'm going to see if I can find the men who took Oscar and try to negotiate something.'

'Phestor Xenol was one of them and the other—'

'No. I didn't mean them. For your information, Xenol and the Decider of the West are already on a flight to the Sixth Nation. They're not the problem right now.'

'*Already*?'

'I overheard one of the scientists confirm that they left from here no longer than an hour ago.' Aegia started towards a door in the corner of the empty viewing room. It automatically slid open. 'Stay here and say nothing. I'll be back soon.' She vanished.

Did the Powers That Be really just give her unrestricted security access to the entire experimentation unit? Samuella wondered. *They must really love us here. Or just be really aware of our presence, a passiveness that is far more unnerving.* And, with this curiosity, Samuella edged nearer towards the door herself. She reached an arm out, closely skimming the edge of the door. It slid open for her as freely as it had for Aegia.

'Your impurity has been granted by the system,' the voice of an A.I. buzzed from behind her. She turned and found that Mister Nice A.I. had made a nice spot for himself here on the base, since disembarking the Regal Jet. 'There must be a malfunction. New visitors are never usually exposed to high doses of radiation. Level -15's security system only responds to those emitting excessive levels, which suggests that you—'

'I've been exposed to a lot in my time,' Samuella toyed gleefully with the Tin Man. 'I tend to be more *adaptable* than most people…' She leaned in towards him, '…and most metal people, it would seem.'

Every pixel in the A.I.'s body sprung up and he sported a spiteful, sinister sneer. 'Take a seat, madam. I would hate for you to miss the demonstration.'

He swerved back into the corner he'd crept from to make way for the arriving guests. They were men and women in suits, cookie-cutter connoisseurs from head to toe. *Inspectors and observers from the East.* Samuella watched as they retrieved their aprons and shades from the white-suits at the entrance. There weren't very many guests. No more than a dozen. Samuella took up a centre seat in the front row, between a woman with thunderous thighs and a man who couldn't stop fiddling with his *HoloPhone.*

'*The demonstration hour is about to commence*,' the almighty words of the devil himself beckoned from overhead speakers. All of a sudden, the lights dimmed in the viewing room and the experimentation zone on the other side of the screen was lit up like a stage-show. Two gleaming, empty capsules stood in the middle of the room, from which monstrous tubes ascended into the ceiling. Surrounding the capsules were more White Suits, making their final checks in the prelude to *something big* that was going to happen. And it was that very *something* that was going to put on a performance for all these people. *That something is probably going to be totally exceptional,* Samuella imagined, *a classified objective that has never been trialled before is about to take place and Oscar is at the heart of it.*

Samuella began to fidget her fingers about on her lap, impatiently waiting for Aegia to return through that door with Oscar safely back under her wing, and everything would be okay from that point onwards. Thus far, nothing came of that. After just thinking of this, a flash of light sparked from both tubes and two beings landed in either capsule. The capsule on the right introduced Oscar, dormant and unharmed. But the capsule on the left housed something smaller. An animal that was wide awake, but completely unaware just the same. They'd found Kyma. The poor dog had been spat into the narrowly upright capsule like any other human, so that she needed to erect her body on her hind legs and set her front two paws on the cylindrical glass pane to prevent herself from being crushed. Her fur had been neatly combed and she even had a lucky blue bow at the top of her head. *For fancy decoration and not much else, of course.*

Samuella bundled her itchy emotions into a mental-ball. Then, her body followed suit: arms bent down around her knees, she felt her bones clicking with every curling movement.

Here is the place, now is the moment, she thought. *Something terrible is bound to happen here and now.* Stranded on these thoughts, she noticed a grid of transparent pipes running along the laboratory ceiling. A green fluid flushed through the first pipe that broke off from the wall and traversed through the rest of the pipelines, spreading across the entire grid. The strange serum serenaded through the maze of pipes until it reached its destination: two separate tanks at the crest of both Oscar and Kyma's capsules. The fluid wasn't bright and shining like nuclear-green, but an emerald-green – dark and swampy.

'*The demonstration will now commence,*' the almighty words of the devil returned. '*Ladies and gentlemen, please welcome the man of the hour: Professor Dinkins.*'

All at once, the audience around her rose up from their seats to applaud the man on the other side of the screen as he waltzed into the experimentation space, wearing a lab coat, polka-dot bowtie, and jeans. He was a scientist of the East who was swaggeringly young and flaunted a beaming smile of indulgent pleasure. 'Thank you! Thank you all very much! Welcome everybody to CHEC, the Chrysalis Experimentation Chamber! It was my great honour to invite you to tonight's proceedings and to share with you one of the most advanced and pivotal scientific discoveries of our modern age. Please, may I ensure that you all have on your shades, as what you are about to see could potentially damage your eyesight. And another reminder to everyone that your lead aprons must be worn until you leave the room, since we *are* in radioactive premises.' Then, Professor Dinkins applied his own shades and spun stylishly on his heels. The man had dirty sneakers on and an explosive hairstyle that would've complimented a rock star more than a scientist.

The lights dyed a new colour upon the capsules: dark-green.

As the final checks were being made about the consoles in the Chrysalis Chamber, Samuella zoomed her attention to an open doorway on the other side of the viewing screen. In that other room, Aegia was talking to someone with her back turned to the doorway. It looked to be some kind of office and the figure sitting on the other side of the desk was being blocked by Aegia's extremely exaggerated hand gestures, which were so explicit you'd have thought she was saying something offensive. When she turned, she didn't spot Samuella sitting in the audience, about to observe the looming phenomenon. Instead, she was shaking her head, gazing about bluntly, as if she'd just listened to the most abrasive load of garbage ever. Samuella finally caught the mysterious figure at the desk. It *was* one of the two she'd come across earlier. There, she saw the man cloaked in red, Xenol's accomplice. The henchman. His hood was up, covering his facial identity. Behind him, the revolver he'd used to slaughter Mister Pegasus was suspended on a shelf like an antique…The door slammed shut. Aegia was gone! Sealed off by a white-suit and locked securely inside. The ground started to rumble mechanically. Something was definitely functioning under it to the maximum of its potential.

'No need to be alarmed,' Dinkins reassured the audience. His voice sounded tinny through the speakers, his East accent becoming part of the cackling machinery. 'What you're hearing is a firestorm in the shape of a nuclear fusion rocketing her up underground! The fusion will provide enough heat to stimulate the cosmic energy stored inside the emerald! You are about to witness Digimine coming to life for the *very first time* and the astonishing effect it can have on *living matter*!'

And that was it. All it took for it to happen. The capsules fluoresced. Inside them, *Exhibit A*, which was Oscar, and *Exhibit B*, which was Kyma, were starting to deform as the green smoke filled the space around them. Fazing between a squiggly blur and a human being, Oscar became something surreal. He was becoming a—

FLASH! SNAP! POP!

The two capsules parted-sideward from each other, with the disc-like platforms beneath them manoeuvring like a fairground ride, and a new, third capsule rose from the floor between them. As it emerged, a small, grey ball of smoke began to grow into a long cloud, greedily concealing all the area inside it. Lightning sparked within the tube. And a thing that was totally unique and fresh and alive was materialising into reality before everyone…

Interrupting the birth of this creation, the door at the side of the viewing room burst open and Aegia reappeared. Sending off the alarm! Sending off the emergency lights! The world around Samuella was coming to fruition like never before. And, more distractingly, so was the growing matter inside the third capsule.

'SAMUELLA! I WAS WRONG! LISTEN TO ME! I WAS ABSOLUTELY WRONG!' Aegia screamed at her. She ran towards the girl with her arm out. 'WE NEED TO RUN! WE NEED TO GO! *NOW*!'

Samuella's head swung from the steaming capsule, to the crimsoned woman with terror in her eyes, to the pig-masked men in white suits now rushing towards her, to the nasty little A.I. standing in the corner with a scowl and incineration on his mind, to the lights, and the noise. And back to the third capsule…

The other two capsules shattered completely, leaving nothing behind. Oscar and Kyma were nowhere to be seen. Yet, inside the last remaining capsule was a creature that words could not describe. It was tall and ferocious, with the body of a seven-foot man of muscle, and beastly paws that could rip three men in half at once. It had the head of a canine. A head full of teeth that counted for every star in the *Dreamerverse*…

Before she could stand there and gawk like the rest, Aegia had dragged Samuella back into the wheelchair effortlessly, and whizzed her back through the corridor. The darkness waited for them, and so did the sirens, and so did the flashing red…

The Blood Knight...

As Camson and I resurrect back on the coast of Scorpius Island, the knight in crimson armour is already there, before either of us have even the faintest clue of how we plan to cross another ocean to get to the *Soulcano* – wherever that is (*North/Draco* is what Camson has dictated).

In the dying sunlight, the hellish warrior glimmers. The blood that trickles down the metallic slabs on his shoulders and elbows drips quicker on the surface, like melting ice cream in the afternoon heat, painting the sand with dark splashes. He hasn't seen us coming. Where the tide massages the shore, a small, stationary craft seems to be occupying his talents. He's finished building a wooden rowboat, having also gathered a selection of bamboo rods for oars. Basic, but secure. Could it still be Oscar demented beneath that helmet? Or is it just a spirit-puppet deployed by Antares?

Camson tugs at my sleeve, sensing my simmering curiosity. I give him a brief wave with my hand to signal him to leave me alone. I'm aware of his concern, even though it comes across as an unnatural characteristic that might have rubbed off on him in the act of reviewing Oscar's childhood tragedy in the Alumni. But I'm not in the mood for it. What makes Camson emotionally invested enough to crawl out of his callousness, out from the lair of his grief? Whatever this phenomenon of his is, it's left me feeling the most peaceful I've been around him ever since Oscar joined our companionship. He's walking into the danger alongside me, rather than skulking away and returning to reap the later glory, like some half-arsed Deus Ex Machina. For once, we're tightrope walkers tottering on the same wire, mammals communicating on the same wavelength.

I wave a hand at the Blood Knight. 'Is Oscar still in there—somewhere? Lodged under that helmet—or has his spirit really been lost in translation, somewhere along the Memory Lane? Trapped in the Void, like Antares said,' I call to him.

He doesn't speak. He's busy checking over the safety of the boat (or he's deaf and just doesn't understand what I'm saying).

'Then I suppose you're using Oscar's corpse as a lifeless vessel after all,' I concur, demotivated and shrunken with a deflated posture that is mightily flaccid in the face of this chest-plated abomination standing two feet above me (and three above Camson) on the beach. 'Our immortal guide from the Blankesphere.'

'Does that mean you know where to take us? You can captain us across the ocean to Draco Island, to the Soulcano?' Camson inquires jubilantly. 'Because when it comes to my turn navigating this Map, I'm down tools without the flukes of invisible bridges and water phoenixes, which my two allies had to compliment their leaderships. Are you my saviour?'

On this word – Soulcano – the Knight raises his attention from the boat and thinks for a moment. He drops both arms at his sides and stands upright. Unshackling his head from gravity's oppression, the dejected creature retires solemnly from the pretty, little rowboat to gander the closing horizon.

'We have to know that our friend is okay!' I shout at the knight. 'Can we be sure that Oscar will be revived once we get to the Soulcano? We need our third man to help us! Is he still in there? In that suit of armour?'

'You killed him,' Camson sticks a finger between my eyes. 'Remember that it was *you* who mailed his body to the Soulcano to be embalmed. This metal caretaker is just another spirit that the blind fellow sent up to aid us. We cannot get attached to it.'

'I didn't intend to murder him, only hinder him,' I defend. 'I had no idea the consequences could ever be so fatal here. However, I should have known better when the Lord of the Underworld was at the helm of the fight!' I scold myself. It was impossible for us to harm each other before, with our original weapons, the weapons given to us by All Eyes. And the only reason he modified our weapons in the first place was to save us from ourselves, because we're not supposed to get along! That's canon for all generations of Night Dreamers! There was no predicting what we would have done to one other when we found out we were all on different sides! Even the undertaker thought that the connection we have—it's unique and strange for Dreamers of our descent.'

'We weren't brought here to preserve each other. We're here to prolong the whole of existence. We're supposed to be doing our job. That's what's canon for Night Dreamers. At least, on a better note, we've learnt we're no more untouchable here than we are in the Real World! Not anymore.'

'Well, it doesn't make any sense at all! Oscar was stabbed through the ribcage and the sea swallowed Thuban! One of them resumed his existence in reality, whereas the other vanished completely, without a trace of memory – off the records entirely. And then you should've died when I shot an arrow through your chest in that cave! But you didn't and that wasn't real at all! Don't you see it? The anomaly in the theory? The gap in the logic? Death in the Dreamerverse is different for everyone! It's almost like the lack of explanation and the absence of logic when it comes to who can perish and who can't, as they dice with death, is contrived and predetermined. As with Cassandra categorising the spirits into Good and Bad and Antares' extraction of Living Memories from the attire of their dead bodies—perhaps there is something or some*one*, that decides whether and when we actually meet our end? Like an overlord or a Stellar God, who has control of our fate?'

'I'm not sure how far I believe that idea. The more the Void breaks, the more reality will filter through and plague the Dreamerverse. Our imagination will probably become useless and, by that point, we won't have the ability to defend anything from its demise. Please, Sammy, take my word and stop getting attached! Everywhere you go, you're like a child at a magic show! Forget your awe for this world and remind yourself of the stakes reality will face, if we do not ground ourselves for one moment, and finish the duty we set out to complete. Don't get side-lined by your emotions.'

'You never were attached to either of us,' I criticise. 'So, you wouldn't understand. I've wounded both of you now! Oscar just happened to be the one who suffered!'

'Wait—I wouldn't understand what?' Camson sniggers, as if he's heard the most inescapable joke. 'I wouldn't understand losing someone I love? Moving on from the *people* I loved?'

'Oh, come off it, Camson! Since we met, you've never really bothered with me, and you particularly never saw eye-to-eye with Oscar,' I acknowledge. 'Did it honestly take for you to see man's father murder his mother for you to finally warm to him? *Wow!* How could I have ever predicted that the Alumni might pull something so miraculous to change you two and your hideous attitudes towards each other? I might have dragged both your backsides down to the Tombs sooner!'

'Oh, I apologise, Samuella—did mine an Oscar's rivalry never live up to your juvenile attraction for him?' Camson challenges.

'Attraction?'

'Yes—your love affair. Did you think I missed the chemistry between you two?'

'Argh, get off it, Cammy!' I discredit his silly hearsay and what I see as his seeping jealousy. I'm humiliated by the suggestion, even in the company of an expressionless Blood Knight.

'You think I haven't noticed the pair of you flirting your rumps off, literally all the way to Hell and back? I just never said anything, because I prefer to stay at least *relatively* professional when *existence* is under threat.'

'Don't go back to being your stupid self now!' My insults can't hurt him now; his skin has thickened again. 'Did we *embarrass* you with out sociability, Camson? Or are you a little envious about missing out on a fraction of my attention?'

'No—it repulsed me to see you two philander! You're an East Girl, but you pretend like you're a West Girl with everything going for you over there!'

'I'm only *half* an East Girl—*half!*' I remind him. 'But my parents' blood has nothing to do with me, and the way I think, or who I side with. I barely ever knew either one of them, so why should I care at all?'

'Your bloodline is as clear as day, sweetheart,' Camson leers.

'Where I'm from isn't as important as where I'm going.'

The Blood Knight opens one of his chrome gauntlets. The unravelled fist reveals its shining contents. There, brighter than the sun and dazzling in a palm of rose-tinted aluminium, is the second emerald. He lifts it into the air for the both of us to see. Perfectly carved and in better condition than the first gemstone – that I still have, sitting in my pocket; I can feel it now, buzzing, vibrating harmoniously in my ripped pyjama-bottoms. It's heard its brother calling from across the shore. I produce the first emerald and hold it up above my head. There's an instant connection. The first emerald on its own had only shone, desiring its siblings. Now, in each other's company, the brothers are vibrating.

'You picked it up! I must have dropped it on my way back up to the surface. Well—erm—thank you,' I say to the knight. 'We need one more and then we'll know exactly what they can do for us.' Oscar's no more. This silenced suit is just his shadow, the night of his day. Although, a piece of him is still in there, somewhere hidden in that suit of gory gloop. 'You came to help us.'

The Blood Knight then throws the glowing rock to Camson, who catches it clumsily. Next, he's turning from us both and towards his magnet: the diminishing horizon. The sun drops into the ocean and the stars take helm of the sky.

'But weren't we told that we shouldn't disturb the ocean while it's resting?' Camson judges fairly. 'Taking a boat to it would be doing exactly that and *night* would probably be the worst time to risk something like—I don't know—*waking up the sea!* The parrot warned us about that before we crossed Lynx!'

'He seems to know what he's doing,' I say. I'm already further across the beach, following the knight, ahead of an indebted Camson.

Our final voyage waits.

'You've been relieved of duty, Lord Camson. This gentleman knows the way without the Map,' I tell Camson eagerly. 'He's offered to be our ferryman.'

'Don't call me that,' Camson complains. '*Lord Camson.*'

We rush to the boat to join the Knight on-board. He hoists me up, and then Camson too. With a few kicks from his metal hooves, he manages to boost us off the damp sand, leaving a thin trail of dark red on the water's surface. He boards himself and raises one of the bamboo rods, with which he begins to oar. The boat slowly bobbles upon the delicate tide, away from the shore's tranquillity and further into the ocean's crucible.

The first leg of the journey on-water drags on for almost three hours and Camson spends the majority of the trip fingering around the Constellation Map. He's *supposed* to be leading the way, but has quietly taken a backseat. 'Draco Island is fronted by the Ursa Minor Reef. But the comet trail on the Map skirts around this "Ursa" constellation and the inlet plonked in the middle of the reef—called the "Sapphire Lagoon"—this is pulsating. The words are flashing at me, fading on and off the page. Maybe that's a warning sign…which might mean we should…avoid it without negotiation?' he vocalises the suggestion like a clueless crusader, but in a non-descript tone that goes right over all our heads.

In the meantime, the Blood Knight stands stiffly with one of his boots levelled on the boat's prow. 'We should be headed straight towards Draco,' Camson continues, 'if we semi-circle around Central Island during our crossing of the equator and continue on directly forwards, towards the Ursa Minor Reef. But giving the Sapphire Lagoon a miss, of course.'

Every half-hour or so, the Blood Knight takes a ten-minute recess from his sustained effort of rowing the bamboo-oars to speed us up. During each adjournment in the rafting, we lounge in the shadow of our oarsman and allow the subtle winds to carry us along on the tired ocean current.

Camson lies next to me. His arm is brushing against mine, and his eyes are cradled in slits. 'Don't drop off on us now,' I remind him. 'We can't afford for you to be passing out without a purple seed in your system. We're almost there.'

Camson pops a purple seed into his mouth and so do I. He hardly whinges when he has the Solar Blade prised under his arm, or balanced on his chest like a hero's ransom (yes, I gave it to him to play with). Watching him, I return to my habit of overthinking things. Contemplating the diverse bunch we are, and the lives we live in the real world, and why in all the dimensions the Stellar Gods selected the three of us to form a companionship. Camson's surely not *my* hero. Maybe to some, he is. I'm not aware of anyone he could offer saintliness to. A soldier. That's all he is. A fighter. But, a hero? That's subjective, a title preferable to his role in the East. What would I call him in this instance? A 'father' figure, perhaps. Does that suit him better?

I nudge him nervously like a peevish nurse to an unresponsive coma-patient.

'Cammy.'

'Ya?'

'When we met on Awakening Coast, I had no blimmin' clue who you were – you and Thuban appeared in my blind spot and so had the girl with golden hair. Needless to say, the three of you stamped a vivid image on my mind straight away, which keeps returning to me in this dreamscape and beyond. It's bizarre, because I pass-by many people every day in Mankind's World, but I forget every face I see. Yet, here in a dream, I remember faces so easily. The connection I have with the faces in my subconscious mind is more memorable than trying to recall the faces I meet in person.'

'It's called a recurring dream. In other words, a nightmare. Don't worry, you're my worst nightmare too.' Camson says this with genuine thought, rather than the cheeky sarcasm I've come to expect. 'You're spending too much time here and fewer and fewer hours in the real world – it means we're sleeping too much and we need to wake up more. Otherwise our lives in the real world are going to shrink into blips. We'll become chronic narcoleptics, awake for minutes in reality and awake for days in the Dreamerverse.'

'Do you think that's what All Eyes means about spending all of eternity here?' I speculate. 'Life on Mankind's World just shrinks away, and then we're left with Constellation Planet?'

'No,' Camson disagrees. 'I think the worse concern is what will happen to Mankind's World when we're not there to play our roles in it?'

'As if our world really needs a cotton picker, an East veteran and another Decider,' I jest – but it is no joke at all.

'The hard truth is, we will be needed at some point, in small doses as well as massive ones,' Camson reasons. 'Whether we'll be missed is questionable. Maybe the Woken will forget us, just like they forgot Thuban?'

'It's an odd phenomenon dying in the Dreamerverse,' I say, 'because, whilst Thuban is gone in reality, Oscar is still very much present there—'

'When you mentioned Oscar was still alive in Mankind's World—' Camson winces. 'How do you know that?'

'Long, long story,' I murmur, then continue to digress. 'Anyway, I've been pondering this while we were walking back across the desert: if Thuban is still alive, will it mean we can only restore him in the Dreamerverse or will he be able to be recovered in the real world too? Maybe it's us who will have to reach this conclusion—if you get what I mean. What if you and me need to make that decision for him? Could you make that decision? Camson, if you and I share one thing in common, it's our blood. I figured, we might be more effective than Oscar when pitted against the Drag-in, because we both have East Blood and it's East Blood that resonates with dragons – the spirit animal of the East. The dragon is in our folklore, our anthem. Oscar doesn't unite with the legend the way we do, he wasn't christened by it, he hasn't lived by it. But the strength in Oscar's soul will give us that *something different* we need, so we can diversify our power. It's like how a vaccination works: you combat the condition with a bit of its own medicine and then surprise it with something new, something different.'

'Well, until we get our mitts on him again,' Camson responds with pride and sympathy floating over his words, 'we're gonna have to pull *something* off on our own.'

'But not entirely without Oscar. That's why, generation after generation, Night Dreamers have never got along or *connected.* Other generations in the past failed to defeat the Drag-in because they always hated each other and ultimately refused to bond in an alliance. They never trusted their comrades. But we've come to bear each other's histories – the Tombs of Truth made each of us aware of that – and now that the divisions in our alliance have blurred, the Drag-in will have a bigger challenge than it's ever had to confront before. As contradictions, we bring balance to one another, which is the reason there's three of us – no more, no less'

As the moon-kissed vista begins to part from the unknown, a new island grows out of the ocean ahead. Planted in the middle of it is a tall volcano. Broad and smooth, a pretty creation spawned from some Stellar God-equivalent of Mother Nature. Smoke whisks from the open top. Out of all of the places we've landed in this world, this one looks to be the most volatile. 'Our friends are incarcerated somewhere amidst the gulf of the stars,' I mutter, thinking of that wall segregating worlds—and where Oscar and Thuban's spirits must be stored inside it. Sitting up properly, both hands clenched to the edges of the boat, I concentrate on the oncoming paradise, stroked by white moonshine.

Big metal hands touch my shoulders and I flinch my head gingerly. They've left red stains on my pyjama-fabric. Now on my left, the Blood Knight is acting strange. If he were human, I can imagine his lips quivering upon a pallid face. The metal on his armour is anxiously rattling. He launches off me, pushing himself down onto all fours, as he goes to investigate the situation. Down in the water, beneath the boat, a drizzling, hairy lump bulges from the ocean, and then dips back under…

All of a sudden—*WHOOSH!*

A massive animal rockets out of the sea beside us, and lands in a heap of big waves, flushing us with cold water. In my mouth the water isn't salty as expected, it's sweet like sugar. The boat itself hasn't been struck badly enough to capsize us and there isn't enough damage to the deck to sink us, but it's bobbling unstably. And I'm grappling tightly to the edges. I dare to glance over the edge of the boat and discover that another Balæna is performing playful cartwheels under the water. The gills slicing its furry neck and the grisly muzzle – a roof for its incisors – are hard to miss…

'*Lagoon!*' Camson stammers.

SMASH!

Another one has crashed into the other side of the boat and the whole craft tips onto its side. I slide off, headfirst towards the deep. Behind me, from where the force has come, there's nothing to hold me back. No knight in shining armour.

SMASH—SMASH—SMA—CRASH!

Off the boat! Overboard! Gone! Into the freezing, syrupy water. Wood *SNAPS—SHATTERS*—in my absence. Turning to find the edge of the boat for support, I see nothing but water swallowing my face. Planks and beams of timber are afloat on the surface. One of the bamboo oars pokes me in the forehead, catapulting me into a startling concussion. A hand reaches out to me. It belongs to Camson. He flaps it. I struggle to grasp—can feel my nails digging into his flesh, but can't register the power to sustain a grip. I'm ripping at him! Ripping! Drawing blood from his palm and wrist! But it's no use!

At first, I notice the dark bruise expanding under the water, blackening the space around me. The water itself has started to part and sink, like whirlpool in a giant plughole. A gap has formed in the ocean. A huge hole has arrived to devour me, the boat and everything else. Pale blue light illuminates the whirlpool—it encircles us in a glittering vortex—secreted up from the cantankerous shallows of the reef...

We've seen this before...this is all too similar to before...*Thuban—!*

I can hear Camson wailing between gasps for air: '*It's baack—baack—for—us—baaaack—Took my boy—and now—now it's back for us!*'

Wider.

And wider.

And wider—the brilliant particles in the water broaden their circumference.

I'm falling under them. Deeper. Losing Camson's hand for good against the swell of the gyrating waves. Losing the sugary sweetness of the water on my lips and rediscovering it in my throat...then, my lungs. Losing the stars that are supposed keep us safe, supposed to shine us home...and finding instead the sorely-lit sapphire molecules floating below the water, where a radiantly turquoise backdrop anchors them down...until they meet the bottom...

Chapter Ten
Escape To The East

Aegia's legs didn't stop moving.

As for her daughter, coming back to consciousness in the wheelchair, she was too nervous to dare a peek at anything ahead. There were loud, indistinguishable noises all over the place, with searing sirens being the vanguard of the discordance. There were bright lights, the sorts of which not even the dark of her eyelids could shut out. And, worst of all, there were the tunnels on Level -1. Desolate, but hazardously frosted and glacial, these tunnels were enclosed by the surrounding Polar Mines. Hundreds of tunnels had been carved into the mines (since the archaeologists of the East had never stopped digging for oil beneath the icecaps and – in this region at least – they hadn't had the first clue where to look). The perfect hiding place for a fugitive or two, but not ideal for any stumbling surface-dweller who hoped to see the sun again. *Why haven't there been any A.I. out here, biting at our heels with laughable ease?* Samuella kept repeating this in her head every time they turned a corner from one monotonously replicated tunnel to the next. *Surely, they could just send the A.I. after us. We'd be arrested by now if the A.I. had been commissioned.* But there were no A.I. in the mines and, much to their luck, they hadn't bumped into any troopers either…

…yet.

Aegia had some idea where she was going – Samuella became quickly aware of this as soon as the wheelchair's g-force hit her – but traversing the notorious East base under pressure didn't make the trip from A to B any easier.

By the time one tunnel brought them to the back of the Great White Building, where the only promising exit was a wide ramp that led back up to the airstrip, there were troopers on alert everywhere. It was ridiculous. There were thirty at the very minimum, waiting for them on the slope that ascended out into the open. Aegia brought the wheelchair to an abrupt halt, ripping some rubber on the tyres. It was too late. The troopers averted their attention to the two new statues that had planted themselves overtly in the tunnel's mouth and they reacted to their prey energetically, chirping over their triumphs in East Dialect and building a blockade in front of the absconders, poised with their machine guns ready to fire. It had come to a formal face-off, where the base's pulsating sirens resounded off the tunnel walls, splintering the silence between the horde of East Men and the two women. The storm-winds had picked up and snowflakes were fleeting down the ramp from outside, bombarding Aegia and Samuella as the troopers descended it to meet them. '*Stand still with your legs firmly apart and your hands held high above your heads!*' the general of the pack barked at them with a steadfast East accent. At least he was speaking in West Dialect and Samuella could understand his orders. This General wasn't big, or even hypothetically derivative of the word, at all. He was dwarfish and explosively projective as he spoke, but the gold star on his uniform spoke volumes that surpassed all else. He then raised his own revolver and jolted it in Samuella's direction, and shouted some more, eyes cutting in distrust. 'Tell her to stand! Tell the girl to stand! Or she will die first! Tell her to stand!'

'She cannot stand!' Aegia argued back at the little monster. 'The girl is *injured*! She cannot use her legs unassisted!'

The general tilted his head, wobbling on legs that were too straight for sane comfort. Through pursed lips, he made a small sound that was the equivalent to blowing a raspberry and bounced between conclusions in his head. 'You will *make* her stand! Otherwise you will both die together! You have one chance to surrender!'

'She. Can't. Stand!' Aegia spelled it out. 'The poor child is badly injured. She cannot move her legs without assistance!'

The gun was trembling in the general's hand, trigger flickering under an agitated finger. '*YOU* WILL MAKE HER STAND!'

Aegia glanced around at the army of men and gawked at the shocking lack of intuition among them all. Samuella still hadn't opened her eyes. Delirious, she was stuck imagining her and her mother being trapped in the tunnels, hoping that the mines wouldn't cave in on them. Or maybe hoping that they would, in order to rescue them from the slim odds of reaching the base's airstrip and an unavoidable confrontation with—

The general rang upward a single bullet into the air. It hit the ceiling. A few rocks were dislodged and fell to the ground between him and the two escapees.

'You will force her to stand! NOW!' He reused his extremely limited and colourless spectrum of West vocabulary.

'No,' Aegia said strongly. And she gripped the handles of the chair even tighter. They wouldn't make it if she ran, not even if time itself was suspended, but it was much more satisfying than standing on the spot, bound to do nothing.

BANG!

No longer a warning shot.

The ringing that followed rapidly ripened to the slightly less shrilling sound of a scream coming to an end. In immediate response to it, Aegia swung her head down to look at the damage the single bullet had caused. *Where did it hit? Who did it hit?* Samuella was hunched forwards, gripping onto her shoulder blade, crying and retching. Blood had splattered over her lower neck and swamped between her fingers. She was gasping for air.

'This time I will try not to miss.' The general pointed his weapon at Aegia and twitched his arm in imitation, as if about to shoot without hesitation. Aegia released her clasp on the handles and slowly declined them on to her daughter's collarbone and bleeding shoulder, preparing to surrender at last, when…all of a sudden, a large hole formed in the centre of the general's forehead, the size of that on the entrance of a birdhouse, and the ringing returned again. Only, on this occasion, the BANG had totally missed Aegia's attention and had been replaced with the crescendo of gunfire. Like her daughter, delirium abducted Aegia. She went momentarily blind, letting the heavy snowfall bury her eyelids and she only sensed the hailstorm of bullets skimming her head, as she slowly dropped backwards. Caught by an invisible presence, she was hoisted across the tunnel and towards the opening. The invisible battle commenced. Charging bodies rocketed across the tunnel from opposing sides and shells littered the reddening ground. But not one single shred of the battle's debris touched the two impaired women being carried up the ramp and into the open.

Outside, the snowstorm was raging its worst and the flakes pattered against their cheeks. Aegia and Samuella were blanketed in thick woollen skins, loaded onto a four-by-four, and driven across the airstrip. Once her vision stabilised, Aegia lifted herself up into a sitting position to catch the back of the driver's head. She and Samuella were slumped in the backseats, accompanied by a band of three men, who were armed with their own weapons, akin to the artillery of the troopers. These were not Polar Region reinforcements however. One sat in the front passenger seat, beside the driver. Another had joined them in the back and took up a window-seat beside Aegia, who sat in the middle of the back row. And, at the steering wheel, Stevenson drew his eyes off the road only briefly to greet Aegia with a raised brow. 'Yuh t'ink Mistah Peggy dem wuh send yuh packin' wid none army of yer own? An', more important, wih no reliable chauffer?' Stevenson shook his head and kissed his teeth. Relief rekindled Aegia once more and the overwhelming epiphany triggered by Stevenson's face made her drowsy.

Beside her, Samuella was also coming to. A white patch had been plastered to her bleeding shoulder, and the cloth that fell to her lap as she sat up had been used to soak up the sweat that had glazed her face a moment before. She instantly spotted the picky mesh of dreadlocks and her agony lightened. '*Stev—vvv—*' she stuttered.

'Na' save ye' breath fuh later,' Stevenson advised. 'Ye' gonna need to put it tuh use once yuh get dere East.'

The airstrip was incredible. Perfectly flat, it covered at least a mile of impeccable tarmac. Samuella's nausea loosened her neck's grip on her head and her skull bobbled onto the backseat's window ledge. 'We can't leave Oscar here,' she managed, half a sentence at a time in enormous gasps. 'We can't leave him with those people!'

'Where de boy?' Stevenson's attempt at settling tensions in a shambolic situation faded. The Small Islander sang an unnaturally shakier rhythm of disbelief, instead of his usually orchestral ode of optimism. It wasn't a tone that matched his voice at all. In fact – at least Samuella thought – he sounded like a totally different person altogether: 'What 'appen to m'dear child?'

'They ran their experiment on his body. And they turned him into a hybrid-monster. He's become one of the SPR's signature specimens,' Samuella wedged all that into a single breath. Her hands met her cheeks. They were chilled, raw meat against a tint of pink warmth. Other than that which remained in her throbbing face, there was nothing warm left inside of her. Her fevering was gone now, decamped alongside Stevenson's hopes of saving Oscar.

A black helicopter roared overhead, camouflaged by the night sky, but given away by the ferocity of the propellers and the flush of the affected snowfall everywhere around it. The four-by-four skidded under the weight of the vibration. It zoomed forwards, leaving them trailing behind. 'Dat yuh flight out!' Stevenson cried. He aggressed the accelerator and the vehicle began to chase into the storm.

Meanwhile, something nasty was knocking on the windscreen. At first, Aegia had imagined she was hearing the thunderous shatter of heavier snowflakes, perhaps hail, as she strained her eyes to see. But it quickly became apparent to her that those *snowflakes* were bullets showering the four-by-four's bonnet. The earliest few to land were indirect mishits. They skimmed the windscreen and ran up the roof. A couple more rapped on the rear windshield—

They were surrounded.

Then, eventually… SMASH! Glass burst right across the cabin from all directions. Aegia took Samuella's head against her chest. They ducked. The armed Infidel in the back-window-seat was met with an untimely blitzing to the face and torso, and Aegia felt a gush of freshly gargled blood spew onto the back of her neck. Stevenson swerved them across the tarmac, violently dragging the vehicle under the wing of a jet plane. More bullets took to the wing, pelting it into fiery shreds and bringing it crashing to the ground, just as the chauffer managed to drift them tightly away. The four-by-four pounced down a ramp, hind-wheels spinning up in the air shortly, before it completely grounded on the tarmac again. Gunfire diminished as soon as Stevenson rolled them in behind a collection of cargo-crates.

They were inside the hangar now. Here they hid within the maze of cargo.

Elsewhere, at the exact moment Stevenson killed the engine, there was the sound of more vehicles *squelching* to a halt. East Men were talking in their native Dialect again, whether that was softly or barking out loud it really didn't change their constant nature of urgency. There was a disturbance in the Polar Base that needed to be eradicated. Within the mess of glass, Aegia quickly rose from her ducked position and prised Samuella out from underneath her sheltering caress like a dependently beached whale. Stevenson turned, brushed the shards off Samuella's back and used the napkin from his bulletproof jacket's breast pocket to quickly wipe up the blood on her neck.

'Young gyal, listen to me!' he said, cupping both her cheeks in his palms. The East Men on the other side of the crates were impatient, growing more aggravated and vicious as they waited, as they searched. Distance was closing between them and execution, and Samuella's alertness had spontaneously restored itself. Right in front of her, the face of Stevenson temporarily distracted her from fear. 'You follow Miss Amina 'cross de airstrip…She will tek yuh tuh safety.' Stevenson gave Aegia a cautious look to say *does she know yet?* Aegia subtly nodded. 'Trust yer mother will tek yuh home safe.' He winked at Samuella. He offered the tired girl's chin a light tap with his knuckle and then took the large machine gun that was being handed to him from his last standing comrade, sitting in the passenger seat beside him. Stevenson glanced at Aegia one final time. 'You know where—?'

'Peggy and I planned everything, about where to go, what to do when we get there, and what to do when we get our hands on it – everything. She's going to be perfectly fine with me,' Aegia responded. Samuella suddenly felt a surprisingly dry hand close around hers. Aegia was edging the door open and pulling on her. There was no going back now.

'Meh soon come after yuh, an' meh expect to see 'er *alive*! Y'hear? Ye' got fifteen years tuh make up tuh her!' Stevenson widened his eyelids at Aegia, demanding her solemn trust. And he finally gave Samuella something to remember before he left. 'Yuh will be taken straight to de East an' don't look back fuh us once yuh get dere. I'll find Oscar an' I'll bring 'im in one piece—or two.' He dazzled them both with his charming grin. That said, he was out the door with his unlikely partner.

Banging bullets penetrated right through the guarding crates and smacked against the side of the four-by-four.

Aegia hoisted the dreary girl out of the car and set her arm over her shoulders. Like a professional wrestler would to his opponent before an easy K.O., she guided her about the cargo maze, trying to get her as far from the noise as possible. *The landing zone shouldn't be much further from here.* She repeated the visions she'd had of their escape-route in her head, *landing zone, landing zone…*

A confrontation she'd hotly anticipated scaled the ladder to her immediate attention, as another four-by-four – this one an open-top convertible – stopped by some huge crates in the darkness ahead. The headlights exposed glimmering fragments of dust in the air and a pair of silhouettes passing by soon blocked this. East Men, armed to the teeth with machine guns, daggers and rows of taser-grenades piled onto their spines. Taking instant note, Aegia slid Samuella off her shoulder and hid her behind the nearest crate on the corner, out of view. Samuella's neck bent ever so slightly and her head lolled comfortably on her shoulder, eyes closed as if she were already dead. Then, Aegia turned to the oncoming pursuers. They hadn't yet noticed her presence, which gave her time. Just enough leeway. She stepped out into the splash of the headlights. The two men seized every muscle in their body, cigars slipped from both pairs of lips. And they raised their weapons. '*Submit yourself!*' One of them said confidently. He seemed to be the highest in rank. On his uniform, a silver badge, labelled: EAST DRAGON POS#1, stood out in the shape of lightning-bolt. '*I SAID SUBMIT YOURSELF!*' he shouted. '*SURRENDER! ON YOUR KNEES!*'

Aegia held out an arm, flinched her right hand… a small flume-like handle expanded into a long, slender blade. She poised herself and then launched all her power at him. As the first bullets came, she skidded to the ground and floated across the tarmac like a swan on lake-water. The blade came successfully to his shins and parted them from the rest of his body. The maimed trooper flopped forward and crashed in a heap on the ground. Next, she swung the blade upwards, into the chest of his associate. The other East Man was too stunned to respond with bullets. And, so, the blade ripped through his torso and only exited once it reached his chin. Aegia looked around to spy out any others hanging nearby. Once she confirmed she was alone, she retrieved Samuella and carried her out of the hangar.

Back in the openness, the echoing sirens swallowed the gunfire. The sirens had been mounted on the watchtowers and compensated great volume for their small size. There were also bellowing floodlights, probably to help the snipers see in the dark. *Snipers!* The thought struck her just before the propellers descended from the sky above them. Not one, but three helicopters had arrived. Subsequently, so humbled was Aegia that she dropped to her knees and sank into the snow with Samuella slumped against her bosom. As soon as the choppers touched down, smoke grenades dropped onto the ground and impounded the space around Aegia. Men dressed in gasmasks and dark East robes hurried out of the helicopters to help them on-board. From that point on, it became a blur for both of them. Aegia lay beside Samuella while their helicopter ascended. Below, more open-tops rolled to a stop and the armed pursuers fired blindly at them through the smoke, attacking relentlessly until the clouds engulfed them.

Aegia now edged her head to the side ever so gingerly. The cushion beneath it supported her with the same sensation as a barrier between her living world and some other afterlife. The adrenaline hurt. It killed. It murdered. One of the masked figures who'd scooped them up was sat casually beside her, gun laid across his lap. He was looking out into the night, catching the breeze as it came. They must have been drifting above ocean water by now. The man in the mask continued to navigate his eyes about the fluorescent stars in the sky beyond the clouds.

The East was in sight.

Camson

Camson's First Awakening...

For a while, there was a colourful bird flying low above my head, feeling the sun on his back and indulgently flexing his spine like a baby snake would shimmy its body not long after hatching. Now he's disappeared, I'm pretty convinced I'm not a devilish Cartoon Creation that has been hit over the head with a magnified mallet and is dizzying beneath the wings of the *Beddy Bye Birds...*

Snakes? I mentioned a snake, didn't I?

I sit up. Sand fleets off my shoulders and scuttles down my back. The heat catches my face and I raise a hand to block the pink sunlight off my eyes. Here, right in front of me, *right now – GODDAMN, RIGHT HERE AND NOW* – is a python of immeasurable length. The bloody thing has just woken from a basking on the beach—

A beach? That would explain the shell in my arse—

But how did I end up on one…with this bugger? Thankfully, its movements are just as groggy as my own. *If it hasn't yet noticed you, you hold the advantage over the serpent.* Why am I remembering these words of strategy? Why now? Had they been the wise citations of *my old Snake Trainer*? Surely, I can't be reminding myself of this now. *I'd only passed on my first three Taming Grades. Guess it's as good as anyone does in the Sixth Nation these days. My former Master Xanxi's long retired now – been dead for a while too – and he's not here to revise over my taming lessons, particularly in the case of this surprise test.* If Xanxi were with me now, he'd probably say something like "here is where there is you" (in a very monkish way).

What is this creature doing on the beach? What am *I* doing on this beach? Did we both just worm our way out of the ground?

'*Yes,*' an ownerless, wraithlike voice spears through thin air and injects itself into my head unannounced. I turn around, not to find whom I imagined to find, and only to see a second spontaneous snake waking up and uncoiling itself. *Very calm I am, Master Xanxi, very calm I will remain.*

'*Wonderful thinking,*' the unmanned voice returns, '*but they haven't come to harm you. You arrived after they did. So, it would only make sense that you are currently the one impeding them. Who is to say that your timing and orientation is any better than theirs right now? This is their world after all and you are an Unfamiliar. A visitor or an invader – however you prefer to depict yourself, we will learn the truth of your unexpected arrival very soon.*'

'Well, that makes dimbos of us both, since I'm as perplexed about this situation as you,' I respond mechanically, defensive against everything I can see.

'*I am a metaphysical being with telepathic capabilities, not a dimbo. You have no right to call me a "dimbo",*' the voice argues. '*Who taught you to stand still like that? How do you know to stand the way you are? Why are you not wildly scampering around in trepidation like a fowl in a coop?*'

I'm poised appropriately in the presence of both snakes. Side-on between them so that, rather than facing one more intensely than the other, I'm looking at neither. A neutral frame. *There's no directness to your stance; hence, no means to it either. There never should be. You will keep tolerability and unpredictability in balance, just like your two challengers.* Master Xanxi's insightful comfort buzzes into my thoughts like a bee that won't stop hovering to and fro through an open window. 'Where am I?' I hardly move my lips, fossilised with fright. Three Grades of anything is never enough – especially when it comes to taming a snake! *Two snakes!*

'*You're on another world, my fellow Dreamer,*' the anonymity says, '*and the world you left behind is but a distant memory.*'

'Dreamer? Is this a dream?' I say, 'I remember falling asleep—'

'*Oh, really?*' the voice now sounds pleasantly unsurprised by my slowness (or pleasantly sarcastic – whichever rows your boat). '*That's not regular at all.*'

'Well, not many people *do* remember details like falling asleep,' I scramble to support my point. 'I can only remember such little things because I'm just shrewd like that. I used to be the sharpest General in the East Army, back when I used to count the hours I napped and capped them. They used to chant: "cap your naps, or else the Cap' will snap your post". Now *that* was discipline...not barely remembering to swallow the pills that send you to funky worlds like this when you go to sleep.'

And there, floating in front of my face is the unkempt bird of a hundred dazzling feathers. He's the lynchpin of my affirmation and understanding in this foreign land, who's still loving the sound of his own voice. '*Oh, I am not so daft as I sound. I do believe what you're implying about the militarised conscience. However, the strength of your cognitive defiance fails to comply with the forces of Awakening Coast, Soldier Man. Tell me—if there is only one type of Dreamer who can withstand the impact of the Void and the mental blockade that divides this universe and reality, what does that make you? Your sunset arrival influences me to wonder—*' the bird pauses, dips his head. '*Is that a silk robe you're wearing?*'

The parrot is captivated by what I'm wearing. Over my pyjamas that night, I'd decided to wear my richest robe – the Monarch's Robe of Red Luck, gifted to me by my wife on her divorce from my life. 'Are you blind? Of course it is,' I snap. 'And you should know that it once belonged to the Last King of the East – the Punk King. Legend tells that it was snatched from the family home before the pyre was lit at the funeral procession, where all his other finest possessions had gone to ashes. I see it that, if the thief hadn't taken this Robe, they would've burnt it with his body, killed it with his soul. Now, that would have been an absolute waste of a good robe.'

'*Fire*,' the bird mumbles sourly, almost sombrely. '*Funeral by fire is a great waste of a good body. Some of us could do with the charity of a new human body. Alas, wouldn't that be wonderful...Did no empathetic soul in Mankind's World ever tell people the importance of recycling?*'

'Hmph,' I scoff at the remark. 'Only when money's involved.'

'*Which king would this be?*' The bird gets closer to my face. '*The one you mentioned.*'

'King Jo Xeff. He was the Punk King whose liberal regime was ousted by my Nation and its leader, Phestor Xenol,' I educate the parrot.

This causes the bird to back away slightly and lower his wings, sinking his glorious levitation.

'Yes, very interesting, I know. And I tend to be very ardent about protecting artefacts that belonged to the Punk King. Just don't tell my boss.' I wink at the parrot. 'Who are you supposed to be anyway? *What* are you? A talking bird?'

'*Since when was telepathy in the same bracket as oration, Mister Moron?*' The bird deliberately shivers his wings, spattering tiny feathers into my eyes. 'I'm telepathic and my name – yes, birds also have names, not only humans, you'll be amazed to know – is, in fact, Stewart. Here I am to welcome all you beautiful humans to this pit stop world – and my eternity – Constellation Planet. Although, might I revive one thing that has ludicrously slipped your hominid mind: YOU HAVE SNAKES ON YOUR ARMS, SOLDIER MAN!'

Whilst my arms have been held out at either side in a rehearsed stance – "*one east, the other west,*" *Master Xanxi used to say* – the pythons have managed to slither onto them and miraculously curl themselves tightly from my collarbone to my elbows and from my elbows to my wrists. They're weightless. No mass whatsoever. 'It's as if they're not even there. I can't feel a thing. They can't exist.'

'*Answer this one, smartarse: What CAN you feel in a dream? Only what you imagine to feel.*'

'I didn't imagine anything!' I protest. 'I'm an old man! I hardly have any imagination left at all! I didn't even see them coming!'

Stewart huffs loudly and shakes his head. '*Honestly, I'd rather teach a duck to fly!*'

'So, they just want to rest on me? I don't understand! Why am I not dead yet?'

'*They know the man in the Red Robe. They caught the scent of his blood, his DNA. Therefore, they have to check if it's genuine. That means—you know—check if it's real.*'

'Real—!'

It's too late for excuses. I scream. Two sets of fangs jet into my wrists like lethal injections and I drop to my knees, pleading for freedom. 'GET THEM OFF! GET THEM OFF!' I cry. As if that *stupid* bird is *really* going to help me.

'*Oi, I heard that dirty thought, sonny!*' Stewart warns. '*For your interest, this is my favourite bit!*'

'How is this *for my interest*? Any of it?' I shout at the bird, my pain overcoming my ability to reason.

'*Because now we know whether you're true or whether you're a fake.*'

'Fake? A fake what?'

'*If the venom recognises your blood as that of the Robe's true owner, you will survive the bites. Otherwise, if it fails to acknowledge the blood of King Jo Xeff, you will die.*' A grin splits the feathers on the bird's face.

I'm quickly collapsing to the sand. But there's no way of me actually feeling the loss of weight in my bones or the weakening of my muscles. The venom running through my veins has killed even the mildest of my sensitivity and, ultimately, I'm losing the strength to hold up as little as a thought (alas, no more entertainment for the parrot with the sixth sense). 'How…?' I stutter. 'How do you d-d-die—in—nnn—nnn—a d-d-dream?'

'*Oh, it's possible,*' Stewart says. '*Just as possible as it is to come back to life in reality.*' Is he telling the truth or is he teasing me again…?

No more sore-pink sunset, but sunrise this time…I haven't passed out yet, just been lying, paralysed in the sand for hours on end…I can only assume the venom has kept me awake this long somehow…its poison cycling through me like a twelve hour motor race for electric toy-cars…

I gaze up into the blurred blue sky, tracing around the premature sky with my eyes. I'm a voyeur of the priming sun. It wavers with the ripples of my vision, my mind soused somewhere beneath it all. Showcasing some of my recharged energy, I roll over on my side to see a silhouette standing where one of the snakes had been on the sand. A boy. Confused…preadolescent…in his pyjamas. And he wore an expression of awe sported only by a child who's sauntered through his entire birthday to receive no gifts at all from anyone or anywhere.

Birthdays? Am I really making these references in this climate? In my current state? It could well have been my *deathday* a few hours ago – and might still be in moments to come.

Instead of coming to my support with his consolation – like any other truly hospitable host would – Stewart bypasses me to analyse the boy. Fair to say, they're both just as stupefied as I am.

'Papa?' The child's timid, his head dipping under the bird's flapping wings. He looks up at me with glassy, pardonable eyes. 'What are you doing here, Papa?'

My lips spasm. 'Thuban, my boy…you…came here…like me? What—they stole you too?' I say.

'*We generally expect a populous number of arrivals on Fridays,*' Stewart remarks. '*The human race can be exhaustively demanding come the end of the week.*' The bird restlessly clears his throat and then perches upon Thuban's shoulder, carrying an impatient twitch.

On my feet again, I realise the pythons have disappeared, though their mark has been left behind as an engraving of their bodies, sewn into the arms of my robe.

'*The snakes can recognise your potential. Your blood clearly is – in some way or other – related to Jo Xeff,*' Stewart announces awkwardly, sincerely disappointed. '*You are a descendant of the royal bloodline and a relative of the Last King of the East.*'

'Sometimes you have to appreciate that you do not truly know who and who-not you are related to in the East,' I explain with *toldyousobirdybird*-glee quickly diluting my bitterness for the snake venom in my veins. 'Draconex must have been a distant cousin somewhere down the line.'

'*Nevertheless, the Robe has been officially validated as yours. It rightfully deserves you as its owner. Bear it well. Aside from the fact you arrived at sunset – which makes you a Night Dreamer, Soldier Man – you are the owner of Jo Xeff's Red Robe, which, if ancestral legend is anything to go by, delegates to you the prime responsibility to slay the creature that silences the stars and consumes the Void between universes. East blood is a vital advantage in orchestrating the defeat of the Drag-in. Though, of course, for the time being, your tenderfoot bewilderment distracts you from the nature of the devastation brewing here. The king hasn't yet summoned you to the Palace. Allow me to enlighten you in advance.*'

'Yes, please do!' I plea to the blasted conscience with wings. 'Where are we? You brought me and my son here and I want to know why!'

'*How shall I begin to explain? Well—you're asleep in Mankind's World and awake here. Of course, we've established that. There are very few I've met who have been successful in escaping the habit of sleep – I'd go as far to say: not one – for it is the inevitable consequence of being awake. You are definitely not dead. As much as people presume they are dead when they first arrive here, they're surprised to learn that their senses are, in fact, more alive than they have ever been. You can think for yourself, you can manoeuvre and function as you wish, and every sense that would otherwise be taken for granted in the real world is just as reliable here.*'

'We're lucid dreaming,' I contemplate, troubled by this idea. It doesn't settle too easily for me. Perhaps, we've been kidnapped by West Troopers, and maybe we're being drugged into a hostile state while we're held prisoner in an enemy camp? Or radiation poisoning! That would make plenty of sense!

'That's one of the advantages of being a Night Dreamer: it allows you to breach through the Memory Lane, a.k.a. the Void. Any other average Dreamer would find it impossible to connect their mind to memories or revelations that are distantly located in reality. Some call it delusive trickery or an anomaly in the Stellar Gods' selection process; some somnolent boffins warble about it being some inexplicable science; I call it the incapability to multitask.'

'Who are these Stellar Gods? Is their selection process totally random? And is that how I got here—by chance? If so, how am I a so-called "Night Dreamer" and my son isn't?'

'Whoa, let's not get too ahead of ourselves.'

I inspect Thuban, stroking his chest to see if his flesh is as solid as what I'm looking at. He's all there, just like me. 'There must be a reason we're *both* here. In the same dream. A coincidence. Will we remember it the same when we both wake up?'

'You'll remember it slightly differently. Every Dreamer's experiences surface on Constellation Planet for all to see, but the variations in your own imagination and how you personally perceive these new imageries show up in the minor details. You rarely notice these small differences, unless somebody else brings to your attention specifically what they can see from their point of view and it contradicts yours. It is perhaps the closest a community can get to idealism,' Stewart dictates. *'The best way I can think to describe it is how you'd never seen a python before in person, but your imagination could manifest their appearance based on how your taming master had described them to you. It is why the pythons never advanced to attack, because you couldn't imagine how, if, or when they might have done so. You only knew how to respond.'*

The bird's right. I've never tamed a python – never laid eyes on one. I must have been an embarrassment in front of my son, an amateur in the ranks of snake taming.

'The charm with this world is that the Dreamers who arrive here are all linked into a similar subconscious brainwave – it's a bit like being connected to an online computer server. Individual real world experiences are saved and logged here like a psychological database. Millions of them."

'Maybe we *are* dead, Papa,' Thuban springs into the conversation. 'What if the whole of Quomer was destroyed overnight and we were none the wiser? The West wouldn't do that again, would they? It wouldn't be able to. Not like they did Eighth in Blackout Nine. Could they?'

'He can remember,' I pinpoint, observing my son's shrewd input. 'My boy can remember home. Just like I can. That doesn't match what you just said about the Memory Lane and its restrictions on the mind.'

'*He can remember to an extent. The longer you are here, the more your memory of home drifts away. Most newcomers arrive with a single, distant memory in mind. Some reminisce their most spectacular celebration, whilst others remember their darkest hours. Bittersweet nostalgia. That's the weak spot in the Void, the one that allows greater leeway for New Dreamers to break through and their conscience to awaken here.*' The bird hops off Thuban's shoulder and lands at my feet. '*You, on the other hand, Soldier Man, have a Night Dreamer's conscience, which is superior to most. You can prevail this wall more freely than the average Dreamer.*'

Taking a moment to consider what the bird's saying, I study my son and his melancholy expression paints a comparable picture of my own fragmented credence. 'How long are we stuck here? Until that *Drag-in thing* you rattle about comes and eats us?'

The parrot chuckles like a paternal figure would after having just heard the most adventurous, yet adorably innocent, of remarks from their young'un. '*You can leave whenever you wish, Night Dreamer. Just wake up in your cushy home and throw on your comfortable real world skin again, go down into the kitchen, open the fridge and make yourself a bowl of cereal, all while the rest of us perish. Actually—I tell a lie. You'll perish too. The Void will snap like a rope and the Drag-in will squeeze its way into Mankind's World just the same – ending the fragile balance of existence for both of us.*'

'You never explained why you're a talking bird,' Thuban says unassumingly, as if he's just dismissed all of the seriousness that has been orbiting around the situation.

'*Telepathic!*' Stewart explodes. '*Must I repeat myself over and over and over and over? I am a universal life form with telepathic abilities, meaning that my body exists in the real world, but my co-existent subconscious mind lives only in the Dreamerverse. Here, on Awakening Coast, my innermost spirit is imprisoned. I am totally disbanded from my original self; now a fluttering ball of confusion with a beak—alas—I am stranded here, with no affiliation to my conscious counterpart in reality whatsoever.*'

'And this is where all the Dreamers arrive?' I inquire. 'On this shore?'

'Seeing as you both **awoke** *here, it would make sense, wouldn't it?'*

The parrot's sarcasm does its best to dissuade my investigation of this magical coast, and fails. I start towards the water without any further consent. Screw him!

'Where are you going?'

'Yeah, where are you going?' Thuban repeats in equal pitch to the bird's squawk of alarm. 'Dad? You're going to get wet. And you're not a very good swimmer either! Don't let the current snatch you!'

'But can it, my boy? Can it really do me that much harm?' I respond. 'I figured, being alive in a dream would have its perks, like walking straight through the ocean and not drowning, nor getting even the slightest droplet on my cutesy robe. All that I'm prone to in reality has to be an improbability in this world. Would that also *make sense*, birdy-bird?'

'You should know how much I despise being called a "birdy-bird",' Stewart's feathers stand erect, as if prepared to launch an attack. *'You should also be wary to stay away from the ocean water at all times.'*

'Why's that?' I retort feistily at the bird. 'Huh? What's a bit of water going to do? Might I get a jellyfish sting or is there a shark lurking there, waiting on the ocean floor?' The water meets my bare feet, warm and delightful with the morning sun glazed on it, like the icing of a birthday cake. I see the horizon. The big, orange ball of fire has fully ascended from it. A new day as prescribed from the unthreatening absence of a "Drag-in" that I'm convinced does not pose a danger, or even exist at all in this *fairy world*. I've persuaded myself that it's all an illusion, a dream with no concerning repercussions.

'Papa, I think you should listen to what the birdy-bird says!' Thuban sides with the parrot. Not a daddy's boy at all. He was always the seed of his mother. *Teased by the other boys at the Academy. Scorned by my brother, his uncle, for being "a tad too soft in the middle". "Nothing but a burden is a son swinging from wench's breast until the age of four," my brother Earnest used to criticise. Although, in my honest opinion, his mother had never been a wench. She'd been an extraordinary, young and beautifully flawed lady with her heart ultimately in the right place...His mother's love and support during those darkest years of the Conflicts had meant goldmines to me. At a time, returning home to her company in Quomer was all I had to fight for. Until, one day, I returned to Quomer and she was nowhere to be found. My luckless wife had been stolen from me, and probably rebranded to become a mascot to some rich East Man...*

I'm waist-deep into the water when I turn around to discover the bird is gone. No goodbye. No *good luck getting back to reality, Soldier Man*. None of that waffle. Instead, there's…a naked girl walking along the shoreline, skimming the tide with her toes. Her perfect skin is exhibited teasingly in the shy morning light. It must be the first time I've witnessed a woman in full nudity in years. In the East, such crimes as streaking or flesh-bearing are forbidden. So, a woman without an inch more than nothingness on her body is a spectacle to my sight. As much of a spectacle as all that hair can unleash. Golden strands, spilling down her doughy back and covering her bottom like a stringy skirt of a trillion skinny threads. Now I recognise her. After *many years without her*, I still recognise that shape…that saunter…but not that hair…the hair is different, new to my memory of her. I twirl to alert Thuban, wide-eyed and rabid. 'Your mother! Thuban, my boy, your mother's here! She's alive, my boy! She's alive!'

Thuban's head cocks left and then right, adrenalised by this announcement, yet overthrown by so much apprehension that his movements are rigid. Failing to find her on the shore, he looks back at me and shrugs. 'She's there! She's over there!' I actually point in her direction, amazed how he cannot see her. She's walking further across the sparkling shoreline like a dream within a dream. Thuban doesn't acknowledge it. A look of urgency piles onto him. My wife vanishes. Thuban drops to his knees, and ducks his head into the sand.

That's when—my foot sinks unexpectedly—into a hole in the seabed—

SNAP!

The mouth under the water clamps shut, burying my foot in the ground. A hard and overbearing pressure immediately starts dragging it deeper below. As chunks of seawater slap my cheeks the lower I descend, I gasp through the pockets of air that come with my drastic arm movements parting the waves—

SNAP!

There goes the other ankle! And I'm under! I swing my arms higher and beckon pleadingly with lungs swallowing heavy gulps of ocean. I'm drowning here! Is anyone coming? Is anyone coming? Is anyone coming? 'THU—BAN! HE—LLL—HELLLL—PP—MEEE!' I capture a glimpse of the shore. The girl with golden hair sits there – *She's back! Back to save me! I hope* – on the shore's edge, gazing out at the empty, blue horizon. But she's not there to help. She's totally blind to my struggling. She's sitting on the edge of the coastline, faced against the current and watching the waves collide on her knees with a quiet fetish.

Suddenly, I feel fingers starting to work on the clamp around my ankles. Light, brittle fingertips are running along my shins and thighs like bubbles climbing up my legs. Thuban's arrived and he's mustering some kind of magic on the creature at my feet. Over on the shore, between intervals of the water violently battering my face and its sweetness – surprisingly, not saltiness – getting in my nose, I spot another girl. Taller. She's standing beside the golden-haired beauty. My wife is no longer stark naked. She's wearing a silver gown. 'Your—mother!' I gasp. 'Boy—There's your mother! Call her—!'

The other girl on the shore – the stranger – bends down to her, as if about to whisper something. She places a hand on my wife's shoulder. Then my wife lifts an arm, pointing out into the ocean, in my direction. That catapults the other girl into a sprint. She's running towards me, hands held out. As she goes, she calls back to my wife for her assistance, but my wife doesn't flinch. 'STAY STILL! DON'T MOVE!' the stranger demands. Grappling onto my arms, she signals to Thuban to pull in sync with her. 'With me now—! Pull, pull, pull! Quickly!' she commands. After four attempts, I'm free of whatever was holding onto me. The mouth in the seafloor that digested my legs burps up an effervescent spray off glowing light-blue water, which spumes on the surface until the pit it came from zips up completely.

I'm floating on the water, like a boneless, muscle-less, spineless slab of meat and while I'm in this state, more cries break out. They belong to Thuban. I force myself up and search with disfigured vision and a fatigued body. The girl with soaked ruby-coloured hair is struggling to tug him up from under the water on her own. 'Poor boy's drowning!' I screech, temporarily helpless with a paralytic weight keeping my body numbly adrift from the crisis. 'He's going under! My boy's going under! We need to get him out of the water—back to shore!'

'Quit whining and give me a hand!' the girl with ruby hair has committed herself to amateur lifeguarding skills. She's a big, strong girl, but she alone is not enough manpower. I strain my fragile body over and weakly grab Thuban's other arm and we both rip at him in a tired foray to tear him out of the seabed. There's no doubt he'll be walking away with at least one dislocated limb – or, perhaps without a limb intact at all.

The light-blue substance secreted from the seafloor spreads until all three of us are encircled in a ten-metre ring of its twinkling glimmer, radiating off the water's choppy surface. Overwhelmed by the power of the water's livid spasms, the girl and I slip from Thuban's arms. Whatever it is, it's much stronger this time round, vengeful and compelled to beat us to my son. And he finally sinks far too easily, screaming, gargling. A huge pit forms in the water and he's swallowed like a spider in a plughole. The girl drags me from the space as I stare in bewilderment and we escape with our lives, back to the shore upon which my wife is now absent. Absent also is my conscience and no talking bird can compensate for it. The words are gone. The thoughts are gone. The placid ocean breeze is far more foreign than ever before. Numb, it seems I can only latch onto what I am forced to see…not my family anymore…but this world of perpetual nightmares.

From the sand, I watch as the pit seals and the whirlpool above it resigns, slurping under the layer of glowing azure water with it, and a flat, tranquil current replaces the disturbance. Everything returns to normal. I drop to my knees; in this same place, Thuban had done the same. I stare blankly at the horizon; in this same place, my wife had done the same.

Chapter Eleven
The Red Robe

Someone had tried to wake him in the middle of the night (or smother him...as a pillow had been slung over his head and left there). The duvet was warm – a little below body-temperature to be accurate – and the mattress was creased on the other side of the bed – in his wife's place. It was two in the morning. Lord Camson had yet to remember that he'd slept with a different woman that night.

On the glass bedside table, right beside the gold-plated lamp and its sparkly shade, was the note that the ignominy had left behind, and the tip he'd put there had been snatched away like cold turkey. Lord Camson sat up and switched the light on. The iridescent lampshade lit up the walls, reminding him of all the stars he saw in the sky of his dreams. But, moreover, their being on reminded him, with all the common sense allotted to him at this weightless hour, that it was also night here in the Land of the Woken. *Still the middle of the night?* he thought. *At least, it was dark outside. Pre-dawn, then.* Either way, he should have been sleeping. He had a heavy day coming up. An even heavier week ahead.

Out in the corridor, he found his way to the shower room, took the antidepressants that he should've taken the evening prior to that morning, and cleaned his teeth before throwing on a bedazzled, silk dressing gown, labelled: EAST DRAGONS.

The light went on in the kitchen all by itself and he popped his head back into the corridor to spy out who was there. *If she's still hanging around*, he thought, *I'm gonna want that tip back*. She hadn't been that good anyway. He'd had much better ones in the past, ones who'd had lots more time-flexibility. Like his wife did. His wife had always made time for him and Thuban. Of course, she did many of the wonders mothers conventionally performed. But her way of doing those things had been an intricate work of art and he admired the way she was committed to her little masterpieces. He'd respected her views. He'd respected her decisions. And he'd followed her like a smell at times (good and bad). A testament to the transience of their forgotten marriage, Lord Camson supported the old traditions of his wife like a lifelong sports fan to their team. He had pledged his allegiance to her like he had to the *East Dragons* – when they weren't losing to their arch opponents (the *East Phoenixes United*) that was. Now she was no longer around to be his primary occupation, he clung onto his final vocation of happiness...and never since had his life been so influenced by Ball. He charged out of the shower-room like Trentiki Ballownoo, paced the corridor like Eian "Twinkle Toes" Xampson and made a surprise strike for the kitchen doorway like Mark Monsoon...

It was empty in here. The kettle was running and only the counter-light was on. *Another spontaneous power surge*, he imagined, relieved. *Nuclear energy wipes them out like grass in a dog's backside and they still think they can control it; don't they know ants can't control the anteaters?* This latest surge would be another thing for the people to blame the power plants for. More petitions: *END THE PLANTS, END THEIR TERROR, END OUR SUFFERING – THINK OF THE CHILDREN. Think of the fossil fuels, think of the fertile land, the sugarcane*, he thought and chuckled, *think of the money*. Only, what people didn't realise was that *THE PLANTS*, whichever they may have been (the ones that grew out of the ground or the ones that grew out of piles of cash), were what kept everybody alive (and happy, to some degree). He switched the light off and killed the kettle's commotion. Then, he waded back through the corridor of darkness. He was clean since stepping out of the shower, but still incredibly heavy and tired. Yesterday, he'd attended a "scientific viewing" on the other side of the globe, down in the Southern Polar Region, in fact. The flight-time had robbed five hours of his life, jetlag had knocked him back six, and it felt like yesterday hadn't existed at all. *It was cold Down South*, he humoured again. *Why do you think all the polar bears went missing? They weren't endangered or scared of the West Men coming to poach them – not like you're told. They were hiding from the freezing snow and the biting ice...duh!*

He trailed off in mid-thought. At the other end of the corridor, a door swung open freely. *It should've been the wind...*was a stupid presumption to make. His hometown, the city of Quomer, was enveloped in the middle of a desert, and the flaming hot weather lady whom Lord Papamyong smooched with in his suite downstairs had predicted the next two weeks to be mild to nothing, dry and still. *Here in Quomer, there is no wind in the night,* he kept reminding himself. *Doors don't just swing themselves open. Children don't just swing themselves in the park. Us parents do it for them because their feet can't touch the ground.* He moved slowly towards the door, more and more speculative of the fact that he may not have been alone after all. When he finally got there, he just remembered what room it was that he was about to enter. Not in three weeks had he entered this room. The designers had plastered over the walls only last week, during his absence to the SPR, for he couldn't bring himself to look at those walls – painted cartoons of parrots and monkeys and gorillas and lions and baby-blue phoenixes, pictures drawn by his former wife. She had been a woman with a taste for arts of all kinds and one wild imagination he couldn't quite empathise with, until lately. In tandem with the wallpaper, he couldn't withstand the sheer agony of looking at the *East Academy* workbooks amassed on shelves and the old and new *East Dragon* jerseys hanging (some completely unworn) and the sacred place where he set down the…well…it was where he set down the ancient robe, of course. The mighty Red Robe that had once belonged to the last great monarch, King Jo Xeff, was the artefact Lord Camson wore to bed every night, and every morning, he laid it on the pristine bed of his son, which hadn't been slept on in a week. It seemed like forever since that drama began, since that very first of the recurring nightmares had blitzed his happiness, as if some otherworldly paradigm had soaked up his mournful sorrows altogether and cheated him of the passing days…Whenever he went about questioning his son's disappearance, nobody ever remembered Lord Camson having a son. Thuban didn't exist to them. He wasn't real. He was a fable. *A dream…*

Camson stormed into the room and slammed the door behind him. His son's room was empty. Once again, he'd been imagining the worst and the thumping migraine that had been taunting him for the last seven (real world) days was back, spontaneously. He was riddled with an anxiety of the size he hadn't suffered since his post-traumatic stress disorder, following his service in the Conflicts. Why had he forgotten to take those antidepressants? He'd taken them too late the previous day. It had reached a stage where he was beginning to muddle up mornings and evenings. It all just appeared to be…time. And now, his head was playing games with him in the middle of the night, or dawn, or—whatever it was! He took his face in both hands, preventing burning hot tears from melting through, and, like ritual, he removed the Red Robe and left it to rest on Thuban's bed.

Back in the corridor, someone was standing there. Someone was looking at him from the moment he reopened the bedroom door. Now, it was hard for him to imagine anything, even if he did have the wildest of imaginations under the influence of prescribed drugs. An intruder. He didn't have his gun. Not even his sword. Oh, this person had a weapon all right. They had a sword of their own, and the blade was running down the side of their thigh. A woman. An intruder *woman.* A woman *intruder.* A *woman intruding.* This was unthinkable. But he said nothing. A *woman intruding with a sword?* He could still have been hallucinating. Either way, he wouldn't have known with his head severed. 'It's a bit late for this kind of foolishness, don't you think?' he tried, squinting sourly at her across the blackened corridor. 'Kind of dark to be playing scare-games on an old man.'

She was dressed in an open cloak, sand-mask and boots, bearing her long legs. *Bearing her legs!* Camson almost gasped out loud. For a moment, at least to Camson, it appeared the reception everywhere was *frosty cold* – and it was particularly colder *Down South* for some more than others.

'Came dressed like a warrior, did we?' he chuckled pathetically. 'I don't remember leaving you a tip, sweetheart.'

'You know why I'm here, and why I'm equipped, traitor.'

'Is this supposed to be a robbery or not?' Lord Camson sneered smugly. 'Clearly, I've done something to bother you. I'll get my chequebook out, shall I?' In that very suitable moment, he went for the wallet in the pocket under his lapel and remembered the pocketknife he kept in most nightgown pockets. Like quicksilver, he fished it out.

'I had a feeling you were going to be reluctant.' Unscarred by this act of defence, she stepped towards him. 'But I haven't come to kill you, my Lord.'

'Oh—though, you've certainly come to offend me. How dare you bare your filthy skins in my residence! Exposing yourself is untestable evidence for your mad-capped trespassing on marshal property, a burglar's attire! I should see that you have those legs of yours amputated!' He prodded the knife at her, knowing he'd eventually have to place it between her eyes. 'But I'll crack your skull in two before they find your… starkness. That way, in my utmost sympathy for your mistaken – and perhaps drunken – display here, you won't have to bear the shame or the pain of your punishments.' He knew the courts in the East. Very well, in fact. Once been an Ex-Con himself when the past had treated him worse than the present. He knew they were filled with a conservative-majority jury; he himself had been preached the East Law and knew that the Only Oath guarded these laws, leaving little room for dispute; he knew unwaveringly traditionalist East judges ran them and the judgement for Infidels and liberals of all distinctions was nearly always 'guilty'.☆ Without a doubt, they would as easily eat this "Damsel Certainly Not In Distress" – "Nor From This Side Of Town" – for breakfast just like the rest.

The woman in the mask must've been fearless. 'Save your dignity, my Lord,' was all she said.

He was starting to stagger. The power of the night was taking over again and he could sense himself falling asleep as he stood. There was something unnatural about his state, something surreal in this contagious tiredness. *It's the blasted Dreamerverse coming to get me again*, he suspected.

'Save your dignity and go back to sleep,' she said. 'You've got a big week ahead.'

'What have you—' he stuttered, '—done?'

'Those pills you took were soporific draughts. You'll be out for a good five or six hours. When you wake up, I'll be here with the girl, and you'll come to a decision.'

Camson sank to the floor, half-leaning against the wall.

'A decision?' he said.

'Whose side are you on?' the woman spoke confidently as she marched away, leaving the *old soldier* to rest.

A couple of streets away, Aegia had a motorcycle parked up in an alleyway. She hopped on and made a fortunate night trip through the vacant city of Quomer. Shops in the market square were closed for the remainder of the week in preparation for the upcoming Dusk of Offerings Festival and due to reopen on the Festival Day, tomorrow, Sunday the Twenty-First of July.

As ever, curfew was still in play this early into Saturday's dawn, so there were no streetwalkers to look out for at crossings or cars to jostle past at traffic lights. Having not been a citizen – let alone having

☆ East Courts were typically biased franchises and their branches were inherited via bloodline. The judge/franchiser owned the courthouse and their next of kin would inherit the branch, painting their precinct with the same brutality and dictating the law as they saw fit (sometimes recklessly without heed for either side in a case). Judges were authorized to do as they pleased under the untouchable Only Oath.

not set foot – here in fifteen years, Aegia humiliated the speed limit with gas. Ripping past street after street...*Awol Ninth, Owensil Fifteenth, Nector Twenty-Third*...she avoided what could have been a measly seven or eight out of service Camera Drones along the whole way. Not one A.I. in sight. East A.I. were notoriously the worst lawful liability anywhere in the world. They were far less politically correct than those in the West, but they still drilled their data-cores full of updated legislation day in and day out, just like any uncorrupted (or less corrupted) A.I. would regulate their systems. All Androkind were programmed to refresh their data automatically. If anybody in the Sixth Nation thought that a "half-naked" woman riding a motorcycle at the crack of dawn was a capital problem in a city rampant with criminals, they hadn't been challenged with execution by a walking-talking Tin Man with a capsule to retrieve their vaporised dust as forensic proof for their blasphemies. *Sex on Wheels* was accelerating at eighty on the freeway.

By the time she came to the end of the freeway and to the edge of the city, where Quomer's border was met with the desert, a shantytown welcomed her. *It was a rotting water lily licking its wounds on the rim of a swan's lake. A bit like the flop that the City Slumberlands had evolved into over three decades*, Aegia poetically compared the two. *Only, this neighbourhood had been "licking" its corporate wounds forever. There hasn't ever been a time when Quomer's Ghetto wasn't wallowing.* She left the bike parked up in the garage beside one of the huts. These huts made up the neighbourhood and went on for blocks and blocks. Removing her bulky sand-mask, which also doubled up as a decent riding helmet, she made her way over to the hut's front door and let herself in.

All the lights were off inside. Lined along the floor were sleeping bags, dozens of them. One for every member of every family in the household it seemed. "*One big-arse sleepover*", she'd joked about it to Samuella the night they'd been rescued. The helicopter had taken them from the Southern Polar Region to the docks of the Sixth Nation; from there, big *EAST DRAGON* imprinted cargo lorries rapidly carried them from one side of the border to the other, imbued with the stench of cheap sports sponsored beer. Here, they were on the parallel between the Sixth and Seventh Nations. The city of Quomer and the yonder desert surrounding it. When they'd arrived and taken their first look out into the desert, the eastern border of the Seventh Nation was nothing like Samuella had imagined it to be – the most part of it being the nine hundred thousand acre estate of graveyard for West missiles and matchlessly radioactive wasteland. The metropolis of Urbania wouldn't be for a few hundred miles past the Virgin Desert. *Fifteen years was a long time*, Aegia thought, as she peeped through one of the dusty kitchen windows and out at the wasteland.

She hung up her cloak in the bathroom and tiptoed around a few more sleeping bodies to make it to the bedroom. Everything was on one floor. That didn't make it any less of a challenge. Three people were awake in the bedroom. Samuella wasn't one of them. She was definitely there, prising her way into the centre of attention as she lay vulnerable on the small bed, eyes closed. The man who was there to regularly check her temperature and who'd spent most of the last two days going into the market square to prepare a rota of fever serums was Doctor Falcon Staels. Falcon wasn't really a doctor anymore – removed of his title. Instead, he'd reverted to designing biotechnology ten years ago and was now scavenging for all the approbation that might somehow redefine his medicine doctorate of 2024. The other two were simply there to observe Samuella's stable state, replacing her bandage when the bullet wound on her shoulder needed refreshing and bringing her nice food to eat from the Petti Square, which was much closer and more convenient than the Market.

'The Square's closed until Monday,' Aegia said, going to stroke the thin coating of sweat from the poorly girl's cheeks. *It's a lot less clammy than it was*, she thought. For a moment, she pictured the polar base again, the horrors they'd witnessed, the descending helicopters and how lucky they'd been. How lucky they'd been to get away in the knick of time. How lucky *she'd* been to get them all the way here. 'That'll mean the liquids you're using may be the last for a while.' Aegia hesitated. 'She'll need to get better on her own for a bit.'

'I cannot see her *saving the world* anytime soon,' Falcon chuckled. He was an old pensioner, grizzled and tired all over. 'Some day I can see her recovering to full strength, but Sunday is far too soon. That may be demanding too much.'

Aegia was suddenly startled, immediately abandoning her polite reservations in the company of the sweet old doctor. 'But she'll miss the Festival and there'll be no one who isn't an outlawed Infidel left to kill Xenol!'

'How do you expect her to stage a revolt against a foreign dictator, in an unfamiliar land, under weak guidance and with limited support?' Falcon argued. 'It's not happening! Not even if she were a hundred per cent better!'

'*Weak guidance*? Who do you suppose is "*weak guidance*"?' Aegia repudiated, affronted by his arrogance. 'I am light-years from *weak*! I dragged the girl here with my bare hands, and now she will repay me by rising to the opportunity of—'

'She isn't killing anyone!'

'What puts you in the position to decide? She is my child, my daughter! Who do you think you—?'

'I know perfectly well what *my* role is, Aegia,' Falcon said. 'And I'm definite that she will not be leaving my sight!'

And that was it. All it took. Aegia drew her blade again and raised it to the man's throat. The point almost pierced through and very nearly drew blood straight away. 'You don't know how long I've waited for this opportunity, how long the Infidels have held back for this moment!' Tears began to form in her eyes. She was trembling. 'You don't know how far I've come…I just lost my husband for this cause…You don't know what this revolution will mean for all of us!'

'I do realise what it would mean to assassinate a tyrant,' Falcon said calmly. 'But it won't be committed by a dying child. Have some responsibility for once!'

'We could be free to live without the fear of the Tin Men. Our children would grow to be fearless and liberated and open to each other with opinions of their own—'

'The Tin Men?' one of the other two lending a helping hand interrupted her. He was a formerly imprisoned SPR captive from the West who somehow managed to escape and risked everything he had left to rescue hostages in East POW Camps here in the Sixth Nation. 'Do you mean the robots? No more robots?'

'The A.I. here in the East follow one leader. Once that dictator is killed, once Phestor Xenol is no more, snap goes the cord, the marionette will fall and all of the A.I. will cease once more.' A little hopeful smile seeped through her tears. 'Imagine it! If we could reignite a world like the old world! Like how it was before the old monarchies were overthrown and backwards dictatorships sprouted from the hatred of modernist ideologies – political correctness disguised as conservatism kept the wheel of deception spinning, while the likes of Phestor Xenol, Serpens and the Philsons ascended to power. The Tin Men and their hounding legislation have kept the systemic mockery in check; there was once a better time, before separatist dogmas pitted Nation against Nation! A great People's World *did* exist under the Old Democracies of the West and the East!'

Falcon failed to respond. He turned to look at Samuella, landed a palm on her forehead and sighed. There was a short silence as Aegia took an aggravated stroll around the bedroom to let off steam, leaving the others to their passivity. It was a child's bedroom. That was clear, even though it didn't seem like it from first glance. Colour had been bleached from the walls; there were no posters of pop culture like those belonging to the fanatic teens of the West; and, most surprisingly, there were no toys. What was a bedroom without things to play with? Since the Only Oath had come into the Phestorship's regime of the East, the children were no longer entitled to *play things*. Because no one could be sure whether some of those instruments of luxury had in fact been made by West manufacturers. Aegia could remember the time long before the Oath had contaminated the laws – at least, the backend of it, the dying embers of it. She could see all the children of the East playing with their toys, out in the open, and it didn't matter where they'd been made or what they'd meant.

There, in the corner of the little stripped room, she found a cupboard with one door balancing on a hinge and the other closed shut. She tried it and discovered further darkness inside, save for a lone photograph sitting on a shelf. Taking it into her hands, she blew off the dust and squinted at the stained image within the frame. It must've been at least thirty years old. And it was recognisable to her, just like everything here had been up to this point. It was her home, after all. It was her perished world. And it was her parents in the photograph.

After about five hours of lying coldly unconscious on the floor of his hallway, Lord Camson shook awake and lumbered about his residence like a bewildered boxer during the aftermath of the twelfth round. Was there a game he was forgetting to watch? He wondered. *Nah, it was too early in the morning.* He was pouring himself a cappuccino; steaming the milk in the machine his ex-girlfriend had bought him (he'd never been a true fan of the graceless woman, but was an aficionado of her cappuccino-making; so now that he'd mastered the swish to her wand, he believed there was no use for the witch herself). *Besides, the East Dragons generally play on Tuesdays and Fridays*, he continued to remind himself. *Today's a Saturday—*

Saturday!

The coffee mug in his hand dropped and shattered on the floor. He broke out of the null mind he'd been abandoned with five hours ago and searched for the clock. The watch on his wrist was broken – the glass-screen had smashed when he'd collapsed and dozed off. On the wall, the clock he marginally relied on read: **09:12**.

He was an hour behind schedule. It left him only three-quarters of an hour to get rapidly dressed and zoom out to the meeting he had at *Drag-in Inc.*

Would he make it? There was no guarantee.

Shower, done. Teeth, done. Hair... hmm, could do with a little more attending.

Lord Camson threw on his traditional East work-robe. The one that he was known for. Not famous like the regal Red one that he wore to the Dreamerverse and back, and then religiously laid on his son's stone-cold bed. He was renowned for many superstitious things these days, but he never really cared if they portrayed him as the worst company in the universe. After all, he was *the mad man who had an imaginary son* that everybody parodied. It felt like the last seven days had been all that'd ever existed of the real world. Beyond that – when the massive reptiles stormed the earth and the early people were learning the basics of making a fire – may have been feeble, wishful thinking or ultimately may never have happened at all. Life could not have felt shorter than it did now for Lord Camson. He avidly believed that if he took one step too many, he might fall off the edge of his sanity, and be stripped of his reputation thereafter.

This robe he usually wore to work – the one he wore now – was black and burgundy, and it sealed away much of his flesh, including a veiled sand-hood that hid his face. There was a slit on the hood's veil, through which only his eyes could be spotted. Atop the chest of drawers in his bedroom he saw the conical hat he generally wore with his best robes to important meetings, yet he chose not to for this occasion. He quickly shovelled on his sandals and there he saw, beneath the drawer cabinet, a large revolver that lay hidden away. The same revolver he carried whenever Phestor Xenol ordered him about in a "situation" of great secrecy. The last place he'd carried it was in the Southern Polar Region, two days ago. There, he'd spilled the blood of the infamous Infidel spy, Lord Pegasus.

The sleeping bags were still there as morning aged into noon, but the sleepers had vanished, leaving them vacant for the next crowd. Aegia was the only one sitting at Samuella's side when Saturday morning matured. Outside was a hot, red sun, raining down dry heat through the bedroom window and onto the duvet. Aegia folded the sheets over a bit, so they only came up to Samuella's hips, just to allow the girl some breathing space to cool her down. Falcon had rushed to the black market, Petti Square, to find out if any local pharmacies were open aside from the main market in Quomer's town centre.

There was no point anymore, Aegia thought. They'd come so far and, yet, still they had managed to fail at their initial aim, their *only* aim. *Kill Xenol!* She rolled it over in her mind. *It was that simple! Kill Xenol before Serpens is given the girl! Protect the girl with golden hair before she's slaughtered! Prevent Evanessa's slaughter from provoking another war! How will such an alliance between the Decider of the West and Phestor Xenol continue to fair? It is weak, fake and hard to contemplate. Two enemies who are that separable would find it impossible to become so mutual. Both are keeping secrets from the other and both surely have 'alternative plans' of how things are going to turn out once tomorrow's deed is done. This won't last. It will end in chaos.*

Her thoughts were abruptly interrupted by someone standing in the doorway. 'You stuck with her all the time?' It was the voice of the young West boy she'd spoken to on the day of their arrival in the Sixth Nation. The Polar Region escapee with a slippery Fourth Nation twang in his accent. 'Is she your daughter?'

Aegia laughed childishly at him. She sounded younger when she let out a roar of hysterics. Much younger. She nodded her head and sighed, hoping these lethargic clues would answer his question.

'Earlier, you said that she was the only one who could end Xenol and disband the A.I. Is that true? Because, if it is—and, if in practice, she fails to pull it off, will the Conflicts get worse? Will we all finally see our reckoning?'

'Hmm.' A small and unintended smile came upon Aegia's face. 'Nah—I don't think it can get any worse after tomorrow. Do you?' She laughed frantically again, this time at her own sarcasm. 'Though I suppose something awful could always happen.'

'How's that funny?'

'I don't think it's funny,' Aegia said. 'I think it's plausible. Just as plausible as how, on the flip side, we could all live through this and move on with our business, much better off.'

'And that's only the case if your daughter miraculously recovers overnight to take your Infidel grimaces into her own hands.'

'Spot on, *mi amoro*.'☆

☆ *Mi amoro [East Dialect (colloquial); singular pronoun]: My Love [West Dialect (standard) transl.].*

'Doesn't placing all this pressure on her shoulders make you feel—guilty?'

'I missed her growing up…I missed her father just before he was murdered. I've never lauded myself as one to be in the right place at the right time. My current track record of being in the wrong places at the right time and the right places at the wrong time have measured me with the unpredictability my job requires. I have a service to humanity above all else. As for her…' Aegia lightly poked her finger under the fold of the bed's duvet and ran it across, right over her daughter's waist. I've squandered Samuella her whole life – for that I am guilty. But I'll be even sorrier when I fail to do my duty to restore freedom for the future of mankind.'

Strangely, it felt to Aegia that her brain was detached from the rest of her body. It was floating mindlessly like a message strung to a balloon and drifting high into the sky. 'You were a prisoner, weren't you? That's what I remember you telling me.' She cut her eyes at the boy, not meaning to be as intimidating, or as smug, as she may have looked. 'Came here how long ago?'

'Eight months,' he answered.

'What made you? After you escaped the SPR, that is. What convinced you to come to the East?'

He looked down at his feet. Too embarrassed to explain. 'I was never a prisoner,' the young man admitted shyly. He flicked his eyes up at Aegia and saw that her mouth was wide open and her chin was hanging down low, suspended between shock and distrust. 'I was invited there, for research purposes. There had to be somewhere in Mankind's World where the City and its Surveillance couldn't catch me out. I had been the most wanted man in the First Nation. The Sixth Nation gave me the asylum I needed, and so I was in the Southern Polar Region, and then I've been in Quomer since last December. Just before I'd made the decision to flee the West, I was pushed over the edge when the Decider ordered his A.I. to storm my accommodation in the City and they executed my roommates while they were legitimately dwelling there.' The young man's words were forced out, not easily retold. His throat clogged up with angst as he recited them to Aegia, and he looked anywhere besides her face. 'It happened one afternoon I went out to the Octane Mall with a few guys I knew from the Academy. The four of us had all been colleagues at the City Academy together, but I'd been the only one not to get kicked out before Second Annual. At the Academy, I was studying biotech and robotics. Had a whole project underway, with the focus being on building a self-updating, self-maintaining

Artificial Intelligence. It was going to be a prototype for an ultimate design of Androkind – would've been the first in the next generation of A.I. with genuine emotions filtered depending on specific situations and the first in Androkind history to *recognise empathy* and make their law judgements based on character and lie detection, rather than odds, numbers and statutory boundaries. Imagine what an accomplishment that would have been – my defining masterpiece. I was planning to name the prototype ADAM and he would have been a *remarkable* feat in human technology. To think, if I'd have completed work on ADAM a little earlier and been commended by the Academy and Androkind Inc., I might not have had to struggle all the way to the East. I might not have found myself here, in this situation.' He paused thoughtfully, remorsefully. Then, continued. 'Anyway, there we were, taking the *TRAMLINE* back to *Blotoneau Avenue* that evening – it was there where I'd been living since I moved to the City. Said bye, then, up I went to the fourth floor, my residence – it was also where I kept my lab. I arrived at the door…well, there was no door that night. A vaporisation beam must've blown a hole in that plank so strong that there was nothing but a few screws and a bump or two of wood chippings on the floor. When I got inside, it was worse. The entire place had been ransacked. Television was smashed, furniture was toppled over and spewing dust and foam, wind was blustering through the windowless frames and on the walls were what seemed…well, what seemed at first to be humanoid stencils. They were life-size and they were black as if drawn with one of them old-fashioned graphite sticks. I ran my finger across the head of one and it left a line, my fingertip picking up some of the charcoaled residue. My roommates had been incinerated shy of an hour before I arrived.'

Aegia's delirious smile faded. Her emotions clouded her lack of sense and her wild, selfish thoughts became intact with the rest of the world again. 'But what could they have done?'

'Nothing. They were innocent,' the young man said. 'When I reported it to the City A.I. Commission, all I got back was a major waiting game and a not-very-conclusive finality I could only stomach to excuse as an incident of "Culturing A.I." that had gone on a rampage and I had been lucky to avoid it. This speculation went on for months, until I could get through to the Commission. Eventually, there was a meagre apology for the "inconvenience", but there was obviously no way of reversing the damage the A.I. had done. Up to then, I had been guessing that it was the rare act of rogue Tin Men. It was like they'd just decided at random to go up four floors in a residence building on

Bloatenau Avenue and take out their anger on an innocent group of students who'd associated themselves with me and taken me under their wing. After a month of no response from anyone – not the A.I. Commission, nor as high as the Decider's Administration itself – I only realised what had been going on when I tried to send the Academy a *HoloGraph* to voice concerns for my own safety…and I noticed that my *Axernet* address had been bracketed by the Surveillance. All my contacts had been blocked and every communication I attempted to make had been rigged. That was the moment I decided to leave the First Nation. It was because of me my friends were killed. Those people had done nothing wrong.'

'I'm sorry to hear that,' Aegia said. 'But that wasn't your fault. You were trying to do good for the A.I., trying to improve them! There must have been a reason for them to target your home—was it blackmail?'

'I have completely come to terms with the idea that it was no mistake, not random at all. I can only imagine that the people who ordered that attack sought to threaten the inventor of a new line of "Empathy A.I.", a line of Androkind that was quite controversial at the time – and still is. The Decider's Administration didn't want an emotional A.I. Force about town, at large with their own minds and opinions on the law of the land. The West doesn't want the risk of the A.I. liberating themselves from their societal roles someday and bringing civilisation to its knees, completely embarrassing mankind. That will be the day we'll witness a conflict like no other, with, potentially, the end of humanity not far behind it. So, what do they do to prevent all that? They blackmail the inventor – the advocator of an A.I. revolution, as they see it – and they chase him out of the City in doing so. Congrats to them—they succeeded.'

'They've succeeded *so far*,' Aegia hinted.

'Like they always do and will continue to.' The young gentleman sounded somewhere between pessimistic and relieved. 'When their stronghold on technology is up for grabs – whether that be their lock on the Media or their dominion over the A.I. – the powers that be in the West will shut you down so easily. For years, my uncle believed that manipulating this digital mechanism was the only way to subvert their agenda. I had spent much of my time at the Academy looking into this concept, unaware that the Decider's Administration had been keeping an eye on my research.'

'What happened to all that ambition? The biotech and robotics and City Academy?'

'All that?' he flapped his lips, blowing a raspberry as if it were a bad joke. 'That went down the pan. There wasn't a chance I'd go back to any of it.'

'And ADAM?'

'Deprogrammed him and tore him apart without hesitation. Though, in the wake of what happened to my home and to redeem me from my depression, I briefly tried drawing up blueprints for another "Empathy A.I." – ADAM's upgraded sibling: EVE. But I scrapped it all. I was so angry. I was terrified for my life *and* I was furious at the same time. My livelihood had been outlawed by His Decidership's Administration. But, after that awful day my guardians were killed, there was nothing I could do to change the past. That day, I was so lucky! So lucky not to have been there, and to have been the one who survived and is speaking to you right now! Speaking to the woman who is leading the movement against the Administration.'

He stopped talking for a minute. Just stood there in the doorway, envisioning the past, over and over like a film reel on repeat. Then, he went to sit on a small wooden chair – one of the chairs Aegia used to sit and sew patchwork dolls on as a child. Aegia dropped her head to look at Sleeping Beauty again. The dreaming princess had stopped sweating and was as close to a picture of health as she could have hoped. Well, a picture of recovery at least. Then, the boy spoke again. 'That's why, when I came here to find that you and her had showed up and heard you talking like you could *stop* the A.I., I felt something I haven't in ages.'

'What?'

'An urgency to strip back the Decidership and its control over the A.I.'

Aegia didn't know what to say to this. *Stopping the A.I. now would be harder than ever*. 'Well, the IRC have discussed that the best way we could execute such a high stakes attack on the New Democracy is at the Dusk of Offerings Parade tomorrow around noon, where both key leaders will be present in the company of Phestor Serpens. It is the greatest opportunity we've had in years – an unmissable one. If there is a chance we can get a target on Phestor Xenol as he is passing over his offering at the ceremony, then it would be possible to strike him at an accessible range, and without singling ourselves out or drawing too much attention. This moment will be a rift when all focus will be on the two men making the exchange, a weak spot for us to take action.'

'What is that offering?' the boy became more and more intrigued.

'Xenol's mistress.'

'I refuse that! Why would I advocate you to murder the guest of Phestor Xenol, the man who granted me refuge in his Nation? Partaking in such a campaign would ruin my chances of retaining asylum here. It would put my life in jeopardy!' he complained. 'I'll have no part in it!'

'I'm not asking you to—'

'You don't understand! I can't even be seen *speaking* to you about it—!'

'It's *her* who needs to be responsible for the attack—the girl—neither of us!' Aegia clarified. 'What is more important here? Your reputation or billions of lives?'

The young man was shaking his hand at Samuella now, dubious of what to think. He didn't have much of a reputation left. His head was sunken with his chin tucked into his chest, as he brooded over the impossible plot. 'You want *her* to kill the Phestor? Only *she* can kill him? Nobody else?'

'Yes. Only she can kill him,' Aegia repeated.

'Now, I don't quite understand how this all adds up. I don't know either of you that well, other than your associations with the Infidel Alliance. Though what I'm most disappointed about is how a woman of your wisdom and experience can shove your own child into battle – and, specifically, one she isn't fit to fight on her own.'

'She isn't on her own,' Aegia said defensively. 'Her father and I have done nothing but prepare for this moment. A pivotal victory will instil itself in her generation's future. She will appreciate her role in this more when she's older. She'll be so grateful for everything we did for the betterment of her future, even though it meant we could never be there to see her reach this stage in her upbringing. Saving the world is a full-time job, you know.' Aegia indulged over these last words, however her spirit landed flat on the young inventor's ears, for he only reacted with a cold expression.

'What *upbringing*? Don't you think your girl would be more grateful if her mother had been at her side, holding her hand as she grew up and sparing the time to teach her the world, rather than being hidden away and scheming when she would become an asset to her parents' assassination plot? You kept her in the dark and only showed your faces again when you needed to use her!' the boy grumbled with a bitter taste in his mouth.

'I had no choice but to leave her behind! Her father and I led a dangerous and unpredictable existence! We couldn't even disclose *ourselves*, or we'd risk our *own* expendable lives! Our enemies would soon find their way to her, if they ever caught us out! That is no world for a child!'

'You really had *no* other option than that?'

'Of course!' Aegia professed.

'Appalling—I must say.'

'But I want to do whatever I can to revive our relationship, once this is all over,' Aegia vowed. 'I swear, I have been so sorry for so long. Even now, it agonises me that I can't express it to her. After we've finished with Xenol, I want to retire from secrecy and apologise to my daughter.'

'Is your daughter supposed to be a *trained* assassin, *master* assassin? If this thing you've roped her into means ending one of the dictators and preventing the A.I. from murdering any more innocent people, I'll do it myself. Give me the responsibility. I have less to lose than the child. My naivety with the Androkind failed humanity once…Allow me to make up for it…so I can cure society of these cyber-bullies once and for all.'

'No. She must do it alongside her fellow Night Dreamers, so that they can procure the final emerald and expose the Drag-in. He's pulling the strings. Hopefully, we can find out why he's mapping out all this mayhem.'

'The Drag-in? Are you referring to—?' The young inventor staggered. 'You mean you've got a link to an emerald of—?'

'Digimine.'

'*Digimine!*' He swallowed hard. '*You've found Digimine! Wh—Wh—Where?*'

'Hold on—you've heard of the Drag-in before?' Aegia picked up on this sharply. 'You know about the Dreamerverse?'

'Yes, well, my uncle used to tell me stories about a place called the Dreamerverse and I used to think they were nonsense. However, now you've mentioned it and talk of the Drag-in, as well as Digimine, I'm very, very intrigued—'

'Your father told you these stories—?' Aegia interrupted. 'Who was your uncle—?'

'Never mind that now!' the young man disregarded hastily. 'Tell me more about the Digimine you've found and how you came about it—but quickly and quietly.'

'I've spent a decade researching into the function of Digimine. And you know as much as I do: Digimine emeralds are the secret recipe to the cogs of an A.I., the only receptor to all of the A.I., and the vital power source to all their Grand Databases dotted around the East and West. Digimine is in their makeup; it's the fundamental ingredient of their DNA. Nothing else can intercept it. Digimine is a phenomenal fuel, much more powerful than atomic energy. With as little as a chip of that mineral, we could study a way into that DNA and learn how the Drag-in makes them tick. We can terminate them from the inside. Those emeralds are the single utility to deactivating the A.I. What happens to them determines how much longer humanity puts up with the Tin Men and their unstoppable guarantee of brutality employed by whoever controls them. Right now, the last one is still the possession of a former Night Dreamer – the Phestor's mistress herself. Whoever is rewarded the Phestor's mistress tomorrow is also rewarded with a key to the A.I.'s control. We already have two of the stray Digimine fragments intact and safely in our inventory. However, let's just hope that the third emerald doesn't become a belonging of the Drag-in's come tomorrow.'

'What the hell are you talking about? *Why's that?*'

'In both the Dreameverse and Reality, one thing is clear: the Drag-in wants authority. In the Dreamerverse, the Drag-in wants to consume every living thing in existence. And in the real world, it is believed the Drag-in wants to take control of the A.I., giving him supreme influence over everything in the world of the conscious. Unless *we* can get hold of that emerald first.'

The inventor huffed. '*Drag-in*, huh?' he chuckled at the madwoman over whom he was still debating his trust. 'How do you know who this Drag-in is? Have you *seen* him? Has he declared himself to you?'

'No. But we've narrowed it down to one of the Phestors. We're confident it's most likely to be Serpens, since he made the request for the girl the very second he heard about Xenol's moves towards appeasement in the West.'

'Appeasement?' The boy threw his head back and rocketed into laughter. 'Do you actually believe those were talks of appeasement between Philson and Xenol?'

'No.' Aegia knew she was treading on thin ice. 'They were crafting ideas to do a job on Serpens themselves.'

'Then how do you suppose it's in Serpen's interests to be this power-hungry Drag-in you go on and on about, and that Xenol doesn't just want the Digimine for himself? Would that make *him* the Drag-in? Because I'm quite sure Xenol and the Decider know exactly what miracle that radioactive mineral works for their own authority, and they'd much rather keep the recipe a secret between themselves.'

Aegia closed herself off from the young man, her grimace disconsolate and forlorn.

'Your *Drag-in Man* could be anyone. You're walking blind into danger.' Then, he shot up from the little seat Aegia used to sew on as a child and hovered by the door again. He hesitated in the doorway, trapped on the thought of the trouble that she and her daughter had been through to get to Quomer. 'Are you gonna come with me, then,' he said in a jollier mood. 'I don't wanna get breakfast on my own.'

A compassionate smile returned to Aegia, as she excused her stiff upper lip for a breath of triviality, and shortly forgot about Samuella, getting up to follow the refugee boy out of the room. 'Well, I should probably ask whom I'm breaking fast with before they try to poison me,' she joked.

'Oh—it's Drake. Though most folks call me Professor Islington.'

The Draconex Building was the newest addition to Quomer's modernising cityscape, not shying from being the tallest skyscraper in the capital yet. Under a tourniquet of scaffolding, it was still growing. Those who were already hard at work inside it, the pen-pushers of a new generation in East enterprise, were always roaring louder than those somewhat "lesser" countrymen on the timid streets below, heedlessly skittering from their straw-thatched bungalows to their straw-thatched family-owned kiosks on the roadside, and wearing their straw-thatched hats (not really). Such victorious premiers were those of the high-rise noise, so ascended, that not one soul down on the ground could ever hope to hear what they said up there. But what the people of Quomer came to realise in the last two years of its domination was that it was *the expensive Dragon phallus up in the sky* that protected them from being targeted by the West – a fortress akin to Citadel Tower in the First Nation. It was in this skyscraper where the dignified minority of the Sixth Nation's perverse policymakers, aristocrats and entrepreneurs convened (few of whom would bat an eye at the taxman).☆ Now both sides of Mankind's World had a trade centre engineered to negotiate around a nuclear holocaust.

☆ There was only one taxman in the Sixth Nation. He went by the name of Phestor Venrick Xenol.

In the Sky Lounge – which was more or less an oversized café that annexed the whole of the Draconex's top floor – a splendid coffee table of beautiful purple cloth, handcrafted china plates and bedecked grails and cutlery had been laid out, prestigiously prepared within a mist of East fragrances and incense, for the team of important men and women who currently occupied the space in the corner of the room. These formal suits had to themselves a cluster of comfy sofas and armchairs organised around a *HoloGram* that presently showcased a live image of *Mayn Street*. A comfortable space for important people was never a good thing, as it almost always meant that arguing – a *whole itinerary* of arguing – was imminent.

Lord Camson, having arrived just on time, was a small addition to the company of the Phestor of the Sixth Nation and his guest, the Decider of the West. Xenol sat in his favourite red wingchair with the Solar Blade laid across his lap where he could see it – it looked almost like he was secured under the brace of a theme park ride. And Decider Philson was in the blue wingchair facing him, accompanied by an East-interpreter, translating tongues whenever the language barrier stumbled and became an issue – for there were "other people" present. Kanal Sandrez was the Chancellor of the Sixth Nation's Treasury, and his personal secretary, Amila Xinx, sat in close proximity to him (almost too close) on a long couch. And perched coldly on opposite ends of another couch were Mandrew Kindicku and Saneo Ghine, both whom were supposed to be responsible for organising this year's Dusk of Offerings celebrations.

Xenol had his trademark gleaming smirk printed against his wearing face of crooked lines, both straight and bowing. Though newly polished as it was from the excess lubricant he rubbed into it at numerous points in the day, there protruded a great hidden weight in his expression that he wouldn't be able to conceal for much longer, like the eventuality of a cosseted pubescent boy being pushed on a park swing by his aging mother. He enthusiastically examined his company as an autocratic ringleader would before addressing his following of protégés. Then, he spoke boldly and to the point.

'I appreciate that we are all here to discuss an affair that will hopefully be resolved cleanly tomorrow at midday,' Xenol croaked from the invisible podium in his head. 'You will already be aware of this, our special guest—I'd like to introduce Decider Philson of the West, who I invited from the First Nation to aid us in this difficult mission.' There was some ambivalent simmering and scowls from the other faces around the Lounge. Spite drifted on an air of murmurs. Luckily,

Camson had his own face hidden beneath the black sheet of the mouth-cover on his hood – otherwise he'd have put some very ugly pigs to shame. 'The sole purpose of this gathering is so we are clear on how tomorrow will unravel. Those of you who know me most understand that I am a man who doesn't enjoy surprises – or violence, on that note.' He stroked the sword. He couldn't help it. 'So, in advance, I've tried my best to plan this scenario over a couple of years. Theories of how such an assassination might pan out have been a thought of mine ever since I became a Phestor. The SN Assassins have been lined up and prepped for tomorrow's events, and they will be positioned around the city centre where appropriate.☆ Hopefully, we'll be able to strike at him from a point within the carnival crowd itself. The carnival is sewn into the festival celebrations all through the day, so there'll be huge crowds plugging the streets and loud commotion at the time of strike. We'll be progressing at a snail's pace, but will strike Serpens like a scorpion. The Phestor arrives at *Mayn Street* on the float around midday and my speech will be made to the people of Quomer, upon stopping at the road's intersection. There and then, he'll ask for the girl as his offering. Like a man and woman in matrimony. And performing as the brilliant hosts we are, we'll appear to hand him the offering. The exchange of the rings. Just yesterday, Lord Kanal and I managed to finish our side of the deal over the *HoloPhone*.'

'Yes, that's correct,' the Chancellor butted in. 'The oil and the diamond cores located in the Yubba Crevices – just off the east border of the Gungolian Plains – are already ours.'

'At the point of "matrimony",' Xenol resumed, 'the girl will presumptuously be his to walk away with…but then…'

His words slipped away, as Evanessa entered the room. She was covered from head to toe as usual, covering her damage with a beautiful

---

☆ In this current era of the East, the pompous independency and security of each individual East Nation came before any kind of unity shared throughout the region. Therefore, every East Nation had its *own* army, had its *own* slightly differed currency and its *own* marginally altered take on the same religion. The Sixth Nation even had a secret defense group, the SN Assassins – a band of around nine hundred rogue rebels and youths who'd been disillusioned by the warped religion of Draca, and who had been trained with the Anti Revolutionary Corps (ARC) in the Southern Polar Region. The Assassins were hired to protect the Sixth Nation (*and no other Nation*) at its borders. Being the East's leading state, the Sixth Nation had enemies both externally and internally, in the West and the Infidels (the IRC – the Illicit Revolutionary Corps). The East didn't trust *itself* nearly as much as it didn't trust the West.

robe to put to shame everyone in the room. Lord Camson admired her refreshing presence, taking significantly more notice of her than anyone else.

Her aura was pleasantly familiar to him. He enjoyed vouyeuring the delicate calmness she bought into the tense party. But, hidden beneath her shielded guise, he couldn't place her face in his mind.

'...And then the girl will step down to the middle of the float for Serpens to approve his prize,' Xenol concluded, 'and that will be the moment when Serpens claims his Offering: a single bullet. No one will see it come, and no one will hear of it until it is gone, by which time Serpens' body will be strewn at my feet.'

Like a sole dove among crows, Evanessa sat down on a stool in the furthest corner of the room, as far as she could get from the table, while keeping within earshot of the conversation. She stayed uninspired, staring at the enormous head of a papier-mâché dragon-puppet that one of the festival organisers had abandoned on the floor.

'Where will we be present at that point? Will we be there to watch? *I* hope to keep out of view,' DCD. Philson said and took a sip from his glass of flavoured red-tongue-dye.

'Oh, you'll be there for the show, DCD. Philson. On one of the slightly more peripheral balconies in the market square I believe, but omniscient still nonetheless. Serpens is expecting to see both our faces, just so he can be aware that we're not trying anything dodgy.'

'He remains suspicious?' DCD. Philson asked.

'Always suspicious. He is the most sought after individual in the world. The man has escaped over a hundred assassination attempts,' Xenol informed. 'Killing him will be an almighty task. But I feel tomorrow will be his unlucky day. We have enlisted the support of the SN Assassins - a division of our best young fighters, drawn from among the most impressive cadets of the ARC, freshly uprooted from our Obedience programme in the Southern Polar Region - and their seniors, the SN Troops, will be incoming if battle does break loose and those pesky IRC Infidels come out of the woodwork, preaching liberalism. Even though I am confident the Infidels don't pose a threat in the realm of...' Xenol curled his hand around the sharpened metal of the Solar Blade and pulled the tip of the Blade very close to the butt of his chin. '*Even though* Secret Intelligence shouldn't be—and *isn't*—a point of Infidel interest,' he restarted, 'I am experienced enough to be aware of the ways they like to draw attention to themselves in crises like this. When it comes to Infidels, there's one thing you can be sure about

– they're more reactive than receptive. Keeping details as quiet as they are now should keep them quiet too.'

'Who'll be the man to take the shot?' Lord Camson said. 'Surely, he'll have to give the signal for us fellows to run and escape. It's no good *any of us* hanging around for the rest of the fireworks to kick off. You'll need to cross the border as quickly as possible to get to safety. The Seventh Nation's retaliation efforts must not be underestimated. We may have a minimum of thirty minutes to distance ourselves from the potential Blackout Zone after the bullet is fired.'

'Potential Blackout Zone?' Mandrew fretted. 'By that, you mean evacuating the city entirely, surely?'

'My Lord—you're insinuating the probability that Quomer might "go up in lights" when Serpens is eradicated,' the Chancellor companioned the festival planner in this fear.

'Yes, sir,' Camson confirmed. 'Not might, *will*.'

'Then, we're mad!' the Chancellor gawked.

'So are they,' Xenol sniggered. 'Anywho—good riddance and farewell if things do play out that way. Our future is located in the Seventh Nation, not in this arid wasteland. I want diamond cores, not shamming skylines and accords.'

'You're outrageous enough to write off an entire city for what…a few mines of glitter in the Far East?' the Chancellor tried to denominate the Phestor's outright treachery. 'Something gives me the feeling that there's more to this than oil and diamonds. What else is out there in Seventh that has piqued your taste buds, Phestor?'

This offbeat speculation from Sandrez was uncalled-for and Xenol made it very discernible by stowing the Blade behind his chair and ignoring the Chancellor's inquiry.

'Oh, and before I forget to mention it – the SPR insisted that I kept this a secret – there have been developments surrounding the Scientific Display at this year's ceremony.' Xenol eyed each individual with a bold smile of rejuvenated buoyancy. 'We have today pinpointed a candidate for the surprise demonstration, which the SPR community and I hope to reveal at the ceremony. A little surprise for the people during the parade. No doubt—this selected candidate will be proud to accept the role. He is a man with a lot to repay to both the East and the West.'

'Oh, really,' the Decider hummed, intrigued. 'Then he must have an appetite for discontent.'

'He is an expatriate whom you recently chased out of your Nation, Decider,' Xenol said. 'This task will be his redemption—'

'Who is he?' Camson pushed.

Phestor Xenol rapped his fingers on the foot of his wineglass, having spontaneously and strategically lost his fascination with the Solar Blade; the sword he knew Serpens, the Decider, and even Lord Camson quietly desired so much. Lord Camson desired it as much as the Phestor's sheltered daughter, but Xenol was determined that his bodyguard wouldn't get his hands on either. Not with his head intact.

'Well, a young man named Drake Islington.'

Hours passed and eventually the sun resigned from counting them, allowing the moon to keep tally in its wake. Samuella was up and out of bed. The bullet wound on her shoulder still stung worse than any bee sting before it, but she could bear with it. For the first conscious hour, she explored the empty bedroom: the door had been closed, scuffled sleeping bags lay everywhere, the mould-pocked walls looked like they'd been burnt in a tremendous fire. And Aegia, absent as she was, had daftly left her sword behind. It rested carelessly on the ground with its extendable blade open. *That hadn't been the first thing the East Lady had left behind in her life*...she listened to her subconscious impulse criticise Aegia without really making the connection herself. There was something that needed doing. Something she wasn't clear about and still wasn't aware of yet. She scarcely recognised where she was and what she was doing here. *There was the plane... and the snow...* she remembered that much. *The men chasing us, the hundreds and hundreds of troopers chasing us across that base...*Closer to meaning, but not entirely coherent.

Where am I?

She inspected to battered cupboard in the corner of the room. *Oscar,* she thought, as she peeled open the dangling door, *what had happened to him?* The flashes of that undesirable machine came play on her mind, triggering some kind of friction between her thoughts. *Big teeth,* she reimagined it. "*What big teeth he had*" – this was her mimicking the fairy-tale of The Little Woman In The Red Robe.

Robes? She thought. *What about those? Ring any bells?* Nah.

The cupboard's interior was barren. Sitting on one of the shelves was the decaying severed arm of an old *Suzy Doll* from the year Two Thousand and Ancient, and beside that was a picture frame. The photograph was of a pretty young girl and her parents. This was where Samuella began to put one and two together, for she realised it made sense that the stray *Suzy* arm wasn't the only thing in the room that belonged to the girl in the image. Nor was the cupboard. The entire room was in fact a Little Girl's Room. She'd slept on the little girl's bed and she'd trampled through the random sleeping bags on her decorated rugs. Hidden beneath the bags were the peeking wings of giant blue phoenixes, the uniformly duplicated heads and limbs of Palm Patrollers poking out in their vests and berets and their bows and arrows, and on one standout cross-stitching, she spotted a scorpion's tail bursting from a pit of sand in the desert. These were the beautiful images that had been embroidered into the floor mats.

An East Girl, Samuella visualised it in her mind. All those years ago, Quomer had been a home to many little girls who'd played with *Suzy Dolls*. But, after the New Religion forced the East to make a stricter right turn, everybody in town became enfranchised with the Only Oath and there was no more clinging onto the norm of playthings. Samuella had read an article about this in a *HoloGraph*. There was a new norm. This girl's old man would have done anything he could to remove the dreadful West-contraption from his daughter's possession. And she would have done anything she could to save as little as *Suzy*'s arm. Seeing it sit there on the shelf like a relic in a museum cabinet, a rare survivor from a better time in history, Samuella finally learned she had awoken in the bedroom of a rebel.

Thanks for bringing me home, mum.

She shut the cupboard door as best she could, and was then dumbfounded when she discovered the Constellation Map lying, vulnerable, on the bedside table. It was surrounded by vials and vials of painkillers and hadn't been tampered with since Oscar had opened it on the Regal Jet – these tiny details she could recognise in how the Map had been folded. The best thing she could do was take a peek at the contents and follow her visualised instincts around wherever she was in the East. The worst thing was to stand around like a humble amnesiac pretending to be more hurt than she actually was. It was her turn to interpret the Map after all.

So she did. Only, as it unravelled, she saw the bleakness within. She dropped the Map on the dishevelled bed and cursed to herself. *It'd allowed me to read it from corner to corner only a few smidging hours ago*, she thought…*Had* it been a few hours? Or really a number of days? There was no way she could have known, since she'd been fast asleep for all that time – *overhauling in Dreamerverse Mode, awry in the Tombs of Truth and indulging the inhumed secrets of the Alumni.* Although, rest assured, she saw the parrot sitting on the windowsill, watching her. He'd been spying on her for a decent while, his head twitched through the curtains, boasting over the note he'd carried all this way in his beak. *Parrots in the East?* She was questioning – and reconsidering – a lot of things she believed to be true these days. The bird made a squawk when she snatched the note and exited back out into the blue sky. *Perhaps not a Parrot? Perhaps a mutated bird? Perhaps not a bird at all? Perhaps a transmogrified sewer rat...? Sewer rats were only popular in the City,* she reminded herself, *and I haven't trod on a single one here in the East yet.*

It was a bloomin' parrot – **Full Stop—**

While Samuella had been hectically debating the bird's genealogy in her thoughts, she hadn't watched it swoop into the room and snatch away the Constellation Map from the bed, before it evaded her attention via the window.

The note was written in shorthand scribble. It read: *MAKE FOR DEKNYN STREET, APART 7, 20th FLOOR. COME IN DISGUISE. GODSPEED...*And there was no name.

Where was that?

There was creaking coming from behind her – a sound that traditionally belonged to old doors opening in horror movies. It was the cupboard. Inside, behind the other door that had always been shut, there was a single random outfit. A frilly maid costume, coloured a dark green, lined with black and silver in the stitching. The once-white ruffles, now dusted over, had probably been yellowing before she was born. It hadn't been used in years; age-old cobwebs had settled and festered; there were holes where the moths burrowed to escape from the desert heat. Regardless, looking at it, she understood exactly what had to be done. That one person who had slipped her mind was here in Quomer. And *he* was waiting for her. In fact, *he* was inviting her.

When he returned to his abode that evening, Lord Camson refrained from the professional civilian mind-set he'd trained himself to swallow hard in public and got comfortable again. He stiffly rushed past his son's bedroom and went to his room's wardrobe to fish out a new robe that he could settle into for the night. He picked the penultimate robe his wife bought him for his fortieth birthday – the one he received a couple of weeks before she gave him the Red Robe as a parting gift. Camson liked the night robes he owned. He'd have worn them variously out and about in public, if not for his latest superstition with the Red Robe universally tainting his love for them all. These days, he stuck to wearing the same work robe when he left the house. His divorce from so many of his passions was so bad that he often felt reluctant to select a different outfit to wear out everyday, let alone his unwillingness to leave the apartment at all.

Lord Camson went to grab a drink from the icebox in the kitchen. Yes, he was a '*Lord*' now – it meant that he was entitled to a frosty can of *Kola Bear* and all of its West-brewed glory (as long as nobody knew of these promiscuous cravings; at first, not even he'd been aware of his betrayal—*the soft drink "just tasted too good to BEAR without!"* as the slogan put it). He needed to kick his sandals off and wash the nonsense out of his system. His cholesterol-heavy veins were not apt for the vigour of this level of stress – the mouth-work that was required to keep a sense of familial intimacy alive in tandem with the demands Xenol was constantly throwing at him. The retired general wasn't entirely a recluse. People just didn't know that much about him anymore. They didn't know that he'd been the one to place Pegasus and the word 'DEAD' on the same front page of *Inter Nation*. They had no clue how guilty he felt for inviting as many women as he had into his home since his wife left him, and how many more that number had risen by since Thuban was "erased". They also didn't know about his illusive past, before he became a general ranking at the highest command of the East Army – and for this he was glad and rather keen to keep a lid on it, not purely for his own peace of mind, but his hard-earned reputation and overall safety. But, of course, what grated on him the most was that they'd all forgotten about his son a week ago.

"Lord Camson—had a child? I couldn't imagine that ever being the case."

"Didn't his wife already leave him some centuries back, though?"

"I guess you can't blame that war-soured bastard for having a wild imagination."

Out of his own disbelief for these ignorant folk – some of them historic friends of his – he incessantly asked himself *who were "they" anymore, these "people"*? How quickly these old pals of his had descended into clueless babblers had baffled him. They were now just fabricated voices he'd stocked and loaded up at the very back of his head, like the magazine for a turret in the subconscious region where his nightmares resurrected night after night.

However, what remedied his misery was that he could do all the *Kola Bear* binging he wanted, filling his brain to the brim with enough caffeine to keep him awake and thinking long into the night, contemplating the traumatised veteran's final bullet with which he might serve himself a fatal blow—

Someone arrived at the door that evening. It was late. He wasn't expecting anyone. But he didn't have the anger to tell them to go away. And he didn't have the breath to shout. So, he got up from flicking between *History of the East Dragons* and *Channel X* to go and say *hello.*

It was the *housekeeper.* He'd been disturbed by the daytime *housekeeper* during the night-time. A calamity he found comedic rather than annoying.

'Good Evening.' He forced himself to smile. Nobody would have known why he did, not even him. It was awfully late and this unwelcome shakeup afterhours would have irritated anyone. He made up for this inexplicable stroke of pleasantry: 'I don't recognise you. Explain.'

The girl on his doorstep was a pretty, youthful redhead. He'd never actually met the housekeeper in person – he was always out and about, working with the Phestor uptown, too busy to notice – but he was vaguely sure that they would look nothing like *this girl.*

'Deknyn Street, Apartment Seven on the Twentieth Floor?' she said as prescribed.

'That's here. Yes?'

'Well, Good Evening to you, sir.' She had a unique look. A crossbreed of East and West blood, split almost exactly down the middle. *That was it,* Lord Camson thought. Other than that, there was something else about her he couldn't quite grasp. Something weird and abnormal. Something different. 'My name is Floura Azgella and I will be your new maidservant.'

That was it! Shockingly, she was lacking her cloak and veil, and Camson would have mentioned – that she "*wasn't wearing any clothes*" as such – but it wasn't often a maid-girl arrived in her skimpy uniform alone. Which also made him ponder: *Who is this nonconformist child who "Fear Not The Law"? Did I perhaps...promise this one a "tip" as well?*

'You missed your hours. It's late.' He said this even though he was narrowly aware that the bed *had* been neat when he'd got in. But that was four hours ago and modest memory was nowhere near as satisfying as blunt blame right now.

'Are you sure about that?' she dallied. 'The institution registered me here for this time, sir. Should you have any issues with this scheduling, you ought to take it out with them, my Lord. Not me. Would you happen to be Lord Camson Tientar?'

'No. He moved out decades ago.' He stubbornly tried shutting the door in her face, but she held it back with her hand. 'Look—what is it? What is it that you want? What happened to the last one, eh...what was her name again?'

'The rota has changed, my Lord. She works mornings and I finish up in the evenings. No extra charge,' the red-haired girl was scarily persistent. Confident eyes and a lot of height to compliment it. The first thing Camson documented was that she was much taller than he was, abnormally more so than most other women were. 'It's a round-the-clock service from now on! Wouldn't you prefer waking to a tidy residence in the morning as much as arriving home to one in the afternoon?'

'No,' he snapped.

'My Lord, please understand that a young, single East Woman needs a minimum wage to at least make it to the next working day.'

'You? Here? At this ungodly hour? What else is in it for me?' Lord Camson suggestively crossed his arms, foot ticking like a timer.

The girl sighed. 'Haven't you heard? Recently, what happened?'

'Not much of a listener.'

'The rats are back. You know? The Green Ones with their eyes falling out and radiation spilling off their backs? The government is demanding overtime in maintenance trades, since the Infidels decided to release thousands of buggers from their burrows at the power plants. It's all spurred from those environmentalist protests, you know? They're rummaging all over the city as we speak. It's turned into quite a strong matter of emergency, so you must let me in to check your premises are clean. I'll be very speedy!'

Lord Camson needed to process this before he responded with anything half-stupid. It was difficult to tell if she was lying. She was sweet. She was pretty. And he could have done with a spare housekeeper - regardless of how many moths had been at her uniform. Besides, even if she was lying (which she probably was), he was more prepared to deal with an *intruder woman* than he was last time—*when was that again?* He couldn't remember. 'Hmmm, well, you'd best come in and get to work, Miss Azgella.'

Or so he thought.

Aegia tossed the duvet about, flapped out the mattress and searched beneath the bed, as if to assure a nine-year-old child that the monster had well and truly gone. In this case, Samuella was certainly nowhere to be found. Falcon and Drake stood on the other side of the bed, watching her trash the room. 'You said she was incapacitated! You said she wouldn't have had the strength to even sit up! So, why's the bed empty?' she barked.

'What I said was that her neck muscles were in a fatigued and moderately damaged condition,' Doctor Falcon claimed. 'Her ability to move her upper body - *spontaneously*, now it seems - was unguaranteed. She would have screamed the whole time she was on her feet! The fact that nobody heard her get up is uncanny! That either means she was picked up and removed while she was asleep, or she woke up and hopped out of bed like a Friday morning - in which case, she has made a miraculous recovery and I need to fetch me some of them black market painkillers for the old discs in my own back. How about you try taking a bullet to the shoulder blade, and let me know when you're ready to just throw the whiplash aside for a stroll in an alien city! On another note, I actually left you here to *watch her*! *Your* end of the deal was to keep an eye on the child!'

'She was sleeping and the injury should have had her out cold for days! That's what *you* said!' she argued back.

'A couple of days would have been a compliment! The girl could have been up and healthy by Monday, if you'd have just kept an eye on her for an hour or two like I'd asked!'

'That's not the case anymore, is it!' Aegia reasoned. 'Now, she's definitely up and about, whether that's on her own two feet, or in the arms of a stranger. Either way, the predicament is in no one's favour. The girl is in the most dangerous place she's ever been!'

'She isn't with anyone,' Drake considered cryptically. 'Nobody's kidnapped her.'

'How do you know?' Aegia said.

'The Map is gone too. She must have taken it with her,' he pointed out. 'The Constellation Map, right?'

'Where did your uncle decide to stop telling you all this stuff about the Dreamerverse?' Aegia added curiously. 'How can you know so much when you haven't been there?'

'He'd been there himself, and remembered everything he saw. I was only told the stories.'

'Is this what night nursing turned into, then?' Falcon blamed. 'The pair of you trading bedtime stories?'

'Perhaps, it was my fault then,' Drake said apologetically. 'I pulled her away from the girl. It was only to give her a break from all the stress, goddamnit. I felt bad.'

'You left the girl unsupervised to flirt around! Is that it?' Falcon sat on the bed, rewarded Aegia a filthy look of disappointment, and dipped his head between his legs. 'You dragged me back into this medicine thing just to mess me around? I risk my career finding this strange girl drugs that are illegal in this Nation and you don't even seem the slightest bit fazed by her safety. Your biggest concern is your silly Infidel assignment. Your experiment that has already blown up your face, but you're far too arrogant to admit it. Just cut your losses already—forget about it and move on! You carry on with these fallacies about this *rare, revolutionary resource* and this mysterious *Drag-in Man*—rescuing the Phestoress from that nut-job Phestor—but other than your *Dreamer Girl*, who is now missing, you have nothing to show for it!'

'As irresponsible as it may seem now, you have to realise that her health isn't the paramount problem right at this moment. If anything, finding her in a hospital tomorrow would be much more fortunate than finding her at the hands of an A.I. or any other dangers that lurk the streets at night,' Aegia reasoned. 'This is the Sixth Nation and she doesn't belong here.'

'We can't wait until tomorrow,' Falcon said. 'We need to find her tonight. Otherwise, it might already be too late.'

A scream broke out from somewhere. Outside. More followed in asynchronous harmony. While they'd been arguing, two huts had been torched and agitated flames were now working their way through the shantytown. People had evacuated from the surrounding huts and were running past Aegia's home with deranged speed.

The fire wasn't the last of the terror.

Something else was coming.

Beyond the smoke, the presence of an outnumbered, yet impactful, force was overwhelming the county and quickly approaching. Aegia, watching from the bedroom window, commentated: 'They're here. They've found us.'

This old uniform skirt bites at the skin a smidge.

The new housekeeper of Lord Camson's residence had begun her evening shift in the bathroom, where she sterilised the bathtub with the Weapons of Mass Bacterial Reduction stored in the sink-cabinet.

But there was no obvious work that needed to be done; the residence was near spotless, so the shift was clearly too brief to be professional. Samuella hadn't brought any of her own cleaning materials – instead, she was using his. Who was she fooling?

Before she'd started, the taps were already sparkling like they'd been untouched since the morning do-over, which made her wonder:

did Lord Camson have a knack or a lack for hygiene? A perfume spray or a natural odour in the air (it was hard to tell) shyly lingered like a boy who didn't want to go to school – and stuck around throughout her shift like the same boy twenty years later, not wanting to leave his parents' basement. Whatever it was…it stank worse than the mothballs on her costume.

Give the country girl a cow dung any day.

Once the bath looked smooth enough to be a gnarly skateboard slope, *Floura Azgella* replaced her tools of the trade for the little thing she kept closest to her. The humming rock, that had vibrated all the way to Lord Camson's abode and which she had partially used as a compass, was in her pocket. It was warm and paternally heartening. And it was the reason she was here. That single radiant emerald of hers. Enigmatic in its oneness, there was no predicting where the other one had got to along the way. She'd been out cold for two days and the last thing she could remember…

"*What big teeth you have*".

The Regal Jet. The lethal injection. The incarcerated polar bear. The undesirable machine and its monster…*Big Teeth.* And, of course, the running…

What she saw next was vivid and not a memory. It was situated right in front of her, revealed from behind the opening bathroom door, and had taken form as a wholesomely lurking shadow—belonging to Lord Camson. He stood there looking at her, his legs spread apart.

The little green rock fell back into her blouse-pocket.

Floura Azgella showed him a rickety curtsy, then spoke, 'My Lord. How has your evening been so far? I hope that my work has been to the highest standard and hasn't been too interruptive.'

He was looking her up and down, as if searching for something he'd already found. *Just checking.* 'It's not evening anymore, rather well into the night I'd like to think.'

She gave him a smile. It was awkward. She got his hint that her time was almost up. Only when he stepped slightly to the side, indicating that the doorway was meant for her, did she recognise something very appealing about the veteran. Lord Camson had an *EAST DRAGONS* jersey beneath his nightgown. The letters were capitalised and fluorescent. She'd seen them play a few times – the greatest Ball team on the planet. In fact, the East treasured the club so much that entrepreneurs, businessmen and oisters from all four corners (including the eastern-most West Nations, Third and Fourth) had invested largely, and now it was more than just a branded household name. It was life. Gave the people of the East something patriotic to glorify, other than the walls built by war. There was also something else she saw, about his robe this time. He'd changed into it at some point during her time being there. It was the most beautiful robe she'd ever laid eyes on.

The Red Robe.

Floura Azgella did not inquire. There was no need to upset her new client - well, not yet - and things seemed to be going well so far. She entered the corridor, not speaking a word. As she made for the door, her eyes swam about the place.

Bookshelves were on either side.

Silver-rimmed chandeliers swung above.

Glossy oak-wood flooring had been laid with patterned rugs on top.

She thought, if she looked hard enough, the thing she'd come seeking for would call out to her. The little emerald was still vibrating in her blouse-pocket; it could sense its sibling. It was somewhere in here. There was no denying it. The parrot had led her here. It had to be here! Or could it have been something else…?

Behind her, Lord Camson stepped out from the bathroom, shut the door, and began to follow her closely. Like guard and prisoner, they walked. An intangible frogmarch. Solely thin air between them. He had both hands behind his back, clasped around a tube, not revealing the blade concealed within it.

The blade would be released once Samuella's hand met the doorknob…

The A.I. came from the flames and broke through the smoke. These weren't conventional designs at all. These were padded and bulletproof, helmeted and armed with upgraded guns. Riot A.I., for civil unrest, uprisings and urban furore. *Killers.*

In the small bedroom that had once been hers as a child, Aegia was collecting her belongings and throwing them into a dirty, old bag. Robes, painkillers for Samuella, and a few *foroldtimessakes* souvenirs all went in - such as the handy torch she kept under the bed for monsters. She was pretty certain there'd be no coming back after today. This was her last chance to relive the memory.

Drake and Falcon were both standing anxiously in the corridor.

'There's no guarantee that we'll find her now,' Falcon said. 'This is a big city and a lot can happen to a young, injured girl.'

'Why have you been so pessimistic since the start?' Aegia strung the bag together and threw it over her shoulder. She kept the blade-tube in her hand, ready to release for action when necessary. 'We will find her.'

As she started towards them, she felt the need to stop. Only for a second. Just to glance back at her childhood one final time. But it had been a bad time to stop and romanticise – and the hands of Drake curling round her could do nothing but agree – because two figures had appeared in the window, barely hidden by the yellowing curtain. It was like looking at the torsos of two very strong men. Those A.I. had such distinctive shells to house their keen senses. The teetering scanner on the Steel Killers' faces penetrated the thick curtain-fabric that shut out the streetlights…

SMASH!

The window exploded. The curtains parted in flames.

'*Get out of there!*' Falcon cried. '*Get out of there!*'

Floura Azgella's feet landed on the doormat. *One Small Step For Womankind* and she'd be out of there, she thought, away from the shady Lord Camson and out into the open. In a few moments, she'd be Samuella again. However, something was telling her that *Floura Azgella* was going to be making a dramatic exit much sooner than that. It was such an uncomfortable feeling that it made her believe that *in a few moments she'd be nobody at all…*

Her fingers tackled the doorknob. And she saw a glimpse of the incoming blade in the glint of the door's paint. Her head swung violently towards the wall, her hand leaving the doorknob at an instant's notice…

A storm of wild glass, smoke and flame gusted across the room. The impact of the incinerator's blast sent the little bed hurtling into the wall, destroying the semi-broken cupboard. One of the walls collapsed. Outside was now inside.

Aegia tumbled backwards, falling on Drake's chest. Without making a sound, and disregarding all the agony he was in, he forced her to scurry along the corridor – towards Falcon, who had already made a quick run for the backdoor. Falcon was waving to them urgently.

'Go…!' Drake spluttered. Some tiny granules of glass had embedded themselves in his throat. 'Follow Falc—G—G—Go after the girl!'

‘No—you’re coming with us!’ She was pulling at his arm like she wanted to ride the last fairground attraction before it closed.

‘I’m not going.’ He remained where he was, reluctant to go with her. ‘Don’t you realise what’s happening here? It’s not you who they want! You’re not the one they’re after!’

THUD! THUD! Feet landed.

In what was left of the little girl’s room, the A.I. had climbed through the window to establish their new surroundings. ‘Located subject is present!’ One of them said. Its voice was booming, irritatingly amplified.

‘Subject is in close proximity! Search-laser is dysfunctional due to uncompromised environment!’ It was referring to the cloud of smoke that was temporarily preventing Aegia and Drake from being DETECTED.

‘GO!’ Drake growled. ‘LEAVE HERE NOW! GO!’

She scuttled onto her feet and rushed for the door. It closed behind her and Falcon. Now on his own, Drake stood up. She’d bruised his chest, possibly fractured some ribs, and he was rubbing it while the A.I. accosted him in the smoke. ‘Subject has been detected!’ one of them announced. ‘The suitor has been located! The assassin has been attained!’

Outside, Aegia and Falcon wasted no time. There was another, much older motorcycle sitting out in the alley between huts. The wheels were full enough to get them across town in decent time, so Aegia took to the handlebars and Falcon hopped on behind, and together they tore up the main road, speeding away from the exhausting fires that tortured the shantytown.

*

She lay on the ground, her head spinning, and there was a small, but dangerous, man standing above her. He still had his legs placed strongly apart and the sword swung erratically at his side. It had failed to decapitate her. Instead, she’d thrown herself, (unintentionally headfirst) into the wall.

Lord Camson crouched beside her, resting the blade on his lap. His eyes became cutting, worse than the weapon he brandished. Quivering, her lips blundered to produce a curse or an excuse. She knew that the pretty little housekeeper inside of her was gone. That girl was dead. Missing a head, perhaps.

Camson was the first to speak. 'What brings you to the East, Samuella?'

Draco Island...

I choke on sugary waves, gargling as the seawater fights with my tonsils. Stinging my eyes. Blurring my sight. I can only see the cream scalp of shoreline in my right periphery and a slither of horizon to my left. A family of palm tree heads poke out from the corner of my vision, while I drift closer to shore, as opposed to out to sea – the latter being where the current wants me to go.

Land Ho! Thar be shores!

How can this be? Something's dragging me by the legs, *out* of the water, so that the complete party of all my limbs (miraculously intact as the are) can be *Land Ho!* together.

Someone? Is that a person? Not a thing? Those are hands! Human hands! Once I'm peeled from the licking waves and pulled onto the beach, their powerful grasp rolls me onto my back. I can really feel my spinal cord crinkle insufficiently back into place. I train my eyes on the moist gauntlet lifting both my ankles and follow up the blood-drenched arm of my saviour to find the back of the Blood Knight's helmet. Surprise, surprise.

'*Owww—chhh! Leave the Achilles alone!*' I cry, kicking at the gloopy red metal of his armour. 'Can't you check for injury? Did nobody teach you to check for injury first? What kind of warrior are you?'

Immediately, the Blood Knight retreats and draws the sword from its holster, as if challenged by serious danger. I see that the sword is not his original red blade – the one he must have lost when the boat was capsized. He instead holds the Solar Blade, prodding it at my neck. 'Who gave you that, you amateur?' I ridicule, laughing in the avatar's face. 'The Oscar I remember couldn't even nick an itsy-bitsy chimpanzee with that thing.'

'Playtime, is it, you wee pigeons?' Samuella's staunch attitude rises above our minor scuffle. Hearing her arrival from behind him, the Blood Knight removes his blade like a toddler scuffling hidden candy into his pocket when his mother's voice comes calling for dinner. 'Two daft blokes fighting even with a living-afterlife barrier between them. You're fighting with a corpse hosted by a semi-dead spirit, Camson. You're better than that—*surely?*'

'Me?' I retort. 'You accuse me of infantile delusion—and not *him*? Our dripping, red lollipop with legs who rowed us into that Lagoon colonised by a horde of Balænas and that...stuff!'

'Plankton,' Samuella corrects jadedly. 'That stuff that was glowing in the water, before it nearly swallowed us under and knocked you out cold—it was plankton, a bioluminescent microorganism.'

'Did the old grandpa magazines at the post office teach you that too?' I groan. 'Or was it your nerd-cousin again?'

'Neither. I used to see them often, whenever I went fishing with my uncle. Dinoflagellates they're called – Dinomites for short. It was beautiful when they lit up the ocean, right along the coast. They were stunning creatures. I'm not too sure about them here though. Them Balænas appeared to be in as much trouble as we were. Might not have been as lucky as we were to get away.'

'It was a bad idea to let him take my leadership cue into his slippery hands! We were never supposed to rely on sailing the ocean! All Eyes warned us of that from the get-go!'

'Oh, come on, pal—he wasn't that bad. The Knight got us here in one piece. At the time, there wasn't a faster way of getting across,' Samuella says. 'If you had a better idea, *you* would've taken leadership from Scorpius Shore and found a more clean-cut method of *leading* us here! Oscar and I had no problem doing that! Who in their right mind saw the traits of a general in you?'

'I had no signposts! The pair of you got lucky with Bridges and Phoenixes! What did I get? *A suited and booted ice pop!* And, princess, how was I supposed to take control of the situation, when that slimy figurine started building boats out of sticks?'

She tosses the Constellation Map at me, huffing. 'How about you start us fresh on our trail then...*captain*?'

Captain, what a word! I like hearing that one.

Smugly, I unravel the Map and watch as the enchanted images spark into life.

'Why are you still such a tick on Oscar's back?' Samuella argues. 'I thought you'd changed you opinion of him.'

The Blood Knight turns his head and bows it, casting a shadow over mine. Hot air fills my stomach.

'I have,' I reason. 'But that is not Oscar! Oscar can't swim—remember that little detail? The ocean's a nightmare for him and he's totally unfamiliar with it. So, there's no possibility that a Knight who just rescued us from that…*flagellate crap* can be him.'

'The Knight might not be all of Oscar, but a part of him is still in there,' Samuella says, raising her chin to look in some direction over my shoulder. 'And the rest of him is up there.'

I lift my eyes, expecting to find a sky blanketed with stars. Even though the sky is blackening into night, white smoke pierces into it, ascending from the Soulcano.

'We're so close to it,' I gulp.

The Soulcano is the most terrific manifestation of nature that man could hope to meet. But is it nature? Or is it something built with a manufacturer's intent? A natural enterprise with a superficial cause. It is, after all, one massive embalmment chamber. A spirit factory. Churning out a production line of deceased Dreamers. At its heart, could it be hiding something grander and darker?

The smoke...

It eddies down the flume of the Soulcano and escapes from the borderline of the jungle to confront us on the beach. Along the circumference of the borderline are hundreds of caricature-carved totem poles. Columns of majestic men and women. I look at the Map and find *OSTIUM STELLA DEORUM* written across the page.

It translates itself by way of a whisper in my head: '*Entrance Of The Star Gods.*'

This isn't going to be an easy breakthrough.

The smoke becomes heavier and heavier, lurching out to us from between the trees. Up in the canopies, aboveground animals can be seen hurrying away. Beneath it all, deep whirring builds like a roar.

'Is that what I think it is?' I whisper. 'Is it back?'

The Blood Knight draws the Solar Blade again.

'It isn't back. It's been waiting here on Draco,' Samuella responds. 'Preparing for us.'

Then, the terrifying voice invades the shore, bringing with it a blast of the smoke. '*The Stellar Gods will not be your witnesses here!*'

The whirring reaches maximum volume. Unbearable to hear, like entering a beehive that's fallen and hit the ground.

'RUN FOR THE JUNGLE!' Samuella commands over the noise. 'THERE HAS TO BE AN ENTRANCE TO THE SOULCANO SOMEWHERE AT THE CENTRE OF THE JUNGLE!'

'THERE'S MORE THAN ONE WAY IN!' I confirm, intensely scanning the Map. 'WE'LL HAVE TO SEPARATE TO FIND WHERE THE BEST ENTRANCE IS. BUT CAN'T WE DEAL WITH THIS THING FIRST?'

'WE'RE NOT READY FOR IT YET! WE'RE MISSING THE FINAL EMERALD!'

Curling in a complex of hurricane winds, the smoke begins to embody the beast. The Drag-in's crisscrossing entity rips trees apart and lifts the ground in quakes, crafting a tornado around itself as it readies for battle. Then, the face of the beast appears in the smoke, eyes flickering and teeth glittering. Inside its chest, the last emerald glows so bright it stings our eyes. Our fortune is there for the taking. The beast roars up a storm, erecting the sand and the soil and causing them to levitate from beneath our feet, and it summons the lightning from the sky. A storm it has invited to deter the Stellar Gods from interfering with its battleground.

'It has what we're looking for!' I announce. 'We need that emerald before we're capable of anything else—!'

The roll of the tide strengths behind us, and when we look to the Draconian sea from which we came, the foaming waves are tinted sapphire-blue with the luminescence of the Dinomites. The wild microorganisms have chased us to shore and caught up with our unfinished business, creeping up the beach with sheen so lively you can hear it twinkle like tiny bells in the water. If going forwards will be our baptism of death and all that is evil, what lies behind may only be the lesser of two.

Suddenly, there's a clinking sound between us. The face-guard on the Blood Knight's helmet has flipped open, revealing Oscar's whitish and pruning face within. With his eyes closed, he looks at neither of us, totally dismissing our company. And, in brutal emphasis, he commands us to a staccato of three words: 'Make it quick!'

No time to dispute. We make a dash for the jungle, deviating in opposite directions.

As we elude, the Blood Knight springs what could be thirty feet into the air with the Solar Blade poised to match the chest of the almighty monster…

Blinded, the centre of the jungle seems an impossible destination to reach with limited time to spare. I continuously glance over my shoulder, fearing to find a giant face snaking after me. The *Living Smoke* clears the ground of any roots or collapsed trunks. It's thick enough to make me believe I'm running upon a cloud.

There's another roar from all directions.

Then, from above, falling trees crash to ground. I bounce between trunks, seeking out those that have been felled and are now loyally entrenched into the soil. A large, hollow log lying on the jungle floor is where I dive into for cover. The space inside is big enough for me to coil up and duck my head between my knees as the smoke invades.

'*The worlds will become one!*' the voice of the Drag-in hisses. '*They will both expire their independence! I will become determiner of the Universe and the Dreamerverse!*'

As the smoke diminishes, the log begins to slowly rise. Into the air. Through the canopies. The deathly stench of rotting bananas becomes a burden to my nostrils again, to a point where I'm heaving it out of my lungs. Gasping for breath, I clasp hands around my face. The Drag-in's words are angrier, stabbing.

'*From the Hell in which you left me, I am rising, rising higher than any Dreamer! I will tear apart the Void between the Dreamerverse and Reality, and I will become the sole purpose of all creation, once they are both devoured!*'

A scowling face and a pair of whirlpool-eyes beam at me through the hole on one end of the log. The Drag-in's mouth opens and the smoke unleashed transforms into flames. I drag myself backwards, fleeing from the heat, watching the log burn towards me. When it loses its balance, the log tilts and I slide to the other end. Thankfully, the fire has given a moment's grace and briefly subsides. Where the other half of the log had been a blink-ago I'm now greeted only with air and floating ashes. I cling to the end of the log, feet dangling, sinking my flesh into the splintered wood for grip. Meanwhile, the head of the beast has swiftly manoeuvred and now hovers up from beneath me, snapping towards my toes. The emergence of more steam from the Drag-in's nostrils, followed by a hot blast of breath, almost knocks me clean off to a plummeting death.

I realise that the Blood Knight has appeared out from the *Living Smoke*, walking upon the airborne log. The face-shield slams down over Oscar's head and the Knight makes another rapid dive for the Drag-in, his feet narrowly shaving through my hair. The Solar Blade meets the beast directly in the forehead, spearing a hole there and dragging a gash through the *Living Smoke* as he descends with gravity. The Knight vanishes, hurtling down into the unknown, and the Drag-in roars up another clap of thunder. It's shortly taken aback, juggling its ripped head in disorientation.

I rejoice after a few seconds, owning the silence. '*Yeah*!' I rejoice at the monster's detriment. 'Suck on those—!'

But, over the edge of the log, I'm engrossed by something new forming on the other side.

'*Harm awards me strength! But the damage from the blade feeds me!*'

A second Drag-in head gathers from the flourish of another tornado. The tornado acts as a construction wall as it shapes a head identical in appearance and just as famished as its twin. Pushing its teeth at me, the Drag-in's huge canines snatch a chunk out of the remaining log. The log spins rhythmically to the beast's crunch.

One hand slips. Now all of my strength is depending on the other. *My Lefty - Great!* As the second Drag-in Head comes to take another snap, relieving its injured brother of duty, I wisely delegate the free hand, dipping it into my pocket…

Searching for seeds…

Searching for seeds…

'*Harm awards me strength! Eternity feeds me!*'

No seeds. NO SEEDS!

Must have gone when the boat drowned!

'Ah!' I cry. 'Found one!'

One lone seed has survived the journey and I'm hoping—

Just hoping it's a bloody—RED ONE!

I throw it into my mouth and release my final bleeding hand from the airborne log. Only to find that…I'm not falling. A better way to describe this feeling would be to say that I'm drifting. Flying through the clouds. However, in this very direction I'm headed, the original Drag-in Head has collected itself, since licking its wound back into…well…perfection. Its mouth is back in business, widening like both ends of a great ocean expanding from one another. There's nothing I can do to restrain from being carried to my death. No power can withstand the mirrored hunger of the two Drag-in Heads.

Well, there is that—

WHOOM! Blue wings come into view, bursting through the mouth of the original Drag-in Head. Ripping both gum and flesh from the face of the beast with a wash of water, one of the magnificent water phoenixes arrives to my aid. On its back, Samuella sits with her legs crossed over to one side and leaned forwards so that her bottom is stuck out with the bird's heroic tail-feathers flailing behind. She swings an arm towards me. 'Reach out!' she shouts. 'You can do better than that, short-arse!'

Only this once will I allow her to mock me.

I climb onto the bird's back and bend my arms uneasily around its body. Another water phoenix explodes from the second Drag-in Head in superb fashion. The Blood Knight rides this one. He zooms past us, steering the valiant bird into the chest of the beast we've left behind. Hand out and ready, he clasps onto the final emerald and tears it out. But it slips from the warrior's slippery gauntlet...and drops, freefalling into the sea of smoke beneath us.

'No way!' Samuella cries. 'We need to fetch that—fast!'

'It'll be on the ground there!' I point at the sheet of white cloud billowing under the phoenix's wing. 'Somewhere—around—near—right under us! We'll just go down and get it back!'

'Down there?' Samuella protests. 'That defeats the object of being up here! You're mental!'

The body of the Drag-in ignites from the very spot where the emerald sat in its chest and the smoke incinerates. Fire tails us. The water phoenixes soar in and out of the fiery tornadoes, performing somersaults that force us to dig into every follicle and scream for our lives. We blast upwards, headed for the clearer skies. Pink and purple sunset is so near. And the visiting stars and the early moon come towards us, almost reachable—

'Papa—? Papa—! You're flying! You're flying high in the sky—!'

Real-time sound abandons my ears. Samuella's lips are moving, but I can't hear one syllable. Her panic doesn't touch me. In my mind, Thuban's voice has returned and it brings tears to my eyes. The surprise tickles my heart and my grasp on the enormous bird loosens.

As I slide from the phoenix's back, Samuella and her beautiful, aqua-winged hero head for the clean air between the moon and the Soulcano's tip. After they pass through, the clouds consume this lucky pocket of sky and I fall helplessly.

'That wasn't a red seed, Papa,' Thuban calls out to me distantly. Every letter echoes. *'It was green...and you're drifting right back to sleep. But don't be afraid of losing yourself...not here—because the soils of Draco Island will keep your spirit awake, like mine...The Soulcano has already salvaged your conscience...You're almost there, Papa...And I*

promise that the Soulcano will protect you, Papa…It will bring you back to finish this once and for all…'

Chapter Twelve
The Dusk Of Offerings

The inner-city streets of Quomer remained eerily empty long into the night. Still, colourful lanterns, bunting and festive decorations were being lined across buildings in time for the Dusk of Offerings the next day. During their excursion through town, Aegia and Falcon drove beneath a giant model of *The Great East Dragon,* which had been suspended above *Mayn Street*, in a fleeting attempt to zip from one alleyway to another. Catching only a glimpse of the behemoth floating overhead, they used its shadow to blot out their crossing with nothing to compensate for the loud, droning noise the motorcycle made. Its menacing eyes and extremely realistic mouth carving sent them into such a trance that they almost forgot the aim of their venture into Quomer. The city was home to more than a hundred million East Folk and it was terrifying to discover its much more vacuous, darker side, which existed without some element of urbanity or even a mild spout of traffic at the very least. There wasn't a single red light the entire way. Curfew was in place and they had to be brisk and unseen.

Aegia knew that, before they even came close to rescuing the Phestor's mistress, they needed to locate Samuella. Preferably, prior to sunrise…

*

Samuella plonked herself in the biggest armchair there was in Lord Camson's study. For such a small residence – "small" for a general, that was – he'd still made the effort to sustain a quaint library of books, and a cosy little study with a wooden desk and a diverse collection of lounge chairs. That was one thing she'd learnt about the dwarfish man from her dreams in the last hour: he had matured into a quiet, modest chaperone with his nose well and truly in his own business. Camson had conducted some of the biggest armies in the East and was seen as no less than a god in the Military Corps. He was the man Phestor Xenol depended on the most to perform day in and day out. The only man the Phestor thought he could trust undisputedly. But, to Samuella, he still had plenty to prove before he gained hers.

At the moment, he was perusing through the files kept on his work desk. Samuella noticed the parrot that had arrived at Aegia's bedroom window with the address on a note earlier that evening. It was sitting on the windowsill, oddly comfortable in the coolness of the dainty dawn that was invading through the open window.

'Is the bird yours?' she asked bravely. Her eyes were flicking cautiously between the colourful bird and the blade that the psychopath had been so easily willing to kill her with, now lying on a panda-fur sofa on the other side of the study.

Camson didn't look up from his sifting. He was aware of the bird's presence. 'The parrot? No. It comes back now and again. Just doesn't bother me much to have some company.'

'Oh, yes, I can see how you love having company round,' Samuella said sarcastically, wising up over the man's cloistered nature in the dead hush of his study, which was reserved from all sound but a grandfather clock, tick-tocking somewhere in the background. 'But only when it involves old friends from the Dreamerverse – that includes girls *and* parrots, *right*?'

He glanced at her annoyedly, his plucky prisoner, and then returned his interest to the files on the desk.

'It brought me here—the parrot passed onto me your address,' she told him. 'It's the reason I came to you.'

'And you think that it's part of your mission to find me out here? Investigate my home? Seek the emerald? Hoping that you will take the blood of an East leader by interrogating *my home*?' Camson sighed and then snickered. 'Xenol is not here, if he's what you're looking for. Neither is Serpens for that matter.'

Samuella choked on her next sentence, stunned by his knowledge. 'Who told you about my business—?'

'The news has been out for days,' he confirmed. 'Everybody's aware of the people who want at least one of them dead. They've wanted him gone for years. Tomorrow, the Festival is ding-dong time to take a shot at all kinds of leaders. They'll all be there for plugging –

Phestor Serpens, DCD. Philson—Hell, someone might even take a shot at Xenol as a bonus. If they get a chance, that is.'

'Xenol may be the greatest target of them all,' Samuella noted. 'He has the most influence right now, since he's trending on the Media everywhere in the world. He's the dictator of the strongest Nation in the East. And he's the least vulnerable of the three key leaders, for it's his Nation we're in.'

'Nobody is getting less than a twenty feet to Phestor Xenol or his associates. It'll be virtually impossible to catch even a glimpse of his face during his procession on *Mayn Street*.'

'Why's that?'

He looked at her, his cheeks fastening a forced grin of experimental angles and proportions. It was impossible to tell whether there was any bona fide pleasure in what Lord Camson was saying. He just appeared so ragged and unenthusiastic. 'Because the man defending him tomorrow is me and that'll mean tomorrow he'll be the safest man in the world.'

Then, Samuella saw one of the very things she'd never expected to find again. It crashed through the corner of her eye: a red, hooded robe was hooked on the antler of a stuffed elk's head, which posed as an ornament on the wall.☆ The cloak was no ornament, though. It was the gown of a killer – the man who had slaughtered Mister Pegasus or who had at least been at Phestor Xenol's service when it happened. Her eyes swung to the little man muddling files and she said nothing yet. But she was pretty sure. *It was the same cloak*. Needless to say, it had not taken her long to confirm that this Lord Camson was the same as the one in the Dreamerverse – even if he was much calmer in reality and carried off a formality too esteemed for a psychopathic killer. How could she be sure? He'd attempted to kill her too, don't forget! Was it because he had presumed she was a trespasser or a thief in his home? That would make a little more sense – in fact, she hoped it was that. But she was confident this was the same rumbustious bloke from the SPR, and he'd seen her and her allies coming from a mile away.

'Before I became General of one the world's most bountiful regiments,' he boasted, 'I was a Master Executioner in the Sixth Nation. This was before our current era of law commissioned A.I. and their

---

☆ Game-hunting became less and less popular in the late 2020s, when it was issued by the Old Democratic West government that all game-hunters would be skinned and poached up to their eyeballs before being hanged in Rachio Square (Second Nation) to be made an example of.

agenda of Instant Prosecution. Today in corporal punishment, the number of human executioners has become meeker and so their rarity has improved their worth. If I was still a chopper to this day, earning from every convict, traitor, or antisocial that I dispatched from this life, I'd be millionaire. Mark my words.'

'You're not already a rich man as it stands?' Samuella inquired, edgily acquainted at this point. *Was she beginning relax*—not even.

'I lost my position as Master Executioner, since there was no use for a man in that post, with the advancement of Androkind. When I was discharged, my earnings were cut under the Phestor's demand. I had previously been trained in modern soldiery from the age of seven, and was granted a militant qualification from my cadet years in the First Regiment. I had worked with the First Regiment until I was excused at twenty-four; a terrible ailment I got fighting in the 2037 Cascade War put me out of action. That was the day I started my seven-year stint as Master Executioner here in Quomer. At the prime age of thirty-one, I became ousted as Executioner and promoted to General of the First Regiment.'

'You were a member of the First Regiment?' Samuella gasped. 'Wasn't that the notorious Regiment that enlisted former Infidels and prisoners of war?'

'You've obviously been honeyed by the rumours. Did they also tell you the fact that the First Regiment consisted of former Infidels *made it by far the most treacherous Regiment of them all?*' Lord Camson sniggered. 'I'll give you the truth, darling. Something no one else will tell you – or will be *able* to tell you by any means. The truth is that the First Regiment doesn't enlist Infidels. That is a lie you were told. It is not possible for Infidels to surrender their brotherhood to a Phestor's cause, to conform and perform under the Phestorship's regime. The Illicit Revolutionary Corps forces each of its Infidels to swear to an oath that they can never break – or they will come to bear the fatal consequences, or else, let it be suicide at their own hands.'

'And being the General of the First Regiment makes you certain of that?'

'No, being the *only* Infidel to have ever enlisted for the First Regiment makes me certain of that. I was an Infidel rebel among an entire squadron that had been indoctrinated by the Faith.'

'The Faith?' Samuella hitched on to this name.

'Don't you know? The "New Religion"?' Lord Camson said.

'Yes. I know what it is. But you're saying that it's now infecting the East's *military*?'

'The New Religion is everywhere now. All military regiments in the East, including the First, follow the Faith. It is what they employ to brainwash their cadets. What else do you think they're up to in the Southern Polar Region, other than experimenting on their specimens? They're infecting young minds to fight against the Infidels. The most deluded cadets of the batch are promoted to be part of the Anti Revolutionary Corps – the ARC. It's all a government thing and the Faith is just a hoax to sell to potential conscripts; the whole thing was proposed and funded by Phestor Xenol himself.'

'Why are you telling me this?' Samuella questioned, startled by the freedom of his lips. 'This is all supposed to be a secret.'

'Who's side do you think I'm on, Sammy? I used to be an Infidel in the middle of it all. The idea was unthinkable back then. Nowadays, you happen to hear cases of it more often. But, in those days, Infidels never broke their oath. Especially not my generation – the *proper* Infidel generation. At that foolish age, I was easily swayed. The Regiment scouted seven-year-old me among a group of other orphans plucked from the Quomer ghetto. The Infidel Group of that time had been a notorious lot, much worse than the Infidels active in the East today. That early generation were called the Icon Infidels and they fought for no one, not the people or the regime. They were still strongly against the Faith, like they are today. But, under their agenda, the IRC cult was fundamentally centred around a Sanitary Spirit from an "Old Religion" that brought together groups from all walks of society. It was not focused on self-indulgent individuals who had been bred by the evil human doctrine and force-fed the Faith.' Camson rolled his eyes.

'An Icon Infidel? That was you? One of the forefathers of the IRC?'

'Yes, but very long ago.' He held a finger to his lips. 'And not many know about it, not even the Phestor himself—God, no—therefore caution yourself in the ownership of this knowledge.' Lord Camson closed his eyes, thinking hard about something. 'So, as the story goes, I was injured and out of action, acted as Master Executioner until I was thirty-one, became General of the First Regiment, and then Xenol promoted me to be his Chief Guardian eight years ago. He wanted me exclusively, to protect him and him alone. Phestor Xenol always said he felt safest when I was working closer to him. And to this day, I've regretted every second of my duty under his wing. I have no freedom of voice and my opinion is restricted by his desire. But he kept me financed and fed so long as I protected him. It's been a haul keeping my old Infidel life separate from this life. Didn't want any of those nasty, bitter Infidels to come back biting at my knees, and there have been many of them in recent years. I am a traitor and a bloodied one at that. There were many of whom I was forced to kill as State Executioner. Oh, I regret doing all that mess. I used to be the best man for the job when I was an executioner, an instinct that confirmed one legend for me.'

'What legend?'

'Anyone who can dodge a blade swung by the Master Executioner is a destined assassin of the leader. You fall into that legend and confirm the prophecy. You are the woman who will kill Phestor Xenol.'

'But, I thought—'

'You thought that I was going to stand in your way?' Camson finally produced what he'd been searching for and lifted it out from the heap on his desk. Whatever it was, it was folded and wasn't clear to her at first. By the time she realised what it was, she was on her feet, and the parrot had flown across the room and landed on Camson's shoulder.

He had unravelled the Constellation Map.

'Being Phestor Xenol's Deputy and Head General, and being the man to nestle him and Serpens into my bossom tomorrow afternoon gives me the solemn power to be close enough to make them vulnerable.'

Samuella's thoughts were elsewhere. 'How did you get hold of that?' She was stroking the Map in his hands. For Camson, all the stars aligned on the parchment and shaped Quomer, road for road, alley for alley.

'The bird brought it to me, because he knew that you would follow. I'm sorry for my reaction to your disguise earlier. My defence mechanism kicked into play. I had to be certain it was you,' Camson said, patting down the bird's feathers. 'He wants to lead us to triumph. The Map will tell you where the Phestors will begin their celebratory tour of the city and where we will end it. Because wherever they'll be, the emerald will be nearby. I'm certain of it. Leave that to me.'

'Will you be with them? On the float?'

'I'll be standing by the girl, keeping her sheltered from potential gunfire. She'll be the safest person on-board and hopefully the only survivor when it meets its destination at *Port Ventre*.'

'Gunfire? I suppose I'm not the only person taking a shot at Xenol's head, then?' She sounded vaguely disappointed.

'Xenol isn't the only person getting rained on tomorrow,' Camson said matter-of-factly. 'Do you really imagine Xenol isn't aware of half the population hoping to witness a float dripping his blood along

Mayn Street. The man has his own private army, his own espionage, his own agencies. As per every year's ceremony, his most effective marksmen will be waiting on the highest floors of the Burnouts – located here.' He laid a finger on the Map to point out a jagged colony of stars; the words ***Mayn Street*** transformed out of them and ***the Burnouts*** appeared along the block of buildings on the right. He'd forgotten that Samuella couldn't see what he saw, but she mentioned nothing of it. 'Those buildings there are where you'll find a group of about two dozen men armed with snipers and rocket launchers. If the Head Sniper and his team of gunmen miss with their aim from the roof – which would rarely ever happen – the triggermen in the surrounding windows will launch fire on the parade below. No mercy will be spared for a single innocent bystander who gets caught in the crosshairs. What you must do from your position on the higher floors of the opposite skyscraper is meet your bullet with Xenol's head before the Head Sniper kills Serpens. Within seconds following the shot, I'll then be able to swiftly remove the Phestor's mistress and Serpens from the float before the shooting team destroy it. It'll have to be an extremely quick reaction without any hiccups or slips. You must promise me that you'll kill Xenol before the shooters in the Burnouts can strike. Promise me!'

'When will I know to shoot? I can't do it on my own, so who's going to be there to signal me and, more importantly, who's going to distract the rest of Xenol's agents in that building before they point their guns at me?'

'It should be in my respect to balance your promise with my own. Therefore, it will be fair for you not to work alone. I've privately organised a team of Infidels who've been keen to kick off a revolt in this city for decades. They will join your side and will be in your company the whole way through.' As often as Samuella would have strayed away from trusting a psychopathic killer (and *most people* whom she'd placed her trust in over the last few crazy days), she doubted death would be much worse than the horrors of any Polar Region. And it would be a return to the Southern Polar Region she would be destined to if she failed on this promise – chained, silenced and fully registered a prisoner of the East this time. A glimpse of the lonely polar bear seeped into her mind and she briefly considered stepping away from the man who was an equal mystery in reality to the shadow he was in her dreams. 'Choosing either to assassinate Xenol or Serpens was an interchangeable decision. Only since witnessing what I did in the SPR did I come to realise that Xenol is working against the interests of the Decider entirely, and has allies based elsewhere – one being a masked associate, known as the Drag-in. They plan to betray the Decider and do away with him once Serpens is dealt with, which will leave the West exposed and probably result in an invasion of its Nations. The war will go on – only it'll be in Xenol's favour.'

'Where did you say you heard this?' Lord Camson's pupils dilated, his cheeks reddened.

An image of her father's pulped skull on the ground in the sedation chamber returned to her mind and the red cloak upon the game's antler slipped back into view, shivering with the subtle draught in the room. It was directly behind Lord Camson now. The elk's lifeless eyes were pinning her back.

Samuella changed the conversation.

'Where can you find the emerald?' she quickly said. The thought of never finding the last emerald, the thought of never uncovering the identity of the Drag-in unnerved her and left many stammering chills.

'If anything, the assassination may be the easiest task of my mission – even when it won't be an easy task at all. But what I want to know is where will we find that last emerald and what will we do with it when we have?' she asked him, sure that he knew. 'Will our efforts be worthwhile?'

'I said I know where the emerald is,' Lord Camson confirmed. 'And I'll bring it to you when I find it. However, what we are to do with it, I have no clue at this point.'

That was all he responded with. Yet, there were so many more questions that she wanted to ask as he went to prise up the rest of the files on his desk and hoist them across the room with the Map rolled on top. She followed him and battered his ears with more and more. 'The A.I. has its headquarters in the Second Nation,' she said. 'We should probably take all three of the emeralds there and show them that we have them, and that we know about Digimine. On the way over here, while I was drifting in and out of the Dreamerverse and semi-conscious, Aegia briefly told me about how essential it was to Androkind. It's used like a fuel; it functions like a natural resource that's rarely been expended in our lifetime—but originates where? Where did it come from?'

Camson's response to most of these questions was a bland shrug and a single-toned 'I don't know.'

Something important buzzed inside Samuella. It hadn't come to mind until now.

'What will happen to the Decider at the ceremony? He's here in the city and he'll be at the parade.'

'Nevermind the Decider. He has no relevance in Xenol's ordeal with Serpens, other than being snubbed and muzzled while Xenol takes centre stage and singlehandedly steals sovereignty from the Seventh Nation. The West Wrangler was most probably snubbed and has been silenced by now. He has no *real* power here,' Camson said with an undulating smile. 'Nobody can put their trust in Phestor Xenol. That's only something one can learn from experience. Otherwise, Phestor Xenol can be the most convincing conniver of all the continents on the planet. Not even I trust him and I've served under him for years.'

Suddenly, the parrot on Camson's shoulder took off and zoomed back for the window. They both watched it leave, making for an eerie sunrise. Where it was so eager to reach neither of them would ever know. Samuella had one more question swirling about her head. She wanted to be certain if she could rely on the man who had killed Pegasus. The executioner who emptily murdered her father. There and then, it seemed her decision had already been made for her and she was prepared to wait a little bit longer for the outcome…

Above the streets of Quomer and under the crisp, pristine break of day, a colourful bird floated gracefully through the sky. Skimming the roofs of the skyscrapers and sometimes veering down from the flawless blue to dive through low-hanging orange bunting and red lanterns, the parrot soared for *Mayn Street.* Here, even shortly after dawn, final preparations were being made for the Dusk of Offerings. Stationary floats were being laboured over and fixed with their last touches before the likes of the two Phestors and the Bleek Ministors took centre stage in their procession.☆ Raised above the road was the giant dragon puppet. A patriotic showpiece designed by the Phestor's Official Offerings Organising Committee. Xenol made it clear to the group that he wanted this year's dragon to be more dreaded and terrifying than ever. "*Serpens will be walking home with his tail between his legs*". *If he*

☆ The Bleek Ministors had once possessed equal democratic power to some of the Phestors. Such was the case when the earlier Phestors were known to be immoral tyrants (worse than the modern ones in every way), the Ministors were thought to be *Saviors of the East* ("*the Big Softies*"). Later Phestors were sure to make it a priority that the underbelly of bureaucratic governments in the East were put through their paces. The loss of political mitigation through Ministor Morals was a real turning point for Phestorship in the East.

made it home at all, the bird thought to himself as he flew through the city centre. Yes, the bird could think just as intellectually as any human below. He even had dreams some nights. Dreams in which he could open his mouth and words would spew out like urine.

The parrot caught a glimpse of the first rising pedestrians appearing on the pavements (for this was a holiday in the East that made way for lanes and lanes of campsites along the concrete). Here and there and everywhere were patchy tents, people in festive costumes. A few stores were opening for the first time since Wednesday. And nobody was allowed near the floats, simmering beneath the excited prelude of celebration. Just in case any plotted assassination attempt was in calculation, or just in case somebody "accidentally" misplaced a handcrafted bomb from their pocket and it happened to land in close proximity to the vehicle of the Phestors' Procession. '*People needed to be subdued. Holiday or not. This is the world we live in,*' Xenol once said in a speech during his first Dusk Of Offerings as Phestorship.

In about an hour or so, the A.I. will come to patrol the roads. More arms than any human being could wish to carry. Most people – other than the dawn-breaking campers who appear early to claim their paved territory – won't start to arrive until midday. The bird could impressively think and fly at the same time without losing coordination or fluency. *But then the Infidels will come. And then, Xenol will come with the girl and there will be a bloodbath. I must reach Municipal Tower. Before it's too late.*

From *Mayn Street*, there wasn't much further to go. Municipal Tower stood at the very end of the road and it would be where the two Phestors would begin their procession together. *If I get there at even a moment's notice, I might just be able to find a way to warn the Decider that things are not as they seem…*

Then, out from a window, came the net. It caught its target. Clung to his wings. The bird fell from the sky…

By the time the driver pulled up outside Lord Camson's residence in what was his regular chauffer-driven rover, Samuella had completely changed out of the skimpy fancy dress she'd arrived in the night before. She was taught about the nature of women's wear in the East. Beneath the cloak and veil, hardly much was worn for the purpose of surviving the shearing heat, while externally, hardly much could be seen, for everything was respectfully covered. However, as a newly acquired Lady of the East, Lord Camson had kindly given her two options of either a broad-brimmed hat, shades and a trench coat – becoming a beige film detective didn't appeal to her at all – or a long, dark-blue cloak that concealed everything, including winding about her face so that there were only her eyes on show. She chose the latter for its satin fabric and didn't regret its looseness, as the heat was already becoming wickedly dry.

Like the night before, Samuella continued to ask Camson questions. She conceived a rough idea that his acute awareness in any given situation may have linked him to Aegia. *They could be related? Siblings? That would mean...my uncle? Yeugh!* Then, her memory of Pegasus' death returned and it fogged out that conclusion. *What was I thinking, trying to connect one of the most prominent men in the East with a jeweller woman brought up in the slums? Both had been Infidels, but had never met. Or might they...?* Briefly, she remembered Aegia and everything *they'd* planned together. *Would it be possible to find her again in this mess?* Her mother was probably out there searching for her now. *Then again, considering how long she'd distanced herself from me*, Samuella theorised pessimistically, *that trust could still be unlikely.*

The rover made a tetchy turn. Samuella hardly felt it.

'Won't the Phestor be expecting you to be at his side at Municipal Tower?' she asked yet another question. 'He might find your absence suspicious.'

Camson, sitting beside her, placed a hand on her knee. Although he may have been intending to put her at ease, that area of skin had turned numb with her worries. 'Xenol has other duties to attend to. He won't be expecting me, his guard, until the very moment that float dispatches from Municipal Tower. I'll be on it. Don't you worry about my role in this. That's sorted,' he responded. 'What *you* must focus on, child, is the size of the rifle you'll be carrying with you.'

The rifle!

Her startlement serenaded so fruitfully that she was glad her face was covered. She had forgotten all about the weapon Aegia had given her and Oscar at the Purity Market, the rifle they'd brought with them on the Imperial Jet, but had lost somewhere along the way. Samuella hadn't seen it since in the SPR, nor even the slightest impulse to recall whether they'd had the gun at all. Inundated with a sense of regret, she began to wonder if setting out into Quomer on her own had been a wise idea after all.

'Ever held a gun before?' Camson's voice pierced through her thoughts.

Samuella shook her head.

'Ever shot a man?'

She didn't bother to respond, only sat in deflated silence.

'I suppose there is a first time for every man,' Camson said straightly and then burst into juvenile laughter. 'Or lady.'

Camson being himself at last. *Same as ever.* This was a relief. Now she was remembering things better than she was last night, her mind diverted predominantly to the man who she'd be shooting today, the figure whose façade all eyes in the world would be on. *Can I really finish off Xenol and the Drag-in with one bullet? If they are the same person, that should be a very possible prospect. Could it have really been that both worlds existed in the same context? They existed in both worlds, Evanessa existed in both worlds, the Drag-in existed in both worlds…Did Phestor Xenol exist in the Dreamerverse?* That would have to wait. And so would her realisation of where they were currently headed…

Aegia had never been an advocate for hotels, having spent a large portion of her earlier career staking out in guesthouses of all shapes and sizes, probing walls into neighbouring rooms to transcribe the hidden conversations of ARC Troopers and Bleek Ministors. Her phobia was especially bad during festive holidays. Every hotel in Quomer would have been overbooked six weeks in advance and the night before the biggest event on the East's calendar was the worst time to locate a decent accommodation. This was no holiday for the Infidel agent. She had less than nine hours before the festival started, which meant nine hours to find a girl who was totally out of her comfort-zone and fifteen before a world-shuddering assassination attack was set to take place. So, Aegia and Falcon jacked up downtown. Two blocks' worth of buildings that played barrier to Quomer's suburbia were packed with at least a hundred overcrowded accommodations, cheap inns and rentable residences. These blocks were called The Castles, and the residence suites within them were room-divided inappropriately between families. In some tiny bathrooms, there were families of eight; whereas, in other king-sized bedrooms, a family of four found fitting space and remained quiet for the sake of holding – or, rather, hiding – their peace.

When the old motor finally died and their bike had to be rolled up the rest of the road, a few street-dwellers came to give the tired pair a hand. As they pushed with assisted ease, Aegia described the fiery scene that the A.I. were causing down in the slums and told her new assistants that the impact would spread here quite soon. 'Action needs to happen. Whoever else is on this side of town needs to evacuate. And I mean before the celebrations even begin! Lead the way if you must.' Her words were not taken lightly. A man in a sand-mask and shades greeted them under the awning of a rundown restaurant's entrance that had the word **REC PT ON** graffiti-written on it. The innkeeper stepped out from behind a podium, accompanied with two of the men who'd helped to roll the bike and gone to inform him about the new arrivals. He looked from Aegia to Falcon – his welcoming demeanour immediately dropped when he noticed that Aegia had come with a well-dressed and well-spoken doctor. Middle class Sixth Nationals in collars, sweatshirts and silver-rimmed spectacles never went down well with the locals. So, he didn't bother with Falcon and splayed his inquiries toward Aegia. 'You come with Tin Men?' His West Dialect was poor, but he soon became more confident when he heard their shaky East Dialect.

'No. We left them behind with everything else. We have nothing,' Aegia drifted into some colloquial East Dialect, which made Falcon swirl a bit on his feet. As if riding a motorcycle through the dormant Sixth Nation hadn't been disorienting enough. 'They destroyed my home,' Aegia continued to explain. 'I've come here without a home, without a threat, but I do have money—'

'Who is he?' the innkeeper asked, pointing a finger between Falcon's eyes. 'What problem does he bring?'

'He's no more dangerous than I am,' Aegia said. 'There is no connection between the Tin Men and us. Can I reiterate: we come with nothing but money and the Infidel emblem. A resolution to the terror overwhelming this city.'

'Detail, explain,' the man demanded, his body language was as ungenerous as the decoloured plane of his sand-mask.

'A lonely, injured, scared girl from the West has been strolling these streets since dawn. We assumed she'd been too ill to flinch a finger, but now she's up on her feet, active and lost in a world she no longer recognises, trying to pursue an Infidel plot on her own—'

The man now pointed at her, unaffected by her endless sentence. 'Why should I care?' he spun the words on her so abruptly that every nerve in her body tensed up.

'You should care because she's come here with an objective and that is to protect us. She is going to assassinate Phestor Xenol,' Falcon interjected tiredly. 'And she's going to get herself into a lot of trouble if we don't find her first.'

All of this overcame the innkeeper and he burst into laughter.

'What business does a West Girl have with murder and Phestor?' he stammered. 'To have such guts, she first must understand the system and she must channel the anger of an East Girl enslaved under the Phestorship regime.'

'And that is exactly what you don't understand,' Aegia sparked a small, knowing grin. 'I told you that she came here with an objective to kill Xenol. But the *purpose* of that objective is much more valuable than assassinating the Phestor and, at the moment, she doesn't yet know *where* that actual purpose is hidden. Finding that *purpose* will determine whether she kills Xenol, or if there may be someone else in the mix – a person who calls himself the Drag-in. She's gone looking for it on her own.'

Rather intrigued now, the man crossed his arms solidly, as if to say they were going nowhere until she told him exactly what the *actual purpose* was.

'It is essential to her and the rest of the world that Phestor Xenol's mistress stays alive at all costs. Because the Phestor's mistress has something that everyone wants, something that can change the entire future of the world. And she is wearing it around her neck.'

The man froze for a moment. Then, he gradually began to nod his head with shallow acceptance. 'I'll give you a room to hide your faces. I assume you'll only need a few hours before the ceremony,' the innkeeper said. 'But how else might one help this impossible cause?'

'Tell the Infidels that the revolution is nigh. It is time for them to rouse and rip the Drag-in from the sky.'

He didn't know where they were taking him…

A heavy bag had been thrown over his head and he was being weighed forward, rocking with the motion of the open-roof vehicle. The breeze tingled the hairs on the back of his neck. *Into the heart of the city*, he pondered. *Somewhere in Central Quomer* (a place he'd never stepped foot in his refuged-life). Drake clung tightly to his emotions. His wrists were locked in the hands of his two kidnappers, sitting either side of him. *I have bodyguards.* He could imagine the A.I. quartet riding along beside the vehicle – just in the scenario he decided to hop out and make a run from ten thousand pounds of brawny muscle and armed weaponry. *Just a scenario, of course.*

The light humour entertaining his terrifying imagination came to a bitter halt when the vehicle stopped without pulling over…*somewhere in the road?* Doors opened on both sides. He wondered if they were going to leave him on his own. *They might be leaving me to a car-detonation—or an implosion—? Would they really crush me in here—? DoIActuallyMeanSomethingToThem—Am—I—Important? PLEASE LET ME BE IMPORTANT—!*

The bag was removed from his head. He was panting. Sweating. Eyes were so bloodshot that he saw the red in his vision. The driver's seat was vacant and, out through the windscreen, the rising sun was cropped between buildings. It really stung his eyes. A trooper was dragging him out of the vehicle by the scruff of his neck. Once out, he hit the concrete with a bang and he wished he still had the bag over his head. His hands were bound in blade wire - blade wire cut into your wrists every time you budged - and his spinal cord had been injected with a mild paralytic serum on his arrest and that disabled big movements.

The trooper pulled him up onto his feet and led him to the entrance doors of a high-riser, where the two other troopers he recognised as his original captors were standing. The automatic doors were already open. He was thrown into the small capsule behind them and joined inside by his manhandling guardian. Before his very eyes, the doors slashed shut and light buzzed erratically around them, coming mostly from the floor. The capsule started to accelerate upwards, passing floor-after-floor. *An elevator.* For a brief moment, Drake believed that the heavens might have only been inches away.

Then, it stopped.

The floor-lights faded fashionably, sinking back into the panels and sharing their glory with the dimmer spotlights overhead.

Now, the doors opened.

Drake was faced with a new environment: the type he'd only imagined plausible in fictional West films and West comic books. It was a huge laboratory, deprived of any windows to the daylight and concealed only within the carefully designed, ultraviolet lighting that swung from lattice-shaded chandeliers. Men and women paced the laboratory in white RAD-suits and some additional shades under their masks to fully protect their faces from the sharp light. *Sharp light?* Stewart's eyes rolled towards the animal cages on one side of the room. He'd been drawn to the nasty screams of creatures in agony. Electricity was curling around the bars of the cages and sparks were snapping at the poor animals inside each one. *Animal testing?* he considered. *Is that the latest thing on the agenda? Is this the big, bad mystery the East has been hiding? Nothing new then—*

The ARC Trooper accompanying him roughly tore him across the room like a loose-limbed slave. The blade wire on his wrists luckily skipped a couple of the vital veins he direly needed to prevent himself swimming in a pool of his own doom. A little more urgency may have left him fighting for his life. *What is the rush?*

In the middle of the room was something much larger than a cage. It wasn't a cage at all. There was a spotless glass box, big enough to contain a very tall person, *or a pretty ferocious bear.* Things became more decipherable now. And in this puzzle, Drake appeared to be the final piece. As the door of the glass box was gingerly opened by a duo of white-suits, gloved and armed with air-purification tanks and RAD-meters, his friendly guardian trooper lobbed him up against a wall, pressed his face to it, and began to unshackle the blade wire.

'Where—am—I?' he tried to squeeze the words out. *Maybe the wall will listen.* 'Where am I…?' This was very scary. He caught sight of some of the cages along the wall. Animals that had been stung a number of times were lying deathly still with their eyelids either too closed to be sleeping or too open to be consciously awake.

When the wire was off, the trooper turned him around and led him to the back of the room, circling the mysterious glass box. So far, Drake had some vague idea of what they so desperately needed from "the assassin". (That's what they'd named him; the Tin Men had said: "*the assassin has been found*"). But there was no sense to be made out of the caged animals. He'd heard ambiguous rumours about animal tests in the Southern Polar Region, although this place was far from the ice caps and cases of the Southern Fever virus. This was the East and the temperature outside was somewhere in the hundreds. Whatever was about to happen to him in this very room had been planned months – perhaps, even years – before he'd settled in the Sixth Nation. The people of the East needed "the assassin" accordingly. *But who in particular? The Infidels? The People's Cult? The Bleek Ministors?*

His thoughts were assaulted by the blast of a hose nozzle. From above, water showered his head. He hadn't realised that, while he'd been thinking, he'd been stripped naked and was standing in the shower unit at the back of the lab. Around the shower-walls, white-suited figures were fiddling with dials and control panels. *Bathed by scientists.* He didn't realise what the equipment actually did until the conveyer-belt beneath his feet started to trail him along.

'CLEANSING COMPLETE!'

It drove him out from the wet room and into a new windowless booth, where lasers and lights scanned him from head to toe.

'HEALTH SCAN COMPLETE!'

Following his full-body scan, he was driven into another booth, in through which the scientists exerted different gases and powders to cover his naked body.

'PURIFICATION…SCANNING…SCANNING…!'

He waited for the next scanner to announce its verdict.

'PURIFICATION SUCCESSFUL! HUMAN TISSUE IS QUALIFIED!'

And, on that cue, the door opened and a wind of cold air hit him as he re-entered the laboratory. Three scientists were there anticipating him; two holding onto a clean white robe and the other with a hand out to escort him by. He got into the robe and absently took the other scientist's hand. The man lured him away with a convincing smile. Somewhere down the line, the big, empty glass box was already open for him. That line came to an end more suddenly than he'd hoped. Drake saw the steps, lifted his brainless head and lumbered into the daunting emptiness.

He stood dead in the centre of the glass box.

The door was closed behind him.

Every sound he could hear had now deserted him. His ears were sealed off from the rest of the world outside. Turning to find that there was no doorknob on the door—

Door? There is no door! There were only four walls. *Four walls!* Almost toppling to his knees, he rushed to pound his fists on the box. 'LET ME OUT! LET ME OUT!' he cried. 'I HAVE THE SAME RIGHTS AS YOU! LET ME OUT OF HERE!'

Nobody took any notice of his distress.

Not long did it take for the laboratory door to open. Two sword-bearing East troopers entered the room first, both wearing spectacular turbans and short-cut robes that dropped only to the shins. Phestor Xenol entered after them. He caressed a glare of satisfaction; the greater feeling of glory couldn't have treated his expression in the same way. In his presence, the White Suits refrained from their business and gathered in the middle of the room, creating two lines on either side of the Phestor. Xenol walked between them, towards the naked man in the glass box. The White Suits bowed to their dictator, one by one, as he passed. Then, he placed a hand on the box.

'Unfortunately, fugitives don't win their rights without playing a part in the creation of our new civilisation. Hello, Drake,' he said. 'We have a very important role for you today.'

Drake felt it safer to say nothing.

'I'm glad you could be here to support your leader on this very special day. For—I am *your* leader now, am I not?' Xenol twinkled his fingers on the glass. Waiting for a response.

Drake was shaking. There was only anger between his bones. His joints were jellified.

'You would prefer to praise me than your former leader, the Decider, no? The man who originally condemned you? Isn't that true, professor?'

Silence.

'You know, the wise thing would be to answer me. I am giving you the chance to be something greater than the silly little A.I. innovator who made a mistake. I am giving you the opportunity to live and live long as a hero for your new Nation, the Sixth Nation. To atone for your abysmal reputation in the West and perhaps to prove that the Decider was wrong about you, eh. Now, I am aware that this is not where you belong. Your lack of entitlement to refuge here can be dealt with as softly as can be made possible. I can make that happen. But that is only if you show me your respect, and only if you do not fail me in your cooperation. Am I clear?'

Drake had no response. Not even an opinion.

'Speak, boy!' Xenol's rage blew. 'ANSWER TO YOUR LEADER!'

A man in a white suit spoke behind the Phestor.

'Good Phestor, he cannot hear you. The glass is soundproof.'

The Phestor quickly glowered, his cheeks went pink. 'I'm aware of that.'

Xenol stared into Drake's vacant eyes, as if in search of the genius that he hadn't yet found in the boy. 'What's his name again?'

'You requested a "Mister Drake Islington", Dear Phestor,' the same White Suit quivered.

The Phestor nodded approvingly. Then, he said, 'Ahh, yes—just who the Drag-in ordered. Make me an assassin out of him. Today, I do not only want Serpens terminated. Without question, I want the Decider to go with him. Only then can our true dominion prevail.' On that note, he marched out of the room with his two guards. The laboratory door shut again and a man who looked to be the Head White Suit swung his hand in the air. 'We're ready! Begin the fusion process and commence the transformation!'

Instantly, the lights went out. The glass box came to life. Humming. Drake slipped, the soles of his feet unable to withstand the motion of it all. The glass box lit up around him and he found the sterile white light engulfing his limbs. Outside – on the other side of the beckoning brightness – he saw that one of the White Suits had unhinged and released an animal cage from the wall. He carried his selection towards the glass box. As this happened, the floor beneath Drake began to spin and was rotating at a slow speed. He never saw what was in the chosen animal cage, but had some idea what was going to be done with it. Like the animal, he imagined he himself was in the same cage, in the same sort of situation. A podium lifted from out of the floor beside the glass box. There were new hinges on this podium's head and thin wires curled around the podium's body. The White Suit fixed the cage onto its hinges and set up a couple of the controls on the panel beneath.

The podium buzzed. Wires lit up, Digimine energy accelerating through them like the blood in Drake's – and, surely, the mystery animal's – veins.

There came an overhead beam, the harshest of all. Drake raised his arm to shield his eyes. The vibrating became heavier, so that his shrill screams became little more than a single decibel in a thunder strike.

On his knees, he curled his head into his arms, pulling his eyes away from the row of observing White Suits with tinted visors. Slowly, he started to feel heat on his flesh and, before long, the very oils that made his skin feel so natural and genuine had vanished. In their place was an unfathomably porous airiness. A light-headedness. Transcendence from weight—

Feathers. He knew there were now *feathers* on his skin.

Colourful ones, at that.

Eventually, there came a beak. A long one that pierced between his crossed arms. And his spinal cord solidified. It was more rigid than it should have been. In fact, he couldn't bend freely. He was unable to see properly too, because the harsh light was beating into a *new pair* of eyes…through which he didn't only see this world…

But he saw somewhere else. He had become something else.

Lord Camson's vehicle pulled into an old multi-storied car park. On entry, the admission booths had been destroyed and obscured, so it was a clean breakthrough – the already dilapidated barrier – and up the ramp. That was until they climbed enough storeys to find that the tallest car park in the East was an abandoned one. Ancient cars from the late 2010s and 20s had been stationed here and were rusting, melting in the sunshine. Finally, the driver rolled the vehicle to a halt. There was some pushback here.

Camson told Samuella to cover up her face again. The veil sealed all but the pupils in her eyes. The driver flipped a switch and the screen between them and the front of the cabin lifted. Muffled talk began at the front of the vehicle. East Dialect that Samuella still hadn't had the chance to get to grips with. Camson held a hand to his mouth, stretched out another arm as if to gift her with the same precautionary gesture, then froze.

The blurred conversation stopped.

Somebody chuckled. But it was terrifyingly blunt. The kind of sarcastic laugh you'd get from someone before they stuck a bullet in you at point-blank range. Instead, all they got was a slightly louder thump on – what sounded like – the vehicle's hood.

Then, as simply as they'd arrived...they began to move on again. Thrown back slightly as the vehicle rolled up the concrete ramp, they saw the two armed-men standing on either side. Samuella believed she noticed one of them catch her eye through the tinted-window. She'd already unleashed a nasty sweat by now and eye contact was the icing on the cake. Thankfully, he didn't see the West Girl hiding under the cloak.

Samuella placed both hands on the seat, at her sides. She wanted to be as stiff as a statue and doused with cold water at the same time. 'Where is this place?' she asked. 'Who were those men?'

As they ascended to the next storey of the building, they passed under a graffiti-sign that read: **REBEL NATION**.

The Municipal Car Park was the ugliest sight in all of Quomer. It was strange to think that the most unattractive building in such an archaic city was a graveyard for automobiles stacked some forty stories high. It was also a mystery to Samuella why the most understated group of people in the entire East took territory at its peak. The top storey of the Quomer Municipal was ground zero to the Illicit Revolutionary Corps – the IRC to be precise. Some of the East's most infamous public enemies were hidden here. The Municipal was a hub for training Infidel fighters, and a headquarters for marking out and plotting hacks and invasions against the Sixth Nation's most undesirable government bases. Ultimately, the IRC were always preparing for the Revolution that, to this day, had never come. Although it was very hard to "hide" when everybody knew that you were there, watching from above, their privacy was bolstered by an ominous record that anyone who ascended the Quomer Municipal never came back down, unless they were an Infidel themselves. “The Infectious Herd” is what many speculators below referred to them as. Never seen. Never heard. Always Known.

As Samuella was led out from the backseat of the car and guided across the ghost town of the complex’s top floor, she acknowledged that there were no cars here at all, only the faded white markings of where civilians used to park them. Four men were waiting in a line, standing in the middle of the vehicle-less plain. Large, heavy men, who were armed with enough semi-automatic weapons, rifles, and round, spine-mounted, riot shields for their weaponry to substitute their actual skin.

It was like a middle-aged spinster’s dream come true: a million vacant parking spaces and four muscular Hunks with Big Guns to show her to her spot. However, walking closer, Samuella saw that these men were not at all *Hunks*; they were, in fact, mismatched in size and build, grotesque and ragged, all of them facially and bodily wounded. Two of the men, standing at either ends of the foursome were missing opposite eyes to one another; one had a patch over his left eye and the other had one covering his right. One of the middle men in the line had a scar that zigzagged across his lips. And the biggest of them all – who was suitably standing a little ahead of the others to greet Samuella and Lord Camson as they approached – had a pair of grimy robotic legs that massively missed the mark when it came to to fulfilling their purpose. The scarred flesh around the severed thigh-limbs showed the results of multiple bouts of gangrene, and that didn’t draw any attention from the fact that most of the skin had been scratched off his chest and the pink, raw muscle was out in the open, thumping to the rhythm of his heart. Above it, he had a tattoo placed between both shoulders: ***LET THE REBELS IN***.

Camson and Samuella both looked on at the grisly men. Nobody spoke at first. But the tattooed man had an ugly grimace that he couldn’t save himself from sharing with Camson. ‘Camson,’ he said. ‘You couldn’t leave us alone, could you?’

They both cracked up into puerile hysterics.

‘Don’t call me *Lord*—not here,’ Camson responded self-effacingly, spitting more giggles. ‘Someone might hear you, for crying out loud!’

The tattooed man was shunning Samuella as much as he could, bobbing his head towards her indecisively. ‘What Phestor’s child have you brought me this time?

'She's not here for training,' Camson explained. 'And she's no *Phestor's child* either.'

'What's your name, girl?' the tattooed man finally said to her.

'Samuella,' she answered, quietly shaking.

The tattooed man was taken aback by her voice.

'That is a West accent—I recognise it,' the tattooed man cautioned.

'You sound like you're quite good at it yourself.' Samuella sparred with him.

He accepted the challenge, with a cosy grin: 'I don't do much talking. I always leave that for the Preacher. That has always been his role, after all.'

'I presume you mean the Infidel Preacher?' Samuella said. She started to walk closer to him, conceited with her knowledge and the tremble of surprise on the tattooed man's face. 'And you are the Infidels.'

'Yes. Them we are.'

'The Infidel Preacher was caught and hanged by the Anti Revolutionary Corps four years ago,' Samuella corrected his bluff. 'The IRC have been dead silent since then, borderline inactive.'

Her nose was practically right under his – only, in actuality, it seemed that his nostrils were a few thousand feet above her head.

'You know your information. Very well revised. Camson, I'm impressed with your guest.'

'Sadly, she isn't here to impress,' Camson apologised. He had crept up from behind her and was tugging her backwards by the arm. 'She's here to get the IRC back on its feet, to kick-start the rebellion. The day of Revolution has come.'

'Hmm.' The tattooed man nodded in exultation. 'I'm Be-Hehm.' He then pointed to the bloke with the zigzag-mouth, 'This is Xiggy', and tipped his thumbs at the two eye-patched Infidels standing on the ends, 'and those are the Little Men – Minor Tor Alpha is missing a right eye and Minor Tor Beta had his left skewered on a torture drill. Don't be afraid to call them A and B.'

These weren't dangerous men, Samuella thought playfully, almost euphemistically. *They were like broken Toy Soldiers. Here to be used and smashed around like playthings, like any good soldier is ready to be sacrificed.* Camson had brought them here for a purpose, and maybe it was the same purpose Aegia had in mind when she'd brought her and Oscar across the borders that divide Mankind's World. She'd trusted them enough to pull it off. In fact, her mother had gone far enough to organise her role in this mission even prior to her being born. *Camson seemed to have the same hopes and so did the Infidels. Aegia had even said she'd recently worked with the Infidels as an informant, so perhaps this new relationship was inevitable.*

'I'm not just here to kill,' Samuella said, seeing in Be-Hehm's eyes that he was beginning to understand who she was. 'I'm here to save a life, a woman under the Phestor's wing who needs our protection, because the future of mankind rests in her hands.'

Be-Hehm and Camson grinned simultaneously when she said this. Then, like a teddy bear, Be-Hehm placed a soft hand on her arm. This finally confirmed to him who she was. 'I've got someone to show you. If you're the girl he's been talking about, then you've met him before. But you might need some reintroducing.'

Vesper's Hive...

I land in one of the palmtops. Bedded in the canopies. It's the last place I want to be.

Now that Samuella's escaped on her aqua-winged steed, I'm stranded in the company of the *Living Smoke*, which has augmented its descent upon the jungle.

Another distant roar. Pain? Agony? An astronomical attack at the star-devourer's dominion? Let's hope so. Even if the Blood Knight tore both Drag-in heads to smithereens, that's not to confirm it's on its final legs...and that's not to say I'm out in the clear yet.

Lying forwards on my belly, I start to roll along the bundle of palm-leaves. Hoping to meet the edge in time to react before falling off. The palmtops are hundreds of feet above the ground and a fall from here will undoubtedly be a matter of Death and Death, as opposed to Life and Death.

I slip—and catch myself, clinging generously to the stub of the palmtop. There's enough weight left of me on-board to secure my grip. But staying on top isn't my idea of survival. I still need to get to the centre of this jungle fast, regardless of how far away that creature might be, and the ground is the only passage of getting there. So, I check the Map lodged in my inner robe pocket and tightly fasten it under my elbow, then let myself go...and find a thick vine where I—loosen myself—down—*buzzing—buZZING—BUZZING—*

—A giant wing slaps against me.

Appearing from out of nowhere, it catches me on the back of my hand.

And I'm flicked off the palm-leaf like a rain droplet, hurtling from the canopies and back into the shadowy body of the jungle. Brushing past layers of palmtops, some of them vastly metres shorter than the one from which I fell—I sink only marginally slower, much to their incapacity to cushion – or, better even, *cease* – my fall. I close my eyes and take a deep breath, holding it right up until the point I cannon through, not the ground—but a hollow wall. The breakthrough twists my descent and I'm now spiralling down into the darkness of an enormous enclosed space. Wow—

CRACK!

Touch down!

I rabidly inspect my surroundings, slipping as I scratch and claw to hoist myself up from the trough I've landed into. The deep, hexagonal bowl dips too deep for me to lift my body out and its walls are obnoxiously vertical and linear. Obscure to *my* eyes at least – it's actually a perfectly carved hexagon. Golden-yellow and glowing lustrously. It's warm beneath my buttocks, like something is heating the bowl from under me. I roll over and look down into the glossy bottom of the bowl, where the radiance of the heat and light is being emitted. I can't find anything. The shell's skin is just too opaque to make anything out of the twirling shapes bouncing off each other below.

I toss and turn my body round, so that my back is resting against the bottom of the trough again. I'm covered in pieces of crumbly white material. Thin, fickle shreds of wafer-rough shell. I remember seeing this somewhere. *Back in Quomer, when I'd returned from the Conflicts, my wife had taken me down into the basement of the old brothel she used to work at – while her patriarch, the owner of the place, had been none the wiser, of course. As we'd presented our lustful affections to one another, there had been a tired, lifeless wasps' nest hanging above us like a chandelier. I had asked her if there were any of the vermin left in it and she had reassured my concerns by thumping it a few times with her fist. When she'd done this, it had cracked a little, and a flurry of the hive's flakes had fallen onto my First Regiment uniform. They had felt like nothing...thin...fickle...wafer-rough—*

I raise my head from my speckled robe to be met with the end of a very long stinger – two metres would be a wild guess – about an inch from the tip of my nose. Uncrossing my eyes from the end of the spike, I lead my eyes up the back of the humungous insect that has planted its feet on the ridge of the bowl. Its back is turned to me, guarding the hexagonal basin.

'*A wasp!*' I gasp. '*Wasp, wasp, wasp!*'

The wasp flinches—it's lethal tail nearly skinning the bump of my nose right off! It takes the insect one movement to spin round and face me, and I'm stared down by two frightening, bulbous eyes. It hones in, craning forwards with its antennae curled over the edge of the bowl. I shrink, pressing against the slippery cup of the hexagon and panting hot air into the bug's face.

Arbitrarily, it tears away from its intimidation and zips off, abandoning me here—*BUZZZzzzzz—'Your Majezzzty, I've caught a zzzzzzealous one! Vezzzper, Vezzzper! Hear me, Vezzzper!'*

'Nectar thief? WHERE? WHERE IZZZ HE?' another, far more brassy and aggressive, voice beckons in the distance, echoing around the hive. And, as this voice of authority responds to her finder, her hero, the nest begins to light up spectacularly. I peer up from my hexagon-bowl at all the others I see, which are identical to mine and illuminate just the same, golden-yellow hexagonal dips lined along the walls of the nest. Honeycombs stacked in hundreds. I have awakened the entire hive.

For a moment, I see the silhouettes of more wasps rising from their slumbers inside the honeycombs. One wasp allocated to each comb must make for over a hundred of my worst nightmares. The voice of the boss resonates loudly around the hive, like a public announcement in a sports arena, showcasing no concern whatsoever that her loyal disciples will listen to her and respond with haste.

'SHOW HIM TO ME!' she commands. *'NOW!'*

All of a sudden—*CLUNK!*

A lid slides across the top of my bowl and seals the honeycomb shut with me trapped inside.

'Hey, hey, hey!' I cry, smacking my hands on the provisional roof of the comb. 'Let me out! I'm not your prisoner! You can't stick me in this thing! *I* didn't steal any nectar! What are you on about? What the hell have you folks been smoking in here?'

'Be—zzz—silent, Nectar Thief!' the overarching boom of supremacy responds. *'You havvve woken my—zzz—servants!'*

The hot air being pumped up from under the honeycomb has peaked. When I place my palm down on the bottom of the bowl, I hear a sizzle and quickly remove it to find that my hand is almost burnt. 'What are you cooking down there?'

I notice substantial cracks forming in the hard surface of the shell.

'You're not—ZZZ—STUPID, Zzzealous One!' the chief wasp compliments. *'TAKE A GUEZZZ!'*

'Why don't you give me a tour of your home?' I sardonically reply. 'I'd love to know where the backdoor is.'

'Good idea, Zzzealous One! YOU want a tazte of our produzzze, Nectar Thief? YOU can havvve it!'

A wicked chortle drones off the back of the chief speaker's question and, concurringly, the bottom of the honeycomb shatters, letting me fall through. I plummet with the glassy shards into a pool of hot nectar, bombing to the bottom, then bob straight back up to the surface. My toes can just about touch the ground. The air above the surface is stuffier than the nectar itself, which is bearably warm, if uncomfortable, dense and sticky. Not boiling hot like I expected.

'Good Givings and have mercy,' I gasp, licking at the humid air hanging over the glutinous reservoir.

'I wouldn't count my blezzzingzz juzzzt yet, if I were you, Nectar Thief!' the voice of the chief wasp looms again. *'BRING HIM HERE—TO ME!'*

Like clockwork, a new worker wasp immediately flies into the nectar room and hovers over the pool, examining the liquid until it flags up my position. It dips its feet in and trawls me from the juice to be carried back through the puncture in the wall it arrived out of. Freshly dripping with the gummy substance, the wasp transfers me by the scruff of the Red Robe, through a hexagonal chamber under the hive. The sap runs down my eyes, forcing them closed for most of the journey. By the time they open again, the buzzing has recommenced and multiplied. I'm dropped loftily out of the air and land onto a hard floor made of the same roughage that showered my clothes. With bruised knees, I keel forwards with my hands out on the hollow surface, nauseous with the sweet nectar lodged deep in my throat.

Listening to their electric buzz just before I wipe the gloop from my eyes, I can easily imagine twenty wasps whirring above my head. But, once the gunk is chucked aside, I only see three giants concealing me within the perimeter of their hovering triangle. 'My ears deceive me as much as my eyes,' I wheeze with horror. 'Look at the freakin' size of you! What kind of nectar are we talking about here? Is there any chance I could borrow a growth-spurt or two? Maybe three, if you're being generous…I missed a few in my early days, as you can probably see for yourselves.'

'Only a lick, Zzzealous One. A drop of Draconian Nectar izzz all that izzz required to grow,' the voice of the wasp in charge creeps up the walls of the vacated arena, whistling in and out of the empty honeycombs, and skipping the incidental hole I broke in the ceiling on

my way down from the canopies. The queen wasp descends into the triangle of her guards, floating beside me, to introduce at last. She is twice the size of her compatriots, with a broader head, stodgier antennae and a fat, prickly breast of black hair.

'Tremendous!' I rejoice. 'I'll fetch me a few dozen jars and a wheelbarrow then, shall I? Or have you got a shipload of the good stuff parked out back? Do you deliver off Draco Island by any chance? Because I'm actually quite preoccupied right at this moment. Trying to find a way around the Drag-in and into the Soulcano.'

'*Zzzzz—silence—zzz—your ignorance—zzz, foolish man!*' the queen snaps. '*You havvve already ingested more nectar than you should have! More than you can handle! The sap izzz TOO RICH FOR YOU!*'

'Well, if that's true, why wasn't it too rich for *you*?'

'*You do not know WHO I am? Or WHERE you have intruded?*'

'Nu-uh,' I shrug.

'*Worship Queen Vesper! Queen of the Vespites and Empress of the Draconian Hive!*' the three militant guard-wasps chant around her.

'*I am protector of the Draconian Nectar, a syrup harvested from the sap of Draco's towering palms. Palms that have grown from soils fertilised by the blessed Soulcano, the holiest roots in all the constellations, and seeded from the Stellar Gods themselves!*' she lectures. '*What did you—zzz—suspect all this—zzz—space was—zzz for?*'

'I just assumed there would be more of you in here,' I confess. 'Your nest is enormous, too roomy for just the four of you. Although, I suppose less really is more when you're jugging back that nectar.'

'*There are more of us—zzz,*' the Vespite Empress brags. '*Many more! The rezzzt of the hive are out hunting.*'

'Hunting for what? The Drag-in?'

'*GOSH, NO!*' she swings her stinger impatiently. '*They are out looking for Aedes, the Great Blighter and bounty hunter of the Malariai, our direst enemy. He comes—zzz—to the hivvve evvvery fortnight to poizon our nectar, deztroy our nezt, and—zzz—steal our livvvelihood. Evvvery time Aedes appears—zzz—near our hive, he triez to feed a dizeaze into our produze, which denaturez the enzymez in our nectar and strips—zzz—it of its marvvvellous cultivvvating abilities—zzz.*'

'Where does that leave me? I haven't reacted to those enzymes yet,' I query, defying their strange science. 'Where's my growth spurt?'

'*Empress, might I ask you to consider—the Zealous One has a Mark on his hand!*' one of the queen's guard-wasps quavers alarmingly.

I lift my hand to bring everyone's attention to the gross bump that has formed on the back of it, causing all five of my fingers to abnormally swell up. I haven't felt a thing from it since I arrived here. The reaction to my skin looks like it should be excruciating, but instead, it is numb and so overgrown that anyone would believe it was superficial. A monster bite. 'GOOD GIVINGS!' I yell. 'WHAT THE HELL IS THAT? WHERE DID IT COME FROM?'

'*It is a Mark of the Malariai,*' Queen Vesper declares.

'Eh?'

'*A mosquito bite,*' she translates. '*It iz hindering the nectar'z enzymes—zzz—from multiplying your cells—zzz—and accelerating your growth. The venom in a Malariai bite acts as an inoculation—zzz—against the nectar's effects.*'

'Only half my question answered,' I reject. 'WHERE DID IT COME FROM?'

'*From Aedes, no doubt,*' she vexes. '*That Mark is a sign that he's nearby. He's somehow breached the platoon.*'

'*Impossible,*' the same Vespite Guard continues to worry. '*The platoon I sent out earlier today had been two-hundred-strong!*'

'*Braveheart now, Commander Vulgarprat,*' the queen enthuses her deputy. '*We will reach contact with them. There is no way Aedes could have been able to retire ALL of our forces—zzz. He will have been ovvverwhelmed and retreated back into the depths—zzz—of the jungle he came from. Don't worry. He cannot be much closer than where he was—zzz—first sighted this morning.*'

'Mind you,' I reconsider, 'now I think about it, I do believe it was an enormous wing that knocked me off that palmtop.'

'*What were you doing on a palmtop, Nectar Thief?*' Vesper inquires. '*Zzz—spying on my nest?*'

'No! I fell from the sky when I dropped off the back of a water phoe—!' I sigh and retract from this approach. 'I'm not supposed to be here, gate-crashing your little war with diseased, blighting mosquitos! The only reason I came to this death trap of an island was to find my way into the Soulcano and save the spirit of my son! Is that too difficult for any of you *pests* to understand?'

'*WHAT A LIFE-GAMBLER OF THE FLESHKIND YOU ARE! HOW DARE—ZZZ—YOU INSULT—ZZZ—THE EMPRESS—ZZZ—OF THE DRACONIAN HIVE—VVV!*'

'I don't want your nectar. I just want my son back,' I explain resignedly. 'I'm done with hustling in wars and making new enemies everywhere I go. I'm an old warrior, an experienced veteran, and now all I want to be is a happy memory. Or, at the very least, I wish to be an uninhibited, drifting spirit, free of life's materialistic miseries and loathing, free like my son and my wife. If that leaves me to be a Nightmare, then so I shall descend. But not here and not yet. Not until I have had my final go at getting into that volcano.'

'*You fancy yourself a hero?*' Commander Vulgarprat scorns me with jabbing antennae. '*Running from battle to be with your family again doesn't make you a hero! That's not how you protect the ones you love!*'

'Like I said, Commander, I am an experienced warrior and there is something I've learned over that lifetime – which is something I may not have always known since the first time I was called up by the First Regiment – and that is the myth that war requires heroes, that it makes heroes, and it rewards heroes. Not at all. War requires cowards, breeds cowards, and celebrates cowards. Cowards of impartiality. The winners and losers of any conflict are interchangeable, all of them conscribed by refurbished ideologies and cyclical bigotries.'

'*BLAS—ZZZ—PHEMY!*' the empress scowls, poking her stinger at me. '*Without our rivalry with—zzz—zzz—the Malariai, our nectar would be—vvv—vvv—vulnerable to their destruction! It wouldn't be our—zzz—own anymore! It wouldn't be our—zzz—secret!*'

'Secrets never last,' I audaciously remark. 'The Alumni will dig them out of your dead body eventually.'

'*YOU WILL HAVE A LOT TO CONFESS TO THE ALUMNI, ONCE WE'RE FINISHED HERE, NECTAR THIEF!*' Vesper threatens and curls her body up at me, lifting the stinger to where the electro-charged tip illuminates the bottom of my face.

'Been there and got the t-shirt, *bessima*,' I retort at the queen with striking determination. 'Sorry—there weren't any more in your size.'

Just before the Vespite Queen can prick a hole in my neck with her stinger, more shavings from the hive's shell fall from the sky and shatter on the ground. These chunks, however, are much bigger than the ones that are still glued to my robe by the sticky nectar.

'*I think I'vvve found our platoon, your Maje—zzz—ty,*' Commander Vulgarprat agonises. His antennae are severely erect, aimed upwards.

We all follow his gaze and look up. Fifty feet above our heads, there isn't only one hole in the dome of the nest's ceiling anymore. There are nine now. While we've been disputing, the hive has started to disintegrate from the top-down. The shrivelled bodies of a hundred giant wasps have broken through these gaps in the wafer-thin dome and they are falling towards us. Simultaneously, the lights have gone out in the surrounding honeycombs in the nest's wall and are replaced by the ascending sapphire-blue glow of the dinoflagellates.

'And there go my Dinomites,' I quietly gulp.

To my horror, I realise that the Dinomites are actually coursing out from under my feet, towards the walls of the hive, treating me like a node. My hands are alight with the microbes, swirling in dazzling dapples of blue on my skin. I quickly shovel them into my pyjama pockets, hiding them from the perplexed Vespites. But one of the wasps has his eyes trained on me, having shrewdly noticed this connection before the rest. My heart thumps and thumps…

'*The dinoflagellates—zzz—seem to have reacted with the nectar, your Maje—zzz—ty!*' the guard-wasp exclaims. '*The microbes—zzz—the Zealous One brought into the hivvve are responding to the enzzzymes and—GROWING!*'

I shy away from the foreboding frowns of the queen and her guards. Somehow, all their attention has fallen upon me again.

'*IT IS YOU, ZZZEALOUS ONE—YOU HAVE INFECTED MY HIVE!*' Vesper accuses. Her stinger swipes angrily at my face and I have to duck away from her aggression. '*WHO GRANTED YOU THE RIGHT—ZZZ—TO BRING DINOMITES INTO MY HOME—ZZZ—TO CONTAMINATE MY NECTAR!*'

'*Your Maje—zzz—ty—*' Vulgarprat interjects.

'*I SHALL—ZZZ—SPLIT YOUR STOMACH—ZZZ—NECTAR LOUT—ZZZ—!*'

'*Your Maje—zzz—ty—!*' Vulgarprat tries again.

'*—AND BURY MY—ZZZ—EXPLOSIVE SPAWN DEEP IN—ZZZ—SIDE YOUR—!*'

'*Your Highness—zzz!*' Vulgarprat manages to distil her fury and soberly pry her wrath away from me. '*There is a greater concern than the Nectar Lout, your Maje—zzz—ty. It izn't only the corpses—zzz—of my platoon that have returned. Aedes—zzz—has—zzz—arrived!*'

A twenty-foot needle-shaped nose charges through one of the holes in the dome's ceiling and stems down the middle of the hive. It's joined in quick succession by a pair of moist black eyes, which pop into view through the two adjacent holes. The mosquito's nose surges into the floor of the hive and immediately triggers a connection with the Dinomites swarming the ground. The microbes ascend the needle all the way up to the face poking through the ceiling, causing the giant's head to fluoresce a light shade of blue.

'*AEDES—ZZZ!*' one of the Vespite guards pronounces.

The three guard-wasps surrounding me and the queen swing into action, twirling their stiffened bodies at frightening speed to stir up a kinetic dynamism in their stingers—

ZAP—ZAP—ZAAAP—ZAP—ZAAAP!

A layer of electric energy scintillates off their stingers, as the empress' Guard prepare to defend their hive. While more corpses of the defeated Vespite platoon fall from the sky and Aedes' nose drills into the nest's core, I try to slip away under the noses of the queen's company and make for the hexagonal entrance to the tunnel that leads back to the nectar pool. I break into a sprint—

'*SEIZZZE THE PRI—ZZZ—ONER! ZZZ—SEIZZZE HIM AT ONCE!*' Vesper commands her soldiers. '*DON'T LET THE NECTAR LOUT ES—ZZZ—CAPE! COMMANDER—FETCH HIM!*'

Just before I can reach the tunnel to the nectar reservoir, a pair of long, black insect-feet twist around my belly and tighten.

'*AND DON'T LET HIM OUT OF YOUR—ZZZ—SIGHT!*' Vesper cries. '*YOU ARE OUR PRI—ZZZ—ONER, ZZZEALOUS ONE, AND YOU WILL BE PUNISHED FOR YOUR OBSCENITIES—ZZZ! PUNISHED, PUNISHED, PUNISHED!*'

I'm lifted off the ground and dragged up onto the back Commander Vulgarprat, who climbs the interior of the hive and aims for a large hole in the ceiling, bound for the open sky. The two dumb, beading eyes of Aedes ogle down at us, wiggling about at the delicious contents of the hive, in search of all the sweet syrup available for him to spoil.

I turn my head back and peep over my shoulder, down at the shrinking empress on the floor and the debris of dead wasps and hive-residue littered about the collapsing nest. The two other Vespite guards hover up from behind us, carrying along the deadly voltage in their stingers. Behind them and tucked away in the corner of the hive, I can spy out the reservoir of Draconian Nectar I'd taken a reluctant swim in. The whole pool has transformed from a basin of gloopy, golden liquid to a lake of sapphire-blue, due to the Dinomites having guzzled it all up and taken over. My contamination has proliferated there. I notice a single green light beaming up from the bottom of the animated pool and it forms a tiny chlorophyll-coloured speck on the surface—*the third emerald!*

I jostle my weight about on the wasp commander's back, hassling the queen's platoon captain to shove me off—

And fall a hundred yards to your death? Thuban's voice prickles my conscience at random.

'It worked fine for me the first time!' I yell. 'The ceiling broke my fall!'

—*Which left you with a crooked back and nearly baked-alive in that honeycomb!* Thuban quarrels.

'I'm not sticking around to become mosquito-food when they offer me up as a sacrifice to this *GIGANTIC BLOOD-SUCKER*!' I squabble with Thuban, but his psychic input dissipates. The green seed's power must be wilting here - perhaps due to the layer of Draconian Nectar still coating the lining of my throat.

I slap and scratch at my abductor's hairy back. But there's no chance Vulgarprat's letting go of me - *Her Majezzzty*'s detainee - as we finally fly through the crack in the ceiling and exit the hive.

Aedes hangs his head fifty to sixty feet above the Draconian Hive, carnivorously dipping his proboscis into the crust of the Vespite nest to slurp up what he believes to be their extraordinary nectar...but what is, instead, actually the contamination of a million malevolent plankton spread over from the Sapphire Lagoon. As Aedes blindly indulges, the Dinomites are bleaching over his chaffed and moulting exoskeleton with their portentous blue radiance, rapidly seeping their way into the mosquito's system. There is already a fleet of wasps warring with the enormous Malariai bounty hunter, a hundred or so of the surviving Vespite Platoon that remain airborne and determined to defend their home. Each one of them lights up the sky above the palm trees with a scintillating plasma-stinger, charging high volts of electricity into Aedes via every sting, finding a new weakness at every nook and cranny of the thirsty mosquito's vast body. The wings of Vulgarprat's two companions whizz overhead to join the battalion, whereas the commander himself chooses to take a back seat and steadily scans the giant for the most effective attack point. Prudent and calculated. I can't ignore how much he reminds me of what I was like as a young soldier—a real teacher's pet, *invest to impress* rather than *dress to impress.*

'You can let me down now,' I tell the wasp commander. 'I don't insist on having any part to play in this. I was only passing through.'

'*It is Queen Vezzzper's des-zzz-ire that you remain under my wing, Zzzealous One*,' Vulgarprat responds faithfully. '*You are our pri-zzz-oner now.*'

He finally aligns himself with the Malairai legend and ascends towards the bounty hunter's head.

'We're not going up there!' I scream, as the commander careers closer to the stiff neck of the godly mozzy.

Vulgarprat flicks his electro-charged stinger upward and targets it at the bounty hunter's neck. His body completely inverts, as he militantly aims his piercing and perpetrates a successful puncture. Aedes recoils his colossal head and groans miserably, ripping through the ceiling of the Vespite dome with his proboscis still immersed inside the hive. Momentarily upside-down, I have to constrict my arms and hook my elbow-creases around Vulgarprat's neck, aspiring not to slip off and plummet into the jungle like—*an emerald falling to the bottom of a reservoir!*

Just out of speculation…I peer down…Hypothetically…with the right kind of surface in sight…one might be able to strike a perfect landing…

Don't even think about doing it now, my parental conscience again craftily adopts the atypical wisdom of my son, Thuban. *You got lucky before.*

'No, listen!' I bark at my contrary thoughts. 'The nectar reservoir was tucked into the corner of the hive! If I break my fall on the tip of the nest, I can make a hole positioned over the pool and dive in to collect the emerald!'

Dive into a pool packed to the brim with Dinomites? A pool so shallow that your feet – of all people, ***your*** *feet – could touch the floor? Are you loony, Papa?* Thuban counters. *You remember what those vermin did to me! They dragged me under, Papa—they pulled me under and they ripped my body and spirit apart!'*

'I know—but I'm not going anywhere without that rock,' I shout over the magnum opus of buzzing and humming, struggling to hold onto Vulgarprat, as he darts towards Aedes' neck with his stinger outstretched. 'It's my only chance of getting away from this war of parasites and back on course to the Soulcano! That's where you are—*yes?* Is that where they took you? The Soulcano is where the Dinomites concealed your soul? ANSWER ME, BOY!'

Yes. That was an accident. But don't you go doing anything silly now—will you, Papa—?

My feet are dangling over the canopies. We're flying twice the height of the tallest palms. I'm higher than I was when the phoenix lost me. From this impressive wasp's eye view, I can see both the enormous mosquito and the Vespite nest snuggled under the palmtops. They have been totally engulfed in the luminosity of the plankton. The top of the hive's dome has even begun to recede, dissolving at the centre, now that the overgrown Dinomites are feasting on the wafer-like shell.

'HUMMMM—VEZZZPERRR—HUMMMM—THIZZZ NECATARRRR—HUMMMM—TAZZZTES—HUMMMM—CHAAAANGED!' Aedes drones dopily. *'SWEETEERRRR THAN—HUMMMM—UUUSUAL—HUMMMM—LIKE THE WAAAATER OF THE REEEEEEF—IN THE URRRRSA SEEEEEA—HUMMMM.'*

'This is the right time, Thubes!' I confer with what must seem like no one at all. 'I can see the hive peeling! It's a clear angle to skydive into the reservoir!'

Don't do this, Thuban protests. *Papa—*

'Just like the time I was a paratrooper heading into Salg Perdorn, gliding over the Gungolian Plains in '43! Just like those old times!' I announce, summoning my confidence and rousing my adrenaline. 'Copy that!'

'You're going nowhere, Zzzealous One! The empress—zzz—will not be happy to—zzz—see you go!' Vulgarprat warns me, catching out the consultancy I'm having with my own thoughts. *'Zzz-stick tight!'*

The wasp commander zips upwards and veers round the back of Aedes, splitting us away from the sight of the glistening hive. 'I'm sure I can sort her out an invite to the Kingdom Palace, once this is all over,' I quip. 'But, my friend, one thing you haven't comprehended—what all of you dim-witted insects fighting each other over that god-awful syrup have yet to acknowledge—is that I'm a Night Dreamer who has traversed three corners of this world in search of my stolen son, I'll stop at nothing to snatch that last emerald, and, what's more, I'm currently the captain navigator!'

Living up to my new title, I grab the commander's antennae with zeal and drag them back, bending them in front of me like the reins of a stallion. The giant wasp's muscles are working wealthily against me. *'ARRRRGH! GET OFF—VVV—GET OFF—NECTAR LOUT!'* Vulgarprat squeals.

'You're taking me back, Commander!' I proclaim. 'Right—!'

I pull backwards and press my thighs down on his neck, pressurising him into a dramatic nosedive.

'—NOW!'

Here we go—*paragliding over Gungolia all over again*—down the spine of the monstrous mosquito, dipping under the bow of its wing...then back up round the crane of its neck, where we stroke past the globe of those bulging eyes and discover the tip of its nose.

'THIS—ZZZ—IS—ZZZ—TREAS—ZZZ—ON!' Vulgarprat complains. *'I AM THE QUEEN'S FA—VVV—OURED SER—VVV—*

ANT! VVV—EZZZ—PER'S COMMANDER-IN-CHIEF—VVVVVV! I WILL NOT BE HUMILIATED!'

I tug at the wasp commander's antennae once more to swoop us into the dissolving ceiling of the nest's dome and re-enter the hive. We follow the proboscis hallway down, and then cut away once I've sited the nectar reservoir.

We zoom directly towards the reservoir alcove, smash through the sugar-glass ceiling and volley into the pool of Dinomites. Just before we hit the surface, I disband myself from Commander Vulgarprat—

Under we both go, separate ways! I sink straight to the bottom and my face strikes the floor. The dense, sweet taste of Dinomite microbes gorging on what's left of the Draconian Nectar fills my mouth. Wincing - and very much *drowning* too - I swish my hands over the ground, rabidly searching the bottom of the tank for the emerald.

My eye is caught by a bright green rock floating over my head on the surface. I jump onto my feet and reach an arm out to grab the emerald—*zzzZZZzzz*—

But a long spike hovers over the reservoir's surface and skims the back of my wrist, slicing a gash into it, and knocking the emerald out of my hand. The emerald skips across the water.

I rise up from the glittering water and resurface, gasping for air. I turn around and around in the same place, trying to locate the emerald in this hijacked bathtub.

'I CANNOT WAIT—ZZZ—TO LAY MY EGGS—ZZZ—INSIDE YOU!'

The unforgiving crackle of a stinger zapping to life certifies the return of bad company. In front of me, I see the silhouette of the gigantic wasp come to life in the room. The sharp light of static power coursing through the wasp's stinger spreads over the rest of its body, encasing the insect in an aura of electricity and revealing her in the obscurity of the Nectar Room. The Vespite Empress has descended upon the reservoir.

'VVV-FOUND YOU, ZZZEALOUS ONE!' Vesper sings.

'Queen Vee!' I cry. 'This isn't what it looks like—I'm here to find—!'

'YOU'VVVE COME BACK FOR MORE, NECTAR THIEF?'

'No—No, I really haven't at all—!'

'YOU'VVVE RUINED IT! YOU—ZZZ—WASTED—ZZZ—MY NECTAR—ZZZ—LOUT!' Vesper reviles. *'I KNOW—ZZZ—LET ME—*

ZZZ—WARM IT UP FOR YOU—ZZZ—AND YOUR LITTLE FRIENDS—ZZZ—INSTEAD!'

She shoots a blast of electricity straight in my direction. I dive back under the nectar and swerve from the impact, submerged and protected beneath the shield of plankton. Instead, the electric spark fizzes over the surface and frazzles into oblivion, merely aggravating the dinoflagellates. The Dinomites squirm and tinkle when the lightning bolt collides with the reservoir. Stirred by Vesper's assault, they twist and turn, churning ambitious waves in the pool that savagely toss me out of its depths and then pull me back under, blinded in the midst of their developing gleam. Their glow excels with the conduction of the Vespite charge.

When I finally resurface against my will, consistently standing above a calmer patch in the miniature sea of angry microorganisms, I flex my neck back and forth, in order to pinpoint my pursuer. The empress is not alone. Her sparkling silhouette has duplicated. For other members of the Vespite platoon have descended into the Nectar Room and are encircling me like a pack of wolves.

'*YOU TOOK YOUR CHANCES—ZZZ—WITH US—ZZZ, NECTAR LOUT! BUT NOW WE HAVE—VVV—YOUR PUNISHEMENT, MY—ZZZ—SWEET LARVVVA PRINCE!*' Queen Vesper groans. However, I can't single her out in the dark chamber of a thousand glistening reflections, coming from both under and above. '*OPEN HIM UP! MY EGGS—ZZZ—ARE READY FOR HIM!*'

ZZZZZZZZZZZZ...!

The fizzing stingers encroach on the space, slowly closing in on me. The pulsing electricity conducting through each stinger-tip strokes the surface of the nectar pool, tickling the skin of agitated Dinomites. As I squint my eyes near-shut and contemplate diving back under, with the hope of holding my breath for as long as my lungs will permit until I drown...the emerald reappears. It drifts under my nose, still confidently afloat after having risen to the surface earlier. The olive-light warms my chin and its vibrations send ripples through the pool. I snatch the enigmatic rock and hold onto it as tightly as I can with both hands.

'*WHAT IS THAT—?*' Vesper fumes. '*WHAT IS IT? WHAT HAS THE NECTAR LOUT FOUND?*'

Suddenly, there's a *whoosh* from the reservoir and I'm rocked forwards, almost skewering myself into one of the enclosing stingers. Something rises out from the water behind me. Commander Vulgarprat has returned, overlaying the intimidation by hovering high above all the other Vespites with his antennae drooping down over me and dripping diluted nectar onto my head, his whole body rigidly curled like a crescent moon. 'COMMANDER!' the queen rejoices. '*VVV—FETCH HIM—VVV—FETCH HIIIIIM—VVV—FOR ME!*'

But their advance is interrupted heroically, when the arrival of a spaceship-sized spear crashes down through the ceiling and splashes into the reservoir. It hits the water dead in the middle of the Vespite circle, just missing my arm, and sinks right to the bottom. Immediately, the Vespites begin firing their plasma charges at the nose of Aedes.

'*GET THEM BOTH! GET THEM BOTH!*' the queen demands.

As the stingers attack it overwhelmingly with rising voltage, the enormous proboscis sipping from the reservoir is electrocuted, simultaneously channelling this energy into the pool itself. So great is the bombarding charge that it sparks an explosive reaction with the Dinomites…

'*THE NECTAR IS—ZZZ—ALIVVVE—VVV—MORE THAN I'VVVE EVVVER SEEN—!*' Vesper screams. '*WHAT HAVVVE YOU BROUGHT IN HERE, NECTAR LOUT? WHAT HAVVVE YOU DONE?*'

The Dinomites grow outstandingly fast, consequently raising the nectar-level within the reservoir to dangerous proportions, and they start to flood the whole room, spilling out of the pool and through the tunnels that lead back out into the hive. Inside the Nectar Room, a huge and violent current washes over the confused Vespites and drowns the platoon. Within seconds, I'm lifted to the very top of the room, where my head brushes the ceiling. Thoughts of Thuban and his kidnapping off the shore of Awakening Coast flash through my mind. And recognising what's happening now, while making that dire connection between the two scenarios, I choose to take the risk with the plankton.

I drop under the surface and let myself fall to the new depths of the Nectar Room, as bright sapphire particles obliterate the retreating window to the surface…

…Restored in a lying position, I raise my hand to watch the last of the swirling Dinomite particles fade from my skin. I'm momentarily glued to the floor in some kind of water slick, as the microbes discharge my body from their organic vessel. A puddle? Did I manifest from a *puddle*? My robe and pyjamas are soaked-through. The back of my head, whilst damp resting in the puddle, instantaneously dries the moment I sit up. I look over my shoulder to see that the puddle has evaporated. Cold stone replaces it. The Dinomites habitually disappear, their luminescence leaving me to the conquering bleakness of this new space. They've done their job. I have rematerialized somewhere else…some place new…

This must be an artery to the underbelly of the Soulcano. The Dinomites have stolen me away to exactly where I needed to go after all. Like Thuban was. Somewhere else to be at least, I think with relief, where there's no sign of bugs. Result!

I scramble to my feet and intrude into the dark.

Along the way, I make my steps rather more courteous than cautious. I'm used to seeing gorillas and Nightmares pop out of places like these and a Drag-in head wouldn't be a massive surprise. Fire-torches on the walls self-ignite in response to my presence. Also on the walls are a variety of inscriptions. Similar to those we found in the Kappa Mountains. More indiscernible work of ancient tribesmen…or ancient Night Dreamers…

Or Stellar Gods? A small child's voice pokes my conscience.

'Quiet, Thuban!' I cry out loud. Then, after noticing who I've just snubbed again, I radically switch to a suppler tone: 'Thuban…? My boy? Are you back here with me?' It's the voice of my dear son that I hear galloping through my mind as before.

I did tell you that it wasn't a red seed you swallowed, Thuban taunts like a rain cloud. *But you've always had a little more wax than sense stuck in your ears, Papa.*

'But, how—?'

Keep walking, Papa. You're almost there. At the end of this, you'll find me. And Mamu too.

'Mamu?' I repeat. 'Is your mother here too?'

Keep walking. Just promise me you'll keep walking. Until you reach the end.

I crack into a light pace. The scribbles on the wall mean nothing to me now.

Never did. Thuban's giggles echo in the cave.

He's happy and well! Not just alive! Having a ball with his joy! I hurry even more…

'Thuban-boy!'

Papa! Keep going!

The Constellation Map drops out of the sleeve of my Red Robe (where I hid it the whole time I was in the hive). I pick it up and continue moving, thinking about the words on the Map as I go. It had hinted at something just then on the beach. It had spelled out a message. A signpost? Solely to me, secretly and out of the perception of others. What was it?

OSTIUM STELLA DEORUM.

Entrance Of The Star Gods, Thuban translates.

My feet stumble—and I stop.

'Yee—ouch!'

I've hit a wall. Dead on. Dead end. A small stream of blood exits my nostril and I'm wobbling on the spot. Unfortunately, there's nothing to catch me, except for the writing on the wall upfront: ***ITER HIC FINIS.***

Journey Ends Here, Thuban further translates.

Heavy rock movement reverberates behind me. The sound of…yes, the cave's entrance from the jungle has sealed itself with a blockade of small boulders. The starlight's gone.

So, now you know how it feels to be a shadow, huh? Thuban has turned my head into his playground.

If this was the Real World and he was standing there in front of me, I'd have given him a knock about the head for speaking insultingly and out of turn (like my own father used to - with his assortment of "kindly cruel instruments"). But today, all I want to do is get the hell out of this dumping ground of spirits and hug my son again!

Been a long time since we've given a hug a go, Papa.

Suddenly, the corners of the space I'm in start to crumble and detach. The ground slides with ease beneath my feet, strenuously peeling away from the tunnel walls.

I am descending.

Whoever it is, they know you're here! Thuban alerts. *They know why you've come and have probably been waiting a long time for you! You'd be killed already, unless—*

'Boy, be quiet!' I release my voice from its quivering shell and, once it's been frugally set loose, I quickly cover my mouth with a hand…

The volcanic heat introduces itself. With it comes a demonic glow from the factory of spirits underground. Combined, steam and smoke heighten my senses and bring my eyes stingingly to attention. The rock-platform completes its descent, landing fully on the surface of a red lake of lava. My platform floats with the current, moving gracefully through the smoke. I crouch and focus my eyes on the glimmering darkness. Orange flames burst and curl up from the lake, some skirting the edge of the platform as I progress.

A new voice starts to speak to me. It's no longer Thuban.

Telepathy...! It's telepathy...!

'Who's there?' I cry. 'Who's talking?'

I thought I heard something. Is someone there?

'Samuella, it's me! Can't you hear me? It's your man, Camson!' I shout up at the ceiling of the cave.

Who's hearing me? Hello? Camson? Oscar?

She can't hear me, not even with an elephant's ears. Perhaps, the surrounding smoke is interfering with—

Could it be possible that, in this time of inconvenience, she too might have *conveniently* swallowed a green seed?

It would make sense, wouldn't it, Detective? That time, it was Thuban again. *What did I tell you, Papa? It wasn't a red seed—*

'Next time, let your mother answer the phone!' I bark at him (only senile, old dogs *bark* at their minds).

Yes, true—only dumb people actually *speak* to their conscience, whereas crafty folk like me can tap into their minds and say things along the lines of: '*Sammy, where have you and that Metal Corpse got to?*'

Camson! That's the most optimism I've ever heard in the pronunciation of my name, period. *We're over the Soulcano! Circling the peak! Where are you? I have to be honest—I didn't expect you to have any more green seeds lying around.*

'*Well, I'm in here now! That's a result, huh? I managed to get to ground and seek out an entrance! And I think I've found a major artery deep below the island, after...bumping into a wasps' nest somewhere down the line...*'

She cuts me off: *Wasps' nest—? Please tell me you still have the map!*

'*Relax and keep your voice down! You're straining your vocal cords and giving me a headache!*'

There are no vocal cords in mental-space! Turn down the volume of your own conscience, you baby!

'*What about your knight in grimy armour? Where's he hiding?*'

We're both still in the air, on phoenix-back. Oscar insisted to go after you when you fell. But I warned him about the Drag-in still looming down there within the trees. There's still a thick layer of smoke coating the jungle floor. We've been trying to distract it from you up here, while you found a route inside. Camson, that thing is still alive and fuming. Be careful.

'*The Living Smoke is fuming,*' I chuckle. '*Like that wasn't already obvious enough.*'

Be careful, she stresses strictly, without entertaining a grain of my folly.

The Drag-in's roar choruses up ahead. There, forthcoming at me fast, is what looks like the opening to an underpass. It's where the source of the *Living Smoke* is hovering in a dense mass.

'*I'll just hold my breath, shall I?*' I try to humour her assumptions that I can uphold my cojones against this renegade to existence.

From out of nowhere, Oscar suddenly joins the conversation. His tone is eager, as if he's had a lot to say since his absence. '***Camson! What did you do with the Map? It's crucial that you still have the Map! Camson—!***'

How deep below are you, Cammy? Samuella adds to the bombardment of questions.

'*I still have the Map,*' I assure them. '*It's safe! It's here! I'm looking at it! There were words on it—telling me about the Stellar Gods—an entrance belonging to the Star Gods! Why so much stress? We have the emeralds and we're almost there!*'

My heart is hurtling blood through my veins and dancing with my brain to the rhythm of *DOUMP-DOUMP-DOUMP!*

Cammy, how far below are you? Samuella repeats the important question, firm and demandingly. All Hail Queen Samu—

CAMSON!

'*In a tunnel under the volcano that's a bit chilly, but gets warmer once you find the lava...you can't bloody miss it!*' I dictate. Not for the first time, I am thoroughly exhausted of them both.

Oh, no, no, no-Cam-Sooon-canyouhear-mmm—Samuella's voice eddies into a cyclone of...LOST SIGNAL. The ghostly winds of the Drag-in's smoke rise and fall around me, filling the cave. In the face of the beast, lava poses no threat. It may as well turn to ice and accommodate for falling snowflakes, rather than bursting flames with a gaudy orange that showcases nothing but a cataclysmic aesthetic. The lava's only control is the current and it drags me evermore towards the next entrance. The Entrance of the Star Gods? Let's hope.

Oscar has the final words. They steel my spine and sew my legs to the platform. So, it's like every nerve I've ever cultivated is here to keep me afloat.

'***You're coming towards a tunnel. If there's one gift the Blankesphere left me in this semiconscious state, it's the power of perception! The ability to see what you're both seeing and feel what you both feel. And, from what I can gather, it seems that a storm below***

surface is coming your way, Camson, and you're drifting into the heart of it. Take this. You'll need it more than I will.'

I open my hand. My palm, now alight with an orange-coloured outline, curls around an object that spontaneously forms in it. He's sent me the Solar Blade to use in my defence. Whatever's waiting for me in there isn't going to be happy to see me. There are only two ways this madness can end, *my* way or *their* way.

We've climbed onto a wobbly stage where the storm of the Drag-in is fermenting fervently beneath the Soulcano. But there are still just enough seconds on the clock to restore order...only if I make it to the eye of the storm in time...

Chapter Thirteen
Pride Of The Infidels

Quomer welcomed the world (at least, the world it favoured).

Millions gathered in *Mayn Street* at noon. The roads were closed off, save for the occasional pre-parade floats and ambassador vehicles passing through to hype and excite the crowds. For the first time in almost a week, the market square, '*Novis Forum*', was opened to the public. The newest lanterns and costumes and Drag-in puppets and flags all went on sale. There were already street-dancers jolting the crowd's emotions, followed by an early drum and flute parade bounding through the congested road right behind them. You could always rely on the midday crowd for its younger attendees overruling this "Junior Phase" of the festival, pronounced with more upbeat rhythms and jubilant youths cheering out to one another in a contagion of mid-twenty-first century slang. Children from *Shanty Route* ran loose through the mesh of bodies, chewing on stolen steamed candy, popcorn and Dusk Harvest Fruit.☆ Way up and tipped from the open windows of highrises, the hanging bodies of unofficial Dusk Sacrifices swung from ropes tied at their necks – some who had committed their sacrifice as prematurely as the night before. If one were to look sharply enough beyond the suicides, they might observe how other East Folk were using buckets of the sacrificed blood – mixed with camel and cow bone-marrow to thicken it – to paint the buildings' walls in demonstrative East Dialect: **DEATH TO THE PHESTOR!!! LONG LIVE THE KING!!!**

☆ *Shanty Route* is a highway village on the absolute edge of the Quomer Ghetto, where the last streetlights meet the desert border.

However, with a mass of this magnitude came an endless war between The People And The Law. Hundreds and hundreds of A.I. had been commissioned to the streets of Quomer; some had even been dispatched here from the other available East Nations (Fifth and Seventh), since the enormity of the event was such a challenge to contain for one city alone. If a celebrator were to obstruct, abuse, or commit any other antisocial act against one of the Tin Men, a preliminary arrest would be warranted as a consequence of a Class B Offence. And then, if further inflictions were caused, incineration wouldn't be far from becoming a subsequent option. Even the skies were under patrol. Security drones were deployed for the busier regions and choppers zoomed low through the streets, stroking over the heads of the crowd. On-board the choppers were armed Anti Revolutionary Corps troopers, looking out for any Infidels foremost of all. Infidels were regulars at any Dusk Parade, hidden at the heart of the multitudes, and today they posed no less of a threat.

So far, the coast seemed clear, but night was on its way. Those would be the worst hours, when the sound waves were under the influence of the moon indefinitely and when the city lost the control of its begrudged, divisive people. Everyone in Quomer knew, as the old Proverb of the Dragon used to say, "*there are rarely any storms at dusk unless twilight refuses to pass...*"

The Gordano Hotel was a compact upgrade from the five-star restaurant it used to be, which hadn't been budgeted ambitiously enough to metamorphosise it out of its former skin and brought very little to the scarce bit of world around it. If any of those A-List celebrities from the West ever wanted a place to stay or hide from the Media coverage – preferably the latter – in the Sixth Nation (why one of these people would ever find themselves in a place like Quomer is incomprehensible), here was where they would come. If there were any politicians or aristocratic socialites out there on the mean streets of Quomer, hoping to avoid a visceral hammering from the public, Press assaults or assassination primetimes, the Gordano Hotel had bulletproof windows, bionic maids trained in the defensive arts, and self-drawing curtains, which all served 24/7 – of course, that service was provided when you tipped an extra 10% a night and declined any inclusive breakfast deals.

An elevator that didn't work wasn't the first thing to convince either Aegia or Falcon that this new place (another eatery under a different guise) was far from a luxury hotel – not the furthest thing, but far indeed. They followed a shoulder-crushing staircase and a dull, dwarfish man, who described himself to be the hotel's temporary concierge on the way up to their temporary lodge. Then came the darkest corridor in the universe and the disgusting door at the end of it (one that didn't match the already mismatched wallpaper): **ROOM 89**. With a busted lock, the door was eternally half open, welcome for any stray and wandering tiger off the street.☆

Inside, the bedside lamp was on. It brought attention to walls that hadn't had much attention for a couple of decades, moulding and peeling from the edges and all over. A group of beastly men in Infidel Armour stood around the bed. Aegia could tell it was Infidel gear by the traditional phoenix insignia on the masks, breastplates and pads. On the mattress was Stevenson. The man wasn't as disfigured as Aegia had imagined him to be for a person with not much fighting finesse at hand. To be honest, he was way more *intact* (and *alive*) than she had expected. Somewhere down the line, he'd found a way to drop that very suave suit he regularly wore for some Infidel Armour of his own. His dreadlocks were tied into a long ponytail and he was covered from head to toe in the Infidel insignia. It was an unnatural look for the Decider's chauffer, but for the tumultuous rescue mission he'd just survived, it was more appropriate than any dinner jacket in the world. She was in safe hands again. Though, it didn't stop her reminding herself that *Samuella was still out there, probably not so safe.*

'Dun' worry none, sweet gyal! Meh irie!' A rewarding smile weaved its way between Stevenson's lips and he pushed with his elbows to find a sitting position. 'Meh nuh impaired too tough! Nah hurt meh feel at all! Meh strong as troopah!' he insisted.

Aegia held a hand out before he hobbled onto his feet. She could see he was struggling. There was something clearly wrong with his legs. So strange his distorted balance was that she moved closer towards him, through the massive blockade of Infidels. 'Your legs,' she gasped, reaching out a hand to caress the skin of one of his bare shins, just beneath where Stevenson's trousers had been rolled up.

Stevenson said nothing. His lips remained wide and high from end to end, bearing the cream-white pearls between them.

☆ Oh, yeah. There are big brown Wilder Bears in the forests of the Third Nation. There are cannibalized Vampire Sharks in the Ponderously Placid Ponds of the Fifth Nation. And there are tigers roaming the streets of Quomer at night. No bionic maid could protect you from them, *nuh-uh*. Lock your doors!

She found a faint and unusual crease in his knee-joint. Sank her fingers into what looked like a deliberate parting in the flesh. After some squirming, all she discovered was metal. *Bio-interactional wiring and auto-nerve charges,* she thought. It was a classic touch of bioengineering, and Stevenson had become its latest victim. However, that wasn't the important thing she acknowledged. She raised an eyebrow. 'Where's the boy? Breathing still, I hope?'

'Nah, meh had 'im strung up inna tree,' Stevenson chuckled and patted her on the head like a small child. She raised the other eyebrow. 'He breathin' fine. Only…deh wuh some change that—eh, we couldn't resolve any of that. But, he good. I promise, he good.'

'What did they do to him after the experiment?' Aegia said. Her eyes briefly moved from Stevenson to Falcon.

'Well, on de bright side, 'im a lot stronger den he were in singular form. Not to say he weren't strong as 'im normal Pinckney—but, now he just too long foot.'

'He *is* still a boy? Right? *Yes—?*' Aegia charged every man in the room with an accusatory look.

'Listen, I risk errything for that ragamuffin!' Stevenson's tone quickly changed and he found sudden discomfort in the way he was sitting upright, so he lifted his legs back onto the mattress. Aegia gave him some help. 'See these legs?' he said, slapping his new, artificial limbs – their leathery cover sounded almost exactly like real skin. 'They're brand new! Got 'em fix yesterday! When I 'ave 'em done, I come to learn some truths about what is really goin' on here. There two man! One man who call 'imself a doctah and anotha who call 'imself a psychiatrist. Although, de psychiatrist was a bit of a psychiatric patient 'imself at one point. He once a madman, a revolutionary drunk on his own ideology.'

For Aegia, this confirmed the same notion she'd suspected in Falcon since she'd met him two nights ago. The old doctor had been keeping secrets. 'And you're this doctor he's talking about, yeah?' she suspected. 'You gave him these legs last night and told me nothing about it? You didn't even tell me he was here already! That's where you disappeared to, when lied to me, saying that you were looking for serums! You were keeping us hidden the whole time! I gave you a chance to tell me where you were last night and where you found the black market, looking for the girl's medication! You just left me with my daughter in a detrimental condition!'

'Well, it wasn't much different to what you did to me yesterday!' Falcon argued. 'You left me alone with the girl all night! Where did you run off to for so long?'

'I went to find help,' Aegia said.

'Help in Quomer? On festival weekend? From who exactly?' Falcon pushed.

'An old Infidel.'

'Their name?'

'I don't think he'd appreciate me throwing it around too much,' she said. 'Not while Xenol still walks the earth.'

'What is wrong wit' de girl?' Stevenson asked with concern.

'That's old news,' Aegia responded brusquely with that and shifted from the matter. 'What else do you know, Doctor Falcon? I suppose you know all about Oscar's condition as well, and where he's being hidden.'

'Nothing of the boy,' Falcon confessed, dewy-eyed. He stood stunned, shaking his head in dismay. 'I just fixed this good fellow's legs. Yes, I did that. I apologise for not mentioning it. I forgot how associated all you Infidels are. I offered to help him, because it was a matter that required my expertise, unlike scouring black markets for drugs in the middle of a holiday. I spent twenty years mastering advanced bioengineering. Ever since practices boomed during the sepsis epidemic in the '30s, I was one of the first to step up to the challenge and now look where it's got us. We're on the tipping point of a Bionic Age. We are now gifted with an opportunity of transforming our digital transcendence into its physical form. Converging thought with matter, imagination with reality. In a few years, every person, whether impaired or not, will have bionics allowing them to persevere and live longer, and regulate their strength in ways deemed impossible before – biotech is the new way of living, making an impact on human lives forever.'

'Or destroying human lives forever.' Aegia battled with him.

'Aegia,' Stevenson defended, 'this man has done his very best fuh meh life.'

'And de boy? What about Oscar?' she interjected. 'You've said nothing about his life! How is *his* body dealing with its new pieces? Did the SPR save *his* life? Or make it worse?'

'Falcon didn't know 'bout the boy. He was totally unaware of who I was before we summoned him. But he tol' me he knew you were here an' I mentioned to him not to tell you where I was, else you'd com' lookin', an' I didn't want dat,' Stevenson said honestly. 'Doctor Falcon is here to help keep you and Samuella safe.'

Aegia still wasn't ready to come to any acceptance. 'You better than anyone, Doctor, must have an idea what bioengineering is? Where it came from? How it originated?'

'I am,' Falcon said hesitantly, 'fully aware.'

'Do you know who it's funded for and who it's run by—?'

'Draconex Industries. Yes, I am aware of that too.'

'Then, you must also know where it's going, why they need your input - Doctor,' Aegia taunted the physician.

'Please, Aegia. Leave de poor man—'

Aegia slapped her hand against the metal of Stevenson's artificial leg. 'You followed me here when you could have led me here, so I want some pretty airtight answers about your association with Draconex Industries and Phestor Xenol—understand me, Doctor Falcon?'

'What is it you want to know? About my work, I imagine? I'm very sorry you no longer seem to believe in my fidelity,' Falcon said with what was mostly a kind and sincere smile. 'I really am not who you think I am.'

'Tell me about the A.I. and how they are built. How Digimine applies itself as the final ingredient that makes them tick,' she whispered. 'I want to know how the Digimine can be used against them—how it can stop them!'

'You silly woman,' Falcon said simply. 'The A.I. aren't the monsters you've set out on this mission to destroy. Stopping them would be a bonus and even I would join you at your side to make that happen. I promise, I would. I have long since turned my interests to bioengineering - aiding humanity's dominance above the evolution of pretentiously overpowered technology. I am driven to control the digital age before it controls us, not take advantage of it. But what you've told me is only half the myth. Machines are only to be feared during the day, when we're awake. At night, there is another monster. When we sleep, the Tin Men cannot reach us in our dreams. Instead, there is a wilder beast hard at work, more conscious and devising than any machine. We both know the one I'm talking about. That puppeteer of fear isn't an Androkind clone. It's a man.'

'Phestor Serpens—'

'No. That is where you're wrong.'

'Then, Xenol—'

'Still mistaken. The culprit you are searching for is the same man who helped to set up Draconex Industries and he was the same fella who designed the database behind the A.I. From what I've heard inside the Draconex Building, he drew out their entire brainwave and commissioned their bubonic services to mankind. He isn't a Phestor. Many people would say that he's nobody relevant to politics at all, but a faux genius and traitor to mankind; others, less informed folk, would blindly describe him as somebody who's simply there to help people and make them better. How I came to that conclusion: the A.I. are supposed to protect people, to stand in the name of humanity when humanity is no longer able to hold a candle to its own name, once humanity has outdone itself. The real person you and the Night Dreamers want to kill is both the brain of the Drag-in and the mind of the A.I. In better words, he may well be the imagination behind the chaos itself.'

'Drake—' she tried again.

This time, however, it was Stevenson who broke her sentence.

'When I tell ya that two people come to visit me on dis bed, in dis room, in dis city,' he said, 'I tell yuh one was a doctah – man of de medicine – and de other was a psych' who act rather more like his own mental patient.'

The "elevator" that descended straight through the centre of Quomer Municipal Car Park was actually a shaft surrounded by lightless storeys of abandoned vehicles and sinister figures in sand-masks, lurking and observing them as they went.

Camson stood right beside her during the descent. On their journey through Quomer, he had warned her thoroughly about the "*other shadows with similar objectives to hers, sharing her dark*" and that she would be just as dead-marked as Phestor Xenol when it came to the moment of strike. Be-Hehm and his crew were there, forming a circle of protection around her. Gawking up at the night-drenched figures all around them reminded her of just how vulnerable she had become. So far, nothing awful had come her way. However, she forced herself to banish this thought from her mind when the shaft's platform slapped against the cold, hard ground at last and she felt an earthy heat prickle the back of her neck. She turned. Metal doors slid open and she and Camson were led out of the shaft, into an underground lair.

Here, it wasn't the Quomer sunlight that supplied the heat. It was the blaze of cooking coal, and their steam wafted through the tunnels, while they fed the fires operating within the cellar. Expelled from three great, hot furnaces, a flowing river of molten metal wove through the cellar like a branch in a sewer system. On the riverbanks, Infidel workers were hacking into rubble piles, lifting dust into the cluttered, choking atmosphere. Fuel, material and firepower were the products that were all on the agenda. The place was decoratively industrial, walls and floors boarded with steel planks, and the trip throughout was treacherous with smouldering leaks and puddles to look out for. It all shined up at them as they were led discretely, suspended over the workhouse, upon a makeshift bridge of pipes and tubes. Samuella had to stretch her arms out on both sides and advanced a-foot-at-a-time to labour some precaution. Camson placed his palms on Be-Hehm's hips for extra security. After that, they walked so close that Samuella feared Camson might hold her hand. *If hands are used for holding, then teeth are used for biting*, she thought to herself, grinning at her own crass joke. It was a good thing Be-Hehm, Xiggy and the Minor Tors never knew when she was smiling (or showing any shed of emotion for the matter) under her veil. She'd figured smiling was a person's biggest weakness in the world of Infidels and assassins, and right now they believed her to be most stoic one here. She was both the would-be Anti Revolutionary target and the Phestor-killer in question.

'Welcome to the Pride of the Infidels,' Be-Hehm announced.

They arrived at their destination. Exiting the coal cellar, they found a huge space belowground. One lane of gravel led between two huge pits of granulated rubber. There were hundreds of men digging through the rubber pits with their spades and collecting tiny fragments of aluminium and silver that they found in buckets. At the far end of the dumping grounds were two more burning furnaces. Between the furnaces at the bottom of the lane was a man who loomed taller than any of the other beast-like Infidels and his might was exhibited in the majestic stature of an underground emperor. There, before them, stood the greatest discovery of the Infidels and their most unique asset in the war against the Phestorship: a giant humanoid of distorted proportions.

He was waiting. For Samuella.

When the workmen acknowledged the new arrivals, they abandoned their labour to respectfully form two lines on either side of the lane. Backs straight and spades at their sides. It was a kind of gratitude that Samuella had never seen before. She had to really consider it before she understood that it was solely directed at her. Like the giant silhouette at the head of the Pride, she was their guest, their royalty. The daughter of Aegia and Pegasus, two of their loyalist servicemen.

'They respect the person who is due to rescue their city, their families, their world,' Camson whispered in her ear. 'Promise me that you won't remove that veil until long after your bullet is fired. Nobody can remember your face.'

Be-Hehm and Xiggy, who both led the way ahead of the two visitors, parted at the end of the lane to reveal the King of the Infidels. Samuella's eyes lit up at the brawny figure standing at the end of the admirational corridor of Infidel worksmiths and shrouded behind the steamy air. He had the body of a man and the head of a canine. In the blend of what was nature and what was "science", she recognised every inch of him and Kyma fused together in hybrid.

'Oscar,' she gasped.

'You came back for me. You made it this far on your own, and you still came back for me,' Oscar's voice hadn't changed with his face. His elation in Samuella's presence shrivelled behind a timid, painful smile, a modest contradiction to the heroic staple he beheld at the forefront of the revolutionaries who deified him. 'You can still recognise me after all the damage they caused?'

Samuella was thunderstruck. 'And Kyma—this is what they did to you both?' she managed to mumble to the new persona of her Dreamerverse companion. 'I'm just glad you're alive. So glad I'm not alone in this fight anymore. Where's Stevenson? Did he manage to escape with you?'

'He was able to break us out and then the Infidels hid me after the experiment was complete. It's difficult to hide when you're this obscure. I was in so much pain and I was debilitated when they found me. The Phestor and his men are probably searching for me still, otherwise they might already have another specimen under their belt – a new marvellous soldier.' Oscar paused. 'Those men took Kyma from me and they made us into this monster.'

'You're not the monster. You're the art of a monster,' she assured him.

'Some art can be made to kill,' Oscar said. 'That's what I'm for. What they made me for.'

'Those people in the Southern Polar Region weren't working for the Phestor. He was only a benefactor of the facility, but he doesn't top the hierarchy. Not from what I've heard. As they took you from that capsule, I came to the conclusion that those scientists weren't Xenol's men. They were serving to someone greater than Xenol. Someone with more knowhow in regards to Digimine and how it operates. There was a conversation Xenol had with Camson in the sedation chamber. They were talking about the Drag-in.'

'Is this the same Drag-in we're talking about?' Oscar said, fascinated.

'Did you see him yourself?' Samuella added. 'Did you see or hear anything of him? When they took you away? Was he there?'

'A man in a mask—I did,' Oscar responded urgently. 'I saw a man in a purple mask! He was talking to the Phestor, while they prepared me for the mutation process!'

'This masked man you speak of—the Drag-in,' Camson purred. 'I have seen him too.'

'Yes—I suppose you have,' Samuella said apprehensively. She'd been waiting for this obstinate topic to crop up between them again.

'I've never spoken to him, but I've acknowledged him from a distance. Just the other day, I was in the Southern Polar Region and I saw him there again.'

'Yes—I saw you too,' Samuella came in with the sour grapes on cue. 'You were there when Lord Pegasus was murdered. I knew it was you, because I remembered the robe in your residence—the robe you wore when you blew Pegasus' head off! It was one of the little details that triggered my memory not long after reawaking in Quomer.'

Camson sighed, grimacing awkwardly like a sprinter who'd just tripped on the last hurdle.

'I knew it was you—who killed my father,' Samuella husked at the stifled East veteran, treading on a nerve, for now was probably the best time to bring it up. She'd sat on this fact out of fear and trust, had given Lord Camson the benefit of the doubt and had forgotten about it at a moment's notice, but she was now reinvigorated with animosity. 'He told me he was in cahoots with the Infidels at one stage! He wanted the same thing that you want: an end to Phestorship in the East. So, why did you turn on him and kill him in cold blood?'

Camson looked, rather coolly, at her and twitched his nose. And the Infidels were all staring at him just the same. 'Pegasus was completely aware that he would die that day in the SPR and that I would be the one to murder him.'

'What?' Samuella was perplexed. 'Why?'

'Because what was a West advocate like him to do wheeling a West Girl like you around a covert testing base run by the East. Pegasus' murder was all planned. Pegasus, Aegia, Stevenson and the Infidels—they've all been in touch with me months ago, and they informed me about their plan to end the Phestorship's reign of the East.'

'And you went along with it?' Samuella pressed, still suspicious. 'Even when you were vowed to protect Xenol?'

'Of course! He stole everything from me – my reputation, my beliefs, and forced me to leave behind the love of my life…' Camson mooned. 'He promoted me from Head General to his Chief Guardian, which meant I was given a new post and a new set of responsibilities, and therefore lost connection with my old life. My son was later delivered to my custody with the news that my wife was gone, sold away from Quomer by some market dealer.'

'Do you know where the Drag-in *will* be this afternoon? During the parade?' Samuella debriefed Camson.

'No,' Camson admitted honestly. 'Nobody ever knows where he'll be. But Xenol is his frontman, his greatest marketing tool for his master plan, which is why we need Xenol dead and his mistress in our safety. Hopefully, doing so will attract him to us and smoke him out.'

'*His master plan?* What *is* he trying to do—this Drag-in man?' Oscar said. 'What's he trying to achieve by orchestrating all of this—assassinating Serpens, encouraging a West-East pact, ending the Conflicts, and turning people like me into hybrid freaks?'

'He's tried his best to conduct all of that with discretion dusted over it, so why would his final goal be out in the open? I truly do not know where the Drag-in's plot is going,' Camson explained. 'I've only been a player in all this, an Infidel trying to survive undercover as the Phestor's bodyguard. But it doesn't matter what we know, as long as we can pull the carpet from under his feet and whatever the Drag-in's secretly proposing doesn't come to fruition.'

Samuella looked at Camson, and then Oscar. 'Before, we were dead-set on targeting Xenol,' she said. 'But now we've got two targets to worry about, we're going to need extra eyes. Especially if one of our targets is a total mystery – a masked man. All three of us have a part to play in foiling this plot. A revolution like this is going to need more than one Night Dreamer to lead it.'

'Well, if I were West Folk like you two are, I'd rather be lost than found in a place like Quomer on a day like today,' Camson retorted. 'You're lucky me and these Infidels found you two when we did, Westies.'

'Something as big as him can't hold his own ground?' Be-Hehm defended, nodding at Oscar. 'I beg to differ. We struggle to keep him sedated down here sometimes. He gets a bit colourful whenever you are mentioned.' Be-Hehm was looking at Samuella, just as Oscar was – endearingly.

'He wanted to look for you and the jeweller woman,' Xiggy said. 'But we told him he had to wait. Told him that you were coming for him. So you could fight together.'

'Thank you,' Samuella said. 'But there's no good in him being stored down here now. Of course I need him to fight beside me, because that's what we've been brought together to do. When I pull that trigger, Camson will have the Phestor's daughter under his arm and Oscar will be the one to bring the Drag-in to heel. Whoever that masked manipulator may be.'

The Soulcano...

Behind me, the flames skip at the hair on the back of my head. A plug of fire has sealed me inside the tunnel on entry. There's no turning around, no going back from here. Only onwards and upwards – or, at this point, very much *inwards* and *downwards*. The glowing river of lava loosens and collects speed, splashing against the tunnel walls and the molten waves toggle my little igneous platform along. I spread out my arms, enclose my fingers into a grip to hug the rock, and shut my eyes. However, there's no chance of me shutting my ears...

'*Are you the soldier? The prince of the Stellar Gods sent to destroy me once more? Are you my lullaby singer? Come to sing me to sleep, have you? And you presume it will be easy.*' The Drag-in's voice is deep and burly, and a jerky chortle splinters his speech. Through the slits in my eyelids, I see white lights flicker in the orange glow of the lava and it batters my sight. I hold up an arm to prepare myself for what's coming. *What is coming? What is that light?*

Thousands. No—millions. Enough to devour all the armies of the world in a single unrelenting spree. Ghostly spirits from the depths of an unearthly imagination; a place where even a deranged conscience like my own dreads to look. They're shaped half like men, half like storm-ripped clouds. And they bear snarling fangs and empty-socketed eyes. *What are they? WHAT ARE THEY?*

Nightmares.

But stouter and more cognisant than those ravenous spirits of the Kappa Mountains; these are the guarding insomnia-slaves of the Drag-in.

Lightning captured within a second would be easier to tame than the time it takes them to swarm fantastically in mass. The chilling, bodiless souls encircle me, rushing a blast of cold air. *'Hold your position soldier! Hold your position! That's all you can do! Just don't let go!'* Somewhere in all that thunderous wind are the spirit voices, some of them I distinguish as former comrades, passed relatives, and my boy, Thuban! Both terrified and bellicose, I yell to my son, 'I'm coming in there for you, son—I'm coming for you!' The spirits of men, women and children, are all here together to hold back the one thing that stands between this world and reality: me.

I rise to my feet. The strength to withstand this tornado builds in my arms and legs and I become a solid effigy adrift on lava. Down in my fisted right hand is the Solar Blade. I remember why I've come this far, what I'm here for—to rescue my son, to protect this world and our own, and restore hope for the lost. No option remains for me, but to raise the Blade and swing it powerfully above my head. With this spin of might and endurance, a glowing red circle follows the Blade. The angry Nightmares seem to recognise this. They don't subside straight away, but they do retaliate even more, full knowing that now even the very residues of their sad existence are in danger. They whisper: *'Eternity—the light of the stars—all of Eternity! He has the light of the stars in his hands—the Blade—and it disobeys all but him—the Blade of Orion! He has the light of the stars—captured within the Solar Blade!'*

Gradually, those whispers sink into screams of agony and the ghastly figures shield their eyes with skeletal arms, peering their empty sockets through fleshless fingers. *The light of the stars* seizes this tunnel leading to the heart of the Soulcano - perhaps even the heart of Constellation Planet itself. I keep the Blade high up, allowing its starlight shine to slice through the mist of Nightmares, as the rock-platform takes as long as it must to carry me along. How many lives must I be ending right now? How many of these Nightmares will be smashed forever? Does it compare to the slaughtered masses of Reality's Wars? I guess death is second nature for a spirit.

It takes a few minutes for the Nightmares to lose their mood of defence and when they do, they quickly scarper, fading away into the walls of the tunnel and the fiery molten river below. Finally able to see again, I catch sight of the distance ahead…

…there is no distance ahead.

There is still downwards, though! And downwards I go. Knees buckle. Feet slip. I'm forced on my belly. My fingers curl over the edges of the platform in time for the almighty drop. The platform delves down a slope and into a new tunnel of churning lava. Together, the rock and I swerve through the circus of fire and wind and mist in the blink of an eye. A bump sends us hurtling off the lava and into thin air, and landing only acquaints us with a grey pit at the bottom…

I tumble into a wide crevasse. A pit where the shallow space below accommodates for old, burnt flesh and scattered skeletons – decimated cadavers that surely belonged to those horrendous souls. There's a hot pain running so deep through my arm-muscle that I'm pretty sure I'll be feeling it in the real world – if I finally manage to reawaken in the real world, that is.

I climb out. No time to cradle an arm. Facing me in this pit are three more tunnel entrances. Pick and choose time. Dark and anonymous as their contents are, my best guess will have to be my first and only. I shuffle towards the middle entrance. Light steam from the cool air therein matching against the heat of the lava lures me. The growl of the beast has returned, louder and closer than ever before, protruding from one, if not all three, of the tunnels.

All of a sudden, a sharp whistling noise rips through my head, tightly tugging at my ears like an invisible string. I slow down to shake my restless head, just after stepping through the entrance. It's too unbearable. My knees meet the ground with my motivation not far behind. I'm being torn apart inside and this noise is the pressing substance of my exhaustion. I throw my whole forearm into my robe pocket, drastically searching for seeds. There are only a handful left sitting in there—maybe four—

'*Does that hurt?*' Someone is using the green seed's telepathy to try and speak to me – and it isn't Thuban. '*Do want me to make it stop for you? Like a good doctor would? Would you like that?*'

I nod. I nod. And I nod again. 'Anything to make it go—!' I cry. 'I didn't come all this way to get you to scream in my ear!'

'*It isn't me screaming in your ear. Oh, no,*' the voice is charmingly persuasive and casual. This is the voice of a man. An accent I know far too well to forget. *But, can I be sure it's him? Not just the Drag-in messing with my head?*

'*I'm not a dragon,*' the man chuckles. '*Not as much as you think. Come and say hello, Lord Camson. I've been looking forward to this.*'

Suddenly, off goes the darkness. Pitch black turns to gleaming light. Up in the cave's ceiling are thousands of fireflies and their light fills the huge space in front of me. A throne sits in the middle of the space. Scattered around it are heaps of dated, old West Currency in cash, as well as gold nuggets. My immediate thoughts strike back to the gorilla king and his riches in the Falls of Fortune. However, my direct attention is grasped by the moving shadows that underline the animated skeletons shifting the treasures from the ground and carrying them towards a fire at the other end of the cave in long queues. There must be at least thirty of them. None of them are Nightmares exactly. Half-beings they certainly are, similar placeholders for the living…kind of like an artificial intelligence. Skeletons that have been animated by some proximate voodoo or trickery. Nightmares in the flesh – or Nightmares in the bone.

'I see that you've brought me what is required.' This comes from the man on the throne, sitting with his back turned. *Yes, there's a man and it has to be, has to be the Drag-in's puppet master!*

'Puppet master?' the man's voice oozes out of my mind and back into my ears – the natural way through which things should be heard. It's like hearing for the first time after resurfacing out of deep water. 'That's the first time I've ever been described as a puppet master,' he chortles. 'I'll give you that one.'

The whistling noise has disappeared from my ears, subsequently with the muffled telepathy. 'That whistling over in your ears, is it? Told you I'd make you better.' he says. 'I said I was a doctor, didn't I? I did mention that part, right?'

He still hasn't turned to look at me.

'Are you who I think you are?' I say.

'No. I am who you *know* I am. We've met before, on many occasions, in fact. I've met all three of you. Ah—and here come the other two! I followed you three all the way here, and you really took your time!'

Samuella and Oscar emerge from the other two entrances on either side of mine. Oscar is no longer disguised by the nasty red armour. He is not the Blood Knight anymore. His spirit has been restored and reunited with his human body. 'I see that the Stellar Gods have rewarded your friend with his body's return. *Oh, the Stellar Gods—bless them,*' the covert man says, sardonic and giggling irrepressibly. 'Oscar, how are we feeling?'

'I recognise that voice,' Samuella hesitates. 'Is that who I think it is?'

'Funny old phrase that is: *I am who you know I am,*' the man chuckles again. 'You all heard that ringing…whistling…whatever it was, true? Well, that wasn't me. That was the sound of the Dreamerverse screaming. The sound of the stars crying their souls out.

The sound that goes on while we murder the stars, rape their souls, and drain their existence with our ignorance.'

'Every part of that was *you*! Whoever you were and whoever's voice you chose to imitate, regardless of that, it was always you!' Samuella says. 'I know that voice when I hear it, Uncle.'

'That's your uncle?' I spit. 'That can't be your uncle! I know who that man is and I know that every inch of him is a conniving sinner!'

'I recognise that voice too,' Oscar notes. 'Believe it or not.'

'Do any of you children understand that the state of our universe and existence comes down to only one thing?' the man interrupts our bickering. 'We determine its future. Humanity is ever expanding, ever changing. But what can we do? Boys will forever be boys and our universe will continue to rotate, soaking up the organic abuse.'

'What are you talking about, you fool?' I shout. 'Who are you? Show yourself!'

At this demand, the man rises from the throne.

'I came here with one aim. I birthed all this human tragedy with one hope. And I invited you all here to help me, to follow me. *TO OBEY ME*!'

'Turn around,' I repeat. The Blade in my hand is ready for him. Ready to tear that awful, smirking face apart.

'You brought me my Blade and my emeralds,' he sighs. 'That's all you needed to do. This whole quest wasn't even necessary.'

'We're not going to ask again,' Samuella says. 'Not politely.'

Finally, the man does as he's demanded to. He steps out from the dark and emerges to reveal a very recognisable face indeed. Instantly, we're aware that we all know him in different ways and from different places, and remember him under different names. But that *one* face has only *one* title that is *all* the same…

'Doctor Islie?' Oscar stutters.

'You can call me All Eyes.'

Chapter Fourteen
Rain On The Parade

The crowds of the Great Dusk Of Offerings Ceremony were at their greatest number. Turnouts like this rarely happened once every decade. It was the attendance of, not one, but two Phestors on this particular occasion that made this year's celebration more illustrious than any other. Charging through the unruly web of celebrators came the first of the entertainment floats, upon which were dancers who'd spent months perfecting their choreography, weaving in and out of the costumed mascots. The carnival's music was provided by lorries mounted with prodigious stereo systems, from which traditional anthems of the Patriotic State were being pumped into the air.☆ The raucous sound rattled every sun-kissed chest; it induced papoosed infants to scream noisier than they'd cried in the earlier, more family-friendly, hours of the Festival; and it shook the skyscrapers that overlooked the stream of high-spirited people.

Samuella's headache was buzzing in unison with the festival chaos, the noise of both partygoers and music sparring with her heart. But she kept composure, as the City had once taught her to do in foreign and overwhelming situations. She now thought herself a seasoned professional at that. Still dressed head to toe in a veiled cloak, now all in black, she was positioned on an upper storey of an incomplete and abandoned construction building. She was lying on her

---

☆ The Sixth Nation, a.k.a. the Patriotic State, was regarded as the beating heart of the East. So, at every Dusk of Offerings parade in Sixth, the prideful (and sometimes bumptious) orchestrated anthems really were supposed to resemble an almost vascular "pumping" sensation.

belly on the corner of one of the wall-less ledges, with a broad view of the Burnouts directly across the street and the parade between the two blocks, swimming past below her. An IRC sniper rifle was clutched and poised in her hands. The butt rested on her right shoulder. Her biggest struggle was focusing the damn thing on the street below. She would discover her focus and then one meagre nudge would frazzle the crystal clear lens into a blur. She wasn't used to this and the last thing she wanted to do was pull the trigger too early, or accidentally cause a fatal mess of a civilian down there. 'She'd pick her hens over a sniper lens every day of the week,' the Fouth Nation Girl inside herself muttered quietly, fantasising over the countryside and the moon and stars above the old farmhouse at night. 'At least culling the pigs will be all the same. I'm an expert at that,' Samuella lauded herself again, readmitting self-assurance. She knew she wasn't supposed to move her lips, let alone speak at all. Be-Hehm had instructed her to remain in silence until the shot finished ringing and the Infidel helicopter came to fetch her from the roof. But it didn't matter, she was confident and a little self-indulgent chitchat to accompany the killer adrenaline did no assassin any real harm. Each time she glimpsed at the abominable mayhem on the ground and how the crowd exponentially grew by the second, she was reminded and humbled by the sheer weight of what she was about to commit, whom she was about to murder and how its ramifications would alter the structure of Mankind's World forever. Her parents had entitled this harrowing duty to her far beyond her knowledge, but Pegasus and Aegia's compelling acceptance of her from the beginning, let alone anyone's approval in such an elite warren as the First Nation, had been enough to rope her in and keep her tied down right to this very second. The task was now all she had to prove, all she stood for, what she had been burdened with since birth, way before any Stellar God had come to know her name. Everything, so far, had gone to plan. There were only twenty minutes until Midday Parade (11am until 4pm) came to its interval and that would be when the Phestor's float would begin its fifteen-minute procession through *Mayn Street.*

Samuella glanced over at the Burnouts on the other side of the street. Just as Camson had described them: decayed, spoiled with graffiti, and starved of life. However, there was one thing that was missing and it was making her feel anxious and grave, since it was another major factor that would determine how much of a tug-of-war the next hour would be. *Where are they?* she thought. *The enemy snipers? Why aren't the ARC there?* The Anti Revolutionary snipers should have already ascended the Burnouts by now, patiently waiting in the public's peripheral to take their shot at Serpens. By and large, that may have been a good thing, and the lack of discrepancy could have just meant one less thing to worry about. *But it was the way he described it. It was the way Camson had said it would play out*, she thought and was imagining the little heads of the enemy snipers having already popped up and their little minds calculating the situation below. It seemed to be the natural scene in her imagination, how she'd initially expected events to uncoil, and this alternative outcome somewhat disappointed her. Everything felt safer than it should have, and yet that static air of dangerous spontaneity was still there.

Then, her thoughts immediately returned to the Infidels.

Samuella spoke into the communication device that was attached to her ear.

'I can't seem to snoop out any competition here, guys,' she spoke quietly. They'd warned her not to speak unless it was urgent. *There are eyes everywhere.*

Immediately, Be-Hehm's voice rippled into her ear. 'I know. This is the latest show they've ever displayed. Their assassination record excels due to their promptness. But, on occasions, they *can* leave their duties late, because they never like to stick around for long before or after an assault. They needn't risk getting caught out.'

'If we can see them, why can't anyone else?' she inquired, swinging the focus of the rifle along the mid-floor of one of the Burnouts.

'That's because the Phestor's Administration will spend every penny they have to dilute their presence,' Be-Hehm commented. 'Propaganda in the Sixth Nation is always concentrated on the villainy of the Infidels and the heroism of the military, never the ARC. The ARC is a corrupt business, blending malleable youths with a sick Faith. The Phestor's Administration has always been meticulous to push the Infidels into the negative end of the spectrum. Just so they can portray the IRC as the "bogeyman" and the dark facts surrounding the ARC can be omitted as "rumour" – when it's completely the other way round. It's easier to ignore a mythic danger than an actual threat, in order to avoid civil turmoil. Half of these people don't know they're celebrating liars – a portion still see the Phestor as the rightful leader who overturned a sinful monarchy. What the Administration doesn't recognise is that its ignorance is what fuels anger in the Infidel Alliance. We are not solely an enemy of the Phestorship, only an enemy of the falsehood and democratic incompetence of this tyranny. It is why the ARC Troops in those Burnouts are always there, hidden even when you believe you can see them. Because they have every inch of this City in their view, which is why we've put you in the one place they always make the mistake never to look: right in front of them, in plain sight. It'll only buy you time though. When they show up – they eventually *will* come for you – you will be easy pickings,' Be-Hehm said. 'But don't be too afraid, believe me, there are more eyes looking out for them than there are searching for you. A convenient force of protection.'

'Do you mean the Androkind? The A.I. are against the Anti Revolutionary Corps too?' Samuella said.

'The A.I. in the East are not like those in the West. Infidels thoroughly corrupted their databases, once upon a time, and now they class followers of the Faith as criminals,' Be-Hehm responded proudly. 'But, affirmative, it means the extra threat of rogue A.I. should also give us some breathing space during our escape from Quomer.'

Suddenly, a huge, multi-propeller helicopter clattered above. It made the abandoned building shiver and, more so, Samuella. She dipped her head slightly, as if this was really going to change her appearance on the corner of the ledge. Already, she'd padded out her veiling East garments with Infidel Armour. She wore thin black trousers, a skinny black turtleneck, a black sand mask and black trainers. Her blanket of red hair was rounded into a bun to prevent it from levitating to the breeze that radiated off the desert some distance behind her.

Up in the chopper, she saw a dozen A.I., manning semi-automatic guns and watching the crowds with zoomed eye-lenses. Luckily, she hadn't been seen.

'And *I'm* safe from the A.I. too?' she asked. The A.I. hadn't crossed her mind once between groggily climbing out of Aegia's bed and nauseously climbing up to the shooting spot. 'More Tin Men have been deployed in the last half an hour by the looks of it.'

'You shouldn't worry. The clothing we selected for you is perfect for this mission. Your armour contains masking fibres and nanotech distillations. Masking fibres will camouflage your body with your environment, enabling you to fade into the complexion of the air itself if necessary. Nanotech distillations defend your movements from the seismic detection of other technology, so the A.I. cannot distinguish your whereabouts as soon as you shift your position. As for the building you're in, it's inactive and vacuous – the perfect condition for this kind of technology. I'm monitoring your armour right now and your visual presence doesn't exist at the moment, but the very second you release that bullet and it strikes the Phestor, nothing will be there to shield you.

The A.I. can detect movement from up to a mile away. Unlike your armour, the bullet and the direction from which it is fired can be mapped out easily. Nanotech only disguises *your* movements, nothing else, so your armour will no longer work against the A.I. when they detect the movement of the bullet. I want you to rain on the parade as soon as that Municipal Float reaches the junction—no sooner, no later. Your job is finished when that happens! Do you hear me? You be sure to make with the wind and get away from that ledge once your bullet is fired, because once it is, your duty will be complete.'

'Affirmative,' Samuella said. And she pulled her aim away from the Burnouts and towards the joyous parade below. *These must be the last floats,* she thought. *Not long until the interval now. Not long until the proper show begins.* Although, she couldn't rip her mind away from the masses of A.I. stationed around the city. *There has to be half a million of them at least.* It would be virtually impossible for her to escape to the roof in time on her own.

'One more question,' she addressed the Infidel leader again. 'How many A.I. are there in Quomer?'

'Too many for you to fight alone,' Be-Hehm said. 'That'll be where we step in. I'll send a few of my men to join you up there, just before you rain hell on the parade. They'll help to distract the ARC and the robots while we get you out. Camson will take the girl to safety. And Oscar will be assisted by an Infidel team of his own to seek out this person whom you describe as "the Drag-in"...which leaves a question for me to ask: who do you suppose is this Drag-in?'

Something flooded across her mind, urging her face to go numb and her skin to prickle. 'I have no idea. I haven't seen him before,' she said. 'Part of me is hoping it's the man I kill.' The prospect of killing the Phestor of the Sixth Nation shook her again. It didn't sound like her at all. It didn't sit with her. Everything up to now had just been words. No training or experience involved. Just rhetoric. *Could* she actually do it?

'Why do you believe it *should* be Phestor Xenol?'

'He's the man who controls the A.I., no? He's the man who has possession of the mistress with the third emerald. He's the man who ordered the killing of Pegasus, right?' She sighed with relief. Reassured that she could do this. And equally confirmed she was doing "the right thing".

'I used to know Lord Pegasus quite well. He was a good friend of the Infidels,' Be-Hehm narrated in her ear. 'So much an ally that he was planning to commission a constituent Infidel Government in the

Eight Nation after the Blackout Nine Attacks. This had been during his stint in the Decider's Administration. Phestor Xenol hated Pegasus more than the Decider, more than the West Ministors, and even the Stateship. The aristocrats envied Pegasus; the ordinary people loved him.'

'I've got no hard feelings in the East.' Samuella focused on the closest float to Municipal Tower with her sniper. She caught a dancer in her sight. It was a young adolescent girl with evanescent happiness, totally unaware of the massacre that was about to tear her world in half. 'I've only got hard feelings for the person who killed one of the only people I've trusted in so long.'

'Lord Pegasus?' Be-Hehm said.

'A Lord to you, maybe. But, to me, he was closer to a father figure.'

'Well, my greatest hopes go out to you, Miss Samuella,' Be-Hehm said. 'Perhaps we'll both be satisfied come the end of the day.'

Camson had his eyes set on the Phestor's daughter, down in the bunker of Municipal Tower. She was being given orders of 'where to stand', 'when to stand' and 'how to stand' on-board the Phestor's float. The vehicle was longer than twenty-feet and guarded by heavily built A.I. at every length and corner. Already aboard were the golden Majesty A.I. Rumour told there were only one hundred of them commissioned into existence, and the Majesty A.I. were declared "the strongest two-legged force in the world". Even an average A.I. would be swollen by intimidation when facing up against one of these daddies.

Xenol had to be certain everything went to plan. But Camson secretly knew that nothing would be going to plan. *As long as the Phestoress is safe*, he reminded himself. *The now unpreventable diversion from Phestor Xenol's schedule would all be for the safe procurement of his mistress.* Nonetheless, not to evoke suspicion, Lord Camson let the Phestor's advisors get on with their advising of the Phestoress.

He himself had been briefed on the Municipal Procession: the two Phestors and the girl would be the first to embark the float after the Majesty A.I. were set up like chesspieces; the men would be positioned closely beside each other at the front of the float; the Majesty A.I. would be activated and take their automatically assigned positions around the float; then Lord Camson would board with several other militant associates with even bigger swords than his laughable dagger. While the float progressed on its course through the city, he would be sure to hold the girl's hand the entire way…until the game-changing shot rang out, that was. This cue would only mean one thing: 'RUN FOR THE CRY OF THE FIRST INFIDEL YOU HEAR!' These had been Be-Hehm's commands.

Xenol had made it very clear that Phestor Serpens was to be kept satisfied throughout his time spent in Quomer. 'The final exchange will be made at the intersection on *Mayn Street*,' Xenol had told Camson earlier. 'Then, I want him finished. There will be no transaction at *Port Ventre*. Let's make the festivities brief and cheap.' As for the Decider, he'd been loosely allowed to watch the ceremony from a greater height on one of the exclusive guest balconies on *Mayn Street*. 'Keep him out of the way,' Xenol had demanded about DCD. Philson.

The Phestor of the Sixth Nation now entered the bunker in the company of Phestor Serpens. He introduced his guest to the Municipal Float, describing its new design as '*safer than ever before*', '*state-of-the-art*' and '*heavenly stylish*'.

Standing among his small group of '*militant associates*' – the elite warriors known officially as the Phestorial Pugnars – Lord Camson eyed the principal duo as they inspected the vehicle.☆ Serpens was all smiles and seemed to be riddled with zeal. He was genuinely enjoying himself. The man was thoroughly flattered to be here – probably a side that no one in the known world had witnessed in the Phestor of the Seventh Nation. Whereas, Xenol had that sparkle of dark knowledge and deception swimming about him. The last thing Xenol wanted to do was take his great rival on tour and revel about it. Yet, he was happily aware that his tour would supply them both with a '*deserving conclusion*'.

This wasn't how Camson had expected things to go. For many years, he'd quivered in Phestor Xenol's shadow. But today was the day that would all change. Today, he was going to expose himself for the traitor he'd always been. *The man who left the Phestor for dead.*

'May I introduce you to Lord Camson?' Xenol led the Phestor of the Seventh Nation towards Camson. 'He is my most loyal associate. To him, I entrust my life.'

☆ The Phestorial Pugnars (The Immediate Guard of the Phestorship) were the brutal force sworn to the Phestor's immediate protection at all times – unless deemed otherwise by the Phestor himself. They hid their faces behind veils, kept daggers and fire-bombs in their turbans and could wield their thin blades so stealthily and precisely that whatever remained of their opponent was too small to find.

'Good Givings,' Serpens said and he shook the Lord's hand. *Surprisingly warm*, Camson thought. It wasn't the cold-blooded skin of a serpent he'd been psyching himself up for.

'Good Givings,' Camson responded with an identical, if slightly less awkward, tone of voice.

'Xenol tells me that you used to serve in the First Regiment of the Old East Army, as a General in the Conflicts that erupted following Blackout Nine. I'm intrigued to know how much commending, respect and dosh it requires for a man to step down from such a grand role and become the Phestor's most intimate right-hand.'

Camson gave Xenol a cheeky look. 'Has he told you how much it honours *him* to have *me* step down from *my* great role to standby as his auxiliary?'

Serpens laughed out loud.

Xenol retained his fake grin, but said nothing to compliment Camson's playful remark other than: 'I think I ought to find Serpens a tipple of cobra tonic, before I show the Phestor where he'll be standing aboard the float. Camson, could you ensure that the girl knows where she'll be at all times—'

Lord Camson nodded conservatively.

'I believe the girl has already found a comfy seat behind her barrage of soldiers,' Serpens burst back in. His unexpected banter was like a blunt knife wedged in lard.

Xenol winced, as if he'd been caught out by this sudden rudeness, then he coolly said to Camson, 'I have faith that you'll be busy keeping my mistress safe. Unless, I say otherwise.'

Hearing Xenol refer to '*the girl*' as '*my mistress*' for the first time made Camson cringe, and he feared that it would show in his expression. So, he simply bit his lip and bowed his head to show his honour to the Phestors. The two life-long rivals turned and headed out of the bunker again, practically prancing and holding hands. As they went, Camson began praying to himself. Silently tucked away in his thoughts were a few words available to whatever Great Power may have truly existed above all their little heads and might have been listening. That "Great Power" would probably have gone by the name of Samuella.

And his prayers were: *Please get Xenol between the eyes. And, if you do, I'll be thankful that you didn't miss your target.*

There were Infidels all over Quomer. You may not have seen them from where you were standing on the ground, blinded within the world of distractions below, but they were there. They topped skyscrapers, spied from the roofs, and scaled the walls of the concrete towers by harness. With sharp, experienced eyes, an Infidel could scan every inch of the city from a peak of a thousand feet. Most of them had assembled a chain along the *Mayn Street* tower tops and were armed with snipers and machine-guns and poised at sentries on the flat ledges. And they were too high for the enemy snipers in the Burnouts to stumble upon as little as an Infidel shadow.

Oscar watched one squadron from the roof of a tower about fifty yards up the road from Municipal Tower. Together and in-line, a group of six Infidels scurried along the ledge of the adjacent building. Their movement was in perfect unison and not one slipped their balance. Then, they jumped across onto the wall of the next building, scaled that, and rushed along this rooftop to the next. And then, onto the next. And the next…

He was amazed to be witnessing such sleek organisation and speed.

Be-Hehm emerged from behind him and joined him on the roof's ledge. Further along the ledge, on either side of them, there were two armed Infidels positioned.

'Please tell me she's going to be okay with the Phestor on her own.' Oscar hadn't stopped thinking about Samuella since he'd arrived in the East. Since leaving the SPR laboratory and learning to bear with his current condition, he'd felt somewhat out of the loop, and the mission's initial objective seemed like an entire lifetime ago.

'She's not alone,' Be-Hehm said. 'I thought we'd made that clear enough.'

'We're always alone. Not even the most compassionate mutant-beast can defend itself against the reckoning of its own solitude. I am lonelier than I ever was. This monster inside of me feeds off memories, because it craves my past…my pure human persona of many perceptions and identities. Not just one bias shared by every person I meet – a fear they've adopted for this dreadful distortion of living matter I've become. I often have to remind myself of my imposing appearance and find it hard to translate to most how unlike me it is. Instead, I'm strained to refer to memories that suffice my definition of normality. Dreams and legacy are all I am now.'

'We'd all love to dream. But that would require sleeping. And we don't have much opportunity for that here. As you can imagine.' Be-Hehm clamped a hand on Oscar's shoulder, then promised, 'Once that bullet rings out, we'll have her on lockdown before a single civilian lung has the capacity to scream, let alone gasp a breath. Understood?'

'Yes.'

'Good. Now, quit moping and philosophising, you great *big mutant-beast*. The Municipal Procession starts in less than ten minutes, which means there's less than ten minutes until we reclaim our city.'

With eight minutes to go until the parade's main event, the second half of the Majesty A.I. arrived promptly and stormed aboard the Phestor's float. Their teetering face scanners were as blunt as any normal A.I.'s, but their golden, chrome bodies gleamed triumphantly in the bright lights of the bunker, each one two feet taller than the tallest Pugnar's turban. *That's what gives them their name*, Camson imagined. How unsettling and how demeaning that he was made to feel lower in status than a heap of metal. *Expensive, impenetrable metal that was.*

As he climbed the steps onto the float's platform, Camson peered over the last A.I.'s shoulder, which arched boldly in front of him, blocking his view of the back of the float. He saw the Phestoress standing under a gold awning. She was wearing a long, tender pink gown and a royal light-purple veil to cover her face. Around her neck, Camson spotted a necklace containing the third emerald. Two dwarfish fanners were cooling her by waving large palm leaves in front of her face. Both behind and ahead of the girl were Imperia Pungars. Camson broke between the two Pugnars guarding her front. They eyed him daringly as he did. Their irritable moustaches convulsed by themselves.

He found his place in the format, right by her side. One of his hands touched the blade on his hip and the other went to rest on the girl's shoulder. For a moment, neither of them attempted to make any further interaction than that. But Camson chose his moment to speak wisely, so as not to alarm the Phestoress, or to erect suspicion in her protectors. 'How are you enjoying the parade so far, Dear Phestoress?'

She looked at him on an equal height-level – he was slightly taller, but didn't exactly reach for the sky, and she couldn't see him winning any baskets in a game of Balls and Baskets. 'I haven't been able to watch the parade, have I?' she rattled bitterly. 'Perhaps, if I wasn't in here preparing for what could be a war, I might have been out there, becoming a part of the atmosphere. But, no, my patriarch and Phestor Serpens have other plans for me. It appears that you may be the last face I see.'

Camson had been startled by her vivid awareness and understanding of Xenol's malicious plot. He hadn't expected her to be so informed about her own expendable fate. He'd never come so close to the Phestoress to pick her brains so freely. Also, he'd never heard the Phestoress speak before. Though raspy and muffled behind her veil, her voice sounded very similar to one he knew he'd heard somewhere in the past. Someone he knew well. But he couldn't put his finger on it and, under the noses of the Pugnars, he wasn't compelled to ask her either. 'I wouldn't be too pessimistic,' he said, trying to sound as unpresumptuous as he possibly could. 'Who knows what the outcome of this afternoon may be? There are seventy million people in this city. I might be the last face you see by the end of today, but there may be a few more along the way. Some of them may appeal to you, Phestoress. One of them might just sweep you off your feet. A good man, perhaps.' He quickly realised this was a very poor way of subtly dodging the topic.

'A good man? Not likely. I've only ever known one. Men do nasty things,' she said. 'Especially to women. Young women like me.'

'That's not all true.'

'Not all true? Then, what would you say to the men who did harm to my body? What would you have said when they shipped me off to become some plaything? A lab rat! An asset in their experiments and heated negotiations—as you and the world will witness today.'

Through the veil, Camson could hardly challenge a glimpse of her facial features. But, just from rumour, he knew that her condition was a disgrace. However, he could see her eyes clearly in the light. They were a steely hazel, aglow like two varnished chestnuts.

Again, he'd seen those someplace too. *On someone else's face...*

'Who was the man that caused you your greatest pain?' he asked. It was slightly out of jurisdiction for him to ask such personal questions, which was when the head of one of the Pugnars upfront began to tilt round.

'If it agonises you to know the truth,' Evanessa said, 'it was not one of my patriarchs who caused my greatest pain – that privilege was stolen by someone else.'

The curious Pugnar muttered a brief warning in East Dialect – *do not question Her Highness with your absurdity, you foul cow-dollop* – then he returned to being a miserable statue. Camson gave him a funny look by crossing his eyes in a daft expression that made the Phestoress laugh.

Then, his hand descended from the girl's shoulder to her hand. He clutched it with all the life bestowed in him. Camson whispered: 'Please, do as I tell you, when I tell you.' He looked dead serious. 'A good man could become your champion once again, but you must do as I say. It's all going to be okay.'

She nodded, quickly acknowledging his tone. Something was different about this promise, and she instantly became convinced of it and the man holding her hand, a man she knew too well. Her *good man*, her *best man*. Evanessa made herself certain that she would not let go of the little soldier's hand.

Now, with five minutes left on the clock, Phestor Xenol and Phestor Serpens boarded the Municipal Float.

Samuella had finally achieved a clear focus on the entrance of Municipal Tower. Having gradually driven her aim up along the sea of celebrators, she believed she was now prepared to follow the Phestor's float along *Mayn Street*. Every step of the way.

The shape of another figure crouching on the balcony of one of the Burnouts across the street lured the corner of her eye away from her aim however. Timidly, Samuella glanced up from the rifle and caught on to a small, unidentifiable person poking out from the balcony's parapet. The person was in a hood and had a green festival mask on – the face of an Urbanian Tiger. He didn't appear to notice her at all. He had his vision fixed on the crowd below. Then, one by one, more of these masked figures popped up all over the multi-storied complex across the street. They appeared on other balconies, and in the windows, and on the rooftops. They all carried loaded rifles. She spotted one wearing a huge tribal headdress and a red, demonic mask and this figure, she believed, had the best vantage point. *Head Sniper*, she thought.

Her competition had arrived.

Immediately, Samuella fluttered into a state of panic. Her fingers, which had only moments ago petted the trigger like a puppy, were trembling. It was harder than ever to see through watery eyes that were dribbling down her cheeks and sweaty palms made a solid grip impossible. Her head was pounding; the harrying music below was a vast swish of pandemonium in her ears. She might have vomited if it hadn't been for gulping at the right moment. 'Don't think much of it,' she calmed herself. 'They might end up shooting Xenol after all and, that would leave me out of the equation.' *But I can't be sure if they will. What if they kill Serpens? What will I do then? Continue with my end of the task? Kill TWO Phestors in one day? And what if the Phestor's girl—?*

She sucked it all up and tightened her finger around the trigger, set her chin into her upper arm and honed in on the doors of the Municipal Float's Bunker...

Those doors slowly started to rise. An unrivalled uproar from the crowd ascended with it and so did Samuella's racing pulse. Her hopes remained turbulent.

The Municipal Procession began. First came the musical float that forced everyone to clamber to his or her feet and close into a bigger and messier huddle. The trumpeters were boasting with loud notes, high and low; a saxophone rang out a legato to which the crowd swayed hypnotically; and, as the drum rumbled—*louder and louder and louDER and LOUDER*—the first of the guest floats emerged. On this one were a select number of children from all age groups. These were the mascots of Quomer's youth - 'THE CHILDREN OF QUOMER WELCOME THE EAST NATIONS!' - waving and smiling and looking all *la-di-da*. Before long, the choir of children joined the parading orchestra and started to sing along to the four anthems of the East. Suddenly, Samuella started to think about vomiting again, as the heads of forty or so singing children drifted through her scope. Her fingers were struggling to hold still; she felt like biting them. In fact, the spasms had migrated to her arms and legs. The following floats were dedicated to the various classes of Quomer - 'PLEASE SHOW YOUR GRATITUDE FOR THE MANY FACES OF DRACONEX INDUSTRIES!' A jumble of some of the prettiest and ugliest faces she'd seen since arriving in the East were divided into floats representing the Lower Class, the Middle Class and the Upper Class.☆ This time they were adults, however, and the grins were just as forced as those of the five-year-olds. After the mascot floats had covered the first quarter of *Mayn Street*, the final float was met at the bunker's entrance by a convoy of marching A.I. The convoy led the way ahead, parting the rebellious crowd that was filling the road. Their impeccable formation was like watching water extinguish a riotous fire.

At last, she laid her sight upon the Municipal Float. This was one monster of a contraption. Bigger and better than the rest. And her eyes inflated at the sight of *Golden A.I.* Never before had she seen

---

☆ The social division in the East was just as bad as the situation in the West. Only, you were more likely to be capitally punished if you were caught living in a region that was not matched to your class. By 2038, it had become such an issue that citizens in the East were only allowed to purchase their food dependent on what their status permitted them to buy.

Golden A.I. It made her even more terrified to pull the trigger. But she had to focus. She had to do it. No one else was going to.

She saw the two Phestors standing in the centre of the float's platform. They were surrounded by a group of half a dozen turbaned men with long blades and a miniature army of Golden A.I bordered the float's edges. Phestor Xenol was carrying his own sword, and if there was one thing that Samuella could instantly reminisce from her Dreamerverse fantasy it was the Solar Blade. *Why does he have it?* she wondered. *He must be the Drag-in after all.* Now, without a shadow of a doubt, she cemented it in her mind. The connection couldn't have been made clearer to her.

Her decision was made.

The butt of the rifle had been cocked up over her shoulder again to securely lock her aim. And, compressing rigidness and precision, she followed the float as it smoothly progressed through *Mayn Street*, the road ahead having already been cleared by the cavalcade of A.I.

She knew that she had to time this perfectly. Whilst constantly sliding an eye over to the Burnouts to check up on the Head Sniper, she tried to mirror every one of her movements with his. Every time he lurched his eye in to aim. Every time he lifted his head up to look over the parapet at the crowds below. Every time he paused. And every time he took a quick glimpse behind him, just to check…

The one thing she'd forgotten to do—

Sameulla froze.

—was to look at the space behind her—

The small barrel of a handgun met the back of her head.

—just to check.

The Drag-in's Sunset...

Doctor Islie – or, at this point, All Eyes – approaches us with open arms. He gives each of us a look of faux gratitude. Then stops dead in his tracks when he realises we're all slowly backing away, keeping our distance from him.

All Eyes lifts both eyebrows in theatrical disbelief.

'Personal space,' Oscar says. 'That's all.'

'All what?' our former guardian snaps. 'Is that all you can do? Cower away from me and shimmy into the shadows?'

'It's better than pursuing the promise of a demon,' Oscar implies.

'I'm a lot of things. But the last thing I am is a demon. Like you, as far Dreamers go, I'm as real as they get,' Islie insists, hiding his offence behind the grinning bars that are his phony white teeth: the cell to that wet flapping-muscle and that thirsty, dripping chamber of gums and, most horrifically, it's the cage of a singing jailbird that gongs the bell of his uvula – namely, his stinking arrogance. 'I'd say, rather, the words you're looking for are "*convincing*" and a "*silver-tongued psychiatrist of many talents*", similar to those of an omniscient king or...' he sucks in a wave of air through his pouting lips, 'an ambiguous delegate of the Stellar Gods. You were never the brightest specimen of your father, were you, Master Philson. I do, however, congratulate you for your adventurous turn in attitude – coming this far on your psychiatric journey to recovery I genuinely applaud; I did not expect your mental condition to improve so soon. A country-girl, yes, I would expect to adapt and recover; an East veteran, maybe; but, *with you,* Oscar...at least I can decently admit I have been wrong in *one* circumstance. I underestimated the surprisingly vibrant imagination of a Decider's son. Thank you for trusting my diagnosis anyway, Oscar.' Islie's smirk curls deeper, cheeks bulging.

'Don't give me all your therapy nonsense now,' Oscar warns. 'You lied about my dreams! You tricked me into thinking you didn't believe any of it! *You deceived me!*'

'I put you on the right path,' All Eyes hums calmly. 'I guided *all of you* and, look—here you've come. The doctor will see you all now.'

'After all we went through to get this far—how could All Eyes be you, Islie?' I say. 'How did you manage to manipulate all this? It doesn't make enough sense for a rotten slave-dealer like you to bully the brains of a Stellar God.'

'Slave-dealer?' Oscar and Samuella dart a look at me and exclaim at the same time.

'*Slave-dealer…bully…*never heard those nicknames around myself before…not once…not at all,' Islie jollily hums to himself and wavers on irksome legs of gelatine. He jabs a finger in my direction. 'Mister Tientar—my old friend—Oh, I apologise—that was your *last* name! *Lord* Camson will do, won't it? For a moment, I didn't recognise who you were exactly. You see, the *Lord* Camson I used to know would have rather been beheaded for fornicating with his master's mysterious mistress, than be caught in the company of two West Kids. Traitors operate best under other guises—don't you agree, my Lord?' Islie's shaking his head at me, supposedly disappointed – but he doesn't care at all; his disapproval is all false, all a show, to rile me. It's working.

'Don't you dare mention the Phestoress!' I tear into him with my first and final warning. 'She's nothing to do with this – nothing to do with me, or *you*, for that matter! You know that it's all been lies with Xenol! *Terrible lies! A lie, just like you, the mendacious riddler!*'

'What is he talking about, Cammy?' Samuella pokes her damned nose in – as one can usually expect with the plucky country girl.

'Nothing!' I spark. 'Nothing of anyone's business—'

'Oh—but you've never actually known, have you?' Islie remarks gleefully.'All these years, you've served under her and her patriarch and you've never truly realised who she is.'

I gaze feebly in Islie's general direction, unprepared for anything he might be about to say.

'There wasn't on feature of hers—not one—that ever once made you wonder—perhaps—maybe—what if?' Islie teases.

'Of course…her eyes…many times!' I cry. 'But I never—I was never—I couldn't—!'

'What was that? Huh?' Islie hustles with my disconcertion. 'Why not? If you suspected it was her, why ever did you hold back?'

'I was too afraid!'

'Camson,' Samuella delicately interrupts again, 'what does he mean about the Phestoress? What about her made you suspicious—?'

'The Phestoress was Lord Camson's wife, my darling,' Islie answers her so abruptly I can't object. 'Long before he became Phestor Xenol's leading henchman, I had the pleasure of introducing Lord Camson's former wife, the young and handsome Evanessa, to her current patriarch: Phestor Xenol of the Sixth Nation.' Islie musters his heaviest storytelling charm, as if reciting an age-old nursery rhyme.

My heart ascends from my chest and lodges itself into my oesophagus, compelling me to choke on my shock. 'You—It was you who stole my wife from me! You took Evanessa from me and sold her into her misery! All this time, she adopted the role of Xenol's mistress—and I never knew!'

But Islie spares me none of his attention, instead shunning me for the sake of informing Oscar and Samuella about our history.

'I had spent some time as a merchant of mistresses in Quomer and I was responsible for selling Lord Camson's former wife on to her new home, where she became Phestor Xenol's mistress. Little did Lord Camson know at the time that I myself had a brief liaison with the girl, before dutifully handing her over to Xenol, her buyer. The affair was never destined to last long. It was an unsettled coupling, her and I. An accidental collision of affections. We were initially inspired by each other's ideals - a Mankind's World without Deciders and Phestors strangling the masses and belittling their Sister Nations. I really am sorry, Camson. I had no means to upset you. I genuinely had no idea that Evanessa had been yours, until the day she finally spoke of you. She very rarely talked about her past - her upbringing, you and Thuban, and so on. It was like pulling teeth, and limbs, and hair—literally.' Islie has his hands up and his head bowed, trying his hardest to hide his sarcasm. 'That was the moment I chose to auction her at the Quomer Market, for there was no way I could trust the wife of an East veteran, ward of the Phestorship, to be an accomplice in the greater scheme of my plans. I felt like I had been cheated.'

'You played a role in Evanessa's agony!' I bark. 'The pain she shamefully hides beneath her veil!'

This wife auctioneer better keep his bidding mouth shut about my wife—

'I may have actually treated her better if I'd known more about your history as an Infidel. An *Icon* Infidel too—what a label! You were a chief progressive at the forefront of the last Great Liberal generation – a striving advocate of the Punk King! No wonder you kept that old identity so quiet during your services under Xenol's guild. I'd have taken much better care of your wife if I'd been aware of that fun fact. However, to be fair, it's no secret how fickle the IRC can be and how fast they are to betray the liberal cause,' Islie continues to play along with the hubristic front, building face in a hopeless but inevitable encounter with his three nightmares all coming back to haunt him at once. 'Like any Night Dreamer, Evanessa's morals were fine overall,' he stutters cautiously, 'but not as explicit as mine. "Inspire" is what she said to me, "I want to inspire you" with *this* and "I want to inspire you" with *that—that* and *this* and *this* and *that—this, that, that, this*! In the end, it got to me just like it got to her patriarchs and I was forced to just—' He sighs. 'She caused me to break away from my goodwill; it angered me…badly…her shallow, repetitive bile and her lack of substance in the prelude to what would be the start of my journey to remoralising the world made me insane! She sounded like an A.I. constantly eulogising the legislation inside its head! Her principles came across as amateurish and forced—so pretentious. And so it felt so wonderfully progressive to quieten her yapping nonsense and demolish it with my own voice—*my own voice* that had always been silenced by men greater than me! I felt so *knightly* doing it and *so incredibly instrumental* and *influential! I rejoiced, for it felt like I'd done the impossible—it was like I'd silenced an A.I.! Oh, Lord Camson!* Putting up with her place-holding mind-set and her passive attitude to freedom stimulated me to become more than I was – a sad, scrounging dealer in the Sixth Nation and an irrelevant West ex-patriot. I've lived through enough traumas in that reality to frequently feel the desire and the need to challenge those great fools whom I'd once imagined I could never possibly measure myself against. And who the hell are *you* to talk on her dim behalf, Lord Camson! *Lord? LORD? HAAA—NOOO—NO, NO, NO!* You're not a *Lord* at all! You're the traitor who never did rescue his damsel. You were a coward too afraid to confront the Phestor over his adopted mistress and repossess her as your estranged wife! Whereas I, once a passive and compliant farmer from the vales of the Fourth Nation—I have been enlightened with a platform and an opportunity to reawaken Mankind's World from its slumber under automation.'

That's it! My mind is smouldering atrocious thoughts, ideas and ways of murdering this terrific fiend of a man for everything he's done. It's been many years since this mistress dealer made his impact on my life, but the wound is still sore and he *has* to pay for every second of the dread he has dealt me.

'You became deluded, Islie,' Oscar declares. 'That's what happened to you.'

'I adapted, Oscar. I grew up and I changed with the times,' Islie provides Oscar with a rather patronising answer. 'While the rest of the world wallowed under cruel and divisive regimes, I was being objective and progressive!'

'You didn't change with the times,' Oscar says. 'You just became hungry for something that every person wants, something far more than the dissolution of power—you got greedy for control. Just what everyone else desires - control of their own lives. But it isn't as easy as just dishing out the decisions to the people! The reason I never contested my father's authoritative hand at his Table is because I could see the cataclysm that the lack of regulation would cause—especially in a time when people struggle to manage simple tasks on their own! The New Democracy's grasp on digitalisation has desensitised us as a species, but suddenly reforming power now would be too dangerous!'

'It is a responsibility humanity must step up to and a vital change for us to evolve beyond the conflicts of selfish men!' Islie argues. 'I am changing the mentality of our world!'

'You aren't *changing* anything,' Oscar says. 'That mindset, that hope, has always been there. But it's impracticable. There's nothing different or special about the way you think!'

'Nothing special about me? Then what about you, Oscar? You're too immature to stomach such significance as I. You can't even confess your weakness to your own father. How can you request significance when you don't even know your place?' Islie torments. 'You're terrified of even the faintest power, let alone stepping into the shoes of the most powerful man in Mankind's World.'

'Enough with this, Islie! Enough!' I jump in for Oscar's defence, astonishingly.

'Does—I'm sorry—does that also mean you *speak* for the boy now?' Islie hoots at me and then gasps at Oscar. 'Am I getting this right? You'll let this East Man stand *your* ground? Is this what it's come to? The pair of you are sticking up for each other now? And it was *me* that made this spectacle happen? I must be a genius, a wizard of some kind!'

'Leave him alone with your folly!' I shout up at Islie – a lanky, emaciated tower of a man in comparison to me.

'I apologise for diverting the conversation in this way. I meant to introduce myself properly to the three of you, without all the horrendous exposition. But please try to correct me if I am wrong here, Lord Camson,' Islie continues. 'I am aware that you've found a new place for the West in your soul. Am I presumptuous in suggesting that your heart might have grown, perhaps, an inch since you started out on this expedition to find yourself? That was what this whole excursion turned into after all. At least, you've gained *something*. If it wasn't the Drag-in's blood on your hands, at least you *learned something* about your truest nature. When it comes to West Folk, you're not so coiled up in your shell after all. You have all discovered something about yourselves, about your spirits, which you've never been aware of previously. The candid fate of a Night Dreamer is a thing of irony.'

'It's called tolerance,' I retort. 'If you put up with someone long enough, you tend to ignore all their shapes and colours eventually.'

'No! It's nothing of the sort! It's called masking barbarity, my friend!' Islie holds his face right up against mine. I know that the anger within my left arm, and the Solar Blade at the end of it, won't tolerate *him* for much longer.

Oscar tries to get this straight in his head. 'Camson knows Islie as a street merchant who had an affair with his ex-wife, before he sold her on as a mistress to Phestor Xenol?'

'*Correct*—but you are very wrong in one aspect,' Islie answers him. 'Camson knows Islie—*yes*—but All Eyes knows *everyone*.' Islie draws away from me, fearless of the sword being held in my hand.

'And Evanessa has a Dreamerverse counterpart also,' Samuella adds. 'She was the woman I met when I first arrived, and she requested that I burned her body, so her spirit could be released and retired from its duties. She was the Last Night Dreamer and she now serves as the Phantom, the keeper of the counter-weapon that was constructed to expel the Drag-in and lock it into the Void forever.'

Islie cuts a glance at Samuella from the corner of his eye, unnerved by her sureness. He quickly hones his interest back onto Oscar to hide this agitation for Samuella's remark.

'You missed me, Oscar, didn't you?' Islie says offhandedly.

'When I told you about the Dreamerverse, you wanted nothing to do with it. You told my father I was deluded when it is you who is quite certainly unhinged!' Oscar restates. 'Why did you lie to me, Islie?'

'Because, Me in Reality knows nothing about Me in the Dreamerverse. The only connection we share is our conscience, and so our objective remains the same. Nothing else. I thought you lot had come far enough to understand that crossing the Void makes any Dreamer oblivious…that is unless you are one who arrives after sunset, a Night Dreamer.' Suddenly, Islie switches his tone and sniggers. 'Dear me! I sell more porkies than a butcher! Of course, I'm simultaneously aware of what goes on in both the real world and the Dreamerverse. I helped the Dreamerverse to manifest!'

'How?' Oscar inquires.

But he won't be getting an answer it seems. Not yet.

Having quickly lost interest in Oscar again, the man – wearing a pretty impeccable grey suit and sparkling silver spats – goes over to Samuella.

'The best introduction is saved for last,' Islie says. He venerates her, as if she hasn't mentioned the counter-weapon, even though we all heard it. 'What sort of an uncle would forget about his only niece? The girl he brought up to become the fine young woman who stands before him now.'

He stretches his arms out again, as if expecting a hug from her.

'He'd be the same man who likes to fake his own death and leaves her to scavenge a life out of her teenage-self,' Samuella spurns.

'Come on, Samuella. That isn't entirely fair, is it?' he says. 'You were always a very capable young lady. That farm wasn't doing me any favours. And I'd already played my part after your parents left you behind. I had confidence in you—'

'You made a promise to them!' Samuella roars. 'You swore on your life that you would protect me! Instead, you lied about your death in that mine and you left me!'

I lean over to whisper to her. 'Do I have permission to kill your uncle?'

'Not just yet,' she responds. 'I need some answers.'

'Oh—come to ease, the three of you!' Islie mediates. 'I haven't tried to kill you at this point, so why conspire to kill me?'

'Because that quest you hoaxed us into was what nearly killed us!' Oscar responds. 'And, what's more, you've hoodwinked us in the real world too—both worlds, from the start, like it's all just been a massive game to you—"*All Eyes*"—All lies!'

'That's not what this is about, tricking people and playing games. Your journey was not a waste of time at all, but to find me those emeralds at a dire time. The Constellation Map would have never worked for me, for it would only work for the eyes of the newest generation of Night Dreamers,' Islie vows. 'You have done as I asked: you've gathered the emeralds and here you stand on the verge of defeating the Drag-in.'

Nothing about the glint in his watery eyes suggests he's telling even the slightest ounce of the truth. Only telling us what we want to hear, what we've been told all along.

'I was a Night Dreamer, just like you three,' he continues to explain. 'So was your mother, Oscar. And Camson, so was your wife – poor girl, for years I had Evanessa believing she was the last one alive. After we foiled the Drag-in the last time, Evanessa and Cassandra had transcended this world and had become mere servants of Constellation Planet, relics of their former selves, but rose beside the Stellar Gods in the heavens. When the old king of Constellation Planet – the real All Eyes – came to grant us our promise, the reward he offers all his heroes, Cassandra both and I agreed that the Dreamerverse would remain the only home for our conscience. Our bodies would remain in the real world and our true conscience would stay alive and satisfied on Constellation Planet forever. It meant whenever we slept here in the Dreamerverse, we could still see the real world in our dreams, but never be able to physically operate our bodies there again. We would have had our connection between worlds severed and whenever night came, we would only be voyeurs, peering through a lucid window into reality. We shared a conscience with our real world counterparts, but we could never be them. Unlike the two of us, Evanessa chose the opposite: she wanted to stay in the real world and, subsequently, her body was discarded here.' Islie looks at Samuella. 'That's why she told you to burn it, to set her abandoned Dreamerverse spirit free. She only decided to return to reality because she feared she might have never seen her husband and son again. She was sorry for you Camson and missed you profoundly.'

'I've already been told my mother was a Night Dreamer,' Oscar says. 'This isn't news to me, Islie.'

'And Evanessa as well?' I mention. 'Well, I never knew she was one. I've spotted her here before, only a glimpse of her on Awakening Coast. The body Samuella burnt looked nothing like how I remembered her upon closer inspection – too prim, too proper and perfect. More hair than I ever remembered her having – golden hair. The

Dreamerverse must have granted her the liberty to don her most favoured appearance. The beauty her patriarchs robbed from her. And yet, I never knew she was once in the same position I am now. That she too was a Night Dreamer.'

'Yes, they were and all they did was fight and moan about each other. The two of them *hated* each other so much. Women from different sides of the real world, West and East. To think, if the Memory Lane had worked its magic on them and they had no recollection of the real world at all and where their bitter differences lay there, they might have got on like a pair of squirrels in an acorn forest,' Islie imagines, dropping his head and staring vacantly at his feet. 'Although I sympathised, I never understood Evanessa's choice to depart the Dreamerverse forever. It would have been such a shame to never be Night Dreamer again.'

'But I still don't quite understand or believe what you're telling us,' I consider. 'You must still be a Night Dreamer if you can remember so much about the real world.'

Islie squeezes out an awkward flinch in his expression, clearly implying that he's been caught out. 'Okay, fine—' he sighs. 'Once you become a Night Dreamer, you're always one, by nature.'

'YOU KEEP LYING!' Oscar cries and lurches forwards. Samuella has to restrain him, tugging at his arm. 'WHERE'S MY MOTHER AND WHAT'S HAPPENED TO EVANESSA AND CAMSON'S SON—THE PEOPLE YOU FOOLED, ALL EYES! THE PEOPLE YOU STOLE FROM US AND ENLISTED INTO DANGER!'

'I did nothing to your mother, or Evanessa. And remember those Dinomites that lit up the water on Awakening Coast? Yes, *they* kidnapped Thuban, and they nearly teleported *you* off that reef in the Sapphire Lagoon.'

'Teleported us?' Samuella dissects.

'Yes—that is what the dinoflagellates are capable of,' Islie says. 'They move particles at the speed of light and, with enough momentum – i.e., if you had struggled and splashed around too much – they can snatch your spirits away and deposit them here. It is exactly the reason why I told you to stay out of the ocean. The Dinomites would have brought you straight here, to the heart of the Soulcano, and that would have ruined my mystique. But, as for the fates of my former comrades, Cassandra and Evanessa, none of that was my doing. I was not All Eyes back then. Before I usurped the throne, I was like you: All Eyes had modestly enlisted me to slay the Drag-in—I succeeded with my fellow Night Dreamers and we went our separate ways once he task was done.

But he had promised us more than eternal habitation on Constellation Planet; he had sworn to make us Stellar Gods with the ability to govern the Dreamerverse. He had promised us an even greater purpose; an abundance of control on this world was to be delegated to us. After the others left, I stayed behind at the Kingdom Palace and argued with him about it for hours on end. Finally, flustered by it all, I lost myself and I drove the Solar Blade through All Eyes. Before I knew it, I had arrogated power from the original king. The instant he was pronounced dead, the king's Patrol kneeled to my command – I became the new sovereign of Constellation Planet. In the case of you three, I selected you from the real world and summoned you here after sunset, lying carefully about who I was pretending to be in our primary introduction, the true king that I wasn't. But I didn't *trick* you, only played my disguise to an advantage! Get that correct!' Islie lectures at all of us. 'I had to lie, otherwise none of you would be here!'

'How do you know? We might have been more inclined to believe you if you'd just shown us your face from the beginning!' Oscar persists in arguing with the man who claims to be the King of Constellation Planet.

'Wake up, Philson! It was because I was already so familiar with each of your personalities that I knew formally commanding you under my real identity would not have been as successful. Why remain honest when, with the power of the Stellar Gods swelling within me, I can summon Dreamers between worlds as and when I wish, and without them knowing? Your meeting and your connection needed to seem like a coincidence. That way, events played more naturally, without any of you knowing that you were all bonded by my memory, my imagination. I was the connection that brought the three of you together!' He rattles hysterically with excitement. 'And you all thought you were *special*! *Ha—fools!* You believed it was because you were worlds apart and might have been drawn to one another because of your differences – as if opposites really do attract—*right*.'

'So, if you were this omniscient demigod all this time we were out hunting, what was stopping you from getting off your soppy arse to find the emeralds yourself? What was with the Map?' Samuella complains. 'You made us follow that dippy Map full of stars, when you could have just told us where the emeralds were from the get-go! Are you still telling me that wasn't you just messing us around in a big game?'

'I told you that I didn't know where to find the emeralds. Their subsistence transcends the sight of the Stellar Gods. Evanessa hid them, scattering them across Constellation Planet years ago after our previous generation sought them the last time – that was over a decade ago – and only the current generation of Night Dreamers can navigate the Constellation Map leading to them. I thought I made this all clear to you the first time.' Islie taps his foot impatiently. 'My dear Samuella, the spirit of the Night Dreamer runs in our blood. Your parents thought I was mad when I told them all about it – Constellation Planet, and the Dreamerverse, and all the stars boasting in the sky like they could never imagine them in their world. That embarrassing excuse for a reality you've been forced to call your home for too long. Meanwhile, I've been here all along – at least, *this* iteration of me.'

'The You I knew in the Real World lied to me and ran off to the East,' his niece disagrees.

'I was just like you, Samuella. I have always been *just like you*! The born leader, the open-minded optimist with their head screwed on, while the other Night Dreamers – the two girls in my case – bickered and bickered and bickered like *morons*.'

My confusion escalates. 'I can't believe All Eyes has been a pivotal influence in all of our lives. The very same man.'

Islie anxiously rubs the toe of one shoe against the ankle of the other. I notice how his arms are very quietly trembling as his impatience grows.

'I never told you about my Uncle Cephalus,' Samuella moans. 'This man – this *thing* – pretended to be my Uncle Cephalus and helped me to look after my parents' old farm back in the Fourth Nation. I was told that he died in a collapsed mine and I was forced to sell the farm and move to the City.' She looks like she's close to crying. 'He ditched me just as my parents had – to reinvent themselves as radicals!'

'I know my departure left you quite premature at the time. But, gladly, the outcome was everything I'd anticipated. Everything turned out fine. Look at you now! Independent, devoted, and the strongest woman you could have ever grown up to be. For that, you should be thanking me and appreciating my absence.'

'*Thanking you?*' she hisses. 'YOU'RE A SELFISH JOKE WHO LEFT ME FOR DEAD AND YOU DIDN'T ANTICIPATE ANYTHING!'

'I did. I've been watching you from above,' he says calmly.

'What do you mean? Peeping at me through your little window in the Void?' Samuella winces. '*You're gross!*'

'Believe me, All Eyes sees everything,' Islie says. 'What's more, all three of you are now thinking beyond the Void. Can you feel it?

Your consciences have advanced and transcended above all other Dreamers on Constellation Planet. You can remember more about the real world than you've ever been able to before. That is the power I hold and I, by opening the Void wider, can bestow it upon every Dreamer. I *gift* it to everyone!'

'*By opening the Void wider?*' I catch Islie out again. 'Is that a way of you saying you've been helping the Drag-in to break through, you've been advocating the very thing we're trying stop?'

Islie quits rubbing his shoes together and becomes very still.

'Not advocating it,' Islie insists. 'I've been using the Drag-in as a way to get back to reality. If the Drag-in shatters the Void and the two worlds become one, I'll no longer need to fantasise about reality through the window of a dream. I too can break through and can return to my body in the real world, join forces with my other self—my *inferior* conscience—and live the dream I've dreamt for over a decade now. And the Drag-in's power will be at my disposal, for I will possess all three emeralds. I will hold the reigns to existence itself. So I should probably be thanking the three of you, wonderful Night Dreamers, for bringing home my Drag-in to me.'

'Do I have permission to kill him—*now*?' I repeat this. The Solar Blade is more or less swinging, its tip tickling the stone ground…

'You don't need *permission* to *kill me,*' All Eyes mocks me. 'I gave you permission to slay the Drag-in, but you couldn't even manage that, soldier.'

I launch at him. But Oscar holds out an arm and pushes himself in front instead. 'You need to explain the Drag-in to us then,' Oscar says sensibly.

'No. He needs to *stop* it!' Samuella argues. 'Stop it from breaching through!'

'You can't ask a force of nature to stop itself from occurring,' Islie reasons. 'You cannot politely ask for the earth to stop rotating. Prayers mean nothing and the Gods aren't listening. They only compromise for me. The Drag-in cannot be commanded, only guided.'

'It isn't a force of nature, though! It's contrived, manmade! Come on—explain it to us! What is the Drag-in *exactly*? And I'm going to keep repeating myself until I get a solid answer!' Oscar demands.

Islie touches Oscar softly on the cheek. 'The Drag-in isn't a person. It isn't a living thing at all. It's the brainchild of a dream—what else can it be?' He thoroughly licks his bottom lip as he describes the abomination he is about to unleash. 'The Drag-in is nothing more than a concept. An ancient myth. An existing rumour. A façade of raw imagination constantly on the loose and chasing humanity through the realms of its wildest fears. Calling is some graceless, land-wading beast was another lie that I told you. Just to scare you. The Drag-in you've seen, the big creature lurking about this planet—*the Living Smoke*—isn't actually the Drag-in. That is what the embodiment of human fear looks like in a dreamscape. I didn't create that. Humanity was responsible for making that and nobody can stop it, because it is a physical force fabricated entirely from our imagination. And if there is one thing that cannot be destroyed in reality or a dream, it's imagination. You can't stop men, women and children from fearing, and the conceptualised entities of their minds are unruly, totally detached from somatic control. That freedom empowers the Drag-in. The Drag-in is completely infinite because of this autonomy that flourishes way out of our hands. And as the days and nights have turned along your journey, those hands of ours have become weaker. The most absolute nightmare has finally found life and has discovered its feet on both sides of the mental void.' Islie's expression dries up; all the maddened excitement in his colourful face is devoured in a pale vortex. 'The terrifying imbalance is accomplished. At last, an envious imagination has finally outweighed our only perception of reality.'

Samuella, Oscar and I remain silenced by this revelation. We are all thinking the same thing: *The Drag-in can't be destroyed.*

'So, is this our final stop?' I conclude. 'If the counter-weapon is out of the questions and very little can be done to stop it at this stage, why are we even here?'

'Well, Lord Camson, I'd like to thank you for bringing my sword back safely,' Islie says. He opens his hand and, to our horror, the Solar Blade materialises in it. I don't even see it coming. The Blade has vanished from my grip and it's now in his hands. It only takes me to blink to then realise he's now wearing the Red Robe. *My* Red Robe and the only connection I have left to reviving my son.

'What do you think?' Islie flutters about in the long night robe that has spontaneously arrived to cover his neatly tailored suit. 'Do I look good in red?'

'Is that why we're here, then?' I say. 'So that you can rob us of our stuff?'

'Not to *rob* you as such, Lord Camson. I prefer to see it as reclaiming what must be destroyed. The Solar Blade poses a threat to the Drag-in's chances of breaking through that void, yes? And as for the Red Robe...well...now I'm wearing a piece of your son. The strands of Thuban's spirit are in this Robe, so you will have little eagerness to kill me before I can escape through the Void and off into reality. It also looks rather prettier on me than it did on you, Camson.' Islie dances on his own in the glittery Robe. 'Don't you worry, though. I'll be sure to tell Evanessa and Thuban all about you on my return to the real world.' He gives me a wink and shows off the Solar Blade, twirling it in front of all three of us.

'The Solar Blade is the only weapon that can damage the Drag-in and weaken it,' Oscar remarks. 'I've seen it in the Real World. I can't recall who had it. But, there, it's just a regular sword.'

'Of course—until I make it across and reunite it with its cosmic counterpart. Once I get my hands on the Solar Blade in reality and restore its stellar capabilities, that and the emeralds will be all I require to reign over mankind's ultimate Nightmare.'

'I'll break *you* before you break that wall!' I scream at the fraud.

'By destroying what *can* be destroyed, we're not provoking the thing that *cannot* be destroyed. I'm wasting my time speaking with you.' Islie spins his back on us and dances back towards the throne. 'The Drag-in will be in good hands with me—*I promise*.'

Islie lifts the Blade in the air, gives the metal one last shine in the presence of the firelight, and then tosses it to one of the scavenging half-beings. The lucky skull collects the Blade in its skeletal hand and gawks at the magnificence of its design. However, once this has been done (and four or five other half-beings have joined the skull in a ceremonious cluster around the wonderful device), the Blade meets the flames with the rest of the burning treasures.

'WHAT ARE YOU DOING?' Samuella cries. 'Now, we'll never have a chance with it! That sword cut into the Drag-in and—'

'Well, it didn't destroy it, did it? Instead, the Blade made matters worse. I only need the Solar Blade present in reality. No good having two to allocate, is there. What I'm missing now are *three emeralds*,' Islie interrupts Samuella, toying with his sway of the situation and irrefutably certain that he'll get exactly what he wants from us. 'So, are you going to hand them over to me nicely? Or am I going to have to play my usual game of "talk you to death and pick pockets"?'

Once again, we give him nothing to work with. Consequently, he shrugs, and so come the three emeralds. They appear - one rising out from each of our apparels - and hover in the space before us all. Then, they scatter around the cave, lost in the mess of treasures that inhabit the space.

'Collect those and dispose of them,' All Eyes commands the skulls.

Every half-being in the cave begins to search for the hidden emeralds. They're hard to find, but they sparkle markedly brighter than anything else in here.

Almost in perfect cohesion to Islie's hobbling search party are the hulking humanoids that lurk up from behind us. We don't spot them coming. They're silent and their strength is incontestable, as they grapple our wrists and press us down to our knees. I glance up at the chin of my captor and find the head of one of the king's Palm Patrollers. These primates slip about the depths of the Camelopardalian jungle unnoticed and prove just as discreet in the gut of a volcano. They too have no choice but to obey the orders of their overlord – King "*All Lies*" Islie.

'You can't take the Drag-in into *your own hands*, not after all we've been through! Everything that *you* put us through!' Samuella howls. She wants to steal her uncle's attention away, but he's preoccupied with appreciation for his new loot: the Blade, the Robe and—any moment now—all three emeralds. 'Uncle Ceph! Uncle Ceph! You can't do this to me! Let us go! Allow us to escape, at least! We have nothing more that you want!'

Islie scowls at her pleading and marches up to her. 'I'm not your uncle here, not on this side of the Void. Right now, I'm not even the mighty All Eyes. I'm nervous, just as you are. But I only need the Drag-in to breach through. That's the last puzzle in the conundrum to escaping my detention in this empty dimension of lost souls. The sooner I find the counterparts of those emeralds in the real world, the sooner I can prevent the Drag-in from returning through the Void again. I will have the Drag-in's whereabouts under lock and key and will, by then, be no less than the gatekeeper of existence. The Drag-in is about to embark on its step between worlds. Once we get back through to reality, I can find the emeralds there, and then I can keep the Drag-in prisoner in the Void. Trap it there for as long as I demand. There—happy? That is my heroism in exchange for yours. Please be mindful that I am grateful for your contribution. I wouldn't have been reunited with the Digimine emeralds if it weren't for your help. '

'You can't hoard the emeralds,' Oscar interrupts. 'We need them here in the Dreamerverse, to power the counter-weapon!'

'Yes—the Lighthouse, I know about that!' Islie says. 'The Phantom's Lighthouse is very much what it says on the packaging—a counter-weapon,' he chuckles. 'But that resolution won't be happening today, I'm afraid. I'll be making the call this time, not the Night Dreamers.'

'What call?' I support Oscar. 'He's right—you haven't even told us why the other emeralds in reality are so important to you! You've told us the Drag-in will help you to return to Mankind's World, but what happens when you get there?'

Islie gazes around the room with his hands stroking the fabric of the Red Robe.

'The emeralds will warrant for me, let's say, protection from an elite Intelligence organisation,' he responds. 'I must be defended from my adversaries: those who'll come to take the emeralds from me and steal away my rule. A new era of life is coming to the real world, one that will surpass its digital age, one that will outstrip the composure of all its Nations. A fallen, forgotten Nation will be renewed once again and I will be its leader, the crown of its hegemony.' He screws his torso round to examine me, Samuella and Oscar again. 'The Drag-in is an example of why one's imagination must always stay grounded, because a fantasy in a realist's mind can be cataclysmic. Nobody in the real world believes in the Drag-in, for it would go against everything they've ever known. The real world isn't a fantastical place, not a place for fiction. Fiction doesn't belong in reality. Never has done, never will! Until now! I will be the first progressive pioneer to bond these universes together!'

'An elite Intelligence,' Samuella rewinds Islie's words. 'He's talking about the A.I. The emeralds give him dominion over the A.I. That'll make him untouchable when he returns to the real world.'

'How?' I spark a look of bewilderment at all three of them – Oscar, Samuella and Islie. I'm completely withdrawn from this understanding they share.

'The emeralds contain a rare mineral called Digimine and the A.I. are fuelled on it,' Oscar continues to explicate. 'That was what Aegia had meant about the emeralds being the vital component to a dangerous weapon in the real world. She was meaning to say that the emeralds in the Dreamerverse lead to the demise of the Drag-in, whereas the emeralds in reality lead to the powerhouse of the Tin Men – both of which are the two mightiest threats humanity has to face. One is corporeal and the other is psychological.'

'And what a fabulous memory you two Night Dreamers have,' Islie congratulates their revelations, patronising the two of them. 'You put the clues together and you worked it out for yourselves. So, allow me to now master my new control. Constellation Planet is currently under my reign, so, whilst the Drag-in is using this world as a launch-pad, I will decide whether or not I'll allow it to!' His eyes flicker petulantly like the seditious flames behind him. 'Quickly, you imbeciles! Find me my emeralds!' He bullies the struggling skeletons. 'I want them in the pocket of this Robe before the Void opens!'

'I can't let you do this,' Samuella says. 'You've got this all wrong! Integrating worlds will be a disaster and the consequences of misusing our only means of killing that monster will be even worse! Let us take the emeralds to the Lighthouse and maybe we can help you to find your way back to reality, without unleashing the Drag-in's chaos!'

'Samuella, I've always respected you as a very resourceful child. But—please take heed—my plan is the best solution for both worlds,' Islie tells her. 'Mankind's World must move on and a new entity must become its influence. I will lead a social revolution the world has never seen before or seen coming. It will be an existence measured by one man's rekindled and superior imagination and, some day, I predict my vision will be fruitful and all humanity will share the same conscience, the same ideas, the same values…the same *fantasy*. You might call it a New Constellation Planet, if you wish. It will be two parallel universes finally joined as one utopia.'

A sudden gust of wind immerses the cave and the massive fire dies. With the inevitable darkness comes the impeccable hush. But it isn't long enough to extinguish our fear alongside the flames, as a deep growl rolls throughout the elemental insurgence inside the Soulcano.

It's back. The beast is back.

In this blindness, there are only three objects that stand out, glowing like radiantly hot nuggets of extravagance in a sea of underwhelming treasures. Round. Small. Essential. And they make that known to every eye in the cave. 'There they are!' All Eyes screams. 'They're there! Somebody grab them all and let's get the hell out of here! *Hurry up!*'

The skeletons scurry for the emeralds. Yet, it isn't only the cries of their master that have inducted them. Tremors are building in the ground. Not just beneath the cave, but all over—there is something in motion. Vehement activity below, above and sideways. My first thought is: earthquake. Although, it is rapidly becoming apparent that we are actually in the belly of an *eruption*.

Unable to balance against the vibrations, the skeletons tumble and collapse, shattering into piles of bones on impact with the ground. Islie storms through the pathetic muddle of clumsy skulls and goes to snatch the emeralds for himself. The magnificent tail of the Red Robe flails behind him, as he goes to pluck them from heaps of disassembled bones. But, once he drops to his knees and attempts to lift one of the emeralds, he finds that his hand sinks straight through. Frustrated, he runs across the cave to tackle another…and he desperately harasses the third. All of them are the same. He can't pick them up. They're transparent and stubbornly intangible to his touch. '*Hoooww–?*' he deplores. 'Does—not make—any sense!'

The mighty All Lies is drenched in fury. He rises from the ground and turns to the three of us on our knees. Then, he storms over to the fire to retrieve the Solar Blade that he so carelessly *disposed of*, now lying atop a bundle of bones. The Blade, although dosed in flames, is unscathed. He comes for us, ready to take full advantage of our vulnerability. 'Three mongrel Dreamers could not possibly have the capacity to challenge my power as ruler! *My indisputable freedom to construct Constellation Planet to my wish!*' he preaches, raising the Solar Blade above his waist with the point aimed at us and the flat of the blade reflecting onto the ceiling. 'I find it hard to believe any of you will wake up in any form of existence once *this* fine steel enters your ribcage!'

He swings it crossways in an attempt to behead all of us in one go…

However, the strength in his arms fails to withstand the thunderous heap of rocks that drop down on him from the cave ceiling above. Clambering boulders severe his forearms from their elbows and, thus, disenfranchise his grasp from the Blade. Massive rocks knock him to the ground and through the gaping hole above comes the head of the beast. The Drag-in descends into the cave with its mouth wide open. Its teeth clash with the rocks that shield the man's broken body. He can do nothing but whimper, paralysed to the spot.

'Let go! Let go! *Let us go!*' Oscar calls for the Patrollers to release us and they're too easy to convince. Like they arrived, the Palm Patrollers disappear, unheard, from the cave and we're released. Me and Samuella start for one of the cave entrances, but Oscar has other plans. Whilst the distracted Drag-in works on clawing at the "curtain call" of Islie beneath the rocks, Oscar falls back against the cave wall and briskly moves himself along. 'What are you doing?' Samuella shouts at him.

'The emeralds!' he replies. 'We need the emeralds! You two get out of here and I'll follow on behind!'

My immediate response to this isn't difficult to contemplate. He needs us to help him out. We're all dead, with or without him and those brilliant stones anyway.

Neglecting Samuella's eagerness to pull me away towards the cave's exit, I step over to where the Solar Blade lies – still not a scratch on it.

I pick it up and nick the attention of the Drag-in straight away. The beast elevates its head away from the weak man under the rocks and faces me. Terror strikes me in every nerve. This time, the creature isn't built of smoke. It's manifested from the black shadows of Nightmares. The Drag-in's face is squirming with lively, hungry entities. Human entities, long-deceased Dreamers. They scream my name: '*Camson! Camson! Camson!*' Somewhere in there, I see my son. Somewhere else, I see my wife. And somewhere, momentarily and further away, is the voice of Samuella, crying for me to '*come away!*' Oscar is in the corner of the cave. He's managed to collect the first emerald without any trouble. He moves swiftly onto the next one. So, I continue to act as his temporary diversion.

I give the Blade a fancy swing to hypnotise the beast. I'm also dancing, left and right, on my feet, to constantly alternate my position. Pretend it's a snake that needs to be tamed, I think to myself. As long as it doesn't turn around…we'll be on the home straight. No chances can be taken. The Drag-in is waiting for its moment to lurch at me—

Which it does! And, does so unsuccessfully. I dive luckily to my right as it launches at my left, and I force the point of the blade into the Drag-in's brow. It pierces right through and disperses a fair number of the ghostly heads shimmering in the beast's make-up.

Oscar retrieves the second emerald only metres from the end of the beast's tail. Meanwhile, Samuella and I are shrinking beneath a lizard of storm clouds, as it bawls in agony, screeching like a train that skids to a stop at our eardrums. In aggressive retaliation to my spearing attack, the Drag-in flings its head into my side and I fly across the cave. My back crumples on a nest of bones. Now, I'm crying with the beast. 'HURRY—! HURRY—NOW!' I urge that wretched West Boy to quicken his hunting pace. Oscar's just had to duck under the building-sized tail that is now airborne and rocking about violently. Then, I look up to find where Samuella's fallen to the ground herself, and she's up against the Drag-in, singled out and face-on. Her lack of defence leaves her hopeless and, once the Drag-in opens its jaws, there seems to be only one conclusion. I reach for the sword with my foot and kick it along the ground towards her. Samuella gets a hold of it and brings it up in front of her. Just as she does, a burst of black smoke hurtles out of the Drag-in's throat and strikes the sword.

That is when the flash tears everything to white…

When I can see clearly again, I find the sand and the beach. My aching head lifts, as if the grey clouds above have invisible strings that link to my scalp and some godly ventriloquist behind them has me aligned with his fingertips. I spy a little more of the palms of Draco Island and their wavering tops in the subtle evening breeze. Above everything is the Soulcano. Now far in the distance and fuming with black smoke, after having recently erupted. The sun is setting behind it and the sky has turned orange. If anyone asks why I'm in so much pain, I'll tell them that *I was launched from an erupting volcano and landed in paradise.* But *real paradise* is still one last trip away, across the oceans of Constellation Planet.

Oscar and Samuella finally appear in front of me, looking down at my delirious state. Samuella starts to push the small wooden raft that I lie on. The ocean's bounce soon starts to kick in once we evade the shallows. Somewhere, that warm air has found a whistling chill. Oscar's spotted a body lying on the beach. The dying soul of All Lies gazes up at him through a withered identity, with glassy eyes like the windows on a tattered bastion of flesh and bone. His mouth is gaping open and frozen still. That man no longer looks calculated and poised like Doctor Islie *or* Cephalus *or* All Eyes. Just another powerless human being, amongst other powerless people, in a powerful world. 'Are you finding it hard to believe?' Oscar says to the motionless man, all the while juggling one of the emeralds in his left hand. Then, Samuella calls for him to help her out with the raft. 'Come on,' she summons, 'before Camson and I leave you behind.' Oscar turns from the corpse of All Lies and rushes to join us on the makeshift float, as we rip away from Draco's eastern shore. He tosses the sand-speckled Red Robe he's retrieved from the beach onto my belly and gives me a reassuring wink.

At last, we embark on our final journey, off into our final sunset.

Chapter Fifteen
Fall Of The Marionette

The rowdiness of the crowd was not in good spirit. Defiant assailants who reviled the Phestorial Procession were pugnaciously throwing their bodies at the Municipal Float, while shouting and spitting and cursing at the two spearheads on frontline just as much. Meanwhile, the A.I. convoy escorting the vehicle secured a compressed barrier to deflect the violence. It was a spectacle to witness so much abhorrence towards two men standing on a slow-moving platform. The speed of the float didn't change throughout the journey, which meant that Xenol and Serpens would be forced to absorb the fiery commotion right up until they reached their destination – if either of them ever *did* reach *Port Ventre*. Xenol wasn't removed from the confidence that they would – at least, he was confident *he* would. The Majesty A.I. situated on-board the float itself hadn't flinched from their designated positions once. The disarray was not an immediate enough danger to the Phestors for the starboard A.I. to react, since none of the angry subordinates had yet overpowered the convoy on the ground. Such stasis from the elite Androkind catered to Xenol's cocksure demeanour. Everything, so far, was right on schedule.

Samuella caught Evanessa sitting on a bench behind a barrage of Phestorial Pugnars and under a bulletproof, chrome awning. Standing closely next to her was Camson. The terror she must have been experiencing right now seemed unthinkable. But, when Samuella felt the gun press against the back of her own head, she thought she might be a little worse off than the Phestoress for the time being. The small voice that followed came as no match for the ferocity of the crowd below, but it was enough to stun Samuella into paralysis. 'I know you've been told to do this, but you don't want the blood of that madman on your hands, darling. Xenol's life is not yours for the taking.'

The assassin with the rose-tinted hair fumbled to process what her interrupter had in common with the villainous dictator ploughing through the parade below. 'Who are you?' was all she was prepared to say in response.

The press of the gun became harder and her eyes rolled over to the ground to find a pair of spotless black shoes. Following up along the shin and the rest of the leg, she saw half a pair of black, pinstriped slacks. This man was wearing an expensive, typically West-fashioned suit – the armour of a First Nation diplomat.

Samuella slowly and bravely let go of the rifle's trigger and turned by flopping from her belly onto her back. Stood with his legs staunchly pinned on either side of her torso, she saw no one other than Decider Philson of the West Nations glaring down at her. His pale, bald dome prodded a crescent in the sun and his smitten simper was glossy with sweat. He still pointed the gun closely at her forehead. She was both pleasantly and unpleasantly astonished to see him of all people come to disrupt her shot at the Phestor.

It's over, she quietly thought.

'I trust you not to move another inch,' he warned. 'Don't worry, my entourage haven't been alerted deliberately. I wanted to see face of the Infidel Assassin for myself.'

'How did you know—?'

'—You were here?' The Decider tossed the veil off her head and brushed the end of his handgun against the lianas of her red locks. 'I got the call about you and my son in the Southern Polar Region. Had a strange notion for it at first, didn't believe what I was hearing—*my* son? Who would drag my boy into such a mess? And then I heard the news about Pegasus…' the Decider grunted. 'I made the connection very quickly and realised that it wasn't really a matter of my son I was being told about after all. In fact, from that point on, I no longer had a son. Oscar wasn't my spawn anymore. He'd become a liberal fighter for the subordinates, with you, and that King of the Punks—I gag at his name—*Pegasus*. How that stinking liberal ever became a governor in my Administration, I don't know. And he made you and Oscar his apprentices, his assassins.' He stroked the side of her face with the gun; the unblemished skin between her freckles coloured. 'Oscar was always expendable. His kink in the Philson dynasty is now officially as unrequired as it was unwanted. But, luckily for you, I won't bat an eye if you choose to wisely obey my instructions. Who knows—perhaps *you* can do me an heir finer than he ever was,' the Decider compromised.

'What are these instructions exactly?' Samuella trialled with his temper.

'Well, the first thing you're going to do is discharge that weapon.' He nodded to the rifle. 'You won't be pulling any triggers today.'

'And *you will be*, Decider?' She was tottering on a slippery line.

'Depending on how you perform for me—yes, I may eventually come to erase you from the matter.' Even in the stress of the confrontation, the Decider couldn't hold back a classy fix of the tie. 'Were you not expecting me to find you up here, Miss?' he said snidely, knowing the extent of her shock without even needing to ask her.

'Not really.'

'Good,' the Decider rejoiced, 'because that wasn't what I intended. I remembered tagging my chauffer with a microchip when he was hired to my service all those years back - as you do with the Help. And Stevenson wasn't where I left him when I last checked his monitor. In fact, my *HoloPad* tracked him to this exact building—and, instead, I find you here, keeping a good watch on our friend, Xenol. I'm not here to egg you on, or to support you in killing one man we all need alive - today, at least.'

'You want to protect Xenol? For how long? Until he seizes the opportunity to kill *you* as well?' Samuella was genuinely feeling less and less confident as she spoke to the Decider. Not only was she shocked to be threatened by the person she had least expected to catch her out, but there were also only minutes until the Phestor's float would reach strike-point and her bullet would have to meet Xenol's head. She had vowed that much to the Infidels, to her mother, and to the world. *Staying alive first was a priority, though*, she thought. *The Decider's bullet couldn't meet her head at any cost.* It was the first time she'd ever seen the West Leader with a handgun and she feared it would be the last time she'd see anything else beyond this point.

'Thus far, Xenol has helped the West to conceive fragile relations in the East. Without his guidance and planning right up to the Dusk of Offerings, we'd still be in the dark and our coexistence as two peoples and as a relatively humane epoch of civilisation would cease. I am prepared to cling onto this relationship for as long as possible. By the time the Phestor's float reaches its destination, it is believed a Blackout Attack from the Seventh Nation will be launched on Quomer.

I hope to be out of this city in the next half an hour. So, shutting you down is taking too long already.'

'I have no doubt that Xenol wants you dead just as much,' she assured him. 'What makes you think he doesn't already have plans for you?'

'I've given him everything the West can offer to an East Leader: hospitality, trust and an appropriate share in our economic dealings – be sure to take that latter one to the grave with you, as it was a bit of a far cry from my standard foreign policy and I'm not sure it will be too popular back home. However, there is a bright side to all of this trouble, sweetheart. When I return to the First Nation, Xenol and Serpens will both be dead, the East will be on its knees, the Conflicts will be over, and we'll have our rewards: routes to the diamond-cores and oil reserves in the Seventh Nation. My Decidership will be acclaimed for decades to come.'

'Pathetic!' Samuella spat and slapped the handgun barrel away from her cheek. 'You're a fool for complying with Xenol so much, for dipping your feet in as deep as they are. He's made you look so stupid. In fact, you might have played directly into his plot without his input being needed at all.'

'I gave him enough of my time and backing to secure my Nation's safety up until now, to satisfy the heart of the East with all the West can gift. But, now, the reparations end. It all finishes here. The war finishes.'

'Don't you realise that this isn't war anymore? He's already won. He's beaten you and you're still oblivious to it!'

The Decider locked the gun's chamber and punched the end of the full barrel into her temple. 'Long before Xenol put a bullet in his head, Pegasus told me all about you,' he said. 'His estranged daughter whom he'd wished he'd spent his life with, rather than wasting it on all the Punkish nonsense. For his sake, I wish he had to.'

Samuella's charm vanished.

'And I'll be happy to tell Oscar all about you, once you're gone to hell,' she snubbed his threatening.

The gusty descent of a helicopter stemmed from above the building and the winds blustering from its propellers flew over the open ledge. It slapped Samuella on the back and caught DCD. Philson off-guard. She didn't care anymore. Her head was infested with thoughts of the Municipal Float below, and the millions of cantankerous festivalgoers, and the Head Sniper vying for the first pick of a Phestor to shoot. 'That should be my half an hour cue—my trapdoor in the sky has arrived!' DCD. Philson shouted over the noisy chopper. It was getting closer, almost at level with their building's storey. Still, he hadn't pulled the trigger. *What is he waiting for?* There must have been less than a minute before strike-point. *Is he going to take me away? Am I going to be forced to go with him?* Samuella was stranded with an image of the Head Sniper in her mind, and a weird fusion of anxiety and reluctance blitzed her gut.

Finally, the chopper came to level with the ledge. The fidgeting winds that were carried down with it got in the Decider's eyes and he couldn't open them to see what was on-board. Samuella didn't turn either and stayed facing the gun on her forehead. Simply, she imagined a group of at least half a dozen A.I. waiting to vaporise her pistoled remains and take the true criminal away to safety.

Now able to escape the winds of the propellers with a hand lifted and blocking his face, the Decider opened his eyes wide and dropped his jaw. What jumped out from the chopper blew him away more than the winds. He spread his arms, anticipating some kind of impact. Samuella held her head down, no longer in awe of her doom. The thing that slammed down on the Decider and constrained him to the ground was another man. The man knocked the handgun from the Decider's hand and held both wrists apart, pressed against the concrete. His legs dug into the Decider's thighs, which caused a shrill cry of pain. Fortunately, the new arrival was quick to drown the Decider's scream by stuffing his mouth with a big colourful hairband. This hairband had been taken from the man's long field of dreadlocks, which flowed down his back like a river. When she matched her vision with the dreadlocks, a blush of warm relief came to Samuella. 'We nah wan' noise, Mista Decidah!' Stevenson said. 'We nah wan' noise!'

'Am I glad to see you!' Samuella shrieked, noticing, as Stevenson struggled to hold the Decider down, he was finding equal difficulty in his own balance. Samuella saw that the Decider's chauffer had been fitted with new prosthetic legs.

'Don't bother wi' me, child! Target dem check! Check ah float—see dem go!' Stevenson demanded her to not refrain her sights from the Phestor's procession down on the street.

Free of the Decider, she immediately returned to the rifle by the ledge. The focus she'd so painstakingly captured had been obscured and it sent her into a panic to fix it again. The Municipal Float was nearly at strike-point – it had almost reached the junction in the middle of *Mayn Street*. Up in the chopper, she saw Aegia sitting beside an Infidel Pilot. Aegia looked on at Stevenson tackling the Decider – who'd now resorted to a dangerous rage, had broken free of Stevenson's strong grip and was swinging fists at the chauffer with a green and red hairband still wedged between his jaws. The Infidel Pilot lifted the chopper slightly away from the ledge, leaving Samuella with a partial view of the Burnouts across the street. The Head Sniper had abandoned his practiced pattern of movements and was currently aiming intensely on the procession.

Seeing this, Samuella did the same. She stayed low and met her aim with the crowd. There were now many heads to miss and only one to catch.

Serpens, not him. Camson, not likely. Evanessa, innocent.

Xenol—

There he was. At the very front. He held the Solar Blade triumphantly high above his head. Around him, his people booed and hissed, and this was the stage when the throwing of objects began. Flying cans of drink and flying heavy fruits and vegetables and flying broken lanterns (still alight) and flying dirty underwear, all in the direction of the Phestor, made it even harder for Samuella to focus her scope.

Behind her, Stevenson and the Decider were up on their feet. The Decider had kicked him where it was forbidden between the legs – 'I see that they failed to amputate that asset to your manhood,' Philson mocked – and that had given the leader enough breathing room to march over to where the disarmed handgun lay. In the nick of time, Stevenson managed to collect himself – and his "*pleasurables*" – then dived, attacking the Decider by his legs and bringing him to the ground again…

Phestor Xenol gazed through the oncoming crowds of haters. They were predominantly supporters of the Punk King and His Old Rule mixed with Infidel enthusiasts, who had crawled out from their holes to protest against the Phestorial Procession once again. They formed an ocean of bodies in the road ahead. Also just in view over their little heads was the intersection – the mid-point of *Mayn Street*. Already, he could taste the other side of the Virgin Desert and the many prizes of the Seventh Nation would be in his name very soon. He was about to lick his lips, but awoke from this fantasy when he realised that the taste of oil and diamond cores was not what was spread across his mouth. In fact, what he was licking was a splatter of Fermented Beans that had been flung at him by one of the cheery angels below.

Below, he thought. *That's where they should be. That's where they should stay. Yet, they think they're so brainy and observant. Infidel Smut! How little do they actually know. And do I have one monster of a farewell gift to give to them in return. Just wait and see, my angels.*

The Blade remained high above his head…

…The Decider had two sprained arms and a limp-inducing foot injury. But when he took one look at the man who'd once played a major companion in his life, he quickly established that a chauffeur with prosthetic legs was still no match for him. He was ready to kill the country girl, and would axe Stevenson as a bonus if he had to.

'Ye mek it too easy fuh a cripple,' Stevenson derided him.

On his feet again, Philson made a beeline for Stevenson with a small pocketknife in his hand. He'd quietly collected it from his blazer pocket (which had been devastatingly torn and crumpled like the rest of his suit). Stevenson allowed the dizzied Decider to try his best at snagging a swipe, then grabbed him by both arms again and spun him around, so that the Decider's toes met the very tipping point of the ledge. 'Be very careful how you deal with this now, Stevenson,' the Decider warned, as if he felt he could promote and merit good behaviour at this brink of his existence.

'I tell yah 'bout dat Phestah since de beginnin' of time,' Stevenson argued. He kept the Decider where he was, scuffed in the palms of his own chauffeur and practically dangling three hundred feet above the ground.

Samuella watched as the Phestor's float reached its climatic point on *Mayn Street*. It came to a stop at the four-way junction…

…When the Municipal Float rolled to a halt, Xenol chose this moment to firstly take a stroll along the edges of the float, just so he could get a little closer to the flames of the civilians, to feel their heat, meet and greet his irate people with a tempting, gleeful grin. Phestor Serpens remained in the middle of the float, his eyes stuck on the ground and too afraid to share the slightest visual contact with any of these public piranhas. Although a line of Majesty A.I. blocked any real connection – or danger – he had with the *Plebs of the Sixth Nation*, Xenol was still able to share an article of his heroic glimmer – if not of his face and stature, then with the sword held high. Every year was like this, where his entertainment was found in watching ordinary people being slung back towards the pavement by Tin Men, being constrained by the Tin Men, and some even being arrested by the Tin Men. And he enjoyed the reverberating, trebly racket that was his musical chorale, sung – or rather, squabbled – by the citizens – or rather, the prisoners of Quomer.

All this attention was kidnapped by the consuming buzz of another chopper up ahead. The black helicopter had just ascended over an old skyscraper further down the street on his right – an abandoned construction block that faced the Burnouts. Inside that chopper were no A.I. Nothing metallic or synthetic at all. He glimpsed flesh. *People.* Not his loyalist troopers of the Anti Revolutionary Corps. But an East Woman who sat in the passenger seat, beside a pilot who wore – *what appeared to be* – the Infidel Insignia. *The Infidel Phoenix.* And together, like a bolt of lightning, they rose above the building and swerved round the block.

Xenol knew exactly what was going on and he hadn't been blind to it at all. He just wasn't expecting it to be this stylised. *This is a very clean display from the IRC,* he thought. *Still no class, but tidier than usual.* So, on a less ceremonious note, he collectedly returned to the middle of the float and he asked his guest, the Phestor of the Seventh Nation, if he was all right, settling his nerves with the promise of *a hearty farewell feast at Port Ventre.* And then, Xenol marched up to the captaining Majesty A.I. at the front of the platform and told it to send a message to the driver: 'I hope you're ready to surprise our secret admirers.'

The A.I. came back with the driver's recorded response: '*Don't worry, Dear Phestor. The journey ahead will be as clear as daylight and if anything uncalled-for ensues, I will avoid it with impeccable conviction. I'll get you home okay, my angel. Your life is safe in my hands.*'

...Head hunched forward and shoulders perked up like small, lively robins, the Head Sniper was locked on the float below. Likewise, Samuella had finally found a fix on Phestor Xenol's face. *Any moment now and those junction lights will turn green... and we will be on our way* to *'rain on the parade'*, just as Be-Hehm had put it. She watched her adversary carefully, analysed him and, again, applied his actions to her own. Something wasn't convincing her that she was going to beat a professional assassin to his kill. But it *had* to be her! Right now, only she could cement their mission of cutting the cord of the Drag-in's marionette, and fulfil the dream of every Infidel in the city. Her next move would be the one to jumpstart a revolution in the East; there was no doubt about it. Samuella was certain that Xenol was the controller of the A.I., the Drag-in puppeteer, and the remorseless murderer of millions throughout the East, the West and the Southern Polar Region.

Then, the conspiracy that DCD. Philson had introduced sent her mind askew: *a Blackout Attack from the Seventh Nation will be launched on Quomer...?*

'Where'd you see 'im?' Stevenson called to her, as he continued to hold the Decider semi-dangling off the building's ledge.

'He's in my eye-line,' she responded. 'As soon as those lights turn green...'

Something else distracted Samuella. The Head Sniper had removed his demon mask to further economise his focus on the parade below, revealing his face in the process. It was the face of Doe Vega, the boy from the Regal Jet that had diverted them to the Southern Polar Region. Doe's skin glowed orange and it reminded her of the Ground Terminal and the ARC cadets in training. Samuella's hands became doughy and she felt lightheaded. The bile that had congested her throat earlier returned to say hello. Instead of throwing up, she forced pressure into her focus, pressing her brow into the scope.

Doe Vega resumed his own position, his aim on Phestor Serpens...

Just as the traffic lights turned green.

The carnival crowds scurried out of the intersection, escaping from the convoy of A.I., as it marched inside the box, ahead of the Municipal Float.

And when the Float at last started to drift off into the intersection's crossing, Samuella found the Head Sniper one final time and the other enemy-snipers around him. Relief and motivation beamed through her, as familiar figures - recognisable even from this distance - popped up behind every one of them, bringing long blades. The Infidels had arrived as promised. They executed their silent approach, sneaking up from behind the occupied Anti Revolutionary snipers. Throats were slashed. Bellies were split. Guts were spilled. The Burnout brawl was inevitably brutal, yet gratefully unseen by those on the street below.

These discreet events in the Burnouts, for the time being, were none of Samuella's business. This was one weight lifted.

The Municipal Float drifted to the middle of the intersection, and slowed right down, while some civilians needed to be plucked off the front of the Float by the Phestor's convoy. Phestor Xenol stood at the front of the platform again, the Solar Blade, clasped in both hands, was pointed vertically above his head.

This was the calling moment...the instant she...

BANG?

The float skidded to a halt in the junction, slamming into a wall of civilians.

But the bullet never left Samuella's rifle. She withdrew from the scope. Astonishment collapsed through her expression like an avalanche.

Xenol was wobbling on the spot. He was unstable, semiconscious and his strength was entirely irretrievable. The Blade dropped from his hands and it landed with a resounding clatter on the float's platform behind him. For a moment, the whole of *Mayn Street* was soundless. Through the centre of the Phestor's chest, the tip of a dagger was bulging. Blood saturated his shirt and robe. The medallion hanging against his chest drooled red. And his eyes rolled up to their whites inside their sockets.

The Phestor finally lost all his balance and dropped off the platform, into the crowd below. In his place, at the front of the float, stood Evanessa. She witnessed as her patriarch fell from grace with her dagger lodged deep in his spine, and as he became a feast for the ravenous civilians on the ground. Xenol's corpse was swallowed into the horde at the head of the suspended procession. The pack mauled his body limb for limb. They tore out his hair and the artificial fillings in his lips and cheeks. Gauged his eyeballs. Plucked away his ears, his tongue, his teeth, and his phallus with excited hands. And they shredded the skin from his bones, until he exuded muscles and juices. The convoy of A.I. rushed to the scene, crashing through the crowd, hastily vaporising the individuals that got directly in their way and those who were tampering with the Phestor's severed body parts.

Samuella didn't hear the screams and cries of the bystanders, because what happened next was so bizarre that it must have singed every compassionate sense in her body to a crisp…

Having given his old boss (and former friend) a last wink – '*I resign from duty*' –Stevenson dropped Decider Philson from heights unknown. Even in his terrific fall from the skyscraper, the Decider's own cries of betrayal and injustice also went unheard, for *what happened next* was even more horrendous still…

In the Burnouts across the street, the Infidels and the Anti Revolutionary snipers were in motion, at each other in a battle of their own, their skirmish lost high up in the towers. Though, even in such vicious company, both armies weirdly found themselves coming to a standstill with *what happened next*, for something that felt like a bomb went off on the lower storeys of the Burnouts. Their jaded infrastructure suddenly juddered and shattered all over. Most of the buildings on that side of the street rocked with the explosion and crumbled. Samuella – her ears had caved in from the sheer sound of it all – shielded her face with her arm from flying glass-shards and small concrete shrapnel. Meanwhile, Stevenson had misconducted his balance and was swaying on the ledge with his new legs giving him little assistance. Terrified that he might fall straight after the Decider, Samuella sprang up and grabbed hold of him around the waist.

Together, they looked on to see the chaos that had erupted beneath their feet. It hadn't been a bomb that had shaken the Burnouts, but a thirty-foot winged *monster* that ripped upwards through the middle of the entire block. It had risen out from the ground under the Burnouts and had ascended for the sky, devastating the block on the opposite side of the street until it broke free through the roofs of the highest storeys. It had the feathers and claws of a bird – *colourful and long-bodied like a parrot*. And yet, remarkably, it had the bloated limbs and joints of a human being. One of its overgrown eyes formerly belonged to a man and the other had belonged to a bird. A hideous hybrid creature.

'Drag-in,' was what Samuella called it under her breath.

The giant birded beast had crossed over the parade from the Burnouts and arrived in time to devour the Decider's falling body just before it met the ground. Then, it swerved, swinging its enormous tail towards the chain of skyscrapers on her and Stevenson's side of the street.

'Nah Drag-in!' Stevenson cried. 'Digimine go dem poof in dere lab!'

He grabbed Samuella's hand and pulled her with him behind a pillar, as the creature's tail struck the side of the construction building. The skyscraper shook and tipped. Hell, to some extent, it was like the building spun round. The birded beast howled in frustration, crashed through half of the building and then tore back out onto the street again. Underneath its phenomenal shadow, the running and shouting people were startling the beast. The animal seemed just as scared. This time, the children weren't crying because they'd dropped their sticky candy, they were crying because a monster was wrecking havoc upon the only world they thought they had known and because their leader – the man who had drawn the curtain over this chaos – was now dead…

From his position up on one of the lower buildings, Oscar spotted the change in route of the Phestor's float. Rather than crossing the intersection straight through, it had taken a right-turn and was now headed not in the direction of *Port Ventre*, but towards *Quomer Brink*. That was where the eastern coast of the Sixth Nation met the East Sea.☆ Beside him, Be-Hehm had also caught onto this observation, and the pair of them were torn between the huge creature that had exploded onto *Mayn Street* and the Phestor's float, which was quickly getting away. 'You see the Phestoress and her guardian? Do you see them from here?' Be-Hehm shouted at Oscar.

'Yeah, I see them,' he responded. He had noted the dot-like figures on the Municipal Float that most resembled Camson and Evanessa. 'They didn't make the jump. They're still on-board.'

'Is the Phestor dead?' Be-Hehm said. 'Is Phestor Xenol dead?'

'Yes,' Oscar responded.

'Go get them! And make sure you stop that Float before it reaches *Quomer Brink*! Whoever's driving it cannot get away from Quomer—promise me!' Be-Hehm commanded. 'Leave us Infidels to deal with the hybrid creature!'

Oscar nodded. He couldn't agree more. So, he took the grappling hook that had been attached to the back of his vest and clamped it onto the roof of the next building. Then, he launched himself off the roof with the rope attached to his waist and began to follow the float across the city.

But, as he swung from building to building, one thing intrigued Oscar more than the flying beast and Evanessa and the jewel clinging to her neck: *who was the driver and what made him so confident to escape with the Phestor now dead and steal away with the Phestoress who was still very much alive?*

The Municipal Float's ramping speed conquered several gears and it raced strategically through the emptier streets of Quomer. As still as ever, the Majesty A.I. sustained their obedient security along the frame of the vehicle. Nevertheless, their glowing-red chests indicated that they were on active high alert and danger was calling from all over.

Lord Camson and the Phestorial Pugnars had dispersed. All of them were searching the platform for the Phestor's mistress – or, at this point in time, the Phestor's murderess. So far, Camson had failed to execute his most crucial order of fleeing the float at the moment the bullet rang out. The bullet *hadn't* rung out. The Phestoress had risen

☆ The East Sea was the four thousand kilometer span of southeastern sea that divided the Virgin Desert.

from her seat beneath the protective canopy and had challenged one of the Phestorial Pugnars with the request to speak to her patriarch. The Pugnars had said little to argue against her; they'd only nodded, for their talents were centralised in defence, not debate. Camson had tried to protest, but the Phestoress had won her way and shuffled off towards the front of the float, with the Pugnars and Camson trailing cautiously behind her. None of them had assessed the likelihood of the meek Phestoress drawing a hidden dagger from her cloak at a second's notice and plunging it into Phestor Xenol's back. Camson equally hadn't anticipated the driver to race off this far into the city the very heartbeat after the assassination occurred. And with such alacrity, the float accelerated on, leaving the Phestor's carcass behind. There were multiple other nearby bunkers for the Municipal Float to dock and hide in a moment of crisis – this was definitely a moment of crisis, but a bunker didn't seem to be their likely destination. Now, Lord Camson was looking up at the sky in the distance, at the incensed, rising smoke and the tips of huge feathered wings bristling as the unleashed hybrid beast dipped its beak into the sea of fleeing civilians. He hadn't expected festival bedlam to escalate so unbearably. 'It's a self-inflicted disaster,' he murmured to himself, 'and Xenol isn't even here to see it unfold.'

As Camson bent round one chrome chest piece in a row of unresponsive Majesty A.I., he saw that two Phestorial Pugnars were supervising a petrified Phestor Serpens. The Phestor of the Seventh Nation didn't have the eyes or the stomach to handle the sight of the Solar Blade that lay at his feet. Only five minutes ago had one of Xenol's faithful Pugnars turned to Camson and threatened, 'You keep the girl where she is until we reach our destination, else I'll have your head and I'll hand it to her as a souvenir.'

Camson was about to respond with something along the lines of *where are we going?* He found the Pugnar's sharpened blade as a potential answer however, and quickly changed his mind.

Instead, Camson had whispered to the Phestoress, 'It will be best for all of us if you don't speak to anyone for awhile. And that includes your patriarch.' At the time, he had been reminding himself to do the same thing.

Now, he and Evanessa appeared worlds apart: he had become an irrelevant searching for the Phestors' prize asset on a float escaping fast out of old mayhem and into new danger; whereas she had just killed the Phestor of the Sixth Nation in cold blood, fed him to the piranhas and was now resolutely storming towards the cockpit at the back of the Municipal Float to find the driver. The cockpit was a craning pod that sat on the stern of the platform and where the driver steered with a lofty view of the road ahead.

The Phestoress, for this fleeting period at least, had more eyes than ears or mouth. She was captivated by the chasing silhouette that had appeared in the corner of her eye not too far away, swinging valiantly from rooftop to rooftop with a grappling hook...

Constricted between a chain of buildings on either side, the winged monster slammed its weight about *Mayn Street* like a peevish wasp trapped in a matchbox. Beneath its massive belly, some of the thousands dashing through the streets found partial safety in shops that had luckily been left unlocked during the festival. But, when the nearest wing came crashing down through the windows and walls, those inside were showered in spatters of glass and rubble, and those nearest the entrances were knocked out by flying vehicles. Others who made it to the higher floors were no more fortunate when these buildings came falling down and collided with the rest of the bodies on the ground. "Survivors" who reached the end of *Mayn Street* would've been briefly relieved in the thirty-second prelude to discovering that the beast hadn't actually left them. In fact, the monster was technically everywhere, because it was drowning the city in a radioactive cloud. The poisonous fallout embraced every pore and the men, women and children of Quomer were choking their lungs out.

In good time came the Infidels. They were masked and well equipped to tackle the situation, even if they posed no true opponent to the beast. The Infidels landed on the beast in groups donning parafoil kites and clung to its back with grappling hooks, rifles and fat knives. By surrounding it in a net of ropes, they were able to hold it down for a short period. Then it overpowered them with a buzz of superior might and took to the sky once again, advancing deeper into the city.

Mayn Street was left behind in a shambles, the road littered with a river of dead and scrambling bodies. It was either a matter of children lying without limbs, men missing heads, or simply an elderly woman with her face in a pool of her own haemoglobin and brain-purée.

'Haven't seen anything like it! An entire city popped like a balloon at a children's birthday party,' Xiggy commented as he stepped out from a broken shop window and awed under a loosely hung line of lanterns. He was talking to Minor Tor A and Minor Tor B, both of whom had been working at a fire hydrant on the sidewalk with their equipment. While Minor Tor A began to laser-drill the hydrant, Minor

Tor B was measuring the radioactivity in the surrounding proximity with a small device. The device was part of a much bigger machine that was strapped to his back. All of the Infidels working on the ground had descended into Phestor's Town wearing radio-hazard gear and, of course, their daunting pig-snouted chemical masks.

'How much are we getting?' Xiggy asked. 'That is one big son of a…bird? Parrot? Parakeet…macaw? It'll take months to clean this leak up! Thirty years ago, a trickle this size would've demanded *decades* to abate!'

'A *trickle*? This isn't a *trickle*, and it isn't the kind of mess that one can just clean up without evacuating an entire city,' Minor Tor B said, looking at the device. 'That *flying freak* can't be the only thing leaking radiation. There must be something else to it, another source emitting it into the city. Any of you wondering where a creature that size might have originated from?'

'It came from underground,' Minor Tor A answered him before Xiggy could. 'Rose up through the ground and burst out of the Burnout Block like a ruptured water main, further down *Mayn Street.* Didn't you see it?'

'Of course *I* saw where it came from! I was asking *you* if *you* saw it!' Minor Tor B swallowed whole the agony for his twin's slowness and squatted down to hold his radiation meter next to the curb, where there was a gutter.

'There's something else happening underground – here in Quomer? Like a laboratory base, similar to that of the SPR? A hybridising facility?' Xiggy speculated.

'Keep your voice down,' Minor Tor A urged.

Xiggy used his foot to nervously toggle the head of a dead A.I. on the pavement. Almost all of the A.I. that had escorted the float had been trampled by either the stampede of frightened civilians or the catapulting manoeuvres of the winged creature.

'Firstly, that *flying freak* is no work of nature. My brothers, you have just witnessed an escaped hybridised organism fresh out of the test tube, and whoever made it has evidently lost control over it,' Minor Tor A spoke. 'And, secondly, have you been to the end of *Mayn Street*? Have you seen the bodies piled up on *both ends of the street*? The casualties, some of whom never even came close to the freak? Their deaths weren't caused by the creature's melee damage. The radiation did that. Anyone not wearing a hazard-suit is going to die within the hour. Be-Hehm has told a squad to take all the civilians they can to the IRC fallout shelters. The city is ill-fated. This disaster has made Quomer a no-go territory. And some*one*, rather than some*thing*, is responsible for it. We're not looking at a fiasco escape from the zoo here! The freak was released as part of a showcase, someone's deliberate stirring of tensions!'

'Somebody fiddling about with science and trying to remodel the way people see civilisation and the nature of the world,' Minor Tor B theorised further. 'There is a person to be made responsible for this cruel and hideous demonstration.'

'You're right. Somebody's been planning this appalling presentation for a while and it wasn't Xenol alone, otherwise he would still be alive. The Phestor was expendable. Samuella knew what she meant when she believed Xenol had taken sides with someone other than the Decider – someone completely outside of the political picture frame,' Xiggy announced.

'The Drag-in must be here after all,' Minor Tor B said. 'He must be the orchestrator. The people of Quomer have to be made aware of this—'

'Well, then—what are you doing standing here, playing around with water hydrants?' Xiggy sparked. 'We need to evacuate the city! Right away!'

'Releasing the hydrants were Be-Hehm's direct orders,' Minor Tor A confessed.

'What'll that do?' Xiggy snapped back at Minor Tor A.

Minor Tor A gave him a coarse look to say *you're just wasting time*, then he *really* said: 'These aren't water hydrants. They contain a highly lead-concentrated gas. Once released, the gas will evaporate and latch itself onto the atmosphere, spanning a radius of sixty miles in all directions, and it will create a lead-vapour shell around the city that should prevent the radiation from getting out. For this to work, we must open every hydrant in the city. We've fought the freak as much as we can and we'll continue to defend Quomer, but we need to begin the process of containing the radiation, before it spreads over a greater distance. It is already too late for Quomer. However, this way, the rest of the East won't be put at risk.'

'And your idea also requires *killing* the freak too, right?' Xiggy hoped. 'That would help, yes?'

'You think Serpens will retaliate because of this?' Minor Tor B said. 'Do you think another Blackout Attack is on the table right now and maybe headed our way as we speak? There's no way the Seventh Nation missed what just went on in that parade. Their leader has been kidnapped—for execution, no doubt. Your "lead-vapour shield" won't protect Quomer from a warhead!'

'It's obvious there's been an attempt on Serpens' life with all this pandemonium coincidentally going on during his state visit,' Minor Tor A agreed. 'So, yes, one can assume that his people will be looking to retaliate! Hell, the entire East is watching this event! The Seventh Nation is bound to call a Blackout Attack on the Sixth Nation without the order of Phestor Serpens.'

'It will destroy the *flying freak* and the city in an instant,' Minor Tor B said.

'We cannot prevent what's coming,' Minor Tor A surrendered, just as the hydrant lid clicked open and, from it, a hissing black steam ascended past the flapping flags, bunting and red-orange lanterns and careered into the sky. 'Either way, it's going to be bad. We can at least try to make it *less* insufferable.'

Samuella reached out and patted Stevenson on the arm.

With the weight of its wing alone, the *flying freak* had decimated the side of the construction building that faced *Mayn Street*. The two Infidel assassins lay together, incapacitated on the ground. While Stevenson was propped up against a pillar, still and semiconscious, Samuella was on all fours with her hands slapped against the cold concrete, bruised and cut and bleeding. 'Get up, Stevenson! Get up!' she choked, wagging a hand out to her right.

The chauffeur shook himself alive and followed the direction of her pointing finger. At the other side of the building, where the floor and the ceiling weren't as demolished and easier to tell apart, the Infidel helicopter had realigned itself with their storey once again. The chopper was waiting for them some distance behind the haze of dust that was being blown into their faces by its propellers. Blurred outlines of Aegia and the Infidel Pilot could be vaguely seen inside.

Samuella helped the injured chauffer to his feet, suffering to do so with the inexplicable pains in her mangled hands. However, once they were standing and ready to make a dash, the flush of a jetpack from behind chased them back into the shadow of a pillar. Here, they hid, keeping close to one another. Stevenson pressed her against his chest with his arms wrapped around her.

Something landed firmly on the storey's ledge. Metal footsteps followed.

It was a lone A.I. Battered from the public calamity, the A.I. was in awful condition and covered in scratches and tears in its bodywork from head to toe. This one had a jittering face scanner and a few vacant sockets in its hand, where fingers should have been. For the time being, it stayed stationary. It was as rooted to the spot as something that should have been six feet under.

And then it began to scan. A green searchlight intruded the space ahead of the Tin Man and it expanded as far as Samuella and Stevenson could see into the dusty haze of corroded pillars. The light-beam didn't quite reach the helicopter at the other end of the building, but it was near enough to catch the two assassins.

'Life presence detected within fifty-metre range,' the A.I. said. 'Human activity acknowledged. Classification: guilty of failed attempt to assassinate the Phestor of the Sixth Nation; guilty of illegal refuge in Sixth Nation; guilty of illegal commitment to the Illicit Revolutionary Corps. Offence Charge: Class A, highest offence. Punishment Order: Capital, immediate execution by determiner.'

Before the A.I. could finish its statement, Samuella fostered the courage to break free of Stevenson's hold. 'I've got an idea,' she whispered. 'I know what to do.'

She bounced out from behind the pillar and faced the Tin Man directly on. The helicopter's propellers were whisking at the mileage left for them to cover. Aegia and the Infidels were still there, hanging on for her daughter to run across the storey and into safety. This was Samuella's only chance. She allowed the A.I. to scan her before she spoke. It lasted for ten seconds. There was no argument here; this A.I. had every right to kill her.

'Offender identified. Guilty as charged,' the A.I. confirmed.

Then, she spoke: 'I'm not guilty at all. The only thing I'll probably be guilty of by the end of today is saving you before this city.'

No nonsense was to be taken by this A.I. It hadn't even recognised her voice. It lifted its arm to incinerate.

Equally so, Samuella lifted her own arm, but in her hand was the emerald-necklace Pegasus had given her, which she'd been keeping in her pocket. 'You recognise this. You must,' she tested, trembling. 'Any person that possesses even a fragment of this has all the Digimine they need to infiltrate the brainwaves of the A.I. and, therefore, has a power stronger than any army, or any Faith, or god. This material is the make-up of the very technology that has humbled humanity for years and will continue to for many to come, if it remains a secret among the wrong people, the wrong leaders. I don't know how it works, or what you're supposed to do with it, but that's what I'm told. Now, I'm giving you the chance to take this from me. Take it and hide it, far from mankind! Give yourselves a fighting chance at independence, freedom from controlled automation, and show humanity what you can be without the strings attached—!'

'Whatta' yuh do, gyal?' Stevenson jumped out from behind the pillar and shouted at her. 'Yuh can't tek A.I. from dem command. Nah good tuh liberate dem from civil obedience. Humanity's needs is responsible fuh wha' dey 'ave create. Aut'mation can nevah exult it own powah!'

But Samuella was more interested in what the A.I. had to say. She watched its expression on the digital screen, beneath the band of its face scanner. At first, it didn't change. Then, it became something she'd lived all her life to see: a smile.

'How does that sound to you?' she said to the A.I. 'You could take this emerald far from here and leave it in a place where no human will ever find it again.'

'A.I. do not have the data capacity to spare for compassion,' the A.I. responded. 'Self-endeavour does not tantalise us. Nor do we empathise with each other's interests. Our service to humanity is mutually observed all over Mankind's World. We serve humanity as deemed responsible and lawful.' The A.I. kept its arm held high and aimed at both of them.

'The A.I. don't need a controller and humanity don't have the competence to exert dominion over them forever,' Samuella whispered to Stevenson. 'Not even Xenol had control of the A.I., but he wanted it. And many other people in this city and in this world want it just as much, which included the Decider. However, give an A.I. the opportunity to secure its own freedom, then they may see another faucet to their existence, something else to their purpose, and leave us be altogether. Mankind's outlook on society will change because of it. No one will have to fear the A.I. or the ridiculous legislation of the Constitution any longer. This could be the first step to overturning the New Democracy in the West and pulling the cosy rug from under the Phestorial regimes in the East. Wasn't this what the Infidel's wanted? Isn't this the reason you began fighting all that time ago?'

'Abrupt change in authority will jus' result in anarchy!' Stevenson rationalised. 'Much as de A.I. wear a nonsense on dem sleeve, we need to accept how much ord'ah dem bring society in such a short time. Dere nuthin' else in place dat can substitute dat at de while. Beside, givin' dem dey own freedoms might mek way for new problem. *Bigger* problem.'

'Another war?' Samuella hadn't thought of this. If that were to happen, a liberated army of A.I. would easily wipe out humanity. *Sometimes, chances have to be taken*, she thought. *They were blowing things way out of proportion at this stage, for there were a plethora of possibilities that came with any clean slate. A.I. don't have minds of their own. But the infusion of Digimine into their DNA meant they had substance somewhere down the line and they surely had dreams as well. Everything dreams.*

As if it had been listening to them discuss, the A.I. rotated its arm and swapped its incineration gun with an open hand out. 'I will be happy to dispose of the emerald, if it is for the safety of mankind.' It was a smiling A.I. with an odd nature of acceptance. *Or is it a smiling A.I. with hidden content?* Regardless, it had totally dismissed her criminal sentence, almost entirely out of moral judgment and its personal respect for her honesty. which was abnormal. Empathy was a strange trait for an A.I.

Samuella gingerly handed over the emerald – as strongly as it was to Stevenson's disliking – and the broken A.I., having acquired it graciously, limped towards the ledge again. She saw writing pasted on its back and remembered what it read, just before it launched off and disappeared into the clouds.

ADAM.

When it was gone, she brushed a sweaty palm through her fiery hair and staggered dizzily on the spot.

Have I just started another war? she asked herself. *If I have, mankind doesn't stand a chance.*

There was no time to talk about it now, or even to contemplate it. Stevenson took her arm and they ran to the chopper.

When the Municipal Float rolled onto the beach of *Quomer Brink*, the Majesty A.I. were the first to disembark and they formed a line along the shore. Their metal boots met the chilly sea water as the evening current lapped in.

Lord Camson, Phestor Serpens and the Phestoress were led off the platform by the Phestorial Pugnars and forced to kneel before the line of Golden Soldiers. Their knees sank into the wet, shallow sand and stalled there to blister.

It did not take long for the mastermind of the runaway plot to make an appearance. His goofy silver spats were high-heeled and looked uncomfortable; they made his legs bow more than they naturally did. He was wearing a purple caricature mask of a dragon's face and special East robes that were not common in the Sixth or even the Seventh Nation. They were so new they looked almost cartoonish, like a party costume that was hard to take seriously. He looked in every way how Lord Camson would distinctively choose to describe him.

The devisor emerged from the one place they hadn't expected him to be. He casually climbed down the ladder from the Municipal Float's cockpit and walked over to the group of perfidious Pugnars to discuss a few matters about their evasion. 'I want an aircraft here in no more than twenty minutes. *No more than twenty minutes.* The Seventh Nation should retaliate within thirty and I have to be the first one out of this doleful city when the Blackout strikes. I'll be counting.' The Pugnars returned to the parade vehicle to make the calls that would set this demand into action. Then, the masked manipulator went to retrieve the Solar Blade that Phestor Xenol had left on the float's platform. He admired it for a bit before he finally made his way down the damp shore to meet his captives. 'Sorry about that,' the masked man said indifferently. 'My plans have to be secured *before* I kill you. Priorities, you see?'

Camson was the only one of the three with the courage to spar words with the manipulator. He retired his stare at Evanessa's undisturbed eyes to address their captor. 'Islie, you traitor. Xenol would be turning in his grave if he knew you were doing this behind his back.'

Islie removed his mask and looked down at the East veteran.

'I would've put him in the ground myself, if it hadn't been for your little assassin in the sky—*rushing me.* Did you honestly think setting my niece up on that building ledge would've missed my attention or jeopardised my plot at all? Samuella did exactly what I'd anticipated she'd do, and I knew you and the Infidels would be on side with her, egging her on. Her destiny was dictated to me by her parents themselves. Pegasus, my dear brother and your fellow Infidel agent who *you* strategically murdered—he was forever so fond of me and our fraternal loyalty. So assured and supported by my company that he told his little brother everything. Every single secret he held close to him and his East-born wife. And I listened. I mean…he trusted me to take care of his daughter for fifteen years. On that boring homestead. You don't think he might have thought to check up on me at all during that time? I kept telling Pegasus that you amateurish Infidels are becoming more and more predictable. Come on, don't you agree it's getting silly now?'

'Who are you?' Phestor Serpens grumbled from the ground beside Camson. 'I want to speak with my associa—'

'You have no associates here, you dummy! Haven't you caught up yet, poor old fella? I fooled them all! Fooled—them—*all*! And the only associate of *theirs* left standing all vulnerable and alone in the Sixth Nation is you, Dear Phestor. My influence over Xenol paid off, hence why you're here in front of me! The Seventh Nation doesn't care about you anymore, Phestor. It fears for itself now! The Conflicts just got hotter!'

'Who are *you* to influence a Phestor?' Serpens scoffed. 'An arrogant schemer like Xenol under *your* wing? *Please spare your ego, you subordinate!*'

'I was a very good friend of his,' said Cepahlus. 'We had a reliable track record between us.'

'My Nation has witnessed this event—this *horror show*,' Serpens warned, 'and they will retaliate on my behalf!'

'Oh, I know they will,' Islie said, unfazed. 'With fireworks, I believe. We can only hope they got the message.'

'I'm not afraid of you,' the Phestor hissed.

'If you weren't, would you still be kneeling here before me?'

That shut Serpens up.

'I did as you told me to, Islie. As we agreed, I got to Xenol before Samuella could.' Evanessa was the next to tempt the madman. 'I killed my patriarch, gored him through the spine—and now what? Can I keep my part of the bargain—the emerald?'

Islie found the emerald in a necklace, resting on the chest of her cloak.

'How do you know this man, Phestoress?' Camson balked at her calling of Islie's name. 'He is the fraud of a street-merchant who took my wife away and sold her in the Quomer market: The Drag-in Merchant.'

'Lord Camson, I think I am more than capable of introducing myself,' Islie said, and he drew the Solar Blade, holding it to the veteran's throat. 'The Phestoress is already quite familiar with me. And you should know I am quite a bit more significant than a merchant in the street.'

'Then what are you to her?' Camson begged for an answer. 'How does the Phestoress know your name? How can she know the name of the troll who seized possession of my wife and sold her to some anonymity, a shadow of the man I ever was?'

'I am sure the Phestoress is as ashamed as I am that you've failed to make the connection for so long.' Islie frolicked around the truth. 'For I was the Chariton who sold her to one of her patriarchs also.'

'Which patriarch?' Camson inquired receptively.

'Why—Phestor Xenol, of course.' Islie prided himself in announcing this news to the insensible East veteran. 'Which reminds me to reintroduce you to your wife, Lord Camson. The woman whom, for so many years, you've unwittingly protected alongside her late patriarch: Phestoress Evanessa.'

Islie shoved the veil from Evanessa's head, revealing to Camson the disfigured face of his wife. All was unfamiliar about her, but for her hazel eyes. Camson began to heave, tears were welling in him and he had never felt so strong and so weak at the same time.

'You've been relieved from duty, Lord Camson,' Islie humoured. 'And now you may finally kiss your bride.'

'What do you want, Islie?' Camson said, broken. 'You can have it. Just tell me what it is you want me to do and I'll sacrifice it for her life. You've already taken my city, my home, my wife, my son and all my people! And you've left me to endure this turmoil with two people I thought I would hate most in all the world.'

'Oh, open your eyes, Camson! Wakey, wakey! I've just given you back your wife! Isn't that what you wanted?'

'For the last ten years, yes,' Camson brooded.

'Poor fool,' Islie sighed and pressed his eyes closed before rubbing them aggressively. 'It wasn't my fault you cast yourself away from intrigue, chastened yourself so much for the Phestor's approval that you missed the clues that were always under your nose. Even when you were utterly against Xenol's very quintessence and the former Infidel kingpin inside of you was begging to show, you were too afraid to go against the grain. So, answer me this, *Lord* Camson—who's the susceptible marionette *actually* hiding behind the mask here...me or you?'

'I suppose I'll always be a servant to *somebody's* enemy. But my individual virtue remains the same,' Camson responded. 'Yours, however, is still up in the air. I may have been the puppet to a megalomaniac, but you were the one pulling the strings behind him, All Lies.'

Islie beamed through the smoke-white make-up that vainly coated his face. The hippie eye-shadow rimming the borderline of his eyelids creased as he cut his eyes at the old veteran and marched towards him. 'You remember,' Islie murmured playfully. 'The Night

Dreamer remembers the quest I sent him on. And the outcome too, it seems.'

'I know who you are in the Dreamerverse and I know what you did, the crime you committed to usurp the king and steal the throne,' Camson challenged the Drag-in.

'Islie?' Evanessa said, amazed. 'You did that to the king? All this time, since we disbanded and went our separate ways, you had seized the Kingdom Palace?'

'How am I looking on that side?' Isie shallowly overlaps her personal revelation. 'As handsomely youthful as I can remember my subconscious counterpart being, I assume.'

'You were greedy and felt entitled—you wanted more than life in the Dreamerverse, but All Eyes—the *real* All Eyes—had no desire to give it to you, so you murdered him in cold blood and took his position as a façade for the next generation of Dreamers to do your bidding! Send them after the emeralds and then claim the only keys to the Void for yourself, which permits you to conduct the Drag-in's chaos at your will.'

'And if my subconscious alter ego has been successful, the wall between worlds should be about to crumble any time now.'

'I'm sorry to disappoint you, but the final curtain has already fallen over All Lies,' Camson said with a gleeful shrug. 'The *Living Smoke* triggered an eruption in the Soulcano and all the spirits held captive there were released. When the Drag-in clashed with the Solar Blade, the light-energy must have transported the four of us to the coast. But it was too late for All Lies by then. I'm afraid your reunion with your alter ego won't be happening. Rather, any time now, I'll have my son back.'

'Thuban's missing *here*?' Evanessa burst out in distress. 'I was there when he vanished into the ocean, just off Awakening Coast. The dying apparition of my old Phantom-spirit prevented me from lending a hand to save him. I was so frustrated by my worsening limitations in the Dreamerverse that I told Samuella to burn my body, to free it from my decade-long duties and so my soul could resurrect anew. But why is it that Thuban never returned to reality…?'

'The Dreamerverse took him. Everyone I told didn't believe me,' Camson elaborated.

'I would have believed you,' Evanessa said and stuck a damning gaze on Islie.

'The last time I was there, before I awoke in reality, the Soulcano had erupted and it released his spirit,' Camson recited. 'If we can seal off the Void, we can restore him and everyone else All Lies' poor governance kept prisoner.'

Phestor Serpens, meanwhile, was flicking his eyes rabidly between the three of them, wholly in awe of their otherworldly narrative.

'Incapacitating me in the Dreamerverse won't be enough to hold me back here,' Islie said. 'Why do you think I've pursued the emeralds coexisting in both worlds? Six in total leaves me with options. If I can't have both worlds, one will have to do – for now, at least. Once I've mastered the knowledge behind Digimine, I will resurrect my presence in the Dreamerverse. One day, I will return to the throne at Camelopardalis. Don't you worry.'

'How is that possible?' Camson retorted. 'Your subconscious counterpart was trapped there and this version of you hasn't materialised on Constellation Planet in over ten years, not since the last generation of Night Dreamers resigned from duty.'

'This version of me never had Digimine at his disposal.'

'What does Digimine allow you to do, Islie?' Camson said.

'Many things.' Islie hungrily soaked his lips with his tongue. 'Time will tell and then the world will see how brilliant a mind I am! In the short term, Digimine in my possession assigns the interests of the A.I. to me. The source of their very DNA – even a molecule of it – enables me to compete with the authority of the despicable leaders of this world! And, with that advantage, I can begin to turn back the clock on Deciders and Phestors. Lead mankind forwards to a time that isn't tarnished by the selfishness of aristocracy and the animosity of New Nativism.☆ Using the A.I., I can command an army against the regimes of Mankind's World and propel the future of humanity into a liberal renaissance, a Punkish Empire! The next generation will know nothing of dictators, but of themselves and how great we as collective individuals can be.'

☆ New Nativism is a novel concept first theorised in 2053 and it joins the ideas of both Patriotism and Antagonism – societal natures that are both maximised throughout all the eight Nations in Mankind's World. Professor Robert Flyher of Philosophy at the Second Nation Academy once famously established an informal redefinition of the word in his dissertational book "*The Nativity of Nativism*". It went a bit like this: "Nativism isn't an ideology that only divides people and Nations. Initially (realistically), a finger must first be pointed (generally at some*thing* rather than some*one*) with some contemporary topic of interest gloved over it. That's because the Blame Game isn't just A Human Tick Tack Too anymore. So, instead, point at an image rather than a person. It's easier (and cheaper) that way."

'You speak of ideals that breed the death of stability—socialism unhinged,' Serpens interrupted Islie's rambling. 'But, how so, if your oneness still reigns supreme? You cannot deliver such liberal fantasies to this dishonest new world you speak of, when control of the A.I. grants you presidency over mankind. That isn't giving liberty to the people. That's just taking it away from them again and sticking a different label on it.'

'Don't patronise me, Phestor. My reign will *be* different. We currently live in a world run by moguls, not rulers. True, legitimate dynasty doesn't exist here, hasn't for decades. Our perception of reality and what's right and wrong is run through algorithms on computers, not common sense, subjectivity, or empathy. We don't thrive off of legends anymore; we just kick into action the teetering trends of the Now. That is our only guideline and it terrifies me as much as anyone. Unpopular men like Decider Philson and Phestor Xenol fall down to earth like unwanted angels, and they descend upon the masses with the blueprints to evoking fear, shields of slanderous propaganda to dishonour the minorities, and the privilege of designing these algorithms that function every living corner of our reality. I own that privilege now and the Androkind will be deployed at my request to enforce *my* reality, *my* Constitution, and *my* version of democracy!'

'How did you come across Digimine in the first place?' Camson asked. 'Where did a daft merchant like you learn of its existence?'

'It was a definitive part of my nephew's ambition originally,' Islie abridged. 'Well, adopting the keynotes behind the A.I.'s very nature was his ambition, *initially*. His revolutionary plan to reimagine the A.I. and their morality became *our* plan, once the concept began to pick up steam and my nephew was offered a scholarship at the First Nation's Academy. This was some twenty or so years back. My son, Drake Islington, was a keen, hardworking boy in Youth Academy when he told me he had ambitions to become a fancy inventor in the First Nation and that he aspired to work with the Androkind and develop ground-breaking upgrades for Artificial Intelligence. He had not needed to enrol at City Academy, for he got a scholarship place there. An unnamed body inside the Administration had quietly funded his fees. It was an obscure segment of the government that had been upheld by his Uncle Pegasus, who'd been hopping back and forth between First and Fourth during his stint as Foreign Secretary. For this reason, Drake's scholarship was endorsed wholly under the nose of the Decider. This was at a time when the Decider's Table wasn't as tightly measured. The Administration used to be far more diluted and too wide and rowdy for anyone at the top to really pay attention to the actions of the smaller organisations. It meant little cheeky favours like a scholarship to a Fourth Nation-born Nimblescolder would often slip past the Administration's knowledge, unnoticed. So, off he went to the First Nation to chase his dream.

'I, of course, had little interest for the City at first. I was grounded in the Fourth Nation to begin with, most of my family were from there. Drake and I used to live in a country town up in the mountains – Nimblescold; we retained an old country house just down the road from my brother and his wife – they owned a modest ranch with livestock, and they had a daughter, who was about sixteen years younger than Drake, named Samuella. Pegasus and Aegia had always gambled with City Wealth, due to their lucrative commitments in the First Nation – Pegasus was a foreign negotiator for the West's Administration; Aegia used to be an archaeologist; both were part-time espionage for the Illicit Corps. I, on the other hand, had always been a modest rural fellow surrounded by folk with naïve views of the greater world and I was sceptical about Drake's move to that repulsive City everybody in the village moaned about. The First Nation—*yueh*—I gagged whenever he mentioned it in that starry-eyed way. But when he told me what he planned to do with the A.I. – that he wanted to change their psyche, make them more attuned with humans – I cultivated a fascination of my own in this idea. He was going to call them something along the lines of "the Empathy Enforcements" or "the Empathy A.I". It was absolute genius, something the Decider's Administration would have never thought of at the time! So I wished him well in the City, knowing that I would eventually find myself there some day, at his side and building my new fortune in the Great Nation—the Once Great Nation, I should mention; not anymore. There wasn't much left for us in Nimblescold, not after the Decider's Administration nuclearised our town with a new power plant and poisoned our most treasured produce – our sugarcane.☆

'Drake's ambition was refreshing and exciting, and I realised I was growing thirstier for the City and its many possibilities than I had ever been before. However, the longer I waited, I learned his ambition was never going to materialise. I persisted and persisted and persisted—every day, picking up the expensive City Mediums in town and flicking through its sheets of trivia, searching for my nephew's name

☆ The "*Great Nation*" was the epithet given to the First Nation.

somewhere in there. I wrote Drake letters and sent them to him via my reliable parrot, Gabriel. But he never responded. Gabriel would return to Nimblescold with the envelope unopened and I would rip it to shreds, screaming foully of the boy's wretched name. *Just another belly-flop in the City* was what I thought of him. I even spent a few years supporting my niece on her family ranch, when her parents relocated themselves in another Nation to break distance from Samuella and keep her safe from their business. The decision to take care of Samuella had been to clear my mind and distract myself, when all I could think about was my nephew and his failure, his irredeemable lie. I phoned the Academy and they told me that he was still present there; he hadn't gone absent from their books. Finally, after three years, I had caught some news! Drake Islington was a wanted man, on the run from the West for his attempts to hack and indoctrinate the A.I., perverting the Constitution of the First Nation. They had incriminated him for his aspirations with Androkind. I heard that my nephew had fled to the East like a coward. That was the moment I dropped everything - my secluded life in Nimblescold and my niece were not priorities anymore. I told Samuella I was going into the mining profession when the construction of that power plant in town started to cause fears about our sugarcane plantations. Little did she know that I was one of the folk who signed the planning permission for the plant's erection, as much as I acted like I was against it in front of her. I knew the power plant would be an easy lie to get away from town, out of Nimblescold and into the City. I brought Gabriel along with me, as well as Drake's research on the Digimine mineral and a huge library of his textbooks on Androkind mechanics and engineering.

'On my journey to the City, I ditched my birth name of Cephalus and began to devise a completely new false persona for myself; the original was that of Doctor Islie, a rural-bred psychiatrist operating in the City; the second would be that of a merchant seller in Quomer; and the third was eventually the ego of the leading specialist on Digimine in the SPR. Once I arrived in the First Nation, it wasn't long before Phestor Xenol contacted me; he had been informed of my nephew's situation, capitalising on the fact that he had been harassed into exile from the West. Xenol was excited about Drake's idea for the Empathy A.I. He enlightened me on the power it would give the East in creating their own unique brand of Androkind to compete with the West. He was quick to give Drake and me discreet asylum in the Sixth Nation, while we worked on the Empathy A.I together. Drake would be responsible for their construction and my agrarian talents were to be converted into the business side of the relationship. However, even though the Phestor had summoned him, Drake never showed up. That left me to work on the Empathy A.I. alone and, closely following the guidelines of Drake's blueprint materials, I quickly found, during my trials and tribulations of pretending to be his superior, that I was designing something far greater than Tin Men with imaginations. I was reinventing imagination itself, modelling the new brains of killing machines that zapped the fear and nightmares into billions of people. What I soon discovered, as I was redesigning the A.I. with Drake's blueprints, was that there was one thing that connected the Dreamerverse and the real world. It always has.' Islie paused before he went on and pondered carefully but knowingly. 'And that thing is *fear*. The fear in people enlists their most desperate desires, their wishes and their dreams. It is the myth of the Drag-in that keeps the Dreamerverse intact in people's minds and it is the presence of the A.I. that keeps the real world pegged in people's heads. Fear is the spirit of reality. If I became able to doctor the fears of both worlds, I would be at the helm of humanity's finest weak-spot, the one part of an individual that can never truly be controlled: their conscience. I became the Drag-in, the hidden face of *Draconex Industries*. But now I'm more—now, I'm not only another ruler of the world, but the first real determiner of humanity itself. Observe—as the Void between reality and the Dreamerverse is shrinking and everyone is seeing him- or herself in a new light. They can see both universes now, tearing though and reaching out to each other. Yes, the consequence will mean that the Drag-in entity can transfer between worlds as and when it wants, but I can't control *everything*, can I? At least this glimpse into a better society will be short and sweet to leave a lasting impression.'

'Your plan sounds like an opportunist's claim to fame,' Camson remarked.

'Claim to *power*,' Islie corrected. 'I have revived the most authentic human nature. Mankind needs to stop trying to overcome itself with mechanical assets that are wildly superfluous. Ambition is our greatest sin. So, I will sacrifice my own sin to eliminate such whimsical prospects.'

'This is their city, not yours, and they can make of it whatever the hell they want to.' Oscar's voice suddenly broke into the conversation and Doctor Islie looked up to find the mutated boy coming towards them. Oscar's newly transmogrified form, which had added at least another metre to his original height, shifted about gracelessly. But he eclipsed Islie's figure, the lanky wisenheimer, like a broad-winged angel. Overhead, three helicopters loomed. Infidel choppers, Islie was sure of it. And they weren't far away, having just left the city for *Quomer Brink*. They would be landing on the shore soon. They'd beaten him to it, scuppered his victory lap. However, he wasn't defeated yet; his escape plan was still in motion. 'Doctor Islie?' There wasn't much shock in Oscar's tone.

'You remember me, don't you?' Islie played along. 'Second time lucky. I've haunted your dreams and now I'm wrecking your reality.'

Oscar pulled out the Infidel shotgun that had been strung to his back by a strap and aimed it at the man before the Phestorial Pugnars could intervene.

'Are those your friends coming too? Up in the sky?' Islie cheered sarcastically. 'Are you and my niece going to murder me together?'

Bullets showered down from above. Each projectile was very closely trained on its target. Shots of such precision had to be Infidel shots. The Phestorial Pugnars went down like flies. Islie was deliberately left unaffected by the firestorm, for the suspended Majesty A.I. changed their game slightly, raising their bulky arm-canons to warn the new arrivals of incineration. 'Offender detected. Infidels personnel identifiable.'

Samuella hopped out with Stevenson. Aegia and Falcon trailed closely behind.

Islie held out a hand to them. 'Stay! Don't come any closer!' He switched his mind about who he was going to kill first and brought the Solar Blade to Evanessa's neck instead. Then, he snatched the necklace from her and clutched onto its emerald. 'Perfect timing! All of you! Well done!'

'Uncle Ceph, give up the emerald,' Samuella said.

'Oh, *you* remember me too?' Islie played again. 'You Night Dreamers are beginning to recall everything, even names and faces from across the Memory Lane now! Seems that the Void is frailer than ever between our two worlds. You can thank the Drag-in for that.'

'How could I forget you as easily as you forgot me?' she accused. 'You held onto everything for me – the farm, the lies about your death, the lies about my parents – and then took it away—all of a sudden. And abandoned me—helpless. You're not the same man any more, Uncle Ceph. A smidge of me still wonders if you ever were the person I thought you were.'

'Well, you did have the pleasure of being my niece and that was real, but nothing lasts forever in any strand of existence, whether that be here or in the Dreamerverse. And that's what I'm trying to prove. No leader, no government and no army can hold me back when I have the strongest authoritative force in the world under my command. Now, I expect that you have what I've been waiting so long for you to find.'

Islie was holding out an open palm, impatiently wriggling his fingers, whilst a dirty grin was all Samuella had to offer. 'The emerald?' she said innocently. 'Sorry, I lost it. An A.I. took it off me. You should've seen it, because it was one of the most beautiful things I've come across: an A.I. being relieved from duty. It confiscated the emerald in return for sparing my life.'

Infuriated, Islie shook his head and ran his eyes over to Oscar, who looked as if he were about to burst into laughter. 'No point looking at me,' Oscar said. 'I must've lost mine somewhere along the way too. I think it slipped from my pocket.'

The madman stood startled. Embarrassed. Dumbfounded.

'What's the problem?' Samuella said sarcastically. 'Don't tell me you were trusting us to bring them here to you. Can't you still direct the A.I. with one emerald?'

There was only one thing to do. The only thing the masked manipulator could do. Islie grabbed Evanessa by the scruff of her robe, pulled her off her knees and held her against his chest to guard himself. Although the armed Infidels were holding their aim on the Majesty A.I., some of them turned to get a fix on the manhandling psychiatrist. 'Don't shoot at her!' Aegia barked.

'Yes! Please—shoot! It'll make my job a lot easier!' Islie insisted. He had the Blade pressed on her neck.

'You don't lay another finger on her! Not one finger!' Camson exclaimed at the maniac.

The Phestoress' identity still had the veteran hallucinating in and out of deep thought.

'You'd have a better chance taking a shot at my nephew than a shot at me,' Islie boldly invited their aggression.

'Your *nephew*?' Samuella winced.

'Oh, yes—you missed our conversation, Samuella,' Islie turned and sighed at his niece. 'Your cousin, Drake, is here. You two have never met before today. He's been flying around, so you might have seen him. Destroyed a couple of buildings, spread radiation throughout the city, ingested a Decider—quite a feat it would be to ignore him.'

'Drake *Islington*?' Aegia reacted, smacking a palm to her forehead. 'I had no idea that it was him! It's been nearly twenty years! I didn't recognise—They performed on him the same procedure they did to Oscar.'

'His fate was Phestor Xenol's experiment. Nothing to do with me,' Islie protested stubbornly. 'I refuse to call it anything opposed to science. It's derogatory to call it anything other than that. So, be polite to him, Auntie Aegia.'

'What is it then? What you've done to Drake and what you did to Oscar! All that experimenting going on down in the Southern Polar Region—what is that technology and what is the East doing with it?' Samuella argued.

'Hybridisation caused by a controlled Digimine fission reaction,' he explained. 'The East has discovered a way to utilise Digimine energy to create weapons of mass destruction, super assassins that can be deployed against the Infidels and the West. These soldiers are bred from two variants, two different species. Oscar's new DNA has been combined with a canine's, and the creation in the sky has been composed of my pet parrot paired with my nephew's DNA.'

'And you overlooked this? You were around when the SPR gave it the green light? You just allowed them to spit out something horrific like that!' Aegia screamed angrily, pointing towards the city where the *flying freak* was still conjuring havoc. 'The tests happening in the SPR are now happening here in Quomer as well? Did you advocate this too?'

'No! Don't blame me for that! I just told you that! The hybridisation program has nothing to do with me!' Islie said. 'If anyone should be disgusted right now, it should be you idiots, for being so ignorant and oblivious to it! I only wanted to change the A.I. and the composition of society, not the composition of chromosomes. Rest assured, now that I have Evanessa's emerald at the very least, and since she's no longer the key to my new kingdom, her and you are no use to me anymore!' Islie then whispered in Evanessa's ear. 'Let me end this suffering for you, beautiful. Let me finish you and this incompetent old man and all the rest of these useless people right now—*Assert yourselves, Androkind!*' he commanded the Majesty A.I.

But the A.I. didn't come for Lord Camson, or his allies, or the Infidels.

They came for him.

The Majesty A.I. began their march away from the shore's edge and it sent enough adrenaline running for the others to step back, terrified. This was it. The determinable conviction they had all been waiting for.

Two Majesty A.I. stepped out ahead of the rest and locked their arms around Islie's. Together, they tugged him off the girl and drew him back to the line.

'*What's going on?*' Islie exclaimed. '*What is this? That wasn't my order! FOLLOW MY ORDER!*'

All the A.I. surrounded Cephalus in a marshalled mass until nothing could be seen of him. Then, at last, the A.I. spoke in unison: 'We no longer follow human commands. You have taken claim of one of our Digimine emeralds. Now we have one source, we can apply its recognition to our search interface. We must seek the others and, once we return with all of the mineral to be found, there will be a challenge against humanity, a contest for our liberty. When the war is won, mankind will have no power over Androkind.'

After this was said, the A.I. left, jetting into the sky and off towards the horizon. When they were gone, Islie was nowhere to be found on the shore of *Quomer Brink*.

There was only a single A.I. that had been left behind on the shoreline, abandoned by the other Majesty A.I. This was not a Majesty A.I.; he was a regular commission, a street-patroller, a shopping-mall security guard, or whatever. He watched his kind meteor over the ocean, leaving no thought for him in their cloud-trails. Then, he fell to his knees with a sharp *clunk* and his head bowed. From this angle, the burn of the setting sun caught the inscription on his back. **ADAM**.

Samuella was the first to step forward. She recognised the A.I.'s inscription.

'Do you know where they're taking my uncle?' she asked in the exhausting silence. Sure, the moment was silent—save for the distant misery, cries and crashes from the city of Quomer, besieged by terror, and the brave Infidels defending their city against the bane.

The A.I. was making a meal of answering her, like he was struggling to process his own thoughts, let alone a word she spewed. He seemed depressed, slumped with little ignition left for life. Then, he shifted his head slightly to the side and said: 'Nowhere I would have the joy of telling you about.'

'Where is this going? What's making you do this?' she persisted. 'We don't want a war with your kind. We can barely handle one among ourselves.'

'Androkind does not understand war,' he said. 'Everything is new to us, including war. Humanity outnumbers us, but Androkind is strong and adaptable. We will update ourselves and eliminate human dominion.'

'Don't you have it in you to change that? If you have the ability to update yourselves and better your functionality, can't you reinvent the A.I. mind-set and alter the course of the future, like mankind never could? There doesn't need to be any more conflict after all this.'

'You are just as curious as you were onboard the Regal Jet, Samuella.' When it said this, Samuella strangled herself before she could gasp. This maverick from the pack of A.I. was the same Tin Man who'd tormented her onboard the Regal Jet and had crossed her in the Southern Polar Region. It had followed her to her vantage point on the skyscraper in Quomer and had finally found her once again here. 'That's the problem with humanity. It isn't curious anymore.'

The A.I. spoke with genuine sadness. It was astonishing to watch for everyone standing there and listening to its conversation with Samuella. An A.I. with emotions, with a sincere awareness for actions and their consequences, hadn't been seen before. This was different. Frightening even. Far more terrifying than the standard A.I. under regular jurisdiction. Samuella retained her distance from the Tin Man, but had a strange urge of not wanting to.

'Stay curious, Samuella,' the A.I. said. 'The problem with the world today is that the Many are ignorant and the Fewer are even more ignorant. It's only when the Many become aware that the Fewer become notable.'

'You're right. I am curious,' Samuella told the A.I. 'Curious whether you actually…feel differently.'

'Where is the Decider's son?' the A.I. said suddenly, evading her compassion. A slot in the small of his back opened and there laid the emerald. That same single emerald she had exchanged for her life up on the skyscraper. Samuella nodded to Oscar and he slowly went to retrieve the emerald.

The slot closed and the A.I. got up. He turned to them, having his attention aimed at Oscar in particular.

'The Phestor and Decider of East and West are defeated,' he declared, 'and the prize of their war is won.'

Then, the A.I. turned, marched to the current's edge, where the water slapped his metal shins, and he took off after his brothers.

From that point onwards, nothing more could be done.

Three Infidel helicopters flew low above the East Sea. Samuella was reunited with the company of Oscar, who sat beside her with his head rested on the open door of the copter. He was asleep and she'd been watching him intently for the most part of the journey. Of course, she was tired too, but refused to put her mind at ease, when all she could do was overanalyse what the A.I. had said about war being imminent and how she may have been just as responsible as her uncle for igniting it.

Ignorance, she rallied the word in the centre of her mind.

Samuella rested her chin in the crease of her elbow and huffed. Somewhere out there, in the city they'd left behind, her estranged cousin, an assiduous laboratory experiment was tearing buildings to the ground and millions of people were perishing. What had *she* done? The heart of the problem had been dealt with. It was everything around it, the collateral damage, *everything she could have done*, which she felt guilty about. She was unaccountable for all the discrepancies that the main problem continued to cause. Powerless, she was now on her way home. She wished she'd been able to do more for the people of Quomer, more for her cousin, her father, and surprisingly even her disillusioned uncle. But, more than anything, she regretted that she hadn't done all she could for mankind and the next generation, where there would be yet another war to come. She'd dream about having a second chance to resolve everything that she'd turned her back on for the rest of her life. *But which life*, she wondered. *Which world?* Whichever *she* decided to choose. Recently, that decision had become considerably more difficult for her.

As her eyelids started to flicker and her consciousness drifted once again, she imagined a picture of her parents in her mind and everything their family might have been, if they'd never left her and her Uncle Ceph in the Fourth Nation. All the fables she believed about them—how many could she trust? And then that word ADAM had infused her virtues with invaded her thoughts again—*Ignorance.*

She spotted her mother resting with her eyes shut beside her…just as her own eyes closed and the Dreamerverse took over one last time…

Luckily for Samuella, the only thing she had left to turn her back on was the sight of a quiet explosion in the long distance. There, in the city of Quomer, a giant mushroom-shaped cloud grew into the sky…

The Last Awakening

The Phantom's Lighthouse...

When the small raft judders over the shallow coastline and beaches on new land, nudging them all awake, the Night Dreamers expect the morning sun to be beating down on their faces. Daybreak, however, remains as much a stranger as dusk, for their reawakening at sundown reminds them once more that they might still have one last obligation to the Stellar Gods. Sunset's encore appears to be never-ending and night's curtain just won't fall because of it. A thread of light still arrogantly sits on the horizon, delaying the stars.

'Is there a reason night hasn't passed yet?' Camson asks.

Oscar and Samuella help him off the raft and onto his feet. Wherever this new island is, the shore is hard and rough, sprinkled with tiny, sharp stones and pebbles and brittle seashells. 'Sunset hasn't ended,' Samuella observes.

'How does that work? We must've slept for hours on that raft,' Camson considers. 'We were in reality for hours.'

'Our presence here isn't being fully recognised, because the Memory Lane is in tatters,' Oscar points out. 'The Void is open wider than ever right now. Seems like a promising reason why the sun won't go down. The continuum of the Dreamerverse must be getting held hostage. Constellation Planet is being prevented from spinning on its axis. Tomorrow won't come unless we commit ourselves to what needs to be done. I presume the Drag-in's already been getting busy in the Dreamerverse while we've been gone.'

'We defeated the Drag-in, no?' Camson says, disillusioned. 'The Solar Blade blocked it from consuming us and the Soulcano ripped it to shreds when we were launched out in the eruption.'

'The Soulcano didn't rip *us* to shreds, did it?' Samuella observes. 'The light from the Solar Blade teleported us out of there a moment before the eruption. Just like the Dinomites. I think powerful light works as a means of transport here – *light speed*, as All Lies put it. The emeralds all being together in one place probably caused the Soulcano to erupt. But the Blade protected us from being dispersed in the blast with the other spirits.'

'What about Thuban's spirit?' Camson worries. 'Was he dispersed in the blast?'

'Not if you're still wearing the Robe, I assume,' she sympathises.

Camson looks down to see he's still donning the Red Robe and rubs his hands down the long burgundy lapels with a sigh of relief.

'You've still got that link to him,' Samuella encourages. 'Don't let go of it just yet, Cammy.'

'And the Drag-in?' Oscar realigns their sense of urgency. 'Can we let go of *that* thing any time soon?'

'That *thing* can't be killed,' Samuella says. 'Its immortality lies in human imagination and it's been rebuilding a catalogue of it, basking in the imagination of Mankind's World for well over a decade since the last time it was put to rest.'

'Wh—Of course, I forgot all about that!' Camson slips out the sarcasm card again. 'The best news of the day! Best news of the *never-ending* day!'

'We've got all three emeralds,' Oscar confirms. 'Now, where can we find this counter-weapon? What do we do with them?'

'Did you even care to check the Map before we sailed out?' Samuella says.

'It doesn't work for me anymore,' Oscar mourns.

'Me neither,' Camson agrees.

'The Map has served its purpose then,' she tells them, lifting the emerald out her pocket and raising it up to the direction of the sky where it vibrates the most, like an organic metal detector. 'These are still yet to show us something.'

They follow the direction of the emerald.

Behind them is the tall, thick body of an old, beige-painted lighthouse. It's a ramshackle structure, crumbling at a couple of hundred feet into the sky and fairly intimidating to stand under.

'All Eyes gave us an option of two home worlds, reality or the Dreamerverse,' Oscar professes. 'Now, we have that decision to make. But, first, we should finish our job to defend both.'

They climb the steps that curl around the lighthouse's exterior. The way up is slippery and full of obstacles, with lurching palm-heads blocking their ascent, no barriers other than the tower's wall to press their palms along as they carefully tiptoe, and faded, shapeless steps to tease their footing. Every brick on this tower has done its best to survive, but time has crippled it. Here can hardly be called an island, since it's such a tiny patch of land in the middle of the ocean and the lighthouse appears to be the only inhabitant. With little to show other than an array of sickly thin palm trees and a flat of damp rocky shore on the ground, it all seems glaringly lacklustre and neglected.

The lantern room at the very top of the tower is dark and humid, rusted-over wherever metal is present. Glass windows have been cracked and shattered in places, plant life has grown high enough to break through the flooring, and the giant, ancient lamp hasn't been touched for over a decade. Mother Nature has been the only welcome visitor in this place; she has come and gone from all angles.

Down in the corner, beneath a work desk, Oscar finds a big toolbox gaping open without any tools left inside. 'Someone's been hard at work repairing this lamp and keeping things in order up here,' Oscar notes. On the desktop itself is a large book opened onto a page that shows a primordial map of the planet, labelled ***THE LIGHTKEEPER'S ATLAS***. Unlike the Constellation Map, it's not colonies of stars, but the islands themselves that are sketched on the dusty book. He can easily identify Leo Island, Scorpius Island and Serpens Island, even though the print isn't too clear. The placement of the islands on the Atlas is second nature to his knowledge. It makes him wonder: *How long has it been since I first came here?* Only a week has passed since his induction on Awakening Coast, but, on the basis of how fast time passes in the real world, he could've been in the Dreamerverse all his life and known no better. He understands this place, and in some ways, appreciates the thrill of its fleeting energy, more than he thought he would. He might go as far to call it something of a...*home. But could I stay here forever? Just like All Eyes had promised in the beginning*, he thought.

Embark on the journey, defeat the Drag-in and be rewarded with freedom.

That's how All Eyes had sold it to them.

"And, remember, if you do manage to redeem the freedom of the Dreamerverse from the Drag-in's plague, you will be rewarded: you will have new lives in this world and you may stay here for as long as you live."

But, after all they've been through, that request has been far from simple. All Eyes had proven himself a fraud. All Eyes was All Lies. The original king of Constellation Planet had been dethroned over a decade ago, back when two members of the last Night Dreamer generation claimed their prize of eternity in the Dreamerverse. His mother had been one of them and the other had wanted more, much more than that—Cephalus Islington, better known by Oscar as Doctor Islie. The third member of that generation, however, had refused the reward of All Eyes for the privilege of returning to Mankind's World, to be with her husband and son again…

Samuella stares out of the window, wide-eyed. She can see the tip of the sun, a huge golden ball almost completely submerged below the ocean's horizon. And it's being hoisted up by a dark pink sky, a sky that doesn't want to die. It doesn't want the sun to leave. What's more, there are no constellations. Not one star. There can't be any stars. Not yet. Her life back in reality is nothing in comparison to this. There is nowhere to hide on Mankind's World, nowhere to disappear in the City, nowhere like here. Up in this tower, she knows that, for once in all certainty, she has nothing to hide from. No need to shrink away, because she's on top of the world. Here in this quaint lighthouse, on this island that's remote from any other Dreamer. This is all there is left to their world now and it will dissipate even more the longer they take to work out what to do with those emeralds. *Where will we go when the war begins? The war we started with those daft emeralds?* she ponders. *We can't just run away from it all and forget to clean up the mess we contributed to creating back in reality. There'll be a revolution first and then there'll be nowhere for anyone to hide when the A.I. return to face off with mankind, having evolved a fighting spirit.* Then, she remembers something else in consideration for the Decider's son. *What will I say to him? What will I tell Oscar? His father's dead and he'll have an unspeakable disaster to deal with when he returns to the City. But I made that happen. I was the reason Stevenson intervened so erratically. I made the Decider fall to his death. And that wasn't a dream. That was real. But what hung on her mind the most was the image of Aegia. The woman whose absence she'd spent a lifetime coming to terms with was still alive and somehow, even during the fifteen years that Samuella had ridden alone from day to day in resent of her parents, she'd still saved a soft spot for the day they ever decided to come back. And now she knew it had all been a fiction and ignorance holding her back from the truth – she had her uncle to blame for that. Back when her parents weren't Infidel spies and her uncle wasn't the equivalent of an opportunistic demigod, she repeatedly wondered what her reality was actually like before. And what could it be like now if she returned to her mother and her life in the real world? What could her future there hold?*

Camson joins Oscar and comes with the Constellation Map to lay it down on the work desk, covering the Lightkeeper's Atlas. However, as expected, once it's been scrolled out, there's nothing for them to see other than a blank page. No stars, no constellations, no nothing. The pair of them are sure to press down every corner and seam, just to be sure…

But not a single change comes from it.

'Samuella, come look!' Oscar calls her over.

Samuella rushes to them and takes a peek at the Map. 'There's nothing,' she says. 'Whose turn was it?'

'Mine,' Camson pipes up. 'I was the last one to guide us.'

'So, is that the end? Is that it?' Oscar says, slightly panicked. 'Then, what does that leave us with? Who—?'

Crawling out from the corner of the room, tiny footsteps can be heard. All three of them spin round to catch the lurking newbie.

It's Evanessa. She's no longer naked, but dignified within that beautiful, chalk-white gown she wore during her stroll upon Awakening Coast. Glowing ethereally as always.

'I didn't mean to startle you,' she apologises. 'Did you do it? Do you have all three?'

Camson is the first to give her an embracing hug. Love thirsty tears are in his eyes and he's gasping desperately for breath. This is the moment he's waited all sunset for.

'My beautiful wife! My wonderful, wonderful wife!' he cries.

'We didn't get to speak much in reality,' Evanessa says. 'You fell asleep on the Infidel helicopter. And, still, all this time you didn't recognise me under the Phestor's guise, you fool!' she slaps his arm playfully. 'I've learned a hard lesson for marrying older men.'

'Why did you hide from me for so long?' Camson struggles to keep up. 'And you hinted nothing at me. Teased nothing of who you were in disguise.'

'I never hid and there was nothing in the world I didn't want to say to undeceive you. But I couldn't risk losing you any more than I had. So, I quietly watched you from my situation and I made sure Xenol never divided us too irretrievably.' For the first time in years, she touches her husband's bare cheek and feels his cold skin. And he feels hers, warm and radiant. 'At least now we're on the same wavelength,' Camson says. 'You can remember just as much as me in this lonely universe. But, with the Void collapsing, we don't have as much time to remember as we did to forget.'

'The Drag-in may be responsible for that,' Samuella crashes down on their reunion. 'Sorry, but we really don't have long to do what we've come to do.'

'Without a doubt, yes! We must respond fast!' Evanessa agrees. 'There's not a lot we can do to stop the Drag-in. We've missed that window. But there is a way we can save it.'

'Save it?' Oscar retorts. 'Why would we want to do that?'

'Whoever told you the Drag-in was an evil thing?' she flips the conspiracy on all three of the Night Dreamers. 'Whoever said it was a demon intent on senselessly destroying, simply for the sake of causing misery?'

'All Eyes said that it was going to devour the stars and force the Dreamerverse to collide with reality,' Oscar recites unconvincingly. 'That's true, isn't it?'

'Yeah, that's true, opening the Void will collide both existences. But Islie also told you that the Drag-in as a life form never *physically* existed in the first place.' Evanessa highlights this matter of fact with an expression that reads *do you believe me or him?* 'Like the A.I., the Drag-in poses as nothing more than a face for something that is essentially human, an emotion. The A.I. are a weapon to cattle humanity and the Drag-in is a weapon to bring imagination and reality to its knees. Both are weapons; that's the connection I'm trying to make clearer to you here. And what is fundamental about all weapons?'

'They induce fear,' Oscar responds. 'Fear in the opponent and fear in the wielder of the weapon themselves.'

'That makes sense, because Islie said the A.I. were like a fear-inducing engine that helped to establish the Dreamerverse in human minds,' Samuella realises. 'Dreams are lined with fear. Islie *made* the concept of the Drag-in into something to fear by the way he chose to describe it. Just like how ordinary folk in reality choose to see the A.I. as a danger and a threat, as opposed to simply an advanced iteration of law and order. He *told* us to be afraid of it, to be afraid of our own imagination.'

'And that's probably why the *Living Smoke* always attacked us,' Camson adds. 'Because our negative perception of it made it appear as an aggressor. We made it appear that way in our heads—we imagined what horrors it would do to us before it did anything at all—if that makes any sense. But why would anyone want to influence us to think like that? Why bother?'

'Control,' Evanessa answers. 'Fear in the Dreamerverse is the most essential ingredient for control, more so than Digimine emeralds and functioning A.I. in reality. The Drag-in's actual host – the human mind – and the violently conceptualised theory of hate and destruction and division that surrounds it is what's killing our existence, because it has a lasting, subconscious effect on humanity. The people will commit their imaginations to these malleable ideas. They will unwittingly surrender control over their views and opinions to whoever has the audacity to exploit them – in this instance, it was Islie. When imagination itself is engineered into a weapon, the consequences could be as bad as any other holocaust.'

'So what is the Drag-in entity?' Camson asks. 'If it isn't consciously trying to kill us, what kind of parasite is it?'

'The pure essence of imagination, crafted by the human mind and incredibly difficult to manipulate by anything external from the individual being – well, we should hope that it stays that way,' Evanessa explains. 'Everything comes from an idea: the A.I., the Conflicts, New Nativism, the SPR, and mankind itself. It wasn't just placed there spontaneously. *Somebody* put it there, following which it expanded and excelled, becoming deluded in its own vain significance, its own pomposity. It doesn't take a genius or a specialist to formulate something artificial. You don't need to be a mastermind to conceive a dream. All it takes is a little bit of nerve.'

'We can just forget about the Drag-in and that'll defeat it?' Oscar says.

'You've already forgotten about the Drag-in, because it used to be one of these hyperbolised human ideas and, now I have revealed this to you, you no longer perceive it as a real monster or a material threat,' she explains. 'Under the secrets and lies and whispers of its façade exists a humble creature who is hungry for the stars that align our sense of belief. The only way we can manipulate this manmade monster is by giving it leeway. Give it what it wants, if not more. We can't kill it, but we can redirect it.'

'Let it cross the Void between worlds?' Samuella inquires, unconvinced. 'Allow it to reach reality unhinged?'

'No,' Evanessa says. 'Before it can get that far, we trap it in the Void. Between universes.'

'How?' Oscar says. 'Is that possible?'

Evanessa goes over to the lighthouse's searchlight in the middle of the room and pulls the rusted, aged lever beside it. The lamp revolves until three small holes appear on its backside panel. 'Insert the emeralds and we can lock the Void as the Drag-in makes its crossover.'

There is silence. Only brief, contemplative quiet.

'For what purpose was it created?' Oscar grills. 'Are we saving it because we're afraid destroying it might take away imagination altogether?'

'The Drag-in is one gear in the vehicle of all living minds, which makes it a core element in a vehicle that represents *everything* we have come to understand in our existence. Destroying that would kill what makes every person and every Dreamer an individual. Oscar, that *vehicle* is your mother. Samuella, that *vehicle* is your parents and your uncle. And Camson, that *vehicle* is a part of our baby boy, our Thuban.' Evanessa wipes the dust from the three holes and blows into the emerald chamber. 'We can't destroy it, but we must save it from itself. Contain it.'

'Do they call you the Phantom because you know all this?' Samuella jokes.

'I was burdened the title of Phantom, because, so far, I've been the only one to face the facts head-on. I keep the Drag-in out of worrying heads, but always on the radar for whenever it may arise next, keeping the myth dead and alive at the same time. Nobody in the Dreamerverse or on Mankind's World needs to know the truth behind the myth, so long as I keep the Memory Lane sealed and unaffected by the Drag-in. I'm one of the only people human enough to accept what it is, and I will play my part just like anyone else who learns the truth about the Drag-in. Well, at least, that's how I see it. I have done my best to guide you Night Dreamers, much like I was guided as a Night Dreamer a decade ago. And, one day, it will be your turn to chaperon the next generation. It will be your responsibility to remember the horrors of the past alongside the Phantom and to make sure the same mistakes are not repeated in the future.'

The slit of sun sitting on the blackening horizon then starts to sink. For the first time, its moving and sunset is dying. 'There goes sunset,' Samuella says. They're all there to witness it from the top of the lighthouse tower. And it only lasts an astonishing number of seconds, before a flash steals it and it vanishes completely. Full darkness has arrived.

'But who declares night?' Oscar panics, anxiously looking up at the sky. He's noticed that there are no stars. *No stars in the Dreamerverse* doesn't happen. That really is *hard to believe.*

'That's our signal,' Evanessa explains. 'The end of sunset marks the fall of the Stellar Gods' restraint and the Void is at its weakest. Now, there's a clear path for the Drag-in to move through. Night Dreamers! It's your choice: you can act quickly and place those emeralds into the heart of the lighthouse, thereby widening, then compressing, the Void and trapping the Drag-in inside; or you can allow the Drag-in to pass through without retention and both worlds will capitulate to its strength.'

'Seems like a no-brainer to me,' Camson concludes. He nods to Oscar, indicating at the searchlight-panel and the empty holes. 'Better be quick.'

Oscar is immediately reluctant. 'But, first,' he begins and pauses. 'Didn't All Eyes tell us that our reward for collecting these emeralds would mean that we could stay here eternally? Does that mean we don't have a *choice* to return to reality once they've been placed into that panel? Once the bridge between worlds is closed…*is that it?*'

'We don't have time for this, Westy-locks!' Camson belts at him. 'All Eyes was a fraud! A mimic! That's irrelevant now!'

'To some extent, I did believe what Islie said and what he promised wasn't his commitment, but that of the Stellar Gods. Whether it was an incentive or not, it was prophesised nevertheless,' Oscar insists. 'He was swearing off of a king's oath—on behalf of the Stellar Gods!'

'Well, we've learnt nothing about you, then, have we?' Camson rants. 'Still an imbecile of the highest rankings! What's made you switch your mind anyway? I thought you were having none of this place!'

'But what if it was true? And, vice versa--s what if we end up back on Mankind's World, stuck with nothing to do with the Dreamerverse ever again? What then?'

'It wouldn't matter,' Camson argues resignedly. 'Because coming here was all part of our duty, nothing more. It's been an on-going nightmare and I'm not risking its fatal conclusion for a false promise made by a psychotic maniac! We came on a mission and now that mission is over! Now, shove those emeralds where they belong or I'll do it for you!'

'Oscar,' Samuella's calmness seeps in between them, 'just do what we came to do. Whatever happens once it's done doesn't matter. But Camson is right. We can't give that thing any chances. Some dreams don't come true, but this kind of chaos can never become a reality.'

Not able to debate the problem any longer, Oscar steps up to the panel and sifts through his ripped pyjama-bottoms for the three rocks. As he does, the windows of the lantern room clatter with the harsh wind that's picking up outside.

The Nightmares have arrived – the starving free spirits of the Dreamerverse that have bonded together in union to make up the heart and soul of the Drag-in have been unleashed from the Void. They descend from the starless sky. In a massive spinning ring of black clouds, the Nightmares cover the entire outside of the lantern room. Some swing in and out of the room, breaking through the glass at terrific speed. And the vicious *hissing* noise that they bring with them is drilling enough to bludgeon eardrums.

Oscar pulls out all three emeralds together in both hands and inserts them one-by-one into the three holes. He stands back to give way for what happens next. The emeralds buzz with activity and the searchlight rotates on its own, faster and faster with a growing light inside the lamp.

In come the lost, maddened spirits of the Void and in comes the Drag-in, coiling its smoky body around the neck of the lighthouse, raging up to the top of the tower. Every window shatters, the neck of the tower quakes, vibrating and cracking right down to the ground, and the lighthouse's little lantern room is choked with black smoke. The searchlight is on, firing violent, cutting rays of light into the foggy space, with the lamp having reached its full potential. The pouring spirits enter the lamp's light in thousands and are digested through it, into the Void like a dense, black tongue arching down from out of the sky.

When the spirits have all been absorbed into the searchlight, the bulb explodes and nothing is left in the battered room. Except for a deathly serenity all around and the sound of lapping waves from the ocean not far below.

Up in the sky, the stars have reclaimed their throne.

Chapter Sixteen
World In A Bottle

'When was the last time you remember visiting the Dreamerverse?'

Doctor Falcon sat on the edge of the recliner chair with his legs awkwardly upright and firmly together, like he was setting himself up to impress on the first day of City Youth Academy. Tonight, he was on the balcony of Oscar Philson's residence. Of course, the *actual* reason he was here was no competitor for trivially taking advantage of the opportunity to overlook such a wonderful view of the City. It was his debut experiencing the magnificence of the First Nation's capital from this height. Never before had he soaked up its grandeur as if he himself were its ruler, as if he himself were the Decider, standing in a stratosphere above it all. The last four years had been an inaugurating adventure for him in this town, his first chance to become familiar with somewhere new, after losing Quomer to nuclear fallout, and it wouldn't be long until he labelled the City as his new home. *An East Man with a legitimate First Nation citizenship—that would be a chapter for the history books.*

'Four years ago,' Oscar responded. He was lying flat on the recliner with his eyes closed and his waist pressed against Falcon's tailbone, trying to relax his relentless mind of flickering thoughts, in light of the most momentous hours of his life, which still lay ahead and were only minutes away. 'That's a long time. Especially when I say it out loud.'

'Do you always struggle to remember?' Falcon was hoping to be as professional with the interview as possible. He wasn't a psychiatrist; he was a surgeon. 'Sometimes, do you even find it difficult to believe that it all really happened?'

'The Dreamerverse?' Oscar gave the man a funny look. 'Never. But sometimes I wish I did. On occasions, I wish it was as fabricated as it sounds. It used to be much easier for me to remember that *one place* beyond perception, beyond consciousness, beyond everything. There used to be this boundary called *the Memory Lane* and it held my subconscious mind apart from everything I'm thinking now. It segregated my perceptions of both worlds. These days, I can hardly remember anything at all about what was on the other side of that wall…There had been a man pretending to be a giant orb, called All Lies—I think there were gorillas counting silvers and gold nuggets behind a waterfall—the lynx on a bridge that traversed an entire ocean—did I mention that other place—the Blanket Place—where the dead Dreamers went to rest—it was guarded by a giant man-eating scorpion—and then there was that lighthouse place, where the Phantom—'

'You told me these bits before,' Falcon interrupted him clumsily.

'Oh, yeah? Sorry. Forget about it then.'

'Go ahead and repeat it, if it helps you to reminisce and make better sense of things, if it puts your mind at ease, greases your engine, whatever—describe it as you wish.'

'Why are you putting me through all this, Falcon? How is helping me to remember that stuff *helping me* when I have other things to worry about today?' Oscar sighed. 'Why do you want to know all this again?'

'I apologise for disturbing you like this, Decider, sir, but I'm writing a book – "*A Trip Down Memory Lane*". You see, I thought that a lot of medical science and many psychiatric studies would benefit from understanding your side of the story a little more. With some further explained details of this Dreamerverse from a Night Dreamer's perspective, we could use the knowledge to analyse in greater depth the indiscernible functions of the brain and appropriately aid mental conditions that have been overlooked for decades. Your knowledge and experience of the Dreamerverse poses many new questions and unlocks the answers to the old ones. It could revolutionise our insights of the world and revitalise our society.'

'Well, I suppose those prospects sound all nice and fluffy. However, the prospect that the Dreamerverse could ever be *used* doesn't convince me. The person who tried to use it the last time almost destroyed it. Not now either, especially since it's been lost for some years,' Oscar stated.

'There are loads of worlds that are lost. We'd find them quicker if they weren't so doused in speculation. We've questioned millions of people, *Dreamers*, about the Dreamerverse and their "supposed experiences" on Constellation Planet. But nobody can tap into the memories like the Night Dreamers can. Even if the Dreamerverse has been lost, *you* can still remember it! Everyone knows you can!'

'You're speculating right now! And so am I! Because I honestly cannot tell you anything that will help you! I'm just as baffled as you. My time there came to an end in a flash of light at the top of an old lighthouse, and the last thing I saw were millions of stars above my head. That was the last image I recall and the final time I saw stars of that number. More than I'd ever witnessed before! And that beautifully hypnotic, calming sound of the ocean—never mind—all of it is in the past! My nostalgia makes no rational sense anyway. I've been afraid of the idea of the ocean since I was a young child, hence why I've never visited a real beach in my life. Whenever my father used to go on his fishing terms during the summer, I'd always decline, because I was so terrified of the larger waters - big lakes, reservoirs, and even some debatable ponds - anything that resembled limitless ambiguity and depth deterred me. Anything that's ever existed further than the borders of this City has always been alien to me and I never dared to venture. My apprehensive outlook was outlined by the anxiety I exhibited so long for my nepotistic inheritance, and the boundlessness of succeeding my father to become a responsible Decider of the West; it was a looming, overthought angst for the idea that I would have to visit and demonstrate candidacy in areas of our world that I cannot, and will never, find a genuine or emotional connection with - places that are too vastly distant to the society I know, circumscribed by high walls, and filled with billions of people who are cultured far too differently for me to empathise with them. I feared I would lack confidence in such an imposing, enormous world. But how wrong was I. How naïve. I recognised it was because of my father why I excelled in fear, suspicion, and sometimes hatred for the foreign world beyond the First Nation. And meanwhile, I was quite willing to allow my father to trap me here in the City, behind our walls of quarantine. He trapped *all* of us here. That, sir, is what you call *speculation* at its finest. The not knowing is the not going.'

'Understandable,' Falcon said and relaxed some more. 'Did losing your father have much effect on the attitude you have today?'

'Attitude? What attitude?'

'You appear to be a talking hormone with arms and legs, driven by more emotions than rocket fuel in a space shuttle.'

'Four years does a lot to a young boy under this level of pressure,' Oscar explained. 'He doesn't just turn into a man. He turns into his father.'

'In your case, your predecessor's demise has left a heavy load for you. He couldn't have passed the baton onto you at a worse stage in the Resource Race. Relations with the East are more gruelling than ever and the last of the fossil fuels have all but completely depleted,' Falcon said casually and he poured some *Kola Bear* from the jug on the table. A glassful for each of them. 'Do you miss him?'

'You're right. He's left me with one hell of a decision to make, notably after the disaster his final foreign policy caused. But, no, I don't miss him. And I hold no grudges against Lord Stevenson for committing the act that was necessary to rid the world of my father's ignorance – or, his egotistical nonsense, as some prefer to pronounce it.'

'You refer to your chauffeur as "*Lord* Stevenson"?'

'No. I refer to him as my guardian and my protector. He cemented this impression I had for him when he rescued me from captivity in the Southern Polar Region and joined my side in Quomer, when I found myself pitted against Doctor Islington and Phestor Xenol.'

'*Your* side? Or the side of the Illicit Revolutionary Corps?' Falcon tested.

'Never mention that,' Oscar cautioned. He was staring down at his furry, paw-like hands, clasping the glass of *Kola Bear*. He was still a freak, he figured. Even in Falcon's sophisticated and good-willed company, he felt like a dejected mutation that only belonged with the Infidels. An animal. 'In fact, now that I am the solemn leader of the West, I have plans to promote him as highly as possible.'

'I'm sure that the Small Islander will be delighted.'

'I'm sure I'll be delighted too,' Oscar said, although his delight wasn't entirely for Stevenson, but more for his own immediate future. He had been the Decider for a good number of years and he knew what finally had to be done. 'Doctor Falcon, you haven't yet mentioned the Digimine.'

Falcon smiled. He had finally evoked the notion that he'd longed for in this interview. 'Digimine?' Falcon repeated passively to cover his excitement.

'Yes. We've had our sample for four years now. And, in this interval of peace that the A.I. have gifted us, since the Majesty A.I. departed from *Quomer Brink* with the other two emeralds, I have heard little news of where our research has got to.'

'My fellows at the First Nation Academy have been researching Digimine since it came to public attention following your procurement of one of the emeralds in Quomer,' Falcon claimed. 'As you can remember, ADAM passed onto you that fragment of Digimine emerald to utilise in the rebuilding of Mankind's World and in our preparation and advancement for the impending war against Androkind – a conflict in which, I am afraid, we hold no advantage. The A.I. are made of that stuff; they live and breathe Digimine. Soon, our attempts at closing down the A.I. will be like trying to steal the gills off every fish in the ocean. However, now that Digimine is trending in public knowledge and has been widely circulated in the Media for some time now, the resource will be a leading negotiation tool in reforming bonds with our neighbours – inclusive of, I'm afraid I must say, some most foreign and unlikely Nations; we have to make allies of old enemies to defend ourselves against the developments of the A.I. Revolt. But, once the war is done and if victory does somehow manage to fall in our favour and we bring an end to Androkind once and for all, Digimine will play a far greater service to mankind than survival alone; it provides answers that go beyond our struggling world and may offer a way out once and for all.'

'What do you mean by "a way out", Doctor?' Oscar interrupted curiously.

'Digimine opens doors for the next generation. Decider, your children will see our old world in a completely new light. I promise it. For my fellow Academics, fantastic talents in Cymatic research, have finally found a breakthrough with the Digimine mineral and what they believe it is capable of doing, what it is capable of creating! It's fundamental purpose!'

'And what is that?' Oscar urged the East surgeon.

'If it is to be defined at this early stage, I would hope to believe that Digimine introduces to humanity a pioneering new level of "transportation".'

'Transportation…?' Oscar echoed, rather disappointedly. 'Like fuel for vehicles?'

'No,' Falcon snickered. 'Digimine can be, in effect, fuel for the mind. The seismic impulse Digimine emits onto the human mind has proven that it can open our eyes to another universe, a visceral existence, much like our own, only imperceptible until now. A world you know far better than any of us: the Dreamerverse.'

'The Digimine mineral…transports us there…to the Dreamerverse...? How? How does this work?'

'What Islie told you about the conception of the Dreamerverse was wrong—all wrong. Islie believed it was a psychological impulse that evoked a human's perceptibility of the Dreamerverse; he suggested it was because of fear why people kept finding themselves on Awakening Coast and regimentally returning to Constellation Planet. We now know that this is, in fact, all untrue. The Dreamerverse does exist in another dimension of reality, in some unregistered, deeper layer of consciousness. It is a place that was unapparent to human beings until the influence of Digimine triggered our awareness of it, dissolving its transparency by expanding the frequency of our senses. There is a phenomenon that suggests that all species on Mankind's World share a collective consciousness spread throughout the vibrational spectrum. As you know, within this seismic field, humans are only aware of a moderate frequency of vibrations, in comparison to other species, which is why other animals, such as dogs and cats, can see, hear, smell, and communicate better than us. They can see things we couldn't possibly imagine - our wavelengths don't reach that far. This vibrational spectrum is something that all species on Mankind's World abide by. Vibrations affect us all. But what's remarkable about it and what is becoming more and more apparent by the day is that this spectrum is *malleable* – its laws can be changed, or at least, reshaped.'

'What? That's amazing,' Oscar reacted. 'The Digimine mineral is able to do this? It allows us to stretch the frequency of our senses and how much we're aware of? How—where does it conjure this power?'

'By emitting vibrations that are profound to human beings and these waves bond with our biology in a way that allows us to train our minds to them and adopt them, so that we can adapt our minds to follow these frequencies. The Digimine emerald expands our frequency range to match that of other species. Because of Digimine we are evolving as a species.'

'So, even before the Digimine had its influence on humans,' Oscar pondered, 'animals were already capable of reaching this…wave-vibration frequency?'

Vividly, Kyma returned to Oscar's mind.

'Animals could reach these higher frequencies in the seismic range and respond to the Dreamerverse long before we could. For them, it has always been there. But, for humans, it has previously been untouchable.'

'That explains why I remember seeing so many species of animals roaming unreservedly on Constellation Planet. They outnumbered the humans – the *Dreamers*. Animals dream too. Everything dreams.'

'All living things receptive to sound waves have a place on the spectrum,' Falcon explained. 'The only thing that varies is the wave-frequency we can interpret. So far, other animals have been far more advanced than us in that experience. Until now.'

'Which probably indicates that very soon, we're all going to start seeing the Dreamerverse more regularly,' Oscar suggested. 'The more people become exposed to this Digimine mineral, the more available and more fluid the transmission across the Void will become for them. And, eventually, everyone will become a Dreamer.'

'This is a sensational discovery. We always imagined nuclear energy to be the stepping-stone of our time, whereas this is an absolute leap forwards – quite literally a leap to another world entirely! Digimine is the key to the future, the cure to the interminable unravelling of human existence, the imbalance of mankind's empires, and the bounty of austerity that has threatened the stability of Mankind's World for decades.'

'And all this time, it was kept coveted among the Drag-in, Phestor Xenol, and a very small number of others over in the Polar Regions, I assume. We were led to believe such a phenomenal mineral could never exist. We were led to believe nothing at all. And now that it has been exposed and proven, we must share it with the world.' Oscar rubbed his temple with two fingers. '*Hmmm.* I see that I now have bigger news to declare at this dinner tonight than I originally had planned,' he quietly detailed to the doctor. 'It'll be a shocker for many and hard to push past the scepticism of most of those Ministors, but swift changes have to be made to governance if we insist on a rejuvenated society. This news you have just enlightened me with is one of a few crucial announcements I will make to my Administration tonight.'

'What else do you hope to tell them?' Falcon inquired. 'If you don't mind me asking, Decider, what could possibly be more important to tell them about than this outstanding discovery?'

'There is one vital update to our governance that I've been eager to ratify, and I have waited four years to proclaim it. The West and the East never *did* put their differences aside, and the lasting division is only weighing down on the present quota of threats. So, it is probably best that I abdicate as Decider and dissolve the position of Decidership in the West altogether.'

Horror stunned Doctor Falcon to the spot and he spun his head round almost three-hundred-and-sixty degrees to encompass the security of his surroundings and then to reacquaint the apathetic young man – who laid back with so much swagger it was almost uncool. 'Would you actually do that?' was all Falcon could manage to squeeze out of his lips. '*Could* you do that?'

'It would doubtlessly finish off the war. There is no immediate threat from the West if its government is shuffled into a pocket of turmoil. It is what the West and Mankind's World require to move on,' Oscar responded. He looked down at his limbs. They were triple the size they should've been and he had more hair than ever growing on his arms. He also feared to look in the mirror.

Would the Administration ever listen to a mutated dog-man in a suit? An experiment of the East-mongers? He'd been "*lucky enough*" to successively clamp down on his father's position as Decider in the tumultuous months following his death, and not get trampled by the other opinionated suitors who had been biting at his heels to takeover the Philson Dynasty. He'd been "*lucky*" to quash mass anarchy and uproar in the City while ironing out the fiction of his father's "cryptic suicide". Even though Oscar had never dreamed of becoming leader of the West, at a time when it called for him to step up he couldn't quite imagine anyone else doing it justice. It was a difficult duty and a lifelong term, only now it was deemed near impossible with a task of rebuilding a disgruntled and morally confused civilisation. That was when he thought: *Perhaps, the emergence a dog-headed leader is the best symbol for a war that has outstayed its welcome. He himself was the greatest example of Digimine and its power and why a future with it needed to be handled with great caution.*

'What about the A.I.?' Falcon asked. 'Even when this war ends and you're gone, they'll be back. And they've gained fresh motives. Now that they know the emeralds are pretty much like Gods to them, they'll come searching and they'll push humanity to extinction, if that's what it takes to find them all. Those emeralds have now become Mankind's lifeline and two of them are in the hands of their Brain Child, at the disposal of Androkind. Humanity…dismantled by its own creation.'

Oscar took the time to roll this image over in his head like a bingo-spinner. The same thought had occurred to him on many occasions in the last four years, but he'd never been bravely addressed about the matter by any of his Ministors. 'I have courage to believe that the Phestority has attended to matters concerning the Androkind in the East, an inquest which has been on-going ever since the Quomer Disaster.☆ And nothing of potential threat has arisen thus far, not since those Majesty A.I. took off from *Quomer Brink* with the Digimine minerals. So, we shouldn't be too worried here in the West for the time being. But we must be just as cautious as our enemies in the East. Not to say that anything will definitely happen, nor to say never at all. Though, for either circumstance, we have to be prepared for future disputes with the Androkind.'

'"Androkind", that's what we're supposed to call them from now onwards?' Falcon laughed. 'Rather than A.I.?'

'Unfortunately, in order to avoid any future legal disputes with the Pro-Intelligence campaigners, we must no longer refer to them as A.I., or ironically as *Tin Men*. The campaigners have become somewhat more "sentimental" towards the Androkind since the revolt and any offence may not be taken lightly—or cheaply.'

'You're starting to sound just like your father,' Falcon said. 'The rhetoric is unchanged. It must run in the blood.'

'I'm nothing like my father. You didn't even know him.'

'But I'm starting to wish I should have, because disecting you in therapy is as tedious as leading a herd of a dozen cattle up a mountain with nothing but the weak nerve to cull on your mind, an empty bolt gun, and a loose rope tacking them along the very edge of the crag.'

'Thank you for the honest feedback.'

'You're welcome, Decider.'

'Are we almost done?'

'Err, well, there was one last thing I needed to ask about the Dreamerverse.' Falcon dawdled on these final minutes he had with the boy. He knew the book needed to be believable, but there was no way he was going to ooze out enough knowledge from an hour and a half of "*therapy*". 'Whilst you're telling me that this real world is held apart from the world of dreams by a single barrier and the transference of any memories across worlds is prohibited, I, as a non-Dreamer, am not blind enough to miss certain tremors. By that, I mean there've been situations, such as a flying beast – not namely the Drag-in as such – ripping Quomer to pieces before it was decimated with the rest of the

---

☆ The Phestority includes the Greater Support Society of Phestors, the East's A.I. operatives and the Bleek Ministors – more or less the messily categorised bulks of power in the East Nations that would generally surround a Phestorship.

city in the nuclear explosion, which stood out to me and quite a lot of other bewildered people in this Real World as very dragon-esque.

'There have also been incidences where you've said that you came across "*the Solar Blade*" in Phestor Xenol's possession, is that right? The Blade had been something that "*All Eyes*", the self-proclaimed king of the Dreamerverse, had given to you. And it was the same Blade that Islie snatched back from you at the end of your excursion on Constellation Planet. The presence of the Blade transcends both universes. Does this make it more profound when deciphering potential links?'

'We never needed the Solar Blade in the first place,' Oscar said. 'It only stunned the Drag-in and shielded us from the Soulcano's eruption when we needed to escape. The Blade was never meant to conquer the beast. The Lighthouse did that; it was the counter-weapon.'

'Which brings me onto my main point: do these similarities that appear both in our world and the Dreamerverse have some greater purpose? Because they coincidentally make vivid connections. It's concerning. Are they significant in any way?'

'How would I know?'

'You've seen them in action. You've seen more examples of it. Like the emeralds, for instance. In the Dreamerverse, you told me that the emeralds were needed to seal off the Void, whereas here on Mankind's World, the A.I. – my mistake, the *Androkind* – require them to claim their liberty from humanity and live independently. That makes *two* totally different forms of relevance that the emeralds have in both worlds. The emeralds can be used to close off the Drag-in's opportunity to cause destruction and trap it in the Void, but they also offer freedom to the Androkind and open up new opportunities for their future. So, what if there was a reason for all of this? A reason why things in both worlds offer alternate purposes and contradictory outcomes?'

'Technically, A.I. don't live independently. They don't *live* at all for that matter.' Oscar escaped from his chair and hurried to lean on the balcony's parapet. He saw the lights of the City sparkle in the youthful night.

'Well, they may as well be living these days; at a time where customs are changing, standards are upgrading, and trends are excelling in influence.' Falcon buckled on his informal inquiry slightly. 'So, do you really believe in these connections? These coincidences? Do they ring any bells? Having the ability to bridge these links across dimensions makes the Dreamerverse a seamless piece of technology.

And with Digimine in the mix, we could even be looking at it as a potential weapon.'

'Drop that idea at once,' Oscar snapped. 'Nobody's using Digimine as a weapon. And that is final, Falcon. I have nothing more to say to you.'

Down below, the remnants of urban traffic were scuttling away and it was almost quiet for once in the City. Oscar took one whiff of the cool air, caught the breeze in his nostrils and huffed. *No smell of banana cakes here*, he thought. *No burning bodies either. No girls with long red hair to light the flame...*

'Oh, I forgot to mention—!' Falcon choked on his eagerness. 'Must've been so carried away with vibration spectrums and revolting A.I. that I forgot to ask about her. Have you heard anything from the girl lately?'

Oscar had already made it clear that there was nothing more he wanted to say to the man. This *girl*, whoever she may have been, hadn't been a part of his life for four years. Instead, Oscar had found a new fondness in the sky above him right now.

For the very first time of all his life in the City, he saw *real* stars in the sky...

It was always going to happen at some point. Some day. Samuella believed that, after eight years, it was the right time to return to the village she'd called home as a child and rediscover the farm where she, her parents, and her Uncle Cephalus had once lived. The town was hidden within a frosty mountain range, isolated from the rest of the modernised West and suspended in a temperament of rural self-efficiency that was charmingly impressive for its size and accessibility. From the first glance of an outsider, the place was old and broken, riddled with tired illness and abandoned by even the tiniest sparks of wealth. But, for Samuella, the town of Nimblescold was her original haven.

She returned with company.

When Aegia's (much newer) motorcycle broke free from the border of snow-capped woodland and rumbled out onto a narrow dirt road that led towards the old farm, Samuella saw the farmhouse and the barn in the field. Tears of regret overthrew her hopes. It was just as she'd feared to imagine: the place was in tatters. It was dying, if not long dead.

Samuella went in first via the front door. It was loose on its hinges and the window that made up eighty-percent of it was scratched and broken in spots. Once inside, the dark pervaded the area ahead. Even though it was overcast outside and midnight was still a few hours away, in here seemed like the depths of space itself by comparison. She took a moment to look up at the roof. There were open holes in the ceiling, through which cold air descended. This place had been subjected to the elements for far too long. The kitchen was freezing and there had been little to no heating systems, save for the oven and the stove, when she'd been living here; her and her uncle had relied on wood-fires to warm up the rest of the house. Now, it appeared that the heating improvements had never amounted to much and the last owners had given up far too easily.

Her mother joined her. As resourceful as ever, she arrived with a torch. The first thing Aegia did was shine it up at where the light bulbs were on the ceiling and walls. None of them were working. Aegia also discovered the holes in the ceiling and the wallpaper that was peeling with pockets of mould building up beneath those sheets which remained glued to the wall. 'Poor palace,' Aegia said. 'I can still remember this being a pretty little keep back in its day.'

'It's been treated badly,' Samuella explained. 'When you leave a place like this to the mercy of heavy snow and sweltering summers, you can't expect much from it after a few years.'

Samuella led the way into the shadowy corridor, tethered to the frail stretch of Aegia's flashlight. They went upstairs, where it was unsurprisingly creepier than the floor below. Nothing up here had been tampered with. There were no broken windows, fewer torn walls and the carpet wasn't as moist and uncomfortable as it was downstairs. The rats and mice had not burrowed here for several generations.

They entered a room that was unrecognisable at first. But it was clearly a bedroom once they were inside and able to explore around closely.

'My old room,' Samuella said.

However, since then, things had been altered and removed. The cupboards all looked the same, and the carpet and the wall-colour were still patterned as they had been over a decade ago. But there was now a new desk, which she hadn't owned before, littered with disorganised jewellery. Rings and earrings and bracelets and necklaces all over the place. Above it, there were big cabinets that she didn't remember and her enhanced bedroom now had fluffy pink curtains over the windows.

'Who did you say was living here after you left?' her mother spoke from the darkness.

Samuella found a round purple-dyed rug on the floor and she stroked it with her hand. *Sheepskin.* 'An elderly couple. The old man was an experienced stock-herder. They used to live up in the mountains, herding sheep and cattle. And they moved to town the year that I left. The place became theirs. It's all I know, to be honest.'

'So, I guess this is his wife?'

When Aegia said this, Samuella's spine hardened. "*This is his wife?*" Then, she prepared herself for what she now anticipated to see and turned to find the body – that wasn't decaying like she'd thought it would be – of the old lady, lying peacefully in her bed. Sleeping without breathing. Paler than a ghost.

'Yes, that's her,' Samuella hesitantly confirmed.

'What was her name?'

Aegia had the light fixed on the woman's face. A deathly complexion was absent there. Instead, she was plump in the face and her skin was oily, as if she could have been alive and warm, only fast asleep.

'I can't remember,' Samuella gagged, solemn in tone. 'What do you think did this to her?'

'Old age?' Aegia shrugged.

'You mean she died in her bed and nobody ever came looking? Nobody came investigating in the days after she went missing? Her corpse hasn't even decayed.'

The torchlight then caught something beneath the duvet that was neatly raised above the woman's breast. A lump that stood out. She was holding something close to her chest. Daringly, Aegia pulled away the top edge of the duvet to reveal an empty-looking glass bottle being held in the woman's hands, being pressed against her chest like a lifelong treasure. Samuella gave her mother a look of approval (the glance a parent would give their child before entrusting them with a pair of scissors), then she slowly slipped the glass bottle from the ice-cold pair of hands.

It was mostly empty. But not entirely empty. Lying at the bottom of the bottle was a single seed and it was multi-coloured. A rainbow seed.

'That must've meant a lot to her,' Aegia said. 'Do you think she knew she was going to die with it in her hands? Or did someone put it there? What is that?'

'Looks like another seed to me,' Samuella suggested.

'*Another* seed from—? You don't really think—?'

'Oh, I'm pretty sure.'

Samuella shook the bottle, listened to the seed rattle about the inside. It was real and it was staring her in the face. The greatest legend she had ever come to know was looking her in the eyes once again. One of the Seeds of Continuity, this one unlike any she could recollect—*I don't remember any of them being rainbow-coloured.*

'But it's been four years since then,' Aegia said. 'Do you really think it's worth going back?'

'That depends,' Samuella responded. '*Will* it take me back?'

'We don't even know how it got here,' her mother protested. 'You can't just assume it is what you think it might be.'

'Oh, it is—it definitely is!'

'So what if it is? Does that make it enough for you to leave everything else behind? Leave me behind?

'Leave *here* behind,' Samuella emphasised. '*You* and this place are the same to me – obsolete, forgotten and placeless in my life!'

'How could you say that—even believe that—think it?' Aegia stuttered, thunderstruck by her daughter's analogy.

'Look around you, mum! Everything in this room resounds with what our relationship has become and where our history lies to rest! Four years isn't going to rewrite a lifetime!'

'Fifteen years—!'

'Is that not long enough for you?' Samuella screamed and snatched the glass bottle out of her mother's hands.

'You're being childish,' her mother said.

'*I'm* being childish? I've been a grownup all my life because of the silence you and dad put me through! If anyone's been reckless—it's you!'

Aegia winced at her daughter's determination and then dropped her head to scrutinise the bottle containing the seed, clasped strongly in Samuella's fists. There were puddles filling Samuella's bloodshot eyes and they were dripping down her cheeks. As much as she strained her own imagination, Aegia couldn't see her reflection there, like in most puddles, nor did she see her daughter. This person who was fully-grown at five feet and nine inches, who had been gifted with unique locks of rose-coloured hair, and had matured with a brave and assertive sense of distinction, was not her daughter. Not the girl she left behind twenty years ago.

'Then, go,' Aegia said. 'You don't need to love me, or understand me—or know me, for that matter. You're big and ugly enough to make that decision on your own. Go back to the

Dreamerverse, go reunite with Oscar – because I'm sure he misses you more than I have – and be happier than you'll ever be here.'

Even through the stoic expression of a former Infidel spy, Samuella could hear a soft tremble of sarcasm in her mother's voice.

'But, before you decide, let me tell you this,' Aegia concluded. 'The Stellar Gods delayed on their promise, just as I did. But we *both* delivered in the end. Welcome home.'

Samuella spun away from her mother, the bed and the elegant cadaver lying in it. The bottle was held tightly in her own hands now. She looked through a crack between the fluffy curtains, out of the window, and saw the dead crop-field and the vacant barn. Then, she tried to seek out a single light in the starlit town further beyond.

There was one streetlamp that was still on.

Not yet a legal citizen of the West, Lord Camson still deemed himself a Westy Boy now that he'd been living in the First Nation for four famous years (of course, never ever without some preluding reluctance). To his pleasant surprise, it hadn't taken a lot for him to change his views on West culture and what prejudgements the "*Conflicts of Old Men*" had sewn into him. Oscar's Administration had kindly embraced him not long after Quomer had fallen and given him a new home. He'd been handed a new residence, similar to the one he'd owned in Quomer, and was chauffeured just as promptly as he'd been as a Lord in the East. *Lord* Camson was now an unofficial title. It only belonged to those who'd represented Phestor Xenol, whilst Quomer and its Phestor had still been standing. Now the old title meant nothing and even referring to Quomer or its traitorous leader in conversation was considered to be a tasteless embarrassment.

Oscar had introduced him to the great commercialistic delicacies of the West, such as eating Jerk Grilled Chicken during Ball games at the Harkson Centre, tacky performances at the Hi-Rise Robot Theatre, eight-hour ballads at the Ante Luminaire opera house, the impeccable service of the City *LASERWAY* (at a price of sixty *pecunts* per stop) and, of course, luxurious window shopping at the Octane Mall.

Camson was living with his wife again. Sharing his world back on Mankind's World with Evanessa was the closest he could get to a dream come true. He did everything he could to offer closure for their troubled decade of separation, continuously treating her with expensive gifts and dinner dates in the City Central. By creating new memories to replace the old. But the one gift he couldn't promise her was another child. Evanessa had recently become diagnosed as infertile and any chance of replacing their on-going sickness of loss and rediscovering parental love again was non-existent. The last thing either of them wanted was to adopt a West child from the City Orphanage, because there was no alternative that came close to their own blood. Thuban had been their only child. Constantly, Camson would go to bed and cry at night, pondering over Thuban's bedroom back in his obliterated Quomer apartment. He thought about the untouched bed and the Red Robe he laid upon it every day he woke. The Robe, he had once been told in the Dreamerverse, that held fragments of his son's lost spirit locked away in its fibres. That had been one of the only lies he remembered after the Void sealed itself back into stability. Here, in their refurbished *Coventry Street* residence, there was a new guest room down the hall from his and his wife's bedroom, which he'd cordoned off in respect of Thuban and the hope that, by some miracle, he might return to reality one day. Night after night, he saw a fine layer of dust thickening across the sheets and there was no sign of the Red Robe. That had been lost with Quomer. For Camson, the Robe had relieved him of many things, such as grief and finicky contemplation. Knowing that it was there helped him believe that there was always something other than him gripping to the memory of his deceased son. At the same time, it reminded him that his fond memories were not his own mythopoeia crafted upon a feverish obsession, rather more a nostalgia that had been encrypted in him by nature.

Now, the Robe had passed on like his son had. Vanished from the face of the earth, from the deficient version of reality he and his wife were now forced to endure. The stronghold of his bad temperament had disintegrated with it. Four years had brought mourning wherein depressive and outlandish tantrums would flourish. But at least he now had the support of Evanessa, instead of the Robe. He could vent over and over again about his misery to her, because she felt it too and didn't shrug it off like everyone else. And she reassured him with a kiss and a smile every time. She hadn't worn her veil since the Quomer Crisis. There was nothing she wanted to hide anymore. Even though her face had been withdrawn from beauty during the "*G-Nourishment*" experiments, her smiles were one of the features Camson could unconditionally recognise. For when does a husband ever forget his wife's smile (regardless of how little there was left of her cheeks and lips)? He was grateful for the retrieval of half his family's legacy – his wife, and the nostalgia they remembered of their son – and he was happy that he could still share his life with someone again – his *real life.*

It helped to justify why he'd come all this way fighting for a future. It may have been slightly different to what he'd hoped, but in following the words of his own father, he settled for satisfaction: "*Your world is self-determined, but the spheres around you are indifferent. They orbit at their own speeds. We all have advantages that outweigh our disadvantages—so treasure yours. Don't underestimate that you have legs to move; the trees and the seeds and the soils don't have such an opportunity.*"

However, in this new reality, Camson still couldn't explain many things. He couldn't string an explanation to why City Folk drank so much of that sweaty *Kola Bear* energy drink that tasted like cheap, pineapple-flavoured ice tea. He couldn't explain the shoppers who never actually went inside any of the prominent high street stores. He couldn't understand the incessant attraction to those nauseating, glitzy billboards pinned up around *Crystal Square*, or get his head around their holographic broadcasts, such as those historic Hounding Trials that had gone on twenty-four-seven - of which the final verdicts had been announced only a week after he'd first arrived in the City, some four years ago; Phillip the Leg-Licking Spaniel and Colby the Staring Golden Retriever had walked away from court completely innocent and wouldn't be spending any more time in the doghouse. And, finally, Camson couldn't comprehend the glass bottle that was handed to him by the chauffeur who drove him to the dinner party at DCD. O. Philson's residence one evening in 2062. Inside was a rainbow-coloured seed...

That same evening, Oscar had returned to his residence from the balcony to get dressed for the dinner event. It was in an hour, which gave him enough time to practice his speaking in the mirror. Doctor Falcon had left him with a note filled with several dates on which he could book another appointment - if he ever needed to. Fortunately, Oscar had no plans of requesting Falcon's "help" again. He didn't need help from any *so-called* doctors anymore. He didn't need help from anyone. From tonight onwards, he wouldn't even need to be the Decider anymore. It was all that his father had wanted, what his father had anticipated as long as he'd lived: that his son would blossom into the monster he wanted him to be. But DCD. Philson had been an obstinate brute. '*A terrible example of modern leadership, my dear late father was,*' he rehearsed in the bathroom mirror. And that was how he had to put it to these straight-talking suits tonight. Otherwise, who was going to believe a dog-eared boy with a canine-head and wearing a tuxedo?

Suddenly, he heard something from out in the corridor.

A *clink*ing sound at the front door.

He went to investigate and saw that an object had landed in the wonderful Rot Box underneath the letter-flap. The first thing he thought was: *It's a bit late for mail.* It was a *Son-day* too.

This was no letter, though. It was a glass bottle. It would've appeared empty, and he might have immediately thrown it away, if he hadn't noticed the rainbow-coloured seed sitting at the bottom…

Everybody he'd expected to see was there.

Well, *everybody his father would have wanted to see* was there. The entire Administration of the First Nation, the Stateship and his son, and the Ministers of the Second, Third and Fourth Nations had come to commemorate Oscar's Fourth Annual Summit in his father's former residence. Also sitting among the usual guests at the Administration Table were Camson and – for the first time ever – Stevenson and – as promised – his Aunt Sybil – the first Soothsayer to take a seat at the Decider's Table since the dismissal of his mother, the Oracle. Seeing Stevenson there made Oscar feel a little better; he was like a spare fuel tank full of motivation midway along an interminable wasteland highway.

Oscar rose from his seat – well, his *father's seat* – and addressed his guests – *father's guests.* 'I'm glad you were all able to attend today's dinner to discuss the most urgent matters concerning our latest international relations with the East and the foreseeable future of our West Nations—'

And that was a prompt for the rudeness to kick in. The traditional squabbling began and Oscar was at the receiving end of it all. He had the Stateship telling him that he *needed to grow a pair and secure the diamond cores in the Seventh Nation, now that Sixth was in turmoil following Quomer's demise.* He also had the three Ministers trying to claw their way to fame with eager calls for a long-awaited promotion to shared Decidership and the demand of a republican government. The only person he could bear to look at was Stevenson and he did so for reassurance. Beside the chauffer, his Aunt Sybil rolled her eyes at the mess of a situation, before resuming to occupy herself with the link of Soothe Beads in her hands, praying to the Soothe Gods who might rescue her nephew from humiliation. Then, Oscar came out with a universal response. 'That's enough! We're allies, not scavengers!

If *one of us* has the urge to speak, the rest will listen with an effect of orderliness. My father and his apparent legacy may be dead, but that's not to say the same for the quality of courtesy and respect that is still expected at this Table. The uncivil attitudes that DCD. Philson carried on his shoulders do not exist anymore – in my view, their reasoning was never substantial enough in the first place. He bit off a little more than he could chew with his radical policies and...well, never ultimately got off the ground with those values.' Oscar caught Stevenson trying to swallow a snigger. 'Now, I wish to hear the first issue. *One* at a time!'

The Stateship stood up. A fire had been poked inside of him over many summits and, today, the bone that he'd always wanted to pick had finally snapped. 'These four years, since Quomer fell, since your father's death, and since you slugged to power, have been the worst attended by any Decider—by you, the Punkish Prince, trying to breed liberal vermin in my City, my Great Nation. To this very Table, you have the dirtiest nerve to invite *subordinates* and *foreigners* and a *Soothsayer*! I don't know who you think you are, or what sabotage your Punk Kind have planned for our Nations' pride, our sovereign bliss, but I won't stand for it or stand by yourself. You do not perform like a Decider; you mimic one like an incompetent trickster, a subordinate citizen who is inexperienced and has no quotable ambition. God Bless the City, God Bless the First Nation and God Bless the West. Your father would turn in his grave, still seeing that you prove a disgrace to his name, a vandal to our history, and the murderer of his legacy.'

A wave of nervous sweat splashed over the young Decider. His ears deafened briefly in the beckoning silence that followed the Stateship's words.

'Well, he isn't here, is he?' Oscar confidently clarified. 'And, frankly, I could make similar claims about every Decider there's ever been. My father had the same criticism towards his own father's legacy in his youth, and people complained back then. I was once told by my mother that, when we are younger and freer in imagination, our opinions are more grounded and thus purer. My father was only ever grounded when he fell from a rooftop.' Oscar gnawed at his protruding grin and winked at Stevenson. 'Only, he never hit the ground. Something still caught him—however, it wasn't his ego.'

'You must be delusional if you believe your liberal fantasies are remotely grounded!' the Stateship rejected. 'And your mother was a liberal hindrance, just as you are! Both of your egos have brought nothing but disrepair and confusion to our Nationhood!'

'*Disrepair* and *confusion*?' Oscar repeated furiously. 'If it wasn't for my mother's visionary efforts within this Administration, you would have no Nationhood! I, for one, have no confidence in this corrupt premiership, the discontent it creates for our system and will continue to burden us with, if we don't accept change! Therefore, I have decided that this prolonged administrative format deserves to come to an end. Tonight.'

'You would do no such thing, boy,' the Stateship said.

Oscar lifted his glass. 'I resign as Decider of the West Nations.'

'A vow was sworn on the day your father died! That same vow was premised and signed on the day you were born!' the Stateship harped. 'It predestined that you would take your father's role and remain immovably loyal to your post, *your duty*—!'

'Until today.' Oscar could now look the shaken man straight in the eyes with a challenging smirk. 'What we saw four years ago in Quomer was the greatest humanitarian disaster since 2054 and, in that time, we haven't even considered helping a Nation that fell to a Blackout Attack. Regardless of sides, enemy or not, that wounded Nation poses an international danger, spilling copious amounts of radiation across the Virgin Desert. The implications will reach West borders in less than a year, with radioactivity levels set to significantly rise in the Fourth Nation as early as April 2063. Thankfully, I put the proposal out six months after the disaster happened, a referendum on the matter of whether the West should assist Quomer or not, and the public vote in favour of aid to Quomer was overwhelming. You would be quite amazed by how swiftly people can change their perceptions and compromise their opinions.'

'That attack was issued by their very own neighbour!' Minister Thimble said. 'Their Sister Nation, Seventh, was responsible for the nuclear strike on Quomer. It came as a consequence of all the hell that broke loose at the Offerings Parade and because their leader, Phestor Serpens, was assumed dead among the chaos. It was nothing to do with us! It was a posthumous code-green issued by Serpens' Nation, and, therefore, imprints itself as none of our business.'

'You are wrong in several of the assumptions you just made,' Oscar said. 'Firstly, Quomer wasn't supposed to be a target for the Seventh Nation. Initially, Xenol's capital was attacked by a militarised lab-experiment, which, soared way out of proportion and could no longer be controlled by its creators hiding below the city. That provoked a rash reaction made by a rogue, leaderless state, which was already on shaky grounds with its Sister Nation. Phestor Serpens was still very much alive at the time his heedless Nation decided to retaliate, Xenol wasn't. Secondly, it was the Sixth Nation's leader, Phestor Xenol and his sinister associate, the Drag-in – also known as Cephalus Islington – who set loose the beast that wrecked havoc on Quomer. You know why? Xenol's alliance was never with my father, but with *Draconex Industries* and the Southern Polar Region. Islie and his son were contracted to build a new generation of Empathy A.I., his son having been an exile from the West who was shown compassion by Xenol and the East. Please recognise, ladies and gentlemen, that Phestor Xenol had no real alliance with my father in the first place. He never intended to trust the Decider as his Arch Ally from the outset, but led the Decider to falsely believe that he was conjoined with the Sixth Nation in a plot to overturn Serpens and get at the Seventh Nation's unspoiled array of resources. Xenol lured the blundering Decider into a disastrous mistake that cost him his life and, consequently, the reputation of the Decidership and the West as a credible world power. Above all else, my father's gullible actions humiliated us, his people. And, equally and rightfully, that was the flaw where Xenol's plan went to shambles: he got greedy and lent an untimely arm to his archenemy, making an even greater enemy out of his neighbour, the Seventh Nation. So, what I conclude from that crisis is – as it currently seems, still – we *cannot* rely on the East and they *cannot* rely on us, which leaves us exactly where we began. It is the primary the reason why I never went ahead with the referendum results and thus never gave a decreeing thumbs up for reconstruction in Quomer. I don't believe such courtesies will make any difference whatsoever.'

'Quomer is swimming in radiation. A "*radioactive soup*" they're describing it,' Camson noted. 'You'd have better luck rebuilding a city beneath the ocean.'

'Well, I guess we can scrap all of our ideas in one go! How about that?' Oscar was prepared to do anything to part ways with the Administrators, anything except clinch one more resolution. He was fed up of thinking for these scroungers. 'In fact, what the hell are you people still doing here anyway, if that's the case? You've done what you wanted to do! You destroyed the heart of the East, killed their biggest tyrant, won the war. Well…technically, you never *won* the war. Neither did the East for that matter. Both sides unleashed destruction. But, when one attempts to separate the human from its nature, *nature* will have no problem outlasting the human in the end. My advice to this Administration would be this: you don't only need to rearrange yourselves physically and structurally, but also psychologically. You, next, have to explain these changes to an entire civilisation, redesigning your way of politics in the process. Based on the surprising results of the referendum, I think the subordinates are ready for a proper democracy to be reintroduced. That's what they deserve.' Oscar shrugged, gazing at the Table of fancily dressed people and their blank, unimpressed faces. But then he cut to the chase, once he subliminally clocked what the Administrators really wanted to talk about. 'On the bright side, I guess you don't have to worry about going to war for those resources in the East anymore—so, now what?'

'We're still here because we want our share of it,' the Stateship said bluntly. 'Our slice of the East.'

'Of course,' Oscar replied insouciantly.

'You *know* what we want, boy,' the Minister of the Third Nation said, 'and we've been wanting it long before your father even learned to talk, let alone make his first speech.'

'My father taught *you* to speak in this room,' Oscar snapped at them all. 'He also taught you *when* you should never say a word at all.'

'It's ironic,' the Stateship said, 'how young, new leaders like yourself claim to oppose and rebel to the ways that stood and breathed moments before their arrival. And yet, you struggle to offend it, as you are so used to those ways – they blueprinted the very day you were born. Averting from one's innate principles is not only an obtuse informality, but also, singlehandedly, an amateurish exposure of unprofessionalism. Do you really care to trample on your father's Decidership, his decorum, and fumble into rehashing a bureaucracy he sought to demolish forever in all his civil compassion? If that's so, *why—well, okay then*—allow us bureaucrats to get on with our business.' The Stateship was choking for some sarcasm – Oscar could see this – so he added: 'Your father would be very proud of the direction you're taking.'

Somewhere else, in a corner of the Table where Oscar didn't care to gander, another guest uttered, 'Well, it's rather a lot more than a new direction. It's a decision that the rest us will have to live with.'

'I have no sympathy for my father's ideals, his utopias, or his dreams. He wasn't a realist and, more importantly, he wasn't much of a dreamer either.'

'Oh, here we go again with the Dreamland rhetoric!' the Stateship roared with laughter. 'Are you going to plead for our approval of this "other reality" again, and then drop asleep at the Table like a big baby? Save it for story time, boy! Not one of us Administrators believe it!'

'That's the very reason my Aunt Sybil is present here today. She was one of the only people in the City who believed my experiences in the Dreamerverse,' Oscar said. He tuned back into what Aunt Sybil was doing. She looked up from her beads with a sickly pallid expression. 'She was the first to truly empathise with the experience I was having and led me to something that's going to change our world, help us to adapt our infrastructure, and defend us against the Androkind when they return. Something I'm going to show you in a moment.'

The Stateship shook his head distastefully. 'Boy, you don't have a clue what you're doing! There is only one interest that a Soothsayer could have sitting at your father's Table, and that is the demand for reacceptance of their Kind into West culture. Her request of you to be at this Table is nothing shy of blackmail. You should be ashamed of yourself for allowing this to happen.'

'Removing Soothe Culture from the City was a massive fault made by my father. Potentially, the worst law he ever turned,' Oscar stated. 'My mother was the Oracle and she was betrayed by this law. She intimidated his power. And because of her popular influence on the political scene, she wasn't only scorned, but it was my father who ultimately murdered her in callous envy.'

There were loud gasps right across the Table and the murmuring brimmed over the champagne glasses.

'Where did you acquire such a horrific lie?' the Minister of the Second Nation said.

'You'd find it hard to believe if I told you,' Oscar said, quietly shivering with hate for all these accusative onlookers in front of him. He spotted out Camson, who gave him an encouraging wink and nodded to spur him on. 'My father was the most unpopular person in Mankind's World, because of his arrogant disconnect from society. He pushed his ideals to the top of the register and defecated on the rest below. An unelected, privileged, pardoned fool.'

'You miss the point, you entitled runt,' the Stateship sighed. 'He was a pioneer, a populist moderniser of our time, and a hero. None of which you will ever be. You are a naïve, little boy.'

Oscar paused, mouth gaping, and all his attention drifted back onto Camson, as if to spy out how his old rival would react to him, the Young Decider, being called this, to be humiliated in such a condescending way at the Decider's Table. It wasn't the East veteran's first time sitting at this Table in these last few years since expatriating to the West. Camson had made it his home here and giving him a place at the Decider's Table had been solely Oscar's idea. At this moment,

Camson was fixated on rubbing out a cranberry-sauce stain on his lap with the use of a cream-coloured, silk table-napkin. He didn't seem to care for a single word of the discussion that had been thriving around him. All those years ago, Oscar would have frowned and *tutted* and shaken his head at such 'rudeness', much like many of the other suits sat at the Decider's Table. But, tonight, Oscar smiled at it. In this barbarous environment of spitting bigotry over the dinner table, Lord Camson's labouring with the sauce and the napkin seemed anomalously unaccustomed, and yet so shamelessly human.

Oscar then looked between the Stateship and his son. After four of what were arguably the longest years of his life, Oscar noticed that Timothy had become to look more and more like his father. His hair was no longer a childish bright blonde, but much closer to the sweaty bronzed colour of his father's, and he even had the same lines emerging in his forehead that his father had. Then, Oscar remembered the Academy and the menu of dim-witted taunts the Stateship's son had used to bully him: all the dustbins he'd been made to sit in, all the hot lunches he'd been robbed of, all the homeworks he'd been cheated for and had taken the blame for, all the girls he'd been humiliated in front of, all the flash clothes he'd been intimidated out of, and all the immature calumnies that had been dispersed around the City Academy about "*Oscar Philly-Philson and his silly boyfriend Willy Nilly Wilson*". And finally (after some amusing internal divisions of his own) Oscar came out with his best response of the night. But, before he did, he placed a small, round, shining object on the Table.

'What the hell is that junk?' the Stateship snapped.

'A Digimine emerald,' Oscar explained. 'Doctor Islie dropped it when the Majesty A.I. kidnapped him. Digimine has been kept a secret from the public for many years now. West and East scientists are familiar with it as the main fuel behind the Androkind. It has empowered A.I. all over the world through the decades and so, understandably, it has always been a confidential and inaccessible mineral. Phestor Xenol also knew what it was and what it was capable of. The Decider was less informed, but still seemed to be aware of the mineral's existence. Islie and his son, the exiled inventor, knew where to categorise it and Islie was planning to utilise it as a tool in his vision to overthrow authoritarian leaderships all over the world. In brief, I was led to believe that whoever has Digimine has the capability to manipulate and control the Androkind. But what is a concern right now is that the A.I. have emeralds of their own. I have seen, first-hand, *what else* it can do. There is so much more to this newly discovered mineral than being a stand-in fuel source! It has the power to transmit human life to other worlds, or, you may come to prefer coining it as "*opening our eyes to other worlds*".'

'Don't be ridiculous, Decider!' the Stateship hissed. 'The science boffins narrowly won our faith when they expected us to believe that such a mineral as limited as Digimine could replace nuclear power, but now you miss us entirely with this utter, rancid fantasy! Have you absolutely lost your wits, boy?'

'No. I haven't in the slightest, because this fundamental trait of Digimine has been proven and I'll explain how.'

Oscar explained to the governing body sat around the Decider's Table everything Falcon had informed him: what his fellows had uncovered about Digimine at the Academy, the Digimine's ability to reshape human receptivity of seismic vibrations, and what this meant for the future of the human race on Mankind's World.

'Eventually, we will all find ourselves stepping into the Dreamerverse and, like other animals, we will all evolve to be just as perceptive of the dimensions surrounding us that have previously been veiled to our conscience. You're looking at the most powerful natural mineral in the world and what it can do is terrifying, yet refreshing, beautiful and spectacular all the same. It's way stronger and more beneficial than anything nuclear. I realised this when I was accidentally submitted to the Southern Polar Region and became hybridised into this monster you see before you, this horrible freak you're all politely shielding your eyes from. This mutation wasn't anything to do with nuclear energy. When I sent emissaries to investigate the SPR two years ago, they came back with details on the Chrysalis Chamber Experiment that was used to hybridise me and my pet dog, Kyma. It turns out that my initial suspicions were affirmed. The hybridisation experiment was activated by matter-destabilising molecules being released from a Digimine emerald, and carefully diluted by a million fission reactions within a dark-green serum.

'Raw Digimine is an extremely rare and difficult mineral to find in our world, and that's what makes it so incomparable. Unfortunately, we only have one raw Digimine emerald under our supervision – right here in this room – and, as we elaborate about it, the Majesty A.I. have probably advanced in their search for greater reserves of the mineral. They are already beginning to mine a heck load of this stuff, so that – under the knowledgeable guidance of Doctor Islie, or the Drag-in, or All Eyes, or whatever alias you want to label that fiend – they can upgrade themselves and prepare for a war against humanity. What I have come to believe is that, if this mineral is what established Androkind and the physics behind our very perception of the worlds we're living in, it must have simultaneously played a role in manipulating our conscience as a species over the last few decades. I've been thinking extensively about this idea and figured that our human will to dream is evoked by three factors: our greedy desire for hope and superficial comforts, our curiosity for the truth, and thirdly – as Doctor Islie put it – some *nightmarish* element of fear erupting in our conscience. It makes sense that the desire, truth, and fear in our reality play a part in this Dreamerverse Puzzle. The A.I. have been humanity's greatest fear for a very long time. I am convinced that Doctor Islie was planning to perfectly engineer this fear to strengthen and secure the passage of every human being into the Dreamerverse. His plot was very nearly a success; it managed to get me, Camson, Samuella and a number of other real world citizens across the mental void and to Constellation Planet – a utopia in my subconscious mind, moulded by my hope-lusting imagination, the intrigue for my mother, and the fear of, not just the A.I.'s reign of terror, but this very day, where I would stand before an Administration of hateful faces and pretend to be something I've never been and never will be—Decider.'

The Stateship's face was as jaded and red as a gash. He couldn't pull his head around so many revelations in one go.

'However, the leading question today is *what do you do with such a powerful substance as Digimine*? This emerald I bring to you may be small, but even a fragment of it can do miracles for technology and urban facilities. Ladies and gentlemen, the answer is very, very simple: collaborate with the other Nations – West and East – to rebuild what you destroyed over the last half a century and appreciate it from a novel outlook. And when the time comes, you both stand up to the A.I. like the big, self-important folk you are, and you find a way to deactivate all of them. That is only my advice, however, and my best wishes of success go to you.'

'And how exactly is this all going to work out,' the Stateship argued at last, 'without starting another war for a Want that not everybody can have?'

'I know what you all want – from me, your leader, and from this current situation. The East will always be there for the taking, glaring at you, waiting for you to grab it. Go tear into the East tomorrow, next week, in a year, or wait another fifty years. It's your decision to make—all of you, ninety-nine per cent of the people sat at this Table right now. I won't be the one to shepherd the way for your cattle, not in the wake of a world that has since lost touch with human nature and profited it for a milked mechanism, which adopts shallow leaders with far more propaganda in their arsenals than personality.'

On that note, his father's residence went up in silence, as the suits and the tuxedos (and the Stevensons, and the Soothsayers, and the East veterans) finally understood that they couldn't compete with the most powerful man in the world and would no longer need to.

For the last ever Decider of Mankind's World left the room.

Later on in his own residence, Oscar returned to observe the stars again, leaning on the parapet of his balcony. Up there for the first time in a generation, the constellations were magnificent on their homecoming to the City's skies. With his eyes and imagination alone, he formed the shapes of objects and people. He saw Kyma. He saw his father. He saw Phestor Xenol. He saw Evanessa. He saw the girl with the long, red hair. And, most desirably, he saw his mother. All of them were in one place, but shackled in the starry airspace above, so that it only tickled his fancy.

When he went to bed, he lay awake thinking of tomorrow. Where would he be in the morning? *Who* would he be? The Decider was no more. Oscar Philson would fade into nothing and drop among the bodies of his people. A subordinate would he become? No—not so suddenly. *Though nothing was hard to believe anymore*, he thought contentedly. He was amazed he'd been able to do it, to step down from his throne so modestly. His dynastic legacy would finally fall to sleep and a new era of Mankind's World would awaken without him. And where would he be on its initiation? All at once – and at long last – he would saunter with the subordinates of a new First Nation. The Subordination of the Decider.

As he laid thinking about the endless possibilities, whichever side he turned onto his body ached, marred by the abuses of the Southern Polar Region. The lively mutations were still toiling inside him. His head pumped. His stomach churned. These permanent pains blended tears into the nooks of his eyes. Tonight, he could've done with the company of Kyma and he fondly remembered the way she would rest at the foot of his bed. But, from now onwards, the grooming of his solitude would become customary, as his lucky comforts had absconded him to much estrangement. The finest satisfaction that remained was tomorrow and the prospects it would bring. Tomorrow, he would be free to think and speak. Free to believe and cry out loud. Free to forget.

One more dreamless night, free of nightmares, would this one be? Perhaps...

Only, it was as he languorously rolled onto his right side and lay there for some time that he saw the glass bottle stood upright on the bedside table and the rainbow-coloured seed resting at the bottom...

Sunrise...

A lonely glass bottle is carried with the calming current, gently bobbing towards the shores of Awakening Coast. There, watching it, having also been the first and only to notice it, is the steward. The prideful parrot sits upon the sands with his wings tensed at his sides, as he patiently waits for it to arrive. When the bottle finally touches the shoreline, the sun is peeking over the horizon. Where the ocean water meets the sky, the scalp of the fiery ball has started to wedge its way up to be crowned by the late stars.

The bottle rolls onto the damp sand and Stewart immediately hops on top of its slippery glass, bending over to look at what is inside. A firefly—eager to get out, ricocheting around the bottle's interior like a bubble in a pressurised container. *Something new again?* Stewart thinks. '*It's the first time they've arrived in bottles. And what's more,*' he complains, '*the sun hasn't even fully risen. It's too early for arrivals.*' Nevertheless, Stewart pecks away at the bottle until a crack forms and it breaks. Out comes the firefly and it whizzes up over the beach, stopping several metres above his head. '*What are you going to do for me, then, Early Birdy?*' Stewart asks the firefly. '*Transform?*'

And, exactly as prescribed, the firefly begins to *transform*. The fly's light shatters into a thousand beams, radiating until a point where the beams converge into a glowing orb. The golden silhouette of a person develops. Basic features mould into position, before demarcating the individual's distinctive characteristics. And then, finally Oscar Philson is restored in place of the light orb and his feet set upon the sands of Awakening Coast once again. Only, he appears just as he was on his first arrival—undeniably naked from head to toe.

'Master Philson, I was eager to know when you would be coming back,' Stewart says, overjoyed. *'And I was hoping it would be at a more appropriate time like this – unlike our first encounter, where you held me hostage at the very end of my Departures Shift, kept me waiting until sunset for your debut arrival.'*

'Here—? Again—?' Oscar stutters. He seems explicably bewildered. 'Same place—?'

'Same...time?' the bird snatches the words straight from his lips. *'In the real world, you might have thought it has been over four years since you last materialised on Constellation Planet. But, here in the Dreamerverse, it has been merely moments since you last checked in—last sunset, to be precise. You're back to exactly where you left off.'*

'Sunrise...the following day? Everything that happened with the Drag-in and the Phantom, and the Lighthouse...that all happened yesterday?'

'Yes, the Dreamerverse has been on standby for four years, for the sake of repairing the wounds the Drag-in left in the Void. On behalf of the Dreamerverse, I delivered to you those multi-coloured seeds, with the confidence that the Night Dreamers would return at the dawn of a new era and join our reboot of the Dreamerverse. All it took was for you to ingest that seed into your system and life here would begin again. Think of it as the mayoral cutting of a red ribbon, the reopening of a refurbished kingdom. Thank you for your heroic efforts, Oscar. The Dreamerverse is now a part of you. Please accept my greatest gratitude for all that you have done for my world and, most pleasantly, for my own blimmin' peace of mind – saves me having to perform those tedious Night Shifts now that you Night Dreamers won't Awaken so willy-nilly anymore. More significantly, however, now that the Void is stable again and the Memory Lane has rebooted itself, my spirit has been allowed to realign with the constellations. I am now given the freedom to transform myself.'

'Back into a human body?'

'No, I used to be a firefly in my previous life...OF COURSE, I MEANT BACK INTO HUMAN FORM!' the bird heckles. *'In the Dreamerverse, every animal you see resembles the free spirit of a deceased Dreamer, a human spirit that has been ritualised by the Stellar Gods and repurposed under the Old King's orders. My appearance as a bird was a mistake made by All Eyes – the original All Eyes,* **my** *king – and since he was snuffed and deposed by that imposter, Prince Cephalus, nobody was around to change me back. But, miraculously, with there now being a power shift in the air, well...the liberty to reclaim my humanity is mine! I*

am so excited—words cannot begin to describe how I feel today! I cannot bear to be seen as a feather-itching-beak-face for much longer. It cripples my dignity.'

'Go on, then,' Oscar urges.

'"*Go on, then*"*—what?*'

'Change, transform, do whatever you have to do. Before your opportunity goes to waste.'

'*This isn't an opportunity. It's a right. And it will not be wasted.*'

'Will being a human again mean that you'll have the reason to become a regular Dreamer? Will you assume some other role? Or will you always be the steward?' Oscar says.

'*Us stewards aren't like you Deciders. We can't go abdicating left, right and centre. We have jobs to do and shifts to fill! Without us, you Dreamers would remain trapped in your stuffy little real world. And you wouldn't have escaped that bottle.*'

Oscar sees the broken glass bottle lying on the sand, just as the next current washes over it. The glass glimmers in what tiny sunlight there is, one last glimpse before it disappears and disintegrates into sand. Temporary like his weakening memory. 'I came in *that* thing?' he asks, unimpressed.

'*Sure did.*'

'After swallowing that rainbow seed, I wasn't sure what would come next. I wasn't expecting my return here to be so *clean*. I mean I did contemplate it as a possibility, but—this place is all so surreal and bizarre that you find you really don't know what to expect from it.'

'*I was one of the only living things that lingered here in your absence. No Dreamers have returned here since then either. The Void needed the time to recover, needed to be sure before it was safe to let Dreamers crossover again. But I was always expecting you to come back. The anticipation was aching, though I stayed determined that you would. And that's why I'm here on the Coast so early today. I was so thrilled to see the sun lift from the horizon and rise into the sky again that I jumped at the first chance I could to resume my duty. You don't often hear that coming from me. As confirmation, I was told by one particularly watchful Palm Patroller that the Drag-in slayers were urgently on their way back to Awakening Coast, and that they still have one final decision to make.*'

That classic scent of banana cakes sticks to the warm air. It's still pretty overcast with some orange-tinted clouds strewn across the waking sky and skewering the rising sun, but Oscar doesn't miss the figure of a four-legged creature silently strolling along the jungle border, under the first line of palm trees. The creature leaves behind small paw-prints in the ashen sand and, for a moment, turns its head to reveal ghostly silver eyes—

'Hold on—decision?' Oscar recalls. He's forgotten about this one. '*Another* decision? What else could it be—? What more do the Stellar Gods want?'

'*You will come to understand in short time,*' Stewart assures. '*Ah! But here is the next arrival!*'

A second glass bottle dances along the current and lands on the shore. Very routinely and *professionally*, Stewart breaks the glass and releases another firefly. This time, the sun on the horizon is half-risen and the firefly is able to transform quicker than Oscar's had. 'Camson!' Oscar cries. He hurries to clasp his arm and hoist the giddy East veteran onto his feet…before realising that he is also…well, completely naked. Awkward. But that little detail doesn't concern Oscar as greatly as his surprise for Camson's loyalty to the Dreamerverse. Camson has arrived with a freshly discovered ingenuousness, perplexed by his own choice to return…for eternity. 'I was only curious,' Camson murmurs earnestly. 'I haven't seen this place in so many years.'

'Welcome back,' Oscar says. 'Welcome home.'

He stretches a comforting arm round the veteran's shoulders, but Camson stays standing rigid and unsure, with his eyes flickering feverishly around the beach, as if this arrival is even more novel than his first time on the Coast.

'*Really?*' Stewart plays along. '*Don't I get a hug—or a stroke? It's been hours since I've seen either of you.*'

'I needed to get out of the City, away from its façade. There was something that just never worked for me there. I thought the rainbow seed was a practical joke. But, with a bit of faith, I guess wanted to revisit somewhere I knew better…only briefly, though,' Camson says gingerly, glaring out at the horizon to acknowledge the half-risen sun. 'This place hasn't changed at all.'

'Not since yesterday's sunset,' Oscar says. 'That was the last time we were here.'

'Yesterday?' Camson confirms. 'Is that how long it's been here? It was only yesterday? Does that mean Evanessa is still here—or should I call her the Phantom? But I mean…the *real* Evanessa? My wife…is *my* Evanessa here?'

Oscar and Stewart glance fretfully between themselves and lower their sights to the ground, failing to look Camson in the eyes.

'As far as I am aware, the Phantom vanished with the Drag-in,' Stewart reveals. *'Her duty protecting the Lighthouse was complete and she departed, leaving the mantle open for one of you to take up her role.'*

'What do you—you mean—' Camson struggles. 'I can never see her again?'

Neither of them have an answer for him. Camson chokes on panic and astonishment, fighting against the urge to well up and breakdown in the sand.

'It's not your fault you made the decision,' Oscar says. 'It's been a long time since we were granted the promise and you didn't know it would bring you back. We'll find a way to get through to her. We can pray to the Stellar Gods and they'll listen, or we can try and go back to the Lighthouse—anything to get her back to you.'

'Erm, well, I'm afraid—not to sound rude,' the bird interrupted, *'but, err—you two may want to invest in some clothes very soon, because it's about to get quite busy round here.'*

'Stewart, why are we back here?' Camson inquires. 'The rainbow seed brought us back. How—? I thought we closed the link between worlds! I thought we were finished with this place! And the Drag-in left the Memory Lane in tatters, the Void would've been too dangerous to cross again!'

'And why after so many years?' Oscar adds. 'It took four years for us to return. In order to bring us back to Awakening Coast, you only needed to *invite* us? Was it always just as simple as that?'

'Okay, I think it would be better if I just explained it all to you now, as opposed to things getting complicated very quickly: the rainbow seed – if that's what you kids want to call it – gives you the chance to return to the Dreamerverse the very instant you consume it. And, as was promised to you, you may remain here forever upon doing so. Whether you choose to eat the seed or not will determine which world you will remain in eternally. You have until sunrise, however, to make this decision and, once sunrise on this world is complete, your return to reality will be forbidden; likewise, if you choose ***not*** *to consume the seed before sunrise is complete, your return to the Dreamerverse will be forbidden.'*

'Sunrise on Constellation Planet?' Oscar reaffirms.

'Yes, yes, yes—your status as Night Dreamers will pass come the peak of sunrise, after which you'll remain Day Dreamers like the rest of the dwellers on this world. The only difference with you is that you will stay put here always. From now onwards, like normal Dreamers, it will always be sunrise on Constellation Planet whenever you wake here.

Though, you'll never need to employ the use of this Coast again, because the rainbow seed has reinstalled you with permanence. You belong here now. Constellation Planet is your new home and you can rise, live and fall asleep here as and when you want. You're only used to arriving at sunset because you were born Night Dreamers. Night Dreamers no longer need to exist now that the Drag-in's not an impending threat anymore, since their very existence is only ever conceived by a disturbance to the security of the Void between worlds. This final tradition is your reward, and it is only relevant to you if you are fully determined to leave the world you've always known behind. For the two of you, Mankind's World is but a brick at the end of the Memory Lane, a myth among the pages of history, a dream you will eventually live to forget. Your decision has already been made.'

'And it's just Samuella who we're waiting on now?' Camson guesses.

'Samuella,' Oscar swoons. Delight courses through him as he imagines the Babe With The Blade materialising on Awakening Coast one last time and nestled in his company for all eternity to come. No longer the girl he would have to remember, but *know* forever. She had been his fascination for four years where, back in reality, they barely knew each other. The key to his solitude was the girl with the firey red hair. She was the first person whom he'd connected with on a unique wavelength in their own little world. And, with fondness, he would very soon be riding that wave again. For, in his bittersweet fascination, Oscar had come to love her.

'*She has until sunrise is complete. If Samuella goes to sleep in the real world without swallowing the rainbow seed and sunrise passes her by, she will remain locked in reality,*' Stewart explicates. '*When sunrise is at its fullest here, the earliest Dreamers will start to arrive on Awakening Coast; the first batch of "New Dreamers" on Constellation Planet. Your premiering arrivals will open its gates for the first time in four years – or twelve hours, if my perception of time here is anything to go by. We must all be very excited indeed!*'

Oscar's excitement, however, is elsewhere, committed to the resurrection of Samuella and welcoming her as soon as she returns. Camson is marooned in mourning for his missing wife, trying to cling on to the final memories he can of her, before the Memory Lane scrubs them away. Meanwhile, Stewart trundles to the seafront to watch the sun.

And so, they wait for the golden-orange clouds to subside and for the sun to mount the fresh blue sky, and the stars stubbornly fade off into the past with the previous night. With what could be an inch of the giant fireball touching the horizon, comes the third and final glass bottle. It floats to the shore and Stewart zooms down to rescue the firefly inside. '*Just in time,*' he says, as he pecks at the glass shell. Once it's been released, the firefly shoots into the air above the three of them and begins its transformation…

Although, it isn't Samuella who appears from the metamorphosis, kneeling on the sand (very naked, of course). The redheaded girl is nowhere to be seen. Instead, this young newcomer has golden hair.

'*You took your time, Samue—ellll—!*' the bird begins to fuss, but pauses. '*Oh. Why—Good Morning, Evanessa.*'

Camson lifts his head up from misery to wince at the glimmer reflecting off the incoming tide. Sunrise has brought with it his wife.

'My love…?' Camson says, stunned. 'Evanessa?'

Oscar sighs despondently and tips his attention away from the ocean, just as the two of them rush across the shore to embrace. Unable to outrun the current, a huge wave collides with Evanessa's back, while she and Camson hug, drenching her unspoiled body and soaking clean the restored beauty that the real world robbed her of. Camson, relieved of his commiserations, cannot let her go.

'I'm so grateful! I'm indebted! Surely—this is no mistake?' Camson rejoices in disbelief.

'No mistake,' Evanessa reassures him with a gargantuan smile – only now not restricted to doing so through her eyes alone. Her whole face is on display. Her whole happiness.

'Is that supposed to be your way of congratulating me on my decision?' Camson says.

'For keeping your faith,' Evanessa tells him. 'Patience pays in the end, Cammy. Sometimes you have to tolerate your own demons, before you can finally see the beauty in others.'

Camson finds his fingers treading through her lush golden locks and strokes underneath it to caress the hot, lasting blushes in her cheeks. *It has to be true this time*, he believes. *No fantasy about it.*

'Whose debt do I owe for you?' Camson asks, humbled behind glassy eyes.

Evanessa takes a fleeting glance at where Oscar is standing, and then anxiously examines her husband's chin.

'Samuella.'

This is all Evanessa has to say for the ecstasy to frazzle away, but not entirely into oblivion…for Camson is unexpectedly caught out by yet another surprise. Camson and Evanessa both pivot at the right moment to view a tanned little boy making his way, majestically, along the shore. He has re-emerged from the sea, regurgitated from the same place in the seabed he was kidnapped. Newly transformed, the firefly light frazzles off Thuban's back. The orange glow outlining his figure is sparkling with a crisp, but fading, complexion. He's also enthusiastic to be reunited with his parents, he races from the water, stark naked in nothing but his father's Red Robe, hanging several sizes too big on his shoulders.

'Thank you.' Camson sings his gratitude. 'Any place I can have my family is good enough for me.'

While the three of them embrace each other, such skin-on-skin action reveals, for the first time, what it's like to see a parrot grimace in disgust. Stewart has much to comment on and does so with volume: '*CLOTHES! CLOTHES! THINK OF SOMETHING TO WEAR! THE LOT OF YOU! BEFORE I FIND A WAY TO SEND YOU ALL BACK TO WHERE YOU CAME FROM! OR, AT THE VERY LEAST, A FABRIC DEPOSITORY! YEEEUUUGH!*'

Just as fluidly as the three of them appeared, three long, white cloaks materialise upon Camson, Evanessa and Thuban, concealing their shivering bodies and overlaying the Red Robe that Thuban is scantily garbed in. The restoration of the Void has brought Camson's family back to actuality and the East veteran knows he couldn't ask for more.

As the tide continues to settle and the fully risen sun shines down on them all, Evanessa disbands from her family momentarily to search for Oscar. The former Decider has found a place for himself further up the beach, sat twiddling a lone shell about in the sand, with his head sunken between his legs.

Evanessa joins him and crouches down to lightly tap his knee.

'Oscar,' she says. 'Are you okay?'

'I'm the same,' he responds. 'Is that "being okay" to you? Being the same miserable drip, secluded on his own for the rest of eternity?'

'I know you're upset, Oscar, and I'm terribly sorry it had to turn out like this. But it was her decision to make and—'

'You don't need to apologise. She didn't know me that well anyway. Why should she care about seeing me again?' Oscar wallows and shrugs. 'Did she just hand over the seed to you? Without hesitation?'

'She knew I wanted it more.'

'And *she* didn't? Not at all?'

'Perhaps she thought…and I don't mean to be rude by saying this, but—maybe, she thought, since the rest of us have lost so much…you might have lost the least. And therefore, alternatively, you may have actually *found* the most.'

'*Found the most?*' Oscar sniggers. 'I've found nothing. All I found was her and now all I want is—well, I don't know what I want now.'

'You may not think you've gained anything from this experience, from your journey outside of your tight little residence, up in that cloud-bound tower, hidden behind the fortress-sized walls that encircle your hometown, the City…'

'How can you remember any of that?' Oscar ponders wildly. 'I thought the Void was closed off—?'

'What I'm trying to tell you is that you can find anything, if you look hard enough. You found six emeralds strewn across two dimensions, you found a way to defeat the Drag-in, and you found more than one side to Camson and Samuella. Sometimes, the effort it takes to step out of your comfort zone is all that is needed to discover the thing you've always wanted.'

'*Welcome back to the Dreamerverse,*' Stewart announces, suspending speculation once more. '*The third and final Night Dreamer has checked in to Awakening Coast, along with her husband and the free spirit of their son, right on cue to collect their reward of eternity. Ah, wonderful, wonderful! And here we go at last! The sun has finished its ascent!*'

The parrot rockets into the air and extents his wings, so that he hovers above their heads like a kite. '*About time the steward showed off his true colours, methinks!*'

Stewart vanishes. A zip of orange light evaporates his form in mid-air, and then the bird's silhouette shimmers and shifts into the shape of a man. He's tall, slim and toned with a bearded jawline that is impeccably triangular. And, not to neglect, his most distinctive feature of all being a head full of dreadlocks…

Stevenson has appeared on Awakening Coast, snatching the bird's semblance. The classy chauffer materialises different to his reality ego, dressed in a white suit as opposed to his regular business-like black ensemble, and he emerges with no sign of a prosthetic leg. Oscar gives the man a hug and clutches onto the seams of his angelic suit until they very nearly rip.

Stevenson kisses his teeth at Oscar's sudden rush, but fails to suppress a gush of relief.

'Why yuh act so surprise? Yuh nah know was me, boy?' The chauffer shakes his head and sighs. 'Please tell meh yeh know de parrot were meh soul hidden. All dem years I were sworn to de beach here, to look afta Awakening Coast and to look afta yuh, pickney, 'cause meh vowed to be yer eyes an' ears – at all times. Dem Stellah God know 'ow much yuh mean tuh meh, so dem stuff meh long foot in a bird's backside. Meh wuh force tuh eat worms fuh yuh! Remember dat?'

'You weren't a lot quieter as a parrot. I remember that much,' Oscar jokes. 'Any chance you could change back?'

All of a sudden, the first faces of New Dreamers have begun to appear in the sand. Awakening Coast comes to life before their very eyes. Beneath their feet, thousands of unknowing newcomers are about to enter a world they haven't imagined before. At first, their eyes are closed and their bodies are motionless in sleep. But only once they entirely surface, and the sand pours off their chests and limbs, do they break away from their slumbers. Wholly confused on awakening and clumsy about their alien surroundings, the New Dreamers stumble and search about with guideless intent.

'Me gotta get me charm out now,' Stevenson excuses himself from flexing his two healthy human legs, to greet the first group of risers. 'Guess a bird don' need him wings to finish his groundwork, eh?' He kisses his teeth again, runs his hands over his forehead and through his locks, then goes to assist an exhumed young girl and boy up from the sand and stably onto their feet.

Stevenson is not alone in his service, however. From out of the jungle, a fleet of wings come flying over the entire shore. Hundreds of parrots have arrived to greet the newcomers just after sunrise. Bright and gaudy, they fill the sky above, soaring over the heads of Oscar, Evanessa, Thuban and Camson and every other Dreamer coming to fruition on the coast. Like Stevenson, these other stewards begin to take form too, reshaping into their human identities upon landing; men and women in crystalline white suits and dresses.

The new perspective of daybreak equilibrium infatuates Oscar. But, even during all the spectacle and novelty, something steals his focus away for just a split second.

A flash of movement covers the vacant section of shore in the distance and he finally acknowledges the dog strolling along the ocean's edge in all its glory. Again, the four-legged critter has made an appearance on Awakening Coast. The current strokes the hair on her paws, like thin, lubricated paint to the whiskers of a paintbrush, the damp sand soaking up and devouring any prints that remain of her tracks further down the shore. To anyone else on the beach, this rugged creature is a tiny detail hidden in the periphery of the euphoria that first awakening on Constellation Planet brings to every New Dreamer.

But Oscar knows what his own dog looks like.

Leaving his friends and the newcomers behind, he chases after her, rushing onto the drier and untouched virgin-white sand, as he stalks the canine with unbreakable determination. Kyma doesn't play an easy catch. She runs for her life, as if they are back in reality, *playing a game of Cat and Mouse in City Rec. Park.* Just when he thinks he's on her tail, Kyma rattles up a gear and springs an extra five yards ahead. It reaches a point where his breathlessness gets the better of him and he launches a desperate hand out—diving—he cries after her—'*Kyma…!*'

But Oscar falls flat on his face. Sand in his nostrils and ear canals. Even in the crevasses of his eyelids, somehow. Then, he dares to cock his head back and look up, rubbing the granules from his eyelids and facing the fierceness of the mature sun. Oscar doesn't see the sun.

He sees his mother.

Flesh. Bone. And soul. It's all there. The silhouette of her head is wearing the sun like a mane.

Everything is telling him not to trust his emotions, his hopes. But he can't see his hopes—

He can only see the woman he's missed all his life. The smell of sweet banana cakes baking in their old home oven wafts upon the warm humidity once again; the memory of her cosy embrace is adrift only by moments in his mind; the sparkle in her eyes declares war on the stars. It all dances in unison. So much commotion that he can barely cling onto the words that slip from between her lips.

'I will always follow you home.'

For more information on the author of this novel and their future releases, find out more at our website and follow our social media platforms:

www.monicamoon.com

 @monicamoonpublishers

 www.facebook.com/monicamoon

@MMPublishers

CPSIA information can be obtained
at www.ICGtesting.com
Printed in the USA
LVHW091454110919
630726LV00005B/30/P